Praise for *The ___*

"McMullen's prose is plain but lucid, and, nicely enriched with low human comedy, coincidence and farce, is perfectly suited to explication of his crowded story of heroism and cupidity in this cross between an old-fashioned air-ace adventure and Arthurian Romance. The level of invention of *The Miocene Arrow* may be lower than its predecessor, but there's much to enjoy.... McMullen ties up the numerous plot twists with an admirable facility, and the final pages are imbued with the burgeoning sense that the diptych of *Souls in the Great Machine* and *The Miocene Arrow* is destined to become a classic."

—Paul McAuley, *Interzone*

"With remarkable imagination and insight, McMullen conjures factions, personalities, and plots, including well-placed glimpses of a lost, past America. A complex and lively story, rich with the action and reaction of human treachery, courage, battle-fueled passion, and quiet devotion." —*Booklist* (starred review)

"The tale features labyrinthine politics, a large cast of engaging, thorny and occasionally rather cartoonish characters, and many well-depicted scenes of aerial warfare. The author's inventive use of several oddball technologies is particularly noteworthy, and veteran SF readers may well be reminded of the best work of L. Sprague de Camp." —*Publishers Weekly*

"Set in the same postapocalyptic universe as his groundbreaking *Souls in the Great Machine*, McMullen's latest effort elaborates on the evolution of a strange and, ultimately, mystifying future. Recommended." —*Library Journal*

"Every bit as much ingenious fun as the last book."

—Russell Letson, *Locus*

"A classic 'good read'." —*Analog*

"McMullen has fused the relentless pertinacity of Bruce Sterling with the stylized exoticism of Jack Vance, and, as his command of novelistic technique grows, his neo-medieval tapestry glows with an ever greater speculative intelligence."

—Nick Gevers, *Nova Express*

"[*Souls in the Great Machine*] has some wonderful, sense of wonder-including ideas, and some exciting action and colorful characters. . . . I recommend this novel for the neat stuff. . . . The end is arousing and fairly satisfying. . . . And the book is marked by a definite exuberance that makes it a fun read." —*SF Site*

Praise for *Eyes of the Calculor*
Book Two of the Greatwinter Trilogy

A *Booklist* Top 10 Adult Science Fiction Book of 2001

"McMullen tosses us into the action—of which there is plenty—rarely revealing all aspects of events but instead letting us delightedly discover the full story as the characters do. A captivating conclusion to a brilliant series." —*Booklist* (starred review)

"This is great escape, and great fun."
—*San Diego Union-Tribune*

"Boisterously entertaining . . . the complexity of the books plot is marvelous, like soap opera and Shakespeare, it is filled with fights, romance, wenching, revenge, greed, duplicity and misunderstandings—a cacophony of schemery and slapstick that never fails to entertain." —*Denver Post*

"Beamflash to North American fans: Australia Fowarding Huge Fan by Moonwing." —*Kirkus Reviews*

"One of the best epics I've read. If you've read the first two books, no doubt you need little urging to read this one. If you read it alone, you'll probably enjoy it even without the back story, but you might want to start at the beginning with *Souls in the Great Machine*.

"The Greatwinter Trilogy is certain to become one of science fiction's master story arcs, and the author will no doubt continue to provide us with good reading for some time to come."
—Ernest Lilley, *SF Revu*

"Sean McMullen expands even further the busy, sprawling, and quite engaging series that began with *Souls in the Great Machine* . . . Not many thousand-and-a-half-page adventure epics have managed to hold my attention for the whole span, but this one has left me willing to read more." —Russell Letson, *Locus*

THE
MIOCENE
ARROW

SEAN
McMULLEN

TOR®

A TOM DOHERTY ASSOCIATES BOOK
NEW YORK

THE MIOCENE ARROW

Copyright © 2000 by Sean McMullen

Edited by Jack Dann

A Tor Book
Published by Tom Doherty Associates, LLC
175 Fifth Avenue
New York, NY 10010

www.tor.com

Tor® is a registered trademark of Tom Doherty Associates, LLC.

ISBN: 0-765-34455-6
Library of Congress Catalog Card Number: 00-028624

First edition: August 2000
First mass market edition: May 2003

Printed in the United States of America

0 9 8 7 6 5 4 3 2 1

For my father,
the archetypical
Scottish engineer

THE
MIOCENE
ARROW

PROLOGUE

1 August 3956: North Dorak

Each time that any wing ascended in Mounthaven it was a minor pageant. The tiny aircraft, all with a span of less than thirty feet, formed the basis of the aristocracy and government in mid-fortieth-century America, and were the visible symbol of each airlord's rule. Lamps gleamed on the dark surface of Canyon Lake as the Missouri Wellspring was readied for a night ascent. It was a floatwing regal with two compression engines, capable of carrying as many as four passengers for two hundred miles. The wing was from the North Dorak governor's personal flock, and members of the diplomatic staff of Northmost lined the jetties in parade uniform. The wingcaptain accepted his commission for the flight from the Governor while his passengers looked on. His flight jacket's giltwork and gems gleamed and glinted in the lamplight, highlighting him amid the other nobles on the jetty.

"Your first flight over oblivion?" murmured the Governor.

"Every flight is over oblivion, Sair Governor," replied the young warden, who was eager to begin his first flight as a wingcaptain.

"Remember, when you fly over Callscour lands you fly over certain death. Take no chances."

The wingcaptain and his passengers climbed aboard as a steam engine cart was wheeled up to spin the regal's compression engines. They coughed, caught, and began to idle. The tasseled mooring ropes were cast off, and the floatwing drew away from the jetty to the sound of a brass band and orderly cheers from the onlookers. The adjunct fired a green flare. As it arced through the darkness the wingcaptain revved the compression engines up to full power and the floatwing began plowing through the glassy water, flinging spray behind it. Even under such ideal conditions this was a difficult ascent, and after a run of over two miles the regal was still on the water. The wingcaptain finally pushed the throttle forward to overboost. The floatwing lifted, bounced, bounced again, then clawed its way into the air. Now free of the water's drag, it began to gather speed.

"He should have idled his engines for a while longer," the adjunct said to the Governor. "Overboost can cause damage that will not be obvious until he is flying over death."

"Perhaps you could have delayed the flare a little longer?" the Governor ventured.

"No, no, he would have taken that as an insult, and so he should. He has had a fright. Let us hope that he survives it and remembers the lesson."

The distant floatwing turned northwest, with Mirrorsun's light glinting off its wings; then it merged with the night sky and was gone.

Thirty thousand feet above the lake a huge, matte-black wing was banking, its navigator taking a bearing from the lights of Northmost. It was over half a mile from tip to tip, yet its engines were all but silent and its passage was marked only by the momentary eclipse of an occasional star.

1 August 3956: North Bartolica

There had been no completely dark nights since Mirrorsun had formed twenty years earlier, in 3936. Its coppery glow always hung in the night sky, at the center of a band of darkness from which the stars had been sponged away. When the sun rose, Mirrorsun set, and when the sun set Mirrorsun enacted its own little dawn. To the people of what had once been North America, Mirrorsun was yet another mystery that had been added to plague their lives. The Call tried to lure them to oblivion every few days, the Sentinels spat hellfire at any vehicle larger than twenty-nine and a half feet, and they lived surrounded by land where the deadly Call practically never ceased. These were facts of life, and they had been accepted for two thousand years. At least Mirrorsun was harmless.

Mounthaven was an area in the Rocky Mountains, five hundred miles across and eight hundred miles from north to south. It was the biggest of the three Callhavens in North America, those three areas where the Call came every few days instead of almost continually. In many ways its society and technology were the most advanced on the planet . . . but not in all ways.

High above the mountains the Dorakian floatwing crossed North Bartolica briefly on its short but dangerous flight from Northmost to Kallision Lake in Alberhaven. Eighty miles of its ninety-mile flight would be over Callscour wilderness, where a forced landing meant certain death, yet floatwing flights were the only contact between the three million people of Alberhaven and Mounthaven's fifteen million.

There was teeming life in the Callscour wilderness, but none of the creatures that lived there weighed more than twenty pounds. Anything larger would be lured west, mindlessly wandering away until it died of an accident, or reached wherever the Call led. On the frontiers of the Callhavens, however, the rich but diminutive Callscour wildlife spilled over and could be hunted and trapped by humans in something like safety.

Three Bartolican trappers sat in their hide listening to the floatwing pass overhead, its compression engines laboring to gain height.

"Brave fellas, them wardens," said Zekin, looking in the direction of the sound and stroking the barrel of his carbine.

"That's why we're trappers and they're nobles," responded Jebaz, who was listening for trap bells.

"We's brave too, but wardens is brave *and* crazy," Lemas added, then took a pull from his flask of corn whisky.

"Talk like that's liable to get you flogged for mouthin'," said Jebaz, who was something of a royalist.

"Gah, the Regional Inspector never comes as far as the trap runs. Besides, there's nothin' wrong with bein' a little crazy. Take Zekin, like. He's brave as the airlord's Inner Guard, but he's got crazy ideas."

The drone of the floatwing's compression engines lingered in the distance.

"Have you ever wondered if there's more than wardens and flyers up there?" Zekin said as he looked straight up at the stars. The other two chuckled. "I don't mean all that angel and dragon shit, I mean folk from distant Callhavens with engines for drivin' wings as like we never thought of."

"Folk been talkin' about other Callhavens for thousands of years, Zekin," Lemas scoffed.

"Yeah, and when we got real good compression engines our wardens discovered Mexhaven and Alberhaven," said Zekin.

"And nothin' else in hundreds of years!" cried Lemas.

"Keep your damnshit voice down," hissed Jebaz, "or we'll be trappin' nothin' but demicoons who like to hear philosophy."

For some minutes there was nothing but the diminishing sound of the floatwing in the distance.

"I seen 'em flyin'," said Zekin, who had been brooding on the subject. "Big as a warden's gunwing, but silent."

"Buzzards," concluded Jebaz succinctly.

"Crazy," added Lemas.

"I seen what I seen. They's what made Mirrorsun twenty

years ago. Mirrormen, they are." He gestured to the sky so vehemently that the hide swayed.

"What should I drink afore I can see 'em too?" laughed Lemas.

Jebaz laughed too, Zekin did not. A trap clacked somewhere in the distance and all three men froze and strained for the direction of the jingling bells and the squealing, thrashing animal.

"West six," Jebaz began, but the rest of his sentence died behind his lips.

There was another sound, something unlike anything heard in those mountains for two thousand years: the mosquito-whine of an electric motor. It was away in the distance and from above. A blot of darkness eclipsed stars as it passed overhead; then the whining stopped.

"I seen it, somethin' big," breathed Zekin, "flyin' and all."

"Seen nothin'," chorused the other two, but what they had heard had been enough to make them click back the safety catches of their carbines.

"Got better eyes," said Zekin. "Got eyes to aim at the next one and blast a hole in it so big you can plant your head in it and say 'Well howdo in there Sair Mirrorsun Man.' "

"Meantime we got a trap to clear," began Jebaz, desperate for normality to return.

Something crashed heavily into bushes in the distance. All three men looked around.

"Coon," suggested Jebaz without conviction.

"Mirrorman hit a tree tryin' to land," said Zekin excitedly.

They waited for Lemas' opinion, but he said nothing. In the silence another whine became audible high above them.

"It's another, it's another," babbled Zekin, thumbing the safety catch on his own carbine. "It's gonna be meetin' with its friend what landed hereabout."

Zekin raised his gun and aimed into the star-studded night sky. The whining grew louder, and seemed to move across from east to south. Jebaz and Lemas held their carbines ready, trembling with dread of the unknown.

"Say Zekin, we got no quarrel with no Mirrorman," began Lemas nervously.

"Buckle it!" snapped Zekin.

Lemas saw it first, an eclipse of stars, a hazy outline in Mirrorsun's light. He gasped and pointed, and then Zekin opened fire, blasting at the sky and working the slide action as fast as he could. As the firing pin finally clacked on the empty chamber the echoes of the shots died away among the mountains.

"The whinin's stopped, I'se hit it!" exclaimed Zekin, hurriedly reloading.

"There, it's fallin' there!" shouted Lemas.

Something crashed into the trees to the east, and a large dark shape seemed to collapse down into the branches. Jebaz fired five shots into the forest where it had landed as Zekin reloaded.

"Big as a fir tree," murmured Jebaz in wonder.

"Proof, this time I'se got proof!" said Zekin. "I'm a-takin' one to town an' sure as hell showin' I'm not crazy."

"Big as a tree," echoed Lemas. "How we gonna carry that?"

"Don't care, but we're a-gettin' it into town. Hey, for a fairshow like, and we can get its flyer stuffed. Come on— hey, and bring your trailpacks and Call anchors, you never know how far we may have to chase 'em."

They climbed out of the hide and picked their way across the darkened ground. They knew the area well, so that the weak light of Mirrorsun was enough for them to move almost at a trot.

The shot that dropped Lemas boomed out like a thunderclap and echoed out across the mountains. He fell without a sound, a large hole in his forehead and the back of his head blown away. The other two trappers dropped at once, their reflexes honed by a lifetime of trap run feuds and skirmishes.

"Lemas!" Jebaz hissed.

"Dead," said Zekin, who had a better view of the body. "Half his head gone! What they got for carbines? Cart cannons?"

They lay still for some time, but nothing moved or made a sound.

"Powder, I smell old-style gunpowder," whispered Zekin.

"Mirrormen sure got old guns," replied Jebaz.

"Mirrormen nothin', them's the Bromleys a-tryin' to bag that thing we shot. Get ready, hat trick comin' up."

He raised his hat on a stick. Another booming thunderclap flashed bright from the darkened bushes almost due east. Jebaz was ready and fired three shots back at once. He was rewarded by a cry of pain. He jumped up and ran, working the slide action of his carbine and firing as he went. Zekin jumped up too, but caught his foot on a root and fell almost at once.

Another shot boomed in the darkness, flashing out to the right of the two trappers and from beneath the tree where the first shape had fallen from the sky. Zekin lay still for some time.

"Jebaz!" whispered Zekin over and over. "You okay, Jebaz?"

Each time silence was the eloquent answer, and there was still the scent of gunpowder on the air. Zekin shifted his weight and another shot grazed the shoulder of his jacket. The flash came from the direction of the first shot. Whatever had killed Lemas was wounded but still shooting. Zekin raised his head and peered into the scrub, which was lit only by the dim glow of Mirrorsun. A shot from beneath the tree tore hair from his head as it whizzed past. Zekin considered. There were two of those things out there, and although they seemed to be using muzzle loaders shooting gunpowder, they could definitely see in the dark. He could shoot faster, but they could see to aim.

"You hang low now Jebaz," Zekin called out, more to his conscience than to Jebaz. "I'll get help while you pin 'em down. They can see real good, but their guns is shit. Remember that."

Rolling on his back, he fired a fusillade of shots, then leaped up and ran, dodging back to better cover. Another thundering blast cracked out behind him and a bullet whizzed past his head. Zekin dived for cover just as a second shot sought him. He crawled, wriggled, and scrabbled through the bushes, as if carbineers were shooting at him in broad daylight. He lost track of time, but slowly his panic and desperation subsided as he realized that he was no longer being shot at.

Lying very still and peering through a gap in a lightning-blasted tree, he strained to see movement. Nothing was coming after him. By the glow of Mirrorsun he watched two distant figures separate from the shadows of the forest and hurriedly gather in what seemed to be billows of black cloth. One was limping, yet they worked with efficiency and speed. They walked over to where Jebaz and Lemas were lying, as confidently as if it were broad daylight. Kneeling in the shadows, they began looting the bodies.

Zekin saw one stand up and pull on a jacket. They were taking their clothes, he realized. Something about such personal theft enraged the trapper. He worked the slide action of his carbine and took aim for a long shot. The gun gave a click. No ammunition, and his pack was back with the intruders and dead trappers. By the light of Mirrorsun Zekin watched the figures pack the trappers' gear away and drag the bodies onto a pile of trimmings left by loggers half a decade earlier. They piled together what seemed to be their own clothing and the black cloth beside the bodies; then there was a small flash and smoky flames began dancing and spreading.

Tears of frustration trickled down Zekin's cheeks. Now he could see the intruders but he could not shoot. The two figures from the sky hefted the trappers' packs and strapped them on, then set off for the northeast, moving away across the Callscour frontier and into the wilderness. Behind them the fire blazed brightly, consuming black cloth, cords, clothes, and the bodies of Jebaz and Lemas.

The sunlight of the next morning leached away the mystery of the night before. Zekin returned with the Janberry deputar and municipal militia, and they went over the scene of the deaths in great detail. It soon became clear to the deputar what had probably happened, so he set the appropriate official processes in motion. Late in the afternoon of that same day those processes had run their course, Deputar Bremmel's edict was passed, and his sentence was carried out.

A week later the Regional Inspector arrived as part of a routine tour. At first there was the drone of a compression engine in the sky; then the half-saucer shape of a Bartolican sailwing circled Janberry several times while the local wingfield was cleared of grazing emus and rheas. The crests of the Central Inspectorate and the Hannan wardenate were on the little white aircraft, so that by the time it landed the deputar had his books ready and was frantically sweeping his office.

Vander Hannan climbed out of the tiny sailwing that marked him as more than just another mortal. Being able to fly meant that he was above the Call, that he could go where he pleased, that he was of the nobility, and that he was quite rich. He had the right to duel in the air, fight in wars, and sit in judgment over even the magistrates and deputars. On this day he was in Janberry in his role as an inspector.

"Had a good hangin' here last week," said the wingfield adjunct as Vander supervised the guildsmen pushing his sailwing into a shelter shed.

"Only one?" asked Vander.

"Oh but it was a good one. The yoick said devils dropped out of the sky and shot his partners."

"Devils? Are they in detention?"

"Well, can't say as they are—but at least we hung someone."

Vander was favored with admiring looks from the girls and women of the town as he strode in to make his inspection. He was only twenty-five, unmarried, and his father was the Inspector General. It would have been easy for Vander to live well and do little work, but he took his duties seriously. He visited the frontier towns at least twice a year, and always inspected in field parade uniform. The citizens of the frontier had to be reminded that the airlord took an interest in them, and had a long reach.

"Thing is, I can't figure his reason," Bremmel explained as the Regional Inspector finished reading the Janberry court's proceedings. "He actually came here to fetch us back and all."

"And his companions were both dead by then?"

"Yeh. It's plain as the nose on your face what happened, 'cause both had their guns and silver stole. Their bodies were charred pretty bad, but not so you couldn't see they was shot."

"What did Zekin say about that?"

"Said two devils dropped out of the sky and shot at 'em. Lemas and Jebaz were plugged, so he ran for help."

"What did you find at the site of the murders?"

"Ashes, mainly. He'd burned the evidence. The trappers' blindhide was okay, the fire didn't spread too far. Our tracker terriers found a trail from the shootout to a stream up northeast—but hell, that could have been Lemas and Jebaz just comin' back from fillin' their waterskins. I figure they was returnin' when Zekin dropped 'em, like."

"Just like that? With no warning?"

"Happens. Men go a mite crazy with each other out there. Hell, Inspector, it's dangerous enough without his kind makin' it worse. You capital folk don't know the frontier."

"On the contrary, Deputar Bremmel, as Regional Inspector I spend most of my time on the Callscour frontier and I deal with more crimes in a month than you see in a year."

He jerked his thumb at the body of Zekin dangling on the end of a rope from the loading beam of the general store. Beneath were the charred bodies of Jebaz and Lemas, the latter two covered by blankets in the name of public decency.

"Take the victims' bodies to the town medic's cabin," said the Regional Inspector. "I want to do an autopsy. After that you will escort me to the scene of the shootout."

Two days later Vander Hannan had completed his work and written his report. The report censured Deputar Art Bremmel and his militia for neglect of due process leading to a possible breach of justice. The bullet that had killed Jebaz had not come from Zekin's gun, but the possibility of Zekin's complicity with the real murderers could not be ruled out. The verdict was left open. A fine was imposed on the town for hanging Zekin without a blue Section 19 form signed by a county magistrate or the Regional Inspector, and the deputar and militia were ordered to pay for a memorial service, burial, and tombstone for Zekin.

Vander blotted his report, called for a clerk, and told her to scribe copies for the Governor and the town records. When she had gone he stared at Zekin's weatherbeaten but well maintained carbine, then at a lead ball that he had cut from the charred flesh of Jebaz. It was for a larger bore than Zekin's weapon. Zekin's testimony had mentioned the smell of gunpowder, and the ball-shaped projectile implied a very old-fashioned gun. Regional Inspector Vander Hannan opened his personal journal and began a new entry.

VERACITY ADDENDUM TO THE CASE OF
THE AIRLORD OF GREATER BARTOLICA
VERSUS ZEKIN FELTER:

In my assessment of the evidence tendered, I determined that the victims both died of a single gunshot wound from a primitive flintlock firearm, and that two other persons were at the scene. One of them trailed bloodstains, presumably as a result of being wounded. They escaped along Greenbank Stream, where the terriers lost the scent. My examination of their trail revealed that the wounded man was limping and making use of an improvised crutch. They were wearing the boots belonging to the deceased. This suggests that two members of some frontier tribe attacked the trappers with homemade guns, looted their bodies, then returned to their own trap run. Sair Felter had mentioned that old-style gunpowder was on the air at the time of the shootout. The part of his story that lacked credulity was that the intruders had swooped out of the sky on what looked to be huge black birds as big as houses, and that these hummed like insects.

At the shootout site I found a scrap of cloth and cord beside the fire. It was dyed black and was very finely made. It had survived the flames by being jammed into the splintered end of a log which had burned through and rolled clear of the main fire. The cord can support my full weight, although it is very thin. Its weave is finer and strength greater than I have ever seen in any fabric.

It is possible that these intruders were Dorakian agents that parachuted down from the regular floatwing to Alberhaven, but why Janberry? There are no mineable ruins, fortresses, strategic tramways or wingfields nearby.

Written this 4th day of August, 3956, by the hand of Regional Inspector Vander Hannan of the North Region Inspectorate.

Zekin Felter had been innocent of this crime, of course, but was he blameless of any other wrongdoing throughout his life? Vander wondered. That seemed unlikely. Whatever the truth in this case, justice had probably been done for some crime or the other. The frontier mountains were isolated from the comfortable order of southeastern Bartolica: violence was a part of life, but retribution was also swift, decisive, and very public. Justice had to be seen to be done, and so citizens had to take all the more care to be seen to be innocent.

Even as Hannan was writing his words, two trappers entered Northmost, just over the Dorak border. One had a bandaged leg, and was limping. They were unremarkable as trappers go, except that most trappers who came to town had pelts bundled in great rolls above their packs. These had none. First they went to the tram terminus, where they made inquiries about tickets south in barely intelligible Old Anglian, and then they sat down on a bench and began counting their grimy coins and promissory notes.

Nearby a tramway contractor was addressing a group of newly arrived gangers on their work for the months to come. He was also using the common language, Old Anglian, in deference to the varied nationalities of his recruits.

"Now Northmost is the most northerly town of the Dominion of Dorak, as well as the most northerly town in all Mounthaven," the contractor began.

"Figures," called someone, and the others chuckled.

"I'm glad we have a comedian among us, because where we are going there's not much to laugh about," the contractor responded. "Now then, go one mile north of where we stand and you are in the Callscour lands. Have any of you worked at the Callscour frontier before?"

Three hands were raised.

"You there, sair, with the red hat. Can you tell us your name and what you've done here?"

The youth shambled forward reluctantly, took off his hat

and nervously fiddled with it as he spoke. By now the trappers were listening attentively, although still going through the motions of counting.

"Tartaror Beisel of Yarron, steam tram driver first class. I worked on the Callscour tramway for two months. Last year, that is."

"Tartaror, tell us what goes on, like with the Callscour and all—not the religious bumf, mind, just technical, like."

"Well, to understand the Callscour lands you have to understand the Call," Tartaror began in a soft, educated voice. "The Call began two thousand years ago, during what we call the Chaos War. It's called that because nobody is sure who was fighting who, or even why they were fighting. They had many strange weapons of great power and some still work today. The Call is one of them."

"You mean like the Sentinel Stars in the sky, what burns up anythin' what moves that's thirty feet or longer?" asked a burly youth of about the same age.

"That's it. Lots of Call engines were built under the oceans by folk who did not have Sentinel Stars. Mind you, the priests in some centuries reckoned that the Call came from God, so historians who wrote otherwise were burned along with their books."

"What's oceans?" called someone from the back.

Tartaror scratched the back of his neck, then glanced to the contractor, who nodded.

"Well, from old books we can see that the world is a big ball, mostly covered with water but with some dry land. That's where we live. When the Call weapons were started they put out a kind of sound like a dog whistle or something, and that forced everything bigger than a terrier to come towards it, like as if they were sleepwalking. The Call was meant for someone's enemies, but I reckon they set it too powerful because nearly all dry land has been under the Call ever since."

He paused amid attentive silence. They had lived with

the Call all their lives, but few had ever heard such a technical explanation.

"The Callscour lands are actually the normal sort of Call as a weapon, like because it's full on for three days at a time, then there's a break of thirty or forty minutes, then it's full on again for another three days. That kills folk, nobody can live long like that. It's not completely regular, but we can predict it to about half a day using timetables and charts. Now in the Callhavens, like Mounthaven, the Call comes about every three days for only three hours. Bands of it sweep across the countryside like invisible brooms."

"Why's that?" asked the burly youth.

"We don't know, that's just the way it is. I think someone just set the Call machines wrong during the Chaos War. That's lucky for us, like, or there would be no Callhavens and the world would be run by dirkfang cats and demicoons."

"Okay, Sair Tartaror, that's told it straight," interjected the contractor. "Now then, Northmost is where Dorakian wardens and flyers ascend from Canyon Lake in their floatwings to cross the Callscour lands to Alberhaven. Dorak and Greater Bartolica lease an island in Alberhaven's Flathead Lake, where we have embassies. Only wardens and their most senior servants make the flight, because floatwings are the transport of nobility. Small things like gold, books, medicines, and suchlike are traded right now, but your work will change all that. You boys are important."

He paused to let that sink in, smiling benevolently. Most of the audience were impressed. They had never done anything important before.

"The tramway tracks on this line continue out past Northmost into the Callscour lands, and are being extended by two miles every year. Work is slow because breaks in the Call come for no more than forty minutes or so every three days, but we got ways to work around that. A half day before a break is due you're sent off on a special tram burning low-grade compression spirit and needing no stoker. It hits a special trip lever to stop it just near the railhead, then you wake up when the break comes. After that it's forty minutes of laying tracks and stone like the devil himself's your bossman, then it's back onto the tram before the break ends. Got it?"

"What happens if you don't get back to the tram in time?" asked a quavering voice.

"Your Call anchor stops you wandering too far, and there's specially trained terriers left behind to fight off the dirkfang cats. Three days later you're either dead or you wake up tired and hungry and the next tram's there to take you back here. Another question?"

"How long until the line is through?"

"The gangers from the Alberhaven side should meet us in fifteen years. Wardens have surveyed the route from the air so that it follows old roads which are level, like. Make no mistake, this is hard, dangerous work. Take a look at the folk on your right and left. In two months one of them won't be alive, but the rest of you will have more gold than you could earn in two years. Like I said, welcome to Northmost. Training starts tomorrow at dawn, meantime your tents are over at the rail dump. I'd advise you all to get a good night's sleep."

As the group began to break up, the burly youth came over to Tartaror.

"What you were saying before, like, I was wondering about the other lands beyond the oceans. Could there be Callhavens there too?"

"We know the names of places like England, China, Australia, and Russia from old maps, but if they have Callhavens we shall never know. The Call is most intense near the oceans, and even our best sailwings are too small to even reach them, let alone cross them. I think there probably are other Callhavens, but it's just a guess. I mean, like, we went for centuries before one of our wardens discovered Alberhaven and that's only eighty miles away."

Tartaror pointed north, then put his hat back on. The burly youth bowed and they walked off toward the tents.

"I'm Ceil C'Marl," he said. "Why are you here?"

"I shot someone back in Yarron. What about you?"

"I altered the status of a girl's virginity."

"And you fled here for just that?"

"She was a magistrate's daughter."

The two trappers watched in silence until the youths were out of earshot. By now they were counting their takings for the fifth time.

"Tartaror is bright," said the one with a bandaged leg. "He is right about other Callhavens."

"But wrong about the Call, Fras Sondian."

"*Sair Hambrian Carabas* from now on!" hissed the bandaged trapper sharply. "Get into the habit, *Sair Pyter Kalward.*"

"Sorry Carabas, sorry," Kalward replied quickly. "Still, how fortunate that their common language is still intelligible after two thousand years of isolation."

They sat back and watched the townsfolk going about their business.

"Pretty women, Sair Carabas," remarked Kalward.

"Call in a half hour, Sair Kalward," replied Carabas.

"Like I said, Sair Carabas, pretty women."

Just then a woman strode past dragging a screaming, struggling child behind her. As they drew level with the trappers she stopped and turned on the child.

"If you don't behave the Callwalkers will get you," she shouted in the common tongue, probably thinking that the trappers would not understand.

"Aren't any! They're like ghosts and fairies!" the little boy shrieked back, aiming a kick at her leg but missing.

The trappers sat in silence until they were gone.

"When they briefed us they said there were no aviads on this continent," said Kalward fearfully.

"Get a grip, you heard the brat. To them Callwalkers

are make-believe, like ghosts. The only two aviads in North America are you and me."

Kalward relaxed slowly, then smiled. "I think that child needs to believe in Callwalkers, Fras—uh, Sair Carabas," he declared.

"So you're planning to leave the proof with his mother, Sair Kalward?"

"Just as soon as that Call gets here, Sair Carabas."

It was midafternoon, on a cloudless and calm day. The town deputar noted that the trappers wandered about for some time, asking brief questions of those they met and looking through the store windows. He was about to go over and speak with them when the bell in the east Call-tower began ringing.

A Call had swept over the watchman in the tower, and he had released his deadhand lever and walked east to the barred window of his chamber. With nobody to reset the deadhand lever the mechanism had clattered a short warning that a reset was needed, then engaged the gravity mechanism of the tower's bell. The deputar unclipped his own bell and began striding down the street, ringing it as he went.

"Call in ten minutes, fasten your tethers, secure your children!" he bawled, over and over.

People began to prepare, but it was not a busy time of day. If there had to be a Call, this was as good a time as any for it. Had it arrived an hour later it might have stopped over the town for the night as a Null Zone. That would have been bad for business, and the steam tram was due to leave for the south. As he strode about with his bell the deputar noted that the two trappers had attached themselves to a public tetherbar and were smiling amiably at him.

Within ten minutes the Call arrived, invisible and silent. Everyone turned to mindlessly wander west, but all were tethered. Three hours passed.

Deprian the tailor awoke from the Call, pressed against

the padded west wall of his shop. Turning to the windows, he could see that the shadows had lengthened outside. Hardly any of the day left, he thought, hardly worth staying open. He turned to his workbench to pack up. The bell over the door rang as two trappers entered.

"Sorry boys, I got more pelts than I can handle," Deprian began; then he saw the gold Bartolican crendars in the taller man's hand.

"Want we clothes, traveling, for the purpose of," he said in halting Old Anglian, and with a very heavy accent. "This, payment, for the purpose of."

"Sure son, that ought to do the trick," replied Deprian at once. "When do you need 'em by?"

"Tonight, steam tram, for traveling upon."

It was robbery to be sure, but they were willing to pay and Deprian was willing to miss dinner. Within two hours he had altered two existing suits to fit the trappers while they washed and shaved at the back of his shop. The deputar called in to ask if he had lost any money, as there had been several thefts around the town that had been noticed after the Call had passed. Deprian checked his float but found nothing missing. The deputar moved on.

The chuffing of the steam tram leaving the service shed could be heard in the distance as the trappers had their final fittings. They had burned their reeking clothes and boots in the grate, but Deprian would have done that anyway. He noted that one had a bandage on his calf that was tied in a neat but unfamiliar pattern—almost artistically, he thought. Finally they bought Deprian's own catchbag and fed their greasy packs to the flames. They had their own town boots, he noted, boots with a fine cut in unfamiliar leather, with hook-snap lacing. Deprian wondered where such a style might be the fashion.

It was dusk as Deprian stood watching the trappers walk down the main road to the station, where the steam tram was halted while its wood blocks were loaded aboard and water was pumped into the reserve tank. Those departing embraced their friends and relatives on the platform as the driver blew the whistle. Finally the doors were locked, and with a series of ponderous chugs the steam tram began to ease its way along the tracks with its two dozen passengers, two crew, three carbineer guards, and cargo. People watched from the platform until the squat spruce and canvas tram disappeared around a distant bend. The engine's chuffing echoed for a while amid the mountains before fading into the wind.

Deprian sighed with relief as he turned back into his shop and began to close up for the night. The suits had been worth only a fifth of what the two trappers had paid, yet nobody had pointed that out to them before they boarded the steam tram. The deputar called in again as Deprian was about to climb the stairs to his dwelling.

"You positive nothin's been lifted from your shop?" he asked the tailor.

"Sure as I got two hands. Why's that?"

"Weird stuff been happenin'. There's more than a hundred gold sovereigns and Bartolican crendars reported missin' across the town, from two dozen folk."

"You think them trappers did it?"

"Nah, I watched 'em like a wood hawk, they were steady. There's more too. Semme Thatching says she was, like interfered with during the Call."

Deprian laughed. "More like she's been takin' too long a-buyin' her bread at the bakery."

The deputar did not smile. "Med says three other women have seen him since the Call, all agitated-like and askin' if it's possible to get mounted during a Call—by Call-walkers."

"Callwalkers? They're storybook stuff, Pel."

"I'm not sayin' I got Callwalkers, just a pile of weird shit."

The tailor whistled nervously, thinking of the seven gold crendars in his pocket. There was much that he could have mentioned, but he chose silence. Why should he share in the bad fortune of those who had been robbed?

1 | CORONATION

It was said that no dominion in Mounthaven did coronations and funerals so well as Greater Bartolica. In area it was the biggest of the dominions and Condelor, its beautiful and ancient capital, was the most elegant of the known world's cities. The buildings that lined its streets were built proof against age as well as earthquakes, built with curving walls that tapered gracefully upward, as if striving to rise into the air. The windows were within heavy arches, but there were so many windows in each building that their interiors were never dark or oppressive. The apartment terraces, shops, and storehouses were all encrusted with multicolored stone and glazed tiles. Even the tiles on the roofs were glazed and colored, for it was important that Condelor also be pleasing to the wardens who saw it from the air. Raised aqueducts of sawn black basalt, orange sandstone, and red brick carried water in from the nearby mountains, where it passed down terracotta pipes to power machines before emptying into the canal waterways that interwove the roads and tramways of the city.

As one neared the center of Condelor the parks became bigger, the mansions were more splendid, and the streets and avenues grew wider until the royal palace came into view above the trees. It was built in parkland interlaced with canals, and to the south was the spacious palace wingfield that could accommodate the gunwings of hundreds of visiting wardens and airlords. Even the gunwing halls of the wingfield had stained glass in their arched windows, while the adjunct's tower was surrounded by flying buttresses and encrusted with winged gargoyles.

The coronation of Greater Bartolica's new airlord had attracted wardens and squires with over three hundred sailwings and gunwings, and the field guildsmen and their tents supporting the vast flock of wings had spilled out of the wingfield area and into the surrounding parks. Ground crews could be seen pushing aircraft of every airworthy shape imaginable along the avenues to reach the guild tents where they were to be serviced, tuned, and cleaned. Freelance engineers advertised and displayed their valves, cylinders, rings, bearings, and atomizers at stalls on the mosaic sidewalks. Compression spirit of many caloric blends was available from carts laden with barrels, while other carts carried little steam engines to spin compression engines into life. Freelance gunsmiths did a particularly good trade. The best reaction guns were sold in pairs and were built light—like everything else that had to fly.

Quite apart from its most obvious objective, the coronation was a celebration of travel and class distinction. In fact speed of travel defined Mounthaven society, and one's social status defined whether one had taken months or hours to reach Condelor. At the lowest levels, itinerant workers, poor scholars, outlaws, trappers, and bounty hunters traveled the trails by foot. Such travel was slow and dangerous, but free. At the next level, the farmhands, birdherders, and townsfolk never traveled more than ten miles from where they were born, but they were generally secure and happy, and never attended coronations. The merchants, artisans, and other respectable folk traveled on the steam trams, whose mesh of trackwork linked all the important cities, towns, and estates. The trams were regular and well guarded, but crowded and expensive, and averaged barely three times the pace of a brisk walk. Fuel, raw materials, and equipment were also moved by tram, which meant that everything was expensive unless produced locally. Most estates were self-sufficient, and few cities were bigger than a half-day journey with a farm handcart.

The nobility flew. Airlords, wardens, squires, and a few select guildsmen flew the sailwings, regals, and gunwings that defined the aristocracy. No part of Mounthaven was more than a few hours away from any warden's estate, but even a flock of three or four wings required an estate of two hundred to support, maintain, and fuel them. A new aircraft cost what a prosperous commoner could earn in two decades. Wardens patrolled the land during Calls, fought duels and highly stylized wars, attacked renegade militia strongholds, and monopolized fast communication and travel. The wardens were visible to all, and in turn saw, taxed, and controlled everyone beneath them. They were also free of the Call while in the air. While in many ways less than perfect as political systems went, it had endured since the reinvention of diesel compression engines over a thousand years earlier.

Serjon Feydamor was the lowest of the flying elite, an apprentice guildsman and trainee flyer. The Yarronese youth wore a plain green flight jacket as he explored the multitude of stalls of what might easily have been mistaken for an artisans' festival. On the right and left of his collar he also wore silver flyer blazons signifying that he was qualified to fly armed sailwings in the service of his airlord. He had the crest of his engineers' guild on his cap, but his cap was folded up and hidden in his pocket. Occasionally he was hailed as a squire by the vendors, and each time his heart flushed warm with pride.

Serjon was in a very curious position. After having sired several daughters but no sons, the guildmaster Jeb Feydamor had petitioned his wife and his warden under the tradition of assisted succession. Under this custom, Warden Jannian visited Jeb's wife for several weeks until she became pregnant by him. Were the child another girl, the warden's youngest son would become the nominal heir of the Feydamor guild family. As it happened, Serjon was born of the union, yet he was born with his true father's love of flying and was proving a poor apprentice engineer. In theory, if Warden Jannian and all his other sons were to die, then Serjon could lay claim to the wardenate. Even though he never wished such a disaster to happen, Serjon nevertheless considered himself to be a flyer. The thin, angular, and intense youth of nineteen wore his engineer's crest with reluctance and shame, and only when forced to.

The great gathering of aircraft was not open to the citizens of Condelor, who had to content themselves with merely watching the wings fly in from all points of the compass. Sailwings and gunwings of the Mounthaven wardens soared lazily through the sky while Serjon wandered the streets. They were elegant and stylish aircraft, whose form had often remained unchanged over centuries because their estate guildsmen had decreed that they had achieved perfection already.

There were more ceremonies than just the coronation, which was the actual focus for the gathering. The guildmasters of the engineers, airframists, fuelers, gunsmiths, and instrumenteers had meetings to refine standards, while wingfield adjuncts met to discuss wingfield administration, dueling and war protocols. Members of the guild of meteorologists discussed weather theory and precedent, squires met to arrange marriages for their children, weavers debated the virtues of the new crosswoven airframe silk that promised double strength, and the wardens themselves discussed flying. The competitions were already over, but pinned to Serjon's collar at his throat was a little gold starpoint kite that marked him as the winner of the sailwing division in target kite shooting. Every so often he would caress it, as if reassuring himself that he was born to fly.

Within the palace grounds the Inner Guard and ancillary carbineers all wore parade uniforms, bright, smart, and well tailored for the coronation. The instruments of the bands shone in the sunlight as they marched along the avenues playing bright, precise marches for the parades and processions, but by night string orchestras took over as the nobles and their wives, sons, and daughters danced in the brightly painted and tapestry-laden halls of the palace. An airlord from Senner had once said, "We go to Condelor to fall in love, and to remember how to live." To Serjon, however, the Condelor gathering was an excuse to hide his cap in his pocket and mingle among strangers as a flyer.

Serjon's wanderings had taken him to the palace wingfield when a Calltower bell began ringing. He immediately went to a public rail and clipped his tether to it, then waited to watch the duty warden ascend for his Call patrol.

The duty warden of the palace wingfield heard the ringing of the Calltower bell as he was breakfasting in the adjunct's chambers. Even as he looked up, the guildsmen of his ground crew began shouting to each other. Moments later the compression engine of his sailwing spluttered into life as his engineers spun it with a steam engine on a cart. The warden stood up, buttoned his jacket, then took a steamed towel from his aide and wiped his face and hands. His flight jacket was a blaze of gold thread embroidery on blue and yellow silk quilting, with gilt epaulettes of dirkfang cat skulls and red gemstones inset within each button. Standing in front of a full-length mirror, he pulled on his leather and felt cap with raised domes of giltwork over the ears, laced it tight, then picked up his tassel-fringed gloves. Finally his aide brought a gold cloak with his estate's crest embroidered on the back, and Warden Brantic strode from the room out onto the wingfield.

Along with Serjon there were hundreds of foreign dignitaries outside waiting to watch the warden ascend, ranging from senior wardens to mere merchants. Serjon should have felt pride burning through his body, knowing that even the wealthy merchants alongside him were below a flyer in peerage status, yet something was nagging at his mind. Warden Brantic's flight designator was 13. Serjon stared at the number as if it were a large and dangerous predator, fearful for the warden yet relieved that someone else was about to step into its cage.

Most of the onlookers were in national parade dress, guild uniforms, or their own splendid flight jackets. There were so many dozens of wardens, squires, flyers, guild-masters, and envoys that Warden Brantic found the spec-tacle overwhelming as he emerged. What was usually a routine part of a warden's duties had become a major cer-emony. One hundred and thirty wardens and nine airlords were in the city for the Bartolican Airlord's coronation, and Bartolican prestige and honor rode with every action of every official in even the most mundane of duties. The adjunct and the wingfield's herald were waiting beside the warden's sleek, white sailwing, and the onlookers included guildmasters from Dorak, Senner, and Colandoro, as well as several wardens from Yarron. All wore Call anchors or Call tethers but Brantic: for this day, he alone was to be godlike and above the Call.

"The layabouts are of higher rank than usual today, Sair Jiminay," said the warden quietly as the wingfield herald opened the silver clasps of the Book of Orders.

"A Call now means no Call for three days or more," murmured the herald. "Tomorrow morning's coronation will be free of interruption, so the new airlord can rightly claim divine favor."

"Who knows, perhaps he really does have divine favor," the warden replied.

The herald rang his handbell for attention.

"Hear now, citizens of Greater Bartolica and honored guests, that Warden Hindanal Brantic has been charged by the Airlord Designate of Greater Bartolica to oversee his palace, capital, and all its approaches during the Call that now approaches us. Warden Brantic, you are charged with the responsibility of flying high above Condelor, watching over its people's safety, guarding its approaches, and warn-

ing other wardens and flyers of the peril of the Call. Do
you accept this charge?"

"I do accept this charge and all its responsibilities," replied Brantic.

The warden pinned the Airlord Designate's pennon of
arms to his jacket beside those of his wife, then strode
over to his sailwing and eased himself into the seat. Like
all wardens of means, he had a gunwing for dueling and
a sailwing for Call patrols. The guildsmen of his ground
crew removed the chocks from the wheels and aligned the
aircraft on the wingstrip; then the warden was flagged clear
to ascend. He tried all the flaps and control surfaces,
opened the throttle, and rolled off along the rammed gravel
surface. The sailwing lacked the power of a gunwing, but
was lighter and more delicately built so that it could stay
in the air for over four hours. The warden's sailwing ascended smoothly, and then he cranked in his wheels and
banked to the north. The ordeal was over, he was up. He
had not made a fool of himself in front of the assembled
nobles of Mounthaven.

The Call was approaching from the east, luring every
mammal larger than a terrier to wander mindlessly west.
The warden flew over the city walls and out over the irrigated farmlands, aqueducts, canals, and trackways. Sure
enough, the birdherders were milling about against the
west fences of their fields, yet their rheas, emus, and os-
triches were grazing normally. The Call did not affect birds
of any size; neither did it affect people if they flew free in
the air. Nine miles through the Call's depth he flew over
fields where its effect had passed. There were no outlaw
packs hurrying along in this Call's wake to raid the capital.
The warden turned back.

The Call had still not reached Condelor as he flew back
over its walls, but the people were prepared. The streets
were almost deserted, smoke was less thick from the myr-
iad chimneys, and only the canal barges and gravity trams
were still running. The warden noted several buildings that

had not run up their flags: the owners would be fined in due course. He pressed the lever that released the sail-wing's siren, then methodically patterned the city so that none but the deaf could have missed its blare.

The front of the Call finally arrived, and presently Bran-tic was the only human awake in a strip nine miles deep and thirty miles wide. The truth was that the capital did not need the sailwings to patrol its skies during a Call. There was an adequate network of signal towers, warning stations, and Call bulwarks, so that people were seldom lost through accidents or lack of warning. The patrols were symbolic; they were to be seen rather than to protect. The sailwing was a plain statement that the nobility were above the Call in every sense of the word, as it had been for many centuries.

The movement that caught Brantic's eye was within the palace grounds. A figure was walking briskly, diagonal to the Call's direction and allure. One of the ornamental birds, the warden told himself as it vanished behind a bush; then the figure was in sight again. Through his field glasses he could see arms swinging, and the bright blue of a mer-chant carbineer uniform. A man! The figure vanished into a doorway.

The warden lowered his field glasses and rubbed his eyes. An illusion, he told himself. A shadow, a machine, a trick of the light. He hesitated, then made a note in his log. "Figure walking across direction of Call/ palace ad-ministrative wing/ ornamental rhea bird may be loose there."

He was circling for another look when he noticed a gun-wing over the city, approaching the palace wingfield with its wheels cranked out. Brantic pushed his sailwing's throt-tle forward to full power and stood the aircraft on its wingtip as he came around to warn it off. The red double wedge grew until he could see that it was painted with the East Region's colors. He flew right across its path, but its warden ignored him.

"Idiot, can't you see the flags?" exclaimed Brantic aloud as he released his siren and came around again.

The red gunwing trainer was dropping fast as he caught up, and although the airscrew was spinning, he suspected that it had been feathered. Brantic dipped his wings and pointed east of the city to where the Call had already passed. The other warden stared grimly ahead at the palace wingfield. Now Brantic noticed two other heads through the glass of the narrow cockpit. All that weight, no wonder he's in trouble, the warden thought. He must have ascended with a bare minimum of compression spirit to get off the ground at all.

At fifty feet the Call's effect cut in, even though the aircraft was flying free. The warden had done the alignment well, he was on course to land smoothly and roll to a stop on the flightstrip, even if insensible with the Call. The Bartolican heralds would declare another triumph of Bartolican wardens' skill at flying.

The gust of wind that caught the gunwing trainer would have been nothing to a warden free of the Call, but the red aircraft was gliding deadstick. It tipped, then righted, but it was now parallel to the flightstrip as it continued its descent. It flew over the tents, gunwings, and stores of the assembled wardens, and a wheel passed only inches above the insensible Serjon Feydamor's head as he mindlessly strove against his Call tether to wander west. Finally the gunwing slammed into the compression spirit barrels of the Pangaver wardens. The resulting explosion was all billowing black smoke and arcing fragments, yet nobody on the ground reacted.

Brantic climbed, his head spinning with shock and dismay. A Bartolican warden had crashed during *his* Call patrol. There would be hell to pay, the Airlord Designate himself would be shouting for blood, and the wardens would all be clamoring for an inquisition when he landed.

"Fool!" Brantic shouted at the column of smoke that was slanting up into the sky; then he turned his sailwing to

sweep the airspace over the city for other gunwings. There
was none. For the briefest of moments Brantic contem-
plated a vertical dive at full power into the distant waters
of Saltlake, but his training and sense of honor would not
allow it. He circled until the Call was past, and although
the two remaining hours dragged, they were not slow
enough for Brantic. Call flags were being lowered throughout the capital as he began his descent to the palace wingfield.

The Governor of East Region, his wife, and Warden
Darris of Pocatello had crammed themselves aboard the
red gunwing, intent on making a grand entrance at the
coronation. Even with the extra three hundred pounds of
passengers and their luggage there should have been fuel
to spare, yet there had apparently been headwinds that ate
away the margin for safety during the brief ninety-mile
flight. Perhaps pride had dictated that they try to land at
the capital, rather than coming down on some cart track
where the Call had passed already. Whatever the reason,
all aboard had died. Fortunately nobody on the ground had
been killed, and apart from the fuel dump there had been
no other damage. Pangaver was a small and unimportant
Dominion, and merely being the center of attention was a
matter of satisfaction to its nobles. To Brantic's surprise,
nobody had realized exactly what had happened until he
had landed. Serjon had helped to fight the last of the flames
once the Call had passed and freed him, yet the Yarronese
flyer had thought he was attending the crash site of Warden
Brantic's gunwing—doomed by the 13 of its designator.

The duty warden was suspended from all further Call
patrol flights pending a full inquisition, but preparations
for the coronation went on without interruption. The investiture of a new governor for East Region was scheduled
as the new airlord's first official duty, however.

Some miles to the south a steam tram chuffed across the
pastures and farmlands that were still under the Call. The

driver was in the grip of the Call and had released his deadhand brake and firebox quench, yet another man was gripping the deadhand lever with his left hand while holding a small telescope to his eye with his right. While not totally oblivious of the allure of the Call, he was still in full control of both his mind and body.

Juan Glasken was far less in awe of the distant outline of Condelor than the vast majority of the Bartolican capital's visitors, but unlike that vast majority he had traveled far, far further. Sometimes the big, middle-aged man had been in search of fortune and sometimes city constables had been hot on his heels. On one occasion he had even been in command of the squad of musketeers whose flint-locks were all that stood between the Southern Alliance Mayorates and an overwhelming army of Southmoors.

But there were no musketeers in the four American Call-havens, and not a single army or militia still used flint-locks. Neither were there any Southmoors, and the American nations were called dominions rather than mayorates. Glasken was good at learning new languages, was used to travel, and could handle himself well in a fight. This made him a good choice for a long and dangerous mission to the other side of the world from which there could be no return, but there was something else which made him a truly ideal choice: he was under a sentence of death in his very distant homeland. A friend had once described Glasken as not completely human in some ways, yet far more human than any human had a right to be.

Glasken released the deadhand lever, and automatic mechanisms began to slow the tram. He walked back to the passenger compartment where a woman sat reading while two others strained mindlessly against their Call tethers to follow the allure west into a nearby salt lake.

"The tram is slowing, Fras Glasken," said the middle-aged but still strikingly beautiful woman, looking up from her book.

"There is a Call upon us and we are approaching Condelor, Frelle Theresla," he replied.

"So?"

"So these people have wardens who fly above the Call's influence. I can see a wing-machine patrolling above the city with my telescope, and if he saw this tram moving he would be suspicious about why the deadhand lever had not been released."

Theresla closed her book and looked out over the flat pastures where rheas and emus grazed, as oblivious of the Call as she.

"It is such a bore to have humans who can defy the Call," she said as the tram shuddered to a halt. Steam began hissing through a valve in the boiler.

"The driver will be surprised to be within sight of Condelor and with a hot boiler too—but then *we* know nothing of that, do we?"

"Of course not, Fras Glasken. As always, I am pleased to have you in charge of such details. Speaking of details, they say that the current Bartolican fashion is for the women to display a great deal of breast."

Glasken twirled the points of his waxed mustache and wiggled his fingers.

"Perhaps I was unduly hasty in releasing the deadhand," he replied, but he sat down and clipped on his Call tether nevertheless. "So, do you still think we will find the aviad radicals in Condelor?"

"Fras Glasken, this coronation is one of the biggest gatherings of Mounthaven leaders that is possible. If they wish to buy allies and hatch plots they will do it here."

"There may be hundreds of them, and they will not be pleased to see us."

"So they may reveal themselves by trying to kill us," Theresla concluded with an open flourish of her arms.

"Frelle Theresla, I have ideas about dying asleep, in bed, as a very old man, and in the company of someone else's wife," Glasken grumbled.

"You will probably die soon, in great pain, and with your body riddled with bullet holes, Fras Glasken, just like the rest of us. In the meantime, are you ready to play the part of a suave lecher with no more moral restraint than a pig in a cakeshop?"

"Oink, oink," replied Glasken. "And will you be spying, stealing, lying, and killing people?"

"Oh yes. Ah, the driver is stirring. Best to speak only Old Anglian from now on."

Serjon Feydamor stood with his father, watching the Inspector General's staff sifting through the still smoking wreckage of the Bartolican gunwing and Pangaver fuel barrels. Serjon was now wearing his cap and guild crest, the gold radial compression engine of the engineers' guild. His crest was dull and grimy, yet every few minutes he took a handkerchief to polish the silver wings on his collar that marked him as a registered flyer.

"Of course this is only to be expected," Serjon pronounced solemnly, wiping at the silver wings yet again.

"What do you mean?" asked guildmaster Jeb Feydamor, wondering what his stepson had seen that everyone else had missed.

"This is thirteen weeks and thirteen years since Warden Darris made his first solo flight, I checked in the adjunct's register. Now he should have—"

"Serjon, give it a rest! We're guildsmen, not astrologers."

With that Feydamor turned away in exasperation, and began to slowly circle around the crash site. Serjon glanced across to Brantic's distant sailwing then went after his father.

"Warden Brantic's sailwing has 13 in its flock designator code," Serjon continued as they paced together. "I tried to warn him yesterday but he called me an ignorant Yarronese peon."

"You *are* an ignorant Yarronese peon," replied Feydamor testily. "You give the rest of us a bad name with your superstitions—*and* that badge!"

Jeb snatched the cap from Serjon, rubbed the gold radial engine crest on his sleeve until it shone out against the dark cloth, then jammed the cap back on his son's head. They passed an officer of the Bartolican merchant carbineers who was standing with his arms folded, also watching the investigation. Once the guildmaster and his stepson had their backs to him he smiled and nodded imperceptibly.

Warden-heir Alion Damaric of Yarron also stood at the crash site, paying his respects to the dead nobles. Thoughts and associations passed through his mind as he searched for a reason for the tragedy. Gunwings were kept in the air by fuel barrels and guildsmen's tents, yet how inglorious it was for a warden to end his life by smashing into a pile of barrels. He became aware of a girl nearby, a Bartolican noble with a loose plait of red hair that reached down to her knees. She had her mouth covered with her hands, and there were tears streaming from her eyes. The tiny pennons sewn onto the shoulders of her sleeves declared that she was of the royal house of the Airlord Designate. Alion walked across to her.

"A tragedy of the very worst kind," he said in Bartolican. "Did you know them?"

"Hardly at all," she replied, staring unfocused into the litter of black char. "I weep for the tragedy, but I weep with joy that they died honorably, in a gunwing. Others say they were fools, dying for the sake of a better view in the coronation, but . . ."

"They died honoring their new airlord, Semme. What better way could they have died? In bed? In a training flight?"

"Oh sair, you *do* understand—"

She turned, then caught sight of the gold Yarronese lacework on Alion's flight jacket. She backed away a step.

"Warden-heir Alion Damaric, at your service, Semme,"

he said, bowing from the waist. "I may be Yarronese, but I am not evil."

The girl recovered her composure, stepped forward again, and took his hand, bowing in turn.

"Please, your pardon, sair. I am Samondel of the Leovor estate. You, you startled me, I do apologize, again. Just now some ignorant Yarronese guildsman was saying that they died because of thirteen in a flock designator or some such rubbish."

"They died through chance, but chance also let them die honorably," Alion said solemnly. "There is nothing more to say."

They wandered away together. Alion gave the Bartolican princess a tour of the gunwings of his father's estate before escorting her back to the palace. As they passed the tents and wings of the Jannian estate a guildsman tapped Serjon's shoulder as he worked with his head beneath an engine cowling, hoping to get grease on his engineer's badge again.

"Always happens," said Pel Jemarial, guildmaster of Jannian's airframe guild. "Whenever there's a gathering of the flocks some young fools from the wrong side of a feud decide to fall in love."

Serjon looked out from the open cowling of the sailwing and glanced at the couple.

"Lucky fools," was all that he had to say to his warden's airframe guildmaster.

In spite of the hundreds of towns and cities that Rosenne Rodriguez had traveled to, she was still astounded by the magnificence of the capital of Greater Bartolica. The interdominion tramway led through the most imposing parts of the city: across wide canals, over boulevards teeming with people, under mighty arches, through tunnels, and finally over a huge stone bridge looking down along the processional avenue to the airlord's palace. The angular Sky Tower of the palace reached up above its other spires, as if standing guard over the ancient throne room's red-tile and stone arch roof, and parklands encircled the palace like a ruff of green lace.

Across the steam tram's cabin the envoy's three servants were observing the city as well. Theresla and Darien were the same age as the envoy, and all three women had their hair bound tightly and wrapped in scarves. Glasken wore a scarlet hat on which an ostrich feather bobbed.

"This is wonderful!" exclaimed Rosenne, clapping her hands as they passed within the flying buttresses of an ornate bridge whose extensions met above the trackway. "Unbelievable, fantastic, enchanting!"

"Wonderful," Theresla replied mechanically, attentive but less enthusiastic than her mistress.

Glasken was attentive too, but in the way that a bodyguard is attentive. The tramways had been laid to a plan, and that was to impress visitors arriving from other dominions. Two thousand years and six dozen generations of masons had made the city what it was, and nothing had been lost for a long time. Mounthaven's wars were not the type that laid cities waste.

The steam tram slowed as it approached the waystation and was switched into the Airlord's platform. The chuffing of the steam engine faded to hissing as the tram stopped amid acrid exhaust fumes and the sweet aroma of alcohol and seed oil. Wood-fired steam trams were banned from Condelor, as their exhausts soiled the stonework. Glasken opened the door and stepped out, then nodded to the envoy that it was safe. Inspector General Roric Hannan was waiting for the envoy, resplendent in the boulevard coat and gold chains that he was wearing for the viewing of the flypast later that day.

"The Airlord Designate's welcome to you, Semme Envoy Rosenne Rodriguez of Veraguay," he said in Old Anglian, with a manner that managed a mix of grace, dignity, deference, and superiority. "I am Inspector General Roric Hannan."

Rosenne bowed slightly, then looked Roric directly in the eyes.

"In all my travels from Veraguay, I have never seen such a beautiful city," she declared.

Hannan bowed again, the trace of a smile on his lips. She had said beautiful rather than magnificent, but she was nonetheless in awe of the capital. Greater Bartolica was indeed magnificent, beautiful, and more. Theresla and Darien stepped onto the stone platform and an official beside Hannan snapped his fingers. Two guards and a liaison clerk came forward.

"Your servants will be sent to prepare your new residence," Hannan told the envoy.

"I advise against it, Ladyship," Glasken rumbled warily. "My place is with you."

"Oh Juan, there is no danger," Rosenne replied. "I have all these Bartolican guards, but Theresla and Darien have only you."

"I was not hired to protect servants," Glasken replied firmly.

Hannan noted that Glasken had preserved his fitness against the years and wondered about the studded leather collar that encircled his neck. He was clean-shaven except for a heavily waxed and dyed mustache that sat like a spindle on his upper lip, and a pointed goatee beard. Theresla was obviously Rosenne's chief servant: she held her head up proudly and had authority in her every gesture. Darien stayed back and kept her eyes down, not saying a word.

Hannan took a deep breath. "Aureate, make sure that the servants of Envoy Rodriguez are taken to their quarters in the Enclave of Dominions. Give them whatever help they need to settle Semme Rodriguez and make her feel at home."

He gestured to a promenade barge that was tied up in the canal that flowed beside the tram station platform. The gilt-painted barge was about twenty-five feet long, and the soft, whispery chuffing of a four-cycle compression engine was coming from somewhere beneath the decking. It was open on the sides, but the sun was held off by a red canopy fringed with green and gold tassels. There was no sign of any crew as the party stepped aboard and clipped their Call tethers to the retaining ring in the middle. One of the guards cast off the ropes and Hannan said simply, "The palace wingfield."

The note of the barge's engine rose a little in pitch as they pulled away from the quay and out into the canal.

"We Bartolicans like to keep the mechanics out of sight," said the guard captain as Glasken looked about in astonishment.

"And why is that, Sair Captain?" he asked in confident Old Anglian.

"So that they will not get ideas about being part of the vista, so that they will remember their places as mere cogs in a greater machine. There are men beneath the decking, although there is little more than a foot of clearance. They crawl about on their bellies, tending the compression engine and peeping through slits in the bow to steer."

"This is an impressive welcome."

"A stranger made welcome is a friend to be. You are just in time for the flypast of wardens and allocation of standing ranks for the coronation tomorrow. We Bartolicans take it very seriously, in fact three nobles died this morning in their efforts to get here in time for those ceremonies."

They glided amid gardens of flowering vines hanging down from the stone sides of the canal and trailing in the water. All the bridges were drawn back, even though the low barge could have cleared them easily. The captain explained to Glasken that they were in one of the fleet of royal barges, and nobody was permitted to be above any barge of the Airlord of Bartolica.

"That's the official story, at any rate. The truth is that a blind beggar named Rinol Harz pissed on Airlord Jumeril the Fourth in 3791. The poor wretch was seized and shot before he'd even had time to lace up, then Jumeril had every bridge in the city put on hinges. The Yarronese later erected a statute honoring Sair Harz in Forian, their capital."

"So the Bartolicans and Yarronese are not on the best of terms?"

"Not for more centuries than the number of my lovers, no. We of Bartolica strive for the glories of the Age of Cybers. We seek to emulate the machines of that glorious time, using servants instead of cybers, all the while striving to rebuild the cyber technology itself. The Yarronese wallow in grease and rivets without remembering what those rivets and that grease are leading toward. What is your level of technical achievement in Veraguay, Fras Glasken?"

Ah, the thin edge of civility that precedes the wedge of espionage, Glasken thought.

"I am only from Mexhaven, but the envoy often speaks of home. The land is mountainous, far more so than yours. They have walled roads, cable-cage railcars, terraced farmlands, and rangepens of cobarci."

"Cobarci?" asked the captain.

"They are like little, fluffy pigs, and are not affected by the Call. The villages are small, and there are only five towns with more than ten thousand souls. The cathedrals and universities are in those towns."

"But where do your artisans work?"

"They go where demand leads them."

"That seems unworkable. What about the governments and armies of their dominions?"

"The roads are built into the sides of mountains and are easily defended by the town militias. The Conciliar members have no specific capital or palace, they travel from town to town. They are artisans of organization, just like blacksmiths or tailors."

They passed the Enclave of Dominions, where the foreign diplomats were housed. Rosenne said that it reminded her of a university: all parkland with ivy-shrouded buildings blending in with the trees. One tower nearby reached high above the trees, a conical structure with a circular gallery near the top. Hannan proudly announced that this was part of his mansion. Presently they passed through a gate in the wall of the outer grounds of the palace, and Hannan noticed a lone figure at one of the stone landings.

"Odd, that's Warden Stanbury," he remarked. "I wonder why he's not over at the wingfield for the flypast."

Warden Stanbury paced restlessly beside the palace canal, hardly believing that his governor was dead. Carabas had promised, and Carabas never broke a promise. "Your way will be clear for honors," he had said. Stanbury had thought the man had the ear of the Airlord Designate, and had not expected the disaster that had followed.

He plucked a sky-blue rose from a bush beside the stone barge quay and began methodically breaking the thorns off the stem and flicking them into the water. Carabas finally appeared in an oargig with another man rowing, and both of them wore the uniform of the merchant carbineers. He beckoned Stanbury to join them. The well-mannered Carabas was in his late forties, and although he walked with a slight limp he was as lean, strong, and fit as any warden in his prime.

"It is chronicled that roses were never blue before the engineers of the twenty-first century took a hand to them," said Carabas with a neat, circular gesture to the bloom in Stanbury's hand.

"What of him?" Stanbury asked, looking to the lean but muscular rower.

"He knows all that I do, Warden Stanbury. You may speak safely in front of him."

Stanbury stepped into the oargig and they pulled out into the center of the canal. There were other boats on the water, all full of noisy excursionists and bedecked with flowers. The rower began to pace a barge in which a brass band was playing.

"Well, how did you do it?" hissed Stanbury, his heart pounding.

"I do a great deal, Sair Stanbury," replied Carabas. "To what do you refer?"

"The gunwing crash that killed the Governor of the East Region!"

"The Inspector General's inquisitors have been over the wreckage but found nothing."

"That's just the field inspection. The guild scrutiny will not be so easy to escape."

"There is nothing obvious to find, a mere pinprick in the bottom of the atomizer's floatwell, nothing more. A stick of wax sealed it shut initially, but the bypass pipe on which the stick rested became hot and caused the wax to melt within a half hour. After that the engine began to burn an unreasonable amount of compression spirit. The fire burned all traces of wax from the engine, and who would notice one tiny hole extra amid all the other damage?"

"So your people *did* do it. That's bad, the hole will be found when the pieces are scrutinized in the guild chamber."

"Good, it is meant to be found."

Stanbury flopped back in his seat and flung the blue rose into the water. The enigmatic carbineer clearly had agendas that he could not even guess at.

"Flight guildsmen guard their wardens' gunwings better than they guard their own balls. How did your people do it, are they Callwalkers?"

"If you learned the truth, Sair Stanbury, your hands would be too unsteady to take your gunwing up for a duel."

Carabas leaned back, waving one hand in time with the music from the barge up ahead. Stanbury folded his arms and shuddered.

"Did you have to kill him?" Stanbury asked in a voice that was barely audible above the music.

Carabas shook his head as if chiding a foolish child. "The Governor killed *himself*, good sair. The sweep of the Call is only nine miles deep, he could easily have glided to a field, road, or pond beyond the sweep and made a forced landing once the compression engine died."

"That would have delayed his governor's arrival until after the coronation seating had been declared."

"Ah yes, but what is a life against an event? Alas, he was determined to land at the palace in time to secure a place that befitted his rank in the coronation ceremony. He paid the price of hubris and ambition."

Stanbury had the look of a dirkfang cat cornered by a gang of birdherders, even though the day was warm, sunny, and tranquil, and Condelor resembled nothing more threatening than one huge carnival.

"The Governor was not a bad man," said Stanbury miserably. "He presented me with my warden bars . . . I even flirted with his wife. I saw her body being carried away. Gah, her hair was burned off and her skin was charred black and oozing blood."

"One way or another, Sair Stanbury, you would have had to destroy him—in reputation if not in body. Your only problem now is that Warden Desondrian is his named successor and will be appointed tomorrow unless you declare him to be unfit."

Stanbury sat forward and hunched his shoulders as a gunwing droned overhead trailing streamers of colored smoke.

"Desondrian is sure to hand the black glove to me if I do that. How will you help me to fight him? We are evenly matched for any duel."

"I do not help, Sair Warden Stanbury, I provide opportunities. You have your opportunity, and now you must cultivate it if you want to seize a magnificent destiny. Remember that chances like this come only once in a lifetime.

Declare an objection to Desondrian's appointment, sair, then fight for what is yours to take."

They were approaching another quay by now, and Warden Stanbury was as anxious to be done with the meeting as he had been to commence it.

"I have been doing some research in the registers," he said, looking up at a gunwing practicing aerobatics. "Your birth, studies, and career are all recorded, but up until four years ago people have trouble recalling you."

Carabas smiled easily, as if he had anticipated the question long before Stanbury had thought to ask it.

"The Marquis de Carabas was a character in a very old fairy tale. He was a man of importance from very far away who did not quite exist. I am all of those things, Warden Stanbury, so I am called Carabas."

Juan Glasken and the captain of Hannan's escort had by now discovered that they shared a strong interest in women. While Hannan pointed out the glories of the ancient palace to the Veraguay envoy, across the barge a rather less tasteful conversation was taking place between the captain and Glasken.

"Your Bartolican women, do they, ah, jiggy jump?" asked Glasken.

The captain blinked at the man's boldness, then smiled knowingly and leaned closer.

"They have strong motherly instincts, Sair Glasken. First make them feel sorry for you. Then—and only then—pay them compliments. Bartolican women tend to be generous of figure, and cleavages in particular are a matter of high fashion just now."

"Cleavages and I are old friends from decades past."

"Mind out, Sair Glasken, that you engage their sympathy first. Otherwise you may find yourself with a slap on the face."

"My face is no stranger to slaps, Captain. Love and war cannot be engaged in without casualties."

"Of course, Glasken, I understand. Seduction is part of my stock-in-trade in the diplomatic service. Public lies are shouted in councils and courts, but secret truths are whispered in beds." The captain gripped Glasken's arm suddenly and inclined his head toward the stone quay that the barge was approaching. "That rather formidable battle tram on the quay is Semme Laurelene Hannan, the Inspector General's wife. Don't waste your time looking for her sympathy."

Glasken looked in the direction he had indicated to see a woman in her mid-forties who was a little above average height and considerably above average weight. She was surveying the canal imperiously. Her hair was bound back tightly to hang in a plait festooned with gold and red tassels, while her blue, ankle-length skirt was cascading with flounces. Obviously meant to disguise her figure yet they expand it all the more, he decided. As was the current Bartolican fashion, she displayed an expanse of cleavage that was to Glasken more awesome than alluring.

The barge docked and Glasken was first to step onto the quay. Laurelene swept grandly along the flagstones, with a little page boy running beside her holding a long-handled parasol high to keep the sun from the flawless white skin of her face and cleavage. She stopped before Glasken.

"Sair Envoy, I am Semme Laurelene Hannan," she declared. "I thought I should meet you at least, but I cannot stay. The Airlord Designate's wife has asked me to—"

By now Glasken had bowed so low over the white expanse of her breasts that the waxed point of his beard had dipped into her cleavage. She let out a squawk of surprise but otherwise retained her composure.

"I regret that I am but the envoy's guard," Glasken explained as he straightened. "The envoy is safe in the company of your good husband."

Hannan was helping Rosenne from the barge. Laurelene stood speechless while the quite beautiful Veraguay envoy swept along the stone quay, escorted by the Inspector General.

"Semme Hannan, my thanks for troubling yourself to meet me here," she said without waiting for her escort's introduction.

A minor diplomatic incident was averted by the arrival of an official of the Airlord Designate, who came clattering down the stone stairs and whispered something to Laurelene.

"I regret that I must leave my husband to look after you," said Laurelene to the envoy in a voice as cold as the north wind. "The wife of my new ruler has need of me."

She cast Hannan a glare that said he would soon suffer for this, then turned and ascended the steps with her parasol boy trotting beside her. Rosenne, Hannan, and Glasken climbed the steps together, then stood watching Laurelene sweeping away down the path.

"An ... extraordinary woman," said Glasken in a language that neither of his companions could understand as they set off along the path to the wingfield.

"Uh, your pardon, Sair Glasken?" said Hannan.

"Ah, she is a gracious woman, mistaking me for an envoy," Glasken replied in Old Anglian.

"Gracious?" snorted Hannan. "I would not even wish her married to my worst enemy. Well, maybe my *worst* enemy, but nobody else."

The envoy took Hannan's hand and squeezed it, smiling warmly at him. Hannan was so startled by the gesture that he stared blankly at her as they walked.

"Poor Inspector General, there is little mercy in your life, is there?" she said gently.

"Why, I—I don't know what you mean."

"I see it in your eyes, in the lines on your face, I hear it in the stiffness of your voice. You were not prepared for this meeting, were you, Sair Hannan?"

"You have a sharp eye, Semme," he admitted wearily.

"Then tell me, dear Sair Hannan, why did you come to

welcome me while the rest of the nobles are making merry
at the palace?"

Hannan gave a sigh that almost turned into a sob. Somehow talking to Rosenne was like collapsing into a soft,
welcoming bed after a very bad day. One simply *wanted*
to trust her and depend on her.

"My wife, Laurelene, was supposed to meet you. She
said she had better things to do than trade grunts with some
barbarian yokel, so I came in her stead."

Rosenne put a hand on Hannan's shoulder and kissed
him on the cheek. "You grunt most charmingly, Sair Hannan. Seeing that your wife is so busy, would you do me
the honor of being my escort on this day?"

The woman admired him. That single fact stood out like
a gunwing in a clear sky. Hannan paused to bow low to
her, sweeping off his hat to reveal a prematurely grey and
seriously balding head.

"Gracious lady, of course, how could I refuse when your
charm all but reduces me to tears?"

Some paces ahead, Glasken and the captain were oblivious of the rapidly flowering romance.

"We are about to see wings and meet wardens," the
captain explained. "Wardens are our warrior nobility. Each
of their families maintains hereditary engineers, airframe
builders, and other such guildsmen to keep their gunwings
and sailwings maintained and flying."

"So being a warden is an expensive business?" asked
Glasken.

"If you need to ask the cost, you are too poor to qualify.
Look, there's another flock of gunwings arriving for the
coronation week."

To the north a wedge of dots was moving across the
sky. There were three of the little aircraft, and Glasken
soon saw that they were awkward, triwing shapes painted
with heraldic symbols and codes. Their compression engines were loud and insistent as they passed overhead.

"Only Yarronese gunwings," the captain said with a

sneer. "Now then, among our dominions the wardens settle the more intractable disputes in duels with their gunwings. They are armed with reaction guns mounted in the nose."

"Ah, what are reaction guns?"

"They are guns that use the reaction of each shot to reload. They can fire hundreds of times in a single minute."

"But should a Call come past while they are flying they would be as good as dead!" Glasken exclaimed innocently.

"Oh no, a gunwing flying above treetop height is not affected by the Call, Sair Glasken. Proximity with the ground or contact with the ground is required, by either rope, building, tree, or whatever. Even should they land during a Call, they would not blank out until they were within about fifty feet of the ground. I—"

He had turned, to see Rosenne with her arm on Hannan's. They were laughing and smiling, oblivious of the crowd and splendor around them.

"Sair Glasken, remember when you most bravely dipped your beard into Semme Laurelene's cleavage just now?" the captain asked, turning away quickly.

"It was something of an accident."

"Well my master is currently doing something far braver."

Flown as the preferred weapon of wardens, the gunwings of Mounthaven's dominions were what the warhorse had been to the European knights of three millennia earlier. While hard to tune, expensive to build and maintain, underpowered, difficult to master, and dangerous to fly, they were nearly invincible to all but another gunwing, as well as being the very soul of wardenly status.

Only the wardens and a few of their support guildsmen flew, looking down on the countryside like gods and traveling between dominions within mere hours.

Serjon Feydamor's family had been in the engineers' guild for centuries, and they worked for the estate of Jannian, one of the principal wardens of Yarron. Warden Jannian had sent his airframe guild, engineers' guild, fuelers, and armorers in advance by steam trams, along with spare parts and tools. Serjon had flown there in a spare sailwing, but Jannian was to arrive in his gunwing. Jannian was well known for making spectacular entrances, however, and he had sworn to fly not from his estate on the border, but all the way from the Yarronese capital.

Jeb Feydamor stood looking up at the sky with Serjon and fueler guildsman Bellaroy on the part of the wingfield assigned to the Yarronese.

"A stupid and dangerous gesture," Bellaroy said yet again. "Flying from Median to here would have been enough in itself, but Warden Jannian just had to fly directly from Forian. After what happened this morning, too."

"It's more than a gesture," said Feydamor with resigned understanding. "It declares superiority. This says that his wealth is such that he can rail in his own complete crews and not depend on Bartolicans, while his gunwings have such a range that no Bartolican gunwing can touch."

The droning of compression engines became distinct above the background bustle of the wingfield tents and stalls, and through his field glasses Feydamor resolved three triwings approaching from the south. The gunwing and two T-class sailwings circled the palace once, then landed in quick succession. Warden Jannian's gunwing taxied to the maintenance tents between its two less powerful companions. The Bartolican officials who had come to greet him gathered around the gunwing as the canopy was raised. The flyer within removed a flight cap, but the head that emerged was that of a girl, no more than eighteen years of age. Her thin, alert face was framed by dark brown, shoulder-length hair, and wary brown eyes regarded them through the twin oval marks left on her face by her goggles.

"Warden Jannian is in the starboard T-class," she said as they stared at her speechlessly.

She hurriedly ducked down out of sight within the cockpit. The outraged officials strode off to Jannian's T-class sailwing just as Serjon arrived to collect the logbooks. He stopped in astonishment when the head of Jemarial's daughter Bronlar reappeared.

"What are you doing here?" he demanded.

"I'm pleased to see you too, Serjon."

"But you're in the warden's gunwing!"

"Sair Serjon, I weigh ninety-one pounds, the warden weighs twice that. An extra tank was rigged just behind my head with a twelve extra gallons of compression spirit for the journey. I landed with nearly a gallon to spare."

"You flew this thing all the way from Forian?" he exclaimed.

"Shush, the warden will hear."

The warden did not hear. There was a loud exchange going on between him and the Bartolican officials as they walked back past the gunwing.

"It is the greatest possible insult to the Airlord of Bartolica to let a mere child, and a *girl*, fly the very symbol of wardenly authority and chivalry," the wingfield adjunct was insisting loudly.

"Bronlar is the daughter of my airframe guildmaster and is an accredited flyer," retorted Jannian. "She is permitted to have flyer status in order to test gunwings after maintenance or alterations."

"That rule applies to *apprentices*!" cried the current duty warden.

"The letter of the rule says 'child': age and sex are not mentioned," Warden Jannian countered.

The adjunct's composure weakened. "That cannot be true," he spluttered.

"It *is* true," said the wingfield herald reluctantly. "The word is 'child' rather than 'son', so that adopted sons and stepsons can be included for guildsmen without sons."

"Why were girls not specifically excluded?" demanded the duty warden.

" 'Son, adopted son, stepson, or any other male deemed

to be the son by law and in line of succession of a guildsman' is twenty-three words, 'child' is but a single word,"
the herald explained while counting out words on his fingers. "When the Guild Charter was simplified last century
such abbreviations became common."

"But nobody dreamed that the intent of the reformers
would be abused like this!" interjected the adjunct.

"Meaning that Bronlar is permitted by law to make any
initial test flight," added Jannian.

"A three-hundred-mile test flight?" scoffed the wingfield
adjunct.

"It was the first flight after the addition of the extra
tank," Jannian assured him.

Bronlar's status as a flyer was known in courtly circles
as a matter of debate rather than fact. Occasionally women
would ascend to the throne as airlords of dominions, and
one could not be an airlord without being able to fly. When
this happened the airlord designate was given sufficient
flight training to ascend solo and fire a practice volley at
a target kite. This done, they would be accredited as a
warden but never ascend again, except as a passenger. A
governor's wife had learned to fly with the issue of female
accreditation still unresolved among Yarronese wardenry,
but she had died in a training accident. The rank of flyer
had been conferred upon her as a gesture of sympathy to
the very popular Governor Sartov—and because she was
safely dead.

On the other hand Bronlar was female, alive, young,
from the artisan class, and superior to most youths with
comparable flight experience. Governor Sartov himself had
pointed out to Jannian the loophole in the inter-dominion
regulations that had allowed Bronlar's accreditation to be
passed, but now debate was raging on whether the loophole should be closed or whether the talented Bronlar
should be allowed to progress to the squires' lists. The
Bartolicans had thought that the girl had been lucky
enough to survive one or two solo flights in a sailwing,

and was just a pawn in some Yarronese political dispute. Now she had arrived in a gunwing, having set a record for gunwing endurance that would probably have to be entered in the inter-dominion Annals of Honor.

The wingfield adjunct looked back to the Yarronese gunwing in time to see the diminutive Yarronese girl climb out of the cockpit. She stood on a wing, hurriedly combing her hair in the chase mirror, then brushed strands from the glittering embroidery of her flight jacket. That slight touch of feminine grooming was too much for the adjunct. His face flushed with anger again, and he threw up his hands in frustration. This was a clear abuse of the intent of the Guild Charter, even though no specific breach had taken place. He strode away in the direction of his tower while Jannian and the duty warden walked off toward the pennant pole, still arguing.

Bronlar jumped to the ground, then gazed after them as their voices faded in the distance. Serjon began an assessment check on the gunwing that she had been flying. He was a year older than she, also lightly built but taller—in fact at an inch below six feet tall, he was a giant among flyers. Wavy black hair covered his ears and collar, while his protuberant green eyes gave him a somewhat manic aspect. His attitude did little to dispel this impression. As Bronlar sat on the grass writing her flight report, Serjon withdrew his head from the access hatch and glared at her, his fists on his hips.

"There's no spare gallon in these tanks, Bronlar," he said firmly. "Your indicator float was ill calibrated. You landed with only the fuel in the feedlines. Thirteen perits of compression spirit, to be exact."

"Yet here I am, alive and—"

"By the grace of fortune alone!" he snapped. "Only this morning some Bartolican idiot managed to kill himself and his two passengers while trying to do less than you just did. Thirteen perits! That's very unlucky."

"Then where is my bad luck?"

Serjon glared at her, then held up the measuring glass.

"Bad luck is bad luck. Today you collected some, to-morrow it will poison you."

"Warden Jannian's judgment was good," said Bronlar. "I do whatever he says. He's always right."

"The warden's luck was good, not his judgment," insisted Serjon through clenched teeth. "Had he been flying this gunwing it would have come down before he'd even crossed the Bartolican border. Besides, *I'm* the neophyte flyer on the estate. *I* should have flown *this* gunwing *here*."

"I know," replied Bronlar. "But you weigh more than me and would have run out of compression spirit over the mountains."

Serjon was annoyed to catch himself practically admitting his jealousy, but a fight was a fight whether the cause was just or not.

"*You* are just a symbol for Jannian's reforms," said Serjon, gesturing up to the gunwing. Bronlar slapped his hand down.

"You and everyone assume that I'm allowed to do what I do because I am a girl and a symbol. Well I'm a skilled flyer too! I'm good at nursing a wing along and traveling great distances. I can hang just above stall speed—"

"I'm better at shooting target kites—"

"Aye, but this was about *distance*."

"You flew here without colors," Serjon now declared. "That's very bad luck, ascending in service or anger without colors."

"Luck is what you make of *opportunities*, Serjon. Besides, I do have colors, see here."

Serjon peered at the bunch of ribbons fastened to a tag on the right arm of Bronlar's red and green leaf pattern flight jacket. One had the embroidered crest of the Jannian estate, another was for the engineers guild, another for an unmarried girl, a three was embroidered on the next for the girl was a third daughter, and on the next was a very familiar family crest. Ramsdel, of the flight fabric division of the airframe guild, sauntered up while Serjon was making his examination.

"Kallien!" exclaimed Serjon as he put the embroidered codes together. "My own sister!"

"She helped me make my jacket. I wear her colors out of thanks."

"Nice needlework on the jacket," said Ramsdel approvingly, "but there should be more and smaller leaves—and in gilt thread. Gilt is definitely you."

"But *I* should wear Kallien's colors," cried Serjon.

"You have another four sisters, you wear their colors in rotation," retorted Bronlar.

"But, but I'm her brother, she should care for me first."

"Would you want me to have ascended in service with no colors, Sair Serjon? That's bad luck, you know."

At a total loss for words, Serjon scanned both Bronlar and the gunwing for thirteen of anything, but to no avail. His shoulders sagged and he scuffed the grass at his feet.

"Perhaps I'd better prepare colors for myself," he said at last, suddenly gloomy with resignation.

"It should be the same as Kallien's," said Ramsdel, missing the sarcasm intended, "except that the maroon ribbon with three will have to be one and . . . what color? No man has ever prepared colors before, there is no precedent in heraldry—not officially at any rate."

"The airlord flies over his estate burning a violet flare on the night a son is born, and maroon for a daughter," suggested Bronlar.

"Oh, congratulations, it's a boy," said Serjon.

"I'll do you a set of colors for another half hour of flight time in the trainer sailwing," offered Ramsdel.

Serjon rolled his eyes. "Why not? If more girls keep ascending it may be the only way I'll get one to notice me."

They were interrupted by the appearance of Bronlar's father, Pel Jemarial, who was striding over and smiling broadly. Serjon thrust his head back into the engine's access hatch.

"Bronlar, darling, what a girl you are!" he cried, hugging her and whirling her around. "Three hundred miles."

"The weather helped, Papa, it was calm nearly all the way."

"Pah, even a raging mountain storm would not have stopped you. Come along now, your mother has your trunk. A flying jacket is hardly suitable for your first coronation."

Serjon withdrew his head from the engine and stared after them as they walked away toward the accommodation tents. Ramsdel was tracing out the current Bartolican ladies' fashion for high, wide cleavages on his own chest, a fashion for which Bronlar was not particularly well endowed. Ramsdel had no invitation to the coronation, but had somehow secured work as a standard-bearer so that he could note the fashions and tailoring at the great ceremony. His small, wiry frame, curly black hair, and olive skin allowed him to pass as someone much younger, although he was actually older than Serjon.

Serjon had no invitation to the coronation; he was just a flyer of the lowest rank. He began pumping compression spirit into the reserve tanks to recalibrate the indicator float of the gunwing, all the while holding his mind in a painless blank.

6 May 3960: Condelor

The coronation of Leovor VII of Greater Bartolica was as successful as a court herald's wildest dreams might conjure. The day had begun overcast. The Airlord Designate arrived in a compression-engine barge and did a circuit of the six-mile canal moat that surrounded the inner gardens of the palace. Children on the banks flung rose petals into the water before him, and chosen Bartolican wardens cir-

cled overhead in their gunwings trailing smoke in the Leovor colors. By the end of Leovor's circuit, the overcast
had broken to show patches of blue, but the weather still
seemed unwilling to provide its blessing. The barge
stopped at the outer bank near the Grand Bridge of As-
cension, and the young heir went ashore, called his name
to the sentries, and demanded that the bridge be lowered.

Fifty thousand citizens watched as the huge ashwood
bridge rumbled down to rest gently on the stone bank of
the canal. Midway across the bridge the Airlord Designate
was challenged by the court herald, who barred his path
with a gilt-handled silk whip. The heir proved his lineage
by a genealogical scroll that he was carrying. The herald
then gave his whip to Leovor, stripped his own court finery
and regalia to the waist, and knelt for nine ceremonial
strokes of the silk whip.

The citizens cheered their approval while the Airlord
Designate symbolically asserted his authority over his own
court with each stroke. Leovor noted with satisfaction that
by a slight flick on the downward stroke he could leave
impressive red marks on the herald's skin without seeming
to be brutal. The ceremonial flogging over, an adjunct
stepped forward with an inlaid, lacquered box, into which
Leovor placed the whip and closed the lid. With an odd
little pang he realized that the next time the lid was raised
he would be dead and his own heir would be about to
whip a herald.

The Airlord Designate walked the rest of the way across
the bridge, through the gates to the palace gardens and
along the promenade between the stone watersteps to the
open doors of the reception plaza. Not once did the sun
break through to shine upon him. He crossed the mosaic
of ninety-five thousand separate stone squares in a full-
color rendering of the gunwing flown four hundred years
earlier by Delvrian II at the Battle of Green River. An-
tiphonal choirs sang a hymn to Leovor's authority and justice, and at last he emerged through the ironbound oak

doors of the throne room. Not one stumble, Leovor thought
with relief.

The assembled nobles of Bartolica and the foreign dignitaries and officials all bowed, prostrated, saluted, curt-
sied, or covered their faces with their hands with a sound
as if a strong wind were rushing through the throne room.
Leovor then walked to the throne, seated himself, and
waited for the Bishop of Greater Bartolica to approach
with the crown. A choir of sons and daughters of Bartolican wardens began to sing to his health and wished him
an improbably long reign while the Bishop approached.
Just then the sun broke through the clouds and shone
through the glass facets and tinted mirrors in the roof and
southern walls, concentrating its rays so that Leovor
gleamed with multicolored lights as he sat on the throne.
The courtiers gasped at the sudden spectacle. The choir
stopped in mid-bar with shock, then quickly resumed.
Even the bishop took a step back and nearly let the crown
drop. Seconds later trumpets blared and choirs all through
the palace sang the anthem of Greater Bartolica as Leovor
was crowned in a blaze of light that the auspiciously lucky
break in the clouds had bestowed.

The Bishop ascended a stone dias bound with strips of
gold. He cleared his throat.

"Your Majesty, nobles of Bartolica, worthy guests from
other dominions, look about you at the splendor of this
palace, and of the mighty yet beautiful city of Condelor.
Stop and consider for a moment how such a magnificent
capital can be maintained in the face of the three scourges.

"The Call sweeps across our land every few days and
seeks to lure us away in a mindless reverie, yet we are still
here when the Call has passed, three hours later. Why are
we here in the face of the mighty, the irresistible Call? The
streets are built to gently guide folk allured by the Call
into curved haven walls, the Call towers ring out a warning
of at least ten minutes as the invisible allure stalks over
from the east, and there are many public tethers and tether

rails. Those in trams or barges are safely tethered, and deadhand brakes and anchors stop them safely. Overhead at least one warden is always flying, watching over this city and above the Call's accursed reach. For all of this you must thank the Airlord.

"The Sentinels are the second scourge. Should anyone be so full of pride and confidence to build a barge, tram, regal, or gunwing of greater length or breadth than twenty-nine feet six inches, what would be its fate? When next a Sentinel Star passed overhead by day or by night, and if that vehicle was moving, it would be seared to ash with such speed that the blink of an eye could well mask its passing. Nevertheless, nobles may fly in safety, steam trams carry merchants and their goods across mountains and deserts on rails of wood shod with steel, barges ply our rivers and canals, and pushdrays rumble along our country roads behind teams of free, hearty laborers. The inspectors, the standardeers, the guildsmen, and the artisans that keep our civilization flourishing within that confinement of twenty-nine feet six inches, all of those men are under the direct patronage of the Airlord of Bartolica.

"And the third scourge, that which kills electrical essence devices: how can it be that we have flourished without the electrical engines and lamps for two thousand years? It is because our Airlord is the patron of workshops, artisan halls, and other such places of research, and these develop ways to climb back to the ancient achievements without electrical essence. Such research gave us the compression engine many centuries ago, and moved war into the sky where it is harmless.

"In the twenty years past that Airlord Parttral the Fourth reigned, there have been less than a thousand Bartolicans lost to the Call. In that same time not a single vehicle has been burned by the Sentinels. Surely this is Divine blessing on both his rule and the Bartolican way. Today the clouds parted to enshrine Airlord Leovor in light as he was crowned, and who can deny that this is a sign of better things to come? Warden noblemen will patrol the skies to keep Greater Bartolica safe from foreign invasion and warned against the Call. Squires, guildsmen, and artisans will keep the wings, compression engines, and guns maintained as they have for uncounted centuries. Inspectors, clerks, and merchants will travel the vastness of Bartolica and preserve its unity, and the estatiers and their tenants will keep our tables laden and our wardrobes full.

"Let us now pray for the blessing of a prosperous and glorious reign under our new ruler, Airlord Leovor the Seventh of Greater Bartolica."

The bishop led the chant, and all but Leovor himself joined in the responses. As he sat presiding over his first grand ceremony it seemed to the new Airlord of Bartolica that the wingfield disaster of the previous day had been such a terrible misfortune that it had sponged up all the bad luck that could possibly befall the coronation ceremony. Heaven itself had obviously—and publicly—blessed his coronation.

Nevertheless, his first official duty of appointing a new governor for the East Region was still to come. His protocol advisers had been frantically coaching him for the Governor's investiture in every spare moment since the very hour that the gunwing crashed, however, and Leovor actually felt relaxed and confident about the words and procedures. The preliminary report from the Inspector General had been presented, and it mentioned that nothing suspicious had been found in the wreckage. Warden Darris, who had also died in the disaster, had been named as the dead governor's recommended successor. In the opinion of the Office of Character and Heraldry, Warden Desondrian of Lemihara was the next in line for the position.

Within the crowd that packed the throne room the envoy from Veraguay and her guard were following the ceremony as best they could. They could understand only Old Anglian, the common scholarly language, but all the coronation's speeches and declarations were in Bartolican.

Glasken felt a tug at his sleeve, and he turned to see a maid from the Hannan household. Although not a short woman by any means, she had to go up on her toes to whisper in Glasken's ear. Never one to miss any opportunity, he bent down to listen and slipped an arm about her waist.

"Oh! Sair, ah, the Inspector General wishes the Veraguay envoy to come to a soiree in five days," she whispered rapidly.

"Why not tell her yourself?" Glasken whispered back, his lips brushing her ear.

"Sair Glasken, the, ah, Inspector General does not want unseemly rumors . . ."

Her voice trailed off. Glasken nodded knowingly.

"So, he has the message delivered as if you and I have a tryst instead. Lucky me."

"Oh Sair, I would never presume such a thing."

"Ah, unlucky me," Glasken sighed.

Her face suddenly displayed a grin, and she gave him a little nudge with her hip.

"Well, we should act the part out I suppose," she said coyly.

"Join me when we go into the gardens later. I shall have a reply from the envoy and . . . we may speak more easily."

"Sair Glasken, ask her only to hold the evening free. A formal invitation will only be delivered with an hour's notice. The wife of the Inspector General is not at all understanding where the Veraguay envoy is concerned."

"I understand," said Glasken, allowing his hand to slide from her waist to caress her rump.

The maid had no more to say, but she lingered for another minute before melting into the close-packed crowd. When she had gone the envoy took Glasken by the arm and whispered to him.

"So you are making friends already, Sair Glasken?"

"Only exploring diplomatic channels, Semme Envoy.

Oh, and by the way, I believe that a certain Bartolican wishes to explore your own diplomatic channel."

"Would he be an Inspector General?"

"He would, and he wishes to invite you to an evening of refined pleasures on May the eleventh. You are advised to keep the evening free and expect a late summoning."

"I am disposed to accept such advice. He is a dear, well-meaning, and vulnerable man. Why can't you be like that, Sair Glasken?"

"Because lecherous, shiftless wretches have a better time of it. I shall pass your disposition on to his maid."

"You must come along and protect me when I attend. His wife is a dragon."

Just then the Bishop ended the prayers. The court herald called for attention, then announced that Airlord Leovor would speak. Fighting an automatic impulse to stand, Leovor declared from the throne his intention to appoint a new governor as his first act of office. The crown had been on his head for only minutes, and it was a great display of statecraft and maturity. His father had merely declared a week of festivities at his own coronation two decades earlier. Leovor enunciated the prescribed words clearly, missing none, and managed quite a commanding tone. When he had finished, the court herald stepped forward and the Airlord relaxed everything but the muscles of his face and his bearing. His part was over, and he was practically melting into the throne with relief. Nothing could go wrong now.

"Warden Alexes Desondrian, come forward in the name of the Airlord!" commanded the court herald, and the noble stepped before the throne and went down on one knee. "In the name of the Airlord I ask if you are willing to accept the honor of this appointment?"

The question was indirect, so as to avoid the chance of a slight to the Airlord in the event of a refusal. In this case there was no such danger.

"I accept," answered Desondrian.

"If any peer of the Convocation of Bartolican Wardens sees fit to warn the Airlord of an impediment to this appointment, let him speak now," declared the court herald, grandly and gravely.

"I do!" cried Warden Stanbury, stepping forward.

The court herald froze with surprise. He had never heard a challenge in a dozen such appointments, and he had to think frantically to remember the form of reply. The Airlord had even less experience in such matters, but knew enough of the ceremony to realize that it was beneath the dignity of a monarch to be directly involved. He remained discreetly impassive and above it all.

"Declare your name and wardenate," ordered the court herald.

"I am Warden Mikal Stanbury of the Wardenate Stanbury."

"Warden Mikal Stanbury, state your grounds or hold your peace."

"The late Governor Movael Merrotin, Semme Merrotin, and Warden Darris were well known to me, and I am sure that they would never have taken such a foolish risk as led to their deaths. I petition for a criminal inquisition before Governor Movael Merrotin's successor ascends to that office. I register my dismay at the unseemly haste with which Sair Alexes Desondrian has accepted the appointment, without the scrutiny chamber's results having cleared Warden Darris' judgment as contributing to his own death."

Desondrian had not in fact wished to ascend to the office so quickly after his friend's death, but the new airlord's courtiers had been anxious to embellish the coronation ceremonies with an appointment. Faced with blaming his airlord for undue haste or defending the insult himself and thereby acting as champion of the Airlord, Desondrian chose the path of honor and sacrifice. He rose to his feet and walked forward, removing the black glove from his right hand. Standing before Stanbury, he held out the glove, then dropped it before the challenger's fingers could close on it. Rather than bend before Desondrian to accept the glove, Stanbury put his hands on his hips and spat, hitting the glove squarely. Desondrian reddened and his lips pressed together. After an exchange of murderous glares both turned and bowed to Leovor.

"The Airlord has deemed that this same day the position of governor is to be filled," the court herald concluded, "so in duty to the Airlord you will fight this very hour. The victor will ascend to the office in dispute. Go to your guildsmen and make ready to duel."

Envoy Alveris Sartov, governor in absentia of North-Yarron, was not the preferred choice of company for most Bartolican nobles, but Regional Inspector Vander Hannan valued his fair and forthright opinions. The man was like a mirror, and if what was reflected therein was not to the taste of the original, then blaming the mirror was hardly sensible. As usual, Sartov was on the way to being drunk by the time that the duel was scheduled to start, but he was still steady on his feet.

"There's nobody else here?" asked Sartov as they climbed the stairs of the observation tower.

"No, there's no Bartolicans for you to insult."

"There's you."

"Ah, but I am not easily insulted."

They stood together on the balcony of the tower at the east corner of the Hannan mansion, which commanded a good view of the southwest of the palace and the wing-field. There the preparations were under way for the duel, the sword that would slash apart the threads of knotted diplomacy. The courtiers and guests had dispersed to their homes and hostelries to watch from the comfort of their own towers. This duel involved the judgment of the Air-lord and thus symbolically had to be held above the city and above his grounds. Such duels were rare, and it was unusual for more than half a dozen to be held in a decade.

There was no wind at all, and sound carried very well

over the holiday-hushed city. A fanfare of massed trumpets sounded in the distance, and was followed by the cheering of thousands of spectators who were gathered in the vicinity of the palace—and who were mostly ignorant of the dispute at the heart of the duel. The sound of compression engines cut through as the cheering subsided. A servant appeared with pairs of field glasses for both the Regional Inspector and his guest, and mounted them on chase frames. Both aircraft were plainly visible on the wingfield, painted in the heraldic colors of the two Bartolican wardens.

"So, the Conciliator has failed," Sartov observed.

"Sometimes a result is more important than justice," replied Vander. "Settlement by combat does at least produce a result."

Down amid the turmoil on the wingfield Stanbury spread his arms wide and addressed a group of noble onlookers.

"I came here with no intent of dueling, so I wear the colors of no lady on my arm," he pleaded. "Will any lady honor me with the warmth of her colors, or must I face the sky with my heart cold and my luck eclipsed?"

Most of the noblewomen present hesitated, but Samondel skipped forward at once, sweeping a bunch of embroidered ribbons from the clip on her sleeve.

"Wear the colors of Samondel of Leovor, Warden Stanbury," she declared, and he accepted them with a bow.

"Wardens may fight for the honor of airlords and ladies, Semme Samondel, but on this day a lady did indeed come to the rescue of a warden's honor," he said with gallant flair.

Away in the serenity of the Inspector General's residence, Sartov strained for sounds of action from the wingfield. The compression engines of the distant aircraft revved briskly, as if impatient to be aloft.

"I heard that they are both using Daimzer engines and

Miscafi guns," Sartov said, as if to show that he took this very seriously.

"That is correct. Stanbury is Desondrian's cousin, so he has the right to use the work of their family guilds. I believe that the Daimzer Guildmaster of Engineers has cursed Stanbury for the affront and commanded all those of his house to render no assistance to him. Gremander had to do all the enhancing and tuning."

The crowd at the distant wingfield cheered as a fanfare sounded again. The guildsmen dispersed from around the two gunwings, and the aircraft were left standing together at a white line across the flightstrip. The city's marshal strode out before the gunwings: from the Hannans' tower he was a bright, tiny figure in scarlet robes. He walked first to Stanbury's gunwing, then to Desondrian's before taking a black flag from his aide and walking down the entire length of the flightstrip.

Vander was still focusing his field glasses as the Marshal began waving the black flag and the Daimzer engines of the two gunwings roared. To Hannan they looked like distant white Vs painted on the wingfield's flightstrip. They climbed into the air, then banked away in opposite directions, each turning for their respective tourney towers. Tournament rules applied to duels, and they had to circle their own tower at less than its height before engaging the opponent. They were evenly matched, and Hannan followed Desondrian as he flew for the tower, his gunwing only a few feet from the ground. At the tower he pulled up steeply, clawing for altitude and circling for the sun. Stanbury sped outward, but in a shallower climb.

Within two minutes Desondrian had the advantage of altitude while Stanbury was better placed to use the sun's glare. Both climbed in tight spirals, but Desondrian was edging closer to his opponent. Desondrian broke and dived, yet Stanbury continued to climb as he approached. Desondrian was trying for a tail pass, but Stanbury rolled his aircraft and turned into an even steeper, straight climb.

"If he stalls, he's dead!" exclaimed Sartov, but Stanbury had judged his speed well. The gunwings swept through a head-on pass, reaction guns chattering, then broke into a chasing circle and again fought for height as they pursued each other.

The Mounthaven epics described how wardens used to duel with unpowered sailwings pushed over cliffs. The object then was to descend more slowly than one's opponent. There was grace and style in such a tournament, but this had no such style and finesse. It was all brute power and speed.

Just then, Stanbury broke out of his circle and arced outward as Desondrian turned to pursue him. Again as the gunwings converged Desondrian found himself facing an almost stalled opponent who was nevertheless facing him and firing. On the other hand, Stanbury presented a far better target, and fragments of fabric scattered into the air as the two aircraft passed. Yet again they ended up in a chasing circle, clawing for height. For a third time Stanbury broke and turned to intercept Desondrian's pursuit, and again the gunwings slashed at each other in a head-on pass before dropping back into a chasing circle five thousand feet lower.

"Stanbury took hits again," said Sartov. "He must have a reason for offering himself as a target like that."

"Inexperience," replied Vander.

Stanbury broke again, but this time instead of diving Desondrian came around in a wide arc, intending to catch Stanbury's gunwing after it had lost altitude in its near-stall. It never happened. Stanbury banked to climb in a counterclockwise circle, gaining precious height.

"Good Lord, he's won!" exclaimed Sartov. Vander nodded gravely in agreement.

Stanbury rolled into a dive, and Desondrian tried to emulate his opponent's ploy of firing from a near-stall. Stanbury had the benefit of practice, however, and confidently raked his cousin's gunwing with his twin Miscafis. Deson-

drian broke into another chasing circle, but there was a
thin streamer of dark smoke trailing from the engine of his
gunwing. Stanbury closed with the advantage of full
power, and within another minute had climbed above Desondrian and cut across the chasing circle. Now only one
pair of Miscafis chattered as Desondrian's gunwing bucked
and swerved within a deadly hail of shots. He dived,
rolled, did a spin-turn, then dived again, but Stanbury
merely dropped back and closed again each time.

"He has height and power, damn him," said Vander.
"Desondrian can do nothing but fly the silk."

At that moment Desondrian's gunwing belched a plume
of black smoke and rolled on its back before dropping into
a steep dive. Stanbury followed without attacking, dropping back and plainly taking a chivalrous aspect. Desondrian's gunwing recovered at rooftop level, gained height,
then leveled out, all the while trailing black smoke. Suddenly his port wing snapped, its structure burned out by
the flames trailing from the engine. The gunwing seemed
to give up like a vanquished warrior. Desondrian leaped
from the gunwing, his parachute streaming behind him.
The canopy opened almost horizontally; then both gunwing and warden crashed into a stand of ancient, ornamental fir trees. Stanbury turned for the wingfield, giving
a single roll. There were cheers and fanfares in the distance. Red and white pennants were displayed at the poles
over the palace gates.

"Had Stanbury but kept doing those head-on passes Desondrian would have shredded him like a target kite," said
Sartov as he turned away to go back inside. Vander followed.

"Desondrian tried to ride his tail, to humiliate him," said
the Regional Inspector. "Those head-on exchanges made
Stanbury look brave and tenacious. Desondrian's family
wanted the enemy discredited, not just beaten. Politics,
Sair Sartov, but politics count for nothing in a duel. Per-

haps Stanbury was counting on Desondrian having a political agenda behind his tactics."

A rocket trailing black smoke rose from where Desondrian had come down. Vander watched it through the open doorway of the gallery.

"So he is dead," Vander declared, although there was not a soul in the city above the age of four who did not know the meaning of a rocket trailing black smoke.

They turned their backs on the scene of the duel and settled into a pair of chairs. A footman waited with a tray of glasses and a jug of wine chilled by ice flown in by some warden for Leovor VII's table, but which had been somehow divided and distributed elsewhere. Vander took a distorted lead ball and rolled it between his fingers. Sartov sat down and pressed the tips of his index fingers against his lips as the footman poured his wine.

"Desondrian died beneath his parachute," said Sartov. "In the public eye he died in the act of surrender—*and* while Stanbury was chivalrously standing off. Stanbury has won more than a duel for his family, he has won honor and influence as well."

"The tone of your voice is dark," Vander observed as he toyed with the musket ball.

"Dark, yes. Stanbury is a fine warrior and warden, but he and his family are ambitious and unpredictable. Although Bartolica's nobles have no love for them, they symbolize glory and honor triumphant for all those who have ever been overlooked or neglected in the interests of good politics."

"You talk in obvious truths, Envoy Sartov, but what could Stanbury and his people do?"

"Shake the peace of the Mounthaven dominions, Regional Inspector Hannan."

"Madness. The wardens of Cosdora and Yarron are both an even match for Greater Bartolica's, and all the southern dominions would rally against us if Senner, Montras, or Westland were attacked. Bartolica would have formal wars with as many as five dominions, yet is scarcely united enough for even one."

"Do you really think so? A chivalric war is a good way to ensure unity among wardens."

"I'm sure of it."

Stanbury was gracious in victory, paying respects and consolation to Desondrian's widow as soon as he landed, then praising the dead warden's skills to the adjunct. He finally returned Samondel's favor with profuse thanks.

"The power of your favor is exceeded only by your beauty and kindness, Semme Samondel of Leovor," he said as a circle of admiring nobles and guildsmen applauded. "Would that it could be available next time I ascend in service or anger."

"Would that a lady be lucky enough to be tied to your heart by then, Governor Stanbury," she countered gracefully.

Alion stood in the background, looking studiously at the toes of his brass-capped parade boots and with his hands clasped firmly beneath the tails of his flight jacket. As the group began to disperse he scarcely noticed. Samondel touched his arm. He looked up.

"My lady, I had no idea!" he exclaimed in a sharp whisper. "Yesterday I thought—no, I mean I hoped that—"

"Alion, hush. The new governor was caught alone and without colors, and I came to his aid. It was the honorable and chivalric thing to do."

"Of course, of course, but—"

"Alion, I would be honored if you would wear my colors when next you ascend in service or anger. Keep them until then."

"My lady, Semme Samondel!" whispered Alion, going down on one knee and kissing the hand that held the bunch of ribbons out to him.

Not far away a group of commoners was watching. The young Yarronese guildsfolk could not hear what words were being spoken, but the expressions on the faces of Alion and Samondel spoke far louder.

"I think they're so sweet and romantic," said Kallien Feydamor, Serjon's youngest sister.

"The stitching on her colors is sound, but lacks imagination," observed Ramsdel.

"I hear she once flew a sailwing trainer," Bronlar said with approval.

"There were thirteen ribbons in her colors," Serjon pointed out. "No good will come of it."

Vander had returned to the window to watch Stanbury's gunwing being mobbed as it landed. Presently he turned to the footman, spoke an order, and went back to his chair. The footman reappeared with a long case and presented it to Sartov, then left the rooftop gallery.

"Please, open it," Vander prompted.

Sartov lifted a beautifully made flintlock pistol from the case. Although there was some damage to the wood of the stock, it looked serviceable, and had been cleaned and oiled recently. Its action was firm and sound.

"What do you think?" Vander asked.

"Not an ornament," was Sartov's verdict. "This is the work of a guildsman who specializes in such weapons, yet to my knowledge no such guildsmen exist. Does it work?"

"I have tested it myself. It has a heavy kick, but shoots true."

"Who made it?" asked Sartov, intrigued.

"I had hoped *you* might help me with that matter. A trapper on the northern Callscour frontier has his terriers trained to follow men lured away by the Call. The dogs bring back items dropped and discarded by the doomed followers of the Call, often after days away."

"It is a living, I suppose, and no less honorable than diplomacy."

"One of his dogs found this four years ago, but the trapper thought it of no importance or value. He added two more pegs to his gunrack, and there it stayed until I happened to pay a visit relating to moonshine whisky production in the area."

Vander took the lead ball that he carried and tossed it to Sartov.

"It probably shot this half-inch ball—which was cut from the body of the man it killed back in 3956. It was fired in near darkness at quite a long range. Whoever used this was very experienced with flintlocks, and beat an opponent on his own ground who had a rapid-fire carbine made by a reputable guildsman. How do you explain that?"

Sartov thought for a moment.

"Logic suggests that an elite warrior from some distant Callhaven has reached Bartolica. In his Callhaven they have very skilled artisans, yet their weapons lag behind ours by centuries."

"Such a visitor should have caused a sensation, yet I, the Regional Inspector, heard nothing. Either this is an elaborate prank, or there really have been visitors from a remote but civilized dominion that fled home at once."

"Or they are known to highly ranked people within Bartolica."

"That is true, and thus worrying. *Why* would a pair of explorers armed with flintlocks be kept such a close secret?"

"I cannot say, but then there are many things that I cannot explain about your dominion, Vander. Why are so many carbineers being recruited by Bartolica's merchants for the tramway militias? Your outlaw problem is no worse than Yarron's, yet your merchant carbineers have increased tenfold in the four years past."

"Why worry? You can't wage war with carbineers," said Vander dismissively.

"The Mexhaven dominions do," said Sartov.

"Maybe so, but their nobles have no gunwings."

Later that afternoon the Inspector General released his scrutiny inquisition ruling on the death of the late governor. He found that the fuel system of Governor Merrotin's gunwing had been tampered with, and as the Daimzer guildsmen serviced both the governor's gunwing and that of Desondrian, suspicion fell upon the house of Daimzer. All field engineers and artisans were ordered to be arrested, and their tools and assets impounded.

Not only had Stanbury been proven right, he was also shown to be an excellent judge of character and behavior. His bravery and skill in the air made him all the more of a hero. The new airlord formally confirmed him as governor of the East Region, and lauded him before his court, the envoys, and the visiting dignitaries as being an example of the finest virtues of Bartolican chivalry.

That evening Vander Hannan was at home having dinner when the mansion's main door slammed. The boom reverberated throughout the large residence. Vander looked up to see the footman wince.

"My mother is in another of her tempers," Vander commented, the forkful of emu meat poised just below his lips.

"Semme Laurelene has been in a continuous temper since the envoy from Veraguay arrived in Condelor, Sair Vander," the footman replied.

"So I have observed, yet what is the problem? My father has had discreet dalliances before."

"They were *discreet*, Sair, and for those which Semme Laurelene discovered he was given a great deal of tongue. With the envoy there is no discretion, and—"

The doors to the dining hall were flung open by Laurelene, who stormed in without breaking stride. She was dressed in an afternoon gown with a skillfully designed and sewn framework supporting an expansive cleavage rimmed with olive-gold frills. The rest was just an impression of gold brocade and ruffles to Vander as she swept up to the table and pounded so hard with her fist that the silverware jingled.

"That filthy, lecherous stoat did it again!" she thundered.

"The Veraguayan guard of that scrawny little hen of an envoy!"

"Sair Glasken is from Sierra Madre in Mexhaven, he—"

"Don't contradict me!" she shouted, pounding the table over and over again. "He, he hung about with Kyleal. I feared for her virtue so I sent her on an errand and remonstrated with him in person. I told him that loose and fast romance was not the Bartolican way, but he replied that he did but learn by example—*that* was a remark about your shameless father, make no mistake. Then he swept off that absurd feathered hat of his and bowed to me so low that the filthy waxed point of his beard dipped into my, my . . . cleavage!"

An adventurous man, thought Vander. He clasped his hands, rested his chin upon them, and tried to look sympathetic.

"Of course I complained to your father but it did no good. That's the second time that Veraguayan guard has shamed me in public. If your father will do nothing then *you* must!"

"My region is the north, I have no authority here," replied Vander hastily.

"But you can challenge him to a duel."

"He is not a warden. As far as I can tell his rank is about that of carbineer yeoman. It is his master who must punish him or duel."

"His master is the envoy."

"The envoy can't fly. You could declare a civil feud and—"

"No! That would shame me because my husband and son did not intervene on my behalf."

"Then what do you want me to do?"

"I want you to arrest Juan Glasken for molesting a noble. Make the envoy accountable in court."

"Mother, the diplomatic protocols—"

"I didn't come here for excuses!"

"Well, why did you come here?"

Laurelene swept up a goblet and flung it at Vander's plate, scattering his dinner along the table and onto the floor. When she had left, slamming the door behind her, the footman suddenly became reanimated and called for a serving man to clean up.

"Semme Laurelene is a loud, intimidating, and forceful woman," observed the footman as he cleaned scraps of food from Vander's dinner coat.

"But the envoy is a soft, sympathetic, and persuasive woman," replied Vander. "With luck I may be back north by the time they square off across my father's body, but then I am not a believer in luck."

11 May 3960: Condelor

Rosenne Rodriguez was not on any of Laurelene's lists of people to invite to Inspectorate gatherings in the days following the coronation, but to her annoyance her husband seemed to find his way into the company of the envoy at every other function. On the evening of May 11th there was no delaying the invitation to the reception for the envoys any longer. Rosenne was an envoy, so Rosenne had to be invited. The invitation was sent out with an hour remaining to the commencement, but the envoy's acceptance came straight back with the message boy.

The Inspectorate mansion had quite a large reception hall, and it was ideal for entertaining the thirty-one envoys from four Callhavens. They talked mainly in Old Anglian out of deference to the Veraguayan envoy, a point that was not lost on the fuming Laurelene. Rosenne's guard Glasken also mingled with the envoys and aides. His clothing was a contrast of tight straps over baggy cloth, with the trousers tucked into his boots. Laurelene knew this to be the Hildago fashion of around a year ago. She also had the impression that his eyes lingered on her breasts whenever he had cause to look in her direction.

"What impressed me most was that pretty little . . . how do you say it, gunbird girl," Rosenne was saying as the platters of delicacies were brought past by the servants. "She was so small and sweet, yet she flew all the way from Yarron in that big war gunbird."

"The word is gunwing, my dear," said Inspector General Hannan, his voice easily familiar, "and as to her flight, well, it was quite impractical as a feat of endurance."

"Impractical? I do not understand," said Rosenne with a simpering smile.

"Oh she was far lighter than a strong, trained warden and thus the gunwing could carry more fuel. She has little strength, however, and strength is required for combat."

"Strength? Oh yes, a warrior must be strong."

She charms men with great facility, thought Laurelene, holding an amiable smile over a sullen glare. She asked intelligent questions, but played the fool with the answers. From her observations of the envoy Laurelene realized that Rosenne reserved her greatest charm for men of the senior nobility. Her husband was just such a man.

"You too have traveled an immense distance, Semme Rosenne, I can barely imagine it," Laurelene interjected, more to defuse an obvious buildup of her own anger than out of interest. "I envy you so much."

"But *you* travel as well," Rosenne replied. "You have said that you go with your husband on some of his trips."

Not when he could help it, thought Laurelene. "All that I have seen is North Bartolica and parts of the Dorak frontier. Oh I have traveled to Senner and Westland too—and Montras, everyone goes to Montras."

"So you like travel?"

"Peasants and peons are much the same everywhere."

"What sorts of guns do you have in Veraguay?" asked Vander, who had said little during their reception so far. "Do they load at the muzzle and have flints to strike sparks when you shoot?"

Rosenne reached beneath her parlor jacket and took out

a small, ornate gun with two barrels and handed it to him. Vander turned it over several times, making a careful appraisal.

"The inlay work is beautiful," said Vander.

The artisan who made it had been wonderfully skilled, but had clearly based the design on one by the Lewistar family of Denver. He removed one of the rounds and saw that it had been made in Cosdora.

"We of Veraguay believe everything that adorns a lady should be a work of art as well as functional. Guns are the weapons of the better classes in Veraguay. Commoners use crossbows and snares for hunting."

"And outlaws?"

"Oh I would not know such things."

Just then Envoy Sartov was announced. Being the Yarronese envoy, he was pointedly late and was dressed in a plain promenade coat instead of formal finery. At the door he registered a request to be presented to the Veraguay envoy.

"Semme Envoy Rodriguez, I am pleased to introduce the envoy from Yarron, Warden Sartov," Hannan said with smooth politeness, making the presentation only to be near Rosenne.

"I am as honored to meet you as I am stunned by your beauty," replied Sartov, bowing low as he took a step back.

Rosenne made a show of being charmed by any compliment and beamed at the Yarronese envoy as he straightened again. His movements, however graceful, were slightly uncoordinated. The Yarronese envoy had arrived drunk.

"Gracious sair, I see you are a warden," she replied. "That means you fly. How brave of you."

"Ah, but you flew in a regal to cross the Callscour from Mexhaven," Sartov replied earnestly. "You are brave as well as beautiful, while I am merely brave."

Rosenne simpered and blushed, but Hannan drained his glass, called for another, and drained that too. This was proving to be a very trying exercise in diplomacy.

"I am envoy to Bartolica for only two months more," Sartov was explaining. "We Yarronese like to share the burden of living in Bartolica, so even though I am a provincial governor and seventh in line for the Yarronese throne, I had to suffer here for six months."

Rosenne leaned forward and examined the tiny badges of gold sewn into his collar. She counted fourteen, and noticed that they were all different.

"Are those your house crests?" she asked, pointing with her two index fingers pressed together.

"No, they are victories in clear air combat. Three in duels and eleven in chivalric wars. Five are Bartolican kills, you will note."

Rosenne squirmed slightly, knowing that Hannan was beside her. She turned to him, meaning to ask about the number of victory badges on his collar, then discovered to her discomfort that he had none. Very hastily she turned back to Sartov.

"Your wife must be very proud of you," she said.

"Alas, my wife died last year in a training accident."

"As a flyer?" Rosenne exclaimed in genuine admiration.

"Yes. She was preparing for accreditation as a flyer. We Yarronese are very advanced in such matters. Her death broke my heart, but I am more proud of her than of all my victories. She was accredited posthumously. I declared myself governor in absentia, then petitioned to be the envoy to Bartolica for six months. I reasoned that the torture of being in Bartolica would distract me from grieving for my wife."

Rosenne had by now decided that the conversation should end before the tipsy envoy said something that caused her host to die of apoplexy.

"Would it be possible for me to be presented at court when I visit Yarron next month, Sair Sartov?"

"Introduce me to your secretary and I shall make the arrangements."

"Ah no, my guard Sair Glasken oversees all my travel plans."

Hannan put on a show of forced sympathy once they had left Sartov with Glasken.

"He may be rude, but he comes from a good family. Their tradition of flying goes all the way back to the dueling kites of the twenty-fifth century. He lost his soul when his wife died, and now he is supremely rude, even by Yarronese standards. He has killed two fine Bartolican wardens in clear air duels since arriving here. Sometimes I think he is looking for an honorable way to die. Most times I wish he would find one."

A handsome, heroic, unmarried envoy compliments her so graciously, yet she spurns him to flirt with my lecherous old stoat of a husband, fumed Laurelene silently. To make matters worse, the guard Glasken was still allowing his eyes to linger on her own cleavage. Theresla had been standing nearby, and Laurelene now noticed that a man in the blue uniform of the merchant carbineers had come up to her.

"What in hell are you doing here?" she heard him demand in a very odd dialect of Old Anglian.

"We were sent to provide an independent perspective," Theresla replied calmly.

Carabas, his name was Carabas, Laurelene recalled. She had met him earlier in the week, but remembered only that he was part of some new tramway militia.

"Our work is sensitive in the extreme," Carabas hissed. "If you betray us, we can never go home."

"Fras Carabas, the Miocene Arrow operation has cost hundreds of thousands of gold royals, yet nobody is willing to say just what it might be—outside the Supreme Assembly of Aviads. We are here to find out."

"How did you get here?"

"Tell me about the Miocene Arrow and I might discuss my transport arrangements."

"You cannot be trusted with the plans of the Supreme Assembly."

"If it's like their plan to murder Highliber Zarvora, then I think it is my duty to save the Supreme Assembly from itself. With a single bullet they cut off our supply of the old technology and set us back centuries."

Carabas clicked his heels and gave the briefest of bows. "I do not believe we have further business, Frelle Theresla," he said, and melted into the crowd without awaiting a reply.

Laurelene had not understood much of their rapidly spoken conversation, but it was obvious that agents of another Callhaven were active in Bartolica. If so, the Veraguay envoy would be part of the conspiracy, and might well be vulnerable to the truth being exposed to daylight. Glasken would know, Laurelene decided, and Glasken was stupid enough to let something slip. She caught sight of the feather in his hat above the crowd and moved toward him. She hailed him and he broke off his conversation with Sartov. Bowing low over Laurelene's cleavage, he again caressed it with the point of his waxed beard. She flinched back, but retained her smile.

Fifty if he's a day, Laurelene thought. No bulging gut, all muscle, and he carried the scars of a lot of action. One ear was partly shot off. Not far behind him Rosenne and Hannan were discussing something earnestly, as they nearly always seemed to be doing. She asked Glasken several questions about Mexhaven, and dropped the words Miocene Arrow quite casually. Glasken did not react at all, yet something about his manner hardened ever so slightly.

"You speak Old Anglian with some facility, Sair Glasken," she remarked. "Have you been in Mounthaven before?"

Glasken, who had been expecting more searching questions from her, relaxed inwardly.

"I have never crossed Mounthaven's Call frontier before now, Semme Hannan. There was a warden's aide from

South Colandoro living in Chihuana. She taught me, ah, the scholarly tongue in this Callhaven. It has a lot in common with our own scholarly language."

"But Hispan is nothing like Old Anglian."

"Ah—but there is also Anglaic."

Laurelene had not heard of Anglaic, yet Glasken could certainly speak Old Anglian well, and had a convincing Hispan accent. Still she knew a lie when she heard one, and he was definitely lying.

"That is a lot of trouble to go to, learning the language of such a remote and distant place as Mounthaven."

"Oh no, Mounthaven is the summit of civilization and learning, great Semme. When the Veraguay envoy announced that she was going to cross the Callscour desert there were dozens of fine bravos coming forward to be in her service. I knew Old Anglian, however, so that put me ahead of all the stronger, younger, and less experienced young men. Besides, I am a guard to the nobility, and nobles travel more than others, even in Mexhaven."

"Are you sure that you are not a noble yourself, traveling in disguise to observe Mounthaven more candidly?" Laurelene asked, batting her eyelashes at him.

The effect was not so much alluring as alarming, as practiced by Laurelene. Glasken managed, "Great Semme, you flatter me."

"I'm sure a great many ladies flatter you, Sair Glasken," she said, turning her head to one side with a simpering smile.

"Maybe so, but I must attend the safety of my envoy," Glasken responded with mechanical charm.

I cannot even charm this yoick who pays better heed to my servants than me, Laurelene thought with a momentary pang of despair. As a parting flourish, Glasken began a low bow over Laurelene's expanse of cleavage. Her patience with everything that was frustrating her snapped without warning, and seizing Glasken by his whole ear and what remained of the other she rammed his face down between her breasts.

"If you like them so much, Glasken, take a *really* good look!" she shouted, then swirled around and stamped away through the crowd—which parted readily at her approach. Total silence blanketed the reception hall until the door slammed behind Laurelene.

"You must forgive my wife, she is a little rough in her affections," said Hannan to the astonished Glasken.

As the reception struggled to regain its genial mood Sartov seemed to materialize beside Glasken. He was swaying alarmingly and holding a pitcher of wine, but the expression on his face was anything but jovial.

"Sair Glasken, the 'spector General's wife . . . attacking the Veraguay envoy . . . through you," he said slowly, maintaining the logic with difficulty.

"A remarkable woman," said Glasken as he straightened the points of his waxed mustache.

"Don't under . . . , ah, estimate. She'll press charges, unseemly conduct . . . against you."

"That may not be all she presses against me."

"Your patroness, Semme Rosenne . . . be exiled, if you lose."

"And what happens to *me* if I lose?"

"Hmmm . . . Could be imprisoned . . . forever. Could get hung on the public scaffold—shorter sentence! Get it? Shorter sentence!"

Sartov elbowed him in the ribs, began laughing uncontrollably, and collapsed. Glasken caught the lightly built Yarronese as he fell and removed the pitcher of wine from his grasp.

"If you flee, poof, no trial," Sartov gasped as Glasken drew him up straight by his collar.

"But that would declare my guilt."

"Think your word's better than, er, 'spector General's wife?"

Glasken swallowed, and needed no more time than that to make up his mind.

"I'll flee—but where?"

"Glasken, I wish to go home but I'm . . . ah, incapable. Navigate me to, er, Yarronese embassy, and I'll point you to Yarron."

Sartov arrived back at his embassy across Glasken's shoulders. The clerk did not respond to his knocking.

"Slack wretch, going Bartolican," Sartov muttered in exasperation as he drew out his keys.

After several minutes of fumbling Glasken took the keys from Sartov and opened the door. The envoy turned up the lamps, then slumped into a chair and regarded his guest.

"You're lean, strong, and fit, Sair Glasken," Sartov pronounced. "You'll make it."

He stood up, tottered to the bell cord, and grasped at it. Somewhere in the distance a bell jangled.

"Announcing Sair Juan Glasken, Sierra Madre," declared Sartov as Glasken guided him back to his chair.

The appointments clerk presently shuffled in wearing a bedrobe and slippers, and looking a little puzzled and drowsy.

"Prepare border passage papers for, er, Juan Glasken of Sierra Madre," said Sartov. "Now."

When the clerk had gone the big man thanked him and bowed slightly, his hands crossed over his chest. He sat down on an imported Yarronese lounge chair, which was high-backed and more firm than the Bartolican variety.

"So, you went where no man would, ah, voluntarily go," said Sartov. "What did you say that Semme Laurelene would, ah, take offense?"

Glasken leaned forward. "I made no lewd suggestions, Envoy Sartov, I do not hunt seductions. I gather up those that are easily available, and Semme Laurelene could not be described thus. We had been speaking of language and travel when she seized me and—"

"Yes, yes, saw it all. Unbelievable. Thought I was drunk. Well, ah, I knew that. And you took no liberties at all?"

"No. Not even a little nip while I was down there. It all happened so fast."

Sartov blinked. "She'll be angry, she'll act quickly. Pack, leave now. You're dangerous. No, Laurelene's dangerous. You're in danger."

"Long experience with angry fathers and husbands has taught me to be prepared to flee at all times. I have a gun, knife, and gold with me, my coat is warm and my boots stout. A blanket and some dried fruit and bread would be welcome, though."

"Done! Pantry's there . . . on the right. Take a wineskin too, hey, and there's Mexhaven condoms in there. You'll need one if Laurelene catches up. Bartolican pox, Bartolican pox; It grabs their menfolk by their cocks; . . . ah shit, what comes next?"

The clerk returned with the papers. Sartov signed without checking the details.

"Anywhere in Yarron you'd like to go—particularly?"

Glasken pointed to a map of Yarron under glass on a low table. "Middle Junction, Median, and Forian. After Forian, to Denver in Colandoro. I have, ah, colleagues there, and a library that I must explore."

"A library? You? You, ah, no scholar."

Glasken draped a leg over the arm of his chair and twirled his mustache. "Scholars can be as rakish as the next man, but they are mostly discreet about it."

"Mostly."

"Mostly. I once tried being discreet. It led to a war."

Sartov shook his head as he endorsed Glasken's papers in a register. He dismissed the clerk, and did not speak again until they were once more alone.

"Can give you papers, Sair Glasken, but steam trams

only leave in the morning. Too late. You'd ... better walk."

"I'm good at that," Glasken replied without a trace of disappointment. "Thank you very sincerely, Envoy Sartov."

They stood up and grasped wrists.

"Just why are you doing this?" Glasken asked as he buttoned his coat and pulled his cap low over his face. "I am not important and I can never hope to repay you."

"You are a jackhare with the whole hunt pack of terriers at your heels: I feel sorry for you. Besides, I'm drunk, and when I'm drunk I annoy Bartolicans. Annoying Bartolicans is ... national sport of Yarron. Semme Laurelene will be exceedingly annoyed by this."

"I don't believe that," said Glasken as they reached the door. "You are friends with her son."

"Ha ha, sharp, very sharp. Vander's fair and reasonable, a good inspector. My friend. I'll not see my friend ... dragged into the gutter. Stupid mother, she'll do that. Force him ... be her advocate. With you gone, poof! No case."

"I presume Semme Laurelene is jealous of her husband's interest in the Veraguay envoy, and seeks to stir bad feelings between the two households."

"Aye. Now promise me to escape, Glasken. You owe me a drink for this."

"I'll fetch you a drink to remember, Sair Envoy."

Again they seized each other's wrists in the Mounthaven greeting. Sartov opened the door and checked for lurking constables or carbineers.

"Take the mountain road east, past Bear Lake. It's rough and steep, but only one hundred miles to Yarron. A fit and desperate man might take ... three days."

"I am that man," replied Glasken, turning up his collar.

12 May 3960: Condelor

The next day marked the official end of the coronation festival, and the capital of Greater Bartolica hung between revelry and normality as the debris of celebration were swept away. The bakers and tailors cleaned their shops and counted their profits, while the churls who swept the streets and hauled the refuse carts moved many loads of faded petals, dry leaves, and shreds of colored paper from the streets. The wreckage of Desondrian's gunwing was recovered by the guildsmen and artisans of his wardenàte. The airframe was cremated, along with Desondrian's body, but the guns and engine were taken away to be stripped down and rebuilt.

The smoke from Desondrian's funeral pyre was rising into the calm air as Carabas met Stanbury on the promenade of the palace wingfield. The new governor of the East Region was on his way to his gunwing to fly back to his capital. There he would formally present his credentials and take charge.

"So, I have my region," he said nervously, aware that many pairs of eyes could see him in the merchant carbineer's company. "What payment do you want in return?"

"The use of an isolated and abandoned estate with a wingfield, and your help to secure the services of several artisans."

Stanbury threw him a sidelong glance but kept walking.

"The first is not hard, the second will raise questions. What will their work be?"

"It will be in support of Dorak against Yarron."

"Against? In what sense?"

"War."

Stanbury stopped in his tracks.

"What?" he exclaimed, louder than he had intended. "The Dorakian and Yarronese wardens have a truce going back decades, they are even developing that small, newly discovered Black Hills Callhaven together."

"Nevertheless, they will soon be making declarations, selecting seconds, petitioning for a council of delegates, and making territorial claims. Bartolica will second Dorak, count on that."

Stanbury thought this through for a moment. His new region shared a border with both Dorak and Yarron, but it was not prime territory.

"How will a few artisans affect the outcome of a war?" he scoffed. "Even a minor war of, say, seventy dueling pairs?".

"They will be guildsmen artisans, and they will be the price of services rendered. Your guilds guard their artisans well, and the people who sent me here have seen little return after four years of expense. The artisans are a symbol, a deposit, a holding fee. Certain factions at home will lose credibility if I can supply gunsmiths who are willing to train our own artisans in the making of reaction guns, for example."

"And will those reaction guns come back to us in the hands of Mexhaven carbineers?"

"Governor, we have a whole continent to conquer, we have no interest in your dry and poor mountains. The reaction guns are for our internal struggles, to make our own sailwings invincible. Remember, our sailwings are far, far in advance of yours."

"I still cannot understand how your people can build sailwings powered by the sun, yet simple reaction guns and compression engines are beyond your skills."

"Look upon it as a mercantile opportunity, Governor Stanbury. You have something that we will pay for generously."

"And the war between Yarron and Dorak: do you mean to involve me?"

"No, Governor, but you would be advised to claim the credit for our involvement. It will greatly enhance your status with Airlord Leovor the Seventh. Advice can be taken or left, but this is your single chance to seize a magnificent destiny."

Carabas bowed, then took his leave. Stanbury continued on to where his gunwing was being made ready. A steam engine on a cart spun the gunwing's compression engine to life, and while it was warming the flight clerk briefed him on weather, Call vectors, and the gunwing's performance in a test flight made an hour earlier. His ascent was untroubled, and Stanbury banked out over the mountains as he climbed, hoping for a boost from thermals. Looking to port as he turned north, he marveled that so much had changed in the capital over the days past, yet from the air it looked the same as when he had arrived.

2 | ASSASSINATION

Rollins had joined the Merchant Tram Service for both prospects and anonymity. As Charlegan Vandarforrin he had been a bright and promising student in the Royal Condelor Academy of Languages until he had stabbed and killed another student. That very night he had decided to forsake his career in the diplomatic service and became Teg Rollins. He had grown a beard as he fled north and been given a job as a wood-block stoker while hitching beside a backwoods tramway. The tramways and merchant carbineers were expanding, he was told by the driver. Guild families were no longer able to supply the demand as dozens of new trams were put into service. Did he want honest work? Rollins joined.

Although a hard worker, Rollins spoke very slowly and kept to himself, lest anyone become friendly and try to go into his background. Within a year he was made a driver, and in another he became a driver first class. A senior officer in the Merchant Carbineers named Carabas interviewed him one day in the marshaling yards. Carabas explained that being a loner who was not very talkative qualified Rollins well to drive a new type of tram, one painted black that rolled only by night. The increased anonymity appealed to Rollins, and he signed on.

In the following weeks he drove almost continually at night, transporting senior officers with names like Warran Glasken, Pyter Kalward, the man known only as Carabas, and once even Governor Stanbury. They traveled all the backwoods tramstops and waystations, recruiting men in their hundreds to the merchant carbineers at very good rates of pay. Rollins never responded to anything but Bartolican, yet he spoke five languages fluently and could follow another eleven. He had also been trained in the elements of codework, in his earlier life as an aspiring diplomat. He listened and understood, but remained as impassive as a statue.

A tram twenty-nine feet six inches long leaves little scope for privacy. Rollins' masters spoke mainly in Old Anglian, and although they were cryptic in what they said, he soon pieced together a startling picture. The Merchant Carbineers, the policing arm of the Bartolican government, were being expanded to twenty times their former size and being made mobile on the new trams. Single men, fugitives, lawbreakers, and the footloose were preferred. They were trained hard and put to a life of near-continual travel on two-tiered red trams that seated fifty carbineers each. A version with roof seats and a canvas cover could even move a hundred carbineers, and all were armed with a two-inch carriage gun at the front and a heavy-caliber reaction gun at the rear. Rollins wondered how the outlaw problem in the backwoods had become so bad as to need such measures.

13 May 3960: The Yarronese border

Laurelene's wrath caught up with Glasken at the Yarronese border. On the evening of the third day of his journey he presented his papers at Kemmerer, on the Bartolican side. Both Bartolican and Yarronese officials approved his transit petition, and as the whistle of an approaching steam tram sounded in the distance he paid the fees and bought maps and guide scrolls.

The trip from Condelor to Kemmerer by the scheduled steam-tram service was twice the distance of that by road, but a tram did not need rest and sleep, and traveled at three times walking pace. Glasken stepped over an iron rail inset in the road and onto Yarronese soil, then presented his papers to the two Yarronese guards on duty, tipped them a silver coin each, and strode east. He was a hundred yards into Yarron when a bell began tolling and the bleat of constables' whistles echoed through the evening. Glasken had beaten his pursuers with just moments to spare. Men with carbines hurried over to the border where the Yarronese guards still stood, ready to process transit papers and accept tips. There was a loud exchange in a mixture of Bartolican and Yarronese, neither of which Glasken understood well, but it was clear that the two Yarronese guards were trying to block the passage of some twenty Bartolicans.

Perhaps what followed seemed like a good idea at the time, perhaps he was just tired of being polite, but Glasken should have known that a beaten enemy is not a vanquished enemy. As the Bartolicans stared angrily after him he unbelted his trousers, raised the flaps of his journeycoat, and bent over to present his pale white buttocks for the Bartolicans' inspection while calling "Full moon!" in Old Anglian.

A shot echoed among the mountains and a bullet

whizzed through Glasken's coat, flaying open his skin and
raking his ribs. There was a scuffle back at the border rail
and the two Yarronese guards were quickly overwhelmed
and pinned down, but by now Glasken was running for a
thick stand of trees, his right hand pressed against his side
and his left holding up his trousers. More than a dozen
Bartolican carbineers ran after him, firing into the air.
There were several more shots amid the trees, but to the
dismay of the Bartolican town constable his men returned
with neither a prisoner nor a body. It was a small consolation for him to learn that the fugitive had been wounded
before he had escaped. A Mexhaven handkerchief stained
with fresh blood was presented to him as proof.

The town constable returned to his office in a downcast
mood. There would be an incursion inquest to be endured,
and he was quite clearly in the wrong. Worse, the fugitive
had escaped in spite of the incursion. Waiting for him was
a senior inspector from Condelor.

"I regret that the man Glasken is now at large in Yarron," the town constable reported. "He was wounded by
one of my guards, however."

The inspector examined the bloodstained handkerchief
and smiled.

"You have done well."

"But I've made a Class Five incursion and have no prisoner to show for it."

"I know my mother, Sair Constable, I know what sat-
isfies and pacifies her. If I tell her that Glasken was shot
as he crossed the border and was left to bleed to death by
our carbineers she will be filled with elation and sponsor
a great revel to celebrate. More to the point, she will cease
nagging me to avenge her honor, and that is all that I am
concerned about."

"Sair Inspector, we don't even know that he is dead."

"Sair Constable, we also know better than to tell her
that."

16 May 3960: Pocatello

Giles Normandier was on hard times. The gunsmith was
forty-four years of age, divorced, close to bankruptcy, and
behind with his contracts to the gunsmith guilds of the East
Region wardens. He was no longer a member of the guilds
himself, having been expelled five years earlier after he
had been jailed by the city inspector for public drunken-
ness. His shop was rented, and the rent was three months
in arrears.

The man who entered his shop had a gauze sunframe
over his eyes, even though the day was well advanced and
quite overcast. Giles looked up and knew at once that it
was the bailiff. His bearing was erect, and his journeycoat
faded but expensive in cloth and cut. Two men in similar
coats had entered with him, and they proceeded through
the shop and on into the back room before anyone had
said a word. Giles stood up very slowly, placing a reamer
on the workbench and keeping his hands visible. One of
his visitor's escorts returned after a few moments and reported that the shop was clear. The man did not sit down.

"Sair Normandier," he began in a hard, commanding
voice, "I have been reviewing your work history in the
guilds' records."

Giles swallowed, cleared his throat, and swallowed
again. Anyone who had access to the archives of the guilds
was at least a magistrate, if not an inspector.

"Circumstances . . . are not good for me, Sair—um,
Sair."

"I know. Your shop is rented, your tools and materials
are on trust against your debts, and even your books and
broadsheets are no longer your own."

"I once had promise, sair. Twelve years ago I was as-
sistant gunsmith to Warden Beecherven of Snyder. I made
six pairs of reaction guns for his flock, all of which are

still in use. Two of 'em brought victory in duels. Fine work, those guns."

The visitor nodded. "I know, I flew one of Beecherven's flock last week."

Giles opened his mouth, then closed it and swallowed. A warden. He tried frantically to think which warden would have cause to deal with him.

"I'll have the general spares contract finished in three days, Warden. I have no apprentices, you see. I can pay nobody because of my circumstances, so I do everything myself."

As Giles stood rubbing his hands together his visitor reached into a pocket and withdrew a leather palmfold, walked over to Giles' workbench, placed it in front of him. Giles picked up the palmfold and looked inside. It contained receipts of discharge for his rent, for all his tools, for nine fines by the Bartolican SuperGuild of Armorers, for metals, materials, even for groceries.

"I—I do not understand. Warden, you must have paid what I couldn't earn in two decades to clear these debts."

"Do any other debts stand between you and serenity?"

"Some moneylenders are due small amounts."

"Write down the names of the moneylenders. It is a wonderful thing to be given another chance at life, is it not, Sair Normandier?"

"Why have you done this?" he asked in astonishment.

"Why, Sair Normandier? You are a good master to apprentices, when you have them. You are a slow worker, but your guns are as good as those from any master alive. You also have no ties, and I need of a teacher who is free to travel."

"Where?"

"Very, very far."

Giles gnawed at the dried skin on his lower lip. "I am a loyal Bartolican, Warden. I cannot help the enemies and rivals of the Airlord."

"Your loyalty is commendable, but your fears are unfounded. My clients are much further away than the enemies and rivals of the Airlord of Bartolica. They are so far away that they could *never* be his enemies and rivals."

Now Giles began to recall scraps of gossip from his clients and suppliers. The coronation had been attended by a woman from the very southernmost nation of the Andean Callhaven—Veraguay, that was the name of the place. She was said to be a roving envoy, and had taken three years to reach Bartolica. More questions tumbled into Giles' mind, but too many questions and too little enthusiasm might lose what was being offered.

"I accept!" he blurted out.

The visitor removed his gauzeframe eyeshades. It was the face of the new portraits in every public building: Governor Stanbury. Giles came around his workbench at once and dropped to one knee. Stanbury hauled him to his feet.

"Begin packing, now. Just tools that you could not rebuild easily. The bags must weigh no more than two hundred pounds."

"Two hundred pounds? A thousand would not—"

"Those which exceed two hundred pounds can be sent later. Hurry now, you leave in five hours."

"But can I have time to drink an ale at the Blue Fox and tell—"

"Absolutely not. Word will be put about that you have gone to the capital on indentured work to clear your debts. There are delicate politics involved, concerning the welfare of Greater Bartolica."

"With all possible respect, Sair Governor, how could the work of a broken-down guildsman carry such worth?"

"No more questions. Pack!"

Some time after midnight Giles arrived at the Pocatello wingfield. A heavy overcast rendered the scene as dark as pitch and there were very few people about. The flightstrip was firm and familiar under his feet as he became aware of a sailwing trainer in front of him. He could just distinguish its looming presence in the light that leaked from a pinlamp carried by one of the Governor's guards.

"Here is the hatchway, your tools are aboard," said Stanbury.

"Sair Governor, I—I don't know what to say. When I ate my lunch I was staring despair in the eyes yet now I, I—"

"Sair Normandier, the cost of sending you to where you are going is several times your weight in gold. Work hard, stay healthy, obey orders, and teach diligently. A lot of people are going to be very angry if they do not get a good return for their investment. The first installment is a dozen apprentices able to build reaction guns."

The compression engine was started, then idled until warm. Someone slapped the side of the cockpit twice and dim shapes ran to pull the chocks from the wheels. The ascent run was in near total darkness and it seemed an eternity to Giles before the aircraft rotated and climbed into the air. It banked as it climbed, and Giles could see the distant lights of Pocatello far below through a pane of the canopy. He did not need to be told that he would never see them again.

Stanbury met with his enigmatic partner after Normandier had left, at a local warden's mansion. Carabas was composed and relaxed, and carried nothing with him.

"I delivered your drunken gunsmith to the wingfield, or are you aware of that already?"

"Oh I know that, and I thank you."

"And is he satisfactory?"

"Yes."

"You know that he must be inspected as present every month, or declared dead."

"You may declare him inspected or declare him dead, Sair Governor."

"I may do that for three months, then the Regional Inspector will arrive in September to inspect my books. He will note that the gunsmith has been inspected by only one man, while the law requires three officials to rotate the inspections. I shall have a lot of explaining to do, and the penalty for trading in weapons guild artisans is death."

"By September you could have Bartolica at war, Sair Governor. Alternately I could arrange a very convenient fire in your palace."

"Fire? War? What is all this? Who *are* you?"

Carabas placed his hands together as if in prayer and sat back.

"Why tell you what you would not believe? How are your carbineer brigades growing?"

"The carbineers have been increasing steadily enough. They train at moving rapidly about on steam trams and pump carts, and can reach a trouble spot on the tramways before any outlaw bands would have time to disperse. Banditry has dropped to almost nothing and the East Region is becoming a popular place for merchants to invest, but . . ."

"But?"

"But this increase in carbineers is costing me five times what I used to spend on tramway defense."

"Money will be made to appear if it is needed. Just keep recruiting and have no doubts. Tell me, who was Fudarvier?"

"Fudarvier? He, ah . . . I know the name. He lived many centuries ago, before the warden system was established. He was governor of Absaroka back when it was part of Greater Bartolica, he, ah, put down some rebellion or other, there's a song that the carbineers still sing about him. Do you want me to get down a volume of military history?"

"No, I obviously know the story better than you. Furdarvier held Absaroka with a garrison of two thousand troops, and in the fifteenth year of his appointment he defeated a well-armed rebellion of eight times as many Absarokans in a series of tactically and strategically brilliant battles. He was called to Condelor to be decorated by the monarch of the time, but died of a fever on the return journey. The brother of a mistress of the monarch was made his replacement, seeing that the locals were obviously able to be kept in order so easily. Within two years the Absorakans had successfully crushed the local garrison and fought off three Bartolican armies sent to reclaim what was now calling itself Dorak. Thirty thousand Bartolicans died before a truce was declared and Dorak was recognized."

"Yes, now I remember my tutors mentioning all that. The land of Absaroka was of little profit to Bartolica, and within a few years they were trading with us again."

"Thirty thousand lives call your words nonsense. The monarch wanted that land kept Bartolican, make no mistake, but he did not realize that Furdarvier was one of the most brilliant commanders in the history of the Mounthaven dominions. Furdarvier had a very peaceful rule for his first fourteen years as governor, however, when he was forced to fight he made it seem so easy that everyone else wanted to take the credit. There are lessons in his life for you."

Stanbury was no fool, and was quick to make extrapolations.

"Is there a rebellion being planned?" he demanded, jumping to his feet.

"Not a rebellion, but something better. Peace is not conducive to military advancement. Furdarvier was a brilliant man, but had he died of a fever one year earlier, who would even bother mentioning him today and what soldier would sing songs about him? Pay a great deal of attention to the military resources of your region, Governor, especially over the month to come. You may be needed to save Bartolica from outlaws. Goodnight to you now."

"Wait! What outlaws?"

"There will be outlaws."

"What makes you think that I am a brilliant commander, anyway? I am good in a gunwing duel, yes, and I have won five skytourneys and two blood duels, but I have never led a flock of gunwings."

"Soon you will do more than just that, Sair Governor, you will lead the whole of Bartolica into battle—and you *will* be brilliant, trust my word for it."

After over an hour of flying, Normandier noticed that they were descending to what looked like mountains. From Mirrorsun's position Giles was able to tell that they were flying almost due west. As he looked down a pair of lights appeared below, then gradually became a twin line of lights as runners lit the torches that flanked a wingfield. The wingfield ended at a precipice.

They landed, and two dark figures helped Giles from the cockpit. The sailwing made its way back down the flight-strip, then turned and ascended into a light breeze.

"So, is this my new home?" asked Giles.

"Waiting, seven days," said one of the men, then they left him with his tools beside a small tent while they smothered the torches flanking the wingfield.

When Giles emerged from his camouflaged tent the next morning he was astounded to see that the wingfield had vanished, covered with scrubby trees and bushes in large pots painted to resemble the surrounding rocks. Going down on one knee he brushed his fingers over the surface of the flightstrip. It was not just secret, it had been graded only recently.

Giles whistled, then stood up, shivering in the morning sunlight. He had never seen a new flightstrip, or even a flightstrip less than five hundred years old. This was not just the theft of a few guns and guild secrets, this was the overturning of something as old and fundamental as the civilization of Mounthaven itself.

18 May 3960: The East Region frontier

Rollins was reassigned back to the black trams in mid-May, after an extended interview with the officer Warran Glasken.

"Would you kill for Greater Bartolica?"

"Yes."

"What languages do you speak?"

"Bartolican."

"Nel hisi optil?"

"Your pardon, sair?"

"Never mind. What do you know about the outlaw problem?"

"They're said to come from Yarron."

The windows of this black tram were boarded over, and small forced-air ventilators were installed in the roof to allow the passengers to breathe. Again Rollins slept by day and drove by night. After a fortnight he noticed that just after a Call had passed over whatever siding the black tram was standing in, the merchant officers would return with a dozen or so outlaws in chains. To Rollins they did not look like outlaws. They were well-groomed and pale-skinned men, more like shopkeepers, bank clerks, and such. The occasional women did not resemble gaudily dressed, raucous outlaw women as much as disheveled and frightened schoolteachers.

They were kept on the upper level of the black tram, and when it was at rest in sidings he could hear the officers taking them through rote lessons in a type of numeric code. Rollins, the stoker, and the two gunners were ordered to have no contact with the prisoners. Rollins was inclined to obey, being uninterested in drawing attention to himself. Not so the front gunner. Caught in the act of fornication with one of the female prisoners during a meal and privy stop, he was shot through the head by Warran Glasken with neither trial nor ceremony. He was buried where he died.

23 May 3960: Pocatello

The decomposing body that was wheeled into the town morgue had been nibbled at by vermin for several days and was unrecognizable. The sub-inspector for the town had just finished quite a pleasant dinner when the runner came to his door, and now he busied himself with the registers of travel and absence while the coroner worked with the stench in the adjoining room. Presently the coroner joined him, still wearing his stained, reeking smock.

"The body was found in an overgrown culvert at the edge of town," reported the coroner, sitting uncomfortably close to the sub-inspector. "A passing farmhand noticed the smell. A handmade pistol of .35 caliber was found in his right hand, and two empty whisky bottles were lying beside the body."

"The clothing and papers belong to Giles Normandier, master gunsmith," said the sub-inspector quickly. "Drunkard, heavily in debt, debts recently bought out in return for a couple of decades of work in Condelor. Registered as traveling with tools in a barrow."

"Neither barrow nor tools were found."

"What was the cause of death?"

"One .35-caliber, hollow-point bullet, administered orally, and at high speed. It removed the back of his skull as it exited, along with most of his brains. The bullet was recovered from the wall of the culvert and matched with the weapon discovered in the right hand of the body. The brains had been consumed by the local fauna by the time of discovery."

By now the sub-inspector was chalk-white, and his hands were shaking.

"So, his tools were stolen as he traveled to a new patron

to work out his debts. Got drunk and shot himself."

"So it seems, but I would like to point out that two teeth were broken, and that bicep and hand development indicate that he was left-handed. There is also evidence of bruising to the arms. It may well be murder."

"How can you tell, when he's so far gone?" snapped the sub-inspector, desperate to leave and annoyed at having his word questioned.

"Oh my good sair, even a child could tell. Come, come, let the body speak for itself."

Ten minutes later, having inspected the corpse, vomited on the floor of the post-mortem room, then fled into the cool night air, the sub-inspector lay gasping on a couch while his wife fanned him and dabbed at his forehead with a damp cloth.

"The misanthropic little turd, he did it on purpose, he made up that murder business just to get me in there and see me retch. He knows I have a weak stomach. When I saw that he'd left his sandwiches on the body, gah! At least he'll have to clean up the mess himself."

"Poor darling, but what about the broken teeth and bruises—"

"Oh, the drunken sot probably struggled with whoever stole the tools."

"But if he had a gun—"

"He was probably too drunk to shoot straight. Melline, whose side are you on? My finding is that Giles Normandier shot himself, and there's an end to the matter. His guild can cross one whisky-soaked wretch off its register and good riddance to him too."

Just over an hour's flight to the west, Giles was being strapped into the observer's seat of a huge, matte-black sailwing. Even in the dark, Giles estimated that its wingspan was over seventy feet. He wondered why the Sentinels did not shoot at it.

"It is proof against the Sentinels," said an accented male

voice beside him, anticipating what he was thinking. "It is also very light for all its size."

There were two thumps at the side of the canopy, and Giles heard the flyer clicking levers in the darkness. A low whining began, which slowly rose in pitch, accompanied by the swish of airscrews to either side of the cockpit. They rolled forward, and even Giles could tell that the sailwing was rolling only slowly compared to a normal sailwing. In Mirrorsun's light he could see that they seemed to be racing toward the line of nothingness that marked the edge of the cliff, yet the wheels were still on the surface. They lurched downward into empty space and Giles shrieked in terror, but the sharp dive soon provided the airspeed for the sailwing to level out. Slowly it began to climb.

"How are you feeling?" asked the flyer, with some stiffness in an otherwise Bartolican accent.

"Surprised," said Giles hoarsely.

"It seemed best not to warn you how we manage to get this thing flying when its night ascent run is twice the length of a standard flightstrip. Now in sunlight, we *can* use a normal wingfield."

"Why sunlight?" asked Giles mechanically.

"Because this sailwing is powered by sunlight. It collects it through its wings: some it stores in essence tanks called capacitance batteries so that it can keep aloft at night, the rest it uses to power those engines you can hear. It is best to ascend during the day while we have stored sunlight as well as what is shining down, but then people would see us and that would never do, would it?"

"It is very smooth, ah, apart from the ascent run—oh and very quiet."

"Yes, it is a very advanced sailwing, it can stay aloft for weeks, or even longer."

"This is rather cramped for the long journey that I was told about."

"This is just the beginning. We shall climb above the

clouds as we fly to the Mounthaven frontier, that is forty miles west. After that we go another two hundred miles before dawn."

"Straight out over the Callscour lands? Are you mad?"

"Mad, yes, suicidal, no. *Fras* means Sair where you are going, by the way. You are to learn the language during the trip. Both of our scholarly languages are based on Old Anglian, and the changes come from two thousand years of isolation."

"What happens when—where we land?"

"When *I* land, Fras Normandier, I shall brief my clerk on this mission, then eat breakfast. *You* shall *not* land. Now returning to your new language, if you meet a girl or goodwife she will be *Frelle*. Pretty is *serie*, a carbine is *rifan*, but until very recently we had no flying machines so we say *gunwing* and *sailwing*, just as Bartolicans do."

After several hours of clouds dimly illuminated by Mirrorsun the sky brightened with dawn. As far as Giles could see there were clouds and mountains below, but even had they been just circling the Pocatello wingfield, nothing would have been familiar from this height. An hour after sunrise he saw the sunwing. It was a long, dark line against the sky which kept growing and growing as they slowly caught up to it. Its sheer size had Giles speechless by the time they were closing on a snagline that trailed from the huge aircraft.

"It's as big as an entire wingfield," Giles finally managed. "There must be hundreds of people aboard."

"There's only one, the wingcaptain," said the sunwing's flyer. "It too is powered by the sun, so it must be big enough to collect sufficient essence of sunlight to fly, and store some for the night. It flies continually and is home to the wingcaptain and passengers for weeks or months. There is plenty of open space, but everything that it carries must be very light because the power from the sun is limited. Hush up, now, this is going to be tricky."

The snagline caught in the sunwing's grapple, and it was

drawn up hard against the underside. The flyer swung the canopy aside and helped Giles unload his bags into a large bare compartment with a floor that was covered with hand-holds. Another man appeared through a circular hatch.

"Brother Meltomley, this is Fras Giles Normandier," said the flyer.

"Tarmen gis," replied Meltomley, who bowed to Giles then helped the flyer back into his sailwing's cockpit and lowered the canopy. "This way, Fras Normandier, we must be out of here when the sailwing is released."

Giles waved to the flyer, but could not see if he waved back. Beyond the circular hatchway was a long corridor with walls like smooth white silk. The air was cold, but Meltomley was wearing only a brown robe and cowl, and his feet were bare. The man is a monk, Giles nearly exclaimed aloud. After at least a hundred feet Meltomley ushered Giles into a small room that had a type of double door and was quite warm compared with the corridor. There was a bunk built into the wall, a wickerwork chair, a scribe board, and a shelf of books in the bedhead.

"This is your bedchamber," Meltomley said as he stood in the doorway. "The privy and ablution cell is within that alcove, and a pane in that curved wall shows the land below. I shall be back soon."

Watching through the circular window Giles saw yet more mountains; then there was a slight lurch as the black sailwing detached. It dropped into his field of view and flew a little ahead before banking to the right and descending.

"Fras Normandier."

Giles gave a gasp and spun around to see the huge craft's flyer standing just inside the door.

"I apologize for startling you, I am not used to company."

"Ah, I see. It's nothing."

"As you may have gathered, I am from a religious order where extensive prayer and contemplation are practiced.

We are ideal caretakers for these sunwings, where long periods of isolation are common."

"I—I'll try to stay out of your way."

"That will not be necessary, I have been ordered to teach you something of the language of your new apprentices during the trip. Normally my passengers sleep for the entire journey, it saves the weight of extra food and prevents boredom."

"Am I confined to this room?"

"No. There is a short corridor and small refectory room where you may go freely. My bedchamber, the main stores lockers, purifiers, and the control cell are barred to you, but if you need to speak to me urgently just press the green stud beside any door."

"The green stud . . . Fras Meltomley, why is there such a small living space in such a huge wingcraft?"

"We are climbing at present, and by late afternoon we shall be at over five times our present height. The air is very thin there, and is cold beyond imagining. These few rooms are heated and sealed, but go anywhere else before we descend and you will be dead within a minute and frozen solid within twenty more. Now then, we shall start with a breakfast of dried figs, chickenwurst and limewater, and after that you will learn a few basic nouns and verbs."

The tiny refectory could have seated ten people at most, and had a larger portal with a view of the landscape that was ahead of them. Giles stared in awe at the view.

"With machines like these, why do you need the skills of a humble gunsmith like me?" Giles said without turning from the incredible vista of clouds and mountains.

"That is a very complex matter, Fras. Far better that you find out for yourself."

1 June 3960: Opal, in Yarron

Six days after being shot in the ribs Glasken crawled out of the woods and into the Jannian estate. News that the

Bartolicans had pursued someone over the border had spread quickly, but the fate of the fugitive had remained a mystery. He was known to have been wounded, but not so badly that he could not run. Terriers were sent after him by the Yarronese, but he used streams to smother his trail and lit no fires.

Glasken was found by oilseed planters, who took him to the estate's infirmary. He had lost much blood and his wound was infected, yet he was tough and recovered after a fortnight's care. By this time Warden Jannian and his guild crew were back from Condelor, and Glasken was flirting with his nurse. The stranger showed his gratitude by offering to work on the estate, and the warden agreed to let him stay. Jeb Feydamor began showing him around on the first day of June.

"In Mexhaven the estates are not like this," Glasken said as they walked. "They are walled, and governed like fortresses within the dominions."

"Not so here: our estates are like little dominions within larger dominions. Wardens hold fealty to the airlords, but the airlord holds the land. Warden Jannian could move his estate over to Bartolica if he wished, and if land was granted to him there."

"Has that happened?"

"Not often. Airlords look after their wardens because wardens provide all the parts that build the wings. The guilds of springmakers and valvesmiths have a big guildhall at Opal, and we grow our own oilseeds and sugar beets for the production of compression spirit. The refinery is those stone buildings at the edge of the wingfield, indeed the Guild of Fuelers has given Opal six awards over the past decade for purity and caloric content. The wingfield needs no explanation. The stone guildhalls and houses date back three hundred years."

"So do you grow anything useful, like wheat or birds?"

Feydamor teetered on the brink of taking offense, then

reminded himself that Glasken had asked the question in innocence.

"Useful? There is no higher, more noble produce than that which keeps the gunwings and sailwings of Yarron flying!" he responded.

"I, ah, meant food and clothing."

"Oh yes, we grow fiberweed and vegetables, as well as some birds and swinelets for the table, but the merchant estates provide most of that sort of thing. We do it better, of course, but they do it in quantity. This is a wardenly estate, Sair Glasken. The Jannian family has a crest on its pennon, not just a number."

They toured the core of Opal, finishing at the engineering guildhall. Here there was a compression engine being tested after a recent rebuild. Glasken watched as a steam engine was fired up, then its trolley was wheeled over to a test rig, to which one of the Feydamors' famous radial compression engines had been bolted. A geared spindle spun a wheel attached to the compression engine, and the diesel cycle engine was spun until it caught and came to life. It was left to run up to its operating temperature.

"That one is Bantros," said Feydamor proudly. "He is over two hundred years old."

"He? Bantros?" asked Glasken, who had considered laughing but thought the better of it.

"Why yes, gunwing engines all have names and are always male. They are big, brash, and powerful, while sailwing engines are female for being smooth, enduring, and steady. Bantros has been in thirty duels and combats, has been burned out nine times in overboost, and has crashed twice."

"And, ah, is he to have a new gunwing?"

"No, he is to power the warden's present gunwing for the foundation celebrations at Forian next July. Bantros has a distinctive voice, you see, and the warden wants to make a strong impression as he lands."

The guildsmen began to run power tests on the engine

with slip-gear measuring jigs. By now the warden had arrived to watch.

"Ha there, Glasken, may your full moon shine forever in Bartolican skies," called Jannian.

"But in Yarron it can stay eclipsed," Glasken replied as they grasped wrists.

The warden was a small, wiry man, as most wardens were, and barely came up to Glasken's ribs. He was wearing a scarlet greatcoat with the family crest at each shoulder, and his boots were polished like mirrors and seemed to repel dust by magic. Feydamor had already explained that wardens were considered to be monarchs on their own estates, and were expected to go about as if continually on parade.

"Have you thought about where you might like to work?" asked Jannian.

"The guildhalls are fascinating, Warden."

The warden and Feydamor exchanged glances. It was a subtle exchange, but Glasken noticed.

"That cannot be," replied Feydamor. "We have an embargo against letting any skills relating to flight artisanry reaching any other Callhavens."

"I see, yes, your pardon please, I did not remember. We do have steam engines in Mexhaven, however, and you also use these for your starters, trams, and millshops. Do you need a stoker and oiler for your steam engines?"

"That is not the most noble of callings," Jannian pointed out.

"Ah, but I am not the most noble of men," responded Glasken.

Warden Jannian and Feydamor burst out laughing, and their laughter echoed through the guildhall above the roar of the compression engine.

"You're right, Glasken," said the warden. "We all have a place. Why, we would disappear beneath our own refuse if Sek did not haul away the trashbins."

"Oh but where I come from the building and tending of

steam engines is the very summit of guild skill," Glasken
assured him.

"He speaks good sense," Feydamor agreed. "Do you
have much skill with steam engines, Sair Glasken?"

"My foundation skills are with weapons and explosives,
but I would guess that these are also restricted artisanry in
Opal."

"You are correct, I regret to say," said the warden. "Still,
if you consider steam to be a noble calling, then how could
we affront you by speaking of it badly? Tend our steam
engines, Sair Glasken. Tend them as a Mexhaven guildmaster, and you may sit at my table as a guildmaster each
night."

7 July 3960: Forian, capital of Yarron

An event capable of overshadowing even the Bartolican
coronation was approaching in Yarron. On August 7, 3961,
the Dominion of Yarron would reach the thousandth anniversary of its founding. During its first five hundred
years it had withstood dozens of attacks and invasions, and
since the wardenate system had been established its wardens had been among the finest in Mounthaven's dominions. Although every square foot of Yarronese soil had
been occupied at some time or another, the Yarronese airlords and wardens had always managed to regroup and win
their land back. Only Bartolica had a comparably long history in Mounthaven, being founded fifteen years after Yarron.

The 999th anniversary celebrations in the Yarronese
capital, Forian, were well attended but less of a spectacle
than those of previous years. The gathering of wardens was
primarily for planning the greater anniversary that was soon
to come.

A procession of the wardens through the capital was
marred by a Call that swept across Forian just before the

climax of the celebrations, and the disruption was compounded by a summer rainshower. The airlord's court took place indoors, and while it did not match the sheer spectacle of the coronation celebrations in Bartolica, the pipe bands were truly stirring as they marched into the throne room flanking the Airlord, who was wearing a flight jacket and trousers ablaze with red and green gems, gold thread embroidery, and tiny white tassels. In contrast, his throne was a plain gunwing seat mounted at the head of a flight of stairs, all of which had been cut into a single granite block. Everything in Mounthaven had symbolism in its form, and the throne of Yarron symbolized that the Airlord ran the dominion as skillfully as he flew his gunwing.

That evening there was a feast for the wardens in an ancient hall that had been the throne room in previous years, a huge building of heavy stone walls and tiled roof supported by massive ironbound oak beams interspersing stone arches. As feasts went it might have been considered dull: this was not a gathering for envoys, children, courtiers, or even wives; this was a working meeting of the Airlord and the three hundred wardens, squires, and merchant nobles who formed the elite of Yarron society, government, and defense.

Mere flyers were not invited. Serjon and his peers remained with the sailwings and gunwings in the maintenance halls and tents, tuning and guarding the machines that gave the wardens their very identity. Serjon had by now accumulated twelve hours aloft in nine flights, all in armed sailwings. As the only son in a family of five, his ambitions did not have the support of his guildmaster stepfather, however.

"*Chivalry and the Art of Dueling*?" sneered Feydamor as he entered the tent where Serjon lay reading against a stack of compression spirit barrels. "Chivalry never got an engine tuned."

"Even guildsmen have standards of chivalry to follow," retorted Serjon, without looking up.

"But guildsmen don't stay guildsmen unless they mind their craft. Just remember how the warden dismissed Falcrick's house after five generations of service tending the Jannian airframes, and even after two years of probation Guildsman Jemarial has not been given articles of service."

"But his daughter has had twenty hours in the air over fifteen flights."

"His daughter also weighs ninety pounds, and the warden has strange ideas about long-range flight. The difference between you and her is about fifty pounds of fuel, and the warden values that difference."

"I can play twelve dances on the keovtar and perform those same dances, I play clock-chess, I speak five languages, I know this book of chivalry down to the very last clause—*and* I can fly. I could qualify as a squire, I could even pass as a warden."

"So all you need is a family fortune five times the size of ours and you could buy the articles of an unattached squire. Serjon, as a flyer you can do test flights. Who could hope for more?"

"Well me, for a start."

"So what happens to the family name in the meantime? You're my only son."

"I'm your stepson. Warden Jannian is my father."

"You must carry on as guildmaster after me."

"And I will. I'm an articled engineer—"

"But you don't *want* to be a guildmaster! I look up with pride when I hear the note of one of my engines overhead. You look up and wish you were flying."

"Papasair, I am doing everything that a good son of an engineer guildmaster ought to. The other warden-heirs and flyers are out drinking with bawdy girls in the taverns or gambling their wages away. I am here, and I am reading a book on chivalric practice. What more could you ask for?"

"But why not a book on mixture boost-charging—"

"Gah, that's enough!" shouted Serjon, struggling stiffly

to his feet. "Even though you want me to drown in grease, and though the warden probably wants Bronlar Jemarial for his next squire, *I* am going to *fly*!"

"Where are you going?"

"Outside, for some fresh air. If I can't fly in it, at least I can breathe it! Oh, and you have thirteen gravy spots on your shirtfront."

Outside, in the weakening light of evening, Serjon glanced around to be sure that his father was not following him, then stopped beside Jannian's triwing. It was a graceless but very functional gunwing. The apprentice from the airframe guild who was standing guard waved idly to him, and Serjon waved back. Farther across the wingfield he could see Bronlar standing beside the sailwing of Jannian's squire. She too waved, and Serjon responded with a courtly bow. The bow was in fact the correct formal greeting for a guildmaster's daughter, but Bronlar turned away at once, fuming.

The issue of female flyers was a topical one in Yarron. Many guild families had no sons, and daughters often carried on the work of airframe maintenance and fueling, including the test flights of some wings. The armorers' and engineers' guilds had been less tolerant, preferring adoption, son-in-law heirs, or even "guested" fathers to supply male children. Bronlar had been brought to the capital by Warden Jannian. He had an idea that women might be introduced to the ranks of the flight guild, first as flyers and later as squires, and he had the support of several other wardens with talented female flyers among their own guild families. The issue had raised considerable debate among the Yarronese wardens, although Bronlar's flight to Condelor and the subsequent outrage of the Bartolican adjunct, herald, and wardens had won her a lot of support.

She stood leaning against a pennant pole beside the sailwing, gazing wistfully over toward the old throne room and wondering what was being said about her fate at that very moment. The sky still glowed with sunset, and Mirrorsun was not yet visible on the opposite horizon.

"So you're what all the fuss is about."

Bronlar turned, and not far away Serjon looked up from the book that he was trying to memorize by lamplight. Several youths of her own age or older formed a half circle around her. By their flight jackets and town hats she could see that they were of the families of wardens and squires, and many were quite probably future wardens themselves.

"Are you speaking to me?" she demanded sharply, so sharply that nobody spoke for a moment.

"Being a flyer is not your place," a very thin but handsome youth of about her age said nervously.

"That decision is not yours to make, Sair Alion," Bronlar replied, stepping so that the thick pole remained between her and the group.

"Flyers have to do more than fly gunwings and sailwings, we must fight on the ground as well as the air," declared a shorter but more heavily built youth who now stepped forward and reached for her.

Bronlar made to walk straight into his outstretched arm, taking him by surprise. She snaked an arm around his, stepping behind him and bending him over double. He gave a cry of surprise and pain. Her knee was in the way as he tried to take a step to balance himself, and he rolled over it and fell heavily, crashing into the pole. As he lay there, stunned, the others got over their surprise and began to circle and close in. Some had drawn the calf-canes from their boots.

Bronlar was armed with a cross-truncheon bound in leather, and had been taught to use it. Enduring a cane stroke across the arm, she lunged, striking Alion in the midriff, then did a blind swing behind herself, catching another youth over the ear. For a moment there was a break in the fighting, but the group was still confident although surprised.

Serjon stepped over Alion to stand beside Bronlar, holding up his book on chivalry.

"Does it take thirteen of you to defeat a girl?" he said. "Is Yarronese chivalry in such a state? If you flyers and wardens of the future need odds like this to go into battle, then your pennants will very soon be painted on the canvas of some foreign warden's gunwing. Besides, thirteen is a very bad number, did you know that?"

"Stay out of this, guildsman," warned Alion, who was fighting to get his breath back. "If she wants to fly she needs to know what happens after forced landings."

"Even flyers are sworn to uphold the basics of chivalry," Serjon insisted, "and I do have the license of a flyer."

"You have only daylight solo, even Bronlar has night ascents and landings appended to her license," called someone behind Serjon.

"Bronlar is from the family of a guildmaster of my warden. As a flyer it is my chivalric duty to protect her against—"

"What?" exclaimed Bronlar, suddenly realizing what Serjon was doing. "I'm a flyer in my own right, and with my own license! I need no protection."

Serjon held up his book and brandished it at them.

"It says here on page forty-seven that flyers must serve their warden in the protection of women and children, especially in matters of honor, safety, and virtue."

"That book is ninety years old!" shouted Bronlar, slapping the volume out of his hands and into the dust. "I'm a flyer and a woman, and what's more I'm a more senior flyer than you!"

"Your status is defined in the wardens' constitution," Serjon pointed out, bristling at the truth that he hated.

"I fight my own battles!" Bronlar retorted indignantly.

"I duel with no girl!" declared the stocky youth, who had lost the thread of the argument long ago.

"By the rules of heraldry you must accept a challenge or be posted on the pennant pole below the Line of Shame," Bronlar insisted.

"Challenge can only be given to a peer," he replied.

"Page forty-seven you say?" asked a youth who had picked up Serjon's book.

"*You* are a woman under threat and *I* am under a clear obligation to defend you, whether your rank exceeds mine or not," Serjon cut in.

"He's right," said the youth with the book.

"Well I reject your defense!" cried Bronlar, slapping Serjon's face, "and I challenge—"

Serjon did not see the explosion that erupted within the old throne room of the Airlord's distant palace, but he whirled at the flash of light on Bronlar's face, then staggered back at the massive blast. The roof and walls collapsed in a cauldron of smoke, dust, flames, and sparks; then all was eerily quiet for a moment except for the echoes of the detonation. Whistles, trumpets, and bells began to come to life, and everyone rushed toward the glowing but horrifyingly flat remains of the old throne room.

By the time Serjon arrived there were still small fires dancing amid the rubble from crushed lamps. The weight of the stones and beams was beyond the strength of those who had dashed across, and it was an hour before the first heavy crane was in place and lifting the stone blocks away to reveal the crushed, burned, and suffocated corpses of the Yarronese wardens and their servants. Thousands of volunteers held torches or formed human chains to carry away the smaller pieces of stone. Nurses and medics came from all over the city, and infirmary tents were pitched in the palace gardens. The Airlord's body was found just after midnight, and by the morning three hundred and twenty bodies had been removed. Nine servants and clerks were pulled out of the ruins alive, and five wardens lived to see the sunrise. Not one of them was expected to be able to take a gunwing into the air again, so terrible were their injuries.

Fieldmajor Gravat was sworn in as regent, and he ordered a dozen courier sailwings into the air at first light. They carried details of the disaster and orders for all surviving wardens to wind up their business within a fortnight and come to Forian. Yarron was placed under martial law until the fifteen survivors of the Yarronese peerage were gathered together to proclaim the Airlord's only son to be Virtrian XII of Yarron. One of Gravat's first acts as regent was to declare all business posted for the wardens' meeting to be passed as a gesture of respect to the dead nobles. This included Jannian's motion that women be admitted to the guild of squires.

The Yarronese Inspector General quickly determined that explosives had been placed in the walls and roof of the old throne room with such skill that the building would not be blown apart, but would collapse on those inside, maximizing the number of deaths. The Airlord's own inspectors had gone over the old throne room that very morning, but even under torture it could not be established that they had been paid to overlook explosives already secreted there. Some scraps of sacking with a Dorak haulier's guild crest were discovered amid the ruins, but this did nothing but provoke outrage from the Dorak envoy when he was summoned and confronted with it.

The days that followed were filled with funerals, flypasts, and mass wakes. Succession disputes erupted right across Yarron as its aristocracy struggled to cope with a disaster that was on the scale of a major duel war in terms of casualties to their ranks. Jannian's body was strapped into the flyer's seat of a gunwing trainer and his son Ricmear flew it back to Middle Junction for burial, with the three sailwings of his house flying a guard of honor.

12 July 3960: East Bartolica

Life on the black tram was exceedingly boring for Rollins, his stoker, and the two gunners throughout June, but in early July that began to change. The gunners practiced shooting at target kites towed by unmarked sailwings, and the crew practiced covering the tram with camouflage netting every time it was at rest. Rollins began to wonder if the outlaws were Yarronese, and if their wardens were backing them! Were that the case, Bartolican carbineers and their trams might be strafed from the sky by sailwings—or even gunwings! The idea of warden outlaws was almost a contradiction in terms, but Rollins always tried to keep an open mind. The tram's reaction gun was fired at the target kites both when the tram was moving and when it was at rest in sidings.

On the 12th of July the black tram was at a siding at Bancroft, on the mountain tramway to the border with Yarron. They had been there all day, cleaning and servicing the tram and exercising the prisoners from the top deck. A store of wood blocks, dried food, and water had been left a hundred yards into the forest near the siding, and the prisoners were made to carry everything to the tram in the afternoon. When the last of sunset had faded from the sky a sailwing droned overhead, then dropped a flare with a parachute. A dozen of the prisoners were sent out with two of the officers, and they presently returned carrying two heavy boxes in slings. They were walking very carefully, under the watchful direction of the merchant officers.

The boxes were unpacked in the darkness by officers wearing odd goggles. Rollins could see little from where he knelt on the roof, boring holes with an auger under instruction from another merchant officer. There was a thing like a pedalframe without wheels, a large plain box, and reels like those used for aircraft bracing wire. The prisoners were moved out of the upper level, the contents of the boxes were carried in, and the officers set to work inside, hammering something into place. Outside the tram Rollins and the stoker stood chopping the boxes and packing into firewood.

In the morning Rollins saw that four poles on hinges had been erected on the roof of the tram. Bracing wire was strung from the poles, and there was an irregular peeping sound coming from the upper level.

"I hear whirrin'," said the stoker.

"Sounds like a spinning wheel turned by pedals," suggested Rollins.

"Why not fire up the steam engine and use that to spin, ah, whatever they want spun?" asked the stoker.

"Perchance they want their machine spun discreetly, in hiding, with no smoke to betray the tram's position."

The stoker raised a finger into the air and gave a great beaming smile of revelation.

"Hey there, now that's clever," he cried. "You smell what's on the air? Like a thunderstorm. I'll bet they're buildin' and storin' thunderbolts in there. New weapon, that's what all the fuss is about. Aye, we're in the thunderbolt carbineers, Sair Rollins! Ain't ye proud?"

Rollins winced at the level of the man's voice. In the distance a merchant officer who was keeping watch turned around, but he could not have heard what they were discussing. Rollins gave a small wave, as if he were scratching his ear.

"Hey now, my brother's on a cart cannon crew. You know, the new big ones with a four-inch bore? Now you got to be there to see the look on his face when I tells him that I'm on a *thunderbolt* crew."

The officer was drifting closer, not obviously listening but close enough to hear the drift of what the stoker was saying. Rollins tried to steer the conversation to speculating on when they might move again, and slowly the stoker calmed down and lowered his voice. The officer locked eyes with Rollins for a moment, and Rollins nodded twice. The officer returned to scanning the valley below them with field glasses.

Rollins slept for most of the day, and in the late afternoon he was woken in his sleeping roll by Kalward. The merchant officer asked about what the stoker had been saying about thunderbolts earlier in the day. Rollins related the conversation with passable accuracy. Kalward listened in impassive silence.

"My impression is that you want discretion for the black trams," Rollins concluded. "Stoker Harrical has little sense of discretion."

Kalward stood in silence, leaning against a pine tree and looking across to the black tram as the prisoners were being given their evening breakfast. He looked down at Rollins, and in his eyes Rollins could see something very cold and hard.

"We do want discretion, Sair Rollins, and we want it as badly as this."

Kalward pushed away from the tree and strode over to where the prisoners were eating. The stoker was tending a cooking fire, feeding it blocks of dry, hard wood that gave off little smoke.

"Sair Harrical?" said Kalward, raising his reaction pistol.

As the stoker turned with his mouth open to reply, the officer emptied half of the spring clip into his face. Later that night Kalward came to stand beside the driver's cage as Rollins drove the tram along the winding mountain tramway and one of the other officers stoked the furnace. He gazed into the darkened mountains ahead for a long time. Rollins said nothing.

"Well?" asked Kalward, without turning away from the view.

"Yes, Sair Kalward?" asked Rollins.

"Are you going to ask what this tram is really used for?"

"No, Sair Kalward."

"You're bright and you work hard. Don't you want promotion?"

"No, Sair Kalward."

"That's because you have a past, isn't it?"

"Yes, Sair Kalward."

Kalward laughed. "Good lad, you have a future with the Merchant Tramway Service."

12 July 3960: The Yarronese border

Laurelene Hannan had chosen a particularly bad morning to begin her journey through Yarron, although she would not realize it for some weeks. When her steam tram reached Kemmerer she disembarked and walked through the town to the place on the eastern outskirts where an iron rail was sunk across the road. A sign read WELCOME TO THE DOMINION OF YARRON in Yarronese, Bartolican, and Old Anglian, and two Yarronese guards flanked the road. Beyond this was a small customs house; then the road wound among rocks and conifers.

A guard walked over to where Laurelene stood with a wreath of flowers, reading her son's report as if it were a requiem prayer.

"Can I help you, Semme?" he asked in Bartolican.

She looked up slowly, as if she did not expect him to be there.

"Ah, yes, thank you. A man, an acquaintance of mine, died here some weeks ago. I wanted to lay this wreath at the place."

The guard shook his head, but his expression was one of sympathy.

"I could take the wreath for you, Semme, but you cannot cross without papers. The border between our dominions is tense, especially after the terrible bombing in Forian."

"But I do have papers," said Laurelene, suddenly gathering her thoughts together. "I am to cross into Yarron by steam tram this very hour."

The guard examined her papers, then took her over to the customs house and signed her in for an excursion crossing.

"I was on duty that very evening," he said as he walked down the road with Laurelene. "The Bartolican carbineers shot at Sair Glasken from the border, then swept us aside and crossed into Yarron in pursuit of him. Ah, this is the very spot."

Laurelene sank to her knees and laid the wreath on the ground, then burst into tears. "It's my fault," she sobbed. "I killed you at this very spot as surely as if I pulled the trigger."

"But he didn't die here," said the guard.

Laurelene paused in mid-sob, her reddened eyes wide and her expression hardening.

"He didn't?"

"No, this is the spot that he lowered his trews and shone full moon at the carbineers. That's when they started shooting and crossed the border. He was running when I last saw him, holding his ribs with one hand and his trews with the other."

Laurelene stood up, slammed the wreath on the ground, and stamped on it. She clutched the guard by the lapels of his jacket.

"Then he's alive? Where is he?"

"I cannot say, Semme," replied the rather alarmed guard. "He did not return here, but that is hardly surprising. He may have tried to reach Middle Junction on foot, but the country is wild."

Laurelene stared down at the remains of her wreath, wondering whether or not to leave it. She finally decided that it reminded her that she had been sorry for Glasken, and that was a somewhat humiliating memory.

"What draws you to Yarron?" asked the guard as she marched back to the border.

"I had a whim to travel where my . . ." Laurelene braced herself to utter a lie. ". . . friend was going."

"An affair of the heart?" asked the guard, who was something of a romantic.

"An affair, yes, but *my* heart is not involved. Thank you for your help, young man. If all Yarronese are as polite as you then my journey will be a pleasant one indeed."

Back in Bartolica, Laurelene met with the five carbineers of her escort at the tramway station.

"He is alive!" she told them. "He must be dragged back to Bartolica."

"Leave it to us, Semme," the captain of her escort began.

"No! I want this done properly. If my menfolk will not avenge my honor then *I'll* do it *myself.*"

12 July 3960: Western Yarron

The twin engine, triwing regal droned slowly over the farmland of the Green River Basin on its 180-mile journey to Dorak territory from northern Cosdora. Wingcaptain Perisonian scanned the gauges amid the filigree and inlay of the instrument board, noting that both engines were at the correct temperature, oil pressure, and rate of spin. The long trip had begun before dawn, and the rising sun was to starboard.

"We are nearing the midway point," the navigator reported. "Were it not for the clouds we would see Middle Junction ahead and a little to port."

"I see it, there's a break. Course correct, less than an hour to go. A half-hour reserve of spirit remains."

The steward rapped at the cockpit door, then entered.

"The Airlord is awake," he reported. "He wants to know when we arrive at the capital."

"Still three hours to go," replied the wingcaptain. "We must land to take on fuel once over the border."

"That would put our arrival at nearly the tenth hour of the morning, and the Airlord has a busy schedule. You have to do better."

"We were ready for flight an hour before he arrived," Perisonian retorted. "If the Airlord needed to arrive earlier you should have roused him."

"The Airlord was not disposed to be roused."

"Ah my, so the Dorak ambassador to the Cosdorans has

been using his wife as an instrument of policy again?"

"If you please, sair, keep your voice down," hissed the steward. "You speak of the Airlord of All Dorak."

"Well? Go back and tell the Airlord of All Dorak that this regal is already flying as fast as is prudent along the shortest route."

"Wingcaptain Perisonian, I cannot take that sort of answer back to the Airlord."

"And I cannot run my engines hotter than they are just now. The Carbearu family does not take kindly to its engines being used for something as ignominious as transport, even if the cargo is our head of state."

"But the Airlord is a warden in his own right."

"You don't have to explain that to my engineers guild. I do. If their compression engines show unreasonable wear, this regal will be declared blackwing for a lunar month and I shall be cooling my heels in the flyers' reserve."

The steward looked longingly to the north.

"I need to tell the Airlord *something*. He wants to reach the capital at 9:30. His consort will be waiting."

"All the more reason to fly slower."

"Be serious, Wingcaptain Perisonian."

"Have you met his consort?"

"Wingcaptain!"

"Well . . . tell him there is an emergency."

"What sort of an emergency?"

He was cut short by a scatter of bullets ripping through the cabin from behind. Perisonian immediately swung the heavy regal into a turn and dived to pick up speed. The steward was flung across the cabin and crashed heavily into the navigator.

"Go aft, strap in!" shouted Perisonian.

"What shall I tell the Airlord?"

"Tell him we're under attack!"

Perisonian caught sight of an oddly shaped, strangely thin gunwing as he banked. Instead of at its wingtips the rudders were at the end of a long boom trailing behind the

main wings. There were two engines mounted in the
wings, but they were impossibly thin. It vanished behind
them, then began shooting again. Perisonian flung the
heavy regal about, but the pursuing flyer was not taken by
surprise again.

"Find me somewhere to land, quickly!" he shouted to
the navigator.

"Middle Junction wingfield is only minutes distant."

"That's a Yarronese wingfield."

"Pinedale is the closest Dorak wingfield, and that's
nearly as far ahead as we've already flown."

"Hell and Callbait! All right, set a course for Middle
Junction. Yarron has a treaty with us for emergencies."

Another burst ripped into the starboard engine, which
lost oil pressure and began to smoke. Perisonian reduced
spirit to the engine, and it spluttered but did not quite die.
Another burst raked the cabin, hitting the navigator in the
leg and spraying glass into Perisonian's face. The bursts
were more frequent now, and there were cries from back
in the cabin where the Airlord and steward sat helplessly.

"Airspeed eighty-seven mph," called Perisonian. "How
much longer to Middle Junction?"

"Minutes. Align on the river and bear south five degrees
west when we get through the clouds."

The navigator unstrapped, took a carbine from the utility
rack, and hobbled to the sidereal steps.

"Where are you going?" shouted Perisonian. "Strap in."

"Just you keep us flying."

There was a roar of wind as the sidereal hatch was
opened, then Perisonian heard the navigator shooting. After five shots he gave a whoop of triumph.

"I took him! I took the bastard! He's dropping behind—
no! Damn, he's coming up under us where I can't see."

"Nearly at the clouds," the wingcaptain called back.

"I see him again, dark blue on top of its wings, with
twin airscrews facing backwards and no air intakes. Damn
thing is like nothing I've ever seen before."

There was another exchange of shots, and the second engine began to run roughly as Perisonian fought for control.

"The Airlord is hit, the Airlord is bleeding!" called the steward from the cabin.

"Clouds, we're nearly at the clouds!" the wingcaptain called.

The navigator fired another clip of bullets at their enigmatic attacker. Both engines were running hot, and there was a fire in the starboard wing.

"He's breaking off!" shouted the navigator. "He's banking to port and—lost him in the clouds."

"Did you hit him again?"

"Maybe . . . I don't think so, but I couldn't tell."

"He may think we're dead in the air, we're trailing enough smoke. There! We're through the clouds, and there's Middle Junction. I'll rev up the starboard engine and try to keep some height before it melts."

The engine roared back into life, but after thirty seconds it seized and died. That was good enough, though, it had bought them a little height. The regal approached Middle Junction on one engine, losing height and on fire, but under a degree of control. The wheels squealed on the surface of the wingfield, the airspeed dropped—then the spine of the starboard wing burned through and snapped. The regal skidded along the runway, its landing gear collapsed, scattering wreckage and spraying burning compression spirit like some huge, gaudy pinwheel.

Perisonian woke up in an infirmary bed in Middle Junction to find that the Dorak consul was maintaining a vigil with the medics and nurses.

"The Airlord . . ." whispered Perisonian. "Is the Airlord . . ."

The consul came over and sat on the edge of the bed. "You are the only survivor of the crash," he said gravely. "The Airlord was hit by three bullets, and two of them remained lodged in his body." The consul held up a bullet between his thumb and forefinger. "It's a ten-millimeter jacketed type, by the Worland guild of Casper, Yarron."

Perisonian thought for a moment.

"We were attacked . . . an unknown gunwing. No crest, no house name, no engineers' guild symbol."

"Did you see it?"

"Only for a moment. It stayed behind, shooting unchivalrously. My navigator . . . climbed into the sidereal, fired at it with a carbine."

"He drove it off? With only a carbine?"

"No . . . perhaps, no. The flyer must have thought that he had done his job as we were burning when we reached the clouds. It—it seems he was right, even though we reached the wingfield."

"Can you hold a pen? Can you sketch the gunwing?"

"I'll try. The navigator saw it clearly. He described it to me."

The consul snapped his fingers and a clerk came forward with a board, paper, and writing kit. Perisonian was helped up in the bed and he made several shaky representations while the clerk took notes and the consul watched. The consul watched and listened, then picked up one of the sketches and stared at it.

"Keep working with him until he has recalled all that he can, Loric. Wingcaptain Perisonian, you are a brave man and a loyal citizen. Tell Loric all that you can remember, then rest well. I shall recommend that you be honored. Good night now, Wingcaptain."

Loric worked patiently with the wingcaptain for another half hour, talking little and noting everything that he said. At last Perisonian could recall no more, and Loric began to pack up.

"I hope that I have been of some help," said Perisonian.

"Oh you have indeed, Wingcaptain. Rest well now."

Loric drew a baffle-tube pistol from his bag and shot him between the eyes.

Minutes later a Call swept in from the Red Desert, moving west.

14 July 3960: Middle Junction

Envoy Sartov had been passing through Middle Junction when the Dorak airlord was assassinated. The wingfield's adjunct briefed him on the crash the day after Perisonian had been murdered. The adjunct's office looked out over the staging area of the wingfield, and the blackened wreckage of the regal was plainly visible from where they sat.

"It is good to see you, Alveris, but not under these circumstances," the adjunct began.

"The bombing shortened my term in Condelor by two weeks, so some good came out of it," Sartov replied. "My replacement is not even a warden."

"Yarronese wardens are now the rarest in Mounthaven. We need you all back to hold the dominion together." The adjunct reached for a rock crystal jar of whisky. "Let us toast your return to Yarron," he said, pouring out a measure.

"Just rainwater for me, Morris. I swore off the drink on the day that I learned of the bombing."

"Well, indeed, that comes as good news too. We were worrying about you." He gestured to the wreckage outside. "The Dorakian consul is screaming as if his piles were being cauterized because of that."

Sartov clasped his hands and leaned over the desk. "He must have your fullest cooperation, too. Dorak's envoy in Condelor was talking about war just before I flew out this morning."

"The more cooperation he gets, the more evidence of a badly concealed Yarronese plot emerges," the adjunct said, waving yet another folder from a scribe box. "I found this in the consul's case. He had dropped it in bushes when a Call caught him outside the wingfield infirmary. I had a scribe copy the more interesting parts before everything was returned. There's a sketch of the sailwing that attacked the regal. Look at its configuration."

"Odd, very odd. Impossibly thin engines, no intakes, huge wings. There is no dominion known with sailwings like this."

"Now look at what the consul was waving about in my office this morning."

"Hmm. Looks more like a Yarronese Squire 1000 sailwing."

"We found Yarronese bullets lodged in the wreckage of the regal. It's an attack over Yarron, and the sole survivor and witness was murdered in a Yarronese hospital. A Yarronese bullet was extracted from his brain. The fact that a sketch of a strange gunwing turned up amid stolen notes will carry no weight beside the fabricated sketch of a far more plausible Yarronese armed sailwing."

"A damning body of evidence," agreed Sartov. "The Dorakians will be even more insulted because we supposedly used a sailwing to kill him, rather than a chivalric gunwing."

"It is neat, very neat, suspiciously neat. The surviving Yarronese wardens are howling for blood and vengeance after what happened at Forian ten days ago, and now this happens. The evidence is overwhelming that Yarron is responsible for the Dorak airlord's death, but our only evidence for Dorak hands behind the Forian bombing are some scraps of sacking from Dorak."

"Morris, I have heard nothing of such a plot."

"Neither have I. Nothing! Not a request to turn a blind eye to strange sailwings, nor an order to leave wingfield beacons burning all night and ignore whatever traffic passes through. Perhaps someone in Dorak wanted their airlord dead and decided to incriminate Yarron."

They sat looking across at the ranks for Yarronese gunwings that no longer had experienced wardens to fly them. Teenage wardens strutted about wearing their new crests and waving their hands in parodies of airborne duels. Their guildsmen sat by the gunwings, looking studiously attentive and saying nothing.

"What can you tell me about the Dorak regional consul?" asked Sartov. "I have not had a chance to meet him as yet."

"A diligent but excitable man, with a long record in the diplomatic service."

"He was the last to see Wingcaptain Perisonian alive."

"Please don't publicly imply that he did it, Sair Sartov, the Dorakians are angry enough already. As this report states, his clerk was about to enter the wingcaptain's ward when he heard a shot, then the Call came."

"But he did not enter?"

"No. He was unarmed and there was apparently a gunman in the room. Instead he ran down the corridor of the infirmary shouting for the guards. Then the Call swept over them."

"Very neat, very innocent. Tell me about him."

"The clerk? Loric d'Kemnef's name appears in diplomatic records going back three years. He got his present appointment a few months ago. He has a Collegian Degree from the Dorakian National Academy, with second-class honors—the sort of person who is not quite a merchant officer, but is doing the next best thing. There is one odd thing about him, though."

"Tell me."

"I was in the Dorakian National Academy back in 3955, as a guest lecturer in three of the subjects in which he gained honors. I do not remember him."

"He may have cribbed your notes from others and missed all your lectures."

"True, but I am good with names and I also kept lists of all my students—one never knows when one can claim profitable association when a student rises to high office. The clerk d'Kemnef is not on my lists. I'm sure he has a degree from somewhere, I mean people often forge degrees

from academies with greater prestige than where they actually studied. He seems very bright and erudite, more so
than the regional consul if you ask me."

Sartov got up and walked across to the window overlooking the Middle Junction wingfield. The remains of the
regal were to the left, under armed guard and with two
Dorakian site inspectors keeping watch over the Yarronese
guards.

13 July 3969: Condelor

The Bartolican court had risen for the evening, and Rosenne was waiting at a stone canal quay for the envoys'
courtesy barge. There was to be a feast that night for no
particular reason, but it was suspected that the death of the
cream of Yarron's nobility had inspired it. The Veraguay
envoy was putting on weight under the onslaught of Bartolican feasting, however. She excused herself, saying that
she could write an account of the distant tragedy.

As she stood leaning against the vine-smothered stone
block wall with Theresla, Roric Hannan came into sight in
a small steam barge. It was a squat, stable little craft of
gilded wood with scenes from the classic *Chronicles of
Seductions* carved into the railings. A servant tended the
little oil-fired steam engine and steered from inside a hide
cabin while Roric languidly called commands, as if to the
boat itself.

Seeing the two women alone and waiting, Roric ordered
his barge over to the quay.

"Ho there, you'd not be waiting for the envoy's barge,
would you Semme?" he called as the barge slowed.

"I am indeed," Rosenne called back.

"It's not to be returning until five hours are past. All
other envoys are going to the feast—except for you and
that new boy from Yarron."

Rosenne put her hands on her hips and looked along the

canal, frowning. Roric's barge slowed and bumped against the quay.

"Well, perhaps I am fated to be at the feast after all," she said. "Theresla and I wanted to write an account of that terrible disaster in Yarron."

"Hah, you could share my humble barge."

"Oh Sair Roric, I could not impose thus," Rosenne said, clasping her hands and smiling broadly.

"No imposition, Semme, none at all. I am returning home, and that's near the Enclave of Dominions anyway. I would be glad of your company."

"But are you not to be at the feast also?"

"Alas, I must attend to some tiresome household details that are normally in Laurelene's care. She's in Yarron, you know."

Rosenne did indeed know, and had known since Laurelene left two days earlier. She had not wanted to seem like an easy prize, but two days was a discreet period to wait.

"Oh, how very lonely for you," she responded. "In that case I *must* share your barge."

Rosenne and Theresla got into the little craft, which moved off smoothly.

"You are indeed fortunate to have a personal barge on the Airlord's own canal," said Rosenne as she seated herself and clipped on her Call tether.

"In his wisdom the Airlord recognizes that someone as busy as his Inspector General needs to move about freely and quickly. I have unlimited run of all canals."

He glanced for a moment to Theresla, who was watching two gunwings trailing colored smoke from their wingtips and weaving green and red spirals.

"Is, ah, your servant learning the ways of Condelor's markets and suchlike?" he asked.

"Theresla?" laughed Rosenne. "No, she just attends clerical matters, now that I have three Bartolican servants who daily tend the garden and haggle at the market."

Roric smiled and nodded, and said that he was pleased that she had settled in so well.

"What news is there of Semme Laurelene, your most forthright wife?" she asked, prompted by the sight of the gunwings flying over the palace. "I have heard that war threatens between Yarron and Dorak."

"Oh I have had no letters yet, but I have no fears," he said without concern in his tone. "War is of no danger to any but wardens, and of no interest to those who are not of their estates or guilds."

"Do you mean that the merchants and other citizens do not care who rules them?"

"Well, did anyone in Bartolica refuse to swear loyalty to our new Airlord just because they were loyal to his late father? Of course not. It is the same with our wars, they are merely duels between dominions, matters of honor for those who are honorable. The estates and farms pay taxes just the same, the steam trams, aqueduct engines, roads, and Call towers run as before."

"Put that way, it hardly sounds like war at all."

"Well, we have to be civilized here in Mounthaven. Our land is so poor that it is a long and difficult task to repair wanton destruction. Now then, perhaps *you* can widen *my* own knowledge," said Roric genially. "What other places have boats such as these?"

"Oh none. In all my travels I have only seen such powered boats in this very city."

"Hah! Thought so. As each day passes I have ever more reasons for never leaving Bartolica. My wife likes to travel: she gads off here and there, yet even she comes back and tells me how good it is to be home."

"Oh but surely she enjoys seeing what is different. I do, and I have traveled more than anyone in the known world."

"She has other reasons, I know it too well. As Chief Inspector I have many informants."

"And what do they inform you of?"

"Semme Laurelene visits . . . friends. Friends of a male nature, if you catch my meaning."

Rosenne caught the meaning, and all the others that Roric Hannan had intended.

"You are very tolerant, Sair Hannan, and that is refreshing. Why, my husband was so jealous that he had spies among my household servants. I not only had to lead a blameless life, I had to be *seen* to do it as well."

Slyly glancing to Theresla, Roric noted that she was writing notes from slates of shorthand script. He reached out and sympathetically patted Rosenne's hand. If Theresla noticed, she gave no sign of it.

"Ah, but the good man is dead now, and you are free to live as you will, Semme," Roric pointed out.

He let his hand rest lightly on hers. At first she jerked it back a fraction, as if to pull away, then stopped herself. She twisted it instead, twining her fingers about those of Roric.

"True, and you are an alluring companion, Sair Roric."

Regional Inspector Vander Hannan treated royal feasts and other such occasions the same way as he did difficult assignments in the backwoods. There was information to be gathered and people were liable to part with it, either to bolster their own self-importance, or to trade, or merely because they were too drunk to mind their tongues. Partly out of concern for his mother, Vander had been probing for the truth behind the catastrophe in Yarron's capital.

"I notice that your father is not to be seen," observed Colliconev, Chancellor of Wardens.

Vander looked around, but assumed that the man's statement was true all the while.

"True, he is gone. Is that significant?"

Colliconev shrugged and sipped at his claret. "He left in some haste, just after the lovely Semme Rosenne Rodriguez of Veraguay was seen to be walking down the path to the barge quay. His own barge is now missing, and

would you believe that there is an order signed by his own
hand that the envoys' barge was not to leave until after the
feast?"

"What is your implication, Sair Colliconev?" Vander
asked impatiently, knowing full well what his father probably had in mind.

"Sair Hannan, the elder, has much in common with the
Veraguay envoy. They are probably discussing the wonders of their respective Callhavens."

Within the comfort of the envoy's bed, thought Vander
with impotent disapproval. He had no illusions about his
father's behavior, he just wished that the man could be
less public about it.

"I am due to leave for the north next week," Vander
said idly.

"Ah, that region is no easy task, it is not settled and
orderly, like the south. I wonder that you do not look for
a transfer here, now that you have proved yourself."

Colliconev sipped at his wine. He always sipped, he
never drank. Vander suspected that no wine ever passed
between his lips. He always reminded Vander of a small,
sharp, poisoned blade.

"If you imply that I am being groomed for some post,
then nobody has told me about it," Vander replied.

"You have spent a lot of time in Condelor lately for
someone with no ambitions here."

A group of singers performed an ode to the wardens of
Bartolica. The text had reputedly been written by the Airlord himself, although the Master of Royal Music had set
it for six voices. The work was boring, and it was with
some relief that Vander felt a tug at his sleeve and looked
around to see one of his father's aides. As they left the
hall Vander could not help but note the bloodless pallor
of the man's face.

"A fire, Sair Hannan, a fire at the Enclave of Dominions," said the aide breathlessly.

"I see, that is very serious," Vander replied, "but this is

not my inspectorate. Have you informed my fa—the Inspector General?"

"That is just it!" exclaimed the aide, clawing at the air in agitation. "The Inspector General is in the building that is burning."

Vander's calm buckled, but held. He gasped an oath in shock, then seized the aide by the arm and marched him down the corridor.

"How do you know he is in there?" he demanded. "And which house is he in, anyway?"

"That of the Veraguay envoy. Her servants have vanished, and the city constables have been alerted to arrest them."

The aide had kept a steam barge waiting for them, and after a short trip they reached the Enclave of Dominions and hurried across to the blaze, flanked by Inspectorate guards. The city orderlies had the fire under control by the time he arrived and members of the Inspectorate were already among the ruins. The truth unfolded quickly: both the envoy from Veraguay and his own father had died in the blaze.

Vander smothered his grief with action. The bodies found in the remains of the envoy's double bed were identified by their rings and the blackened remains of Roric Hannan's gun and coat buttons on the flagstone floor. They had apparently been overcome by the smoke in their sleep before being burned. The fire had been started with jars of sunflower oil, whose shards were strewn about in the charred downstairs rooms. Hannan had all five of the late envoy's servants proclaimed as suspects in the double murder. The suspicions that Laurelene had confided to him about Theresla had finally been borne out.

Of some interest were several pages of writing in a strange script that were found in the grounds of the burned-out house. The script was familiar yet oddly stylized, and while many of the words almost made sense, the concepts behind them did not. Hannan took custody of them and set about having them translated by the Inspectorate's linguists. As it turned out, they made very slow progress.

14 July 3960: East Bartolica

The orders given to Rollins were clear enough: take the black tram to its maximum speed along the length of straight tramway, and do it at night. The night was overcast, shutting out Mirrorsun's light, and the two forward lanterns of the black tram provided illumination for only a dozen feet ahead. Rollins opened the throttle, and the little steam engine gradually pushed the square-front tram up to near its maximum speed of 41 miles per hour, four times its normal cruising speed.

Beside Rollins was Kalward, with the forward shutters of the tram wide open and a grapple pole in his hand. Two other officers were watching, one with a bucket of water. Without warning a flare burst overhead, lighting up the underside of a sailwing. The point of light dropped slowly, and Rollins realized that it was on a line being reeled out. When it was almost level with his eyes Kalward reached out with the grapple pole, swiped at it twice, then caught it the third time.

The interior of the tram was filled with fumes and blinding light as the officer drew the flare inside, but it was immediately quenched in the bucket. With glowing spots before his eyes, Rollins saw that there was a dispatch cannister attached to the flare. While Kalward picked up a flare gun the other two officers detached the flare from the line and secured another cannister in its place. Kalward fired a flare from the gun ahead of the sailwing, and the second cannister was drawn up into the air as the sailwing pulled away.

"We're set!" exclaimed the youngest officer in Old Anglian. "The black trams can move every carbineer in Yarron like a chess piece now."

"Mind your tongue," warned Kalward.

"In front of the yoick? He doesn't speak Old Anglian."

"Mind your tongue in front of *any* yoick," Kalward insisted. "This one has a security clearance, the next one may not."

This gave Rollins a great deal to think about. He had a security clearance, which was a relief. Bartolican carbineers were to operate in Yarron, which was a worry. The black trams were to control them like chess pieces, which was a puzzle. Little of this made sense. The wardenate system forbade any more than a hundred armed carbineers to gather at any point in Mounthaven, and even this was only for the pursuit of outlaws. Carbineers certainly never crossed into another dominion except in the pursuit of outlaws or fugitives, yet the officer had talked as if hundreds, even thousands of carbineers would be in Yarron. This sounded like the primitive style of unchivalric wars that raged in Mexhaven and Alberhaven, yet this was impossible. Wardens of all dominions had rallied a dozen times in the past hundred years to bomb and strafe outlaw buildups, while on the ground town militias and merchant carbineers had rallied to shoot the survivors. The trams were impressive fighting units, but nothing could stand against gunwings and armored sailwings . . . unless the black trams commanded the air as well. He had seen with his own eyes that they had access to at least one sailwing.

Rollins shivered. These were alarming times. A few renegade wardens might fly for the merchant carbineers in secret, but never openly. The wardens had more loyalty to the wardenate system than to any dominion or group. Yes, the waging of war was safely in the hands of the wardens, Rollins assured himself. Mounthaven was poor in resources, and could not afford the waste of unchivalric

war. The system had stood for centuries, it could not now
be flouted by a few hundred carbineers.

15 July 3960: Opal

The new warden of the Jannian estate was sixteen years
old. While he had been well educated and had fifty hours
logged in sailwing trainers and three in a gunwing, he was
not by any means experienced enough to run the estate.
Pressure from his peers quickly persuaded him to ignore
the very reform that his father had won in death. Bronlar
was barred from flight duties on the Jannian estate, in spite
of her flyer's license. Serjon, on the other hand, was a
competent flyer, and was ordered to increase his flight
hours at once. Within a week of Jannian's death he had
another fifteen hours logged in sailwings, and was finally
allowed to ascend in the warden's gunwing.

The flight was not easy. The gunwing was heavy, powerful, and temperamental compared with sailwings. His ascent was far too shallow; then he had tried to climb too
steeply and almost stalled. After several circles of the estate he flew against a target kite, and hit it on the first pass.
When he tried to land, his approach was too fast and steep,
and he had bounced heavily before running off the end of
the flightstrip.

The walk back to the guildhouses was a long and lonely
one for Serjon. The gunwing was immobile, and Bronlar's
father and his guildsmen were working at the edge of the
flightstrip, jacking the aircraft onto a trolley. Serjon's
mother and sisters were waiting to greet him after he had
reported to the wingfield adjunct, and he was swamped by
a bouncy swirl of curls and rustling skirts.

"You're alive, Serjon, you're alive!" squealed Cassender, his youngest sister.

"I landed hard, little sister, but yes, I'm alive," he said

as he stood with his arms around her. "It only gets easier now."

"We Feydamors build engines, flying is not for our guild," his mother reminded him.

"Every guildmaster must fly his own crew's work, Mother. That's the law of our calling."

"But you're learning to fight, not take over from your father. One day you may go to war and never return."

"In many ways, I never returned from my first ascent."

Soon they left him and returned to their work. Bronlar had been watching from the steps of her father's guildhall, and she waved as Serjon walked by.

"Congratulations," she said. "You managed to walk away from that landing."

He stopped and turned to look at her, then came over and sat down, two steps below her.

"There must have been a thirteen in my life this morning," he declared.

"Thirteen grapes on your breakfast plate?"

"No, I counted them, there were sixteen," he said, looking out to where the gunwing was being hauled back along the flightstrip on the trolley.

"Why do you fear thirteens so much? I know it's traditionally a number of ill omen, but I've never known anyone to go on about it like you."

"I am my mother's sixth child and my father's seventh. Between mother and Warden Jannian I am thirteenth. All my life I have noticed thirteens present when ill fortune visited me, so I have learned to avoid them. I'm vulnerable to thirteens. It is my fate, just as it is yours to be a girl who wants to fly."

This subject was a sensitive one for Bronlar. She rested her chin on her knees, pressed her lips together, and stared out across the wingfield.

"I'm sorry you were barred," Serjon added presently.

"Sorry? I thought it was what you wanted."

"I've thought about it. I've thought about how I would

feel if exiled to the ground forever, and I wouldn't wish it on anyone who loves flying. Your sex does pose some problems in chivalric procedures, but ... you don't deserve this."

Serjon and Bronlar walked to where the gunwing had been dragged for repairs to the landing gear. The bent struts and broken springs had saved the rest of the airframe from serious damage, but Serjon was still not popular with the airframe guildsmen. When they reached the hospitaler's table Serjon retrieved his sling bag. He took out a book and handed it to Bronlar.

"This may be of use to you," he said.

She stared at the title. "*Chivalry and the Art of Dueling?*"

"With our airlord and wardens dead, and now the death of the Dorakian airlord ... there could be war. If our warden becomes a mark on some Dorakian gunwing's silk, well you should be prepared. Who knows, Jannian is my real father, after all. I may end up as warden, and then I'd let you fly."

Bronlar clasped her hands around the book and stared at the title on the binding.

"You're sweet. I'm sorry I slapped your face, that night in Forian."

"That's forgiven. It made for good theatre."

"Theatre?"

"I provoked that argument on chivalry deliberately. Better to have shouting and insults than pack rape."

Bronlar's smile vanished.

"Do you think that was planned? What about their chivalric principles?"

"They are written to include all women, but in practice they apply only to the nobility. You are not a noble, Bronlar, and they were hoping to give you a sample of what to expect from enemy carbineers."

"But they could not get away with it. Warden Jannian was my patron."

"Warden Jannian would have been alone against the wardens and squires who were the fathers of that rabble. One or two flyers who were foolish enough to be involved may have been hung, but most would go free and you would have been ravished and humiliated. It was about power, and you threaten their power."

Bronlar put a hand to Serjon's neck and kissed the cheek that she had slapped a week earlier. He closed his eyes and hung his head.

"Better a kiss received than a kiss stolen," he said, rubbing his hands together.

"Is that in this book?" teased Bronlar.

"No, but it's in this one," replied Serjon, taking *The Practice of Romantic Chivalry* out of his sling bag.

16 July 3960: Forian

Three days after returning from Condelor, Sartov was reinstated as Governor of North Yarron Region by the new Yarronese airlord. The ceremony was quick and simple, but then Yarron was in shock and it was more important to fill posts and get the work done than to impress the nobles and envoys with splendid displays.

"The burden is heavy, Alveris, but in such times we have to grow fast or fall out of the sky," said Airlord Virtrian when they met later in the model room of the palace.

Sartov had known Virtrian for five years. The Airlord was in his mid-forties, but was not the typical heir who had been kept waiting decades by a long-lived monarch. Virtrian flew his gunwing every day, and had actually fought in border-confrontation duels with Bartolica and Cosdora.

"I had a good rest in Bartolica, but thank you for rescuing me," said Sartov. "How is your wife?"

"Dying, sair, dying."

"But she has survived ten days."

"She is crushed inside. The slightest move makes the broken bones within her slice flesh. She bleeds within, Alveris, she bleeds without losing blood yet she is almost out of blood. At the very time that I need her most she is slipping away."

"I am sorry, I have heard so much yet I did not know."

"Her condition is not widely known, it is bad for public morale at a time like this. When she dies . . . it will be announced as a surprise. Short and sharp, not a long and draining decline. Now, what is your opinion on the problem with Dorak?"

Sartov bent to examine a model of a Dorakian canard gunwing with an in-line compression engine. They did not have the agility of the Yarronese triwing approach, but their wardens were far more experienced.

"They will petition for the right to attack, and Bartolica will second them. It is to their advantage to attack. Politically the new Dorak airlord needs credibility, while their wardens have not been in a serious fight for three decades. The gossip in Condelor is that Bartolica has convinced them to attack our north. It is far from the Bartolican border, you see."

"So the Bartolican support is all but active?"

"The situation in Bartolica is confused. The new governor of the East Region, Stanbury, is building up a lot of power with his merchant carbineers. I think some manner of coup is not far off."

"A coup? But what about the wardens? The wardens of his own region are loyal to Condelor."

"Correct. I do not understand what is happening, but I sense danger. Greater Bartolica is big and well resourced, and if anything should unify it into an effective dominion . . . it scarcely bears thinking about."

17 July 3960: Sheridan, North Yarron

Fieldmajor Akengar was on the Sheridan wingfield as Sartov landed in his gunwing. Once the ground crews had taken charge of the aircraft, he walked with the returned governor along the edge of the flightstrip, well away from the guildsmen and wardens.

"I am honored that you wish to see a mere fieldmajor of the merchant carbineers," Akengar said as they passed the row of gunwings.

"Very soon nobody will be using 'mere' in the same sentence as merchant carbineers," replied Sartov. "I predict war between Yarron and Dorak."

"War? On what pretext?"

"Just suppose there to be a legitimate pretext. Were you a Dorakian airlord, how would you attack?"

The question was not one that Akengar had anticipated, and he had to consider for some time. While flattered to be asked such strategic questions, and while willing to give opinions among his peers, Fieldmajor Akengar had a sudden loss of nerve when it came to being taken seriously in matters reserved for the heads of states.

"Ah, I'd send gunwings and sailwings to overfly the wingfields of the Airlord's governor, oh and find a dominion to stand second before sending couriers to all major airlords of Mounthaven to petition for a war. After that, set a realistic number of gunwings and sailwings to fight and choose a suitable stretch of land to claim."

"Now pretend that the wardens are no more."

"Ah! Ah . . . war would be impossible."

"Maybe so, Fieldmajor, and maybe not so. I wish to recruit more carbineers, and I want them trained to fight in squads. Quickly."

"Carbineers? But they are not permitted to fight in wars, they are lower class and unchivalric."

"The attack on our Airlord and wardens was lower class and unchivalric too, but it still happened. Trust me, Field-major, I have just spent six months in the Bartolican court circles, and a lot of what I saw made me uneasy. If they are recruiting and training carbineers in quantity, then we should too."

3 | SOWING THE WIND

20 July 3960: North Yarron

Dorak declared war on Yarron on 20 July 3960. The heir to the Dorak airlord's throne had only a limited base of support for his claim, as the dead monarch had no children. A war to unite the dominion's wardens and a successful claim against Yarron seemed the perfect way to secure the throne. Yarron certainly seemed implicated in the Airlord's death, and in reparation he claimed a slice of northern Yarron that extended to Casper from Gannett in the Wind River Range. The claim was rejected by Governor Sartov, but he forwarded it south by sailwing for the Yarron airlord to consider. On the strength of his provisional rejection, Dorak petitioned for an attack.

Bartolicà was Dorak's second, and Montras seconded Yarron. A Council of Delegates from the other dominions flew to North Yarron and selected a battlefield. Billings in Dorak and Sheridan in Yarron were selected as the two base wingfields, with the clash to be over the Bighorn River because Yarron was being invaded. The Dorak strategists had hoped for victory through sheer numbers and experience, and they declared a flock of ninety-one gunwings—every serviceable gunwing in the domain. Yarron had lost so many wardens in the collapse of the palace throne room that the new airlord worked day and night granting deputy status to squires and confirming heirs as wardens. On the appointed day ninety-one Yarronese gunwings ascended in orderly ranks of seven.

"Thirteen times seven," said Serjon glumly as he watched the mass ascent. "That is bad."

"Dorak declared the number," Feydamor pointed out impatiently.

"That's not the point. We could have ascended only ninety gunwings and still been legal."

"That would declare that we're beyond our resources."

"No good will come of this for Yarron."

As generally happened, Serjon was proved wrong. The brash and enthusiastic young wardens and squires who dominated the Yarronese flock attacked in a solid block, disrupting the center of the Dorakian flock's attack configuration in the first pass. While the Dorakians were by far more experienced, they were also a lot older and more set in their tactics. Members of the Council of Delegates watched from their red and white striped sailwings as the formal combat raged above the disputed territory. On the ground, medical teams from the sponsor dominions scurried about to collect the fallen and tend the injured.

The rules of combat were in principle simple. Equal numbers of gunwings ascended with equal fuel and ammunition, and the dominion with the greatest number of gunwings returning to its base wingfield was declared the winner. The formal combat recognized that Mounthaven was a poor area, and that resources could not be squandered on total war if civilization was to be maintained. Spoils were determined in advance and combat was always over sparsely populated areas. Gunwings were expensive and dangerous weapons, but they did not lay cities and towns waste, ruin crops, or slaughter herds of meat birds. The toll among wardenly families could be high, but then wardens had a high and privileged status in Mounthaven as compensation.

Soon streamers of black smoke and parachutes began to mark the fall of wardens from both sides. Through sheer honor some Yarronese chose to ram rather than leave the battlefield once their guns were empty, and overall the toll was a lot higher than in most battles of the previous half century. In all, fifteen Yarronese gunwings returned to Sheridan, while twelve returned to Billings. Many more ran out of fuel and glided safely down to land on roads and in fields, yet thirty-one wardens were dead by sunset and two unaccounted for. Yarron had won.

"Serves them right for choosing an unlucky number," Serjon pronounced as the delegates' liaison read out the result before the pennant pole at the Sheridan wingfield.

"So where is our bad luck for also ascending ninety-one?" sneered his stepfather.

"We lost twenty-six killed," replied Serjon at once. "Thirteen always returns to strike you down."

The spoils of the victor also included the wreckage of all gunwings that crashed or were forced down over the disputed territory. This had the effect of weakening one side or another so much that further hostilities were unlikely for a long time to come. The young warden Jannian did not shoot down any enemy gunwings that day, but he did manage to nurse his burning aircraft all the way back to Sheridan.

The Yarronese people were quick to celebrate the close-fought victory, and it went some way to make up for the tragedy that had killed so many of their wardens. The Airlord Virtrian held court in Sheridan and decorated the heroes of the battle while honoring the dead of both sides, and within a few days the wardens and their guildsmen dispersed back to their estates.

26 July 3960: East Bartolica

Rollins had been to the Yarronese border before, but had never stopped at the nearby village of Sage longer than was needed to exchange mailbags. Now there was a large series of parallel sidings in the forest just outside the militia stockade. Within the complex was a gathering of no less than fifty multidecked red trams and six black trams. His black tram had arrived last, but was backed to the head of a siding branch. A quick mental calculation put the gathering at four thousand carbineers, fifty-six carriage guns, as many heavy reaction guns, and at least two hundred and fifty merchant officers, gunners, and tram crewmen. Even without the slaves who labored in the black trams, that was enough to vanquish any warden or merchant estate in half an hour, and even a regional city the size of Middle Junction would not last more than a day against them. It was forty times larger than the largest gathering of armed carbineers or militia permitted under the wardenate system, and exceeded the number drawing the death penalty by an order of magnitude.

All trams were draped in camouflage netting beneath the trees. A glance at the sidings showed that there was no growth of lichens or weeds, and no washoff of dirt: it had been laid only days earlier. This was very unusual. Rollins had seen new trackwork only twice in his life, and it was well known that tracks were laid only after months, if not years, of deliberations by cost-conscious merchant committees.

At 10 A.M. they were ordered into their trams after removing the netting, and the drivers and stokers told to light their fires and build up steam. Rollins noted that the wood blocks remaining in the bunker had been replaced by anthracite coal, the type that gave off little smoke. By 11 A.M. nothing more had been said, and the carbineers were becoming restive. It was a warm, clear July morning, and the lower decks of the trams were ventilated by motion alone. Rollins could hear cursing and raised voices from the red trams on the parallel siding branches above the hiss of the steam engines as conditions inside grew hot and close. Tender carts were being pushed from tram to tram by the luckier carbineers, topping up coal and water reserves. From time to time there came the whirring of the pedalframe and birdlike peeping from behind him.

By now Rollins had identified forty patterns of peeps, of which some were definitely a twenty-four-letter alphabet, two were 0 and 1 for binary figures, and the rest were special functions of some sort. As far as he could tell there were messages in code, and possibly in an unknown language as well. He had 'suspected for the fortnight past that the device was some type of decoding machine, but now the peeping came at precise intervals of fifteen minutes. Perhaps the code was just words spelled backward in some universal language like Old Anglian, he speculated. The peeping started again.

llac mek ni 0101

Reversed it was "call kem in 5" in Old Anglian. Rollins slapped his thigh in triumph, but kept a poker face. Got it, yet . . . binary would not lead with a 0, so perhaps it was "call kem in 10." Who was Kem, and how was he to be called? Perhaps it was the town Kemmerer, on the border? Perhaps call was the Call? 'The Call arrives at Kemmerer in ten . . . minutes'? A remote signaling device! That was pre-Greatwinter science, how was it possible? A Call would be coming from the east at walking pace if true, though.

An officer came clattering down the steps and ran up to Rollins. Kalward.

"Three long toots on the whistle, then move out!" he ordered. "Straight down the line to Kemmerer, maximum cruise speed."

Rollins tried not to let his anxiety show as he gave three

blasts of the steam whistle then opened the steam to the drive cylinders. As the tram chuffed forward he began to calculate. The Yarronese border was twelve miles away, that would take about twenty minutes at a fast cruise. A Call ten minutes from Kemmerer would be going west at walking pace. When it arrived the tram would be ten minutes from Kemmerer going east at maximum cruise speed, say 35 miles per hour. The trouble was that Calls traveled at speeds that varied with the terrain in the mountains, and Rollins was no Call-vector expert. It might go half a mile west in the ten minutes the tram took to travel to the border . . . simple calculus would give an exact meeting, but Rollins was too agitated to think clearly. A meeting half a mile west of Kemmerer seemed as good an estimate as any.

The mileposts to the border counted down. At two miles Rollins could see a warden's sailwing circling Kemmerer on Call patrol. The warden would see the line of Bartolican trams. What then? Kalward leaned over and told the stoker to go to the rear and make sure that his Call tether was clipped to a rail. An officer joined Kalward, one who often took spells at stoking—and Kalward could drive a tram, Rollins realized! One mile. Two minutes to Kemmerer, but sixty seconds to the Call's front? Rollins began counting slowly, reached sixty-two—and plunged away into a reverie of surrender.

When Rollins woke up he was still in the driver's seat with his Call straps in place. There was a lump on his forehead and a bitter taste in his mouth. He got out of the tram. His watch had been taken from him but the sun was at least three hours farther across the sky. The tram had been halted in a mountain siding near an old quarry, and was alone. Four poles stuck up through camouflage netting that had been laced with uprooted bushes. The peeping, whirring, and clacking from within the tram was almost continuous. An officer sitting in the shade of a large rock waved his assault carbine and told Rollins not to go too

far from the tram. As he returned to the camouflaged tram
he noticed that the stoker was sweeping reaction-gun shells
out of the tram: dozens, hundreds.

"Sair Kalward says the reaction gun musta gone off
durin' the Call, accident-like," the stoker explained. "He
say yer te drop the ashes and tie down fer the night. Oh,
an' he says yer bumped yer head durin' the Call. So did
I. We sorta strayed inter Yarron durin' the Call, like.
That's all."

"Where's my watch?" Rollins asked quite reasonably.

"They's all been taken fer coordin' tests, like they
makes 'em all tick the same or somelike. Sair Kalward
says we get 'em back this evening."

Rollins returned to his cabin, and noted that the tram
had merely been stopped and that the furnace had been
hastily raked down. The tripmeter showed that 34 miles
had been added since the siding outside Sage. Given 12 to
the border, that meant they were 22 miles inside Yarron.
So many shells had been fired that he suspected that a
warden in a Call patrol sailwing had flown too close to
investigate a supposedly runaway steam tram in the middle
of a Call. Kemmerer was a Bartolican town, and the warden would have been Bartolican! An officer had fired the
roof's reaction gun into the sailwing and probably brought
it down . . . an officer who could defy the Call.

A sudden chill pervaded the supposedly warm driver's
cabin. Bigfoot, vampires, werewolves, Callwalkers, dragons, and zombies were meant to be mythical, yet here was
disturbingly good evidence for Callwalkers. Rollins allowed himself a full minute of blind terror, then carefully
blanked out his mind, screwed down the brake blocks, and
began to shovel sand onto the sleepers under the furnace.
The best way to remain safe was to be indispensable, and
he was still the best driver on Black Tram MC5.

In the last days of July the west of Yarron suddenly went
silent. No steam trams appeared from that direction, and a

sailwing sent out from Middle Junction to investigate reported whole towns on fire. More sailwings were dispatched, but these did not return.

2 August 3960: Western Yarron

Stanbury had done the unthinkable when he sent armed steam trams into western Yarron and tiny, neutral Montras, seizing and fortifying all rail posts and closing the line to Yarron's Southfort. Montras was overwhelmed in less than a day, and the Bartolican steam trams continued to shuttle across the Yarronese border, moving in thousands of carbineers.

At first the local Yarronese wardens were merely puzzled and annoyed. The Bartolicans had won no formally declared air battles that entitled them to move onto Yarronese territory, while Yarron had the right to demand thirty gunwings from Bartolica for sponsoring the loser in their war with Dorak. While they debated, drafted dispatches decrying the breach of martial protocol, and sent couriers to Forian for instructions, the massed steam trams and galley carts crammed with carbineers poured into Yarron through Montras and the Kemmerer crossings. Intense groundfire tore into Yarronese sailwings that flew too low while investigating the invaders.

None of the local wardens struck at the Bartolican carbineers as they passed their estates. They were mere carbineers, after all, and wardens did not lower themselves to fight carbineers. Only the merchant carbineers in the towns offered any resistance, and the Bartolicans attacked these with well-coordinated fury. Two days after the first attack, the entire tramway north and south of Middle Junction was lost to Bartolica. Yarronese carbineers were rushed in from Green River and Median by the merchant guilds, but they arrived to find Middle Junction held against them. All the while more Bartolican carbineers were being ferried in.

In Condelor a very odd dispatch arrived from Governor Stanbury of East Region. He reported sending his merchant carbineers into Yarron and Montras in pursuit of several large outlaw gangs, and that his men were then engaged by local carbineers who were protecting the outlaws. Blaming the Montrassians and Yarronese for sending outlaws to plunder Bartolica, he then sent his entire force of carbineers into the battle, along with the wardens of his personal guard. Within an hour of this dispatch arriving at the court another was flown in that declared Montras fallen and under Bartolican rule, along with a slab of western Yarron almost to the edge of the Red Desert and bigger than East Region. Stanbury appealed for wardens and squires to be sent to help secure and administer the territories that he had liberated from outlaw rule.

Throughout Mounthaven it was the wording and legal letter of any declaration that carried most weight. Phrased as an appeal for wardens to help keep order, Stanbury's dispatch produced the perfect reaction. The confused young Airlord of Bartolica sent a hundred wardens and their guildsmen to assist Stanbury: "In any fashion that seems helpful," as he put it. The Bartolican gunwings and sailwings quickly appeared, shooting at Yarronese steam trams crossing the Red Desert and destroying any sailwings that they encountered. Faced with such provocation, the wardens of the western Yarronese estates finally took matters into their own hands and responded by sending their own gunwings up to challenge the unchivalric invaders. A deadly ballet of unsupervised air combat was played out time and again over western Yarron, with both sides considering the others to be common and unchivalric rogues and thus worthy of no mercy.

Serjon had actually been flying near Kemmerer when the main column of steam trams began pouring east, followed by a long line of galley carts. He returned to Opal at once, reported what he had seen to the adjunct, and was gratified to see the Jannian squire sent up to investigate.

He made a wide sweep over western Yarron, and reported the incredible news that the entire town of Southfort was on fire. Bartolican steam trams were crammed along the line north, while groundfire from around Southfort was so intense that he was unable to approach close enough for a proper view. The young warden did not believe what either Serjon or the squire had reported, and which Serjon scarcely believed himself.

Farther east, some Yarronese carbineers commandeered a steam tram and went south, blasting the tramway at quarter-mile intervals. A Bartolican armored tram met them after only five miles and blew the Yarronese tram to matchwood. Bartolican sailwings droned overhead, taking relays to fly south and drop message tubes for those on the ground and return tubes to the black trams. The perfect coordination of the Bartolicans defied belief: they acted as if they were part of a single, huge organism and always struck the weakest Yarronese positions in full strength.

At last the warden of the Jannian estate was convinced that action was required, and he met with his squire to rough out tactics. Whatever his faults and inexperience, Ricmear Jannian was decisive when he made up his mind. A "duress response" could be invoked when air duels were required in undeclared and unrecorded conflicts, and Jannian attached a proclamation to the estate's pennant pole stating that this was the case.

The wingfield adjunct found Serjon with his father and Glasken in the steam machinery sheds.

"Suit up, Serjon, you have to fly in a formal war duel," the adjunct cried from the door, then he rushed on without another word.

"Why don't we just strike back undeclared as the Bartolicans do?" demanded Serjon as Feydamor and Glasken helped him into his flying leathers and ornate flight jacket.

"Because we're winning!" said Feydamor triumphantly. "The Bartolicans have trespassed on a massive scale, they have not offered chivalric combat until this very day, and their carbineers have despoiled Yarronese property without wardenly redress being due to them. This confirms the worst that we have ever said about the Bartolicans."

"No offense intended, sair," said Glasken, "but where I come from a mayorate would be history if it was in a position like Yarron's."

"Barbarian talk," snapped Feydamor. "This is civilization, we fight our wars without destroying property or involving the innocent."

"As I see it, Sair Jeb, the Bartolicans are fighting this war very much like us barbarians, and if this is a barbarian-style war then Yarron is up to its earlobes in emu shit."

"Sair Glasken, watch your tongue, you're talking about matters of honor very close to the heart of the Yarronese nobility. If you cannot maintain respect for the dignity of this conflict, then you can get off this estate."

"With the way things are looking out there, Jeb, I have a feeling that things might be healthier in the woods anyway."

Glasken walked out quickly as Serjon finished getting into his flight gear.

"Such unseemly talk before your first taste of the honor of war, pah, this is not the way I wanted it, Serjon," said Feydamor as they walked out into the sunlight.

"But a lot of his talk made sense," said Serjon. "I've spoken with the other patrol flyers, they said that the skies above all western Yarron are filled with Bartolican wings."

"Serjon! My son, you clamored for years to step into a cockpit, but now you turn coward as soon as you have a chance to fight!"

Serjon bristled at the word "coward" and chose not to reply for the sake of not making things any worse.

"Whatever the case, you will have no more than your sailwing peers to deal with, that is the rule of war and chivalry," Feydamor concluded.

Serjon's mother and sisters were waiting on the path of departure, the point past which only combatants and guild

crews were allowed once a conflict was declared. All but
Kallien had a bunch of embroidered ribbons for him to
wear on his sleeve. Very soon I could be dead and they
will all be here to sorrow for me, he thought as he embraced each in turn. He made for the pennant pole where
the adjunct was briefing the other four flyers. Three sailwings and two gunwings were nearby, their compression
engines warming up and the armorers frantically strapping
reaction guns onto the mounting racks of the sailwings.
The third gunwing was under repair. A sailwing trainer
taxied past as Serjon was attaching his colors to his arm,
and Bronlar called to him from the open canopy.

"Serjon, look here!" she shouted.

"You're flying? As a combatant?"

"The warden can't spare anyone for dispatch flights. I
pointed out that I have a flyer's license and accreditation,
so suddenly he decided that I could be useful after all. I
was classified as an ancillary, which means combat-
capable but not combatant. I've got guns, Serjon, and live
ammunition!"

Serjon was relieved that she would be safe, but to say
as much would have been a hurtful insult.

"What mission are you flying?"

"Liaison to Median. What about you?"

"Duress response above Montras. Challenge to clear air
war duel with sailwing support—that's me."

"Really? Which wardens have challenged?"

"I can't tell you anything. I'm already sworn under the
warden's flock command. Look after yourself, and make
sure you come back. I'll try to come back too."

Bronlar beamed back at him then closed her canopy. As
she ascended from the flightstrip Serjon joined the warden,
his squire and flyers at the pennant pole. He handed his
pennant plaque to the adjunct, who hung it on the pole
below all the others.

"The latest scout reported armed Bartolican sailwings
making strafing runs against steam trams in Montras while

their gunwings patrolled overhead," the adjunct was reporting.

"How many gunwings?" asked Ricmear Jannian.

"Fifteen, young sair, and twenty-five armed sailwings."

The warden considered. A fight against hopeless odds did not daunt him so much as the prospect of an unseen and unacknowledged fight against hopeless odds.

"At my declaration, we fly south," said the young warden. "Ceras will fly at my upper back, and sailwings will attack sailwings while we challenge the Bartolican gunwings for the sun height. Thank you, adjunct. To your wings now."

The adjunct went with Serjon to his sailwing to finish his briefing. The fueler was checking the level in his tank.

"How much is in our tanks?" asked Serjon as he pulled on his fur-lined leather cap embroidered with gold thread.

"Two cruising hours, Sair Serjon. The Warden wants the weight kept down for better handling in duels."

"Then fill mine, I may be in the air a long time."

"The warden will read of it in tonight's report."

"Adjunct, the warden will be dead within an hour. Did anyone explain to our sixteen-year-old warden that the whole of West Yarron is falling out of the sky, that the Bartolicans are breaking every protocol that ever got penned on paper?"

"Ceras tried to tell him, sair, but he is intent on leading a flock into a war duel. The governor's default orders were to fly to the Green River wingfield and assemble a united flock with all the other West Yarron wardens, but only at the discretion of each warden."

"So, this is at his discretion," said Serjon bleakly. "When I was six I never thought that I would fly, when I was sixteen I never thought I would wear a flyer's jacket, and now I'm nineteen and I don't think I'll get back from my first mission."

"The tanks are full now, Sair Serjon," said the fueler.

"Grats, I'll strap in now. Adjunct, what are the current

default orders for returning if the flock breaks up?"

"Home, then Green River wingfield. Now try to return."

"Be wary, adjunct."

"We on the estates are safe, but try to win: owing fealty to Bartolicans would be very galling."

Serjon was last into the air, and he joined up with the other sailwings as they flew in a curve that took them southwest to Southfort on the border of Montras, the tiny mountain dominion. Mountains passed below, throwing up thermals and buffeting currents. The sailwings tossed and pitched as they flew well below the two Yarron gunwings. Probably odds of eight to one, Serjon thought over and over.

The Bartolican wardens had not expected a response from any of the nearby Yarronese wingfields, and any unified response had been forestalled by the invasion of Bartolican carbineers. The Yarronese flock headed straight for Evanston, the Montras capital. The Evanston wingfield was only a half hour from Opal, and to the southwest. The warden dipped his gunwing's left wing three times, the right once, the left once, the right twice more: *Attack wingfield. Skirmish order.* The sailwings were on their own from now on.

The little capital of the mountain dominion appeared ahead as the three sailwings came in abreast. The warden swooped over the palace and dropped a dispatch capsule while trailing twin streamers of red smoke. By protocol a war duel was now declared, with the Montras royalty as the witnesses. The flock of sailwings had meantime arced around to come out of the sun above the occupied wingfield. A regal was in the middle of the flightstrip and well into its ascent run as Serjon left the staging squares, guild tents, and buildings to his two companions. Everything had Bartolican markings and colors, the tents, the pennant poles, the parked gunwings . . . and the regal that was lumbering into the air. Serjon banked on a wingtip and began to lose height alarmingly as he turned to attack. He leveled and closed head on, firing into the regal as its wingcaptain fired its strafing guns. Incandescent rounds streamed past Serjon's sailwing as he fired steadily into the left compression engine—then he was past it and climbing in a wide curve out over the Montras capital.

As he returned to the wingfield Serjon could see that the three patrol gunwings above Montras had engaged the two Yarronese gunwings. Ricmear had attacked from above in a fast dive and caught a Bartolican gunwing that was now trailing smoke and losing height. Ceras was flying behind, covering, but the two other Bartolican wardens had already broken off to climb and come around. A Yarronese sailwing came in low over the wingfield, strafing, but failed to pull out of its shallow dive and exploded through a line of five Bartolican sailwings. The other sailwing from Opal flew over the carnage, trailing flames from one of its own wingtanks. Back above the city a Yarronese gunwing was spinning down out of control while two enemy aircraft engaged the other. Ceras was still flying, but the warden was down. On the wingfield the regal had recovered almost miraculously to circle the wingfield and try to land. Just then a gunwing roared off the dispersal track and onto the flightstrip, but the regal was barely under control and descending fast.

The crippled regal landed on top of the gunwing, crushing it, and the two fully fueled aircraft exploded in a lurid fireball that smeared a tongue of flame and smoke all down the flightstrip.

"There is your victory, Sair Warden," Serjon said aloud.

Somehow he did not feel responsible for the deaths. Now he began to climb a little. He had followed orders and strafed the wingfield in his unarmored sailwing. One parachute was descending over Evanston, probably Ceras', but there were still two Bartolican gunwings in the sky. Serjon turned east for home, hoping not to be noticed. This time luck was with him. The patrolling Bartolican gunwings stayed at their assigned area instead of pursuing, and the fire on the main flightstrip prevented any other gun-wings from ascending to chase him.

For half an hour he flew low among the mountains, pre-ferring to chance the thermals rather than the clear air where the Bartolicans were in such overwhelming num-bers. To his surprise he found himself over Middle Junc-tion, and realized that he had gone far off course. He noted with satisfaction that his tanks were still over two-thirds full as he turned northwest for Opal. Off to the south he noticed four sailwings flying roughly parallel to his direc-tion. High above was a single gunwing, but unlike the unconcerned sailwings it was already turning to intercept him. He's coming to check, he cannot see my markings and colors at this distance, thought Serjon.

Serjon boosted his engine and scrambled for height; then the gunwing's warden realized what colors were on the sailwing and came in for a fast pass. Serjon did a tight turn as bullets riddled his left wing and the diving gunwing hurtled down past him. He was in luck, as the outer wingtanks were empty. Serjon flew on as if undamaged.

The gunwing climbed as Serjon climbed, seeking greater height before coming around for another pass. The warden had assumed that the Yarronese sailwing was carrying ar-mor, and that was his downfall. The greater lift of Serjon's sailwing meant that it could match the gunwing's rate of climb at higher altitudes and as the air thinned. He closed. The warden could have escaped in a fast dive, but he was intent on a quick and easy kill. His gunwing wove into a space where Serjon was already firing and a line of hits walked across the gunwing's fabric and through the cock-pit's canopy. This time there was no dramatic ball of flames; the gunwing just climbed until it stalled, then dropped into a spin and fell toward the mountains. Serjon stayed high but followed its progress until there was a distant flash on a bare ridge.

For a moment Serjon felt an elation that was little short of sexual. This time his guns had not just caused an accident, they had killed. By now the four sailwings were directly below. Serjon dived, raking the trailing sailwing and dropping it out of the flock trailing thin, greyish smoke. By the time he came around again the remaining sailwings had broken formation and scattered, so Serjon chose one that was flying almost directly south and set off after it. After a twenty-five-minute chase he overhauled the sailwing, whose flyer was so terrified that he bailed out as Serjon was closing in. The Yarronese novice fired a short burst into the sailwing and left it falling in flames as he turned north again.

As Serjon flew for Opal he wondered what he was going to tell the families of the four flockmates who would not be returning. Guilt had by now replaced the elation of his first kills. Five wings, and as many as seven men killed. The flock had nearly been wiped out, even though they had destroyed three enemy wings for every one lost. After nearly three hours in the air he caught sight of the river, then the tramway, and finally the Opal estate itself. Before landing he flew back over the tramway, which was packed with steam trams chugging east. The sidings were jammed with empty trams waiting a chance to return west.

Minutes later he was over Opal's wingfield again, and as he circled the wingfield Serjon noticed that another sailwing had survived Ricmear's attack on Evanston and had already landed. There was a lot of its fabric burned away from one wing, but the fire had died before doing enough structural damage to—Abruptly Serjon caught himself and did a quick scan of the sky. It was clear, but the lapse of attention could have cost him his life. Now he noticed that the estate seemed deserted. He circled twice more, wondering why nobody was sending up flares and why there were no guildsmen crowded about the other sailwing.

Suddenly too weary to think and beyond caring about the absence of guildsmen, Serjon landed. As he taxied to the maintenance area near the guildhalls he noted with some anxiety that nobody came out to greet him. He unbuckled his straps, checked the clip in his Raddisan spring action, and released the safety catch. As a precaution he left the compression engine running as he got out, pistol in hand. There were eleven holes in the fabric of his wing.

Serjon walked over to the other sailwing. As he drew close he saw that the canopy had been shattered, and beneath it Kumiar's blood was everywhere. The flyer was gone.

The wingfield's buildings were intact, the pennant pole still had the plaques, everything seemed to have a surreal normality about it. Serjon almost convinced himself to switch off his engine, but even as he reached into the cockpit something made him pause. It was almost as if he wanted a reason to leave, yet . . . perhaps there had been some horrendous crash not far away and everyone had left to help. Aware that he had not eaten for a long time, Serjon left his compression engine still idling and went across to the guild refectory hall. The door was open, and swinging in a light breeze. Serjon took a step inside, then stopped, one foot in midair.

The women and children of the estate were all there, dead. Many had been stripped naked, and some were battered from struggling before they had been killed. Serjon swayed, caught the edge of a table, and held himself up. Finally he forced himself to stand up straight, fought down a horror that he could never hope to articulate, and walked toward the closest body.

He forced himself to look into thirty-nine dead faces, checking each woman and child for signs of life and noting down every name in a scrawl that was scarcely his own writing. Their hands were all cold as he checked each body for a pulse. Cold skin, and no beat of life at a single wrist for body after body. Three times thirteen, he said to himself. A very bad number. His mother and five sisters had died close to each other, as if they had tried to be together at the end. Cassender had died clutching something. Serjon eased back the girl's lifeless fingers and plucked a Bartolican merchant officer's pennant bar from her palm.

"Thank you, Cassender, now sleep well," he said as he kissed his dead sister's cold fingers. "He will die for this, I swear it."

Serjon walked about the hall for some minutes, eyes streaming with tears, wanting to do something for the dead yet feeling as helpless as a ghost himself. Bronlar was not among the dead, he realized with a relief so intense that it caught him by surprise. She had not returned from Median, so she had been spared. To Serjon it made sense: if she had returned there would have been forty women and children, and they would have been safe. Still, he could not blame her, he had not noticed the number himself. Fate lay in wait, crouched ready to strew thirteens into the paths of the unwary. One could never afford to relax.

Back outside, he made for the fabrication house. There he found the missing guildsmen, all neatly bound and shot—but not quite all. The senior guildsmen and guildmasters were gone. The ground showed the mark of hobnails in the softer parts, and carbineers wore hobnail boots with articulated soles of wood and leather. Carbineers had been there. Carbineers in their hundreds. They must have arrived almost as soon as the young warden's little flock had ascended, but why do such monstrous murders? Why not torch the place, disarm the people, and leave them under guard? He checked every body for warmth or a pulse, but found nothing but cold skin.

"Serjon!" The call came from outside. "Serjon, where are you? We have to get out!" The words were Old Anglian and the voice was familiar.

Glasken was standing beside Serjon's sailwing, holding Jeb Feydamor and calling out at the top of his voice. As Serjon came running up he laid Feydamor against a wheel. Kumiar was leaning against his own sailwing, his arm bandaged with strips of shirt through which blood was already seeping.

"They came up the tramway branch line after you as-

cended," babbled Glasken. "I'd just taken my pack and
gun and was walking for the woods. I watched as they
herded your people together and into the halls. The guildmasters were separated and marched down to the steam
trams, where they were bound and clubbed unconscious.
After that the shooting began where the men were being
held. I could hear the women shrieking and screaming
when they realized what was happening, but the doors
were locked. When the carbineers were finished they returned to the refectory. The screams began again, and this
time they went on and on and on."

Glasken reeled with the horror of the recollection, then
shook his head clear and continued.

"Only two carbineers were left to guard the steam trams.
I killed them both, and the screams from the refectory muffled the sound of my shots. Jeb was all that I could carry,
Serjon, he was all that I could carry. We had to get right
away into the forest before the others came back. I'm over
fifty, Serjon, I'm not as strong as I used—"

"Glasken, shut up!" Serjon barked. "You did all you
could, in fact you did more than I might have. Did they
take the compression spirit?"

"No, there's plenty on the trolley."

"Then help me fill the sailwings' tanks."

They pushed the wagon to Serjon's sailwing and Glasken pumped compression spirit while Serjon stripped what
he could from the sailwing to save weight. Jeb recognized
Serjon, but his mumbles made little sense, while Kumiar
had lost so much blood that he could barely stand.

"I made it look like Jeb had freed himself and killed the
guards," Glasken called above the chugging of the compression engine. "There was laughing and cheering mixed
with screams, then there was only one voice left screaming. When she was silenced the carbineers came out. God
in heaven how I despise rapists! A man who cannot allure
a woman has no right to sex, if I could make that law I
surely would. Ah, it was barely ninety minutes in doing,

and at the end it all looked so neat! There were two hundred of them, all carbineers. Nobody from Opal put up any resistance, Serjon."

"But why did they do it, Sair Glasken? Why?"

"I don't know! Don't you think I didn't wonder that myself? About ten minutes before you got back that other sailwing landed. I left Jeb in the woods and crawled over, just in case it was a trap. Kumiar was the flyer, and he was in a worse mess than his sailwing. I got him clear and patched him up."

"My family, Glasken! They murdered my family!" cried Serjon, flopping down in the dust. "Why?"

"Perhaps they were in a hurry. Perhaps they could not bother to spare a few guards."

"I touched so many cold hands. They were all so cold."

"I know, I know, the hands go cold first, I have been a soldier, I have seen a lot of death. Strange, though ... nothing has been looted and there has been no vandalism. Look at the place. It's almost as if the humans were being swept away so that ... someone else could march in and take over! Yes, yes. Those aviad bastards want this place intact!"

"Aviad?" asked Serjon, looking up.

"Don't even ask. Get compression spirit and lamps, we owe it to the dead to burn this place."

"Burn it? Why?"

"Sheer spite."

"My family has been here for centuries."

"Opal was lost with only two shots fired back, and they were *mine*! Come on, lad, help the dead fight back and cheat these bastards of their prize."

It did not take long to set the buildings burning, and with nobody to fight the flames they quickly took a strong hold. Serjon used a linkage strap to spin the compression engine of Kumiar's sailwing from his own until it began chugging.

"Well, Johnny's for the road now," said Glasken as he stood back from the aircraft.

"No, I'll take you," said Kumiar. "You helped me when I landed."

"Me? Fly in *that*?" asked Glasken, pointing at the blackened, battle-flayed sailwing and looking doubtfully at the swaying flyer.

"Prove your bravery, Sair Glasken, the girls will love you for it," said Feydamor, whose head was clearing at last. "Leave your gun and pack, though. Take off your boots, have a piss, anything to save weight."

"Climb in behind the seat, I'll tilt it forward for you," Kumiar offered.

Glasken kept his boots, and took a few things out of his pack before flinging it into the flames of a nearby building. He looked terrified but determined as he crawled into the sailwing; then Serjon helped Kumiar into the cockpit. Kumiar ascended first with Glasken, and then Serjon ascended with his father. They skirted Middle Junction, and quickly covered the extra thirty miles to Green River. Their luck held, and the overloaded sailwings encountered no enemy wings before landing at the wingfield. Here the Yarronese pennons still flew.

In a state of near-exhaustion, Serjon and Kumiar told their stories of the attack on Evanston to the adjunct as Glasken and Feydamor described the atrocities at Opal to the presiding warden.

"Five kills," Serjon added to the story of his warden's death. "A gunwing of Palissendier House, and an unknown gunwing, a regal, and two sailwings."

The adjunct steadied Serjon as he sat down in the short grass where Kumiar was already lying. As a medic came running the adjunct made some quick notes on his board.

"Five for three is good," said the adjunct.

"No, that was just me," replied Serjon. "Five sailwings destroyed on the ground by Lindrin's sailwing crashing into them, and an interpretive kill of a gunwing should be made to Warden Ricmear. I saw no more. Both Yarron gunwings of the Jannian household were shot down."

"Shot up two gunwings on the wingfield, left them burning," said Kumiar in a slurred voice.

"That's thirteen kills for three losses!" exclaimed the amazed adjunct.

"Thirteen?" echoed Serjon in a quavering voice.

"A disaster for the Bartolicans, sair. Thirteen for three."

"Thirteen?" said Serjon again.

"Come now, rest while the sailwings are refueled and rearmed. Five victories on your first day—and two of them wardens! You must lead the flock of surviving sailwings to Median."

"Thirteen?" said Serjon yet again as the adjunct hurried away.

Kumiar propped himself up against his parachute as the medics began sewing up the gash in his arm. Wincing with the pain, he called to Serjon.

"Serjon. They . . . didn't die because . . . we destroyed thirteen. Agh! I can read your thoughts. Careful!"

"You don't understand, Kumiar, it *is* my fault. I amplify the curse of thirteen for all those around me."

He got up and shambled away among the guildsmen and flyers, looking for the adjunct. He counted thirteen wings on the wingfield, and he was definitely not going to lead a flock of thirteen. Near the pennant pole was a group of flyers, all waiting for the adjunct as well.

Serjon had been fighting a feeling of nausea for some minutes, and now it overwhelmed him. He sat down beside a tent with his face in his hands. The world seemed to be spinning. . . .

"Easy, easy, give him room!"

Serjon opened his eyes to find himself laid out on a stretcher, with a medic kneeling over him.

"No injuries, but clammy skin, raised pulse and breathing, and—ah, you're awake. What happened, Sair Feydamor?"

"I was walking, then . . . felt giddy, nauseous."

"His first flight in anger was today," said the adjunct's voice. "He made his first kills—and also discovered the atrocities at the Jannian estate."

"Post-duel shock," the medic pronounced. "Does he have to fly again today?"

"Yes, yes. We need five flyers to be on Call patrol, and another eight to take the damaged sailwings to Median. A Call is on the way, too, it will be here in an hour. The Bartolicans have been dropping firebombs on some towns and wingfields during Calls, so we need the wings that can fight to be patrolling while the rest are evacuated."

The medic took Serjon's pulse again. "Normally I would not let him ascend again today, but all the other rules are being broken so why not?"

Serjon sat up slowly and turned to face the adjunct.

"Do you still want me to lead the flock of eight to Median?" he asked. "I'm feeling better."

The flight to Median took ninety minutes, but the weather was kind to the damaged wings and injured flyers. Below them the tramway was dotted with galley carts and trams traveling east. Here and there were wrecks where the Bartolicans had attacked steam trams, but these had just been pushed aside to burn out. It was dusk when they landed. After another hour of debriefings Serjon finally made his way to the refectory tent. There he found Bronlar, sitting alone at a trestle table. In a world of male wardens, squires, and flyers she was greeted with either bewilderment or hostility, but never welcomed. He sat down opposite her, noting the untouched emu goulash with jasmine rice and beans on her plate.

"So you heard?" Serjon asked.

She nodded, and pushed her plate over to him.

"No thanks, there are thirteen beans."

Bronlar plucked a single bean from the plate and ate it, but Serjon had no more interest in food than she did.

"My father was not on your list of the dead, Serjon. Do you know what happened to him?"

"The senior guildsmen were loaded onto a steam tram before the killing started. Glasken managed to rescue Jeb, but there were hundreds of carbineers and—"

"No! Stop it, no more. They are gone, they were murdered. The Airlord will see that justice is done and return my father to me one day, dead or alive. No more on all that, please."

They picked at her meal from opposite sides of the table for a time, while outside the sound of a gunwing landing cut over the clamor of the crowded wingfield. Bronlar explained that the wardens meant to make a stand at Median and halt the Bartolican advance. Already they were demanding reparations amounting to over half Greater Bartolica's territory.

"So you had five victories today," she added.

"I'd rather have my sisters and mother alive again."

"You shot down a gunwing in clear air combat. You shot down a warden."

"So?"

"Well, it shows that you are a great flyer. Duels are very hard."

"It's luck, just damn, simple luck."

"Not so! It's timing and reaction and tactics, and, and knowing sailwing flight like your own name."

"How would you know? Ever fought clear air?"

"Yes, this morning above the Green River bridge."

Serjon blinked and looked up.

"You fought? Today?"

"If since I last saw you is today, then it's today. I fought an armored sailwing for forty minutes before he misjudged a power dive to escape me and hit trees."

With a mighty cheer Serjon flung the top of the trestle table up into the air and aside, then lifted Bronlar off her bench. The carbineer guards at the door dashed in and several of the diners jumped to their feet before they realized that it was not a fight. The Jannian wardenate had been credited with fourteen victories that day. The finger of guilt had lingered before Serjon, but had moved on without pointing.

"You saved me, you saved me," Serjon cried again and again as he hugged Bronlar and whirled her around. "How can I repay you? Do you need a big brother? I'm very good at being a big brother."

Glasken and Feydamor arrived by galley cart the following day, but soon after that Bronlar and Serjon were sent to Casper in the south of Governor Sartov's new region. The Yarronese wardens did not like the idea of commoner upstarts shooting down enemy wardens, and wanted them out of the way before any more fighting began.

More accounts of atrocities came in with each steam tram of refugees, and they were always against guildsmen and their families, never against merchant or farming estates. Green River fell, and Bartolican steam trams began venturing out along the Red Desert tramway. The gunwings hastily assembled at Median challenged and fought the Bartolicans in the skies above the Red Desert, but left the ground defense to the Yarronese merchant carbineers. The Bartolicans had no qualms about using their wings for ground support, however, and within a week they had taken Creston, just twenty miles east of Median.

Only now did the Yarronese begin blowing up tramway track, digging trenches, and erecting barricades in Median, but it was too late. Bartolican cart cannons began shooting fire shells into Yarron's second-largest city. Airlord Virtrian couriered diplomatic protests to all the other dominions, but the accusations were so fantastic that his peers were either incredulous or uncertain of what to do. While they dithered, Yarron was brought to its knees.

Calls did not scatter the Bartolican carbineers in the field; it was almost as if they could anticipate Calls in open country. A frantic meeting of the Airlord and senior wardens in Forian declared that Median, the domain's second-biggest city, was the keystone of all defense plans. The merchant carbineers that were originally brought in to retake Middle Junction were ordered to stop and defend Median, but yet again the Bartolican invaders were ahead of their enemy.

The Yarronese carbineers were trained for shootouts with outlaw bands of a dozen or so, and the Mexhaven-style mass battles had them at a distinct disadvantage. Yarronese forces were up against a numerically smaller but ruthless enemy that was unbelievably well coordinated. Eight days into the undeclared war Median was under siege and close to falling. The Bartolican merchant carbineers controlled nearly a third of Yarron.

5 August 3960: Middle Junction

Rollins quickly became aware that the campaign had escalated into an invasion of an entire domain of outlaws: Yarron! On the fifth day of August he brought the MC5 east to the regional capital of Middle Junction and stopped in the sidings of the sprawling central depot. Almost immediately the officer he recognized as Warran Glasken came aboard and had an urgent, whispered conversation with Kalward. Dawn was a half hour away, and the lamps of the Middle Junction Tramway Depot were all alight. At least twenty red trams were stopped there. Some trams had battle damage, and most of the carbineers were milling about close by. At Warran Glasken's whistle a squad of officers searched MC5, but left again, apparently without finding anything of note.

Minutes passed. Suddenly there were shouts in the distance, followed by women's screams that were cut short by a burst of automatic fire. Carbineers with reaction pistols summoned all tram commanders and drivers to be addressed by Kalward. So, he's more than just the commander of a black tram, thought Rollins; then he stopped so suddenly that the reaction pistol of the carbineer behind him dug deep into his back. Before the line of drivers and officers lay two dead girls in dirty, torn robes, both shot in the back. All around them on the tramway tracks lay looted gold coins, model gunwings encrusted with gems, ornate ceremonial guns that were all inlay and tracery, bottles of expensive spirits, sacramental goblets and artifacts from various religions, and jewelry of a splendor such as Rollins had not dreamed possible.

"All this was found in Red Tram CT038," said Kalward.

He was standing down on the tracks with the tram commanders and drivers while two carbineers held a driver against the edge of the platform. The prisoner had the patch CT038 sewn onto the left breast of his coat.

"You were given orders back at Sage to take *nothing* with you that was not already on your tram. We are fighting for our lives! We cannot afford to be weighed down with loot of any sort."

"But Sair Kalward, after all we were allowed to do at the Fontwater estate I—or like we thought we could—"

"Enough!" shouted Kalward.

He raised his hand high, snapped his fingers, and pointed to Warran Glasken, who was on the platform. The officer marched forward, drawing his reaction pistol as he advanced, then fired a short burst down into the crown of the driver's head. The carbineers let the body flop to the rails.

"Some trams have been searched, but the rest of you have ten minutes to clean your trams out and add your loot to that pile. In view of our success and your good fighting so far, henceforth each carbineer will be allowed such gleanings that can be carried in a single hand. Officers and drivers can take the equivalent of what will fit in a single coat pocket. Take no more, or death. Take no women, or death. Take no drink, or death. Do what you will on the wardens' estates, as long as you obey your commanders and *don't load down the trams*. Now go!"

Rollins stood clear on the platform while a frantic rummaging and jingling took place on the trams. There were screams, pleas—and three shots. The bodies of another three abducted women were added to the pile, along with five times more plunder from the other trams. In the distance Rollins saw the figures of other women dashing over the tracks for the nearest streets of Middle Junction. Some commanders had apparently been overtaken by conscience, releasing their wretched captives rather than taking Kalward's solution.

The dead were later carried into the canteen of the central depot and carbines were placed in their hands. The building was then set afire and allowed to burn to ashes. Rollins was assigned with a dozen other trusted drivers to load the looted treasure into galley carts, which were then left standing alongside the platform, covered with canvas and under guard.

"You've not taken anything," Kalward observed as Rollins was about to return to his tram.

"Nobody told me to," he replied in a strong but deferential voice.

Kalward lifted a cover and gestured to the pile beneath. Rollins carefully picked out a selection of gold coins out and dropped them into his pocket. He stopped when it was heavy, but not crammed.

"That's all?" asked Kalward. "No jewelry to please a special lady back home?"

"Can't say I want anyone being so special that they learn too much about me."

"How many did you kill before you joined the trams?"

Rollins hesitated, but decided that evasion would neither harm nor help here.

"One man," he said truthfully. "Over a woman."

"I thought so. You take no loot that can be traced, you avoid the town whores when we pull into stations, and you

don't drink. That's steady and clever. I like that in a driver.
I'm going to have field glasses and a gun assigned to you."

"Thank you, sair."

Later that day Rollins saw his first war duel out to the
east of Middle Junction. An armed sailwing with Yarronese markings fought a short engagement with a more
powerful Bartolican sailwing before setting its engine afire.
The Bartolican aircraft crashed into the irrigated fields, but
did not explode. The vanquished sailwing had Bartolican
markings, Rollins thought as he lowered his field glasses.
It was not black or unmarked, but Bartolican. That meant
the nobility of Bartolica were now supporting this fright-
eningly unchivalric war.

20 August 3960

Laurelene Hannan was trapped in Median when the Bartolican forces laid siege. She had been traveling with diplomatic papers, and was therefore identified and taken into
custody very early in the war. At first she was merely held
in protective custody; then, as reports of the Bartolican
atrocities and carbineer attacks came flooding in, she was
questioned, threatened, and increasingly deprived of sleep.
Was she a spy? What was her mission? Where were the
Bartolicans going to strike next? Who had really killed the
Yarronese wardens at Forian?

None of the questions meant anything to Laurelene.
What did alarm her was the endless parade of haggard
eyewitnesses that were brought to tell their stories of murder, rape, abduction, and looting by the Bartolican carbineers. While her Yarronese captors were angry, they had
not as yet sunk to the level that her own side was being
accused of. She wondered how long that might take.

Municipal Prefect Staimar was not a trained interrogator, and as such was all the more dangerous. His son had
just been confirmed dead in the fighting to the west, and

his wife had last been seen in an area that was now under occupation. At first Laurelene had defied him as she had defied all those who had gone before. With Staimar, this was a mistake. He brought in a half-dozen women who had recently been widowed in the fighting, and they had stripped Laurelene naked, even down to her rings and combs. Cold, bare, embarrassingly overweight, and lacking any symbol of her status, she would have gladly told them what she knew, yet she knew nothing. She was given a bathrobe and clogs and handed back to the guards.

"Whatever your cause might be, Semme Hannan, it had better be worthwhile for what is about to happen," Staimar said pointedly as she was led out.

"I have no secrets, I'm just a loyal Bartolican subject, Sair Prefect," she pleaded.

"Well in that case you will be pleased to know that this city has no more than days or even hours left before your carbineers break through our barricades and trenches. When that happens, we know what to expect after what has happened further east. Until then, my word still has the weight of authority and my decision is that you be turned over to the bereaved ladies that you have just met. No more, no less. Semme Laurelene Hannan, you will learn what it is to be the plaything of people who are not bound by the rules of chivalric law or the veneer of civilization, rules that your people have so readily flung aside."

"Sair Prefect, you cannot blame me—"

"Oh but I *can* and I *do*, Semme District Inspector's Wife. A room needs to be prepared, so please be patient. I want no mess on my furniture or carpets in what little time I have left to enjoy them."

Two armed guards flanked Laurelene as she sat waiting in the antechamber. The boom of Bartolican carriage guns and cart cannons continued outside, with four or five shells falling every minute. She knew that if she were free to move and no gates or doors were locked, she could have walked to the Bartolican lines within no more than a quarter hour. So near yet so far. The hatred in the Yarronese women's faces kept returning to haunt her. There had been a basis there, they had not been putting on an act.

Haggard and sometimes wounded officials came and went, and there were ominous sounds of furniture being moved about in a nearby room. A lone member of the Dominion of Yarron's Merchant Carbineers Inspectorate strode past carrying a folder sealed with an impression that made the troops at the door salute smartly and stand aside. There was something about both his face—Glasken! Glasken with shorter hair and clean-shaven.

"Sair Inspector, please, may I speak with you?" Laurelene called in Old Anglian, rising to her feet.

The guards pushed her back down into the chair, but Glasken paused and faced her.

"Yes?" he asked with a slight grin of recognition.

"A Bartolican woman," explained one of the guards crisply. "She is due for another audience with the Prefect in a few minutes."

"I see. Well, she does not concern me. I am here to collect the Bartolican Semme Laurelene Hannan for questioning."

"But Sair Inspector, *this* is Semme Laurelene Hannan."

"Ah—yes, how could I have missed her? There is so much of her, she would be very difficult to miss."

For all her predicament Laurelene bristled before the suave, smirking Glasken. "You filthy swinelet—" she began, but a guard backhanded her across the ear.

"Sair Inspector, she is still in the custody of the Prefect," the guard explained. Glasken held up his folder and displayed the seal.

"No matter, I shall have her back in time. I have an extremely comfortable office downstairs. This way, Semme."

"You monster, I'd rather face those Yarronese women!" shouted Laurelene.

"I prefer to face women too, although approaching from behind has its own allure."

Smirking, the guard who had backhanded Laurelene hauled her to her feet.

"Ten minutes, Sair Inspector, then hand her to the Prefect," he warned as he pushed Laurelene forward to Glasken.

Glasken took her by the arm. "We'll be in Room—ah, I can't remember the number, there's a blue star chalked on the door."

"We'll find it."

Glasken snaked an arm around Laurelene's waist and into the folds of her bathrobe. She tried to slap his face, but he caught her arm and twisted it around behind her back.

"Best approach *her* from behind!" laughed one of the guards as Glasken pushed her to the head of the stairs.

He ushered Laurelene down the stairs and along a side corridor, still holding her arm tightly behind her back.

"You may get your way with me, Glasken, but—" she began.

"Not unless you lose about forty pounds," said Glasken, releasing her and unclipping his dustcape. "Put this on, then take my arm and look as if we've been married three decades."

Astonished, Laurelene stopped and stared blankly back at him.

"What do you mean?" she asked.

"Well, I'll be looking ground down, and as if I haven't had it in years. You could try looking bored—"

She aimed another slap at his face but his hand shot up and blocked the blow again.

"Enough of that, Semme, there are no guards to impress. Now put on that cape. Do it!"

Arm in arm they walked through a side door and into a long, narrow courtyard that led to the front gate.

"We were lucky the guards did not think to speak to me

in Yarronese," he muttered as they walked. "Do you have papers, anything that identifies you as Bartolican?"

"Everything was taken from me."

"Damn! That will make it harder for you when the Bartolican carbineers break in. First let's get you into the streets where you can hide from the Yarronese."

"Sair, you mean your intentions were not, ah, lewd?"

"My intentions are generally lewd, Semme, but in this case staying alive is of more concern. What does this pass say, do you read Yarronese?"

"It says Merchant Inspector Myrel Pregel and husband."

"Good. You're Myrel Pregel, I'm your husband. Act like a prize bitch . . . or maybe 'act' is the wrong word."

"You—but who are these people in the papers?"

"They're both dead, I just killed them. The woman was a man and they weren't human, if that makes a difference. Here's the gate, act arrogant, like an inspector."

They were waved through with hardly a glance. The distant bombardment rumbled on as they walked away down the street, but as they turned a corner whistles shrilled out from the building they had left.

"Run, the guards have missed you!" barked Glasken. "Call's balls, but they didn't give me long to bundle into you."

Glasken appeared to be familiar with the alleyways and lanes, and they were soon in a deserted area amid storehouses. The walls were high and blank, and smoke from nearby fires lay thick on the air.

"Stay low," said Glasken. "Hide amid the rubbish. The city's walls are a thousand years old and are crumbling fast before those carriage guns, and the barricades are not much better. When your Bartolican carbineers come through, wait until a merchant officer appears and go to him. *Not* a carbineer, not any carbineer. Now give back that cape."

"But this bathrobe—"

"It becomes you. Give me the cape!"

He snatched the cape from her then made off into the thickening swirls of smoke from fires started by incendiary shells.

"Glasken, wait!"

"Stay here. Hide."

Laurelene followed him at a distance. There were few women or children about, and most of the people she saw were Yarronese carbineers and civilians with guns. Most of the incoming artillery was pounding one section of the ancient walls, but the incendiaries were fired at random to cause chaos. Enemy gunwings cruised lazily in the thermals high overhead. Glasken was running much faster than Laurelene could, and she soon lost him. She saw a hostelry and stumbled over the cobblestones for the front door, her lungs burning with smoke and exertion, and every breath a wheeze. She entered and found the reception chamber empty.

Outside there was a massive explosion, much larger than the thump of artillery. They must have hit a munitions store, Laurelene thought at first, but then she heard cries from people running past outside that the walls were down. Enemy carbineers poured into the city. The fighting was not intense, the defenders had been beaten long before the section of wall collapsed. Laurelene listened and watched. There were screams and sporadic shots, and a growing pall of smoke. Bartolican carbineers ran past the hostelry and a burning firebrand was tossed through the window, shattering the glass to land smoking against someone's abandoned baggage. Another followed, and then the carbineers ran on.

Have to move outside, hide somewhere that cannot burn, Laurelene thought. Must hide until the fighting stops and there's order again. Glasken appeared on the street, helping a limping man to run. Laurelene dashed outside and went after him, but the smoke soon shrouded him from her view. She stepped into an alley as she heard the clump of boots nearby, then made her way through the drifting smoke.

The city was burning. This was a reward for the victors, a day or so to play with live toys, and with no rule of law. Laurelene sprawled headlong over something—a live Bartolican carbineer looting a body. The man was battle-alert and quick, and his hand snaked out and seized her ankle.

"Let go, I'm Semme Laurelene Hannan, wife of—"

"Don't foul our language with your Yarronese tongue!" he exclaimed, backhanding her across the mouth. Holding her by the hair he began punching her in the face.

The beating soon had Laurelene nearly senseless. The carbineer began to tear away her hempcloth robe and when she tried to crawl away he dragged her back and punched her face until she lay unresisting, her legs bare and apart. He's done this before, so this is what it's like to be violated, she thought as he settled down on top of her with a long, shuddering sigh. Anything, anything, just no more beating, she thought, her eyes closed.

Abruptly the man jerked upward, and something warm splashed onto her face. Sticky, salty. Blood! Laurelene wiped her eyes and stared into the slashed throat of the carbineer. A grizzled Yarronese was standing astride them both with a knife in one hand and the Bartolican man's hair in the other.

He hauled the carbineer's body off Laurelene, then held a finger to his lips.

"Sex is dangerous," he said softly in Yarronese as he let the body fall. "It concentrates the mind, so that danger may approach unseen."

Laurelene drew her torn bathrobe about her as she sat up and shrank back against the wall. Her rescuer had a bandaged leg and head, and as he sat down Glasken appeared. He was wearing part of a Bartolican uniform.

"This way, Jeb, I've found a couple of—you again!"

"You are acquainted?" asked Feydamor.

"Acquainted? She once had me shot!" Glasken exclaimed.

"She was being ravished by a Bartolican."

"She's a Bartolican herself, she's the Bartolican Inspector General's wife."

"One of my own people just tried to rape me," Laurelene retorted.

"Well don't look at me, I'm just wearing their uniform!" snapped Glasken, flinging a bundle of clothing at Feydamor's feet. "Jeb, change into this."

"But these are of Bartolican carbineers."

"Very sharp, one day you might be Airlord."

"In all honor, Juan Glasken, I could never wear a Bartolican coat."

"Honor be screwed! Just do it, you stubborn old goat. Do it for Yarron, do it for the Airlord, do it to impress this Bartolican lady, but *do* it!"

"What is a goat?" muttered Feydamor, sullenly looking at the coats.

"I'm talking to one. Now put them on."

Feydamor reluctantly tried on a coat while Glasken went back into the smoke for something else.

"With women, if a man cannot get his way by charm he is less than a man," said Feydamor as he did up the brass buttons. "That is one of Sair Glasken's sayings. He's quite a remarkable man."

"Aye, never ravished a woman," declared Glasken as he reappeared with carbines and forage packs. "Been damn near ravished by a few myself, though."

"What are you going to do?" Laurelene asked Feydamor.

"Glasken and I are going to flee Median. You . . . well, you are at risk, even though you are Bartolican. You can come if you wish."

"Why yes, yes!"

Glasken dropped the guns and packs in astonishment.

"You have to be joking!" he exclaimed, but Feydamor waved him silent.

"Screaming is required of you, Semme, and fear of being ravished. Can you provide that?"

"I'm in good practice."

"Then come with us and do exactly what you are told."

At sunset they approached the breach in Median's thousand-year-old walls. The two men were dressed as fully kitted Bartolican carbineers, with the brass buttons of their coats undone and Call anchors pinned and dangling at their hips. Feydamor stopped Laurelene and took her by both arms and looked into her bruised face.

"Struggle, scream, *be* a Yarronese woman," he said. "Try to say that you're Bartolican and I'll kill you before the guards can drop me. You will *die* and you will *rot*. Understand?"

Laurelene bobbed her head and said that she did. Glasken bent over and drove his shoulder into her abdomen, scooping her up into the air. Now Laurelene screamed, partly in surprise and partly through fear of being dropped. Nobody had been able to carry her for many, many years. Glasken tottered toward the wall over the rubble, with Feydamor limping behind.

"Get a girl, toss that bag away!" shouted one of the Bartolicans posted at the breach.

"They run too fast," Glasken shouted back in slurred, but passable Bartolican.

He slapped Laurelene on the buttocks with his free hand and she gave an embarrassed squark.

"And this one weighs like five girls," Feydamor added in flawless Bartolican.

Laurelene gasped in outrage, then screamed again rather than not retort at all. They left the guards laughing and were quickly lost in the gathering darkness beyond the Bartolican siege lines and camp. Glasken dropped to his knees and dumped Laurelene at the first opportunity.

"If you want sympathy, don't look to me!" snarled Laurelene, getting to her feet and glaring down at Glasken, who sat wheezing with his hands on his knees.

"Your idea, she is," Glasken gasped to Feydamor.

Glasken led them for some miles until they found a burned-out farmhouse. The bodies of several men and boys were lying nearby, but there were no women to be seen. Feydamor lay down the moment they were through the door.

"You stay here," Glasken said to Laurelene as he began changing into the clothing of one of the dead farmers. "When the city stops burning and the merchant officers arrive, find the most senior of them and get his protection."

Glasken began foraging for food in the blackened ruins. Laurelene regarded him by the glow of the burning city, which was reflected from the clouds.

"Why were you in the prefect's building?" Laurelene ventured.

"If you knew, you would be killed," he muttered. "Forget about me, say nothing. There are people who would kill you for just knowing I exist. Return to Median, it will be better tomorrow. Just stay outside the city until you can find a merchant officer."

He began to dress a dead farmer in a Bartolican uniform. Shots echoed across from Median's ruddy glow in the southwest.

"So you saved me from the Yarronese then saved me from being that carbineer's toy and now you just leave?" she asked presently, her question pointed but her voice full of amazement.

"Wrong. Sair Feydamor saved you from the carbineer." He checked the pistol he was carrying. "Watch for .38 rounds, Jeb, I can take another four."

"Sair Glasken, I disgraced you in Condelor and you were shot," said Laurelene.

He put the gun in his coat pocket and regarded her in the dim, red light that permeated into the ruin.

"I was disgraced long before I met you, Semme Hannan," he said with a leer.

He took a small .22-caliber revolver from his coat.

"None of the chambers has been fired, and this is a lady's weapon," he said, holding it up for Laurelene to see. "I took it from a dead Bartolican. I'd say some Yarronese woman tried to fend him off with it, but he rightly assumed that she would be less frightened of being raped than of killing him. Very foolish of her. Do you know how to shoot one of these?"

"I do, Sair."

"I see," he said, handing the weapon over to her. "Now, having been beaten, flung down, and very nearly ravished, what would you do next time?"

"Sair? I—"

"Shoot him!"

"I—shoot him. Yes."

"And more than that. Shoot him in the head to leave his uniform undamaged, dress in his clothing. Grab a bottle, act drunk, rub your face with dirt, rub your clothes with vomit and turds so that nobody will come near enough for a good look at you. *Fight* and *survive*, Semme! Love life! Too many people would rather be dead than be embarrassed or soiled. That is very foolish. Life is a brilliant and wonderful adventure. Never throw it away, and never hide from it."

The words were odd to hear from someone that Laurelene considered to be both a lecher and stupid, yet they carried a strong ring of sincerity.

"Sair Glasken, what part of you is the act?"

"None of me, Semme Hannan. Can you say as much?"

In the hour that followed Laurelene convinced Feydamor that she was needed to nurse him and help him to walk. She found some women's clothing in a laundry basket that had been dropped in the yard outside. The fit of the smockshirt was loose and comfortable, but the dresses belonged to someone much shorter. An oilcloth cloak hid most of the tight, short dress that Laurelene managed to squeeze into, however, and she arranged a hump of cloth between her shoulders. They set off with Glasken in the lead, and they passed as quite convincing farmhands.

"And who are you, Sair Feydamor?" she asked as she walked with his arm around her shoulder, supporting him on the rough, darkened path.

"A guildmaster engineer, Feydamor Engine Guild."

"Ah, and how were you shot?"

"I was on a steam tram, a Bartolican gunwing fired on it."

"Never! Bartolican wardens have a code of chivalry, they fight only clear-skies duels."

Feydamor began a wheezing laugh. "Shot just below the knee, but . . . tram's steam engine was not hit. Gunwing broke off. Perchance it had no more bullets."

"Why did you not stay with your family on the estate?"

"They're dead, Semme. My wife and five daughters were violated and murdered by Bartolican carbineers."

"Impossible, lies—"

"I was there, you stupid pudding. Only Glasken and I escaped. My son was away fighting, he's a gunwing flyer."

Laurelene did not want to believe any of what he said, but her own experience suggested that he was telling the truth.

"I can hear the barking of a terrier pack," Glasken cut in. "If they are a Call guard we are safe, but they might be trackers. No talking from now on, and if we're challenged Jeb must do the talking."

The surviving wings and estate refugees who could fly were moved out to the eastern city of Casper by Governor Sartov before Median came under siege, leaving other guildsmen and their families to flee on the tramway to Forian. Alion, Ramsdel, Bronlar, and Serjon all flew armed sailwings north to Casper; then they were ferried back on an overloaded regal to fly some surviving gunwings out of Median as well. On their third trip that day they were even joined by the wounded Kumiar, who flew a sailwing. Serjon managed to land his gunwing, but spun it on the flight-strip and came to a stop facing backward.

"I was unlucky," he said as they ate in the refectory at Casper wingfield that night. "It's because I ascended in service without a lady's colors."

"So . . . are all of your sisters dead then?" asked Alion, hesitantly.

Serjon nodded. Ramsdel had no colors at all and Kumiar had colors from another dead girl on the Jannian estate. Bronlar began to sniffle when she thought of Kallien, and of how she had died. Ramsdel pointed out that Alion's colors were from a Bartolican, and that he risked a charge of treason if he ascended in his airlord's service wearing them.

"Well I'm a flyer, I fight and I've got one confirmed victory to prove it, so you can all stop looking at me for colors!" Bronlar stated emphatically.

"Which reminds me, I finished these for you, Serjon," Ramsdel said as he tossed a bundle of ribbons to the thin youth. "Note, violet for boys."

"*You* have *colors*?" exclaimed Alion, aghast. "No man has ever had colors."

"I like to make history," explained Serjon.

"Oo, can I wear them?" asked Bronlar. "I like to make history too."

"Besides, you're the only girl in Mounthaven who is qualified to wear them," Serjon pointed out.

He handed her the colors, and as their fingers touched he flinched away.

"What's the matter?" she asked.

"Cold hands," he muttered. "I'm sorry. I—I touched too many cold hands at Opal. The sensation makes me ill."

Ramsdel helped Bronlar attach Serjon's colors to the tag on her right arm.

"What about the rest of us?" asked Kumiar. "Any more bad luck and I'll be dead."

Ramsdel waved a serving girl over and asked her if she

wanted to honor a brave and wounded flyer with her colors. She explained that she had none. Ramsdel took down her details and promised to sew up a set for her to give to Kumiar. Serjon said that he would carry the colors of no more women after what happened to his mother and sisters.

"You see, luck is all balance, like day and night, good and bad, love and hate," he explained. "There is an equal amount of good luck and bad luck, and the more good fortune I have in the air, the more bad fortune is visited on the lady whose colors I wear. I'd rather have the bad luck than harm a lady."

"What if Bronlar is lucky in war duels?" asked Alion.

"Bronlar doesn't believe in luck," said Serjon. "I'm quite safe."

"What about you and Alion?" Bronlar asked Ramsdel. "There are more serving girls over there."

"They're commoners!" said Alion with great finality.

"They have no dress sense," declared Ramsdel. "I mean look at those aprons over those drab-colored dresses that have bunch-belting instead of proper darts. I want a girl whose clothes will not mortify me on wingfield parades. Bad luck is preferable to bad taste."

"And I would rather have bad luck than forsake true and noble love," said Alion.

Bronlar applauded, then got up and hugged Alion from behind. Ramsdel went over to ask some of the serving girls if they would consider dressing better, and according to his directions—and got his face slapped. Serjon sat gazing down at his meal, then gave a cry of dismay and pushed away from the table. Bronlar came around to his side, stared at his plate for a moment, then picked it up and took it over to the serving counter.

"Could I have one more bean, please?" she asked the serving girl who was to give colors to Kumiar.

"One bean, Semme?"

"One bean, Semme. There are thirteen on this plate, and

it's upsetting the flyer whose colors I wear."

"The *flyer* whose colors *you* wear?"

"Yes," said Bronlar, holding up her right arm. "His name's Serjon—"

"Ah, the warden-killer boy with five victories. And you are the flyer-girl Bronlar with one victory, now I understand. I hear everything, you see."

"I know your name is Liesel."

The girl gasped. "How?"

"I heard you tell Kumiar and Ramsdel back at the table." Liesel laughed, and added a bean to Serjon's plate.

"You're not at all like normal wardens, squires, and flyers," said Liesel. "Are you the new Air Carbineers of Governor Sartov that I've heard whispers about?"

Bronlar winked at her and said, "We just might be." As she carried Serjon's plate with its additional bean back to the table she whispered to herself, "Who knows, we just might be."

Median was marked by a diminishing column of murky smoke on the horizon as Glasken, Feydamor, and Laurelene walked east across the irrigated desert. They stayed in burned-out farmsteads during the day, tethered and with one always awake to keep watch. Feydamor was weak and feverish, but responded to Laurelene's nursing. Glasken cut him a pair of greenwood crutches and helped him learn to walk with them. At one ruin they found a sty that had been torched and discovered two dozen swinelets that had been roasted alive but not badly charred. The meat was tender and succulent after a day of hunger. Bartolican sailwing patrols droned overhead from time to time.

"Pannion's house, but not a Pannion squire," said Feydamor, glaring up at a sailwing that passed almost directly overhead in the late afternoon. "Running a Daimzer engine by the sound of it, but in a Schneider airframe."

The words were his first for the day that were not terse replies to questions.

"Is that important?" asked Glasken.

"It's a clumsy combination of light patrol engine and armored sailwing airframe. The Bartolicans are ramming everything into the air that will stay up by itself. That flyer is short on experience too. Look at the way he wobbles and dips as he turns on the updraft near those hills."

"It's sensible. Why waste wardens on scouting?"

"It is ignoble," hissed Feydamor between grating teeth. "It flies in the face of everything it means to be a warden, squire, or even a flyer. Commoners should not do the work of wardens."

"Have you any word of the Yarronese wardens?" asked Laurelene.

Feydamor scowled uncertainly at hearing such a question coming from a Bartolican, then decided that it was asked in goodwill.

"Only nine original wardens were elsewhere when the bomb was set off at our airlord's palace. We have many gunwings intact, but there are few experienced nobles to fly them. Most of our new wardens are just boys, they have not even got their battle commissions and sashes from the Airlord."

"They stopped the Dorakian wardens," began Glasken.

"Pah, that was a miracle of courage against experience. A single Bartolican governor commands more wardens than the Dorakian Airlord, and the whole of Greater Bartolica is upon us."

"The Bartolican carbineers are the real danger," observed Glasken. "They are sweeping through Yarron like foxes in a chicken coop."

"Foxes?" asked Laurelene.

"Wild terriers, sort of."

"What do you know of the noble and chivalric arts of battle, Sair Glasken?"

"I commanded infantry in the wars of my homeland, er, Mexhaven. You might call me a merchant carbineer. We were not as rabid as the Bartolicans, but not as stupid as the Yarronese."

Feydamor bristled, but was too weary for an angry exchange.

"Then what would you do here?"

"Blind their commanders. Order every Yarron gunwing into the sky, shoot down Bartolican scouts."

"But you can't order wardens to do your bidding, like some commoner swinelet herder!"

"Whoever is flying that wing up there is no warden," said Glasken, pointing up to the sky. "He is taking orders, he is scouting, and Bartolica is winning."

"I'd rather die," Feydamor replied sullenly.

"You nearly did just that. Come now, we must bundle up as much pork as we can carry and be on our way at dusk."

They made good progress that night, traveling another fifteen miles before sheltering for the next day in an irrigated orchard. There were other refugees there, and they got news of the invaders ahead. Yarronese-controlled territory was only ten miles away, and the Bartolicans were inexplicably letting refugees flee to safety.

"It doesn't make sense," said Feydamor, "they're letting carbineers through who can turn and stand against them in the service of Yarron."

"It makes sense," replied Glasken.

"How?"

Glasken shook his head. "You listen, Jeb Feydamor, then you scoff."

"Well, you talk bollix!"

Glasken sighed and seemed wistful for a moment. "Semme Laurelene, what is the condition of the refugees we just met?"

"Like us, sair. Women, children, aged, and wounded."

"There are new rules in use here and neither of you can see them," Glasken explained. "Where I come from it's called total war. Refugees strain the resources of the Yarronese defenders, and also spread tales of slaughter, rape, and the invincibility of the Bartolican carbineers. Yarron does not get fresh fighters from the likes of us, it gets chaos, fear, and a dead weight to carry into battle. There is one thing that puzzles me, though."

"I'm stunned to hear it, you seem to know everything else," said Feydamor.

"The Bartolicans learned these arts almost overnight. They fight in perfect unity, like a team of counterball players, like . . . a machine!"

Glasken frowned and stroked his recently bare chin, deep in thought. Presently he said that he was going to scout around and vanished from sight. Feydamor shook his head and huddled down in his blanket.

"The man is mad, but he has a good heart," he told Laurelene as she changed the dressing on his leg.

"He has the passions of a rutting stoat, and his heart is not the organ he favors."

"Not so, Semme. He may be a lecher, but he has a certain nobility and he stands by his friends."

"The same may be said of you, Sair Feydamor," said Laurelene, idly stroking his leg. "I am the enemy, yet you protected me."

"Yet I am no lecher."

"You are the more attractive because of it."

It would be fair to say that although Laurelene's actions were motivated by guilt for her people's invasion and a vague idea of revenge against Glasken, she did have some genuine affection for the wounded Yarronese engineer. Their lovemaking was a hurried fumble of skirts and lacings by two people who had had little recent practice in furtive seduction, and when it was over they were quick to roll apart and restore their clothing. Neither raised the subject again.

They sheltered in the orchard for most of the day, and in the afternoon a flight of Bartolican gunwings flew by going south. Glasken counted thirty of the aircraft through a gap in the trees. There was sporadic shooting in the distance from cart cannons.

The night's journey was much worse than before. The invaders controlled the roads and paths more tightly in this area, and Feydamor did not progress well over the fields with his crutches. Glasken had to carry him while Laurelene staggered along under the weight of their packs. The front line itself was no more than a chain of invader camps linked by patrol paths and lookout stations. They were stopped by a squad of Bartolican carbineers, but managed to barter their passage across the line with most of their load of cold pork. After all they were only farmers: two grizzled men and a hunchback woman. Once clear of the line they stopped, and Glasken and Feydamor changed into the Yarronese jackets that they had been carrying.

"It's such a relief to stand up straight again," said Laurelene, stretching and thrusting out a very impressive pair of breasts.

She caught Glasken glancing at them, but decided against saying anything. After all, Glasken had had better contact with them than Feydamor and the shame was more hers than his. As dawn broke they met a group of Yarronese militiamen, an aged carbineer veteran commanding six nervous youths armed with hunting rifles.

"Big air battle yes-aday," said the veteran. "Eighty gunwings of the invader met seven of our wardens. We had a great triumph."

"Seven against eighty, yet triumph?" asked Glasken incredulously in broken Yarronese.

"Yair-certs, sair. They took fifteen invader wardens down a-fore the last o'them crashed to earth."

"Glorious," croaked Feydamor, who was lying exhausted against a tree.

"Aye, two o'them for each Yarronese wing to fall."

"Hah. Sixty-five Bartolican wardens flying. Rule sky."

"But they won without honor," insisted Feydamor. "Yarron triumphed."

"Yarronese wardens, all shwhit!" Glasken made a slicing motion across his throat, re-framing the Yarronese moral victory for what it was.

25 August 3960: Casper

Governor Sartov's gunwing was so low on compression spirit that he did not even circle the adjunct's tower to check the flags before landing. His engine died on the dispersal track and his guildsmen had to push the gunwing while he walked ahead to report to the adjunct.

"Three Bartolican sailwings," he declared, and the adjunct chalked them on his board. "All of them dual-seat trainers making observations."

"A fine day, sair, and it brings your tally to—"

"Damn my tally, this is about saving Yarron, not my reputation. The Bartolicans were fools, they were flying well beyond the range of their own gunwings to spy on us."

"Perhaps they expected no danger."

"What do you mean?"

"All seven wardens of the Airlord's Guard were killed in a battle over the Saratoga Springs wingfield. These dispatches were flown in before you landed."

Sartov took the proclamation and began to read. Not far away the guildsmen were already working on his gunwing.

"Glorious moral victory . . . triumphant defeat . . . flower of Yarronese chivalry . . . Bartolican scum . . . touching memorial service in Forian Cathedral."

Sartov crumpled the proclamation and dropped it. The adjunct handed him another proclamation. Three bandsmen and a dozen guildsmen and flyers gathered behind Sartov as he squinted at the writing in the fading light.

"Governor Sartov . . . hereby relieved of his posting— ah yes, I was expecting this. I'm being punished for refusing to get myself killed with the rest of the Airlord's

Guard. And Bromley Avondel is replacing me. Brave, but no experience. Adjunct?"

"Sair?"

"We are commanded by fools and incompetents."

"Sair!"

The adjunct handed one more proclamation to Sartov.

"Be it known to all . . . Warden Alveris Sartov . . . *commander of all forces north of the Laramie River and Chancellor of Governors!*"

The proclamation slipped from Sartov's fingers as the three bandsmen standing behind him struck up the Yarronese dominion anthem. Sartov turned as the adjunct picked up the proclamation, and at the end of the tune the assembled guildsmen gave three cheers and fired a volley from their carbines.

The celebratory feast in the adjunct's briefing hall was modest by any dominion's standards, but that hardly mattered. Sartov was reading dispatches and appointment lists even as he ate.

"It makes sense now," he told the adjunct. "The disaster at Saratoga Springs killed the last senior traditionalists from court. The new airlord must have had this planned for weeks, he's actually going to fight back intelligently."

"Would an airlord murder his own wardens, Chancellor?"

"I would call it taking constructive advantage of their own stupidity for the greater good of Yarron. Finish up, now. I want every sailwing on the field ready to ascend at dawn, and I have a lot of decrees to dictate before that."

That evening Glasken and his companions reached Kennyville, where the Yarronese pennon streamers still flew above the Governor's hall. As Glasken had suspected, it was a shambles of refugee guild families, wounded carbineers, reinforcements, and war supplies. He registered as a refugee from Median under the name John Walker and added Laurelene as his sister. Feydamor used his own name. There was little privacy at the refugee staging ground beside the tramway depot, yet the people were too absorbed with the events that had shattered their lives to eavesdrop.

"You're a wounded guildsman, Jeb, which means you can go to Forian on a hospital tram," Glasken told the exhausted engineer. "The next convoy goes in a half hour, you may get a place."

"Where is Laurel—er, Semme Hannan?"

"She is to go in the women's tram. The steam whistle is broken, so she volunteered to scream whenever the driver grabs her bottom."

"Do I detect annoyance in your tone, Sair Glasken?"

"Now that she no longer depends on me to stay alive, she's behaving like a vindictive cow."

"What is a cow?"

"They're large, they bellow, they have horns."

"Laurelene has no horns."

"Give her time."

"I'd like to see her off."

"Not half as much as I would."

He helped Feydamor to his feet and they went to the tramway station where people were boarding the convoy. Laurelene was still on the platform as they approached.

"Sair Glasken, I would lay bets that you would like to travel on the women's tram," declared Laurelene with a smirk.

"I'm no woman," replied Glasken, pulling his trousers forward and peering down. "Would you like to check the evidence?"

Laurelene inclined her head away.

"You know, you could charm a lady with ease if you but took the trouble to ply her with little pleasantries. Why if I were you—"

"—you would be walking to Forian, and it would do wonders for your figure."

"Let me finish. If I were interested in you—"

"Then it would be to prove something to me, or your-self, or both of us, or your husband, or Envoy Rosenne," Glasken declared, ticking off names on an imaginary chalkboard. He dropped to one knee, a hand against his forehead, the other gesturing above his head. "You have no interest in passion, Semme. You want to be desired, you want attention, you want to be taken seriously, and you want to possess hearts." Glasken rose to his feet, swirled the dead farmer's field cloak about himself, raised his nose, and dabbed delicately at his forehead with a rag-ged handkerchief. "But you don't want something so taste-less or messy as passion stirring within your ample, aristocratic body."

Laurelene whipped a stinging slap at his face, but Glas-ken did a delicate twist-step and her hand missed him al-together, sending her spinning. Feydamor shuffled backward, making a show of leaning on his cane.

"Well, yes, fury may be identified as passion, but it's hardly alluring," Glasken observed as Laurelene heaved herself out of the dust.

"Glasken!" Laurelene barked back. "You want me to prove it with *you*, don't you? Well I can prove it and I don't need your help."

"Don't try to prove it for my sake, Semme, I wouldn't wish that sort of suffering on any poor yoick."

Feydamor closed his eyes and cringed, hoping not to be called upon as her champion. Laurelene aimed another slap at Glasken, but this time he plucked her hand out of the air, spun her around three times, then stepped back in a deep bow. A small crowd was gathering by now, unsure of whether it was a dance or a fight. Some clapped.

"You took me with you from Median, you only did that for hope of bedding me!" Laurelene shouted.

"Feydamor did that."

"Ah, took you from Median, that is," added Feydamor.

"You consented to it, Glasken!" retorted Laurelene.

"If I had piles I would consent to have them lanced, but

I would neither enjoy it nor have any say in the matter. Pile aboard now."

Laurelene turned away and stamped across to the tram. It swayed on its springs as she climbed aboard and sat down. Her face was shining with fury and she was gasping for breath. She did not see Feydamor turned away from the fully loaded hospital tram.

The steam trams whistled consecutively and began to chug forward. Laurelene sat thinking of what she would say to Feydamor when they reached Forian. He had not supported her against Glasken's insults, and now she wondered whether or not it would be wise to extend their brief and furtive liaison. The thought of the look on Glasken's face when he found out made it almost worthwhile, however.

At the town of Cairnstop the convoy was halted and members of the Yarronese Inspectorate came aboard her tram. They took each woman aside in turn and asked them about a little sketch. Presently it was Laurelene's turn.

"He's a tall, strongly built man of about fifty," said the inspector. "His companion was limping when they were last seen at Median. Have you seen him?"

The charsketch was a good likeness of Glasken.

"No, but he's a handsome scruff," Laurelene replied with a wink.

"The rogue has unbridled lusts," the inspector responded uncomfortably. "He may approach you and make unseemly suggestions in Old Anglian. He speaks a little of Yarronese."

"I should be so lucky," replied Laurelene, batting her eyelashes at him.

The inspector took a step back, still holding up the sketch.

"Well if you are, report it to the tram driver at once," he said determinedly. "This man, Juan Glasken, is one of the traitors who are betraying our homeland in this war."

"I have met no man of unbridled lusts since escaping Median, sair, but I live in hope."

Laurelene watched the inspectors go from tram to tram, but noted that Glasken was not found. He had said he would walk to Forian, but he was very resourceful, of course, and a master of disguise—and with a spasm of horror Laurelene found herself admiring Glasken. She drove the thought away.

With the line of trams searched, the inspectors set the signal to proceed, and Laurelene's tram chugged back up to cruising speed. They won't have you, Glasken, she thought as she watched the hills passing in the distance. Not until all of your insults have been returned with the very best rate of interest.

29 August 3960: Condelor

Condelor remained aloof from the tortures that were being inflicted on the dominion to the west. Cities, estates, and the families of guildsmen and nobles should have been exempt from the proceedings of chivalric war, but this war was being conducted in a manner not seen in Mounthaven for a very long time.

Under instruction from his merchant carbineer advisers, Stanbury issued more than a dozen reports each day. He declared that in Yarron the Bartolican carbineers were being welcomed for driving away the outlaws and corrupt Yarronese wardens. He complained to Carabas that nobody would believe that defecting Yarronese wardens were encouraging the Bartolicans to press on and take Forian, but went ahead and released the report anyway. To his surprise it was accepted. The Bartolican court wanted it to be true, so the Bartolican court believed it.

The Bartolican wardens had little to do with the fighting on the ground, while their squires were merely concerned with securing wingfields and supplies for their operations.

The Bartolican carbineers were allowed no letters home, while the wounded were treated in camps on Yarronese soil and kept at work repairing equipment or doing whatever light work suited them. Because they continued to draw full pay, there were few complaints.

The militia couriers were a separate branch of the air companies besides wardens and their people. Officially under the direct command of the Bartolican Airlord himself, they were originally a squadron of two dozen masterless squires and flyers who flew errands and deliveries in sailwings for the palace. In this war they quickly expanded by means of the captured Yarronese and Montrassian sailwings, until their number was over seventy. They were painted in strange patterns under their wings, and were assigned long and complex identifiers. The best of them were said to be able to drop a message capsule into the hatch of a speeding steam tram.

In spite of the best efforts of the censors and commanders, some stories of strafed merchant steam trams and plundered estates found their way west to Condelor. Stanbury's Condelor office gave frequent briefings for the envoys and wardens' advisers in the palace, and a sanitized version of the war's progress was presented to the Bartolican Airlord's autumn court every week. On August 21st the orderly appropriation of Median was announced. The Yarronese were not displaying the forms of chivalry, the Warden of Forms pointed out in a long and indignant speech. There were none to meet the Bartolican airlords in duels over the city, in fact there were no Yarronese nobles or their carbineers to keep the ruffians of the city from burning and looting. The Bartolicans had barely arrived in time to save Median from destruction. They had been welcomed as heroes by all honest folk in the place.

1 September 3960: Kennyville, Yarron

Glasken had been waiting at the tramway station with Fey-damor when a flock of gunwings became audible. The guildmaster identified them as Bartolican while they were still distant dots in the northwest, and followed them as they began circling the town.

"All wardens, gunwings all," said Feydamor. "The estates of Simfield, Dunnely, Ridgewhite, Silvereye, and Clintpeal. Five of the finest Bartolican wardens who ever strapped in."

"Then what are they doing here?" asked Glasken, his hand dropping automatically to his carbine. "Do they want lessons in unchivalric fighting?"

"Sair Glasken, for shame. The brotherhood of the war-denate may be slow sometimes, but it's exceedingly fair. These wardens have come to see for themselves what the carbineers are doing in Yarron. You note my words, retribution is on the way."

The flock broke their circle and the pitch of the droning from their compression engines rose. The idea of attack from the air was still so incredible that some of the refugees just stood watching in the open. Wardens only fought in clear air combat, war was the preserve of the nobility. Glasken was less of an idealist. Pulling Feydamor off balance, he dragged the cursing guildmaster off the platform and behind a stone and timber buffer.

"What are you doing?" cried Feydamor as Glasken held him down. "They're wardens!"

Glasken did not have to reply; the steady hammering of reaction guns said it all. The gunwings came in, strafing the trams and the piles of supplies beside the loading sidings. Feydamor shouted incoherently and tried to wave the Bartolican wardens off as Glasken held him down, and then they were past. The station and tram sidings were

alive with running carbineers and tramway workers. Two
trams were burning.

"Seems as the wardens have come for lessons in unchivalric warfare after all," said Glasken as he watched the
gunwings climbing in a long arc.

"They were wardens," said Feydamor, devastated.

"Aye, and from the noble and revered estates of Simfield, Dunnely, Ridgewhite, Silvereye, and Clintpeal, if I
recall correctly."

"Madness! This is like an airlord pissing on his own
throne."

"Greater madness to keep your head up as they do another tour of inspection. Get down here!"

Once more the gunwings came in together, barely a
wingspan apart, shooting methodically into the trams and
stockpiled barrels of compression spirit. Suddenly everything erupted around them. There was a soundless flash,
followed by a thunderclap as the ground heaved. Rocks,
dust, and wreckage showered down, and Glasken saw a
gunwing come cartwheeling out of the sky to crash into
the nearby Kennyville market. He clambered over the
wreckage of the tramway station buildings with Feydamor,
warily scanning the sky through the smoke and dust.

"Two still flying," said Feydamor between coughs.

"Don't think they'll be back," suggested Glasken.

Two gunwings had been blown to pieces when a munitions tram had blown up, but another had crash-landed
in the main street beside the station. Glasken and Feydamor watched the warden dragged out of the aircraft by
enraged carbineers, a tiny, glittering doll being mobbed by
a swarm of dark ants. They began to beat the warden to
death while those farther back in the crowd cheered and
fired their carbines into the air.

Fifteen trams had been destroyed or damaged in the attack, along with a large amount of trackwork. Spilled and
burning compression spirit had set most of the stockpiles
of weapons and supplies blazing, and Glasken gave up

trying to count the dead and injured. The two surviving gunwings circled the town at a safe height, making an estimate of the unhoped-for damage, so Glasken remained wary and made Feydamor shelter beside an abandoned handcart filled with salt chicken sausage. The vendor lay dead beneath the pushbars, his chest bloodied by a large-caliber reaction gun bullet. At last the gunwings broke off and flew west. Glasken hurried away to examine the station. When he returned, Feydamor had limped over to the wreckage of the Bartolican gunwing. The warden's head was at the top of a sharpened pole that the carbineers had wedged into the wreck.

"That's Warden Silvereye, even through the beating I can recognize him," Feydamor conceded reluctantly.

"They got the shells for the cart cannons," Glasken panted. "Soon the Bartolican carbineers will be arriving here. This place is doomed, we just lost fifteen trams!"

"We can do nothing but hold out here and try to slow them," said Feydamor stoically.

"Pox to that," snorted Glasken, taking him by the arm and walking him back toward the cart. "There's wurst in that cart, see?"

"So?"

"So we have something to eat or trade. You can ride the cart while your leg heals."

"I want to fight, not flee!" declared Feydamor, brandishing his carbine in the air.

They regarded the dead vendor lying behind the cart. Glasken selected a length of preserved sausage and nibbled at it. He raised an eyebrow and nodded, then offered the sausage to Feydamor.

"Nice, and this will be worth more than gold soon," Glasken pronounced. "Jeb, if you're alive and free you can return to fight. Stay here, and you're dead."

"But we need to slow the Bartolicans now, else they will be at Forian before the week is out."

"We can help Yarron better by going to Sartov and advising him."

"Sartov? He's just been made chancellor, he'll not listen to you. Sair Glasken, in a day or so new track will be laid, and galley carts can leave for Forian."

"Bartolican gunwings will be shooting up anything that moves on the tramway."

"You can never convince me—" began Feydamor, but Glasken seized him and spun him to the ground.

Kneeling on his back, he tied the guildsman's hands, then gagged him. Once his legs were tied as well, Glasken heaved him up into the sausage cart and spread his field cloak over him. He started down the road north, and they were not alone as they fled Kennyville. A refugee column of merchant carbineers, guild and warden families formed quickly. At first progress was easy, but in the evening there was a thunderstorm that turned the desert road to mud. When Glasken finally stopped and untied Feydamor they were twenty miles from Kennyville.

"You should have fled without me, there was no need to share your cowardice," grumbled Feydamor as they sat eating the chicken sausage and some cold roast potatoes that Glasken had bartered for among the other refugee guild families. "Tomorrow I take my carbine and I return to Kennyville to do serious shooting."

"At anyone I know?"

"One dead Bartolican carbineer is one less invader on Yarron's back."

"And one dead guildmaster engineer is one massive loss to Yarron and an equally big gain for Bartolica. Yarron needs your skills with compression engines to fight back."

"What?" shouted Feydamor. "Us fight like Bartolicans? Never—and even if we did, I'd never be part of it."

"Not *like* the Bartolicans, *better* than that. With my strategies—"

"*Your* strategies? Pah! Take cover, run away, wear a

disguise, loot food, sleep by day and run by night. You even escaped the Prefect's building in Median behind the skirts of an enemy woman."

"Aye but who rogered that same enemy woman in that orchard near—"

"How did you know—"

Feydamor clamped a hand over his own mouth. Glasken drew a small telescope from his coat, extended it, and turned it upon Feydamor's eye.

"Why patrol the ground when a tree will provide a better view of what may attack and what is being guarded?"

Feydamor sat in silence, unmoving. After some time Glasken began to pack the cart. Slowly Feydamor lowered his hand to join the other in his lap. Glasken sat down in front of him.

"What was she like?" asked Glasken with a leer as he clasped his hands and rested his chin on them.

"None of your business."

"Jeb, I was serious when I said that I need to see Chancellor Sartov. I could help Yarron save itself, I could help Yarron the same way that . . . other people are helping the Bartolicans."

"Then why didn't you tell someone earlier, if you're so very wise?"

"I did!" snapped Glasken, his face coloring as his patience ran down to nothing. "Why do you think I went to the Palace of the Inspectorate in Median, then the Prefect's building? Alas, the infiltrators were there before me, and I was lucky to escape alive. Sartov I already know, and trust. He will listen."

Feydamor crawled under the cart with a blanket. He clipped his Call tether to the frame of the cart, then tried to get comfortable.

"In the morning I'll be gone," he declared.

"Then go," Glasken replied after nearly a full minute, as if he had taken time deciding whether Feydamor was worth the trouble.

The sky was still quite bright, and some people were still tramping along the road. Glasken began to clean his carbine.

"Do you have a family?" asked Feydamor, who had expected more argument, and was uneasy with the silence.

"My family thinks I'm dead, they think I died three years ago. Both of my wives betrayed me, Jeb, could you imagine that? Semme Laurelene is like a combination of their worst features."

"Both? Are you a Mormon?"

"No, a Gentheist."

Feydamor rolled over and scratched his head at the word. Glasken clipped his Call tether to the wheel of the cart. High above them a sailwing droned smoothly across the darkening sky.

"Mortical Guild," said Feydamor automatically.

"Uh, sorry?"

"The engine: it was made by the Mortical Guild of Bartolica."

"Ha ha, a wing spotter," Glasken said, shaking his head.

"A what?"

"In my homeland, there are wind train and galley train spotters: people who stand by the tracks and note down what rolls past."

"For enemy intelligence?"

"No, for diversion. Like with you and gunwing engines, they can tell a train in darkness, just by the sound it makes and its running lights."

"What are trains?"

"They are . . . like many trams chained together. Only one has an engine."

"Pah, what a lie. Even *two* steam trams together would bring down the fire of the Sentinels."

Glasken chuckled. Feydamor hawked and spat.

"Why are they killing us, Sair Glasken? Do the Bartolicans want Yarron as an empty land, sponged clean of my people?"

Glasken lay back with his head resting on his hands, looking up at the stars. "It's worse than that, Sair Feydamor," he replied, but did not elaborate.

Feydamor scratched his thinning hair and shrugged. The man seemed to come from a very advanced dominion, but where was it?

"Why do your land's trams use wind to drive them?" Feydamor asked.

"Trains, not trams. It is a very flat land, only a little wind power is needed to drive the rotors of a train and keep it moving. Besides, most of our religions prohibit steam or compression engines. There's a strictly enforced death penalty as incentive to obey."

"I have never heard of such a land."

"Indeed. Its main names are Australica, Austranian, and Centravas."

"So how was the journey here?"

"Don't know. I was asleep."

It sounded like the ravings of a lunatic, yet Glasken had a steady confidence that made his words convincing. His stories were somehow too grand in their scope to be lies.

2 September 3960: Casper wingfield

"It's too late in the season for war duels," Serjon told the other flyers as they left the refectory tent of Casper wingfield.

"You sound disappointed," said Ramsdel.

"I want a dead Bartolican for every cold hand that I touched at Opal. That means a lot of dead Bartolicans."

It was a windy evening in early September. Kumiar had the serving girl Liesel on his arm as the group set off for the nearby town. Refugees had started to arrive in Casper along the road from Kennyville, and the streets were filled with shabby, ragged guild families and Yarronese carbineers. The young flyers, who by now had been officially made part of the chancellor's new Air Carbineers, were booed several times by angry but exhausted men, and one carbineer shouted at them to ascend and fight. Serjon began to give away the coins in his pockets, and by the time they reached a coffee tavern he had to borrow the price of his drink from Alion.

"I feel very lower-class being in the Air Carbineers," muttered Alion. "I am a warden-heir, and I once carried the colors of a princess fifteenth in line to the Bartolican throne."

"Seventeenth," said Ramsdel, "and it's your choice to be with us."

"If I had my own wing I'd be with my father in Forian."

"Oh but you will have a new Air Carbineer gunwing soon," said Liesel. "Serjon and Bronlar will get them too. Newly built gunwings."

For some moments there was shocked silence. Liesel had acute hearing, and she spent her working day serving very senior people who were discussing highly secret matters. This time she had heard the adjunct talking.

"I shall name mine Princess!" exclaimed Alion eagerly.

"It's bad luck for anyone but a female to name your wing," said Serjon just as eagerly.

"To the Call with luck. Princess it stays."

"Are you sure Serjon is included?" asked Bronlar. "He's crash-landed every gunwing he has ascended in."

"For that I name your gunwing, ah, Slash," said Serjon.

"You can't, you're a boy."

"You wear my colors."

"Then I name yours Starflower."

"Starflower? That sounds like I'm a night courier."

Liesel knew some of the nurses who were at a nearby table. Although pale and wrung-out from tending countless injured refugees all day, they joined the group of flyers. A rangalin fiddler began playing, and some couples began to dance. To everyone's surprise Alion departed early with a pretty nurse who was half a head taller than him.

"What happened to true love, faithfulness, and class distinction?" Bronlar asked Ramsdel as they watched the others dancing.

"They're no match for a girl who offers a tour of her underwear. The nurses see lives slipping away all day, now they want to celebrate life."

Bronlar spun her empty cup on its edge, then pressed it between her two thumbs, spun it in the air, caught it between her thumbs again, and set it on the table upside down.

"Jealous?" asked Ramsdel.

"I'm—I'm a girl among all you males. I *must* be one of you, I *can't* be a girl. Do you understand?"

"I understand, but that's no excuse for not looking smart. Can I borrow your shirts to take them in at the waist and under the arms? You look to be wearing flour sacks as they are."

"Ah, er, why not?" replied Bronlar, unsure whether or not to be insulted.

"I'm seeing a very nice girl, a smart dresser who tailors her own uniforms. Oh, and she has a wonderful figure and incredible brunette hair that sets off simply anything she wears. It might be hard to get her to parade, though, because she's the wingfield medic and very busy."

Bronlar realized that Ramsdel was friendly with the only female wingfield medic in North Yarron. Just then the sound of an argument reached them. Serjon was having words with a nurse around whose back he had had an arm draped only minutes earlier. Bronlar stared through the dim light: sure enough, there were thirteen buttons down the back of her blouse. The nurse snatched her coat from a chair, then took a jar of soy cream and emptied it into Serjon's open collar. She flounced out of the coffee tavern alone.

"And he wonders what girls don't like about him," sighed Ramsdel. "I keep telling him, but do you think he can be told?"

"I hope fate spares him," Bronlar replied. "Who else could make us laugh in these times?"

3 September 3960: Laramie Mountains

Feydamor decided not to return to Kennyville. In spite of the mud, he and Glasken managed to maintain their place in the column. Glasken pushed the cart and Feydamor stubbornly swung along on crutches. They passed people frantically trying to repair broken carts, and others who had just stopped, their spirits broken. The abandoned debris from those ahead of them littered the roadside everywhere, and every so often there were the dead. Those that disturbed Feydamor most were the young, pretty women and the children. They looked as if they should have been alive, they did not seem old, diseased, or guilty enough to be dead. Glasken's stories about his homeland played on his mind. The place was so real and consistent.

"Wish I was riding," Glasken said after they had been walking for three hours.

"What is ride?"

"Ride? Just sit on a horse and—ah, I'm forgetting. You have no horses or camels in America. No big animals at all."

"You use the name America, the old name for Mounthaven."

"That was our only word for this place for two thousand years."

"How did you discover us?"

"By accident, while testing a new weapon during our last great war."

"What weapon?"

"You'd not understand."

"I'm a master guildsman!"

"It was a modulated induction transceiver."

"I don't understand."

A Bartolican gunwing droned overhead, observing the column from a thousand feet above. The miserable stream of humanity had no military significance, so nobody gave the gunwing much heed. Presently the gunwing broke off and flew away to the west. Feydamor and Glasken stopped beside an overturned cart and traded wurst for dried fruit and curd that the owner was bartering.

They were near the top of a large, low hill, and as they ate and rested they watched a flock of nine sailwings flying out of the west in a V formation. Slowly the V was transformed into a long line.

"Get away from the cart!" warned Glasken suddenly. "Hurry! It's a target."

He was right. The sailwings lazily cruised up the refugee column, reaction guns blazing. People screamed and shouted as they dived for cover, and within moments the road was clear. Glasken fired several shots from his carbine, and by the time the fifth sailwing was passing overhead Feydamor had his carbine out and was shooting too.

"They can't do this!" shouted the guildmaster as the last sailwing passed.

"They've done worse, you of all people should know."

The flock was circling in a wide, lazy arc as Glasken stood up and began shouting at the top of his voice, in Old Anglian.

"Everybody with a carbine, over here! Hurry! Ten carbines together are as good as a reaction gun!"

There were shouts of assent, and carbineers began to stand up alongside the road.

"Come on, over here!" Glasken cried, waving his carbine. "Show we can hurt them."

A scatter of men came loping over, some with the dustcloths still over their carbines. A few more just had heavy-caliber pistols. Glasken organized them into rows and told them to aim slightly ahead of the sailwings. The flock had circled around by now, and was on a second strafing run.

The first sailwing roared over, and Glasken's cart shuddered and splintered as the reaction gun shots ripped through the wooden boards. The scratch force of carbineers opened fire, but it passed unharmed. Some turned to shoot at its tail.

"Leave it, always shoot at the next one!" shouted Glasken, but the second sailwing swooped over with hardly a shot fired at it.

They were united again as the third sailwing approached. The carbines fired in a staccato rattle, and abruptly the sailwing nosedived into the road and blew up, showering dirt, rocks, and burning compression spirit over huddled refugees. Cheers pealed out amid the cries from those beating out flames in their clothing. The next two sailwings tore through the cloud of smoke; then Glasken's force was shooting again. A sailwing flew off trailing smoke from its compression engine but managed to stay in the air. The flock did not return for another pass.

Glasken abandoned the cart after packing as much wurst as he could into his pockets and sling bag. Now people pointed him out and cheered as he passed, and a lot more carbines were in evidence among the refugees. In the days that followed there were several more attacks on the refugee column, but at the cost of five Bartolican sailwings. In a small and subtle way, the war had changed direction.

7 September 3960: Casper

On the Casper wingfield it was as if there were no war going on. Even though refugees were streaming into the town and Bartolican sailwings made occasional flights overhead, there were no ascents in anger. The wingfield was a staging and refueling point between the artisan shops of Sheridan and the capital.

"I heard about your father dying," Ramsdel said to Alion as they sat ready for Call patrol near the sailwings. "I'm sorry."

"He was shot down in a war duel, he died with honor," Alion replied, then lapsed into thought and the silence that went with it.

"So you're a warden now," Ramsdel said eventually.

"Yes, I have that burden."

Ramsdel sat embroidering a starflower on a black ribbon. He was hopeful that Bronlar would give colors to Serjon, and that he would accept them.

"I could make you a set of colors for that tall nurse to give you," Ramsdel suggested as an idle thought flashed into his mind.

"Her? She's nothing to me," Alion said smoothly, but the color had left his face. "She's just a nurse."

"Warden Alion, really! And after you played humpy-jig in the dormitories with her."

"That's a lie," said Alion, just as smoothly as before.

"I have it from nurses who were woken as she cried out 'Warden Alion, fly me again! Fly me! Fly me!' "

"Who knows about that?" quavered Alion, losing all guile. "If Samondel should learn—"

"The whole wingfield knows!" snapped Ramsdel, who was becoming impatient with his attitude, and had poked his fingertip with a needle. "Look, Alion, Princess Samondel once gave her colors to the Governor who is said to have launched this hideous invasion of our dominion. The next Bartolican warden that you ascend to fight may be wearing her colors and be shooting at you!"

Alion clasped his hands and hung his head. "Then how could I shoot back?" he said in dreamy anguish. "It would be like shooting at Samondel."

Ramsdel finished the starflower, corked his needle, and put both ribbon and needle into his flight jacket pocket. He stood up, stretched, and sucked the end of his finger.

Compression engines sounded in the distance and they both jumped to their feet. No siren wailed, however, so they were not Bartolican. Presently three triwing gunwings came into view, circled the wingfield, and landed. An adjunct's clerk came running up and told Alion to report to the pennant pole at once. When he arrived he found Serjon and Bronlar already there and being briefed.

7 September 3960: The road to Casper

Feydamor and Glasken sat resting in the ruins of the wind-mill tower of an aqueduct pumping station. It had been hastily dynamited by Yarronese carbineers to deny water to the advancing Bartolicans, yet the water that it might have provided was now denied to the Yarronese refugees.

Feydamor had been learning to use his crutches better, in spite of the chafing under his arms that was now seeping blood through his jacket. Their progress was nevertheless slow, and the stops for rest more frequent. Even though they had started out near the head of the column, they were now back a long way. Glasken had remained loyal to his friend, even though he needed less rest and could easily have trudged much faster. As they sat in the shade their conversation became philosophical.

"Remember when you met Laurelene?" began Glasken lazily. "Sair Feydamor, you need not have slashed that Bartolican's throat as he attempted to mount her."

"Yes I did, it's my code," Feydamor replied firmly. "What would you have done?"

"Oh, the very same," Glasken admitted.

"Do you miss your loved ones?"

"No. I miss having loved ones, but I do not miss my loved ones."

"Hah! I wager you still carry pictures of them."

Glasken looked at him for a moment, then smiled sadly. "Pictures, ah yes. I carry pictures." He touched a stud on what Feydamor had assumed to be a brown leather neck-band. A scene solidified in the air between them, a view of a rotund but quite attractive woman reclining in sheer, silk-like robes on a pile of cushions, eating chocolates and sipping some thick, gold drink from a chunky crystal glass. Someone was lying asleep beside her, a man with a hairy chest and golden brown skin.

"Her name is Varsellia. She has a tendency to weight, and one day it will lead her to an early grave. The crystal eye device that spies upon her is in a glass case. She prizes it greatly as jewelry and wears it on very special occasions."

The scene winked out of existence as Glasken tapped another stud. Feydamor blinked and shook his head.

"That . . . that was wonderful."

"That is what ghosts see, Jeb. Ghosts are silent, invisible, and powerless."

"But they were alive. That woman on the bed was unbelievable."

"Hah, Varsellia was a lot better in her twenties, when I first met her. Now Varsellia's face on Jemli's body, ah, that would have been perfection—Jemli was my first wife, you know."

"No, no, I mean your machine."

"Pah, it's become a means to torture me. A lady named Zarvora gave it to me a couple of years after she died. She probably meant well."

"*After* she died? More riddles?"

"No, truth. It's also true that I once had the rank of your airlords, but my title was mayor. Strange, but my wives and I changed roles as we grew older. While I became less of a lecher, mellowed and became fond of study and good living, they began taking lovers and dabbling in politics. I had ruled well for a year, then I found myself charged with blasphemy."

"Blasphemy, Sair Glasken?"

"Blasphemy, Sair Feydamor. Certain philosophers in my pay were experimenting with steam engines, and even diesel engines—the things you call compression engines."

"Yes, yes, and you mentioned that engines are forbidden by your religions?"

"Only engines that burn fuel. Christians, Islamics, Genthiests, all of our major religions have words against them in their Greatwinter scriptures. An alliance of fundamentalists raided the city university of my mayorate and discovered the experimental engines. The philosophers tending them were executed just as soon as the torturers were done, but I was somehow implicated. I'd known about them, of course, but nothing could have been proved. Alas, my friends feared to speak on my behalf, my eldest son denounced me, and my trial went very, very badly. I was convicted and condemned to death."

"And here you are, dead?" Feydamor laughed.

"I was in the very cell of the condemned. I escaped."

"I've noticed that you are resourceful."

"At first I fled to my mansion, sure that my wives would hide me. There, through a leadlight window, I saw my first and principal wife, Jemli, with the prosecutor. He had bent her over a footstool and was exercising her feminine attributes. Ah, it was then that I began to *really* feel dead and powerless, like a ghost. I slipped away to a place that nobody would ever consider searching, a dour and joyless place, yet the only place that had a welcome for me—my old monastery."

"You? A monk?" exclaimed Feydamor.

"Reluctantly, yes. It was there that I was recruited by a woman who eats marinated mice roasted on skewers. Such a strange one, Theresla. She did some unspeakable experiments on me a quarter century ago."

"Yet you work for her now?"

"She never betrayed me, which is more than I can say for my family. She warned that forces were gathering to unleash a war that would make the Milderellen Invasion look like a tavern brawl by comparison."

"I have never heard of the Milderellen Invasion."

"It was big, Jeb, a quarter of a million people died."

"A quarter of a million dead! In our wars we sometimes lose a hundred wardens and squires, but . . . a quarter of a million! Why, some entire dominions are not as big as that. Sair Glasken, why are you and your people here? What could you possibly want from us?"

"The answer to that could get you killed."

Feydamor scratched his head. Glasken stretched.

"On your feet, Jeb. Time we were marching again."

Glasken stood and picked up his pack.

"So, is Theresla your lover now?"

"No, just my friend. Strange, but she is the only woman who has really been my friend."

As they began walking Feydamor heard the sound of a distant flock of gunwings; then he caught sight of a distant V of three aircraft approaching from the direction of Casper. Not only were they Yarronese triwings, they were using Feydamor engines.

4 THE MIOCENE ARROW

7 September 3960: Casper wingfield

The adjunct of Casper wingfield stood at the pennant pole with Serjon, Alion, and Bronlar beside him. Before them, at the head of the dispersal track, guildsmen were preparing three wings with ungainly braces and struts grafted in around the engine mounts. Each featured twin heavy reaction guns.

"So these are the hybrids that people have been whispering about," said Alion.

"They look like ordinary gunwings that have been built in a hurry," Serjon observed, shielding his eyes against the sun. "Rough-looking finish, no pokerwork on the wood, unpolished engine metal."

"They are Chancellor Sartov's idea," explained the adjunct. "Sailwing weight with gunwing power and configuration. They carry a lot of extra fuel and reaction gun ammunition."

"Please explain why these are not gunwings," asked Alion.

"They are far lighter, giving them fantastic range, but they have no plating."

"No plating!" the two youths chorused together.

"None. They are fast, powerful, and heavily armed, but they can absorb very little damage. An attack from in front will hit the engine first, so you have a chance to jump out and fly the silk."

"But if a warden gets onto your tail there's nothing but tentcloth, wood, and seat padding between us and his guns," said Bronlar.

"Yes, so you have good incentive to keep your eyes sharp."

"They strike me as being very fast," Bronlar pointed out. "I imagine they can exceed a hundred and twenty-five miles per hour very easily. That will bring down fire from the Sentinels."

"That is another of Chancellor Sartov's ideas. If you use prohibited speeds only sparingly and when in danger, the Sentinels may not notice."

"May not?" asked Alion. "Only once is enough, and it's a dishonorable way to die."

"That is what you are to find out for us today," the adjunct explained further, keeping his tone cheery.

"What?" exclaimed Serjon. "We've done no conversion training."

"They will be like a very agile gunwing with incredible range and firepower. Warden Sartov thinks that they can be used to blind the enemy by attacking his courier and spy sailwings."

"But chivalric protocols demand—" began Alion.

"Damn the protocols!" shouted the haggard adjunct, his fists clenched. "The Bartolicans have flouted every protocol while our carbineers fight back like guildschool children. Flockleader Serjon Feydamor, you are to lead a patrol along the road to Kennyville. Good hunting."

"Flockleader?" exclaimed Serjon. "But that was only temporary."

"Not anymore. The symbol is being painted on your canvas as we speak."

Serjon looked to his companions, then to the hybrid triwings. Sure enough, the flockleader symbol was being painted beneath his number, along with the word STARFLOWER. He had survived twenty-six missions in sailwings and destroyed seven Bartolican aircraft, three of them gunwings flown by wardens. The guildsmen at Casper called him Serjon Warden Killer. Practically speaking, there was nobody better to lead the flock of three.

"Warden Alion is, well, a warden," said Serjon. "And what about the men who flew these in?"

"Warden Alion has three sailwings down, as has Semme Bronlar, they are ideal companions, but you are Serjon Warden Killer. The flyers who brought the hybrids from Sheridan have never been in combat . . ." He paused, took a deep breath, and then another. "That is why they are lying bound and gagged in my operations tent."

There was no question that could follow an admission like that. The three young flyers stared at the adjunct in silence, all with mouths slightly open, none sure that they had heard correctly.

"These hybrids were being ferried to Forian, I commandeered them," admitted the adjunct. "I cannot bear the refugees to continue being shot up on the road from Kennyville, day after day. Please, ascend these miracles and try to help, Flockleader Feydamor. My family is in that column of misery!"

He threw open his greatcoat, to show a pencil-on-card

portrait of a woman and two girls pinned over his heart
under a cover of greasepaper. Without another word he
whirled the greatcoat about him again, turned on his heel,
and strode off. They watched him walking back the way
they had come. This was his way of fighting back, this
was his way of helping. He was throwing away seniority,
position, and wealth, and perhaps risking a confrontation
with a firing squad to do this. The expression of entreaty
on his face still hung before Serjon.

"It is a brave and honorable thing that he does," said
Alion. "We should do as much."

"Well, looks like we both die virgins," said Bronlar,
slapping Serjon on the back.

"Thirteen kills between us," sighed Serjon. "This will
be a bad day."

The triwing hybrids were tricky to handle on the ground,
being so light yet overpowered. Guildsmen ran alongside,
aligning them and helping to steer until they were on the
flightstrip. They ascended in single file, Serjon first, followed by Bronlar, then Alion. It was a calm day, with
scattered cloud to the south. They formed into a tiered
patrol, with Serjon at the point of an inclined V, following
the road through the Laramie Mountains. Thermals and
drafts tossed and buffeted them at their low height, but it
seemed important to let the North Yarron Air Carbineer
markings be seen.

The refugee column wound out beneath them, the misery and despair lost at even such a modest height. The fast,
skittish gunwings flashed past the fifteen remaining miles
of the column in a few minutes; then all three climbed and
made for the broken clouds above. The hybrid gunwings
could climb at a rate unheard of and were as agile as swal-
lows, yet the three flyers felt curiously vulnerable in their
frail, flimsy war machines.

Far below and to the northeast, Serjon's father stopped to
listen as he and Glasken shuffled along in the column. The

droning of compression engines came from up ahead as the flock of three Yarronese gunwings flew along the column.

"The markings are Yarronese," observed Feydamor as they passed overhead. "Two inverted Vs in white and a Pole Star, that's North Yarron. Nothing more. No wardens' arms, no pennants, no squire symbols, only DK 1, DK 2 and DK 3."

"They're gunwings, and the engines sound hefty," Glasken observed.

"They're *my* engines!" Feydamor snarled in a surly tone. "Guardian Class 3T gunwing compression engines. They're Hailbeater, Volkar, and Borsklo. My guild built them last century. Just look at those airframes! What a disgrace."

Feydamor shouted abuse up at the aircraft, which continued on to the southwest.

"Is there a problem?" asked Glasken.

"Damn them to hell, my finest dueling engines in such rough, unpainted airframes!" Feydamor cried. "Yarron is lost, now my honor is lost too!"

The Yarronese aircraft climbed, soon becoming lost amid the light cloud.

"I've got eleven shells left, unless I can barter wurst for a few more," said Glasken as he rummaged in a pouch.

"Feydamor compression engines in unpainted airframes! I should never have allowed their loan."

"Another week to reach Casper at this rate," Glasken remarked wistfully. "The mountains and mud are no help, nor are the Bartolicans with their little visits."

"If we can survive for much longer," said Feydamor

"Your fever has gone and both your wounds are healing, sair. Just avoid any further bullets and women like Laurelene and, well, you could live to, ah, reasonable expectations."

"Avoid further bullets! Do you think I've not tried to—

Hah!" Feydamor stopped in his tracks. "Listen, can you hear that?"

The drone of distant engines was clearly audible. Other refugees had stopped to listen as well.

"It's just your people's patrol flying home," suggested Glasken.

"They're Bartolican, and there's a lot of them. There! Over to the southwest and wheeling this way."

"Take cover!" shouted Glasken. "Take cover, leave the carts. Carbines, form ranks about me and stay low."

Away to the west a flight of gunwings and armored sailwings was approaching at about two thousand feet. Feydamor counted twenty-five aircraft as Glasken hastily unslung his carbine and checked the magazine.

"That's a Bartolican attack flock!" said Feydamor.

"Should I celebrate?" asked Glasken.

"They probably seek some wingfield up ahead, not us."

"Don't place money on it," said Glasken grimly. "The sailwings are breaking off and diving. Chivalry is not the fashion, Jeb, and *we* are on the menu."

The entire refugee column had already swarmed off the road for cover among the rocks. The sailwings swept unopposed along the road, firing in long bursts. Feydamor fired his carbine as each aircraft roared past, but Glasken saved his depleted ammunition for more realistic targets. They had cover, after all, and the sailwings did little more than shoot up the handcarts and bundles left abandoned on the road.

Bronlar was the first to notice the attack on the refugee column. She pulled ahead and rolled for attention, then banked across to the southeast. The other two followed. Serjon waved to Alion, pointed to Bronlar, then across to the Bartolican sailwings. He patted his own head and pointed up at the gunwings.

An attack, thought the incredulous Bronlar. Three

against twenty-five. Serjon was committing them to engaging a full attack flock.

"I was hoping to do a bit better than eighteen years," muttered Bronlar as she released the master safety lever for her two guns.

Bronlar had never flown into engagement with Serjon before, and the adjunct's illegal orders were clear: no head-on challenge passes. Serjon led them in a long arc that took them through broken cloud and behind the approach of the Bartolican gunwings. As they came around they saw the enemy sailwings strafing the road. Serjon began dipping his wings to pass his orders.

Alion was to follow him against the wardens while Bronlar shot up the sailwings. That meant two hybrids against five gunwings! Time seemed to slow down. Some things in Bronlar's field of view became blurred, while others were focused as sharply as the edge of a razor. Her mouth tasted of something bitter, and she could smell her own fear in the scarf that muffled her face. The twenty sailwings were in two groups of ten, making alternate strafing runs in a line.

Bronlar attacked in a shallow dive. The form of a sailwing danced and expanded in her gunsights. The man is unaware of me—the *target* is unaware of me, she corrected herself. Closer, closer, today you die, Bronlar, but you charge a fee first. She pressed the trigger bar with her thumb.

The sailwing erupted into a comet of fire and fragments, then Bronlar streaked past.

Momentary elation flooded through her. She was alive, and an enemy was dead. That's it, there's fourteen kills between us three, Serjon, you can stop worrying about thirteen, Bronlar told herself. Another sailwing was ahead, framed by dancing mountains and a toy road littered with flecks of color. She fired again. This time her aim was wild, but she was so close that a second burst killed the sailwing's engine and shattered its propellor. A third sail-

wing was beginning to strafe the road as Bronlar opened
fire, flaying the fabric from his starboard wing root and
setting the compression spirit tanks ablaze.

By now the sub-flock was curving up and around for
another strafing run, but the leaders had realized that they
were under attack. Bronlar slashed pieces out of her fourth
victim, which turned on its back and plunged earthward.

"Just as easy as killing Opal's unarmed families, don't
you think?" Bronlar shouted at the unhearing Bartolicans,
exhilarated with revenge.

Feydamor and Glasken did not notice the gunwings with
Yarronese markings until they were already attacking. One
moment a Bartolican sailwing was sweeping along in triumph, the next it had slewed into the ground, where it
cartwheeled and exploded. A gunwing with DK 2 on the
wings and a red claw on the engine's cowling roared over
them and banked to starboard, coming around in a tight
turn. A Bartolican sailwing leveled out for its strafing run,
oblivious of the danger, and a moment later it bellyflopped
onto the roadway and erupted into a fireball of compression spirit. Glasken glanced about. Two more Yaronese
sailwings had engaged the Bartolican wardens high above.
Already one invader gunwing was trailing black smoke.

"This is beyond words," said Feydamor. His mouth
hung open as he sought more words, but none came.

"Twenty-five against three, another glorious Yarronese
defeat, eh?" said Glasken.

Feydamor scanned higher battle in the sky for a moment. Now two Bartolican wardens were trailing smoke
and losing height.

"That's nine—" A sailwing to the right crumpled and
began falling, out of control. "Make that ten Bartolicans
destroyed. Glasken, our hybrids are tearing them to
pieces!"

As they watched another trail of smoke was written
across the sky, yet the invader sailwings lower down were

still trying to make strafing runs. Two more came in to attack, pursued by DK 3. Both crashed into the fields beside the road and burned in smoky pyres.

A Bartolican warden descended with his motor spluttering. Three of the Bartolican flock tried to cover him as he landed on the deserted road. A sailwing landed nearby to rescue the warden, but a Yarronese hybrid cut through at full speed to rake the two airborne sailwings with reaction-gun fire, drawing the defenders after him. They could not match his rate of climb, however, and he pulled away from them easily. Another long, black trail had formed in the sky over to the south, a comet with a tail of black and a head of fire.

"That's eleven," said Glasken.

Feydamor was watching the two grounded Bartolicans being beaten to the ground by Yarronese refugees. Glasken followed his gaze when he made no reply. The proud invaders were on the ground, unmoving, but still the refugees continued to beat and kick.

"Bad form, Sair Feydamor?" asked Glasken, looking back up at the sky.

"They murdered my sympathy long ago, Sair Glasken."

Another six Bartolican sailwings were shot out of the sky before the surviving eight broke and fled, two trailing thin streams of black smoke. Feydamor noted who had fled, noting especially which was the warden who was running from commoners. A lone Yarronese was flying in pursuit, and at a speed that should have brought the fire of the Sentinels down upon him.

"I suppose this is a disgrace because commoners defeated wardens," Glasken said as they made their way back onto the road.

"I should think that, Sair Glasken," Feydamor said, his eyes burning with triumph, "but I can't."

Serjon's hybrid was out of ammunition as he bounced through the mountain thermals back to Casper. Bronlar was flying tatters of fabric from her port wing, and Alion had a streamer of pale smoke trailing from his engine. They passed Casper Mountain, then began to descend. At Casper wingfield there were sailwings on patrol, but the Call signals were down so it was safe to land.

Alion descended first, bounced twice in an overhasty landing, then stopped in a cloud of smoke near the end of the flightstrip. Guildsmen came running up pushing a fire cart and by the time Bronlar made her approach the hybrid had been pushed clear and the fire was out. She landed smoothly and taxied onto a dispersal track, heading for the guild tents. Serjon followed her example, but as he turned onto the dispersal track his mind began to slip out of combat mode and his demons returned. He had returned with one very significant thirteen hanging over him.

As he neared the pennant pole the adjunct came running up, followed by two clerks.

"Bullet holes," observed the adjunct as Serjon unbuckled his straps. "Did you see clear air combat, or was it ground fire?"

"Combat, Sair Adjunct, though the air was a bit smoky."

Serjon climbed out onto the ground and stood clutching the hybrid's wing while his knees trembled visibly. Not far away Ramsdel was shouting at the top of his voice, gesturing to the holes in Princess' compression engine's cowling and a large oil stain on the gold and crimson needlework of a new flight jacket that he had lent Alion. Several guildsmen looked on, puzzled but sympathetic. Bronlar was on her knees beside her hybrid, vomiting her last meal into the dust.

"Are they all right?" Serjon asked the adjunct, gesturing to the rest of his flock.

"If you mean are they injured: not badly. Did you have any victories in these new wonder wings?" the adjunct asked hopefully.

"Three wardens and two sailwings."

The adjunct dropped his board.

"I now have twelve victories, Sair Adjunct," Serjon began babbling. "My next will be thirteen. That's my nemesis. I will die."

Ramsdel came striding over. There were tears in his eyes.

"Fourteen gold circars and just look at this sleeve!" he said, holding up the flight jacket that he lent Alion to go with the new gunwing.

The embroidered cloth was soaked in oil, torn by the passage of a bullet, and bloodied by the graze on Alion's upper arm. Alion stood behind him, his lips pressed together and clearly unimpressed by Ramsdel's histrionics.

"Have you anything to report?" asked the adjunct, motioning Ramsdel aside and looking to Alion.

"Ah, two sailwings and one gunwing destroyed, with two damaged but flying," said Alion with a crisp salute.

"One of those was forced down on the road," Serjon added.

The adjunct chalked the figures that he did not believe. Bronlar was still on her knees retching. A medic and his nurses were attending her.

"And Semme Jemarial, was she in the combat too?"

"Nine sailwings . . . and a warden!" said Serjon after a moment's thought.

"Ten," whispered the adjunct in wonder as he noted the figures.

"She shot up her thirteenth today, she's safe now!" said Serjon with undisguised envy.

The adjunct watched as Serjon took Alion over to where the medic was treating Bronlar. The young warden's arm was not badly hurt, and was soon cleaned up and bandaged. Serjon knelt beside Bronlar and began a conversation that featured the word thirteen very heavily.

"Nineteen victories," said the adjunct to his clerks. "No losses."

"Chancellor Sartov may be pleased," said a clerk optimistically.

The adjunct handed him the board, then crossed the dispersal track to the two flyers. Flopping down in the grass beside them he threw his arms around Serjon and burst into tears. Nothing that anyone could do would stop his weeping.

"Ah, there now, sair, we understand," babbled the embarrassed Serjon. "I lost my mother and five sisters, and Bronlar lost her parents and one of my sisters. I mean, she borrowed my sister because she didn't have any colors and now—"

"When did you hear that they died?" asked Bronlar after taking the adjunct's hand.

"We walked in just as you ascended," said a hoarse voice behind them.

A gaunt, hollow-eyed woman was standing in the adjunct's greatcoat, with a girl of about eight clinging to her ragged skirts and a toddler in her arms.

"He was frantic for the whole time you were away," the woman continued. "He thought he'd sent you to your deaths while we were safe."

15 September 3960: Casper

There were no more Bartolican attacks on the refugee column before Glasken and Feydamor reached Casper, but as they reached the little city they found themselves among the last of six thousand arrivals. The welcome for the refugees was wearing decidedly thin.

A cluster of tents and a clerk with a few carbineers comprised the checking post, and the queue took longer to negotiate than the previous day's walk. As they declared themselves, Glasken and Feydamor were suddenly surprised by the way the jaded clerk's head jerked up.

"Guildmaster Feydamor!" he exclaimed. "You're listed as dead!"

"That's a little extreme," said Feydamor, holding up his arm and feeling his pulse.

The clerk sent one of the carbineers on an errand while he processed their papers, and the man returned with a lieutenant of the local merchant carbineers. They soon found themselves in a small room at the tram station, tasting coffee for the first time since leaving Opal.

"I should begin with the good news after all you've been through," began the officer. "Your son has had twelve victories against the Bartolicans, six of them against wardens."

Elation and amusement pulled in different directions at Feydamor's features.

"So he's facing his thirteenth?" Feydamor laughed. "He should be rattled about that. And is he safe, uninjured?"

"He's on patrol, and as safe as any flockleader can be in a war."

"Serjon? A flockleader?" Feydamor exclaimed, delighted.

"Yes, worthy sair. He's one of the finest flyers in Mounthaven's history. Serjon Warden Killer, that's what they call him."

Glasken now leaned forward and cleared his throat.

"By your leave and all, Sair Lieutenant, but what is to be our fate now that we're in Casper?"

"Well now, that is up to my discretion. Sair Feydamor, you are quite clearly needed at the regional capital, Sheridan, where the Chancellor is directing our war effort. As for you, Sair Glasken, these papers state that you are a diplomatic courier from a very distant dominion in the south."

"Yes. I was told to seek an audience with your airlord on behalf of my mistress the envoy, but I have learned this day that your capital—and airlord—are under siege."

"That is so. The Bartolicans' carbineers moved with the speed of a windsquall and surrounded our capital."

"In that case I must see Chancellor Sartov."

"Ho ho! Chancellor Sartov is a very busy man, Sair Glasken. But tell me your message and I'll have a courier take it to him by steam tram."

"With all possible respect, Lieutenant, if my message was so trivial that I could pass it to you, it would be of no interest to Chancellor Sartov."

"Which tells me nothing," sighed the merchant officer. "Sair Glasken, space in the steam trams is so scarce that passengers must discard their bedrolls, bags, and even water bottles. You may be genuine, but you may be lying. I cannot tell which, so I can provide no authority for you. All I can suggest is that Sair Feydamor sees the Chancellor on your behalf."

Outside the office Feydamor was more hopeful.

"I cannot tell you the message," said Glasken. "Please understand that and take no offense."

Feydamor nodded and clapped Glasken on the shoulder. "Sair Glasken, I'll have a word to Chancellor Sartov when I arrive, I swear it."

Later that day a Call swept over the refugee camp, but most people were just sitting about and securely tethered. Shortly after it had passed, the next steam tram was cleared to leave for Sheridan. Its seats had been ripped out to allow room for a few more passengers, and there were even passengers sharing the driver's booth. To Feydamor's surprise Glasken came running up waving a permission that bore an official seal with the lieutenant's stamp. The station guard scowled and muttered that the merchant officer was breaking his own rules by overloading the tram, but Glasken was still allowed aboard. Amid clouds of steam and wood smoke mixed with vegetable oil lubricant, the tram began chuffing slowly through the depot sidings and rattling over the points. Those aboard were almost all young men.

"So why are so many lads of fighting age being moved to Sheridan?" Feydamor asked the youth beside him.

"I'm to lay rails, but I've not been told where," he replied. "That's like for all of us, what say?"

There was a chorus of assent at his words. Nearly everyone else aboard had been recruited to go lay rails. Some were miners, others had backgrounds in flightstrip preparation.

"It seems a misplaced effort with the Bartolicans swarming over us," said Feydamor.

"Chancellor Sartov decreed it, and he has lost no battles."

"His region is furthest from the fighting," Feydamor pointed out. "Where is the track to be laid?"

"And why would you want to know, Sair Stranger with a Bartolican lilt in your Yarronese?"

All eyes were upon Feydamor as other conversations fell away into silence.

"From Opal, border, mostly family killed," Glasken barked awkwardly in Yarronese.

"And how would you know, foreigner?" Feydamor's interrogator asked.

"Flockleader Serjon Feydamor, he father of," Glasken said, ignoring the question. "Papers having."

"The Warden Killer?" said the youth. "Half the fogeys in Yarron would claim him as their son to beg an ale."

Just then there was a shout from behind the tram and someone exclaimed that there was a flyer running after them. When Feydamor heard his name called he suddenly burst into a thrashing blur of arms and legs as he fought his way to a window and punched out the glass. The tram driver was putting on steam, thinking that an illegal passenger was in pursuit.

"Serjon!" Feydamor shouted to the figure in a flying jacket running about fifty feet behind the tram.

"Dad!" panted Serjon. "You hurt?"

"No, I'm fit and fighting. Serjy boy, I'm proud of you. I mean it."

"Love you, Dad."

"Now you stop and set your Call anchor, you hear?"

Serjon slowed, but they called and waved to each other until the tram rounded a bend and was lost behind a kiln-works. The mood in the tram had by now made a shift from dangerous menace to unquestioning awe and good-will.

"My apologies, guildmaster," said the youth who had been speaking to Feydamor. "And to answer your question, we really don't know where the new tramway is to be laid."

18 September 3960: Sheridan

The wilderness of the Wind River Range was of no interest to any but the most hardy of settlers, but owing to the war there was no shortage of refugee labor when Sartov called for volunteers to work there. Years earlier a tramway to southern Dorak had been laid to the border, but a dispute over tolls and costs caused the Dorakians to abandon the work on their side. Now it was a tramway into wilderness, but as such it made a perfect and easily defensible fastness for Sartov. Navvy men laid track for staging yards and dug earth bunkers for storage, while others graded flightstrips.

Refugees began streaming across to the sanctuary in the mountains of northwest Yarron, walking alongside narrow-gauge trams crammed with tools, weapons, and people. When the first flightstrip was declared finished Chancellor Sartov arranged a hasty ceremony to mark the first flight from Sheridan, and found a chaplain to bless the regal that was to be used—in a break from tending the wounded and praying for the dead. At the ceremony he was watched by a great number of refugee guild families and carbineers who were to go to the new estate. There were prayers for a speedy end to the unchivalric and illegal war, and Sartov made a short speech about how the Bartolicans won only by breaking the rules. He then held a copy of the Code of Chivalric Warfare high in the air.

"Let us see if their triumphs continue when *we* fight that way too!" he declared, then he tossed the book through the air and behind a stack of compression spirit barrels.

The crowd applauded politely and softly, stunned by what amounted to chivalric heresy.

"So they fight us with merchant carbineers? We shall hit back with my new air carbineers!"

This time there were ragged cheers of assent.

"Air Carbineer Bronlar Jemarial has destroyed nine sailwings! Air Carbineer Serjon Feydamor has shot down six wardens. Imagine what a hundred like them will do to the Bartolicans."

Cries of "Mother Cat!" and "Warden Killer!" were mixed with the roar of assent that was returned to Sartov.

"And that's not all. Yarron has extra carbineers in training, carbineers that will make the Bartolicans curse the day they crossed our border, carbineers that will laugh at odds of ten to one."

"Good . enough for Bronlar, good enough for us!" shouted a carbineer from the Bighorn Mountains. "We'll shit on 'em, Chancellor Sartov!" drawled the man beside him. There was more cheering, and hats were flung into the air. Glasken and Feydamor watched from a distance.

"The man impresses me," Glasken pronounced, as if judging an examination candidate.

"He's throwing away everything I ever believed in," said Feydamor sullenly, "but a dead wife and five dead daughters tell me to follow him." After a moment he added, "Did you hear the way they cheered Serjon?" His eyes were shining with pride.

Sartov heard the clanging of the local Call tower as he sat in his chambers, watching a regal being prepared to make the first flight to Wind River.

"At least it arrived once we were finished," he said to his aide.

"Yes, Chancellor. Fifteen minutes, now."

The man left his office and hurried away to tether himself in the common padded room. Sartov locked his door, strapped himself into his chair, and tidied some papers as he waited. Outside the compression engines of the regal revved up, and soon Sartov heard it ascend. He worked on. Just before 11 A.M. the barely perceptible moment of surrender washed over him, and he plunged away into an abandonment that he would only remember as scraps of dreams. He awoke with the clock on just before 2 P.M.

The clock! The clock was the regional palace tower clock, and he was sitting in the guttering between two roofs. Sartov's hands were tied, and a gag was in his mouth. A man that he had seen somewhere once before was sitting in front of him, and there was a bottle of Colandoro frostwine and a cut of chickenwurst nearby. The Veraguayan's guard. Glasken. The man he had helped escape the wrath of Laurelene Hannan four months ago.

"Chancellor Sartov, I see you are back."

Glasken was wearing a Yarronese carbineer's uniform which had seen a lot of action.

"Forgive me for tying you and bringing you here, but I had to demonstrate that I could indeed move about during a Call."

A Callwalker! The word of fancy, fairytale, and legend echoed through Sartov's mind . . . yet here he was, face-to-face with very convincing proof. Did Callwalkers drink blood? No, that was vampires.

"Before being too outraged by my attack on your person, bear this in mind. Real Callwalkers have been sabotaging Yarronese defenses and gunwings during each Call that passes. If you want proof, remember that I have just abducted you, the best-guarded noble in North Yarron. Do you wish to talk?"

Sartov nodded. Glasken untied his hands, but left him to take off the gag himself.

"Glasken and, and . . . how?" Sartov had started angrily, but ended with a strangled whisper. "Uh, are you really . . ." He hesitated over the word from the fairytale nightmares of his childhood. "Are you a Callwalker?"

Glasken leaned back against the slate tiles and stretched.

"Callwalkers, I've read your fairytales about them. They're usually men, and during Calls they steal gold, read secret papers, change words in registers and records, abduct children, murder the innocent by cutting their Call tethers, and raise the skirts of honest, virtuous women—thus seeding the next generation of Callwalkers. One of my human lady friends once asked me to take advantage of her during a Call."

"Did you?"

"It was uninteresting, in fact it was quite hard work. All she wanted to do was walk south, there was not the slightest response on her part."

"But where do you come from?"

"From another continent, Australica. We were invented there, Chancellor. We think that aviads are a synthetic type of human, invented as a last, desperate measure against the Call by ancient Australican engineers. The gift only manifests itself at puberty, which may have led the ancients to think that they had failed when the experimental children were found to follow the Call. A few survived to interbreed among humans as barbarism descended. Our name for ourselves is aviads, although the earliest records refer to us as avians. We have something of the essence of birds bred into us, and our hair looks like very fine feathers under magnification. Except for mine, that is. I must have been descended from a failed experiment, because my hair looks normal and I had to be trained to resist the Call."

Sartov shook his head. "Are you telling me that Mounthaven has been invaded by Australica?"

"Not quite. For the past two thousand years the Aus-

tralican humans have feared aviads and slaughtered them
whenever they were discovered. In the past few decades
the aviads have become organized and set up colonies in
our Callscour lands. There are not many of them, and originally they just wanted to live in peace, but recently a
radical faction has gained power. The radicals want revenge for two thousand years of genocide, and the reaction
guns and gunwings of Mounthaven could make one aviad
warrior the equal of a hundred humans. A deal has apparently been done in the Bartolican court: aviads help to
annihilate Yarron in return for weapons."

"So that's how Bartolica wins so easily," said Sartov
slowly, as if weighing the words for worth. "Did you really
keep your will during that Call?"

"I may have, Sair Chancellor, but then I may have been
just as mesmerized by the Call as yourself. I may have had
help from someone else who can defy the Call who drew
both of us up here, then drugged you to stay insensible a
little longer than me. The point is that there *are* individuals
who can defy the Call."

The tower clock played the first few bars of "The Birds
Are in the Corn," then struck twice for the hour. Sartov
ran his fingers along the slate tiles and greymetal guttering,
trying to accept that the place where he had awoken was
real. He crawled to the edge of the roof, looked down for
a moment, then shuddered and returned to Glasken.

"I cannot believe this . . . yet here we sit."

Glasken took two tin mugs from his jacket pocket and
reached for the bottle.

"I once promised to fetch you a drink to remember, Sair
Chancellor."

"I gave up drinking when I returned to Yarron, but as
sure as hell I'll make an exception now."

They sipped the wine in silence. A large steam engine
chuffed into life somewhere in the distance. Glasken held
up a hand to one ear at the sound.

"Callwalkers," said Sartov yet again. "I'll have terriers

trained to attack them with poison blades strapped to their
jaws. I'll have traps set, sailwings will be ascended to
shoot at them from the air. Sair Glasken, this will change
the war."

Glasken shook his head. "The aviads—Callwalkers—
supporting Bartolica would have no trouble shooting dogs,
avoiding traps, and hiding from air attack. They are the
elite of our elite. There are other ways to fight the Bartolicans, however. Did you know that your steam trams can
haul ten, twenty, even thirty carts?"

"Only until the next Sentinel Star passes over and burns
the tram and all thirty carts to cinders and slag. Nothing
may move that is longer than twenty-nine feet and six
inches. No tram, no regal, no gunwing, no sailwing, no
crane and no canal barge."

"Have you tried it lately?"

Sartov chuckled and sipped his wine. "Have you tried
setting your arse on fire lately? Why bother? Machines are
expensive, and Mounthaven is poor in resources. That is
why our wars are—or were—so stylized and contained.
That is the basis of our chivalric system: the Call confines
us here, and the Sentinels constrain what we can do."

Glasken gestured to the sky. "Two decades ago you may
have noticed some odd bursts of light in the sky. Mirrorsun
split, then re-formed, and the Sentinels flashed and shim-
mered."

"Yes, I saw all that. There was much talk about the end
of the world and church attendance soared to nine souls
out of ten within most parishes."

"What you saw was a war between the Sentinels and
Mirrorsun. The Sentinels were roasted, they're dead
hulks."

Sartov took out his knife and sliced off a chunk of wurst,
then listened while Glasken explained about trains. He had
a great need for transport, and this was a gift from heaven
if true. Thousands of guild families and carbineers could
be transported to his new estate at Wind River, and he

could even build another wingbase at Gannett. Whole artisan workshops could be transported without being dismantled to fit into trams, thousands of tons of supplies could be moved, in fact every barrel of compression spirit in North Yarron could be hauled out of Bartolican reach.

"It occurs to me, Sair Glasken, that the Sentinels also limited the speed of our gunwings to below a hundred twenty-five miles per hour."

"Not any longer. Your Air Carbineers can get away with whatever speed they can manage."

Sartov felt like Faust being tempted by Mephistopheles. His new hybrid gunwings could do 180 miles per hour, in theory; they were light and powerful. The Bartolican Callwalkers would be no more than a minor nuisance if Yarron was first to use tram-drawn lines of carts and to build gunwings that could exceed 200 miles per hour ... or even giant regals with wings a hundred feet across. He held out his mug for more wine and grinned cannily. The strangest of physical sensations swept over him, and he wondered if Glasken could see the lines fading from his face and his hair turning black again. It was too good to be true. There had to be a catch.

"Why did the Callwalkers, the aviads, not tell the Bartolicans about the Sentinels?" Sartov asked, staring Glasken in the eyes.

"You are more suspicious than my former banker. Suppose *you* answer the question."

Sartov thought carefully. "By making Bartolica depend on them, the Callwalkers gain control of Bartolica. It is in their interest to keep the Bartolicans ignorant of the Sentinels being dead."

"Indeed. They just want war and chaos to cloak them as they go about their work. Bartolica's fate probably means nothing to them."

Again, this was fair and reasonable, but Sartov did not want to admit it yet.

"As the engineers say, Sair Glasken, there comes a time

to shut up and cut metal. Centuries ago a warden named Alsek attached a steam tram to a galley cart by two hundred feet of thin gunwing bracing wire. He thought to fool the Sentinels into thinking the cart was moving by itself."

"Were they fooled?"

"No. The next Sentinel to pass overhead annihilated the galley cart, the wire, the steam tram, the trackwork between them, and Alsek. He had such faith in his scheme that he had been driving. Would *you* care to repeat his experiment?"

"Show me how to drive an steam tram and I'll use it to haul thirty galley carts."

Sartov had meant to call Glasken's bluff. Now he shook his head. "I cannot risk a steam tram. I have only fifty in service and two more under repair. The Bartolicans make a point of shooting them up at every opportunity."

"I am offering my life, Chancellor."

"Your life," echoed Sartov. "What are you getting out of this?"

"I might help shorten a war between people that I am learning to like. I might also help prevent your weapons being used in the genocide of humans back on my own continent."

Sartov poured out another drink. From far below came voices calling for Sartov and shouting that the Call had taken the Chancellor.

"I must return, my staff are in search of me," Sartov said as he held up the little mug. "Very well, I consent. This, Glasken, is to be the last drink of my life. Join me in a toast to your experiment, and let us hope that it is not the last drink of your life as well."

That evening several dozen carbineers moved thirty galley carts onto a disused length of track beside the railmuster yards and tied them together with rope. Glasken backed a steam tram down the track with the help of a driver, and it was tied to the lead galley cart. The driver then retreated to a safe distance and joined Sartov and his senior staff. The Sentinel that passed overhead some minutes later gleamed brilliantly as it moved among the stars. Glasken opened the steam lines to the drive cylinders. The ropes between the carts were pulled taut in turn, and the improvised train began to move. It chuffed down the track, gathering speed. No fire poured down from the Sentinel.

They had been so sure that Glasken would die that nobody had shown him the brake. The red lamp of an approaching buffer warned him of disaster and he frantically hauled on levers and spun taps. The buffer loomed in the glow of its own lantern. Without even pausing to curse Glasken wrenched open the forward door and leaped to safety a moment before the tram was annihilated between the buffer and the combined momentum of the thirty galley carts that piled up upon the wreck with a sound like rolling thunder.

The experiment was repeated with another improvised train just before dawn, as a brightly gleaming Sentinel cruised among the stars. The bold provocation brought no retribution from above, and this time an experienced driver was at the controls.

By the time the sun appeared on the horizon the Archaic Anglian word "train" was again in use in North America and designs for the first of five hundred flatbed wagons were on the drafting boards. In the meantime Sartov ordered two makeshift trains of thirty galley carts drawn by steam trams to leave for Gannett that very morning, and by the afternoon a thousand refugees, eleven gunwing engines, and three hundred barrels of compression spirit were on their way to Wind River. The line was soon running day and night at its logistical capacity of a train every four hours.

When Glasken returned to see Sartov some days later, the Chancellor wanted to honor him before his entire diplomatic and strategic staff. Because he was suddenly the most important man in all of North Yarron, the reception was in the ballroom of the Governor's palace. Here Sartov had assembled his senior administrative and tactical staff to meet Glasken, and they were by now restive at the long delay. Glasken noticed that the parade uniforms of the Yarronese were cleanly tailored and smart, rather than opulent in the Bartolican style. The colors were mainly green and orange, with much gilt thread embroidery.

"Can't I give you any reward?" Sartov asked as the guards and servants were being sent outside. "A bag of gold, guildmaster status among the engineers? Learn to fly and I could have you made a ward—"

"No!! No. No, no, no." Glasken had gone sheet white at the memory of his flight out of Opal in a badly damaged sailwing with a barely conscious flyer. "Passage to Denver is enough."

"You have that."

"Well . . . trust me, just one more time," said Glasken as he surveyed the gathering.

Sartov began his address by explaining something of what Glasken had told him. The Yarronese could now do more than just assemble trains. Fast combat wings and giant regals could be used safely.

"Now you may smile at the word Callwalker," Sartov continued after bracing himself with a gulp of rainwater.

Several of the men did smile reflexively, and some shuffled uneasily on the spot. Fieldmajor Gravat took a sudden and intense interest in a plate of emu pate, but Sasentor of the Tramways Corporate remained loyally attentive. Glasken stepped forward, his hand held up.

"Great and wise sairs, may I first provide a small and edifying demonstration?" he asked, taking a very ordinary carbineer's revolver from his coat.

Sartov gave him the floor, and Glasken held the gun up for inspection between his thumb and forefinger. It was just a gun, a Lemnidor of .38-caliber. He now grasped it by the handle and trained it across the faces of the senior civil and military leaders of North Yarron. Most shuffled uneasily. The chambers appeared to be loaded with hollow-point rounds.

"Now there is one remarkably reassuring thing about this gun," Glasken declared, then let his words hang.

Several of the men glanced at each other, others shrugged. Whatever his point, it was an obscure one. Glasken shot Sasentor through the forehead.

Pandemonium was already firmly established before the liaisory of the Yarronese Tramways Corporate hit the floor. Glasken was seized and disarmed, and the guards burst into the ballroom to find him being held spread-eagled on the floor with the tip of Fieldmajor Gravat's ceremonial sword at his throat.

"If I could finish," cried Glasken. "The reassuring thing about any gun is that it will kill Callwalkers as readily as humans. Take a strand of his hair, Chancellor, examine it under a microscope. It will look like a long, fine feather— and remember that birds are immune to the Call. I watched him at work while I hid during the last Call. He never expected another Callwalker to be here."

The microscope confirmed Glasken's words. That night the entire local diplomatic staff and high command was checked and another aviad was discovered. A short, intense, and very vindictive bout of torture extracted the names of two more aviads; then all three were put on a train under Gravat's personal supervision. Sartov would not speak of their fate.

The following evening Glasken met Sartov at the wingfield, as the chancellor climbed out of a hybrid gunwing. He had just become the first human in nearly two millennia to exceed 200 miles per hour.

"I still need to get to Denver," said Glasken as soon as they were alone.

"Sair Glasken, it's getting dangerously late in the flying season. You should wait until spring."

"Feydamor has educated me about such things. It's late in the season, but not dangerously late."

"I'd have to have you flown there at night and parachuted down."

At the word "parachute" Glasken lost some of his composure and all of his color.

"Parachute? Night? Can't your flyer use a wingfield in daylight?"

"Colandoro is neutral territory, Sair Glasken. Any Yarronese sailwing landing at a wingfield would be seized and I don't want to lose a single one—even for you. Only a sailwing could make the distance, and that distance is over occupied Yarron. To avoid the Bartolican gunwings you would have to fly at night."

Glasken drew out a pair of goggles such as a warden might use while flying. He handed them to Sartov.

"Expose those to sunlight for a few hours during the day and you will be able to use them to see in the dark all night. They have been in the sun for most of the afternoon."

Sartov examined them closely. They were grey-black in color, and made of a pliant, soft material. When he put them on he could see through the darkened lenses as clearly as if they were polished glass—and the dusk-darkened wingfield was as brightly illuminated as at noon on an overcast day. Sartov cried out in surprise, then took the goggles off and gazed around again.

"You can have them if you fly me to the outskirts of Denver tonight and land me on a straight stretch of road," Glasken offered.

"Done!" replied Sartov. "What luggage do you have?"

"I'm standing up in it. I can leave now."

After a stop to refuel at Casper they flew out over the mountains and into occupied airspace. They were flying an armed sailwing trainer which had been hastily painted black. As they traveled Glasken told Sartov all that he knew about the infiltrating invaders, and something of his own civilization as well. Sartov had chosen to fly beneath the clouds, so that to Glasken the scene was of unrelieved darkness.

"I see the Laramie River down there," said the Chancellor. "These goggles are worth a flock of gunwings, Glasken. How do they work?"

"I don't know."

"But your people made them."

"No, they were made in Mirrorsun's factories, on the moon."

"What? Your people command forces like that and they still covet our miserable gunwings?"

"It's not so simple as that. About twenty years ago Zarvora Cybeline, a great engineer from Australica, deduced that Mirrorsun was a vast, intelligent machine, designed by ancient engineers to moderate the Earth's climate."

"But Mirrorsun has only been in the sky for about thirty years."

"The automatic factories on the moon were not set up properly when the Call first began. They took a hundred times longer than they were designed to, but they got the job finished. Both the factories and Mirrorsun are intelligent, after a fashion. Zarvora tricked Mirrorsun into fighting the Sentinels, then learned to talk to it using a machine driven by electrical essence."

"Ha yes, the Sentinels destroyed active electrical machines as well. She had to destroy the Sentinels so that she could contact Mirrorsun. Brilliant."

"She was also the most ruthless autocrat in Australica's history, but I digress. Mirrorsun controls the mines and factories on the moon where its own fabric was built, but these also contained templates for building machines for use on Earth. Zarvora thought it was also an experiment in moving dirty, dangerous factories off the Earth. She persuaded it to manufacture certain devices from an inventory of templates, and to transport them to Australica.

They landed in ceramic shells beneath parachutes. Some shells were the size of baskets, others were bigger than a town hall. The Ozone Regeneration Sunwings came in the big ones."

"The what?"

"Sailwings half a mile across, powered by electrical essence and sunlight. They were easy to assemble, but we left out some gas production machinery that didn't seem to do anything useful. The aviad universities were meant to use them to explore the world, but then the radicals took over."

"Did Zarvora take that lying down?"

"She had to, she was dead. All contact with Mirrorsun had been through Zarvora, but this did not suit some of her fellow aviads. They were confined to a thin strip of Callscour land around the Australican coast, while true humans lived everywhere else. It was the very opposite of the situation over here. When the aviad radicals had come to power, they wanted to exterminate the humans, even though it was like tiny Montras declaring war on the rest of Mounthaven. They tried to force Zarvora to build a fleet of sunwings in the Mirrorsun factories so that they could bomb human cities. When she refused they shot her. It did them no good, because Zarvora had set up her communication machine with a secret code. Mirrorsun has been uncontactable ever since."

Sartov laughed mirthlessly. "So, Mounthaven is to replace Mirrorsun as a weapons factory. We should be flattered."

"Australica has no reaction guns at all, our artisans can only make flintlocks. Our sunwings and ferrywings came from Mirrorsun, and two have been lost in accidents already. All we have is a few dozen primitive steam engines; human religions forbid anything not powered by wind, water, or muscle. Your guildsmen and artisans are centuries ahead in engine design and gunsmithery."

Sartov thought back to what Regional Inspector Hannan

had told him about an incident four years ago in northern Bartolica. Mysterious strangers had supposedly dropped out of the sky wielding high-quality flintlocks.

"If I said Morelac to you, what would you say?" Sartov asked.

"Morelac? It's a family Australican of gunsmiths going back centuries. How do you know the name?"

"I have my own sources, Sair Glasken. I suspect that the Callwalkers—the aviads—landed in Bartolica first, four years ago."

"Four years . . . yes, probably."

"Some ambitious Bartolican noble was the obviously first to be offered unimaginable wealth and power, and he accepted. The aviad radicals needed a total, unchivalric war as a cover to plunder our gunwings and reaction guns, and Yarron is Bartolica's traditional enemy—Hang on!"

Abruptly Sartov stood the sailwing on its wingtip and opened the throttle. Glasken screamed incoherently, cursed in an Australican language, then began to pray in Latin.

"Bartolican sailwing!" shouted Sartov. "I've been watching him sneak up on us in the chase mirror."

"Mea culpa, mea culpa, mea maxima culpa. In nomine patri—"

"Glasken! Snap out of it!"

"Gah."

"There's a lever with a safety catch by your left hand. Flick the catch off."

"Done. Now what?"

The enemy flyer had been taken by surprise, but tried to follow Sartov. His turning circle was wider, much wider than that of the Yarronese sailwing. Moments later Sartov was closing in on his tail.

"Fire!"

At Sartov's command Glasken pulled on the lever and the reaction gun spat a stream of jacketed lead into the pitch blackness before him. His burst went wild, but the terrified flyer in the Bartolican sailwing went into a dive immediately. Sartov followed.

"Lock the bloody gun straight ahead, Glasken."

"How?"

"The double ring grip below the lever."

Now Sartov aimed with the whole sailwing and Glasken just pulled the lever at Sartov's command. After five more bursts he saw small, faint flames in the darkness ahead; then Sartov began to drop back. Glasken stared at the diminishing, flickering lights until they suddenly blossomed into a bright fireball. Sartov banked away to resume a course south.

"Near thing," gasped Glasken.

"Sitting duck," replied Sartov. "He too could see in the dark, but he flew like a tram driver. That was a newly trained aviad flyer, wearing goggles like these."

An hour later they landed on a road on the outskirts of Denver. Glasken clambered out of the cockpit, collapsed in a heap, then pulled himself to his feet again.

"Congratulations, Sair Glasken, you can paint a Bartolican crest on the trophy panel of your gunwing," Sartov called above the idling engine.

"Don't have one."

"After the war, you can have mine."

"I'll never set foot in one of these bloody things again."

"One day Yarron will raise a statue to you, I promise that. Have a drink for me, when you reach Denver."

Glasken watched as the dim shape of the sailwing ascended from the road, briefly eclipsing the distant lights of Denver. He waved in the direction of the compression engine's drone then set off for the ancient city, savoring every footfall on solid ground.

23–24 September 3960: Casper wingfield

Serjon did not bother to tell anyone that October 24th was his twentieth birthday. He awoke two hours before dawn, then ascended alone and opened his orders. The mission was a massive 250-mile arc around Median and over the tramway through the Red Desert and the mountains beyond until he crossed the Cosdoran border and reached the regional capital, Vernal. The Cosdoran Airlord was scheduled to hold the first of his traveling winter courts there during that week, and Chancellor Sartov had a dispatch to be delivered. It being so late in the flying season, there was little danger of encountering Bartolican gunwing flocks, and in any case Serjon could outrun them if he wanted to take his chances with the Sentinels and exceed 125 miles per hour. It would be a quick end, he thought philosophically, in fact he would probably not even notice the blast of fire.

It was calm and relatively warm weather for the time of year, and ideal for flying. He saw sunrise over the desert, caught sight of the tramway, then droned out over the wilderness. The compression engine was all that stood between him and a walk back to Casper that could take months, but it never missed. He landed at Vernal's wingfield, noting that there were three Bartolican sailwings and a gunwing parked near the pennant pole. As he taxied in along the dispersal track the adjunct came running up with two bearded mountain carbineers and a score of curious guildsmen trailing after him.

"Warden, Warden, you cannot stop here!" called the adjunct.

Serjon unstrapped and climbed out of the cockpit, leaving the compression engine idling.

"I have a dispatch for the Airlord of Bartolica," Serjon explained. "It is from Chancellor Sartov in North Yarron."

"Warden, we can give no assistance to Yarronese armed wings. There is a new treaty with the Bartolicans, signed just last night. If you stop your compression engine, we cannot restart it for you. Neither can we provide you with fuel, or even breakfast unless you surrender your gunwing to internment in this neutral domain."

After loud words from Serjon and much arm waving from the Cosdorans, the dispatch was accepted and put on a rail galley cart to be taken the two miles to Vernal and the local governor's palace. Starflower's engine continued to idle, and Serjon stayed near the gunwing, a reaction pistol strapped just below his knee. Bartolicans gathered and pointed in the distance, but thought the better of attacking him and causing an incident on neutral soil. Serjon moved to the flightstrip side of the gunwing, unbuttoned, and pissed. As he buttoned up again he noticed that he had an audience.

"Well, am I allowed to piss on your soil?" he asked a chubby, fresh-faced guildsman who was watching.

"The spot where Serjon Warden Killer pissed will be marked with a stone and honored," the youth replied with deference.

Serjon wondered if he was serious as he came around the gunwing again. Six more Cosdorans, all young free guildsmen, were gathered near the tail. He shooed them clear.

"Why was Vernal honored with a diplomatic visit by the famed Warden Killer?" the youth asked.

"Nobody else in my flock speaks Cosdoran," replied Serjon, who was unused to being addressed as anything but his rank title and real name.

The group decided that he had made a joke, and they laughed and clapped. No fuel, no breakfast, no warm coffee, but still they want a tramstop circus, thought Serjon. They introduced themselves, and the names Farrasond, Monterbil, and Ryban lodged in his memory as those three were of near-identical height and stature. Farrasond was more muscular than the others, and wore a free guildmaster's patch. Monterbil, who had been speaking to him, had a tin whistle in his belt and Serjon guessed that he was the wingfield bard, official or otherwise. Ryban was more cleanly groomed than the others, and had a small, wedge-shaped comb dangling from one ear by a gold ring.

A Bartolican love comb, Serjon realized after a moment's thought. In centuries past, a Bartolican bride's husband would have removed such a comb from her pubic hair as a symbol of raising the bars of a portcullis on what lay beyond. Now they were given out more casually and sometimes even with lovers' names and family crests thereon. Wearing a girl's comb so blatantly would have been considered tasteless in Bartolica, but this was Cosdoran mountain country. Each of the guildsmen wore a brass button on the outside of his trouser fly. This meant that they were available, and new lovers were meant to rip the buttons off. Lucky the Yarronese have no such customs, thought Serjon, who was squeamish about such displays and rituals.

The distant Bartolicans now had field glasses out, and were apparently making sketches of Starflower. Serjon glanced at his watch, reached into the cockpit, and drew out a biscuit.

"Are they your victories?" asked Ryban, pointing to twelve symbols of Bartolican gunwings and sailwings on Starflower's side.

"Yes."

"Bet the girls go for a warden."

"They do, but I'm not a warden. Just a flyer."

This answer was clearly a disappointment to the adoring circle of guildsmen, who were in search of a hero to worship.

"Do they, like, horn up because you're a killer?"

"Not the sort of girl that I like to be seen with."

Serjon was saved by the return of the galley cart along the wingfield tramway, and the adjunct hurried over as Serjon checked his watch. Another ten minutes of idling would have cut deeply into his fuel margin.

"The reply dispatch is sealed, but I can tell you that the Airlord was inclined to favor Yarron," the adjunct fussily explained, waving a finger and smiling with the good news. "The Bartolican envoy has been very, shall we say, presumptuous since the signing of the treaty last night and rather than deny service to Yarronese armed wings alone, the Airlord has decided to deny service to armed Bartolican wings as well. The envoy put on *such* a scene, you have no idea."

Serjon accepted the dispatch and climbed back into his gunwing.

"So if I unscrewed my reaction guns and laid them on the ground, Starflower would be unarmed and so eligible for service?" he asked as he put on his goggles.

"Ah, why yes! You could have a meal, use the steam engine trolley to restart, and even buy compression spirit," cried the adjunct with delight.

Serjon glanced at the youth from the fuelers' guild with the comb dangling from his ear, shuddered with distaste at the idea of him pumping compression spirit into Starflower, then waved the adjunct clear and revved his engine.

On the way back he flew high over the Red Desert again to avoid the gunwing interceptors of Median. Having particularly good eyes, he noticed an odd shape moving on the tramway. The air was otherwise clear, so he shed height and fell in behind. Eventually it resolved into a dark-painted tram and a sailwing traveling very close together. They had matched speeds, and the sailwing was a little ahead. Neither was aware of Serjon, or else they were ignoring him. Through field glasses he could see no more than that the sailwing was unmarked, but of a Bartolican canard design. Someone was leaning out of the tram and waving a stick, but the figure was antlike at this distance.

Serjon considered diving at power and attacking, but he had been instructed to avoid combat and his fuel was dangerously low for the hundred miles remaining between him and Casper. He was about to turn and climb when the sailwing suddenly broke off. Serjon thought he had been seen, but the distant sailwing was banking in a leisurely manner. A document drop, and to a moving tram, he realized. This might be a clue to the vaunted Bartolican communications system that had moved their carbineers with such precision and left Yarron reeling. Serjon checked the sky yet again, returned to his northeast arc, and began making detailed notes on what he had seen taking place.

The boom of cart cannons echoed among the peaks and valleys near Casper from the none too distant fighting as Serjon landed. The tramway had been smashed as far as Morton Pass near Forian, so Bartolican carbineers had marched along the road from Kennyville until Yarronese carbineers had halted them in an intense, bloody battle at Seminoe Pass. For the first time in the war, the Bartolican carbineers found themselves stalled.

In the early afternoon Serjon lay dozing near his gun-wing. The guildsmen of his ground crew were ever-present, checking the highly tuned compression engine and looking for wear or damage in the airframe. With twelve air victories he was a warrior for them to be proud of, even if he was a mere flyer.

He was roused when a senior guildmaster arrived from Sheridan in a regal and began walking among the gun-wings with a team of guildsmen. At each aircraft he stopped and took a small black ovaloid from his bag. The guildsmen drilled holes in the engine cowling and attached it with metal clamps. Serjon watched closely, noting that the thing looked like obsidian bored out to take quartz crystal inserts.

"A new device from the Sheridan research guilds," the guildmaster told Serjon quietly. "It is powered by the heat of the compression engine, and it cloaks your gunwing from the Sentinels."

Serjon swallowed, instantly translating this into tactics to use in clear air combat.

"Have you seen it work?" he asked.

"Chancellor Sartov himself put a hybrid into a dive with a Sentinel directly overhead. He touched two hundred and five miles per hour before pulling out, but the Sentinel did nothing."

"The Chancellor?" echoed Serjon, impressed. "That was very brave of him."

Alion volunteered to be first, and all flyers of the Air Carbineers watched as he took his gunwing up and practiced fighting maneuvers at the higher speeds. The almanac stated that a Sentinel was overhead, but his gunwing was not destroyed. Soon everyone was in the air, elated and eager for a clear air war duel, but the adjunct would not let them go out in search of a fight. He had already been reprimanded for the incident over his family, and was now bound by an oath of good behavior. Sartov had meantime decided that Casper was more defensible than Forian and had supplied another six hybrid gunwings.

It was late in the flying season. Soon there would be storms, wind, and ice, but for now the weather remained stubbornly fine. The Air Carbineers spent a very restive evening meal speculating on whether the Bartolicans would be good enough to attack again before the weather closed in and snow covered the wingfield. Afterward Serjon sat in a gunwing hall watching Ramsdel teach Bronlar how to sew, then took a lantern and went out to his own gunwing. He counted the number of inset crystals in the ovaloid cloaking device, but there were only twelve.

"Still looking for thirteens, Big Brother?" Bronlar's voice asked out of the darkness.

Serjon climbed down and joined her, lantern in hand. He snuffed the flame and they began walking across the wingfield in the general direction of the tents.

"I wanted a closer look at the Sentinel device," Serjon improvised. "I was wondering how it might work."

"Do you know now?"

"No."

The wind was light but chilly as they walked in the darkness. Ragged cloud was obscuring Mirrorsun.

"It's late in the season, there may be no more war duels until spring," Bronlar pointed out.

"That's all I need, Little Sister. Thirteen hanging over me until spring."

"I'll be glad of it. No more chilly tents and drafty cockpits for five months. Brrr, what a wind!"

Serjon opened his greatcoat and put an arm around her shoulders. Bronlar stiffened at his touch.

"I wish you wouldn't," she said after a few steps, then pushed his arm away.

Serjon slipped off his coat and draped it over her shoulders.

"I suppose that shoots down any chance of us warming a bunk together through the long, cold winter," Serjon remarked, trying to sound no more concerned than if he had only missed dinner.

"Big Brother, it's because of my position among all these men. I know a lot of them dote on me. The guildsmen who service my gunwing, Ramsdel, Alion, Kumiar, they've all had amorous duelwords with me on that matter."

"Oh my, the flockleader was last into the air," Serjon joked, but the shock was plain in his voice.

"I can't afford to favor anyone," Bronlar said after responding with a forced giggle. "Men get jealous about me, so I must live as if neuter. Ramsdel is seeing that medic girl, and Alion still overnights in the nurses' hostel and returns looking guilty. Some girls do admire you, so why not—?"

"No. No, it's you I fancy, not a body for a body's sake. I've worried about you for years, that's why I . . . bothered you, I suppose. When you came back with nine clear air victories I was so proud of you, I wanted to hug you, vomit and all."

"I never knew. I'm . . . sorry."

"Would you consider me for after the war, or at least let me be in the queue?"

Bronlar walked in silence for a time. She loved Serjon, but not like this. His sudden declaration was unexpected, and almost annoying.

"One day I'll be in the courting mood. Until then I make no promises to anyone and I live as one of the boys. It's my defense."

Now Serjon walked in silence, considering.

"Stepfather Jeb used to tell me that women spend their courtship years picking and choosing and testing to find the ideal man, then marry whoever is to hand when the mood to marry visits them."

"Did he say what men do?" asked Bronlar, unimpressed.

"They spend years hunting an ideal spouse, then grow weary and beg to be hunted."

They were close to the tents by now, and Bronlar stopped at the edge of the lamplight's reach.

"What do *you* think?" she asked.

"I think it's foolish to court a stranger when you could court a friend. You know what you're getting with a friend."

"With some friends that's a good reason not to court, Big Brother. Here is your coat. Thank you, and night's compliments."

Her fingers brushed against his, warm and dry in the darkness. Warm fingers: Serjon found that intensely alluring. He stood with the greatcoat in his hands until Bronlar was out of earshot, then softly said, "Ouch." As he put the greatcoat on he noticed that her warmth and body scent lingered in it, and he wandered back into the darkness to be alone with that trace of Bronlar.

In the morning they were still waiting. The sky now featured scattered cloud, but the air was mild again. Were I a Bartolican, I might attack our carbineer defenders at Seminoe Pass on a day like this, Serjon thought with a mixture of eagerness and dread. Guildsmen kept the compression engines warm with hot air bellows, and every flyer, warden, and squire on the wingfield was within a few steps of a wing. A sailwing droned into view, high overhead. It did a series of rolls, then dropped a cannister trailing red smoke.

As one, the Air Carbineers scrambled into their wings as their guildsmen set the engines spinning with compression charges. The wingfield's adjunct had set off on his pedalframe before the cannister had even hit the ground and all eyes were on him as he opened the message and read. A moment later he raised a signal gun and began to fire off red flares. Serjon counted five as he buckled his straps.

"Air attack, class five!" shouted his guildmaster above the engine.

"Very large air attack!" Serjon shouted back.

"Mind your turns, sair, you've got higher speeds now," his guildmaster called. "Every circle will be wider, and pulling out of a dive too late could buy you a synthetic funeral."

The chocks were pulled away and the gunwing rolled forward. Serjon pulled the glass laminate canopy down and clamped it. A siren sounded, but every gunwing and sailwing on the wingfield was already in motion.

As Serjon buckled his harness straps he saw the adjunct waving the old Jannian estate pennant on the flightstrip. Serjon was flockleader. The red flag in his other hand came up, then slashed horizontally. General order, ascend and intercept. Serjon gunned the compression engine and began rolling down the dusty flightstrip, and as he reached the pace line he opened the throttle. The gunwing rolled faster and faster, tilted, and lifted into the air.

This attack was not expected by the traditionalists, as it was late in the dueling season. A sudden change in the weather was as likely to drop aircraft out of the sky as the enemy. Serjon climbed quickly to gain height over the approaching Bartolican flock, not mindful of saving fuel. The flock was clearly visible, circling the Seminoe Pass, where

the Yarronese carbineers had the Bartolicans pinned down.
The Bartolicans were at least nine dozen gunwings and
sailwings strong, while a mere thirty sailwings and ten
gunwings were ascending to engage them. Starflower was
very responsive to the higher power and Serjon found himself ascending faster than any gunwing should have been
able to. The Yarronese circled for the east, distancing
themselves from the wingfield and looking to put the sun
at their backs. Serjon led the dive, directly at the gunwing
escort, but to the surprise of the Bartolicans all but five of
the Yarron sailwings followed them.

The swirling melee of aircraft allowed none of the tactics that the Yarronese had used over the weeks past.
Serjon made a side attack first, slashing at a turning gunwing, which puffed black smoke as he passed. He came up
behind another gunwing, walked shots across to its engine,
and pulled away to the sight of a splintering propellor.

"That's fourteen!" he suddenly realized. "And I'm alive.
I'm free, I'm safe!"

The minutes that followed were desperate and deadly
for both sides, but the far lighter Yarronese wings proved
to be difficult targets with very superior rates of climb.
The Bartolican wardens continued with the attack, thinking
that their scheme of drawing the Yarron aircraft away from
the mountain pass was working. As the sailwings laid
down supporting fire, the Bartolican carbineers attacked.

The fight in the air drifted down, and near the mountains. Both sides were attacking, but there were only fifty
Bartolican gunwings in the flock, and the Yarronese gunwings were proving to be impossible targets due to their
speed. Serjon banked to the left, cutting around a rocky
peak smeared with gleaming snow, then came in low
through a patch of cloud. Nine gunwings were ahead, turning in a leisurely sweep and climbing. He opened the throttle wide, came up behind the hindmost, and fired a short,
well-placed burst. The enemy gunwing's engine died at
once. His winger was just turning for a better look when

Serjon's second burst slashed through his engine and cockpit. The gunwing slewed away toward the ground, the warden already dead. His third burst was too well placed, and the gunwing burst into a gout of messy smoke and wreckage in midair. Three of the other wardens noticed and banked sharply for the open air. Serjon sat for several seconds on overboost, went for a long deflection shot, and was rewarded by a streamer of smoke and fire trailing from the fourth warden to cross his sights.

Serjon was now aware of a problem with his engine. The long, damaging seconds on overboost had burned or melted something, for the power was down and its response sluggish. The whole Bartolican sub-flock was alerted now, and the surviving gunwings were wheeling and swooping for a dangerously low battle. With all five surviving wardens now swarming after the lone gunwing the advantage was actually with Serjon. He doggedly stayed within their wheeling, roiling flock, making sure that they were never able to get him in the open and chase him like hounds after a hare. They do not fight well as a team, he thought with something like serene detachment. Another burst from his guns tore harmlessly through wing fabric until it ruptured a fuel tank. The warden's gunwing did not catch fire, but compression spirit poured into the air. The warden broke off at once to flee south for Kennyville. Serjon let him go. With that volume of fuel gone he would not get twenty miles; the reserve tank was good for only a few minutes.

Some miles away the main battle was still roiling in the sky like a fantastic fireworks display, but Serjon did not heed it. Inevitably one of the gunwings pursuing him clipped a treetop, crumpled, then vanished amid the branches only to reappear as a ball of flame. Six down, thought Serjon as he rolled on open throttle, then banked sharply, the sky and mountains gyrating insanely. Stall turn, shudder as bullets thudded through his port wing's empty outer tank, dark shape ahead, shoot, roll, bank, climb. That had been a miss, and his arms were aching by now. They were getting the feel of the fight, Serjon realized, while the peak had been sliced off his engine's performance. Farewell to certainty, time for chances.

Selecting a warden almost at random, he cut around as he dived for him and plunged after him with his engine screaming on open throttle. He flew through a shallower dive than the Bartolican, catching him as he was climbing again, closing in and firing a sustained burst into the gunwing until it became a comet of dark smoke. The others were behind him now and stray shots tore through the gunwing's fabric with dull thuds as he rolled and broke, rolled and broke. The damage to the wings would snap them if the punishment continued. One more trick, one trick for a light, struggling gunwing.

He dived out of a roll. The three wardens came after him as he plunged for a wooded plateau, gaining distance before their superior diving speed closed the gap again. Rocks and trees swayed and danced before him like a diorama of jelly. Standing on the plate and heaving back on the stick Serjon dragged the gunwing out of its dive in time to skim the needles of the tallest pines as bullets zipped past and sprayed dirt up from a bare stretch of ground. Serjon gained enough height for a stall turn and counted two gunwings. Two. Down to the right a column of smoke was rising from the plateau where one of the heavier but less powerful gunwings had not been able to pull out of its dive. Serjon's arms were heavy and glowing with fatigue, but he banked and closed to get among the Bartolicans again, only to see them go into a dive and flee. Their nerve was gone, they thought they were being lured into a trap by a demon that was just playing with them.

Now Serjon found himself lost amid broken cloud, and the battle was somewhere out of sight. He looked for reference peaks, checked his compass, fuel, and ammunition, then began to climb for the trip back to the wingfield. Far below him he noticed something moving rapidly, a flock of birds perhaps, or . . . he dived. The Bartolican sailwings had lost hardly any of their number to groundfire, and were still circling the battlefield on the ground.

Serjon lined up behind the stragglers. His ammunition was low, so he had to be careful. Approaching to within no more than a wingspan's distance, he fired a brief, economical burst at the sailwing's pusher engine.

The day was not kind to the Bartolican flock. Thirty-one wardens had been lost, and another forty armored sailwings for the price of eleven Yarronese aircraft. The Yarronese adjunct was making his assessment when the sound of an approaching gunwing engine became audible. Serjon's name was scratched from the list of those missing as the gunwing circled once and landed. It was riddled with holes and trailing strips of fabric. The adjunct ran across as the guildsmen helped the flyer out of the cockpit. Serjon stood by himself, although chalky with strain and exhaustion. He focused on the adjunct.

"Seven wardens down or seen falling," he reported, after thinking for a moment.

The adjunct looked from Serjon to the ravaged gunwing, then back to the flyer.

"Anything else?" the adjunct asked in astonishment.

"Ah, six sailwings," Serjon muttered through clenched teeth, shifting his weight from foot to foot.

"Thirteen victories!" the adjunct exclaimed.

"Can you keep your humping voice down!" hissed Serjon, but people were already gathering and pointing. "I ran out of ammunition. I hit one more sailwing, but he kept flying."

Yarronese carbineers later reported an amazing battle between one gunwing and two dozen armored sailwings while the ground battle raged. They confirmed six sailwings brought down. A Yarronese agent at the Kennyville wingfield reported just three sailwings returning. Serjon was adamant that fourteen had escaped him. After all, would he lie about anything that would have given him even one more kill, and rescued him from the hated thirteen? Bad weather had not brought them down, the winds had been light and it was cloudless south of Casper.

At Seminoe Pass the Bartolican carbineers had meantime made the biggest mistake that one possibly can in warfare: they had believed their own propaganda. They were footsore after marching through the mountains for days, for it was fifty miles from the Kennyville tram station. Many had never marched fifty miles in their lives, as they were tram-based. Even attacking the Yarronese with sailwing support was not enough when faced with a well-armed enemy almost blind with rage over what had been happening in Yarron for the past two months. The Bartolicans wanted an objective, but the Yarronese wanted revenge. If such a thing is possible in war, it was a fair fight, and even with initial air support the Bartolicans broke and fell back after forty minutes of bloody and ferocious fighting. Serjon's help was welcome, but not vital.

The Casper adjunct was tempted to assign twenty-five victories to Serjon for that day but the figure was plainly ludicrous, even for Serjon Feydamor in a hybrid gunwing. The figure 13 appeared beside his name on the pennant board, but the possibility that he had caused another twelve sailwings to be lost was appended to the report that went to Chancellor Sartov. Sartov read the report when he arrived at Casper the following day.

"So twelve sailwings are unaccounted for, Chancellor," the adjunct concluded as Sartov handed the report back to him.

"Ah, but they *are* accounted for, Sair Adjunct," replied Sartov. "I had been expecting this since speaking with a man named . . . since speaking with a very helpful man. Now kindly provide my aide with a strand of your hair."

"Your pardon, Chancellor?"

"A hair, if you please?" demanded the aide, who was

flanked by two armed carbineers with the safety catches of their assault carbines released.

Later that day the weather abruptly closed in. Serjon, Bronlar, and Ramsdel were sheltering from a fall of freezing rain in one of the maintenance tents when a regal with Air Carbineer markings but no number made a dangerously rough landing and taxied up the dispersal track. Two men were marched through the rain by the Chancellor's own guards. Their heads were hooded and their hands were bound.

"Is that to do with the little man who asked everyone for a hair?" asked Serjon.

"Yes, Big Brother. Liesel heard they found traces of Bartolican dye in their hair," Bronlar explained.

Ramsdel was embroidering the symbol of another Bartolican warden on Serjon's detachable collar while Bronlar watched closely.

"They were probably spying on our Sentinel cloaking things," ventured Serjon.

"I was thinking of green plush for your collar's underlining," declared Ramsdel, holding up his jacket with the collar clipped back on. "Where can I get green plush with Forian under siege?"

29 September 3960: Condelor

Even after nearly a month of work by his linguists, Vander Hannan knew no more about the documents found at the scene of his father's death. Although many of the words and grammatical conventions had echoes in his own language, they were like nothing in any of the known domains in any of the four known Callhavens. Certain words were underlined, and these words were particularly strange. Hannan's linguists guessed that the language was based on Old Anglian, but was highly evolved.

"As from a Callhaven cut off for two thousand years?"

Vander asked the linguist who had presented him with the status report.

"There could be no such Callhaven," the woman replied.

The weather was cool and blustery as he strode across the plaza before the Convocation Galleria. He entered the administrative chambers behind the auditorium where the envoys met formally once a week. A clerk bowed as he reached the office of the Warden of Envoys and explained that although the warden was not there, instructions had been left to show the acting Inspector General all possible cooperation.

"As I have said before, I only want to trace three Bartolican servants of the late envoy from Veraguay," said Vander with ill-disguised impatience. "Jeb Feytr, Martyn Harrit and Zoster Wragge."

"They made statements after the fire," the clerk said without even checking the files.

"As I said yesterday and the day before that, I've read the statements and I want to question them further. I'm the acting Inspector General, I believe it could affect the dominion's security."

The clerk tapped a decree by the Bartolican Airlord allowing merchant carbineer recruits to register under false names if they volunteered for front-line duty.

"It's a fine way to dispose of those with a past while boosting carbineer ranks," suggested the clerk.

"So three men with a past work in the envoy's house, it burns to the ground, then they vanish into the carbineers and get sent to the war."

"Inspector! It is a pursuit of Yarronese outlaws, not a formal war."

"Forty thousand carbineers with two thousand cart cannons and carriage guns have Forian under siege!" said Vander angrily, banging the clerk's desk at every phrase. "The palace decrees that it is an orderly operation, yet nobody can tell whether my mother is alive or dead."

"You have my condolences, Inspector, but we all know

that Yarron is a lawless land, full of outlaws."

"Just how many outlaws does Yarron harbor?"

"There's no end of them, Inspector," said the clerk with respectful calm.

The Call that swept over Condelor early that afternoon was flagged as always by the sentinel towers, and the bells of the city rang an hour in advance to warn of its approach. Vander Hannan had returned home with copies of the city's court records for the year past. He had only reached April by then and cursed at the impending interruption. Taking the records, he went downstairs to his Call suite.

"Forlet, I don't want any interruptions while I'm in here," he told his footman. "Either before or after the Call passes."

He closed the door behind him. The lower six feet of the western wall of the suite was padded in red emu leather, and the floor thickly carpeted. At the eastern wall was a desk and chair, and a lightwell in the roof allowed him to keep working on his reports.

A sailwing droned overhead as the duty warden began his rounds above the city. The time passed quickly as Vander worked through the lists. He had reached September when his house crier shouted "Ten minutes! Lock up and tether!" somewhere in the distance. With a reluctant sigh Hannan reached down for a tether bolted to the floor and clipped it to his belt. If an earthquake brought down the western wall while the Call gripped him he might require the tether, yet any earthquake as severe as that was liable to kill him anyway.

He had been looking for three names, but now he idly read the synopses of the hearings. A mason had stabbed his banker seconds before a Call then stepped into the street and been allured to walk five miles west until a public Call barrier stopped him. Had he not neglected to clean the blood from beneath his fingernails he might not have been convicted.

"One minute!" bellowed the house crier.

Vander scratched scraps of wax from the seal on his father's ring of office. Dying in the bed of a mistress was probably how the old devil would have liked to have gone, Vander decided—at least after thirty years with Laurelene shouting at him. At that moment the Call rolled over the house and something within Vander surrendered and betrayed itself.

When Vander awoke the bells were ringing again to announce the Call's passing. He was tired from three hours of wandering mindlessly along the padded western wall, but he also felt strangely uncomfortable. It was a subtle feeling, somehow itchy and clinging. He wriggled and squirmed within his clothes, scratching at himself. Suddenly he realized that his ring was missing! It had been a tight fit, and not easily removed. He went down on all fours and crawled along the western wall. No ring.

Vander stood up and pressed his hands against his temples. He distinctly remembered touching the ring just before the Call, and he was positive that he had not removed it. He began walking toward the door and stopped: there was a bowl on the table, placed on the papers that he had been reading before the Call. Peering into the bowl he discovered that it contained green jelly. He picked it up, and noticed that it was lukewarm. It must have been made about an hour ago, he estimated, yet that would have been during the Call! Then he saw it, dimly, at the bottom of the bowl: a ring. A ring suspiciously similar in shape to his ring of office.

He nearly dropped the bowl, but recovered and placed it carefully on the table. Now he noticed something odd about his clothing. His coat was inside-out, as was his shirt, and his trousers! He began to strip. His baseshirt was inside-out as well, and even his stockings. By the time he reached his underbriefs he was not surprised to discover them inside out, but as he began to step out of them he discovered a blue ribbon tied in a neat bow around his penis! With trembling hands he removed the ribbon. Embroidered on it with white thread was *South Bartolica District Fair, First Prize, 3958*.

Vander was a long time dressing himself again. He was about to dig his ring out of the jelly when there was a knock at the door.

"Enter!" snapped Vander, annoyed and alarmed that he could not deduce how the tricks had been played.

At his word Theresla and Darien entered, the former holding a reaction pistol with a large silencer.

"We did not kill your father," said Theresla in Old Anglian, coming straight to the point.

She closed the door behind her and locked it, then motioned Vander to a chair.

"Where have you been hiding?" Vander asked, grasping at the first of many questions clamoring for an answer.

"That is nobody's business, Sair Acting Inspector General. You want to arrest us, which would be inconvenient. The men who killed your father want to murder us, which is rather more inconvenient."

"Why should I believe you?"

"Because it is in your best interests, and because you are a patriot. Bartolica is under the control of men who can move freely during the Call. Callwalkers is your term for them, I believe."

Vander began to laugh.

"I trust the ribbon around your penis was not too tight," Theresla added.

Vander was silenced in an instant, the smile wiped from his face. The ribbon in question lay on the table beside the bowl of jelly. Vander stared at it for some seconds.

"I trust you washed your hands?" he asked with an eyebrow raised.

Theresla walked forward and picked up the ribbon. She dangled it before Vander's face.

"I did some terribly undignified things to you just now, Sair Hannan, yet I could not have done them unless I was a Callwalker, able to defy the Call. Others in this dominion can do it too, but we are all from far beyond Mounthaven."

"Veraguay?"

"No, much farther."

Darien picked up the bowl and carried it over to Vander. He pushed his fingers into the almost cool jelly and withdrew them with his ring. Theresla scooped a piece of jelly into her mouth and pronounced it "Good."

Darien set the bowl down, took a sheet of his own notepaper, and scribbled some lines, which she handed to Vander.

"Sair Hannan, unless you are very stupid you must realize that some people can remain in control, aware, and free to move about during a Call. Callwalkers exist. Do you believe it now?"

Vander nodded. "Do you come from a distant Callhaven?" he asked.

"We come from a distant continent," Theresla replied. "Australica is our name for it."

Slowly, aware that a gun was pointed at his head, Hannan reached over to his desk and picked up another sheet of paper.

"My linguists have translated the first few lines of some pages found in the grounds of the Veraguay envoy's mansion after the fire. Does this mean anything to you? 'Day of Judgment was not felt on the ground. Slow, round warming was making/made the Miocene climate more comfortable, and it was cold, dry and cutting edge at high mountains.' "

"Do you have the original of the script?" asked Theresla as she handed the reaction pistol to Darien.

"Here is a copy, word for word," he said, handing another sheet of paper to Theresla.

Theresla held the page up and blinked at the awkwardly formed letters, which showed the influence of Bartolican cursive.

"Darien is the better linguist, but she cannot speak so I

shall have to try," Theresla explained. " 'Armageddon passed unfelt on the land. Slow global cooling was moderating the mid-Miocene climate, making it drier and sharpening the chill at high latitudes. The ice sheets in Antarctica expanded and became permanent, while small glaciers developed in Alaska and Siberia. Adaptable species had an advantage during the changes, while those which had fitted too well into fragile ecological niches went into decline. In Africa, several species of apes had learned to use stones to break the eggs of the large, flightless birds, and sticks to extract honey from beehives. These were the most advanced tools in use on the planet, yet in the oceans two marine superpowers and a host of their allies were fighting the war to end all wars with no tools at all.' "

She paused. Vander was perplexed, but she seemed confident in her translation, far more so than his own linguists.

"Miocene means a long time ago," Theresla explained. "Ten million years, we think. Apes are thought to be hairy animals that could walk upright as we can. Marine is to do with the great waters where the Call comes from. The other words are ancient names of places."

"What does all this mean?" asked Vander. "Who wrote this?"

"A man named James Brennan, in the early twenty-first century as you date years."

Hannan put a hand to his mouth, partly to hide his surprise.

"It was found in a ruined city in the Calldeath lands of my homeland, on the Australican continent," Theresla added.

"Which is not Veraguay."

"Correct. Only the late envoy was from Veraguay. We recruited her as a convenience while we traveled, but we kept our real names. We were trying to attract the wrong sort of attention but not attract suspicion, you see."

"No I don't see. You say you did not kill my father or the envoy?"

"No. We were saddened by their deaths, they were both fine, interesting people."

Hannan had heard his father, the late Inspector General, described in many ways, but never as interesting. Still, the word did seem to encompass him better than any other single word might.

"Can you tell me who the murderers are?"

Darien stared at him through her eyelashes, lips pressed together as she trained the silenced gun on him. Theresla returned the two sheets of paper to Hannan's desk, then rubbed her hands together.

"I can tell you about them in the most general terms, but I can provide no specific names. Yet. You need education, but you are in luck for we are both former edutors—that's a type of teacher."

"Well, go on."

"You need a great deal of background to comprehend who the murderers are—and *what* they are, Sair Hannan. We need you working with us, for you are a powerful and influential Bartolican. Are you willing to suspend your disbelief and read a very, very strange story?"

"I . . . shall seriously consider anything that you show me, I can promise no more than that. One last question, though: Why didn't you tell me all this earlier? Why hide so long?"

"Darien has been translating a long document into your language while I have been, ah, going about unseen and checking possibilities. Now I have decided that you are our only hope, so here we are."

It was only now that Vander noticed the cotton slingbag over Darien's shoulder. While Darien continued to train the gun on him, Theresla removed a thick folder of the type that the envoys used for dispatches. She handed it to Vander. The text was in Bartolican, and the script was well formed and legible. He began to read.

Our home continent of Australica was spared the worst of the war and anarchy that broke out with the coming of the Call, but the times were still very bad. We have no records other than folk tales of the two centuries following 2022, but one thing is clear even from our earliest recorded weather observations. The climate was slowly warming. What we call Greatwinter was the normal climate in the pre-Call centuries. It was much cooler back then.

Australica is totally surrounded by ocean, however, so that the few bird-people who could resist the Call have never ventured beyond Australica before now. Only two decades ago the aviads, as we call them, began to organize themselves in the Calldeath lands where humans could not venture. Now, as you can see, aviads have been able to cross the oceans and reach Mounthaven, which was once known as North America.

The implications of what he had just read were difficult for Vander to accept.

"How long have these . . . aviads, these Callwalkers been here?" he asked.

"Four years," Theresla replied.

"What is their business?"

"To start wars. Wars make chaos, and aviads profit by chaos."

Vander noted that Darien was still holding the gun steady, and was as alert as when she had entered. Theresla added that all the religions of Australica's humans prohibited fueled machines, possibly as a result of being shot at for centuries by the Sentinels. In North America the Sentinels' limits had been discovered and they had taken a different path.

"So you are an aviad," concluded Vander.

"Yes," said Theresla. "But not Darien."

"And the envoy?"

"The envoy was our cover, she really did come from Veraguay."

"And Glasken?"

"Glasken . . . Glasken is very strange. Nobody understands Glasken, not even Glasken. Glasken is a Callwalker, but not a true aviad. He has human hair."

Vander raised the thick sheaf of papers and flourished it in the air.

"It's late. Do we need to stay here while I read all of this?"

"Yes. Certain servants of yours are not to be trusted."

Vander bristled.

"What? Which ones?"

"Later, later. Now, be pleased to begin reading. Oh, and you will need this glossary folder for many of the terms used. Some of them we could only guess at, of course."

Vander opened the glossary at random. "Television: a public communications system like our street corner notice boards which could display sounds and moving pictures." Leaving the glossary lying open on his desk he sat down and wearily opened the folder of the main text, but soon found that most of it was not as obscure as the writing on the enigmatic pages that he had chanced upon after the fire. Soon he was completely engrossed and unaware of Darien's gun.

My name is Dr. James Francis Brennan, and I work for the Miocene Institute in New South Wales. At least I used to work for the Miocene Institute. The Institute's staff are all dead, apart from me. Even New South Wales no longer exists in quite the form that it did just nine days ago.

Nine days ago.

Only nine days to end the world. Nine days ago it was November 14, 2022. That means today is November 23. From November 14 to November 19, for five entire days, the whole of the state, maybe the whole of Australia, or even the world, mindlessly walked toward the sea. I was locked in a room, and could not get out without thinking enough to enter a password on a touchpad. Now I sit in the Director's office, writing these notes in his expensive new, gilt-edge, 2023 diary. The Director was old-fashioned about that sort of thing, no voice-pad DDS for him. Just as well. With care this acid-free paper will last for centuries, but in a few years I doubt that a single DDS will be working anywhere in the world.

It may not surprise you to know that I have been drinking. The late Director had a generous supply of wines and spirits in his private drinks cabinet, but I have been working hard to ensure that it does not go to waste before I die. The poor man is nine days dead. His window is smashed, and his body lies where it has fallen. With his field glasses I can study the shore, where there are rotting bodies as far as I can see. The smell is considerable. No, that is not a good word, but who is there to sue me? I can see a few horses too, some sheep, and a lot of big dogs. Mostly I can see people. Men, women and children, all drowned and washed up again. Birds are feeding on them. Funny, but no birds are dead. No cats either, and no rats. Rats have been nibbling at the Director's body, I have seen them by torchlight. I spend a lot time in his office. Being the only member of the Miocene Institute's staff still alive, I must be the new Director. My life's ambition, fulfilled! I must drink to that.

24 November 2022:

The late Director's drinks cabinet must have run out last night. I have been very ill for most of the morning, but after brewing up some coffee in one of the laboratories and eating a tin of peaches I feel a lot better. Late this morning I saw a contrail high overhead, and through the field glasses I saw that it was some type of fighter heading east, out to sea. About twenty minutes later I heard four heavy explosions and saw smoke on the horizon. Then the contrail appeared again, heading west, in the direction of the Richmond Air Force Base. So, someone heard my radio message on November 19, they know where the enemy is to be found. The enemy is not so easily killed, however, and the enemy can strike back with far more deadly force than four smart bombs. I have chained myself to the desk, and am eating a hearty lunch even as I write. I have left water, fruit and biscuits within reach of the end of my chains because—

11 December 2022:

Fifteen days of that accursed call-to-the-sea! Damn those cetezoids, damn them to hell and damn them even lower. Maybe the smart bombs really did kill a few whales, so they hit back. I was in pretty bad shape when the sea-call lifted, but I had eaten the fruit and biscuits that I left in reach and drunk the water. Basic instincts to eat and drink seem to persist, even under the sea-call's influence.

Five hours have passed, and it is 3pm. The wind is blowing the stench from the shore out to sea and the weather is very mild. It is the sort of day that I love to take off to walk along the beach, but I doubt that I shall ever do that again.

I managed to get some of the radios working. The Internet has been dead since the first sea-call. On the shortwave bands I learned some alarming news. There have been nuclear exchanges between several nations in the northern hemisphere, and although only a few dozen bombs were involved, they set off vast fires. The crews of the Orbital Battle Units are now shooting down anything larger than a small plane or going faster than 200 klicks, so I don't think we will end up with a world war. Hey, what am I talking about? We already had World War

Three and we got our fundamentals kicked to the moon and back.

Now it is evening. I can see one of the OBUs moving through the sky like a brilliant star. Not long ago a message was relayed from General Takahashi, who commands the stations. Fancy, a name like Takahashi, yet he's a seventh-generation American: what a world. There was a rebellion among his crews, but he had some sort of master override to kill life support on any of the stations and he used it. Now all OBUs except OBU Alpha are on automatic, with nanotek maintenance mobiles to keep the equipment working and clean up the bodies. Takahashi has decreed that anything larger than 9 metres or a speed above 200 klicks that's got an engine driving it will activate the auto-targeting on his laser cannons. That should stop anyone flinging bombs around, I suppose, but it worries me to have someone who has killed most of his own people in charge of so much power.

21 December 2022:

Happy Equinox and Merry Christmas, all in one! Yesterday I made radio contact with a research group out in the Blue Mountains. We had an extensive exchange of data. Marianne Landini is in charge there, and I gave her my background and theories on the cetezoids and their weapon from nine million years ago. We call it the Miocene Arrow, pretty obviously. Well, she liked my theories, but I only told her part of the story. Some of what makes up the sea-call is of a highly personal nature, and not what one would wish to have broadcast on an unencrypted channel.

She says that birds are not affected. They set up video cameras on several pens of animals and birds—she had the foresight to assume that the sea-call would be used again. All mammals under about 8 to 10 kilograms are immune, as are all birds and reptiles. She is now working on the assumption that there is something in bird DNA that protects them from the sea-call. It seems like a good assumption. After all, the cetezoids are genetically closer to humans and other mammals than emus or sparrows. Landini hopes to splice certain bird DNA into the germ plasm of fertilised human eggs. Members of her own staff have volunteered to be the parents.

Another remarkable finding of hers is that the sea-call loses its grip if one is very, very deep underground. She has moved her equipment into the Jenolan caves to guard against the next attack. The woman is a fantastic leader, I really long to meet her.

2 January 2023:

As I write I can see the remains of OBU Theta dispersing among the stars like a strange little mobile constellation. Someone in North America managed to destroy it, but I can't say how. According to the BBC, Takahashi responded with at least six EMP bombs detonated in orbit after trashing the launch site on the ground. Not one piece of equipment with a circuit in it will be working from Canada to Mexico, unless it was shielded. He has EMP cannons aboard those OBUs as well, to pick off anything electrical that emerges in the aftermath. Now the BBC has gone silent. Is he going to knock out every electrical circuit in the world? That would include all cars and trucks. Maybe I should get moving.

There was a sea-call from December 27 to December 30, so I presume that there will not be another for some time. What I must do is take my life in my hands, cross the parkland to the suburbs, and find a car. No, make that a truck. I need to load everything that I can move before leaving for the caves. A new dark age is descending, nothing high-tech will be built for another thousand years, if ever. Can I do it, I wonder? I live in fear of being in the open with that psychic Sword of Damocles suspended above me. Will I *ever* have the courage to cross the park? The beach is lined with whitening bones and putrid flesh. I am reminded of that crust on the edge of the ocean with every breath that I take.

15 January 2023:

So much has happened in so few days, I scarcely know where to begin. OBUs Delta and Epsilon have been destroyed now, but an EMP bomb has been detonated above Sydney as part of Takahashi's retaliation. Fortunately I had sealed all the equipment that I really need into EMP-proof metal cases and drums. I suppose it was my way of putting off my walk across the parkland. That was on January 7. The next day another sea-call swept over, and I did not awake until January 14. Even though I was starving, dehydrated and exhausted, I grabbed a backpack of tools and provisions and started jogging across the park. I was reduced to a shuffle after about a hundred steps, for I am neither young nor fit, but I made it. I tried to start a car, but its electronics had been fried. Instead I took a mountain bike and rode five miles to an army depot, and there I found a big, lovely diesel truck with mesh-shielded lights and electronics.

As I write the truck is in the Miocene Institute's parking lot, with my equipment, data, computer gear and video records. I also took some automatic weapons: two heavy machine guns, a trajectory mortar and several boxes of ammunition. I am dressed in combat gear too, with the rank of captain. Somehow I always fancied myself in the army. Tomorrow at first light I shall set off for the Jenolan caves. There I shall present Doctor Landini with my truckload of gifts. Provided that I get there, of course.

In case I do not get through, I must trust that some day

someone will attempt to reach the Miocene Institute. After all, it is the gate through which the deadly arrow from the past entered our world. If and when they do, they must find my full and honest story, because it is the key to understanding the sea-call. Indeed, I suspect that I was the subject of the original experiment by which it was tuned to work on land mammals. Okay then, for better or worse, here is my story!

When I was at university I was a shy, withdrawn and inhibited sort of dork, but before that I had been a bright and outgoing kid. The change came when I became a regular on a children's TV show in the 1960s. It was called the Miss Wonderful Show, can you believe it? Well, Australian television was still in its first decade and some pretty crass programmes were able to make it to air. As I said, I was only a kid at the time, and I was really approval-conscious as well. I adored Miss Wonderful, and she was a really sophisticated, beautiful, fairy godmother figure. I don't know the woman's real name, but she would have been in her early thirties.

One night us regulars were on camera and live to air, trading riddles with Miss Wonderful. One of the girls asked:

"Why did the tomato go red?"

"I don't know, Kerrie," Miss Wonderful replied sweetly.

"Because it saw the salad dressing," the girlie replied rather smugly.

"Why Kerrie, how embarrassing for the tomato," replied Miss Wonderful after giving a gasp.

I had overheard my brothers exchanging a version of this joke the day before, and they had laughed until one had had a coughing fit. I did not understand their answer, but it just had to be better than Kerrie's.

"Please Miss, I thought it was because it saw the beet-root," I interjected.

There was instant pandemonium. Miss Wonderful and some of the more knowledgeable children shrieked with shock, the producer tried to shield us from the camera with his body, and off in the background someone was shouting "Cut to commercials! Cut to commercials!"

Of course I was now aware that I had unwittingly said something unspeakably rude, but I was too frightened and confused to even apologize. Just before I was dragged away to the tumbril by my father Miss Wonderful came up to me, bent over, put her face very close to mine and said "You *dirty*, *dirty* little boy!"

I was at university before I could even bring myself to watch a television again, so great had my mortification been. I was soon told by my brothers that 'beetroot' was really 'beet root' for the purposes of the riddle, and that root was one of the many euphemisms for sex. What is sex, I asked, fearing the worst. My elder brother explained, aided by an illustrated pamphlet that he produced from under the cabinet of his record player. My sense of horror and self-loathing now went into free fall, and from that day on I went from being a bright, brash little boy to being a shy, studious little boy.

During my first year at university I met up with a girl named Jillian. She was a bit of a prude and had no dress sense at all, so she probably suited me at the time. She was very like me, in that she had enough pride to want to be seen holding hands with someone and to have someone to eat lunch with in the cafeteria, but as for going back to her room for a bit of privacy? No way.

Now why, you may ask, am I telling you all the sordid details of my childhood mortifications and lack of undergraduate sex life? The truth is that in 2014 I began to have luridly vivid recollections of them. At that time I had been involved with the frozen cetezoid for a decade. In 2004 an echolocator survey working a patch of trapped, ancient ice in Antarctica found the body of a small whale. It had been frozen since the Miocene, for nine million years, and was a species known as Zipiidae or beaked whale. It was fourteen feet long, weighed about a ton and a half, and had the characteristic two fighting tusks of the males of its species. It also had an unusually large brain.

Scientifically it was a sensation. Some very fancy genetic engineering techniques were used to make male clones from its tissues, and some even fancier techniques involving DNA from modern beaked whales produced sister/daughters from the tissues as well. There was no hope of reviving the frozen body, the freezing process would have damaged its tissues beyond hope of recovery, but then someone came up with the idea of doing a section-by-section scan of its brain and mapping that in turn into one of its clones. The idea was to revive a whale with the memories of the original, and then study how it had been using that huge brain in the Miocene oceans.

By 2014 our groundbreaking experiment was showing signs of success. The male cetezoid was displaying signs of intelligence and language, and was teaching things to a female companion. It either wouldn't or couldn't communicate with us, but then we were probably rather daunting to it—or so we thought. If only we had known.

I began to have utterly vivid recollections of my past life, particularly of incidents that were excruciatingly embarrassing or stressful. The Miss Wonderful show played itself through several times as I sat at my desk, trying to work, and then one night I drifted away into a fantasy-recollection about a girl named Rosie.

It had been the end of the academic year, and one of my labwork partners invited me to his post-exam party. Jillian had been still studying for some honors component of a subject, but I was done for the year. I was not such a prude that I did not drink at all, but I limited it to two beers per hour and timed myself with my watch. Whatever my hangups, I did like to fit in with those I had to work with. It was only later that I discovered that someone had spiked all the open beer bottles with vodka. I was not a sufficiently seasoned drinker to tell the difference.

Rosie had just graduated as a student teacher. The night

had been hot, just like this one, and she was wearing a short cotton dress that showed off her figure to the best possible advantage. It was a really great figure, and her legs were more closely shaved than my cheeks. Jillian, by contrast, wore checked flannel shirts and jeans like a uniform. Rosie had homed in on me soon after she arrived, by which time I was just sufficiently drunk to relax a few of my defenses and inhibitions. She had a tanned and flawless skin, and was very pretty. While the party raged around us, she gave me all of her attention. I had had no experience dealing with charming, pretty women, and I was easily swept away.

She led me outside, supposedly to get away from the noise, and in the hot, dark air beneath the gleaming stars I realized that I could touch and fondle whatever I liked without any rejection. She caressed and fondled too, and I knew that I was already totally out of control by the time her tongue licked my ear and she whispered that her place was only a few streets away. We slipped out through the back gate and walked quickly, furtively, through the narrow streets and lanes.

The first time was across her bed, with my jeans around my ankles. Coins, keys and ballpoint pens went jingling onto the carpet. She was soft, she was marvellous, it actually felt good, better than my tethered imagination had ever dreamed possible.

That was an accident, I told myself the next morning as I walked home with my hangover in the bright sunlight. I rumpled my bedding to make it look slept in, swallowed aspirins and coffee, then tried to think things through. After even resorting to flowcharts to work out how Rosie had relieved me of my fidelity to Jillian so easily, I concluded that my inexperience was to blame rather than myself. I had been drinking, I was relaxing after months of tension, I had limited experience of the paths to seduction. Jillian dropped in for morning coffee, and innocently talked of nothing but her exams and what the questions might be.

Normality came screaming around my head, desperate to take me back into the fold. The night before had been a tipsy aberration, nothing more: I had to explain that to Rosie. I had to swear her to discretion, because if Jillian ever found out . . .

I had left a bag with my notes and books at the party house, and I called in at noon to get it back. Big Ed, my lab partner, still had a hangover as he answered my knock at the door. He guiltily told me about the vodka in the beer, then remembered something that he had been meaning to ask me.

"Jamie Brennan . . . I remember that name from somewhere, long, long ago. Been meaning to ask you about it."

I cringed inwardly, wondering if Ed had been a fan of the Miss Wonderful Show, and assuring myself that he could not possibly have been.

"That's it, the Miss Wonderful Show, back in the sixties! You told that joke about the tomato going red and she nearly wet herself. Hey, I laughed so much I fell off the chair."

"That was a long time ago," I began, but Big Ed slapped me on the back.

"Nuts to that, I thought you were great. I only watched the show because my older sisters hogged the TV and wouldn't let me watch Superman reruns. I always wanted to see that stuck up bitch of a Miss Wonderful get hers."

"You—you did?"

"Yeah! Man, that must have taken real guts. You were just a little kid and yet—oh wow!"

"My old man took the hairbrush to me for it."

"Hey, what did Miss Wonderful say?"

"She only called me a dirty little boy, but she was really pissed off."

"Great, great," laughed Big Ed, slapping his knee. "Let's have a beer to celebrate. No vodka this time, I promise."

"Thanks, but let me pop the can myself."

"Hey, how was Rosie?"

"What? Oh no—I—er, didn't . . ."

"You didn't? Don't try that one on me. You get her half peeled in my backyard, you sneak out the back gate with her so fast that you forget your bag, then you come back and try to tell me that you didn't even prong the woman! Hah."

"I, I—"

"Lucky bastard! *I* put it to her earlier and she poured a beer down my fly. Hey Jamie, you're up there with the winners. You know what else?"

"I'm not sure I'm strong enough to know."

"She phoned here this morning and got your address. She left *her* phone number too, and wants you to call her."

Discovering that I had been a hero for over a decade without knowing it came as quite a shock. As I left Big Ed's place and went looking for the discretion of a public phone I felt curiously elated. For the first time ever I could think back on the Miss Wonderful incident and laugh. I did not stop to reflect that my moral underpinnings had moved from rock-solid foundations to a thin plank over oblivion. I dialed Rosie's number, and she arranged to meet me for lunch at Poynton's Bar and Grill.

It was a hot, sweltry afternoon. Rosie was already there when I entered, at a table for two by the window. I sat down. We drank some wine and talked about minor details of our backgrounds, including my age. She bought us lunch, two juicy, underdone steaks with French salad. We drank more wine. The conversation kept trailing away into long silences. If I say nothing, maybe this will all go away, I thought, yet I needed to tell her about Jillian.

"You were just super last night," she said, her voice a silky contralto, barely more than a whisper. We were sitting at right angles, her legs now pressed against my knees.

"Don't get much practice," I replied, staring into the pale fluid cradled by a film of glass between my fingers. Such a thin, frail barrier, but not as thin as the cotton dress that exposed so much of her breasts and which ended at mid-thigh. "Things between me and my girlfriend, Jillian, are, er, not like that."

Be firm with her, my subconscious cried in despair. Last night could be excused, but to do it again would be the end of everything: my self-respect, my good name, my very self as I knew it. Tell her how sorry you are, my inner voice clamored. Tell her you love Jillian too much to betray her like that again.

"So there's trouble with Jillian?" Rosie asked, stroking the back of my hand. An occasional hand under the shirt was as far as I ever got with Jillian, and even that was a big concession for her.

"No trouble, things are always quiet with Jillian."

I let the words hang in the balance, yet did I hope that they would tip the scales in Rosie's direction?

"I know that you love her, I accept that," she answered. "She must be a really nice girl, and I do envy her in a way."

Now she turned her gaze to me, and lifted my face to hers with a fingertip. The words said that she would go, yet her smile said 'follow.' She was like the steaks we just had eaten . . . succulent. Grilled meat as a proposition! The rate of my pulse shot up again at the idea.

"Look, it really was nice, with you. Nicer than . . . well anything. I just can't explain it."

"Jamie, I'm sure it was better than it *ever* could be with Jillian, and do you know why?"

I was taken off guard. I opened my mouth to protest, then closed it and shook my head instead.

"Because it was naughty, it was just a little wicked. You need a little guilt for something to be really nice. Jamie, I've had a lot of boyfriends, but they tried to hold me down, take me over. Now I'm my own boss, yet I like a bit of steady company with some spice thrown in. You're nice, you're really bright, and you're a good screw as well. Too good to hold back. I bet you're getting nothing from Jillian, that's what you meant before, isn't it?"

"Rosie, it's not that sort of—"

"Yes, I know, but I'll tell you what: keep your true romance with her, but come over to my place for a night or two every week and let the animal out to have a run."

This was my watershed, this was where the battered knight could polish his armor as bright as the sun itself, or slip from his saddle and wallow in the mud. This was the difference between a hero redeemed and a filthy betrayer. I was on the balance. If I did nothing for long enough her composure would crack. She would cry, or get annoyed, or flirt with the barman. All you have to do is nothing, shouted my inner voice.

I slowly raised my hand . . . and as it descended the scales tipped, and I tumbled from my saddle. My hand came down on her thigh, with my thumb on bare flesh and my fingers on cotton fabric.

"Can the animal have a run on afternoons too?" I asked, aware that I was falling freely, irredeemably, yet savouring that lush and heady moment of surrender that stretched into hours. She nodded.

It was my second seduction by Rosie. No, I had done the seducing that time, because she had made it very clear that I had to ask—even though the answer was an assured yes. We walked from Poynton's Bar and Grill to her place without holding hands, and at a brisk pace.

We were not at all like lovers.

That moment, that hand descending to that thigh, was a turning point in my life. The fairytale relationship with Jillian dragged on for a few months more while I indulged in a great deal of sex with Rosie at every opportunity. On the surface it was an ideal way to have things, and when it finally became unstuck the parting was amicable.

My affair with Rosie lasted two years, until she went to a school overseas on some teacher exchange scheme. Even now—well, until the sea-call at any rate—we remained friends. Jillian's prudery grew steadily into more of a contrast with my own new attitudes. I began to insist on more intimate fondlings, then consummation. She resisted, she said the idea was disgusting. We began to drift apart. She finally struck up a strange relationship with the class nerd in Biochemistry 2, and they were still happily together when I lost touch with them in the early 1990s.

There now, my unknown reader, you have it all. As I see it, the cetezoid that we reconstructed had telepathic powers, and he was probing about in my memory to find a weakness common to all humans. The basic sea-call seems to depend on body mass alone, but humans could probably resist it. The cetezoid needed a second weakness. He found it, too, but it is not what you probably think. It was not fear of ridicule, or even sheer lust, but the willingness to change one's mind and try a new idea. All of us have that ability, all of us would rather let our hand drop to Rosie's thigh than wave farewell. Figuratively, at any rate.

A few days after my brain replayed the start of my affair with Rosie, the cetezoids escaped. Every so often they were transported in a truck to a university lab where they would be examined in certain benchmark tests. On this trip, our truck failed to take a bend, crashed through a safety rail and landed in a deep tidal gorge. All humans on the truck were drowned, but no trace was ever found of the two cetezoids.

As well as being a tragedy it was also a great setback to the project. Another clone was prepared for the memory transfer and the experiment started all over again. Eight months went by.

One morning I arrived at work and let myself into a high-security room in the computer centre. I felt an odd, almost sensual twinge of pleasure and surrender, then I awoke, battered and famished. My digital watch showed that five days had passed: five days in the secure room, five days while I did . . . what? My fingernails were torn, and the east wall was smeared with blood, as if I had been trying to claw and batter my way through it. I hobbled stiffly across the room and tapped the exit code into the door's touchpad. It opened at once. Outside, the corridors were empty and the phones were dead.

Glass in some windows was broken and bloodied, always those facing east. The sea was to the east. The drop from many of the broken windows was considerable. Crumpled heaps that had been my colleagues lay at the bases of several east walls.

I went to the Director's office suite. It was empty, and the glass door to the observation patio overlooking the beach was open. Taking a pair of field glasses from a rack I walked out to the rail and looked down. There was a sheer drop to the sand, and sand was blowing over a body wearing a familiar suit, directly below. A sea breeze wafted a sickly scent to me, something far more ominous than rotting seaweed. There was a scum on the water, and it extended a long way offshore. The field glasses resolved human corpses, the tide was thick with bodies. I had been lucky. Not many people had been in a place where they had to think to get out, and they had mindlessly obeyed a call to walk east into the sea.

I lowered the field glasses and shambled inside, flopping heavily into the Director's chair and shutting the world out with my hands while I first absorbed the shock, then tried to think it through. There was the memory of a memory . . . I tried to think calmly. It was impossible. I gave up, surrendered, accepted that I was doomed . . . and piece by piece ideas and memories began to fall into place.

A hand wavering, then descending to a thigh: it was an act of deliberate surrender, something that I would do again if given the option. For someone else it might be reversed: the abandoning of lechery for religion, for example. Eight years ago I had thought a lot about that incident, and it was not long before the inexplicable accident when two cetezoids had escaped. The cetezoids! Thousands, perhaps millions of people had been called to the sea. My lapses eight years earlier had stopped not long before the cetezoids had escaped.

Subsequent research with the remaining pair and new clones suggested that the species once had a very advanced society. There were indications of complex rituals and behavior, and an advanced language full of unintelligible concepts. If they had reached such a level of sophistication, and if individuals bore scars from fighting . . . did they have wars? If so, what were their weapons? Could I recognize them as such? An ancient Greek might know a spear-wound when he saw one, but what would he make of radiation burns, or a human shadow burned into the wall of a building? If cetezoid tusks were only for formal duels, their weapons of war might be unrecognizable. They could not have bred great numbers in eight years, but they probably rallied the existing populations of whales and dolphins and taught them to fight us.

Concentrating very hard, I tried to recall what I had been thinking of in the secure room before the oblivion. There it was, as faint as the distant gleam of an OBU in the evening sky: the memory of a hand descending to a thigh. Surrender.

Surrender to new ideas is the glory of the human race, it is the powerhouse of creativity. Einstein had once surrendered his belief in Newtonian mechanics, in fact all progress is due to abandoning old ideas for something better. I refused to feel guilt about my surrender in Poynton's Bar and Grill on that hot afternoon in the mid-seventies— yet right or wrong, it is a weak point in the human mind. Everyone has their own private watersheds, moments when they have abandoned something. The cetezoids somehow used that moment of surrender.

Human dominance of the material world had dipped us in the waters of the Styx and made us as invulnerable as Achilles with heel armor . . . yet Achilles' brain, too, had not been in contact with the enchanted waters. A single, well-aimed arrow from an unrecognizable Miocene weapon would sink straight in. I could have waved good-bye to Rosie instead of touching her thigh, but my hand descended. When I woke up from the sea-call it had been descending for five days.

Ideas flicked through my mind, like abstracts in a scanner. This was like a neutron bomb, it destroyed people but left buildings intact. Intact for what? Cetezoids could not leave the water and take over our cities. Still, it was an answer, even if it was incomplete. I took out my pocket diary and scribbled a few lines of explanation. Where to leave the message? In the Director's office? Yes, in the middle of the desk, held down by his meteorite paper-weight. When they came they would check his office first ... when *who* came? I left it there anyway.

I found two lengths of chain touchlocks, and as I moved about the Institute I kept myself chained to at least one fixture at all times. If a second strike came I would be rendered mindless again by the cetezoids' weapon, but I could not unchain myself without thinking.

I decided that my next warning would be broadcast to the world. I tried several hand-held cell-comms, but although the batteries were charged, I got no replies. Still, I broadcast my message, hoping that someone would hear even if I could not receive them. Each truck owned by the Institute had a radio, so I decided to chain myself to the steering column, then drive slowly inland, broadcasting my message as I went. I had to think to steer, so I would be safe. I would rig up a dead hand switch for the brakes in case a sea-call came while I was driving.

If people were walking they could cover no more than 300 miles in five days, so there were bound to be many people still left. I could tell them what was really happening, show them how to tether themselves against the oblivion of a sea-call. I went to the cafeteria, found some sealed health bars and ate them quickly, then packed food for a week. Next I went looking for a truck. The parking lot was empty.

The nearest suburb was a mile away, and along an un-fenced road through a flat, open stretch of parkland. There was nothing to chain myself to, not a tree, not a fencepost. The only other road followed the coastline to the university, and walking that one was out of the question. My next thought was to join together a mile of chain, but that would also allow me to reach the sea if the cetezoids used their weapon again.

I stared down the road from the perimeter of the Miocene Institute with tears on my cheeks. I would have to walk it without being tethered, and if another sea-call came, my mind would be seized by the Miocene Arrow through that window of surrender . . . unless I could close it.

Could I bring myself not to let my hand drop to Rosie's leg? Could I deny my watershed, the turning point in my whole outlook? In a facile sense it was easy to say yes, yet I had to *really* believe it if I wanted immunity from the cetezoids' sea-call. I needed that immunity if I wanted to walk untethered down the road from the Miocene Institute to relative safety. "It wasn't wrong!" I shouted down the road, yet I knew that it was not a case of right or wrong. I was vulnerable because I was willing to question my own beliefs in some circumstances. My own pride and self-respect would never let me give up the right to do that, and an incorporeal hand would always be poised to seize me. I clung to the bars of the Institute's gate, shouting obscenities at the sea and at myself.

Well, now I have come full circle with my story. A grubby little episode of student infidelity has brought down civilisation as we know it. The sea-call now works on all large mammals, but I suspect that humans had not been susceptible until I provided a window. Dear reader, if it is any comfort to you, my days and nights in Rosie's bed were truly wonderful.

Ah, the sky is getting light outside, and it is time that I

was getting into my truck and releasing the safety catch on my fully automatic, gas-operated, magazine-fed assault rifle. I shall exchange this diary with my earlier rough notes beneath the late Director's meteorite paperweight, and most likely I shall vanish from the pages of history forever. Maybe I'll live though, in DNA with avian genes spliced in to make my descendants immune to the sea-call.

Goodbye, reader, and wish me luck. They say the only truly brave people are the frightened ones who overcome their fears. Just now I am very, very frightened.

Dr. James Brennan: BSc, MSc, PhD.

"Good fortune go with you, James Brennan," said Vander Hannan as he closed the folder on the sheaf of pages.

Darien had given the gun to Theresla and was massaging her stiff fingers, but she stared at him and arched her eyebrows as if to say, Well, what did you think? Vander sat back in the chair and closed his eyes for a moment.

"There are many legends of how the Call came into being, Semme Darien. Why should I believe this one in particular?"

"Because it is true," Theresla answered for her.

"Truth needs proof, or it might as well be a lie."

Theresla considered for some moments.

"Ask me some mysteries."

"Does my mother live?"

"Yes, she is south of Forian and seems to be traveling to the Colandoro border."

"What? How do you know?"

"Uh-uh. Proof may be obtained by sending a dispatch to the Bartolican envoy in Denver. Tell her to write when she arrives. Next question?"

"What about an explanation of why inexperienced teen-age Yarronese flyers can match Bartolican wardens victory for victory, while our carbineers triumph in every battle?"

"The Yarronese youths supposedly have six victories for every loss. One of them has twenty-five."

Vander went white, but did not react otherwise. The true losses were known to only a dozen men west of the Yarronese border. How could she have known? That was a question she would not answer, of course.

"Then tell me why," said Vander.

"The Yarronese are good, but not as good as that. There is an aviad wingfield in the eastern Callscour lands. Your wings are being stolen and flown there while being written off as battle losses. I think they are to be used in Australican wars, but even I don't know everything. I keep hearing the term Miocene Arrow in connection with your wings. Have you heard it as well?"

"No," Vander admitted. "Were you serious about my mother being alive?"

"She must be at least forty pounds lighter, but she is alive and uninjured. Write to Denver, check for yourself."

"And if you convince me, then what? What do you want?"

Theresla sauntered across and leaned on the back of Vander's chair.

"You are regarded as too patriotic for some of the secrets that are currently being whispered in the Condelor palace, Sair Hannan. This war is *not* in Bartolica's interests, you see. We can provide you with those secrets, and a few more besides."

"What do you want in return?"

"Acting Inspector General, we want you to do what any loyal Bartolican warden and patriot would do."

5 | BROTHER GLASKEN

4 October 3960: Forian

Rollins' first view of Forian filled him with a mixture of awe and dismay. It was a bigger and older city than Median, and while it also had the advantage of ancient city walls, the walls of Forian were many times thicker and twice as high. Built in an age when the cart cannon ruled, they had long been swamped by outer suburbs of the Yarronese capital. Houses, towers, churches, and picturesque footbridges had encrusted the massive and ancient walls since the wardenate system had begun, but now there were only the stumps of all that left, and the walls again stood clear above the outer city in defense of the Airlord's palace and inner suburbs. A hundred and twenty trams were in the marshaling yards, with their carriage guns concentrated on the western walls, while cart cannons were dispersed through the outer city, adding their heavier shells to the bombardment.

Since the war began the Bartolicans had become renowned for taking advantage of a Call's passage. Although Calls disrupted both sides equally on the Mexhaven battlefields, in this war the Bartolican carbineers always recovered faster. This was the way that they had taken Middle Junction, Green River, Median, Kennyville, and the whole of Montras. Forian proved a lot harder. The city had been given time by the brief death struggles of the western and middle cities, and the Bartolicans were greeted with mines, booby traps, and ancient stone walls defended by

thousands of well-supplied reaction guns and more cart
cannons than the Bartolicans could bring to bear.

A Call blanketed the city battlefield a week after Rollins
arrived with his black tram. It was a sign of desperation
that the Bartolicans were willing to risk their precious and
enigmatic black trams merely for the sake of their additional roof guns. Now that it was early October the high
command wanted a result from the fighting. Rollins heard
Call handbells being rung in the distance and strapped
himself into the driver's seat of the tram.

The world stopped.

He awoke, as usual, to find the day more advanced and
his body fatigued with three hours of trying to mindlessly
escape his straps and walk west. As Rollins watched the
Bartolican guns began firing again. The tram's four-inch
carriage gun added its voice to the barrage; then all was
drowned by a massive explosion that seemed to lift a section of the city's walls and dump it to shatter like a clod
of earth. When the pall of dust and smoke had cleared a
smoothly sloping pile of rubble beckoned to the besieging
Bartolicans. Rollins quickly climbed to the roof of his tram
for a better view.

"There they go, as usual our carbineers were in the right
place at the right time again," said one of the men working
the carriage gun.

"What was that huge explosion?" asked Rollins.

"Hah, same as at Median. Those dead-hump Yarronese
store their shells in the walls to save on the real estate for
a proper bunker. We only had to land one shell on it, and
it's come on in folks."

In some ways it made sense. Centuries of having wardens and squires fight limited, chivalric wars in the air had
replaced the military common sense of the ancients with
practical economic expediency. Why prepare for a besieging army that would not ever arrive?

The bull-ant swarm of Bartolican carbineers ran unim-
peded over the rubble of the wall, went over the top, and

vanished from view. Of course there would be days of fighting to tame the rest of the inner city.

The massed chattering of reaction guns rolled out over the city like hail on a slate roof. Heavy reaction guns, the type that carbineers did not carry. The swarm on the rubble of the wall slowed and stopped as the carbineers sought cover. The chatter of reaction guns continued as the carbineers already inside either hid or fought for their lives against overwhelming firepower. At a mirrorflash signal from the Bartolican command center the two gunners loaded another four-inch shell and aimed just behind the walls of Forian. The bombardment from the tram sidings began again.

"Someone must've learned their lesson in Median," said the gunner's jack as he cranked another shell up from below.

"How's the supply holding?" asked the gunner.

"Crayon code says we got nineteen after this one."

"Nineteen! What happened to the hundred we started with?"

"Fifteen at Median, the rest hereabouts. They don't grow on bushes, Lek. We should ease off."

"We can't ease off. You know what shit we get for doing our own act, even if we're right sometimes. If they want to fight on empty, that's orders. Hey, we're like wheels in a machine. One wheel might think it's a good idea to go faster or slower, but then your whole machine's got a problem."

By late afternoon the Bartolican attack had been repulsed after the carriage guns had exhausted their shells in close synchronization. The cart cannons boomed on for a short time, then were silent as well. Rumors circulated that two thousand carbineers had died. Official word was that the attack had achieved its aims. There was still an hour of light left when the cart cannons of the Yarronese opened fire from behind the walls. The range was extreme, but the rain of shells was intense while it lasted. The Yarronese were letting the Bartolicans know that they were in full control behind the walls. To an untutored eye the damage was minimal, but one black tram received a direct hit and was blown apart.

The area was cleared of all carbineers as merchant officers collected the snowstorm of paper, cards, and fragments of machines amid the scattered remains of the prisoners. Carabas was in charge of the operation, and because he was trusted Rollins was posted as a guard and given an assault carbine. He walked amid scattered cards punched with holes. Littering the place were thousands of little wooden beads, some still strung on lengths of wire. The pedalframe was draped with a sheet while two dozen bodies went untouched, but the wounded were quickly taken away on stretchers, all with gags over their mouths.

Rollins knew that guards watched the guards, and that he was sure to be searched. He picked up nothing, he touched nothing. Later that night he was told to take his black tram south of Forian, and it was stationed in a siding system that was still under construction. Nearby was a village named Somergate, a recreation reserve for officers with high security clearances. The local Yarronese had been completely cleared out—whether they had been shot or just sent packing Rollins never knew. He was to spend the winter there, sharing a cottage with three other drivers, who drank a lot of ale and played cards for looted coins. They were amiable enough and left him alone to read and think.

At night he would lie awake in bed running through his mental logbook of messages sent in the peeping language.

/4 October 3960, leaving Forian, going south/
* calculor hurt in siege and lobe 9 destroyed
# what about Forian
* Forian stands attack failed
# condelor airlord asking for victory date

* tell condelor to go hump—never expose calculor
   again
what to tell condelor airlord
* to save carbineers we will starve forian over winter
(pause)
what about another attack
* we lost 2117 carbineers killed and used all our
   shells
so many?
* more but wounded not included
(pause)
siege carbineers will have to be supplied over winter
* we will send a tramload of gold to pay
(pause)
airlord agrees but not happy

It was obvious that the two signalers had thrown procedures to the winds in the panic after the loss of the black
tram. In all his time as driver Rollins had never heard such
plain speaking encoded as when he was driving out of
Forian and listening to the peeping of the machine behind
and above him. What was abundantly clear was that the
Airlord Leovor the VII of Greater Bartolica had answered
a proposal from Carabas almost instantly while over three
hundred miles away in Condelor. What was equally obvious was that the black trams were somehow a single unit,
which was almost alive.

5 October 3960: Casper

Even for the victors, there is death in warfare. War does
not reward the just and virtuous any more than it punishes
the unjust and evil. There are simply victors, vanquished,
and the dead. A week after the battle above Seminoe Pass
the victors gathered at the Casper wingfield to honor the
known and presumed dead of both sides. The day was

overcast and windy, and although light rain spattered the mourners from time to time, the chill on the air meant that the end of the flying season was not far away.

"This youth Serjon, these battles, they all say the same thing," Sartov mused as he stood watching the field heralds prepare the death pennants that were about to be burned. "We are far better in the air."

Fieldmajor Gravat was beside him, adjusting his pennant sash. The cold wind tugged at their clothing as it blustered across the Casper wingfield, and even the honor guard of gunwings was being tied and pegged down by the guildsmen.

"True, they lose three, four, even five wings for every one of ours," Gravat replied.

"On the ground their forces maul ours with a tenth as many carbineers, but not at Seminoe Pass. There they were far from any tramway, and there we stopped them."

"The Bartolicans have Callwalkers among us to spy and cause mayhem. Could it be that they are somehow tied to the tramways?"

It was not an idea that had crossed Sartov's mind, and he thought it over as lines of guildsmen came marching through the light rain to stand behind the glittering figures of the air carbineers.

"Spying and sabotage would be useless without a strong fighting force that can sweep in and seize control," Sartov finally decided. "No, there is something more than Callwalkers here. Where am I going wrong, Fieldmajor, what am I missing?"

"Bartolican tactical control is nothing less than inspired. True, our people have made blunders and had disasters, but credit to the Bartolican merchant commanders cannot be denied. It is as if they see everything like the players at a chessboard."

Sartov liked the analogy and stood considering it as the spots of rain continued to patter down on him and a distant brass band played a march for the dead. Chess was all tactics, bluff, and logic, yet chess was also the ability to peer godlike down on a diorama. Both sides had scout sailwings to gather information, yet the Bartolicans made better use of what they learned and their forces were always optimized at any battle—except for Seminoe Pass.

"Are you wondering if the Callwalkers may be doing more than spying and sabotage?" asked Gravat.

"I am not wondering, Fieldmajor, I am certain. Come now, time to honor the dead."

One by one Sartov fed the pennants of the dead to the flames of boost spirit in the wingfield's torch of remembrance.

"As the flames of compression spirit took you to the clouds, so now do the flames of compression spirit take you back to the clouds," the chaplain intoned over the torch as each pennant burned. The commoner flyers were represented by a name written on a strip of parachute silk, but they were given the same time and deference. Finally the pennants of the Bartolicans were burned. A squad of carbineers fired a volley into the air and the patrol sailwing swooped low over the ranks of Yarronese mourners and the Bartolican wardens and flyers who had survived being shot down. A trumpeter played "Dirge of the Warden"; then the chaplain led prayers for a quick end to the war.

As Bronlar was walking back to the guild tents she heard someone call her name. She turned to see Chancellor Sartov approaching.

"How are you feeling?" he asked as he caught up with her and steered her toward a line of gunwings. "I hear you have a cold."

"My head is clear, Chancellor," she replied briskly, as close to being at attention as she could be while still being at ease. "I can ascend without hurt to my eardrums."

"That's good, we need you in the air. Two wardens are on your tally of vanquished wings, and you are a worthy match for anyone over Yarron."

"Thank you."

Serjon was standing beside one of the gunwings, shivering and miserable as he pulled a greatcoat over his flight jacket. Fieldmajor Gravat and several officers and wardens were waiting with him.

"This is Flockleader Serjon Feydamor," said Gravat as the Chancellor and Bronlar stopped before them.

"They call you Warden Killer, you have had twenty-five victories in clear air war duels," said Sartov.

"I have been lucky," began Serjon.

"Pah! Nobody has twenty-five lucky victories. Serjon, Bronlar, we *should* honor your skill and bravery, we *should* parade you before our weary flyers and carbineers to give them heart. The truth is that we are fighting for our very survival. We need you up there and fighting or in the guild tents teaching other flyers."

"Ah, very sensible, Chancellor," said Bronlar.

"The Bartolican prisoners complained about the silks of commoners being burned before those of the Bartolican wardens. I ordered that they be loaded with chains and be made to walk from Casper to Sheridan with the refugees."

"Appropriate and fair," replied Bronlar.

"Now I have orders for you, Semme Bronlar Jemarial and Sair Serjon Feydamor. This morning a coded order was flown in by pigeon from Forian. It was from the Airlord of Yarron himself. He wants the services of our two finest flyers to get something out of the capital. I have chosen you two."

Serjon and Bronlar glanced at each other.

"With respect, sair, others have more victories over wardens than me," responded Bronlar.

"But you weigh very little, Semme Bronlar, and your load of fuel and cargo will be heavy. Serjon will provide you an escort in his gunwing."

Bronlar was slightly taken aback that her weight seemed more important than her worth to the Chancellor, but she let it pass.

"With respect, Chancellor, Forian is under siege and

aswarm with enemy sailwings and gunwings," Serjon now pointed out. "A whole flock of gunwings might do better than two."

"A flock would attract a lot of unwelcome attention. Two is better. I have arranged for a sailwing to be stripped down to a single tank and pair of reaction guns. Say the word and I shall have your pennant painted on the nose, Bronlar. Well? I want volunteers, even though I want the best."

A Calltower bell began to ring in the distance, signaling that a Call would be there in fifteen minutes. Guildsmen began to untie five of the patrol sailwings, and disconsolate flyers trudged out of their tents to prepare to ascend into the cold and turbulent sky.

Serjon shrugged and spread his gloved hands. "When do we leave?"

"Before the paint is dry."

Bronlar gasped.

"You want me to fly in a sailwing that my guildsmen have not checked?" she said. "The insult to them would be profound."

"The guildsmen doing the work are mine, and when you are in the air I shall go to your guildmasters and tender my personal apologies."

"The weather is not exactly optimal," Serjon pointed out.

"You are free to decline," said Sartov.

"No, no, I, ah, just like people to know, ah, what they may not know—but probably do know."

It was only ten minutes later that one sailwing and one gunwing with Yarronese markings ascended for the trip to Forian. The winds were difficult at first, but the weather improved as they flew south. The Laramie Mountains rolled below them for a time, then they followed the tramway rails to the besieged city, flew over the ancient walls, and aligned on the massive towers of the palace. They landed without incident, but although a crew of guildsmen rushed out to meet them and drag the wings to shelter, there was no official on hand except for the adjunct and some guildmasters.

"What are we to do now?" Bronlar asked the adjunct.

"Attend court, Semme. A cloak, swordrig, and feather-drew are awaiting you at the palace entrance, and you must present the credentials that Chancellor Sartov gave you—but you are not needed yet, Semme. Court was only called when your sailwing landed."

"And me?" asked Serjon.

"Why, you are the escort flockleader!" declared the adjunct as if Serjon had uttered the silliest words imaginable. "You must keep watch over the sailwing with these guildsmen."

Serjon shrugged, folded his arms, and stared intently at Bronlar's sailwing until the adjunct muttered something about commoners and went away. Guildsmen refueled the wings and installed a wicker seat where the central tanks had been in Bronlar's aircraft.

"It is a fact that wingtanks get hit six times more often than central tanks," said Bronlar.

"And you only have wingtanks," Serjon pointed out on cue. "Does this worry you?"

"Yes."

A liaisory arrived, read Bronlar's credentials, and led her away through the shell-pocked gardens to the palace itself. The place was already bleak with autumn, and cart cannons were firing in the distance every minute or so. The liaisory told her to wait in an antechamber just outside the throne hall, then entered and was soon lost from sight amid the crowd. A middle-aged man walked up from behind Bronlar and stood waiting with her. He had only one arm, but wore the pennant sash of a warden.

"I only have to do this once more," he said, twirling a large, silver circlet on his wrist. "Are you Bronlar Jemarial?"

"Yes. Ah, are you another liaisory?" she replied tentatively.

"Oh sorry, I'm Virtrian the Twelfth, Airlord of Yarron," he said, extending his hand, the circlet of office still dangling from his wrist.

Bronlar goggled. His hand was vertical, not horizontal, so he probably meant it to be shaken, not kissed. She shook his hand.

"I apologize, I'm sorry for not recognizing you," she stammered, waving her hands like the propellers of a regal.

"Why? The coronation medallions are not a good likeness. So, you are the Bronlar who shot down sixteen Bartolican wings. You must be good."

"I, ah, survive well, and ah, just a bit more."

"Yarron should follow your example. Now *there's* a good phrase. To survive, Yarron must do more than merely survive. I'm planning to make you a warden, Semme Bronlar. Does that please you?"

"A warden!" Bronlar's thoughts boiled for a moment. "The intention pleases me beyond words, your, er, Airlord, sair—"

"Virtrian is my name. Lordship is the casual term of address for nobles."

"Ah, Lordship, I . . . would rather you did not. I'm sorry—"

"Explain please, oh and please address me as Saireme Airlord out in court or the heralds will get all twitchy."

Bronlar giggled for a moment, and the Airlord pressed his lips together as if holding back a smile.

"Lordship, the air defense of the realm has been carried by Air Carbineers in the fighting of the weeks past. They are a mix of wardens, squires, and flyers, but they are mainly commoner flyers. If you make me a warden, you honor *me* but that's all. If you grant me an insignia as a commoner flyer, you establish royal favor for all your loyal Yarronese commoner flyers."

He placed the silver circlet on his head, then grasped

the stump of his left arm and stood staring at her.

"Where were you when I was appointing my Centrium of Advisers, Semme Bronlar? You are loyal, brave, honest, and intelligent: I have never seen all four of those virtues in one person before. Are there other girls in the Air Carbineers?"

"Only two, and three in training."

"Sartov is a clever man, that is why . . ." His expression was downcast for a moment, but he quickly brightened. "Shall we go in now, together? Take my arm and we— no, that would imply that we are to be engaged and we hardly know each other. Tell what, put your right hand on your sword pommel and keep your left out like this for me to hold. That is processional form for my defense advisers, you see—and take off that stupid cloak and featherdrew hat. Why dress as a mere courtier when you are a warrior? Be proud of the gold threadwork on that flight jacket, girl, put your chest out, raise your nose into the air, and *be superior*!"

Numb with astonishment, Bronlar walked into the throne hall with the Airlord of Yarron. He did not lead her to the place indicated by the liaisory, or even to the arc of advisers, but up the steps to stand on the right of his throne. He sat down, slumped weary but alert before his court, and made a gesture to the presiding herald. Bronlar stood with her feet apart and her hand on the sword, staring intently at a pennon over the doors at the other end of the throne hall and trying to pretend that the place was empty.

"Attend the Airlord," the herald cried out clearly after banging his ornate mace three times on the floor.

The Airlord did not stand, but stayed slouched in the throne looking as if he had had three hours' sleep in as many days. At last he spoke.

"Loyal subjects of the dominion, the citizens of Yarron, I wish to introduce my newest military adviser, Air Carbineer Bronlar Jemarial, who with sixteen air victories is one of Yarron's greatest living air warriors. Before we entered, Semme Bronlar gave me these words for you and for all loyal citizens of Yarron: *To survive, Yarron needs to do more than merely survive.*"

He let the words sink in, and allowed the court scribe to catch up before going on.

"Accordingly, I have decided to make two pronouncements. First, *all* flyers will have royal favor henceforth. They have been fighting with dedication and valor, and they are all that stand between Yarron and oblivion. Air Carbineer Bronlar Jemarial, I grant you an insignia: crossed feline claws, argent—Bronlar, would you like the white rose of my house between the claws?"

He got it wrong, the claws on my engine's cowling are red, I'll have to have them repainted, screamed a voice within Bronlar's head. "I would be honored, Saireme Airlord," Bronlar replied crisply, staring straight ahead.

"Note that down in whatever the correct wording may be, herald. Secondly . . . as your Airlord I have failed to drive back the Bartolican invaders at nearly every battle, and now their cart cannons bombard Forian's very walls even as I speak."

From anyone else the words would have been treason, and there were stifled gasps from some of the courtiers.

"Accordingly, I shall now board a sailwing and be flown to Casper by Semme Jemarial. There I shall abdicate in favor of Chancellor Sartov. Sartov presided over our victory against Dorak, and has formed the Air Carbineers that have slashed the cream of Bartolican wardenry out of the skies and trained the carbineers who halted the Bartolicans at Seminoe Pass. *He* is the leader that Yarron needs in this black hour. I shall request that I be allowed to return here as City Chancellor of Forian. My intention had been to surrender Forian to the besiegers, to avoid the obscenity of slaughter, violation, pillage, and vandalism that marked the fall of Median. Semme Jemarial's words brought me to my senses, however: *To survive, Yarron needs to do more than merely survive.* I shall advise Airlord Sartov that

I am willing to lead Forian's resistance against the Bartolicans, and bleed them white for as long as possible. If my citizens are willing to stand with me, we may yet save Yarron. Herald, close proceedings."

So that's why he was so offhanded and casual, Bronlar realized. The ashen-faced herald banged his mace on the floor again.

"The words of the Airlord Virtrian have been spoken," he said in a steady but higher-pitched voice.

The Airlord now stood up and unpinned his cloak, letting it fall to the floor to reveal a flight jacket. The jacket was a blaze of paisley swirls in gold thread on purple, with dark green jade bullets lining the shoulder greaves. The thin circlet of office remained on his head as he descended the steps with Bronlar. As they stood waiting at the base of the throne dais the crowded throne hall was in absolute silence. The scribe appeared moments later with a scroll of proceedings, wax was poured, and the Airlord impressed his ring onto his final decree. He then marched from the throne hall with Bronlar beside him. No others followed.

"I apologize for putting you to so much trouble, Semme, but this is the best I can do for Yarron."

Bronlar was too astonished to reply.

"Back there, was that a sensible decision?" he asked as they emerged into the open air.

"I—I am a guildmaster's daughter, and you are an airlord. Your decisions are to be followed, not questioned."

"But were you pleased?"

"You acted with bravery and wisdom, Saireme—ah, Lordship Virtrian. That pleased me."

The guildsmen fluttered about the Airlord as they arrived at the wingfield. Bronlar quickly went up to Serjon, who was standing by his gunwing, and explained what had happened in court.

"That should have been *you* in there, being honored by the Airlord," she said as she took his hand. Serjon did not

seem concerned, but he flinched at the touch of her cold
fingers.

"I'm not good in crowds. Besides, I spoke with the
guildmaster of the ground crew while you were gone. The
Airlord asked for you in particular."

"And I know why. He was using me to humiliate his
own nobles and courtiers. I'm a girl as well as a commoner
flyer, I made the perfect rod to beat them with. In a way
I was insulted, Serjon."

"You're the Airlord's weapon, whether flying a sailwing
or standing around in court," said Serjon, still seeming to
genuinely not care. "I'm touched that you thought of me,
but really I think that the Airlord chose wisely."

"But Serjon—"

"But nothing. Let's plan how to get back to Casper
alive."

The weather was no better on the way back, but Bronlar
and Serjon successfully flew the Airlord to Casper wingfield by the evening. Sartov was made Airlord of Yarron
in the City Chancellor's palace, and next morning Bronlar
and Serjon flew the abdicant back to Forian.

Chancellor Virtrian went on to lead the capital's defense
through the autumn, winter, and early spring. The five
months of desperate, bloody struggle stalled and weakened
the entire Bartolican advance in eastern Yarron, and when
the Bartolican carbineers finally broke through the battered, ruined city's walls it was no glittering prize for all
their trouble.

5 October 3960: Wind River

Maesterrin had not been allowed to sleep for more than
minutes since he had been taken prisoner in Casper. It
might have been ten days ago, it might have been fifteen,
it might have even been a month: he had no way of knowing. He had been gagged and hooded before being put

aboard a regal and flown west. He knew it to be west, because aviads had a birdlike magnetic sense that allowed them to "feel" direction. Maesterrin had counted slowly for the whole trip, and he knew the cruising speed of regals. From all this he estimated that he was somewhere just east of the Wind River Range and north of the Red Desert. This would be of use when he escaped. *When* he escaped. Like all the aviad infiltrators he held humans in contempt and had no doubt that he would quickly outwit them.

He was proved wrong. There was the scent of pine trees and recent rain on the air when the regal landed, and the walk to his prison was 1,670 steps northeast of the wing-field. He was untied, changed into a light bushfiber smock, then tied again. At last his blindfold was removed. The room was cold, but brightly lit by high lamps. An inter-rogator entered, a well-spoken but thickset man wearing a tight-fitting knitted hood. His eyes were blue, Maesterrin could see that.

The Yarronese knew his name, place in the tramway system, and details since arriving at Casper. They also knew that he was what they called a Callwalker. They had somehow worked out the hair test—or there was a traitor among his comrades. Maesterrin refused to even acknowledge his name at first, but the Yarronese were masters at applying pain. A slight squeeze to his elbow would send a thunderflash of agony through his body, and they could do worse with his knees. He eked out information, some true, some false. The interrogator took it all down: how he came from north of Alberhaven, where he had grown up in a lost tribe of Callwalkers. When they had wandered into Alberhaven in search of new hunting grounds the humans there had captured them, then convinced them to become part of a scheme to conquer Yarron in return for gunwing technology from Bartolica.

Maesterrin ate his meager meals of watery soup and dried fruit straight from the bowl, as his hands remained tied at all times. His legs were untied, so that he could visit the privy pot in one corner at will. It was seldom emptied.

One night—or day—the interrogator came in with a clipboard and left the door open behind him. Maesterrin wondered if security was growing slack, but when the interrogator took him by the arm and led him outside he saw that three very alert carbineers were waiting to guard him.

"We are disappointed with you, Fras Maesterrin," said the interrogator as they walked.

Maesterrin flinched at the form of address from the other side of the world. He pressed his lips together as the interrogator went on.

"Little of what you have told us bears any resemblance to the truth, but that is of no concern to us. We have most of the truth already, thanks to your friends."

The aviad had been warned about such tactics in basic training, and Captain Harmondes had drilled his squad over and over in interrogation methods. What they could understand they could resist. The Yarronese were splitting up the prisoners, and trying to turn them against each other. Some would break, but the others could not afford to verify the betrayals of their weaker comrades. They emerged from the starkly bare internment area of the building into a warmer corridor, with carpets on the floors and tapestries on the walls. There was darkness beyond the windows, so it was night. There were guards here too, but the atmosphere was more relaxed. The scent of roast bird was on the air, and onions, and herbs. They passed through a heavily guarded door into an apartment whose table contained the remains of a rich and elegant dinner. Even the cooling scraps made Maesterrin's mouth water.

"You disappoint us, Fras Maesterrin, we are only trying to be friendly—and thorough," said the interrogator, who now stepped behind Maesterrin and tied a gag firmly over his mouth.

A carbineer unlocked yet another door, but this one was

lit by only a dim, blue light within. The interrogator guided the aviad in, and the guard locked the door behind them. There were two comfortable chairs facing a drawn curtain.

"The window behind this is triple glazed, so no sound can pass. A one-way mirror faces the, ah, subjects on the other side, however."

He drew the curtain. There, in a brightly lit bedchamber, Captain Harmondes sprawled naked as a woman straddled him, moving rhythmically, her breasts brushing his chest with erect nipples. Maesterrin sat up with a muffled squark, his eyes wide. She had wavy, unbound brown hair that bounced like long springs as she moved.

"We don't really need your information at all, Fras Maesterrin, we already have more than you probably know. This place is actually a breeding center for little Callwalkers—or aviads, as you call yourselves."

Harmondes reached his arms around the woman and held her close, then rolled over on top of her. Maesterrin wanted to close his eyes, yet could not help but watch.

"It would never do to have uncooperative Callwalker fathers, I mean what woman wants memories of some tortured, pathetic enemy as the father of her child? It would be rape of the father, nothing more and nothing less. You will never go free, Fras Maesterrin, but each captured Callwalker is invited to join this program by proving his goodwill toward us. That proof is full disclosure of all that you know."

Maesterrin watched the scene beyond the one-way window. His captain had considerable endurance, in spite of the heavy meal that the couple had enjoyed. The interrogator explained that each woman stayed with the Callwalkers for three days, at her most fertile time of month.

"There is currently a backlog, but Harmondes has been good enough to do some, ah, matinee work to keep the program on schedule. Your help would be appreciated by all concerned."

Maesterrin collapsed on the way back to his cell, and

the carbineers had to carry him. He was placed on the stone floor, his eyes staring but unfocused. The interrogator untied his gag and stood back.

"I've ordered an extra handful of Sennerese dates to be included with your next bowl of soup, just as a gesture of goodwill on my own part."

Maesterrin pushed himself up from the floor, turning to look up at the interrogator. It took some seconds for him to blink the tears out of his eyes and focus on the man's hooded face.

"My name is Fras Micael Maesterrin, Lieutenant First Class in the Macedon Infiltration Unit. I was born in the Mayorate of Rochester on the ninth of August in the Year of Greatwinter's Waning 1705. That's 3941 in your calendar. Rochester is on a continent on the other side of the world, Australica. I was recruited to the Infiltration Unit while studying at the University of Technology in Macedon, but it was not until I was trained and put aboard a very large wing powered by sunlight to come here that I was told my mission . . ."

Maesterrin was taken out of the cell and bathed, clothed, and fed a small but tasty meal while he continued to pour out his background. The hooded interrogator stayed with him all the while, prompting and asking for clarifications from time to time. As dawn lit up the hills outside the window two silent footmen brought in breakfast and set it out with polished silver and tablecloths.

"Not all of what you have said is entirely correct, Fras Maesterrin," concluded the interrogator as the aviad ate, "but you may have been making honest mistakes. Do not trouble yourself, though, we shall return and do counterchecks with your story and those of the others until all is consistent. The important thing is goodwill, you see. Now I must go. Even interrogators get tired."

Maesterrin paused between mouthfuls of toast, puzzled. There was a second setting at the table. The interrogator closed a door behind him. Presently another door opened.

A woman entered. She was wearing a calf-length pleated skirt of the style currently popular in Yarron, and long, black curls framed a delicate, round face. Her eyes were shining and her expression eager; she reminded Maesterrin more of a patriot than a whore.

"Are you really a Callwalker?" she asked breathlessly as she reached the table.

The aviad swallowed a piece of toast unchewed. "Yes, but that is not our name for ourselves."

"Oh I'm sorry, my name is Demelkie. I volunteered for—oh, this is so embarrassing. I was told some real Callwalkers had come from a distant place to help us, and that the Bartolicans are trying to kill them. I would be so proud to be the mother of a Callwalker. My husband and I have discussed this all, and, ah, we really want to raise your Callwalker child for Yarron."

When Maesterrin eventually fell asleep in her arms he was quite unaware that Captain Harmondes had never admitted anything but his name. The captain had merely been asked to participate in the Callwalker breeding program—then been covertly displayed to the other prisoners.

The interrogator was not in bed, however. He was writing a report while a gunwing was being warmed up outside.

To Saireme Airlord Sartov the First of Yarron. The third prisoner has broken, and his story confirms what the other two have told us. He agrees that calculor trams are the key to Bartolica's success. He appears to genuinely not know what they are, except that they can calculate the best strategies for winning battles. The difference with Sair Maesterrin is that he was once a red tram driver, and he received some of his orders by watching unmarked sailwings dip their wings in a coded pattern. He has given us a current code, but apparently it changes every few days. My thought is that the tramloads of Bartolican carbineers

are rallied and directed by the calculor trams. That is
how their carbineers can fight in units of several thousand, even though they have never trained in groups
larger than a few dozen. My advice would be to send
your long-range hybrid gunwings out over tramways
in Bartolican-occupied Yarron with orders to pick off
any sailwing without markings. This could only be
when the weather permits for now, but in spring a
full-scale hunt for unmarked sailwings could play
havoc with the Bartolican carbineers. I shall now con-
centrate on getting a description of the calculor trams,
but the senior Callwalkers appear to keep these well
disguised. The captain may know, so I have decided
to suspend his work in the breeding program and have
a series of rather intensive chats.

By my hand on this 6th day of October, 3961,
Warden Harney of Windridge.

3 November 3960: Denver

Laurelene's journey through Yarron had made her more
resourceful than she ever realized she could be. At the
Yarronese capital she passed herself off as a warden's
widow and obtained a pass to go south, just before the
siege began. She reached the Colandoro border on foot
after weeks trekking through pasture disguised as a feather
gleaner, and once over the border she was apprehended by
a patrol of Colandoro carbineers. Because she had little
money, she was sent to a refugee camp. More weeks
passed. Laurelene started doing laundry for other refugees,
then for the guards. Presently the officers began to employ
her to clean their quarters. One evening she showed the
guards at the camp gate her work pass, told them that one
of the off-duty officers wanted her for some all-night
housework, then winked. She was allowed out, and in the

next five days walked sixty miles south to Denver through mushy snow.

When she arrived at the offices of the Bartolican envoy to Colandoro she was trim, fit, and very, very angry.

"My own countryman!" she raged, flinging yet another ornamental vase across the office to smash against a portrait of Airlord Leovor as the envoy cringed behind his desk. "He pounded my face to red mince so that I could not even speak to plead, then ripped open my clothing and knelt between my legs. I remember his weight pressing down on me and he—he actually kissed and licked the bloody bruises that he had just pounded into my face. I actually *wanted* him to have his way with me so that the beating and humiliation would just stop! Can you imagine that, Sair Envoy?"

"But, ah, you escaped," whispered the envoy.

"A stranger, a *Yarronese* stranger, killed him and helped me escape."

"Even the ranks of our own carbineers are not free of occasional deviants," suggested the envoy.

"*Occasional*, Sair Envoy? I saw much, I heard even more. I *felt* a great deal too," she shouted, pointing at her face.

"There are realities of war—ah, actions against outlaws that women do not know."

"Women on the winning side, you mean," Laurelene corrected, picking up another vase and slapping it against her free hand. "Now I am here and alive—and it's more by accident and Yarronese goodwill. I want sixty orbens and official papers and passes from your office. Debit it from my husband's service account."

"Of course, and you are welcome to stay in the diplomatic lodgings."

"I need no rooms. There are people that I must visit."

"But I have no consulate guards to spare, what with the war—"

"I have a spring-clip pistol, and the Yarronese taught

me how to use it. Would you like to know how many Bartolican carbineers I have killed, Sair Envoy?" she asked, tossing the vase to smash through a window and drawing the pistol.

The man's jaw worked several times as he stared down the barrel, but he could muster no words that seemed suited to the occasion. Suddenly he remembered the folder on the desk before him. With a convulsive movement he seized and opened it, producing a sealed letter with a flourish.

"This—this arrived before the border was closed due to the outlaws—"

Laurelene snatched it out of his hand.

"I shall read it at my leisure," she said as she slipped it into her bag. "The affairs of home are made a lot less urgent by distance."

"But the sender—"

"Is my son. I can read. It is doubtless full of news of what and who my husband is getting up to while I am away. Good morning to you, Sair Envoy."

When she had stamped out of his office and slammed the door the envoy lay back in his chair and blew a long, gusty breath between pursed lips. In her fury Laurelene had not noticed that the seal on her son's letter was that of the Inspector General. The envoy had learned of the elder Hannan's death through other channels, but after what he had endured for the previous twenty minutes he was in no mood to prolong any interview with Semme Laurelene Hannan. With luck she would be a long way away when she finally opened the letter.

The Monastery of the Holy Wisdom was fifteen miles from the city walls of Denver, but not far from a steam-tram hailstop. Laurelene walked to the gates carrying her own bags, introduced herself to the monk on guard, and declared that she was not expected. He rang for a liaisory monk, Brother James, who hurried out to meet Laurelene.

"This is a scholarly monastery, not a contemplative retreat," he explained as they walked the snow-bordered path to the guesthouse. "We get few visitors who are of your rank, Semme Hannan, our attraction is mainly to scholars."

"Brother James, I survived the siege of Median, fought my way to Yarronese lines, then walked here from Forian. If your rooms are more comfortable than a burned-out farmhouse or the shelter of a hedgerow then I shall be quite content."

"I see, yes, well, they are superior to all that. They have a little grate, and a bunk with featherdown quilts."

"Wonderful. I'll make a donation as soon as I put my bags down."

They entered the guesthouse and Laurelene stood beside a fire in the parlor as Brother James stepped out to arrange a room for her. Presently he returned and announced that her room was being made up, and that she could go to it in ten minutes.

"Might I inquire as to the nature of your studies here?" he asked, rubbing his hands together. "We have several libraries and archives, including one of the finest collections of pre-Call books in Mounthaven."

"I had arranged to meet an itinerant here, a man not of your order. His name is Brother Glasken."

"Ah, Brother Glasken, *everyone* knows Brother Glasken," Brother James replied, beaming. "What a brash and naughty soul he is. Why in the six weeks since he arrived he has told us gossip of all the courts of Hildago and the Andean Callhavens, and even of the coronation at Condelor. Did you know he has actually been flying in a sailwing? What a man!"

"Indeed, quite a man," Laurelene agreed.

"He has been teaching some of us the arts of defense without injuring one's opponent, and the use of simple sticks as weapons—they can be more deadly than swords, you know. Ah, but he likes the wines in our cellars, too, and has shown us some *very* fine ways to mull them with herbs and spices that would never have crossed my mind. Ah, such a wag that Brother Glasken."

"Can I see him now?"

"Well, not precisely now. The Sisters of the Divine Codex have been inviting him across to their nunnery for, ah, well, he seems to walk over there every second or third evening and returns in the morning. I believe that he is reciting certain Andean prayers and hymns while the nuns transcribe, and he is also conducting tutorials in denial theology and practice. It is nearly noon, so he should not be long." The little monk gave Laurelene a wink. "He gets along very, very well with the sisters, Semme Laurelene."

"He stays there overnight? The Reverend Mother Superior actually allows it?"

"Oh yes, he has been instructing Mother Virginia in Gentheist denial theology. You see, Gentheists believe that self-denial can be made all the more worthy if whoever is practicing that self-denial actually has experience of what is being denied!"

Laurelene swallowed, and clasped her hands behind her back so that Brother James could not see that they were shaking.

"Mother Virginia," said Laurelene flatly.

"I used to find her quite formidable, but Brother Glasken sees the good in every person. He calls her a fine, strapping, and generous woman. He likes big women."

"That sounds like Brother Glasken," she muttered.

"Ah, your pardon?"

"He . . . is known to be a diligent teacher in such matters, Brother James. Have you ever, ah, participated in Glasken's denial tutorials?"

"Oh no, Semme, but Brother Glasken's teachings are being studied by the theological committee of our order. A ruling is expected by the end of the year, but it *is* December, you know."

Laurelene sat down, quite overcome by what she had been hearing. Another monk entered and announced that her room was now ready. She stood up and set off, with Brother James carrying her bags.

Glasken returned soon after noon. Laurelene watched him returning over the fields, wearing a cassock of the monastery's order and trudging through the snow as if quite weary. He paused to speak to two monks working in the vegetable greenhouse, then continued to the library. Laurelene sought out Brother James.

"I see on the slateboard that Brother Glasken is to give a talk tonight," she said.

"Ah yes, and a talk of great importance, he says."

"It's upon denial and the virtues of learning the foundations of temptation, I suppose?"

"He did not say that, Semme."

Laurelene considered for some moments, then nodded as she composed a plan in her mind.

"If you please, Brother, do not mention to Brother Glasken that I am here. Oh, and could you allow me to listen to the talk from some secluded place where he cannot see me?"

"I can do all that, Semme, but why?"

"Brother Glasken likes surprises, and I am certainly about to surprise him."

That evening Glasken arrived at the refectory after dinner to give his lecture to the monks, along with a dozen nuns who had journeyed over and were to stay the night in the guesthouse. To Laurelene's surprise she discovered that it was not to be on sexual experimentation for celibates, but natural philosophy. She sat in the shadows at the back, but had a clear view of Glasken.

The monastery's expert on physical sciences, Brother Alex, had died four years earlier. The circumstances had been suspicious, yet there was no proof of murder. Brother Alex had had a laboratory where he experimented with electrical essence. He had been doing it for decades, and using a passive system of coils, crystals, and metal plates that were powered by the signals that they received. He could listen to the sounds of thunderstorms beyond the horizon, and he had hoped to develop tools that would determine a storm's direction, distance, and speed.

Brother James used to clean out the scraps in his workshop, and the researcher had taught him a little of his electrical essence techniques. He had fragments of books that dated back two thousand years and more, and these had strange codes of numerals and symbols in Archaic Anglian.

"Electrical devices grow unusable from a buildup of reiterative humors after a few hours," said Brother Lariac, another researcher in the ancient physical sciences. "The buildup is theorized to come from the wandering stars we call the Sentinels. Perhaps it is an ancient weapon, designed to destroy earthly weapons of electrical essence, but now it destroys all electrical devices. How did he cope with that?"

"Twenty years ago the Sentinels were destroyed in a celestial war," Glasken replied. "Their mechanisms were burned by Mirrorsun, and now only their shells remain."

"But, but large or fast gunwings get burned out of the sky," protested the monk.

"And who would bother to build a large gunwing, or dare to fly one?" Glasken asked in turn. "Brother James, would you tell us what you know?"

Brother James explained that two decades earlier the scholar and researcher had discovered that the Sentinels were no longer active. In May 3939 one of his receivers detected signals from beyond the Callscour lands and the legendary oceans. Brother Alex built a transmitting device from clues in one of his ancient texts, studied the old languages and transmission protocols, and made contact.

"But, but why did he not tell anyone?" spluttered the incredulous abbot.

"At first he intended to. He certainly told me, his unofficial apprentice. There was a war going on in that con-

tinent, whose name is Australica. It was on a scale that
staggered Brother Alex, in fact he could scarcely believe
that the people at the other end were telling him the truth.
He told them about our ritualized wars, fought between
wardens in gunwings. They showed great interest in our
type of limited conflict, but it soon became clear that they
were seeking details of reaction guns, compression engines, and gunwings. They wanted them in order to fight
even more destructive wars. Brother Alex was horrified.
He dismantled his induction transmitter machine and
burned his notebooks, lest Mounthaven's dominions be
contaminated by such terrible evils. I made copies of some
notes from memory, though. It seemed such a pity to waste
such incredible discoveries."

The monk held up a sheet of paper and began writing
on the slateboard:

MIRRORSUN & WANDERERS WAR—FEBRUARY
   3939
MILDERELLEN INVASION—FEBRUARY 3939
MIRRORSUN VICTORY—MAY 3939
MILDERELLEN INVASION DEFEATED—JUNE
   3939

"This here, MIRRORSUN & WANDERERS WAR—
FEBRUARY 3939, this is nearly twenty-two years ago. It
was about the time that Mirrorsun broke asunder in the
sky and we all thought that the end of the world was upon
us. Then here, three months later, mention of a victory.
We know that Mirrorsun had healed itself by then, and
that there were odd lights about the Sentinels. They
seemed to be surrounded by twinkling starlets for a time."

At the end of the evening Laurelene's head was in a whirl
from what had come to light in the hours past. As she lay
on her bed, she watched the stars through the window. The
universe had not merely changed that night, it had been

changed for two decades without anyone in Mounthaven realizing it.

The universe had changed. The Sentinels were dead. Anything with an engine could now be longer or broader than 29 feet 6 inches, and there was no speed limit on any powered vehicle. Gunwings could be of unlimited size, power, and speed, and steam trams could be coupled to a long string of unpowered trolleys and called trains.

When she was fairly sure that the monastery was quiet, she left her room and padded down to the men's level of the guesthouse. Glasken was in the only occupied room. His door was open as she approached, and she rounded the doorway to find him flat on his back in his bunk with his eyes closed.

"The night's compliments to you, Mother Virginia," he said as Laurelene stood in the doorway.

"You *dirty*, *lecherous* old man," said Laurelene slowly, every word perfectly enunciated and spat out with venom.

Glasken sat bolt upright, and for nearly a minute they stared at each other in the weak light from the coals in his room's grate.

"I wash thrice daily, and fifty is not old," he replied at last. "Lecherous is a little harder to defend, but give me time."

"You deceive and pervert these poor, holy folk."

Glasken lay back.

"Nothing of the sort, I *am* a monk and there *is* a Gentheist order that practices the knowledge of pleasure followed by denial. I may not be a member of that particular order, but—"

"How surprising."

"—but I've studied their rules in great detail."

"How predictable."

Glasken closed his eyes.

"Did you attend my talk?"

"Yes, but just now we have other business unfinished."

"Ah, I see. So, how did you fare once we parted?" he asked wearily, the words a little slurred.

"I walked one hundred and thirty miles through to snow to get here!" Laurelene burst out as she marched into the room and stood over Glasken's bunk with her hands on her hips. "I slept in open fields while you lay abed with some fat, religious tart and relieved her of that which she was named after."

"Well?"

"What do you mean, well? Are you not ashamed?" demanded Laurelene.

"No. It was your choice."

"I'll reveal your background to the monks."

"They know all that you do, and quite a lot more."

Laurelene considered storming off to her room, then returning to Denver in the morning and shouting at the envoy, but there was nothing in that but empty distraction. She turned her back on Glasken and glared at the coals in the fire, her arms folded.

Glasken slipped a Winsworth 9mm pistol from his robes and silently eased the safety catch free. He raised the barrel to point at her back, which was so close that he did not even have to take proper aim.

Laurelene swayed, then leaned against the wall and slowly sank to the floor, still facing away from Glasken. For a moment he looked at his gun, wondering if he had somehow shot her with a silent phantom of a bullet. She began to sob, not angry flamboyant sobs or hysterical sobs, but the sobs of one who has reached a goal after immense distance and suffering, only to find it a mirage. Glasken eased back the safety catch and put the gun away.

"I'm so lonely," she said after some minutes.

"That is a good admission, Semme, but I doubt that I could help."

"And I'm pregnant!"

Glasken jerked up in the bunk, pulling the covers up to his neck. "It wasn't me!" he blurted out by reflex.

Laurelene turned slowly to stare at him for a moment, then both of them burst out laughing. Glasken got out of the bunk and lifted her to sit on the edge, then he hunkered by the grate and began feeding in blocks of wood.

"I thought I was too old, I was careless," she confessed.

"Anyone I know?" he asked sympathetically.

"Jeb."

"A good man. I approve."

"You seemed such a transparent, slippery toad at first, Glasken, yet somehow people love you and care for you."

"And you wanted me for a pawn. Well, it's not the first time I've been a pawn."

A chant began in the distant chapel. Glasken got up and sat beside her on the edge of the bunk. He ran a hand over her stomach.

"Pregnant or not, you lost weight," he said, his words slurring again. "It suits you."

Laurelene took his hand and placed it squarely over her right breast. "I've maintained it in all the right places," she pointed out.

"That suits you too," he replied with a squeeze.

Laurelene hunched over, shivering a little. The distant chanting continued, and she found herself humming along with it.

"You need people to depend on you, Semme Laurelene," Glasken pointed out, draping an arm over her shoulders. "A bit less shouting might help them turn to you."

"I shout to keep the horrors away, Sair Glasken, but now I have grown tired of facing them alone and they are never far away." She stood up slowly. "Sleep well now, Juan. You look terrible: one nun too many, I'd wager. We can talk tomorrow, you old devil."

She leaned over Glasken and kissed him on the forehead.

"Jeb Feydamor is alone, except for his stepson," said Glasken, sitting with his hands clasped between his knees.

"He is a fine gentleman, Sair Glasken. But I'm a married woman."

"A married woman, three months pregnant, who last bedded her husband . . ."

"Before the coronation. All right, Glasken, you win. As usual, you leave me with something to think about."

The following day Laurelene and Glasken went walking in the snow-covered monastery garden. Nearby a mixed brass band of nuns and monks was practicing for the first time, while the axes of monks cutting wood in the distance echoed like gunshots.

"Tell me a secret," said Laurelene teasingly.

"My name is Johnny Glasken."

"I like just Glasken better. It has the ring of a lover about it, it's silky with romance."

Glasken stopped to look up at the overcast sky, as if it reminded him of something.

"Two decades ago I was seduced by a fine and lovely woman. Like you she had a husband at a convenient distance."

Laurelene flinched, then took his hand.

"And what came after that?"

"We married."

"I see. Is she now at a convenient distance as well?"

"She betrayed me to the constables. I was charged, tried, and condemned to die. I escaped and hid. Certain . . . certain powers required the use of an able fugitive, so here I am."

Laurelene thought about the story for a time, and Glasken honored the silence. Snow crunched beneath their feet as they walked, both with their hands behind their backs. Laurelene reached across and took Glasken's arm.

"You visit the convent every two days," she pointed out. "So tonight you are staying here?"

"Yes. Maybe tomorrow night too."

"Because I am here?"

Glasken shrugged, but did not reply.

"Three months is not very pregnant," Laurelene suggested.

Glasken began a shrug, but it turned into a cringe.

"You think that I'll betray you as well, Glasken, I can tell that," Laurelene burst out, pulling his arm tightly against her. "Well I'm *not* about to betray you."

"Words are cheap, Semme, and there is a scar on my ribs with your compliments."

"I'm sorry, I'm sorry, if I could change the past I would and you know it."

Laurelene was long out of practice at being tender, as Glasken discovered as she hugged him amid the seclusion of the snow-shrouded evergreens in the garden.

"What was the Milderellen Invasion?" she asked as they began walking again.

"It was terrible—and without need, just cause, or good result. In a sense I caused it, and it badly shook the mayorates of my part of the world. Other forces moved in to seek power. Some of those forces turned rogue, and forged plans to dominate the entire world."

"Oh surely not, Glasken," said Laurelene, leaning against him. "It is hard enough to even travel the world, let alone conquer it."

"Laurelene, these people are real Callwalkers."

She raised her head and stared at him, eyes wide and smile gone.

"Sair Glasken, have you been at the monks' wine so early in the day? Next you will say that they walk on water too."

"They are part bird, the product of ancient experiments on my continent. I can do it too, although I am not a true . . . aviad is their name for themselves. The Call is based in desire, you see, and that is also its weakness."

"I know that, Glasken. The Call is punishment sent by heaven for excesses of desire, all churches and faiths teach that."

"Not from heaven, Semme. As for desire, in me it burned far brighter than in practically any other human, and an aviad woman conducted certain experiments with me. Slowly I learned to resist the Call through the denial of what I would otherwise do as readily as breathe."

"So . . . Yes, it makes a little sense. During Calls you could go where you would to spy."

"Yes, most surely."

Laurelene looked up at the sky, facing south. "This day must be late spring in your homeland."

"Why yes, and in December there is the summer solstice. We have many carnivals, fairs, and religious festivities. Ah, but here it is autumn. Where I come from autumn is celebrated at the March equinox. Log fires are lit in every hearth, and mulled mead and other wines are drunk to celebrate the long nights indoors during winter. Whole towns are decked out for festivals. Half a year later children set off fireworks to frighten old man winter away and houses are covered in greenery and bunting to welcome summer back. In Mounthaven the equinox is little more than an equality of day and night."

"Glasken, I shall hold a great feast on my estate on every solstice, I promise you. Bartolicans like an excuse to revel, in fact I cannot think why they have overlooked the solstices for so long."

By now they were getting cold, and Glasken suggested that they warm themselves by the library fire. They entered, but found it deserted. That was unusual, for there was always a monk on duty when the door was unlocked. It was Glasken who found Brother James lying bleeding on the floor behind the register desk. He had been shot in the abdomen.

"Brother James!" exclaimed Glasken. "Who did this?"

"Five men, sair," Brother James whispered. "Cold eyes. Asked . . . about you."

"Australican Callwalkers," Glasken said grimly. "In a

way I marvel that they took so long to get here. Come now, Brother, let's see your wound."

"But this man needs a physician," said Laurelene.

"I've tended my share of wounds in the decades past, and most of my patients have lived."

He looked up when Laurelene did not reply. Five gun barrels were pointed at them.

Laurelene was soon bound and gagged in a reading chair. She gave muffled squeals of fury as one of the men ran his hands up her legs and under her skirts. He withdrew them to display a small pistol. He turned his attention back to Glasken.

"You dirty, evil old man," said the lean, muscular aviad.

"I am neither dirty nor evil, and fifty is merely middle-aged," Glasken replied smoothly, as if he faced this sort of accusation several times a day. "Brother James, I believe you have already met my son Warran."

Warran Glasken returned his gun to a holster beneath his coat and stood with his fists on his hips.

"Chorteau, close the door and bolt it," barked Warran. "Glasken, get away from the monk."

"Only when Brother James is bandaged shall I move away from him," replied Glasken, tearing a strip of cloth from his own robe. "Besides, since when have I been *Glasken* instead of *Father*?"

Warran's eyes blazed with fury at the word "father," but he let Glasken bind the monk's wound.

"He's bandaged, that's enough!" snapped Warran. "Now move away."

Glasken did as he was told, moving well away from the monk.

"At least have one of your men tend his wound properly," pleaded Glasken.

"My men open wounds, not heal them. Sablek, search him."

Sablek ran his hands through Glasken's clothing quickly

and methodically. He drew out the clip-spring pistol and two daggers.

"Is that all?" demanded Warran. "What about another gun? He always carries two guns."

"Both daggers are for throwing," Sablek pointed out. "Perhaps his second gun was that which we found in the woman's garter."

"You're right. So, *Brother* Glasken, where are your notes?"

"Notes? I have no notes."

"You study at this monastery! What did you scribe from their books?"

"I merely entered the holy cloisters for some weeks of quiet contemplation. I did no study."

"I think otherwise. You gave a lecture last night, I know that!"

"Oh, yes, on denial theology—"

"Don't give me that drivel, you lecherous, adulterous old goat! I know *everything*! Everything that you did with every nun in that convent, and the names of every monk who has followed your example. Even this fat Bartolican tart went to your room long enough for a quick one last night, I know that as well!"

"If that's your story, then you know nothing. Laurelene is my friend Jeb's lady, and I'd not betray—"

Warran backhanded him across the face.

"Don't talk to me about betrayal! You betrayed your wives more often than I've drunk hot coffee. It was your fault that they started following your example. You all shamed me!" He took one of Glasken's daggers from Sablek and pressed the point lightly against Glasken's nose. "I could threaten the monk, I could threaten your whore, *Father*, but there are three other things that I know you treasure far more. Chorteau, Sablek, fetch rope and a chair. I have a very slow operation to perform."

Chorteau and Sablek holstered their weapons. Brother James had been moaning softly and clutching at his bandaged wound beneath his robes, but as soon as the two aviads had put their weapons away he drew Glasken's missing pistol and opened fire on the two other aviads. Glasken kneed Warran in the crotch and dived for a fallen pistol as Chorteau and Sablek drew their guns and sprayed the monk with bullets. Rolling across the floor, Glasken opened fire on them. In the withering, unshielded exchange that followed all three were hit, but Glasken's aim was better. Laurelene tried to scream through her gag, and the sound was enough to get Glasken's attention. He turned to see Warran, almost doubled over with agony, raise his own gun. His shot hit Glasken high in the chest. Laurelene, still bound and gagged, surged out of the armchair, crashing into Warran's legs and sending him sprawling. He rose to his knees, his gun pointed at her forehead.

"You dare to touch me, you filthy, perverted whore—"

Warran's head exploded as Glasken squeezed off one last shot, then dropped the gun and lay still across the Dorakian carpet covering the library floor. Laurelene writhed her way across the floor to Glasken's fallen dagger. With much fumbling she managed to cut her hands free, then removed the rest of her bonds. Outside in the yard the woodcutters continued to chop. Nobody thought the shots from the library were anything else but axe blows.

Seven bodies lay sprawled on the library floor, but only Glasken was still alive. He was hanging by a thread when Laurelene reached him.

"Glasken, lie still," Laurelene said urgently as she began cutting the clothing away over his chest.

"Easily done," he whispered.

"We have to stop the bleeding first, then I'll get the monks—"

"No use. Frelle Laurelene. Two favors . . ."

"Anything! Anything!"

"When I die, press gold stud . . . remove collar."

"Yes, yes. What else?"

"Tell me I'm . . . handsome devil."

"You're a handsome devil, Glasken," Laurelene managed, but as she winked a tear was squeezed from her eye.

Slowly, carefully she knelt, straddling his body. She bent down low over his face.

"I shall never, never forget you, Glasken," she said, her voice breaking up. "Many women may have said that, but I mean it."

"No better way to go . . ."

She kissed him for a moment that lingered and lingered, tasting blood in his mouth. As she pulled back he was no longer breathing.

"No better way to go than between a woman's legs," she whispered, finishing his last sentence for him.

For a long time Laurelene lay sobbing on Glasken's body. At last she got up. She cut a lock of Glasken's hair with the dagger, then wrapped it about her fingers and stood. She shuffled over to the armchair and flopped down into it with her bloodied hands over her face. Soon she had to raise the alarm. Soon, but not yet. She could share a few minutes more with Glasken, that much she felt she was owed.

A flickering filled the library, intense enough to be evident past Laurelene's closed eyes and fingers. She opened her eyes. Glasken's body was glowing brightly—then the glowing image of something human-shaped began to rise free of him. She cowered, scrabbling back into the chair, but it was not facing her. The image stood, yet its feet were clear of the floor. The profile of a much younger Glasken's face looked down at his body.

"Hah! Za'be liv-te Morthet post," the image said.

A second image began to materialize in front of the Glasken wraith. It too began as flickering light, then defined itself into a tall woman of about thirty-five. She had thick, bushy hair and intense, protuberant eyes.

"Fras Glasken, va'sen hale," she said casually.

"Zarvora! So, za'be devil! Diz'be hell?" Glasken's image gasped.

The image of the woman named Zarvora folded her arms and shrugged.

"Advan, reprobart, Mirrorsun liqu-to var'aq," she replied, holding out her hand.

Glasken's image took a last look at his dead body; then the two images faded.

"Did I dream?" Laurelene asked herself as she walked over to Glasken's body and knelt beside it. "The gold stud, you say? Well, how better to remember a randy old dog than by his collar?"

The collar looked to be leather, yet the material felt more like silk. A seam appeared as she touched the gold stud, but as she peeled the collar away she saw that dozens of gossamer filaments ran from it into the back of Glasken's neck. She hesitated, then pulled gently. The filaments slowly withdrew from Glasken, to hang in a limp bundle two handspans long. As she watched they were drawn back into the collar by some unseen mechanism, until all that was left was a damp mark on the collar's inner lining.

"I'll keep it, but I'll not wear it," Laurelene decided, then slipped the collar between her breasts.

Raising the alarm was not quite the same in the monastery as it was in Condelor. There was no ringing of bells, no cries of "Bloody murder!" and no cloaked inspectors arriving to examine the scene. The abbot was summoned, the bodies were examined, and Laurelene told her story while a scribe transcribed it onto paper. Mother Virginia and the visiting nuns led Laurelene away and comforted her—or more accurately they comforted each other, as Glasken had been close to them all.

It was sometime after sunset that Laurelene finally found herself alone in her room. Bone-weary, she began to undress before the meager heat of the little fire in the grate. Released from her cleavage, Glasken's collar fell to the floor. She picked it up and put it on the washbasin stand, then pulled her downfiber nightgown on and sat on the edge of her bunk. She closed her eyes, dreading the thought of lying down in her bunk alone, for that night and forever after.

Laurelene opened her eyes to find a flickering image standing before her. The coals of the fire were quite distinct through it, and the form and face were familiar. Theresla.

For a moment Laurelene was dumbfounded. "Are you dead too?" she asked.

"I am not a ghost. This image is . . . is like a very advanced semaphore system. It is Mirrorsun technology, not like the primitive induction transmitter radios of the aviads. At this moment I am four hundred miles away in Condelor, and I am very much alive. I have been listening to what you and the nuns were saying for the hour past and no, I'll not repeat it to anyone. The world has lost a strange and capable man."

Laurelene was too wrung out to feel shame or anger.

"I—I fancied that I saw his ghost after he died."

"Glasken is truly dead, Semme Laurelene, but for three years he has been wearing that collar. It is the machine that is now projecting my voice and image, but it also communicated Glasken's . . . essence, habits, and memories to Mirrorsun. An image, a shadow, a pale copy of Glasken lives on within Mirrorsun. It is not Glasken's ghost or soul, but it is a likeness of Glasken."

Laurelene shook her head, as if that would make Theresla's image vanish. It did not. Now she had to come to terms with the image of someone that she had never liked yet would not go away.

"You say that Glasken is dead, yet he lives," she said, looking down at the bare floorboards and shaking her head.

"His soul has gone to . . . wherever it is destined to go. I could speculate, but I shall not. What remains is an image, a mold taken while he was alive and stored in the fabric of the huge machine that is Mirrorsun. The collar that you took from his body is a machine too, built by Mirrorsun."

Most of what she said was lost on Laurelene, who sat absolutely still and scarcely breathed.

"So you wear one too? Are threads buried in your skin?"

"I wear mine with a padded copper plate over the bio-cybernetic interface."

"The what?"

"The place where the tendrils come out. That way I can use it for speaking like this, but my soul will not be copied out and stored on a machine."

"So Glasken lives, or exists, ah—can I speak to him?"

"Glasken is not my concern, Semme Laurelene. You are. You must not return to Condelor until spring, and you must not breathe a word of today's deaths to anyone outside this monastery."

"But there are seven dead men in the next building. That cannot be hidden from the inspectors for long."

"It can indeed. The five Callwalkers were not known to the Denver city inspector, and neither was Glasken. Brother James will be marked in the register as going on a long pilgrimage. Glasken could have killed you, Semme, but he never takes the easy way out. Do not waste the sacrifice of his life by returning to Condelor and telling all who will listen that the Sentinels are long dead."

"But why?"

"To survive, the Bartolican people must lose this war."

"What?" gasped Laurelene.

"Greater Bartolica is under the control of Callwalkers such as myself. They are stealing gunwings under the shroud of war's anarchy. There may be more, but as yet I do not know."

"So you *are* a spy. Against your own people."

"Indeed. Now, will you stay in this place for the winter, and not return to Condelor until at least the equinox?"

"The local envoy knows I am here, he will mention it

to my husband in dispatch letters. He will inquire after me."

"Your husband is dead," Theresla said bluntly. "He has been dead for months."

"What? No! Lies! The envoy would have—"

Suddenly Laurelene remembered the unopened envelope that the envoy had handed her. She rummaged in her bag and drew it out. Tearing it open, she dropped to her knees beside the grate and read the message by its red glow. Theresla had been right. Roric was indeed dead.

"I'll stay," Laurelene said as she slowly stood up and then slumped back onto the bunk. "It's as good a place as any to give birth."

"Good," said Theresla as she started to fade. "If you wish to wear Glasken's collar but do not fancy spending eternity within Mirrorsun, have one of the monks glue a copper plate over the interface spot. If you do not wear it, it will cease working tomorrow. It is powered by a mixture of body heat, sweat, and motion."

When Laurelene got into bed it took her only moments to plunge into the sleep of one utterly exhausted. The suggestion of an image of Theresla lingered to watch for a few minutes, then faded completely.

Glasken, Brother James, and the five aviads were buried in the monastery cemetery by the monks. Laurelene stood among the graves as Glasken's large and heavy coffin was lowered into the ground, standing aside from the rest while prayers were chanted.

On Glasken's the headstone was written HERE RESTS JOHN GLASKEN. BRAVE, LOYAL, AND LOVED BY MANY. ANNO DOMINE 3909–3960.

Lied about his age, Laurelene thought, then noticed that there were sparkles before her eyes. They vanished as she blinked.

"What a disaster," muttered a familiar whisper close by her ear.

"Glasken?" whispered Laurelene.

"Wander away by yourself. Pretend to pray in private."

Laurelene opened a little book of prayers and slowly walked away from the seven open graves.

"Did you really think about killing me?" she asked, a little resentfully.

"Yes, and so did Theresla. There's a power store in the collar that can be overloaded remotely. Had you said that you were returning to Condelor before March . . ."

"Bang?"

"Very big bang. Bartolica *must* lose the war."

"Glasken, what could make such a chivalrous man as you contemplate murder?"

"Mounthaven is being invaded by Callwalkers from my continent. They see themselves as a master race, and I have learned that they have rebuilt a war coordination machine called an internet. Bartolica is under their control, as is Montras. Dorak will be next. Yarron has put up a better fight, but it can do no more than buy time for other dominions with its death struggles."

"What do you want me to do?"

"Nothing, I just wanted you to know, to understand. Laurelene, later today certain monks will begin pilgrimages to all Mounthaven dominions not yet in the war or conquered. There they will deliver secret messages to the Airlords, messages telling them that trains and wings of any size and speed are now possible, that Callwalkers are among us and that dominions have already fallen to them. That's why I came here, to organize a message to go out to all dominions at once. They will be warned at the same time, and be given designs for better weapons than Bartolica has."

"Sair Glasken, this is very hard for me to tell you, but—"

"Don't say you love me, Semme, please. I'm in a strange, shimmering place, I can feel nothing, I'm dead yet

I'm going to live forever, and having no body has ruined my sex life."

"I was going to offer to betray my dominion and airlord, Sair Glasken."

"Oh."

"When I eventually return to Bartolica, just say the word and I'll do what I can."

"You are a truer patriot than most, Semme Laurelene."

By now the monks were shoveling soil into Glasken's grave. Laurelene nodded, and they said goodbye. Glasken's secret was better kept than he could have realized. Laurelene wrote to the local envoy that she was staying at the monastery for several months to mourn her husband, and would not return to Condelor until April. The monks all dutifully left on their missions to warn of the aviad menace, but only in Yarron did the seeds that Glasken had already planted take root and grow. Even in death, Warran Glasken was a little ahead of his father.

6 REAPING THE WHIRLWIND

Forian stubbornly refused to yield throughout the winter. It had one advantage that was shared by no other inhabited city in Mounthaven: massive, ancient walls, sixteen hundred years old and five miles across. They had been maintained for their sheer magnificence after the wardenate system was established, but were still proof against direct attack. Amid snow and freezing rain the Yarronese defenders drove the Bartolicans back through their breaches in the walls time and again, then fought from rooftops, sewers, canals, and alleyways after the center was finally taken. When aviad infiltrators were detected they were shot dead where they stood.

The Airlord abdicate, Chancellor Virtrian, was taken alive in the spring and was forced to sign the articles of surrender. Unfortunately for the Bartolicans, his powers only extended to surrendering the capital. The whole of the north was still in Yarronese control and ruled by the new Airlord, Sartov. The former Airlord was put aboard a steam tram for the trip west to Condelor. There were great celebrations planned in the Bartolican capital, and the vanquished leader was to be the centerpiece of them.

During the winter the Bartolicans divided Yarron into three portions. The western third was directly annexed to Bartolica, the northern third would be isolated, and the remainder was declared the independent dominion of Bartolica-Yarron. In a secret pact, Dorak was charged with conquering North Yarron alone, in return for being granted all its territory. Strategically it was a stroke of genius by Stanbury, as Dorak was destined to be bled dry by what became a very difficult late-spring campaign. It would be an exhausted, minor power at the end of the war. Like all brilliant plans, however, it did not credit the enemy with sufficient ingenuity and tenacity. The winter campaign had also cost Bartolica dearly, and there were increasingly loud questions being asked in the Airlord's Condelor palace.

In the west of Mounthaven, Bartolica forced Westland to join Montras as a Bartolican protectorate, then annexed eastern Senner in a campaign that lasted only five days. Senner had an alliance with Cosdora, however, and to the surprise of many in the Bartolican court Cosdora's Airlord declared chivalric war in defense of its vanquished ally and gave sanctuary to the surviving Sennerese carbineers and wardens. Cosdora was a bad enemy to acquire, being nearly as powerful as prewar Yarron.

Thus Bartolica was forced to open a second front before the life had been squeezed from Yarron. Aviad agents were hurriedly withdrawn from the vicinity of Forian for use in

Cosdora, but it took time for them to infiltrate into positions of trust in that dominion. The war slowed to a standoff on both fronts. Greater Bartolica was once again great, and Stanbury's popularity had never been stronger, yet it had all been bought with easy, glorious victories. What even Stanbury failed to realize was that the supply of soft, easy targets had now run out.

Having become Airlord of Yarron, Sartov lost no time in organizing a new strategic approach to the war. Knowing that Bartolica would be extended for some months to come, he evacuated twenty thousand people and thousands of tons of materials and tools west to Gannett and Wind River. There he set up new factory towns built into the hills or disguised within forests.

On the 30th day of April, 3961, Sartov was brought news of the fall of Forian. He ordered that all flags be lowered to half-mast, then called Fieldmajor Gravat to his briefing room. They surveyed a map of the whole of Yarron. Much of it was covered with black hatching where the invaders had taken control, and their bases were marked by red circles. In his hands were reports on the battles of the previous four months, and spread out on the map were lists of names.

"Us Yarronese 'outlaws' are biting back hard," he said to Gravat, who had been directing the northern defenses.

"The odds are better with the Callwalker featherheads removed from behind our lines. We just may survive."

"Remember what Virtrian said, we must do more than survive," responded Sartov. "For now I suspect that we are secure, so I have a very special strike planned."

"A strike, Warden? All our victories have been defensive."

"On the ground, yes, but in the air we have better latitude." He tapped at the map, deep within the shaded area. "I have some potent weapons at Gannett and Wind River. The area has difficult approaches and a loyal, well-organized militia. The Bartolican merchant service has posted garrisons on the western approaches and left them to be conquered later. The eastern approaches are all ours for now, and there are good, long wingfields there. We have been doing a lot of development work, and have thirty new gunwings stationed in the area. More are being built."

"Good, good. From there our patrols could shoot up those unmarked Bartolican sailwings over the Red Desert and harass their trams on the main tramway."

Sartov smiled. Gravat had reached a good conclusion, but one that was also wrong.

"A stripped-down regal with a five-hundred-pound air-bomb could fly two hundred and sixty miles without re-fuelling. How far could it get with a crew of four and three Klasmikar guild double reaction guns?"

The fieldmajor thought for a moment.

"It could perhaps get into the air with such a load, but it could carry no more fuel than that to circle the wingfield and land again."

"What about a giant regal with a wingspan of over a hundred feet and six gunwing engines?"

"What? I—impossible, the Sentinels would destroy—"

"Ah, but our improvised trains now go unmolested, they have done so for five months."

"That is true," Gravat conceded.

"I trace logical paths out for myself, Fieldmajor. Five months ago I sent the airframe guilds—or what remained of them—to the Wind River Range. There they were charged with developing a new type of regal, one that could fly an immense distance with a very heavy load. I thought to bomb the besieging Bartolicans around Forian, but now, alas, Forian has been crushed. I nevertheless have six super-regals with a return circle of . . . an impressive number of miles."

Gravat whistled. "How fast are they?" he asked.

"Not fast by any means, but each has two carbineers

with reaction guns for protection, and we have also developed a method to extend the range of the hybrid gunwings. There are twelve converted already. They have even been tested in combat. They are good. Very good."

"A dark view will be taken by the wardens—but I do favor such innovations," Gravat hastily added.

"I am now Airlord, the wardens will obey me. The six super-regals have been practicing bombing runs in the Wind River Range for the past week, Fieldmajor. Further, one of our known Callwalker spies was slipped intelligence that all remaining Yarronese wings will be used to bomb the rail approaches to Forian. This will be meant as a gesture of defiance, in the face of the capture of the city."

"And the real target?"

"Fieldmajor Gravat, even the flyers will not know that until they ascend from Wind River."

"Ah, the railway bridges between Middle Junction and Median, then?"

"What makes you say that?"

"They would need a range of just over two hundred miles to bomb the place and return. If they are such an immense size they just may able to carry all that load and still fly such a distance."

"True, Fieldmajor, and you may be right. What is important is that the Bartolicans expect a massed attack on a plausible target. I want you to set sailwings practicing strafing runs against rail bridges and steam trams. Make sure that Bartolica's agents know of it, too."

24 April 3961: Bartolica

Although beaten, Yarron's power was by no means broken. Two days after the fall of Forian an armed sailwing was cruising high over the Snake River Plains in western Bartolica, flying so high that the engine also drove a little compressor to give the flyer enough air to breathe. The sun was not yet up on the ground, and he intended to turn and make a pass after surface dawn, when the shadows were at their most revealing.

As his compression engine droned steadily he scanned the great assembly grounds near Richfield, where hundreds of new gunwings were being built. The area was sealed off, even to ordinary Bartolicans, and was of great interest to Sartov.

Then he saw it, flying some distance above him and across to port. It was a sailwing of some sort, but of an odd configuration. Even as he watched, he noticed another sailwing, apparently much closer although still above him. The flyer released the catches on his reaction guns. They had obviously seen him . . . yet they were not diving to intercept. Then he noticed another of the odd sailwings, and another, all in a row.

The texture of the aircraft was odd, blending with the sky so as to make them scarcely noticeable. It had only been the sharper contrast with the Bartolican sailwing that had caught his attention in the first place. He scanned them with his field glasses, and he noticed long, thin lines that converged to—the gunwing!

Suddenly the Yarronese flyer had it. The three odd sailwings were not close and small, they were distant and immense. The gunwing was at the same height as they were, and he noted that its propellor was not spinning.

The Yarronese flyer could not make out anything else at such a distance. He trailed the strange convoy for another thirty miles until it flew west out over the Callscour lands; then he turned back and resumed his original mission.

The Yarronese flyer had made detailed sketches and notes as he flew. He estimated the span of the giant sailwings to be at least half a mile.

24 April 3961: Denver

It was a few weeks after the birth of her son that Laurelene decided to return to Condelor. A wet nurse was available to feed the baby, and she knew that she had work to do in the Bartolican capital. Like all the others who had left the monastery, Laurelene decided that she wished to do so with discretion. The Callwalkers knew of something going on there and the place was certainly being watched, but their numbers were small and they could not afford to lose another five so readily. The way out was as subtle as it was shameful to the eyes of the world.

One afternoon Laurelene dressed in a monk's cassock and set off across the fields with two others for the convent. . . . Glasken's preaching of knowing pleasure so that one could resist temptation in better knowledge had caught on, and overnight visits took place in small groups every week. Mother Virginia met Laurelene when she arrived, and the two women sat reminiscing about Glasken for some time.

"But now what brings you here?" asked Mother Virginia. "If you wished to initiate one of the holy brothers into those things that he must avoid you could do that in the comfort of the guesthouse at the monastery."

"I mean to return to Condelor," replied Laurelene. "As you smuggled the monks away to Denver, so you must smuggle me too."

Mother Virginia explained that she disguised herself as a farmer's wife and the monks as farmers or itinerants; and then they walked to a nearby hamlet, where they took a canal barge into the capital. There they stayed as man and wife in a hostelry for a day or two until the monk quietly slipped away. Mother Virginia stayed on at the hostelry, pretending that her husband was still about, then left by herself a few days later.

"In your case we could well be sisters," suggested Mother Virginia.

"I have no small experience at being one of the riffraff," agreed Laurelene.

With some forethought Laurelene had kept the clothing in which she had escaped Yarron many months before. She and Mother Virginia changed into their disguises around sunset; then the nun left Laurelene in her room while she went to tell her deputy what was happening.

Laurelene looked for somewhere to hang the cassock. She was surprised to see that Mother Virginia's wardrobe held several fine gowns, and she recognized the embroidered marks of Dagraci and Lingor. A sliding panel on the dresser opened to reveal bottles of perfumes from Santarita and Parribi of Hildago, and several others that she did not recognize. She did recognize several darkwood pubic combs inlaid with gold and silver, along with sundry silk undergarments.

Leaving everything as she had found it, Laurelene took out Glasken's pistol, checked the rounds in the clip, then screwed the silencer barrel onto the muzzle. She had just put it into the roughweave coat that she now wore when Mother Virginia returned.

"You have some very fine robes and perfumes," remarked Laurelene as she swung her bag over her shoulder.

"Well Semme, the painted women of the city have fine robes and perfumes, so if we are to show temptation in its true guise we should do at least as well."

"Very good, I do approve," giggled Laurelene. "A true pupil of Glasken."

They set off for the tram station after dark, and within an hour were on a steam barge and chugging through the night toward the glow on the horizon that was Denver. Mother Virginia led the way to a hostelry near the center of the city. It was in a bustling but seedy area, the sort of place where one could easily lose oneself. She signed them both in, winking and giggling with the manager as she paid for the room in advance, and then he led them to a ground-floor room. Mother Virginia sat down on the bunk nearest the door.

"So, do we go out and sample the delights of the wicked city?" asked Laurelene. "I've not eaten since lunchtime."

"Oh, we can occupy ourselves delightfully in here," the nun replied with a wink.

"How so? I want to eat."

"All in good time. I have arranged for company."

"Company?" asked Laurelene, turning to look through a window that opened onto a dingy lane.

"Male company. They're men worth waiting for."

Laurelene whirled and fired her silenced pistol in a string of muted pops. Mother Virginia slowly toppled from the bunk, already dead, and hit the floor with a loud thump.

"Dagraci and Lingor gowns, perfumes by Santarita and Parribi of Hildago, crafted love combs by Brugervit himself!" Laurelene whispered sharply down at the corpse. "There were four thousand orbels' worth of clothing, perfume, and jewelry in your room, Reverend Mother Virginia. Your servile nuns and monk lovers might not recognize the height of expensive fashion, but *I do*!"

She climbed out through the window, dragging her bag with her. It was none too soon. Crouched outside she heard the door open and a male voice curse. There were more footsteps following.

"Ah good, you—what! This is the wrong one, Callbait! You shot the wrong one!"

"I shot nobody!" another voice cut in.

"Can't you tell one fat pudding from another?"

"I didn't do it."

"Don't lie to me!"

"I swear it, sair. Check my gun's clip."

"Idiot, pash-head! You saw this one every time we killed a monk. Now those foreign gentlemen will have our balls in brandy. . . ."

Laurelene padded quietly away down the lane and out

into the street. She walked past the tram station, out onto the main arterial highway, over the barge canal bridge, and through the ancient city gate. Stopping only to buy a stick of roast potatoes and dried emu meat from a vendor, she walked on into the night by the light of Mirrorsun, going north, alone. She walked all night, not sleeping, and she covered more ground than she had when the snow had been thick and slushy. It was sixty miles to the border, but by sunset the next day she was on Yarronese soil.

18 April 3961: Wind River

The Wind River wingfield had been untouched by the Bartolicans not because it was so very unlikely as a threat, but because it was a hard target. At some time in the distant past glaciers had combined to grind a level stretch of valley floor that suddenly dropped away sharply. The result was the site for a wingfield that was difficult to find and difficult to attack, but easy to hide and easy to defend.

In early spring Sartov had his adjuncts interview all flockleaders about volunteering for service over Bartolica. When Serjon asked the rest of the flock, Alion accepted before he had finished the sentence. After all, they would be based 130 miles closer to Condelor and thus Samondel. Bronlar also accepted without hesitation, but with a strange, wistful look to Alion. Ramsdel and Kumiar were more reluctant, but accepted to be part of the same strong flock.

On the 18th of April they ascended an hour before sunrise for Wind River, leaving their guildsmen to follow by steam tram. They landed just before dawn, at a wingfield that seemed to be no more than a flightstrip in hilly wilderness, serviced by a tramway. On closer inspection it was a very large, camouflaged complex of huge tents, backfill bunkers, and barracks. Leaving the five gunwings with the pool guildsmen they registered with the adjunct and passed in their pennant plaques. They then break-fasted.

When they emerged from the refectory to look for the wingfield hospitalier they were stopped by a warden and six carbineers with assault carbines. Alion was arrested and marched off into detention.

The charge against Alion was very serious. A diplomatic drop cannister had been found concealed in his gunwing by one of the pool guildsmen. When the message within was decoded it was sent to his guildmaster, and it quickly traveled all the way up to Airlord Sartov. Late in the morning Serjon was summoned to testify before the Warden Inspectorate of Wind River, being the youthful warden's flockleader. Alion cited Bronlar and Ramsdel as the two character witnesses that he was allowed.

Sartov began by reading out Alion's decoded message in full.

My dearest and only love Samondel,
Cruel and unchivalric war spreads his cold shadow before Princess as I fly her to your side. He loads ice upon her leading edges until she is forced from the sky to stand helpless in the wasteland while I lie as dead at her wheels. Melt the ice with the warmth of your smile, my darling love, and spin her engine into life as the sparkle in your eyes spins my head with reverie. Wrap me, your faithful lover, in the cascading flames of your hair and bind me that I may never leave your side again.

Your loving and faithful warden,
Alion of the Damaric estate

"The signalers' guildsmen have been over it in great detail, and it appears to be nothing more than it reads as: a love letter to the seventeenth in line to the throne of Greater Bartolica. Warden Alion is known to have had a liaison with Samondel Leovor at the coronation in Condelor last year."

Sartov sat down. The presiding warden called the red advocate to the floor, and he asked Serjon for his opinion.

"Well I think 'faithful' is a rather strong word, given what he was doing with a certain nurse from Casper until a month ago."

Alion put his face in his hands and Bronlar closed her eyes while trying to think of interesting air battles of the last few months.

"So you think that his supposed love for the Bartolican is a blind to hide treason against Yarron?"

"No, I do think he's in love, sair—I mean if faithful means love. Not if it extends to other parts of his anatomy, though. I mean he was not kind to that nurse, and a truly chivalric warden would have remained faithful in mind *and* body to Princess Samondel while leaving the nurse to someone more suitable like, ah . . ."

"Go on."

"His flockleader," suggested Bronlar.

"Order!" called the presiding warden.

It took a few moments for the red advocate to get his breath back. "But what do you think of the message as a whole?" he asked next.

"Oh it's the most awful drivel I've ever seen. It scans terribly and the imagery is the sort of thing that makes drunks throw up during bards' hour in the taverns. He reads it out to me all day on the operations bench, then people wonder why I hate poetry."

The presiding magistrate swallowed. Sartov snapped a pencil between three fingers.

"If there's a suicide mission leaving in five seconds then I volunteer," muttered Ramsdel to Bronlar.

"Order!" the presiding warden barked at Ramsdel.

The red advocate had no more questions. The white advocate took the floor.

"Flockleader Feydamor, aesthetics and morals aside, do

you think that this letter is anything more than a desperate bid to contact a lover who happens to be an enemy noble?"

"No. It was probably one reason why he volunteered for work over Bartolica."

Bronlar and Ramsdel confirmed Serjon's testimony with somewhat more taste and discretion, and Alion was acquitted with a severe reprimand. Outside on the wingfield Bronlar hugged the limp and mortified Alion while Ramsdel told Serjon that his testimony had been the greatest animal act since the Archwarden of Cosdora had blown his nose in the colors of the Airlord's consort.

"And you were simply heartless about Alion's sense of romance and affection," sniffed Bronlar in sympathy with Alion.

"I was trivializing the charge," insisted Serjon dismissively. "Don't all thank me at once. Besides, what about that nurse? I stayed up all night persuading Jenina not to suicide after he gave her the heave. I mean I didn't so much as get a hand on a boob out of it, and at the end of everything she said she'd never trust another warden, flyer, or squire again as long as she lived and threw me out."

"Well so she should have!" snapped Bronlar. "And while the subject is open, I can do without these!"

Bronlar ripped Serjon's colors from her sleeve and flung them down to the gravel. She and Alion walked off together with arms linked and were lost to sight among the tents.

"If she turns into his next Samondel substitute it's all your fault," chided Ramsdel. "She fancies you, did you know that?"

"Me? You have to be joking."

"She wears your colors."

"Not anymore," he said as he scooped the bunch of ribbons from the ground.

"She named your gunwing."

"She named yours too. Sartorial, what a name."

"Bronlar speaks well of you when you're not there, Serjon. She can name every warden you shot down, and she thinks you're wonderful fun."

"As my old stepdaddy says, women like either strong men, or steady men, or interesting men, or pathetic men. Bronlar's taste is for pathetics, but I'm definitely classed as interesting. I mean, does anyone want to know if *I* like *her*?"

"Well?"

"Ramsdel, I've come to realize something. The girls I really like are the sort who like interesting men. Now they're rare, and the ones I've met have all been taken, but it's better than collecting clever and sensitive brush-offs from those who like the strong, steady or pathetic— *and* having to put up with being their light comic relief."

About an hour later Bronlar sought out Ramsdel as he was handing out embroidered overall collars to his temporary guildsmen.

"Alion kissed me rather too ardently as I sat with him behind the compression spirit store," she explained as they walked out onto the flightstrip to inspect its surface. "He wants us to go on a picnic tomorrow and . . . I need to be in your company, if you know what I mean."

"If you wish to be one of the boys, then comfort him as one of the boys," Ramsdel replied, dropping a knife from waist height to see how far it penetrated the flightstrip surface. "Embraces and kisses are also used in courtship, or had you not heard?"

"He should not have taken all that the wrong way."

"Ah, but he was liable to, and he did. What now?"

Bronlar withdrew the knife with her finger at the penetration line, then gave it back to Ramsdel. It was a firm, well-laid clay and gravel surface.

"I . . . I might like him. The war will not last forever, and I do not want him to just drift away to some other because I had to seem cold. He has a vulnerable aspect, and, well, he has nobody strong to guide him. That nurse, she was just a girl with dreams of being a warden's lady."

"She was two years older than you, and a warden's niece."

Bronlar had managed to forget that.

"Alion needs someone to look up to, Ramsdel, that's why that princess infatuates him. I'm deputy flockleader, and I have four times more victories than him on my pennant board plaque."

"Wonderful, just the very foundations to build true love upon."

A siren wailed three short bursts, warning them to get clear of the wingfield, and Ramsdel said that he could hear a flight of gunwings. What appeared out of the north was a single sailwing of monowing design, with two dots to either side. They stood at the perimeter of the ascent strip, watching it approach and wondering where the additional sound was coming from. It was a single wing, lacking fuselage or tail, and it grew and grew. Six spinning disks pushed it from behind. The dots resolved into hybrid gunwings flying escort.

Ramsdel exclaimed when he realized that the three aircraft were actually together. The single wing was at least a hundred feet across, he estimated. Its wheels were wound down, and it landed with a series of lumbering hops. The gunwing escort stayed aloft, warily circling the wingfield.

"The flaps alone are as big as Sartorial's wings!" exclaimed Ramsdel in amazement as it passed them.

They jogged along the dispersal track behind the monstrous wing until it was steered into one of the larger tents. Serjon was standing to one side of the tent munching on a bread roll and looking surprisingly calm.

"Did you see it land?" shouted Bronlar as they ran up to him.

"It's a super-regal, number SR-5. It carries a crew of four, a thousand-pound bomb, two pairs of reaction guns on universal joints, and has a range of a thousand miles on standard tanks."

"How do you know all that?" asked Ramsdel.

"I volunteered to be wingcaptain of that one," Serjon said in a cold, hard tone that Ramsdel had not noticed before. "I would like you, Bronlar, Alion, and Kumiar to fly escort when we are sent out to strike at Bartolica."

4 May 3961: Condelor

The former Yarronese Airlord was already in the palace dungeons as Laurelene arrived back in Condelor. Vander had her whirled from the tram station to a revel on a canal barge to celebrate her return. The capital had changed a great deal while she had been away. It was as if a new type of pride in the place had grown up with the victory over Yarron. The Airlord wanted Bartolica to seem mighty in war, yet untouched by war, so a massive campaign of repairs, rebuilding, and cleaning had polished the city until it looked like some idealized painting of the place.

Laurelene had the impression of a city whose stonework was brand-new. Lichens and mosses had been scoured away, and weeds had been cleared out of the gutters and crevices. Some ivy was still tolerated, but only barely. After the traumas of her trip through Yarron, the city almost made her think that the war had never happened.

The barge revel traveled all the way up to the wide canal that ran around the palace grounds and separated them from the wingfields. Here the barge turned to port, and presently arrived at the quay beside the palace gates. A senior courtier came aboard and invited Laurelene to come with him to meet the Airlord.

Laurelene had been presented to the Airlord before, but had never exchanged more than ritual courtesies with him. As it turned out, he was taking the spring air only a short distance from the stone quay. In a shaded pavilion amid topiaried bushes and trees, the monarch of all Bartolica lay reclining on a wickerwork couch while a string quartet of girls played courtly dance music. Laurelene's reception was informal, and he bade her listen to the variations being played—his own composition, she immediately guessed. Sitting on the wickerwork couch beside the Airlord, she remarked on the grace of the music, and then made a show of surprise when told that her own monarch had penned the notes. The mood relaxed further.

"I have been thinking of visiting Yarron," the Airlord announced. "Do you recommend the journey, Semme Laurelene?"

"Yarron is no longer in any sort of order," she began.

"Oh but to the contrary, Semme, it is under Bartolican order!" he admonished.

"Your pardon, Lordship, I chose my words badly. Yarron's towns and cities are in ruins as a result of the war. Accommodation and provisions are not to the standard of Condelor."

"That will not be a problem, Semme. I am a warrior, trained to endure the chill of flying a gunwing and happy to eat no better than my own loyal wardens and carbineers in the field of battle."

"Battle is yet another matter, Lordship. The new Airlord of Yarron still controls most of the north. The central tramway through Yarron is well within the range of his sailwings, and there have been several attacks on Bartolican steam trams."

"Once again, Semme Laurelene, any danger that I ask my wardens to face I would not shirk from myself."

To her surprise, Laurelene found herself thinking how tiresome the conversation had become, and wishing that the Airlord of Greater Bartolica would dismiss her.

"Lordship, I am neither a warrior nor young, so I found Yarron dangerous and trying. You asked my opinion, and that is Yarron as I found it."

"I see, yes. What manner of Airlord would I be if I dared not go where Semme Laurelene Hannan had already set foot, eh?"

"It is not my place to say, Lordship."

After the Airlord had spoken to her, Laurelene was taken to Stanbury. He met her on the stone quay beside the barge, and was wearing his sashes and uniform as Archwarden. The whole of the company on the revel barge was watching.

"Semme Laurelene Hannan, it gives me so much pleasure to welcome you back, alive and well," Stanbury began. "For your treatment and suffering during the fall of Median I can only offer my most sincere apologies. I shall do my best to ensure that those who mistreated you from both sides will be punished."

"You are generous and just," Laurelene replied in a clear but indifferent-sounding voice. Something about her tone unnerved Stanbury, however, and he went on hastily.

"May I also offer my condolences on the tragic death of your husband. The investigation into the circumstances is continuing, but the unseemly rumors that have been circulating in the aftermath have been discredited. The reputation of your house has been restored."

"If you mean that he died abed in the act of infidelity, I doubt that anyone's efforts will ever cover that up. Besides, I was no better."

In the stunned silence that followed Stanbury took a step back, his eyes bulging and his mouth agape. The barge was filled with gasps and titters, so that it sounded like a park full of birds at dawn. Stanbury's shock turned to fury, and the color drained from his face. Vander Hannan had arrived at the head of the stone steps of the quay just as Stanbury and Laurelene had begun to speak. His first inclination was to cheer, but he managed to press his lips together and clap a hand over his mouth to hide the smile.

Without another word Stanbury literally turned on his heel and hastened up the stone steps. He stopped as he reached Vander.

"The horrors of your mother's journey and losses have clearly turned her brain, sair *Acting* Inspector General. Be so good as to convey her from the palace grounds and do *not* allow her to return until a committee of palace physicians pronounces her fit again."

Minor courtiers jumped from the barge and sprinted away to spread Laurelene's words to whoever would listen. Vander and Laurelene waited for his barge to be brought around, and in that time a crowd of minor nobles, servants, and groundsmen gathered. There were hisses and catcalls, but nothing more threatening. Laurelene was triumphant. She had successfully become an outcast.

6 May 3961: Condelor

Two days after Laurelene returned home the Airlord was due to formally declare Yarron defeated and have Virtrian paraded in to be charged as an outlaw. Because he had abdicated, it would not be before a Council of Airlords, but a Bartolican magistrate.

Samondel had become a warden during the conflict in Yarron. With the deaths of several wardens in line for the throne she had to either renounce her claim in line, or get a warden's flight qualifications. With the legends about Bronlar leaking into Bartolica, Stanbury wanted some type of public figure to be visible in Bartolica as a counter. Much to her surprise he encouraged her to take sailwing training, and in April she finally managed to take a gunwing aloft and bring it down again in one piece. There was no thought of sending her to Yarron, it was a matter of Bartolica having a female warden while North Yarron had none.

Samondel was made the presiding warden at the victory parade to the palace. Virtrian and two hundred other senior Yarronese prisoners were marched all the length of the grand parade road and into the palace grounds by a squad of carbineer veterans while a band played a march written for the occasion by the Airlord of Bartolica. Lining the road were girls flinging rose petals at Virtrian in a parody of the force needed to vanquish Yarron. Samondel marched before the prisoners in a flight jacket and trews that blazed with gold embroidery and jewels, with her long hair unbound and flowing out behind her like a red cloak. Flanking her were Archwarden Stanbury and Acting Inspector General Vander Hannan, representing the courtly and civil arms of Bartolican government.

Vander had been allowed back into the court in spite of the indiscretion of his mother, but it was clear that someone else would be appointed as the permanent Inspector General. He thanked fortune that he would probably retain the post of Regional Inspector, although that would remove him from the capital at a time when Theresla was using his house as her base of operations and he was finding her very educational company. The permanent appointments were due to be distributed at that same day, and many would be rewards for military achievements and bravery. As Vander had not been in Yarron, he was conveniently not in line for such a reward.

The court was called to assemble while the parade was still approaching. The first matter of business was the welcome of the victorious wardens by their airlord, and these were assembled in the throne hall already. Across at the palace wingfield Laurelene was standing with the envoys' aides, guildsmen, and duty wardens. Having disgraced herself, she was not on the invitation list for Bartolica's day of triumph, but she was still nobility and thus had duties to perform. By the very nature of their duties, the wardens who were flying in the skies above the palace were excluded from court, so Laurelene presided over an extension of the court on the wingfield. There was a timber stand for the nobles to sit in, and this was decked with strings of flags and pennants. Laurelene read out announcements and proclamations without any real enthusiasm, and watched the streamers of colored smoke being woven in the sky by the gunwings.

None of them were aware that the war was far from over, least of all the former Airlord of Yarron.

6 May 3961: Wind River

Eighteen days of intensive training followed the arrival of the super-regals at Wind River. The super-regal crews were pushed hard, especially those converting from the small and agile gunwings. Ramsdel was chosen as Serjon's backup wingcaptain, but the other three of the flock did no more than normal patrols. Serjon also volunteered for night patrols over the Green River Basin, and the other member of his flock began to wonder when he slept, if at all. He could not speak of Bartolicans without cursing, and it was as if he was winding himself up into a frenzy.

"Bronlar's really worried about you," said Ramsdel as he and Serjon shaved behind the outdoor ablutions screen. "I mean we all are, but—"

"That's because I look a bit tired and pathetic."

"Ah, so this is a play for her?"

"No. One good night's sleep and she'll be back on Alion's knee. Big assembly this morning, have you seen how the guildsmen have been working on the super-regals?"

"Yes, we may be off to our first real target today."

The assembly was postponed several times owing to mechanical problems with one of the super-regals, but at last a trumpet blared for flock assembly. In the spring noon's chill the wingcaptains and their crews gathered around Sartov. They had already been given an early lunch after exercise drills, which suggested that they would soon be leaving on a mission. The engines of the five huge super-regals were being started by the guildsmen while Sartov was speaking, as were those of twenty gunwings.

"Long flight, I'd say," Serjon whispered to Bronlar as they watched Sartov handing out sealed envelopes himself.

"Look at what they're loading," she replied, and Serjon turned to see a line of trailers with the huge thousand-pound bombs being taken over to the super-regals.

"I'm wagering it's a strategic tramway bridge," he said. "All crews have been practicing at low-level, precision drops."

"Attend the Airlord of Yarron!" cried the wingfield adjunct for a second time. Everyone snapped to attention.

"Within those envelopes are your orders and maps," he said crisply. "Keep them sealed until you are inside your aircraft. The authority is from me, Airlord Sartov, you can check the seal. You are to proceed to Montpellier with four gunwings to each super-regal as escort. At Montpellier you will rendezvous with the gunwings of the Air Carbineer Guildsmen of North Yarron, who will escort you all the way to your target. There will be sixty of them. All of you have served with them before being posted here, so you know they are to be trusted."

There were whistles and exclamations of amazement at the size of the force.

"The Air Carbineers have orders that match your own. Are there any questions?"

Serjon raised his hand.

"Yes?"

"With all deference and humility, Lordship, but if a super-regal should be separated from the flock, what then?"

"If you are separated, then release your bombs and rockets on whatever target that presents and return here. Proceeding to the primary target alone would mean the almost certain loss of an expensive super-regal and crew, and I have other work planned for you all. Any other questions? No? Good. Good fortune and clement weather be with you."

They began to disperse. Serjon walked beside Bronlar, Ramsdel, Kumiar, and Alion for a way as they made for their gunwings.

"All us escorts have wing extenders, and thus a range of six hundred miles or so," observed Ramsdel. "Why you could fly to Condelor and back with a reach like that and still have fuel left for a war duel. What target needs such penetration?"

"The guildsmen have put those strafing rocket racks on our gunwings as well as the super-regals," said Bronlar. "I'd like to see our orders."

"This is a mighty and noble endeavor, I hope the target is be equal to it," said Alion.

"Aye, you're right there, Alion," said Ramsdel. "Over half of the compression engines available to Yarron will be in the sky today. Should we be shot up, there will be precious few to hold Yarron for the Airlord."

"Pray for light winds," advised Serjon. "This is shaping into a very long mission. Six hundred miles at most."

"Why bother guessing at what you will learn once you are inside your super-regal and able to open your orders?" asked Kumiar.

"A good warrior should be able to guess his commander's strategy," Ramsdel replied. "My guess is that we are striking the tramway junction yards at Idaho Falls."

"That is within range of a light gunwing," said Serjon.

"But it's different if we have to duel," countered Ramsdel. "Bad headwinds, or a long duel, and we would use up our reserve margin, leaving you on your own."

"Agreed, agreed," said Serjon, stopping as they drew level with the cockpit of the huge super-regal. "Good hunting, gentlefolk, and watch your fuel mixtures."

"Good hunting, Serjon, and watch your mirror."

"I don't have one, I use a tail gunner."

The engines of all their wings were idling and the fuel tanks were being topped up from handcarts. The three other crewmen were already aboard as Serjon clambered inside.

"Here are the orders, sairs," he said, flourishing the sealed package. "Let's get this thing ascended and see whose revel we get to spoil. Guildsman Perric?"

"Present."

"Gunner Lurmant?"

"Present."

"Gunner Vortiel?"

"Present."

"Very well, to your posts. Perric, how are the engines?" Serjon asked as they strapped into their seats.

"Steady so far," said the guildsman, who was by nature gloomy about any device operating reliably for long. "Oil pressure within normal range in all, temperature reads orange in Port 1."

"Once we get an airstream over the fins that should drop, what do you say?"

"You may be right, Wingcaptain Feydamor."

The adjunct waved the green flag, and the gunwings began to file out to the airstrip along the dispersal tracks. Bronlar's aircraft labored to gain speed with its load of fuel and ammunition strips. It shot out over the fallaway, dropped, then rose sluggishly into the thin air of Wind River. She climbed, banked, and circled the wingfield.

Serjon's super-regal was next onto the strip. Perric brought all six engines up to boost and the enormous wing began gathering speed. Like the gunwings, it was overloaded. Serjon had persuaded the wing to ascend with such a weight in practice runs, but it was tricky. That was why there were now only five super-regals and not six.

The super-regal rotated and its wheels spun clear of the strip as it heaved into the air just before the fallaway. The two gunners unlatched the main wheel frames and began winding them up while Perric worked on the nosewheel. Serjon banked gently to the left and circled the wingfield, watching the next super-regal ascending. In only minutes the five super-regals were in a shallow V formation and climbing to clear the peaks of the Wind River Range as they headed southwest.

Serjon broke the seal on his orders and divided his pa-

pers from those of the bombardier-guildsman. They were
to rendezvous at Montpellier and turn north slightly to
avoid the Weston and Pocatello wingfields to fly on to . . .
Twin Falls! Serjon whistled. That was nearly a six-
hundred-mile return journey. They were to bomb and
strafe a secret assembly field for Bartolican gunwings.

Perric returned to his seat and noticed Serjon reading
the orders.

"All wheels locked for flight, Wingcaptain," he reported
crisply.

"Very good. Our orders are to proceed to Montpellier,
where we rendezvous with a flock of sixty gunwings."

"May I ask our target, Wingcaptain?"

Serjon hesitated, and made a show of checking his orders again.

"No, Guildsman Perric. If the mission should be abandoned for any reason, we want as few as possible knowing
that we had designs on the target."

"Very good, Wingcaptain."

Also circling Wind River was the flyer of gunwing Blackfeather, who broke open his pack of orders and scanned
them. Cavos Lester's pulse quickened as he read. The assembly field at Twin Falls, but they were not going there
in a straight line. Sensible. They would have a different
route home, a straight and direct route.

Slowly Lester dropped back as they circled; then he
broke away and headed almost due west, his engine on
overboost as he vented fuel to save weight. Blackfeather
only had to reach Twin Falls fast, it did not have to get
back. By flying the direct route he could be there with as
much as a half-hour margin—ample time to warn the res-
ident wardens of the impending attack and have them into
the air. He prayed silently that a Call would not be sweeping over Twin Falls as he arrived.

He changed the mixture back to a fast cruise setting as
he flew up among the mountains and the gunwing rocked

in the thermals. He pulled out his map plates and discarded several in turn, then adjusted his course. Ahead of him the sky was clear and the landmark peaks were clearly visible.

Bullets suddenly ripped through the fabric of the gun-wing and the engine lost power. The horrified flyer broke off into a sluggish dive at once, catching a glance of the gunwing that was pursuing. A Yarronese gunwing!

The fast, short-range gunwing was behind him. It was more than a match for a gunwing lumbering along with extenders at 130 mph. Lester thought frantically. Gannett Peak was to port and the Bartolican border only minutes away, but no wingfield or town was nearby.

The gunwing fired again, sending a hailstorm of bullets through Lester's gunwing. Lester unbuckled himself and released the catches on the sailwing's canopy. It tore free and was sucked away as he released the last catch; then he clambered out and jumped without hesitation. His gun-wing flew on in a shallow dive, but the pursuing gunwing broke off and circled. Suddenly terrified, Lester spilled air from his parachute to drop faster. The gunwing closed with its guns chattering.

In the attacking gunwing Air Carbineer Tallier watched dark fragments being torn from the body of the man beneath the parachute; then he swooped past.

"May I never, never have to do that again!" he said to himself.

Circling, he saw that most of his victim's skull was gone; he was dead in his harness. Tallier broke off from the descending corpse and went after the empty gunwing again. As he caught up Tallier could see smoke leaking in a thin stream from the engine. Two more bursts sent the gunwing into a spin. It struck a mountainside, spilling a long streamer of flame from its compression spirit tanks. Tallier now turned east and set a zigzag course for Gannett wingfield. Far below a puzzled party of Bartolican troops set off to capture the enemy flyer who had been shot at by one of his own side's gunwings. It was two days before they found the body, and another five before a sailwing courier brought the flyer's papers to Condelor for decoding.

Off to the southwest the five super-regals droned steadily along, with their watchful escort of nineteen gunwings trailing along behind. By now they were over Bartolican territory, but they were too high to be in danger from groundfire. In any case, the area was sparsely populated.

"Wyoming Peak to starboard," Serjon called to the guildsman.

"That's where it ought to be, Wingcaptain. Estimated greeting with the sailwing flock, twenty minutes and three."

A whistle came over the speaker pipe. Serjon shouted "Wingcaptain!" and held it to his ear.

"Gunner Vortiel here, Wingcaptain. Flock of gunwings in sight, bearing to third quarter and a fifth positive."

"Third quarter and a fifth positive?" asked Serjon.

"Confirmed."

"The gunwing flock should approach from starboard, and second quarter nil. What guild are the airframes? Those of the Air Carbineers?"

"Not triwing types, Wingcaptain, canards. They're Bartolican wardens."

The Bartolican wardens were on their way back from Yarron to Condelor for a meeting to assess the strategy for destroying the rest of the Yarron's forces. Taking the example of the Yarronese, they climbed for a high attack.

"Relay engine throttles to master panel," called Serjon.

The clank-clank of levers being moved clacked out six times.

"Confirmed, engine throttles to master panel," shouted Perric.

"Gunners Lurmant and Vortiel, repair to your posts and report."

"Vortiel at rear," came a voice, followed by "Lurmant at dome."

"Guildsman Perric, are you at damage control and strapped in?"

"Confirmed at damage control, sair Wingcaptain."

"Gunwings, diving," shouted Vortiel and Lurmant together.

"One at a time on that pipe," shouted Serjon back. "Gunners, fire at your discretion."

The Bartolican gunwings had by now been tuned for higher speeds, and were nearly twice as fast in a dive than the Yarronese super-regals. They roared down through the defending shield of gunwings and fired into the super-regals before sweeping on past. Port 3 engine began to lose power.

"Reporting loss of power in Port 3," shouted Perric above the engines and reaction guns. "Suggest mixture boost."

"Boost at maximum now," Serjon lied.

"Gunwing flocks engaging," Lurmant reported from the dome. "The super-regals are on their own, but we're dropping back and losing height."

"Gunwing, rear, starboard, climbing," Vortiel shouted into the tube above the chatter of his reaction guns.

Off to port Serjon saw an attack wedge of Bartolicans closing with them in a shallow dive. Almost at once Kumiar and Ramsdel cut across the super-regal into the Bartolicans' path. They converged, guns chattering; the Bartolicans broke and scattered. One of them swerved right into Kumiar's path, and there was a lurid starburst of flames, smoke, wreckage, and exploding ammunition. Ramsdel plunged through the debris, then pulled into a long, banking dive. He was trailing smoke and fighting for control, shedding his pod tanks and rockets. Serjon lost sight of him.

"Sleep in clouds, my friends," whispered Serjon. "You will be with me as I tear the Bartolican heart out."

that warden girl, Bronlar. Oh, and Pel Jemarial was reported as being alive at the aviad wingfield."

"Pel, ah, Pel, back from the dead. Did Bronlar and Serjon seem, er, happy?"

"Yes, and I'd not bother looking for them until the morning."

Sartov gave a brief account of the attack on the aviad bases. Only five sailwings had escaped south before the surrender at Sioux City, and there was a report of a Sandhawk gunwing linking up with one of the huge sunwings over the Red Desert.

"Six stolen wings are not going to bring Mounthaven down," Sartov concluded. "We have beaten them."

Although exhausted, Feydamor now began the long explanation of what had happened a thousand miles to the west that day. Suddenly it became clear to Sartov why the Call had ceased.

"This is the end of Yarron, of Mounthaven, of the wardenate system," Sartov said, looking as if something inside him had collapsed. The shadows accentuated the lines on his face, and he looked decades older. "Everything I fought for, all that our people died for, all gone."

"But with the Callscour gone we can expand east," said Feydamor. "We have the wings with the greatest range, and we have over a million displaced people who can move into the wilderness and build new lives."

"But it won't be Yarron, Jeb. The rabble from Mexhaven will be there too. How can we fight their style of unchivalric war?"

"We just spent a year learning to do just that."

Sartov waved the suggestion away.

"I wanted to go back to gunwings and chivalry. I smashed on the code of chivalry to save the code of chivalry, and—gah, Jeb, I'd nearly restored it when the one Callwalker woman in all of Mounthaven thwarted me. Mounthaven is gone, broken like an egg. Now the chicken will leave the pieces of shell and never return. No more duels, no more parades, and why bother with having a pennant pole at a wingfield if the flyers are going to take their wings out over the frontier and never return?"

Feydamor sipped at his drink, tired and wrung out but unable to share in his airlord's depression.

"The world has changed, Alveris, like it or not," he said as he heard Laurelene shouting at someone in the distance and stood up to go. "You led Yarron out of hell, nobody else could have done it. Are you going to desert your people now, when they need your help and leadership even more?"

Sartov tried to put his mug on the low table, but misjudged the distance to the edge through fatigue and it fell to the ground.

"Do you really think I can do any good?" asked Sartov.

Feydamor extended his hand and drew Sartov up from his chair. "Alveris, nobody else is even in your class," he said as they walked out of the command tent.

The running battle raged for only a few minutes, but it was costly for both sides. Five Bartolican gunwings went down for three Yarronese destroyed and two damaged, including Ramsdel's wing. Increasing cloud added to the confusion, but Bear Lake was by now visible to the south. Low on fuel even when they attacked, the Bartolicans broke off.

Four super-regals stayed together, holding their course until they met with the flock of Air Carbineers from Gannett. Ramsdel launched his pair of wing rockets and began the trip back to Wind River, too busy keeping in the air to worry about where Bronlar and Alion were. They were, in fact, still heading southwest.

Bronlar knew that she was now outside the mission profile, but Serjon's super-regal had an engine that was apparently damaged. It was not losing height as she went after it, but its course did not match anything in her orders. Still, the giant wing could absorb more damage than a gunwing, and Serjon's orders probably included targets of opportunity. Alion stayed with the super-regal as well, sharing Bronlar's reasoning.

"Gentlefolk, we appear to be alone," Serjon announced over the pipe as he adjusted the engines back to proper tuning. "We also appear to have full power again."

"Two gunwings from Wind River still flying escort," reported Lurmant. "The crests are of Warden Damaric and Air Carbineer Jemarial."

Serjon cursed softly, then caught himself. None but him on the super-regal knew that the official target was at Twin Falls. Perhaps Bronlar and Alion would assume he had extra orders that they did not. His own target was much closer, and the gunwings could easily get back to Wind River. They would be welcome as an escort, of course.

"Gentlefolk, the target in this mission is the royal palace of Condelor, the seat of the Bartolican Airlord," he announced, then sat back to whistles and "Humping Call-walkers!"

"Just now we're separated from the main flock, but we're fully functional and on course. We shall come in from the north. The target is the large stained-glass window above the main steps of the palace and just back from the fountains."

Serjon had done this in his fantasies time and again in the month past, and now he called the measurements, distances, and perspective frame settings to Perric as he strapped himself into the observation bunk in the nose. The idea had been born when he had seen a super-regal for the first time, and it was why he had abandoned gun-wings. His career in the air would be over the moment that he stepped back onto Yarronese soil, but the Bartolican nobility would at last be really hurt for what had happened at Opal and uncounted other wardens' estates. They cleared the mountains and flew out over the irrigated farm-lands.

"Bear River in sight," Perric reported from the nose viewport.

"Releasing ballistic rocket arming bars one, two, three, and four," Serjon called.

"Condelor to Pocatello tramway in sight," Perric echoed. "Change heading to due south, less five."

"Banking . . . due south less five, confirmed."

"Twenty miles to target."

"Guildsman Perric, proceed to the bomb chamber. Arm the bomb and connect the flyer's release lever cables."

There was a pause of more than a minute while Perric left the nose and carried out his orders. Serjon continued to lose height until they were only a few hundred feet from the irrigated farmland below.

"Perric from nose. Bomb armed and release connected to the flyer lines. Grid indicates twelve miles."

"Gun tests," ordered Serjon. "Tail and dome."

There was a brief burst from the reaction guns at the tail, followed by another from the dome.

"All functioning, Wingcaptain," the gunners reported in order.

"Status of escort, tail gunner?"

"Both at four hundred behind and fifty high. Ah—one, no, both have dropped their wing extenders."

"Ten miles—Condelor outskirts in sight!" cried Perric.

Condelor! None aboard but Serjon had ever seen the ancient and magnificent capital of Greater Bartolica. Serjon shed a little more height. Bronlar and Alion compensated, still guarding his back. He was the flockleader, after all, and they had to provide protection no matter what he did.

They came around low and fast, their compression engines roaring as they flew over a ridge that screened inner Condelor from sight. The ridge loomed, bare rock passed close beneath their wings. Small, dark things scurried for cover as the nightmare shapes of predator birds bore down on them, then passed on. The city unfolded before them, a patchwork of roads and stone dwellings beneath a light haze of smoke. They banked over the eastern quarter, which was all market gardens and terraces dotted with reservoir cisterns and aqueducts. Figures far below pointed, some even waved.

"Three miles!" warned Perric.

"Duel status?" asked Serjon.

"Clear skies," both gunners reported back.

"Two miles, target in sight."

Serjon had seen all this before; he had overflown Condelor at the Airlord's coronation. There were the gardens, the wingfield, the palace spires with parade and court colors flying—court was in session! That was too much to hope for, but . . .

"Gunwings to southeast, burning aerobatic flares," reported the dome gunner. "I'd say four miles, no threat for now."

"One mile!" called Perric. "Down—point, point. Port—

point. Steady . . . Aim reference in crosshairs. Down—
point. Steady."

They were over the gardens, Serjon ached to pull the
release lever but he had to trust the guildsman. There were
a lot of nobles about in the gardens. Some dived for the
ground, others ran. Nobles and royalty at an afternoon picnic, thought Serjon, but most of his attention was on the
looming palace.

"Drop!"

The super-regal lurched up as Serjon released its bomb,
roaring over the roof of the Great Hall of the Throne and
barely clearing the central tower behind it. The bomb
smashed neatly through the stained-glass centerpiece window of the Great Hall. A bright flash burst glass and flames
from every window; tiles lifted, then crashed back and
down into the carnage below in a roiling cloud of smoke
and dust. The tower teetered, the keystones at its base
blown away; then it collapsed down into the ruins.

"A very good hit," reported the tail gunner.

The bomb had detonated a few feet behind the throne
of the Airlord of Greater Bartolica, and if one could discuss differences in terms of millionths of a second, he was
one of the first to die. The blast, the falling roof, then the
collapsing tower annihilated the assembled nobility of
Greater Bartolica before they were aware of what had happened.

The super-regal banked over the city, then began another approach on the palace gardens. A part of Bronlar's
mind watched in wonder as the rest of her prepared for the
next pass on the palace. The palace had been hit and that
had to be the target. The Great Hall of the Throne had
been hit while the Airlord's personal colors and pennants
flew from the masts of the shattered tower. He had been
humiliated . . . he had probably been killed. On the palace
wingfield several gunwings were scrambling onto the ascent strip while the aerobatics display continued in the dis-

tance. She broke off for the wingfield, leaving the super-regal in Alion's care.

Alion was numb with shock. He had dropped lower than Bronlar and had seen the palace and its gardens very clearly. They passed over a parade with bands and marchers—and then he saw a tall girl with long, red hair unbound at the head of the parade. The bomb flew free.

Alion flew through the debris of the blast, fighting for control in the turbulent smoke and dust, and cursing Serjon and Sartov to hell. He followed the great super-regal around as it came in for another pass. Ahead, Bronlar broke off, heading for the wingfield. Ballistic rockets began streaming from the super-regal. The terrified groups of nobles in the gardens were in Serjon's sights now, and again there was a tiny figure running with long red hair streaming out behind her.

Alion tugged at a lever and his two ballistic rockets streaked into the super-regal's starboard wing.

The super-regal belched flame and smoke from the ravaged wing, lost height, and sliced the top from an ornamental tree while Alion stayed behind, firing his reaction guns into the central body. Incredibly, Serjon managed to level out, then ease the super-regal up slowly as he dumped a plume of fuel from ruptured tanks. He gunned the surviving port engines to overboost and cleared the palace garden walls, but began to clip more trees in the park beyond.

Serjon fought for height, but each tree that he touched robbed momentum. The enormous wing lost more power as the outer port engine seized; then it began dropping in a shallow glide. It clipped a gargoyle from the roof of a mansion and slid along a street. The wings were torn from the central body as it plowed its way through poles, carts, and garden fences before it demolished a low wall and splashed half into a canal.

Alion flew over the wreck. He had sacrificed everything

in the defense of his beloved. Now it was time to go to her side.

Bronlar had not seen Alion fire at Serjon. She had flown across to the palace wingfield, shooting two ballistic rockets into a gunwing that was ascending and strewing wreckage all over the flightstrip. She came around again, shooting her reaction guns at the other gunwings getting ready to ascend, then climbed to look for Serjon. She circled over the city in a tight curve, banking near-vertically and losing height as she came about to scan for Serjon. Beyond the palace there was a long smear of flame and wreckage that ended in a canal. By the sheer scale it could only have been the super-regal. Serjon was down, Serjon had to be dead.

The former Airlord of Yarron was left alone in the middle of the plaza before the steps to the Great Hall of the Throne. The carbineers who had been marching beside him scattered as a monstrous sailwing with Yarronese markings lumbered overhead. Musicians flung down their instruments and dived for cover, people in full parade regalia lay sprawled and cowering on the lawns or dived for bushes. The six-engine giant released a dark teardrop that arced down and smashed neatly through the colored leadlight glass of the Great Hall of the Throne. For a moment there was only a hole in the window; then glass, tiles, flames, and smoke belched from the windows and roof, followed by a blast of sound that doubled Virtrian over like a punch to the stomach.

Somehow the former Airlord was spared the shards of glass and debris that hurtled past him. The remains of the roof collapsed with a mighty rumble, parts of the walls began to tumble as well, some out and some inward, and then the tower came down in a fantastic cascade of bricks, stone and masonry. Virtrian fell to his knees, his fist raised, cheering.

Yarron was undefeated, Yarron was being avenged.

* * *

Stanbury watched in horror as the tower collapsed. This was the very hour of triumph for the Airlord of Bartolica, yet an infernal monster of a sailwing had appeared from nowhere to hit the Great Hall itself.

"You say they are vanquished, yet they can still do *that*?" cried Vander, stabbing a finger up at the stump of the shattered palace tower.

"An act of wanton terrorism, nothing more," Stanbury shouted back. "They're suicidal fanatics and assassins."

"Those fanatics and assassins seem to have some very advanced sailwings," replied Hannan.

Stanbury looked north and wondered where the defending Bartolican gunwings were that should have been rising into the air. Distant shots thumped and crackled as the palace defenses fired at an enemy triwing-type gunwing circling far beyond the range of their guns. He had counted three wings, one an enormous type of regal. How had they flown so far? Kalward had said the Sentinels were now harmless, that the aviads had disarmed them to aid Mounthaven in the war. The aid obviously worked both ways.

"This looks bad, but it's nothing," said Stanbury dismissively, flapping a hand in the air as if the attack were a poorly fought clear air duel. "We knew they had two big regals and a dozen or so gunwings. We spared them out of mercy, but we should have crushed them. See there, at the south. Our own wardens are coming to slash them to pieces."

Somehow it was all so unreal to Bronlar. She was still alive while so many had died. Serjon in particular. She flew over his super-regal's wreckage, then turned away once she was satisfied that nothing could be done. Looking back to the palace, she could see that fires had started.

Her orders were unclear now. Off to the south there were gunwings approaching. Dragonfly-class gunwings, trainers. Bronlar counted, estimated twelve gunwings in the air. She banked, gaining height over the city as she turned north. Impossible odds, deadly odds. The dragonfly flyers were fresh, while she had been in the air nearly two hours—she attacked head-on.

Pieces were flayed off her first target, which rolled on its back and fell away as she flew past. The ragged formation broke up, some scattering, others trying to ram her. Bronlar banked and streaked up behind a second dragonfly with her reaction guns blazing. A wing tank ruptured and ignited, trailing a plume of fire as the warden bailed out. Now she realized that these gunwings were unarmed.

By now armed gunwings were ascending and Bronlar turned east to flee. Another dragonfly blundered up past her gunsights and she fired again. This time there were no dramatic fireworks, but the dragonfly continued to climb until it dropped back into a stall: the flyer was dead. Two dragonfly wings collided and fell circling, locked together.

All at once the sky seemed to be clear as Bronlar looked around. A dragonfly was trying to circle and climb behind her. She put her gunwing into a sharp turn and closed, taking advantage of her much larger engine, then fired a sustained burst at the dragonfly. Her guns suddenly began clicking, but the enemy's engine was trailing black smoke as it began to drop. Bronlar banked, caught sight of the looming dark form of a biwing gunwing, tried to swerve, and smashed into it with massive, wrenching impact.

Red curtained her vision, all balance was gone, and cold air howled past her head. Bronlar pulled out of a steep dive, wiped at the blood on her face, then looked for her compass. Its housing was bent, and it was useless. I'm unarmed and damaged, she thought. The mountains were ahead and her compression engine was droning steadily. She blacked out.

Laurelene turned away from the sky, folding her arms and staring expectantly at the wingfield adjunct, yet it was Warden Cadrice of Dorak who spoke.

"One Yarronese gunwing just destroyed six of your gun-wings and rammed another," said Cadrice. "It might have destroyed them all had they not fled."

"They—were in pursuit of the enemy sailwing—ah, regal!" retorted Adjunct Stanceous.

"The regal was down long before your gunwings flew west."

Adjunct Stanceous sucked breath in great gusts, as if pumping and stoking his fury.

"This is but the last thrashings of a mortally wounded maniac," he finally managed. "They will wish they had passed away quietly instead, I swear to it."

Bronlar awoke from a stupor, her compression engine still purring obediently. Blood had flowed down over her goggles. She pulled them away, shivering in the air that was whistling through the smashed glass-laminate plates of her canopy. Below were bare mountains with no familiar landmarks. The sky above was hazy, tinted red by blood that had trickled into her eyes. The dashclock was shattered, the fuel gauge read empty. The sun was high in the sky and to her right. Going east, then, and over mountains, she thought. Can't have been blacked out for more than a few minutes, so I'm still over Bartolica, or maybe occupied Montras. Where might I find Montrassian rebels, if there are any?

The engine spluttered, then caught again. Reflexively she reached up and switched to another wing tank. Again she blacked out.

When she revived again she was shivering and there was yet more blood in her eyes. The blood was cold and caked hard. It seemed as if she had been asleep for hours—and bleeding all the while. The gunwing had been flying level, true to the guidance of the autobalance. The mountains were unfamiliar and bare, but they were giving way to more gently undulating country ahead.

Off to starboard was a Call tower, and near that was a

well-maintained wallroad and tramway. There were few trees, this was all mountains and grazing land. The reserve held five minutes of fuel, even hanging just above stall speed; she had to decide what to do quickly. A Call tower meant a town nearby. With lethargy weighing down on her limbs she leaned forward and peered about. No town. But the town would be to the west of a Call tower anyway. A flash of color caught her eye on a plateau to the left. A wind pennant, and that meant a wing-field.

She banked sluggishly and approached, then circled once. Red and gold on the wind pennant meant a regional capital's wingfield. She straightened, reduced power, dropped. The wind was light and steady, the surface seemed to be rammed gravel in clay. Her wheels touched, shrieked and spun. As she rolled to a stop she cut the engine. Nobody there. She unclipped her harness, tried to move—and blacked out.

Bronlar awoke with her canopy off and two men lifting her out of the cockpit. Their language was familiar but she only recognized occasional words.

"Girl!" and "Squire girl!" were being repeated over and over.

"Does anyone speak Yarronese?" she whispered.

"Speaking, yairs," replied one of the men lowering her onto a stretcher.

"Where is this, what dominion?"

"This is the Vernal wingfield in the dominion of Glorious Cosdora. Lying very still now, if it is to please."

Cosdora, a neutral dominion. Tears of relief trickled from Bronlar's eyes and mixed with the blood caking her face.

"As an Air Carbineer of Yarron I request asylum and sanctuary in the wardenate of Cosdora," she said firmly.

"Young Semme, adjunct is sent for and granting is likely. You are out of war."

*   *   *

Hours later the four surviving super-regals and their escort returned to Wind River. The flockleader reported a great victory: Twin Falls assembly wingfield had been bombed, rocketed, and left in flames. The Bartolicans had been caught completely off-guard. The shatter-bombs had hit the central area; then the ballistic rockets and reaction guns had strafed without mercy for a full ten minutes. One super-regal had not returned, and nine gunwings had been lost as well as the two that had returned earlier.

"But the super-regal and two of the gunwings were not lost in the attack on Twin Falls," the adjunct reported to Sartov as he flicked through the pages on his board.

"Then what happened?" Sartov asked.

"They became separated quite early in the flight, after the Bartolican flock attacked. They were last seen flying southwest."

"They might have landed in neutral territory," said Sartov, turning to a map on the wall of the adjunct's tent.

The adjunct traced the likely flight path. "It takes them quite close to Condelor, and all its wingfields. Does that look hopeful?"

"Feydamor was the super-regal's wingcaptain, and the escorts were Wardens Damaric and Jemarial. Why did it have to be them? The whole of Serjon's flock gone, apart from young Ramsdel."

"If it is any comfort, they were not confirmed destroyed."

"Well, if they were killed, let us hope that they died bravely and took a few Bartolicans with them."

In the distance someone in a flight jacket waved then saluted. Sartov beckoned him over, and they saw that it was Ramsdel.

"You should be with the medic," said Sartov as the limping flyer approached.

"I've just come from the medic. It's Semme Liesel."

"Kumiar's girl?"

"Yes. She just shot herself."

It was not until the following day that strange rumors of Condelar being bombed by a huge Yarronese regal found their way to Sartov. It was even said that the Bartolican Airlord himself had been killed and that his palace was destroyed. Sartov dismissed the reports as nonsense, but he nevertheless decided to send one of the high-altitude sailwings over. Such extensive damage should have been visible from the air . . . and it certainly was.

6 May 3961: Eastern Yarron

Yarron had come back from the dead as Rollins' tram sat concealed in a siding in eastern Yarron on the cool May afternoon. He heard the peeping code begin, and then he memorized the message exchange word for word. The content was ominous, and Rollins decided that it was now worth his while to jump from the Bartolican war machine at the first opportunity. He did not realize how literally he would have to do just that.

    # palace bombed by Yarronese regal as big as a town
    # Airlord dead thousands dead aviad liaisons dead
    # need orders no liaisons left
    * who is Commander in Chief
    # Carabas

The hysteria in the distant signaler's words could not be masked by the uniform, shrill peeping. What was in his head might not get Rollins anything but a spray of bullets from his present masters, but the Yarronese might see him as a hero. It was all a matter of getting his head intact to the Yarronese lines.

That night the black tram was proceeding unescorted through the late evening, burning smoky, cinder-laden wood of very poor quality. A Yarronese sailwing came in low, and was not seen by the roof gunner until it was too late. There was a prolonged exchange of reaction gun fire that riddled the black tram and holed its boiler. The sail-wing swooped away trailing smoke and went into a wide, shallow banking turn.

Rollins saw flames playing about the engine as it came around for another pass and headed in at a shallow angle to the tramway. The flyer was very low, thought Rollins . . . or was mortally wounded. He undid his Call straps in a moment, flung open the forward door, and leaped into the darkness. Crashing through bushes on a steep embank-ment, he came to rest with a splintering thunderclap in his ears.

The gunwing had knocked the black tram neatly from the tramway and down an embankment shadowed from Mirror-sun. They were west of Douglas and ten miles from an unmarked siding behind the North Yarronese front, and through some miracle the gunwing's load of compression spirit had not caught fire. Everyone but Rollins seemed dead. The broken bodies of a Yarronese girl in a glittering flying jacket and her observer remained in the gunwing. He found a handful of glowbars in the flyer's pocket and bent one until light began to leak out. The mangled sail-wing was almost unidentifiable as a two-seat type. Almost. Had Rollins been a coward he might not have yielded to temptation, but he was in fact a seasoned warrior and brave man. He was also a mercenary, and his masters had re-ceived some very serious reversals.

For the first time Rollins explored the black tram's shat-tered forbidden chambers, selecting what were hopefully significant samples of cards and papers, and scratching likenesses of the smashed machines with a pencil. A tram passed above, then another. The wreckage remained hid-den in shadows. Here was a treasure trove that he could never get to Yarronese lines—but he could carry and hide paper. There would be manuals and repair diagrams, code books, and training notes.

Rollins spent an hour carrying armloads of paper and

dumping them into a rocky grotto. He also dropped the sunwing's mangled reaction gun and mounting in before rolling rocks over onto the hoard of secrets. Returning to the wreckage, he dragged the observer's body into the tram and draped his own jacket over it; then, as an introduction to the Yarronese, he removed the flight jacket collar and colors from the dead flyer girl. Finally he set fire to the spilled compression spirit.

Carabas was on a red tram that came back to investigate the fire by the trackside later that night. Anyone could see that the wrecked Yarronese gunwing had been responsible for destroying the black tram, and all that remained to be gathered and removed were a few scattered papers that had survived the blaze.

"There were no looters," an officer reported. "There was gold scattered everywhere, left untouched."

"Just as well," said Carabas in a dangerously cold voice. "How many bodies did you find?"

"The pieces add up."

"Indeed? Have you identified them?"

"The charring makes that hard. The components, guards, and comms died in their seats. The stoker's head was found thrown clear of the fire, so we're sure of him. The sailwing hit the driver's cabin so hard that we can't even identify its configuration. No reaction guns were found, so we think it was some new type armed only with rockets. Here are the buttons of the driver, Rollins, and part of his skull."

The charred fragment of bone was still warm as Carabas turned it over in his fingers.

"So, the death sentence that he fled for so long has caught up at last."

"It burned like a haystack," said the red tram's driver.

"The black trams are designed to burn," explained Carabas. "It is a security feature." He tossed the piece of bone into the lamplit wreckage.

"Shall I have tracker terriers brought in?" asked the officer.

Rollins' blood went cold. Tracker terriers. If he stayed they would find him, if he ran they would still find him. They would also lead Carabas to the cache of papers.

"No, no," sighed Carabas. "The bits add up, Fras Merrick. One complete crew for the black tram, and one flyer for the sailwing."

Rollins slipped away, shivering with relief. He traveled only by night across the open, rocky woodland and slept in trees, tied against any Call that swept over. He was unprepared for life in the open, in spite of all his time with the tramways, but using a compass and crawling more than walking to avoid Bartolican carbineer patrols and snipers, the defector took a week to cover the fifteen miles to Yarronese-held land.

7 May 3961: Vernal, Cosdora

Bronlar did not wake for fifteen hours. Her gunwing was being repaired as she began to walk about, and even after half a day of work the damage was still appalling. Even more appalling was the amount of blood in the cockpit. No wonder I passed out, she thought. The cut went along her hairline and down across one temple, but it had not been deep.

Reports on the attack on Condelor's palace were confused and contradictory, but her hosts seemed to think that three hundred Yarron gunwings had escorted fifty regals to the Bartolican capital, where they had bombed the Airlord's palace and shattered the Airlord's flock of wardens. Other reports claimed that a single, heroic wing had done it all—Bronlar's! On one point all the stories agreed, however. The court had been in session at the time of the attack, and the Airlord of Greater Bartolica and the most

senior nobles of his retinue had been killed when the roof
of the throne hall and tower collapsed.

Bronlar was hailed as a great hero by the Cosdoran
ground crew, yet the sheer magnitude of what she had
helped achieve chilled her as she sat drinking hot chicken
broth with a compression spirit barrel for a table and
watching the repairs to her gunwing. Every one of the
mechanics had a strip of blood-soaked fabric cut from her
gunwing pinned to his arm. Her parents had been avenged,
Serjon's family had been avenged, yet why did she feel so
hollow, she wondered. War duels in the air were combat,
why should not an attack on the Airlord be combat? Nausea, her old enemy, clutched at her stomach, as it had the
day she had shot down a warden and nine sailwings near
Casper. Only two of those flyers had lived. She blanked
her mind against the miasma of guilt and blood, and pic-
tured Serjon arguing with Liesel about finding thirteen
pieces of emu meat in his serving of goulash.

A guildsman came over, a chubby but presentable youth
in his early twenties. He had an open, cheerful face, and
wore a pottery gunwing around his neck on a length of
hair braid.

"Semme Bronlar, you look so much better," he said,
taking a stool and sitting beside her.

Bronlar squirmed inwardly. Such familiarity was pro-
scribed by the code of conduct of Mounthaven guildsmen, yet this place was remote and relaxed. The guildsmen
tending her gunwing were all volunteers, and she was not
inclined to demand formal deference.

"How is Slash?" she asked, standing up and walking
toward the gunwing. The guildsman bounded up and followed her.

"Pah, not bad, not bad at all. Canopy panes and frame
smashed, damage to most cockpit instruments, and a third
of your right upper wing torn away. I'm Ryban of the
Cosdoran Fuelers' Cooperative."

The upper wing had been removed and was laid out on

a dropcloth. An airframe guildsman named Farrasond had been proclaimed guildmaster by the nine youths who were working on Slash. He was almost as short as Bronlar, but very well developed across the shoulders. Farrasond seemed a good leader, but was painfully shy with girls.

"We're comparing ribs from the left with those from stores," he chattered, unable to look her in the face. "We can trim them down and get a good match. Five days, with two more for the bonding to cure."

"Thank you for all this effort," Bronlar replied, "but I'll not be allowed to fly again, this is a neutral dominion relative to Yarron."

"Ah, but Semme, we might arrange a little test flight where someone disguised as Sair Rewlon gets into the cockpit and flies away to Yarron," suggested Ryban.

"None of that, I'll not get you into trouble," said Bronlar firmly.

"The compression engine is in fine tune," declared a guildsman in his late twenties who was introduced as Holdrik. "May I know the name?"

"Hailbeater, and he's about a century old. What can I do to repay all this? I'm a prisoner, I have nothing to offer."

"Oh, your story can be payment!" an airframe guildsman named Monterbil declared at once. "Ryban and I are, well, we fancy ourselves as bards. To serve a legendary hero is the stuff of our wildest dreams, but to set her story to epic verse is almost beyond imagining."

For some reason it crossed her mind that Serjon did not like poets of any description—but Serjon was dead.

"Call me at lunchtime, I'll begin to tell whatever I can recall."

As had happened in Forian many months before, the Bartolican guards frantically scrabbled through the ruins of the throne hall in the search of the Airlord and his retinue. As had also happened in Forian, there were very few survivors. There were a lot more dead.

Yarron was very much alive and very, very dangerous. Stanbury was there when the few recognizable fragments of the Airlord were being collected. His younger brother, his consort, his closer relations, all had been in the Great Hall of the Throne to celebrate Bartolica's great triumph. All had been killed.

Herald Jitres came scrambling across the litter of smashed red tiles and beams.

"Great tidings, Archwarden. The city constables have captured two of the Yarronese assassins!"

"Two? Just two? That's meant to be great tidings?"

"Surely—"

"Sair Jitres, the Yarronese have stabbed the very heart of Bartolica! There were no armed defenders aloft until it was too late, and even then they were slashed from the sky—those of them who did not flee first."

"The best wardens were trailing colors for the victory court."

"And how many Yarronese were shot down with colored smoke? How many by girls throwing rose petals?"

"We caught two—"

"Why are two Yarronese so very significant?"

"Archwarden, one of them has defected and asked for asylum. He is Warden Alion Damaric of the Timberwing house. His gunwing is at the palace wingfield. He craves the favor of the Airlord."

"Well he won't find any Airlords in Bartolica. Samondel appears to be the new Airlord Designate, she was lucky enough to be out in the gardens when the bomb burst."

"A woman as Airlord, Archwarden?"

"A woman, sair Herald Jitres. You had better have a coronation festival prepared, she is a warden and can take the coronation oath."

"She has actually flown? I thought it was a joke. Can a woman do such a thing?"

"Yarronese women can, by all accounts."

7 May 3961: Condelor

Serjon was lying on a padded stone slab in a cell when he awoke. His face had several gashes which had been stitched up, and his right arm was splinted and bandaged. He took a deep breath, and immediately winced with pain. Broken rib, he thought.

As he sat up and swung his legs to the floor he saw that there was a tin mug of water, half a loaf of rough-ground bread, and some cuts of cheese. At the sight of food he realized that he was quite hungry and began to eat. Whatever the Bartolicans thought of him, they at least wanted him alive—for now. He drank. There was a trace of lime in the water, probably to ward off jail scurvy without giving him the luxury of fresh fruit. Every swallow hurt, and he began to cough.

"So you are awake, then?" called a voice from beyond the door.

Serjon's first thought was that it was a guard, but the man was speaking in cultured Yarronese.

"Are you another prisoner of war?" Serjon asked back.

"In truth, you might say that. I am Virtrian, ex-Chancellor of Forian."

Serjon thought for a moment. This was either a monstrous hoax, or . . .

"The girl who flew you to Casper to abdicate: what did she ask for when you were returned to Forian?"

"That was Bronlar Jemarial, and she asked for a length of green plush. I called a herald over and cut some from his jacket for her."

Very few people could have replied instantly to the question, Serjon was sure of that.

"I am Wingcaptain Serjon Feydamor of the Yarronese Third Special Air Carbineers."

There was a pause before the other replied.

"Serjon, Serjon Feydamor. You flew into Forian with Bronlar when it was under siege. So, Yarronese chivalry has been replaced with Air Carbineers. Your attack on the palace was very effective."

"It may give the Airlord something to think about."

"The Airlord of Bartolica is unlikely to think about anything, Wingcaptain Feydamor. Grand court was in session when you dropped your little tribute through his stained-glass window. Luckily I was being marched in late. I saw it all, though, and I later learned that over a thousand nobles perished. The very cream of Bartolican nobility and their airlord are dead."

The impact of this revelation took some time to register with Serjon. He had had revenge for his family, and far beyond his wildest dreams. Had just a dozen or two people died he would have been more shaken, but a thousand! The number put a glaze over the loss of individual lives, but tiny, impotent voices seemed to chirp at him from some cold and distant place. Multitudes of incorporeal cold hands reached out to him.

"Are you all right?" called Virtrian when the silence began to lengthen.

"Yes, yes. Thank you for your concern."

"I shall not ask you about the Yarronese forces still fighting, they are obviously in better strength than Bartolica's wardens would have me believe. Besides, someone is sure to be listening to us. That giant sailwing! Sartov made some very effective preparations during the winter, that's obvious. I don't know how it escapes the fire from the Sentinels, though."

"We have developed a shielding device of polished crystals, but I don't understand how it works."

"I expect so. You will be questioned, however. I heard the guards talking when you were brought in—they didn't realize that I know enough Bartolican to follow a conversation. Your survival has been kept a secret from the people of Condelor. An announcement was made that all the attackers were killed after what was called your 'cowardly surprise attack.' "

"So, I'm not being held under chivalric conventions?"

"No, and you will be tortured, there is nothing more certain."

A dark thought crossed Serjon's mind.

"Are there any more survivors?"

"Both gunwings of your escort appeared to be flying and undamaged when I last saw them. Do you have any recollection of what happened?"

"One or both of my escort may have opened fire on my super-regal as I returned for a rocket attack. Is that so?"

"It shames me to accuse a fellow Yarronese of it, but yes. I saw one gunwing open fire, but I could not see his markings and the engine notes were masked by the giant regal's six engines. There was only one gunwing near your super-regal at the time."

As Serjon ate the rest of his bread and cheese he realized that the traitor would pose a problem for the Bartolicans. On the one hand he—or she—would be a hero, but on the other the shooting down of the super-regal by a trusted escort was the most gross breach of chivalric convention possible. Serjon could not have known how much more trouble the traitor was really causing.

In another, and far more comfortable, part of the palace, Stanbury was gathering together what was left of the Bartolican nobility. Warden Samondel was the clear and undisputed successor to the Airlord owing to the other contenders being dead, while the only other nearby wardens to have survived the bomb were the dozen or so who had been performing patrol and aerobatic duties. Two of these had died after being shot down by the escaping Yarronese gunwing.

"The coronation will take place in five days, in the Hall of Morning Light," Stanbury said to Vander Hannan, a junior herald, three nobles, and a frantically scribbling clerk. "A façade of tentcloth is to be assembled and painted brown, then erected over the ruins. The least traces possible of the Yarronese attack are to be visible."

"What of security?" asked Vander, who was once again Acting Inspector General.

"Sailwings have already been dispatched to gather three hundred gunwings and sailwings to mass in the sky during the coronation. It will be the greatest display of air power in history, late though it is."

"What of the court lists?" asked the herald. "The heads of the better estates are dead and their people are in mourning."

"Well get them out of mourning!" shouted Stanbury. "Grandmothers, children, maiden aunts, wastrel uncles, mistresses, get them *all* into the hall and dressed in their glittering best for the coronation. Bartolica will *not* be brought low by three wings! Understand?"

"Yes, Commander," they said together.

Kalward entered once they had left. He sat on the table where the clerk had been writing.

"Did you hear all that?" asked Stanbury.

"Yes, and you were right. This is a heavy blow, but not a death wound. As I see it, your only problem is one of unity," Kalward said urgently, tapping the table with one finger while gesturing to a map on the wall.

"My main problem was one of claiming victory when it was in sight, but not in hand," Stanbury said between clenched teeth. "Yarronese wardens still control enough land and resources to ascend those monstrous six-engine regals. Why didn't you warn me about them? Where were your unstoppable Callwalker spies?"

"Wind River is dangerous and remote. Some of my best agents have vanished while trying to journey there."

"That thing was a over hundred feet across!" Stanbury burst out. "Why can't *we* build the like?"

"You can," Kalward replied smoothly. "I warned you that the Sentinels had been neutralized by my colleagues.

Your gunwings and sailwings are mostly still within the old limits, and the Yarronese tear them to pieces."

"The wardens didn't want to listen!" Stanbury shouted back, exasperated beyond bearing. "For centuries our chivalry has operated within those limits: twenty-nine feet six inches in length or wingspan, and one hundred and twenty-five miles per hour in speed. Now they can't give the limits up without losing their souls. People love the bars that confine them, sair Kalward."

Kalward looked down at the table for a moment, still tapping it lightly with his finger.

"So, think on what has really been lost. Only some hundreds of nobles, courtiers, and bishops—"

"And wardens!"

"Wardens who were besotted with the old limits. The guilds are easier to manipulate, you can have the biggest, fastest gunwings in all Mounthaven built, you can build a super-regal twice the wingspan of the one that came down in Lilyflower Canal."

"Two hundred of the dead wardens were there to be decorated for valor during the war. They were our best. Raglamal with twenty-seven victories. Kalfior, with four of their hybrid gunwings among his twenty-four clear air victories. Most were *my people*, those ready for honors and those being groomed for my new administration. The survivors are those who have had least to do with the war effort: the mediocre, the inexperienced, the dissenters, the rebels, the cowards, and the fools."

Stanbury glared at Kalward, as if to say that he fitted the last-named category.

"It is not as bad as that," Kalward replied innocently. "There are still many good and loyal wardens in Bartolica. Even better, there is a girl on the throne now, so you will have near-absolute control. You can blame the lack of advancement of the surviving wardens on the previous airlord, or on any number of the dead nobles. No tragedy is without opportunity, Archwarden Stanbury."

"What about the four hundred sailwings and gunwings left idle? Have we enough flyers to fly them?"

"My auxiliary training program has been effective—"

"But *how* effective? Can the flyers be relied upon in battle?"

"There is an easy way to find out, sair Stanbury. We shall give your people a glorious victory in the hour of their greatest sorrow and despondency. I note that you are assembling three hundred armed wings for the coronation. Suppose we divert two-thirds of them for some special work on their way back to Yarron."

Kalward was given authority to appropriate guildsmen for a special project, and so it was that two hundred guildsmen began work on a Bartolican hybrid: a ground-attack gunwing. Its wingspan was nearly forty feet and it had four engines on the upper wing. Merchant carbineers kept the guildsmen docile at gunpoint, and what had once been regals became something far faster but able to carry large bombs as well.

12 May 3961: Vernal

Bronlar's fortunes deteriorated quickly with the arrival of the local presiding warden. He had been away in the capital when she had arrived, but when he returned he was less admiring than his ground crew. A list of crimes were drawn up:

* She was flying a wing that flouted the Sentinels' limits.
* She was a commoner, yet she flew without a warden.
* She had killed at least five Bartolican wardens.
* She had murdered Bartolican nobility.
* All but two of her war duels had been without chivalric challenge.

* She was female, but had fought in two chivalric
　war duels.

As Vernal was a regional capital, she was taken to the
town and locked within a tower of the Governor's palace
while the regional wardens and the Airlord of Cosdora flew
in from elsewhere. Envoy Gilcron of Yarron arrived in a
steam tram and went to interview the prisoner while a sitting of the supreme judicial court was being prepared in
the assembly hall of the palace. He was a warden, but well
past flying age.

"I have been hearing some conflicting stories of the raid
on Condelor," the envoy began. "Be good enough to give
me your version, but remember that these walls are almost
certainly listening."

"The raid was sanctioned by Airlord Sartov of Yarron,"
Bronlar replied in a stiff and awkward tone. "We became
separated from the main flock during a war duel. Our orders were to support our super-regal in whatever attack it
made. That turned out to be the Airlord's palace in Condelor. We achieved this, at the cost of the super-regal.
Wingcaptain Serjon Feydamor and his three crewmen died
when the super-regal was hit by groundfire and crashed
into a canal. My gunwing was damaged during another
war duel over Condelor, and as you can see I was
wounded." She lifted her unbound hair to show the long
scar. "I blacked out, flew off course, and awoke to find
myself near Vernal."

The envoy made notes as she spoke, muttering and exclaiming from time to time. He then related how a courier
from Wind River had landed in the Cosdoran capital some
days earlier with the Yarronese version of events. Natu-
rally there was also a version from the Bartolican embassy
that bordered on the hysterical. Serjon had managed to kill
the Bartolican Airlord and wipe out most of his court. A
distant cousin, Warden Samondel, was now Airlord. Yarron admitted the loss of the super-regal and one gunwing,

while the Bartolicans claimed more Yarronese down than
had been in the entire flock and twenty losses of their own.

"I'm not that good," said Bronlar without hesitation. "I
destroyed three in clear air and three on the ground, then
collided with another—but I don't know its fate. Two
more collided while trying to avoid me. That's nine down,
but only three in duel conditions. Why do the Bartolicans
always attribute so many losses to me? Now Alion might
have shot—Alion! He is a warden, he flew with our flock.
That makes our raid an act of chivalric war."

"Indeed, Semme Bronlar, but he flew a sailwing, as did
you."

"Rubbish. Our aircraft have gunwing engines and gunwing reaction guns. All that they lack is the armor of gunwings."

"To get from Wind River to Condelor and all the way
here your supposed gunwing must have flown over three
hundred and fifty miles. That's double the range of a classic gunwing."

"Yes, but ours are special."

"The ground crews confirmed that. The engine has been
bored out and supercharged to give half as much power
again over the original design. The wingspan is thirty-three
feet, and there are strange slots and grooves at the end of
the wings. It's almost as if you had disposable wing extensions which were dropped just before the attack—yet
you should have been destroyed by the Sentinels were that
the case. Is the glass and crystal thing bolted to the engine
something to do with that?"

"Perhaps. Security binds my lips on such matters."

"I understand. Remember, though, that this is not a
game, Semme. Every one of the charges against you carries the death sentence."

"Every mission that I have ever flown has carried a possible death sentence, sair Envoy."

*   *   *

The court convened the following day. The ground crews
who had tended Bronlar and her gunwing were called first.
They testified that the wing's configuration was very odd
but that it could be called a gunwing as it currently stood
on the wingfield. There was nothing to forbid such a wing,
it was just that nobody had ever dared to fly one. The
presence of Alion in the flock nullified the second charge.
The dead wardens of the months past were harder to explain.

"That is a clear breach of squire discipline," declared
the Chancellor of the Convocation of Cosdoran Wardens.

"Objection!" cried the Yarronese envoy. "That discipline should be meted out by Warden Alion Damaric, the
presiding warden in her flock within the Air Carbineers."

"Objection upheld," agreed the Airlord. "That charge is
outside the domain of this court unless the accused admits
to it directly. Proceed."

The bloodstained orders were tendered next. They were
difficult to read, but they clearly showed the seal and signature of Airlord Sartov. Bronlar was unquestionably flying under the orders of her monarch, and that monarch
was certainly at war with the Airlord of Bartolica. There
was an order to attack a wingfield at Twin Falls, but default orders told her to support the super-regal no matter
what.

Fortunately for Bronlar, Bartolican atrocities and viola-
tions of the months past had eroded sympathy for them in
neighboring dominions. Cosdoran nationals had given
firsthand accounts of unprovoked duels and unchivalric
ground attacks. Under the circumstances it was judged that
the Bartolicans deserved what they got from the Yarronese,
who were responding in kind.

The remaining charge was rather more difficult to answer. During the course of the war she had certainly fought
in two of the rare but documented war duels that had been
conducted under chivalric rules. Names of victims and de-
scriptions of engagements were read out by the Bartolican

envoy while Bronlar and the envoy sat in silence. Everything that he said was true, but within Yarronese law. Women were specifically forbidden to engage in clear air combat in Cosdora, however. It was a new law, drafted by conservatives in response to the Yarronese liberalization of the previous year.

At around noon a distant Calltower's bell sounded and the people of Vernal began to retire to their homes and Callshelters while those in the palace adjourned to endure the Call in the comfort and safety of their rooms. Oblivion followed, and lasted three hours. It was past three in the afternoon when the sitting of the court resumed. At the end of the presentation of evidence the Yarronese envoy took the floor to conclude the case for the defense.

"Airlord, Chancellors, Wardens, we live in dark and extraordinary times," he began, holding the lapels of his judicial gown, whose hood was thrown back to emphasize the authority of his white hair. "Within these times there are certain truths that cannot be ignored. Facts are facts. One fact is that the new Yarronese superwings have a wingspan of one hundred feet and six gunwing engines. Clearly the Sentinels do not burn them out of the sky. Clearly Air Carbineer First Class Semme Bronlar Jemarial flew a gunwing that had disposable wing extenders that increased its span and more than doubled its range, yet the Sentinels did not burn it out of the sky.

"There are other extraordinary facts that are less apparent. One is that while Yarronese flyers shoot seven Bartolicans out of the sky for every Yarronese wing lost, the Bartolicans usually triumph on the ground. There are lucky explosions of ammunition stores, mysterious explosions under fortifications, whole battalions of Yarronese found to have faulty Call tethers after a Call has passed. Why? Airlord, I contend that Bartolicans make use of Callwalkers, agents that can defy the Call."

The courtroom erupted into bedlam for many minutes,

and it was only with difficulty that order was restored. The envoy concluded the defense.

"Yarron contests that Bartolica has violated the most basic tenets of warfare and chivalry. Thus, as a rogue directorate it should be considered outside the rules of civilized warfare. Yarron did not violate a single law of chivalry in the conflict with Dorak, you must concede. It is only with Bartolica that the problem exists. Airlord Sartov is justified in using Bartolican tactics against Bartolica, and Semme Bronlar Jemarial is thus innocent of any crime in fighting as Airlord Sartov decrees her to."

The envoy sat down amid a buzz of voices. These ceased as the Airlord's herald banged the floor with his mace.

"Chancellors, Wardens, you have heard the evidence and testimonies both attacking and in support of Semme Bronlar Jemarial. It is now up to you to advise me in the pronouncing of my verdict. I warn you in advance, however, that the most serious of the charges has been answered with no better than a vague theory that the legendary Callwalkers have in fact stepped out of their legends and into the war on the side of Bartolica. I shall be displeased if serious consideration is given to this matter in your advice."

The court rose and the Airlord took his leave. Bronlar was escorted by two guards to a holding chamber, and the envoy joined her there.

"So my chances are not good?" she asked as he stood before her with his head hung.

"On all charges save those of being female your chances are extremely good. Yarron's justification for going beyond the rules of chivalry is a matter of great controversy among the neutral dominions, however, and here we have a serious problem. Some surviving Yarronese wardens have continued to fight in a chivalric fashion, while the vast majority of others destroy Bartolican aircraft in whatever way they can. Technically, all such flyers are rogues and felons, and as such are criminals in the eyes of the Council of Mounthaven Airlords. Being female and fighting flouts an exclusively Cosdoran law, and just now you are in Cosdora."

"But the Bartolicans fight that way too."

"Were you a Bartolican, your predicament would be no different."

"So what is to become of me?"

"I can make a plea for mercy, Bronlar, given your unquestioned bravery. That may make the difference between being hung as a commoner felon and being shot as a rogue warrior."

"Neither has much appeal."

"Like it or not, we are forced to work within the rules this time, my dear Semme. I note that you are a Lateric Christian. You could pray for a miracle, just as I shall be praying to Allah."

The court was scheduled to reconvene at the fifth hour past noon, and several minutes before that time the guards came to Bronlar's door, unlocked it, and ushered her out. As they walked along the corridor Bronlar noticed that a lot of commoners were flanking them, most wearing the guild crests of the ground crews. The faces of most were familiar, as many had worked for free to repair her gunwing. Some still wore the strips of silk or canvas stained with her blood on their arms.

At some unseen signal the guildsmen moved forward as one to overwhelm the guards and seize Bronlar. She was hurried back the way they had come and out into the open. As they made for the gate tower the alarm bells began to ring and the gates rumbled shut on weight-loaded pulleys. The defenses were primarily designed to keep intruders out, however, and the ground crew swarmed up the steps and into the gatehouse. There was an exchange of shots that took the lives of several guards and guildsmen, but the gatehouse was quickly taken.

The nobles and their airlord had been in the throne hall when Bronlar had been rescued, but now they came out and gathered in the ante-yard behind the gate.

"What is the meaning of this outrage?" demanded the Airlord. "Return the prisoner at once."

"With deference, Lordship, we be the ground crew of Semme Bronlar, who be Yarronese in turn," Farrasond declared, terrified but determined.

"What?" shouted the Chancellor of Vernal. "You're ancillaries of my air guilds."

"We're freemen, Warden, we can choose to forsake your service and enter that of another if a majority vote holds it so. We've voted to enter the service of the refugee Bronlar Jemarial and come hell's thunderbolts or eternal Call we'll stand with her."

"You are taking no more than a right to die with her," cried the Airlord. "You—"

He was cut off by a deafening blast behind them, and the throne hall belched smoke, glass, and debris before collapsing in upon itself. Dust and smoke roiled out over them and the alarm bells began ringing again as the nobles scrambled for cover. The Airlord found himself huddling beside the Yarronese envoy.

"God in heaven, were it not for those guildsmen we would have been in there," gasped the Airlord.

"This is just as it happened in Forian," said the Yarronese envoy. "The cream of Yarronese chivalry were under a single roof when a bomb murdered them. It was just after a Call, too."

"Callwalkers!" whispered the Airlord. "Are they real, and not just bogies of nursery stories?"

Just then a distant droning became audible from the north. The Airlord shouted for a runner to go to the lookout tower, then noticed that the guildsmen of the ground crew was escorting Bronlar out of the gate tower.

"We had nothing to do wi' that, Lordship," began Farrasond, but a lookout began calling from one of the towers.

"Eight dozen Bartolican gunwings and five regals! They're coming straight for the palace!"

The Airlord took only a moment to ponder the situation.

"Run up flagstrings for the squires at the wingfield!" he shouted back. "On my authority as Airlord of Cosdora they are to ascend in whatever gunwings are to hand and engage the Bartolicans. By my *express* order, they are free to use nonchivalric tactics."

"Your pardon, Lordship?"

"You heard me! Nonchivalric!! Now! Do it!"

The Bartolican regals came in over the palace in a line, flying at about six hundred feet. Each dropped a single improvised bomb, while the gunwings came in low to strafe. The palace guards fired their assault reaction guns back, but to no effect. The Airlord's prompt warning had allowed several Cosdoran gunwings to get into the air, however, and these came in like hawks among pigeons. The lumbering regals were cut down ruthlessly as they tried to flee north, and the Bartolican gunwings coming in to strafe the wingfield found themselves being set upon from behind.

More and more Cosdoran gunwings ascended while angry wardens took the galley carts on the tramway or ran the two miles to the wingfield in a frenzy of outrage and hatred. The Airlord pointed down the road as he stood beside Bronlar and the Yarronese ambassador.

"Sair Envoy, as Airlord of Cosdora I declare war on Bartolica. Will you be good enough to order your Air Carbineer into the air in the defense of the Dominion of Cosdora?"

"With all my heart, Lordship. Semme Bronlar, get to your gunwing and ascend."

Bronlar was still weak from all the blood she had lost, so she was pushed to the wingfield by her ground crew in an abandoned costermonger's cart. The compression engine was warm by the time she arrived, but by then the Bartolican wings were either destroyed or gone. The warden in command led ten gunwings north along the tramway tracks for the Yarronese border, and was rewarded with the sight of three dozen steam trams crossing the border from occupied Yarron.

The gunwings attacked, strafing the steam trams and halting the Bartolican advance south in its very first steps. The leading and trailing trams were destroyed first; then the others were picked off as the carbineers that they had been transporting fled for the cover of the fields, firing skyward in no real order. By sunset Bronlar was back in Vernal, and the Airlord had convened a makeshift court on the wingfield. Nine Bartolican gunwings, five regals, and thirty-six trams had been destroyed for the loss of twenty-eight Cosdoran gunwings on the ground or in the air.

"The remains of the Bartolican envoy were found in the ruins," the Airlord announced to an open-air court. "Evidently he had returned to the roof to try to reset the bomb when he realized that we had all gone outside. He had not been in time. The envoy for Yarron was right. Bartolican Callwalkers do exist, and they plant bombs in the palaces of their enemies while the rest of us are in the Call's oblivion.

"Semme Bronlar Jemarial, my judgment is that you are innocent of all charges. Further, I extend clemency to your guildsmen. It was their brave defense of you that drew me and my nobles out of the throne hall in time to escape the blast that would otherwise have wiped us out."

Bronlar was invited to stay and teach the Cosdorans the arts of unchivalric air combat. She accepted after a decree arrived from Sartov appointing her as a war liaisory to Cosdora. Far from surgically conquering yet another easy dominion for Bartolica, the bungled strike had made an enemy which boasted a major wingfield just eighty miles from the Bartolican capital and considerable resources. Unoccupied Senner quickly allied itself with Cosdora and Yarron against the Bartolicans, and Airlord Samondel was

faced with a war on four fronts. At the suggestion of Stanbury she decreed that the remains of Yarronese resistance
were to be crushed as a matter of the very highest priority.

Being a Bartolican had not endeared Rollins to the Yarronese carbineers who captured him, but he had been careful to empty his pockets of looted gold beforehand, leaving
only a few more innocent silver coins. The dead flyer's
collar and colors tipped the balance in his favor, however,
and he lied that she was lying wounded behind enemy
lines. He was taken to see a merchant officer, then to a
more senior officer, then to a warden in Casper. When he
was finally taken to the adjunct at Casper wingfield he
poured out the truth about who and what he really was at
last.

   Three more days passed, and a squad of elite woodsmen
carbineers returned from the crash site with the hidden
papers and smashed machines from the black tram. By
now a Bartolican invasion from the north was in full cry,
and although Rollins and his papers were guarded with
great care there were higher priorities for shipment to
Wind River.

7 | THE WINGS OF RETRIBUTION

14 June 3961

A month after the attack on Condelor, Bartolica proved
that it could still roar. With coordination and precision that
defied belief, the Bartolican carbineers stationed in Dorak
for protection against Yarronese "outlaws" suddenly turned

against the local estates and towns. The Dorakians had chosen not to believe the Yarronese claims of Bartolican atrocities until then, but the proof was soon lying dead in their streets and buildings while smoke rose into the sky.

A week later came Stanbury's massive ground attack on northern Yarron via Dorak. This met with greater success than the debacle at Cosdora. The massive Bartolican attack was directed at Sheridan, and by now the Bartolicans were also using improvised trains to move fifteen and sometimes twenty unpowered rail trucks crammed with carbineers. The shocked Dorakians watched from the fields and forests. Dorakian gunwings and sailwings ascended occasionally, but flew southeast without trying to engage the Bartolican trains or garrisons. In Condelor the invasion was decreed to be an alliance with Dorak.

Stanbury's victories were not satisfying in terms of propaganda. The Yarronese retreated in good order, important bridges were destroyed, towns, fields, and forests were burned, and the trackwork of the tramways was ripped up. Traps and tripwire bombs were left everywhere, and not a pint of compression spirit was left by the retreating Yarronese. Worse, the Yarronese timed their confrontations and battles to be just after a Call had swept past, so that having Callwalker agents was no help for the Bartolicans. When Calls were due, the Yarronese would always be well dug in, and behind heavily booby-trapped defenses. Yarronese sailwing patrols were always particularly frequent during Calls, and anything that moved was cut down with reaction-gun fire from above or hit with flaybombs.

In spite of the attrition against the Bartolican advance through Dorak, the advance continued. If slow, it was relentless. The Yarronese did not have the numbers or equipment to fight an enemy whose farms and artisan shops were virtually undamaged, and the Bartolicans were sure of themselves. By the end of spring the cart-cannon fire from the front could be heard in Sheridan, and all tramway links had been long severed.

21 June 3961: Sheridan

Airlord Sartov stayed in Sheridan until the first shells began landing on the wingfield. The city had already been stripped of everything useful, and what remained was ready to be burned or riddled with traps. The last meeting of the Council of Governors was held on June 21st, although only three of Yarron's five governors were there to attend the Airlord.

"I'll open by saying that your gunwings are out on the wingfield being warmed up by volunteers," Sartov began. "Good luck in your flights to Wind River."

"And what of the volunteers?" asked Governor Bennett of the South.

"I have an extended regal on hand. It can lift the three extra men, so they go to Wind River with me after sunset."

"With respect, Lordship, I request permission to remain," said Governor Springwright of the Northeast.

Looking haggard and unsympathetic, Sartov glanced up from his maps and notes. "Explain, sair."

"I do not want to run away and lead a few thousand exiles in Wind River. The people whom I govern and lead are here, and I want to stay here and lead them."

"If caught, you will be taken back to Bartolica for a public hanging just as soon as they can arrange a tram," replied Sartov.

"Only if I am caught, Lordship. I have fought behind the lines before, I'll not be caught."

"Granted," said Sartov without emotion. "One of the ground crew can take your gunwing to Wind River."

"Lordship, thank you. Thank you on behalf of everyone in the Northeast."

"Governor Enzor of the Northwest, are you ready to become my new host?" asked Sartov.

"As ready as ever, Lordship. My province may be poor, but it's still under your rule."

"Then there is nothing more for us to say. Gentlemen, my order to Governor Springwright is 'Collapse and orderly dispersal for armed harassment.' Governors Bennett and Enzor, you shall proceed to Wind River as soon as we rise. This meeting is at an end."

"Lordship, could we not stay and escort your regal to Wind River?" asked Bennett.

"Not unless you can see in the dark. There's an overcast forecast for tonight."

"Then fly out with us now, before dusk," said Enzor.

"No, I have reasons for staying until after dark. Stunningly important reasons."

The compression engines of Airlord Sartov's regal did not chug into life until Mirrorsun was the only illumination in the sky. The predicted forecast had been wrong, but the predicted forecast had been made deliberately wrong on Sartov's order. Sartov was the last to climb aboard the regal.

"We are not beaten, we are just moving the battlefield somewhere else," he said to Governor Springwright as they stood together on the wingfield. "Good fortune go with the resistance attrition, sair."

"Give them hellfire, Lordship. Go in safety."

Sartov swung up into the regal's hatch and the door was fastened from inside. The compression engines gunned and the oversize regal began moving away along the wingfield. A stray incoming shell exploded in the Air Guild Hospitality House, starting a fire, but now the Bartolicans were just destroying facilities that they would soon be taking over. The compression engines roared up to full power, and the regal ascended into the mild spring night.

*　　*　　*

The regal was well tuned, and droned steadily through the light winds as it headed southwest to Wind River. The journey was only 170 miles, and was all over Yarronese-held territory. The Bartolican patrols seldom operated by night, and tried to avoid the aggressive and deadly Yarronese gunwings of the northern area.

Only a few minutes into the journey Sartov went aft to the rear gunner.

"Should be a quiet trip, Lordship," said the gunner. "Anyone trying to target us by Mirrorsun's light will need a big hand from lady fortune."

"Or these," said Sartov, holding a pair of oddly shaped goggles up to his face in the gloom.

"What are they?"

"Put them on and find out."

The gunner exclaimed in surprise at the way the landscape below lit up before his eyes as he peered through the goggles.

"It's like daylight!" he cried, scanning the Bighorn Mountains that were by now below them. "I see a river, and peaks, and, and—"

"And at some time soon you may well see an enemy gunwing out there. Its flyer will almost certainly be wearing a pair of goggles just like these, and to him this regal will stand out in the night sky like a tomcat's testicles."

"Hell's gunsmoke!" said the gunner, aghast. "I'm glad we all got these."

"Not all, Gunner Melstar. You are wearing the only such goggles in Yarronese hands. Be diligent, our lives may depend upon it."

In spite of his warning, the next hour went very quietly. They cleared the Bighorn Mountains, crossed the tramway from Lovell to Bonneville, and then flew above the tramway as it too ran southwest for two dozen miles. A sprinkle of lights marked Winchester, where the tramway turned south again, but the regal continued southwest over the edge of the Absaroka Range.

Sartov rode in the cockpit with the warden who was his wingcaptain, scanning the dusky highlands below in Mirrorsun's dim light.

"Less than an hour to go," reported the wingcaptain. "No Bartolican could ever catch us here."

"None of that!" said Sartov. "Bartolicans are the least of my concerns at the moment."

At that instant there was a whistle from the communications pipe to the rear gunner. Sartov held it up.

"Airlord Sartov."

"Lordship, there's something way, way behind and high. It's after us. A wing, for sure, but I can't tell which type at this distance."

"Closing slowly or fast?" asked Sartov.

"Slowly, so far."

"Good, I'll be with you soon. Keep watching it." Sartov unstrapped and turned to the wingcaptain. "A sailwing of unknown design follows us, and I think that its flyer has night-eyes."

"Lordship, how can you be sure?"

"Because I gave night-eyes to our own rear gunner."

"We might outrun a sailwing, Lordship."

"Do not try; do nothing to alarm him."

"Alarm *him*?" the wingcaptain exclaimed. "*He* is stalking *us*!"

Another twenty miles rolled below as the regal lumbered along at 95 mph. The sailwing continued to close, but at a steeper angle of descent. He was trading height for speed and was catching up.

"I see him better," reported the gunner to Sartov. "A very wide but very thin wing, that one."

Sartov took back the goggles for a moment and looked out at the approaching aircraft.

"Assume a wingspan of about seventy feet," said Sartov as he handed back the goggles. "Use that for your deflection offset."

"Seventy feet? Are the Bartolicans so very advanced already?"

"That is not a Bartolican. Do as I say and assume seventy feet. Set your rangestaff to one hundred fifty yards, and as soon as he is within that range, spray him. Hit the cockpit first, then the left engine."

"Lordship, I can't see *any* engine, just the spin of two props."

"The engine will be thin, so just aim at the center of the airscrew. I want the flyer dead and one engine disabled. Understood?"

"Understood, Lordship."

Another minute went by, and then the gunner began to call out distances.

"One hundred seventy, one sixty-five, gap slowly closing . . . one sixty . . . one fifty-five."

"Is it one fifty as yet?"

"No, it's one fifty-five, drifting back a little to one sixty if—"

"Fire!"

The two aircraft opened fire together, but the regal had a heavier than standard pair of reaction guns in the rear. There was a violet flash within the cockpit of the pursuer. Sartov called for reduced speed over the pipe as shots tore through the regal's fabric all around him.

"The cockpit, keep aiming for the cockpit!" he barked, then cursed as a shot passed through his arm and lodged in his thigh.

The regal's reaction guns flayed sparkling fragments from the cockpit; then the sailwing began to go into a dive.

"Stay with him!" shouted Sartov to the wingcaptain through the communications pipe. "I'm coming forward with the goggles."

Sartov crawled through the regal holding his arm and trailing blood from his thigh, crying out or cursing at every move. A guildsman was already scrambling over with bandages as Sartov gave the goggles to the wingcaptain.

The regal followed the stricken sailwing down. The mountains loomed all around, but the sailwing flew on a steady, descending line.

"The man is probably dead," said the wingcaptain.

"Either that or he wants us to think as much and back away," said Sartov. "Keep close, but don't hit when he does."

It was another ten miles before the sailwing crashed. It raised a cloud of dust and leaves, but there was no explosion or fire. Sartov ordered the warden to circle the wreck.

"Can you land?" asked Sartov.

"Lordship, this thing can slow to almost a brisk walking pace before it stalls, but those are hills down there. We need somewhere flat to land."

The Airlord of Yarron thought quickly, then piped for the rear gunner.

"Prepare to bail out," he ordered. "Take survival rations, assault kit, and a dozen flares."

"A dozen, Lordship?"

"A dozen, gunner. We shall drop lighted flares as you descend. Guard that wreck until you see this regal return in the morning. Set off your flares then, and light a fire. Now get ready."

"He could use these goggles," said the warden.

"No, you need them to note where we are and find our way back. I want that wreck, Wingcaptain."

As the sun rose the following day the regal was back over the site, which turned out to be just five miles from the tramway to Wind River. Six men parachuted down, including the heavily bandaged and splinted Airlord Sartov. Two days later the wreckage of the strange aircraft was dismantled, and over the following week another hundred men arrived on foot. The pieces were carried out wrapped in tentcloth. Sartov was carried out too, on a stretcher and running a fever. The secrecy was so great that rumors even began to spread that Sartov had been killed.

On June 29th Sartov inspected the pieces from a wicker wheelchair in a huge tent at Gannett wingfield. The guildmaster in charge was trembling with loss of sleep, yet bright-eyed with fascination. His name was Jeb Feydamor.

"Not a fragment of wood is within it, nor of cloth."

"What does it teach us?" asked Sartov.

"Nothing, yet everything. The design is competent, but nothing special. The construction and materials are beyond belief, though. They are all so light, strong, and flexible, and the engines are . . . well . . ."

"Yes?"

"They may be powered by electrical essence. How could the Bartolicans have developed such an engine?"

"The Bartolicans did not."

"Then who was flying it?"

"A very unusual man, sair. Only your finest guildsmen are to work on this thing. Study it, then repair it as best you can."

"What? I mean all deference, Lordship, but electrical essence has been the study of none but historical theorists for nearly two thousand years."

"Then find one. Find two! Bring them here—in chains if needs be—but one way or another I want that thing's secrets. Have the tent guarded day and night. Any found inside other than those working directly on the, the Callwalker sailwing are to be shot on sight."

3 July 3961: Condelor

With the news of the Fall of Northern Yarron a public holiday was declared in Bartolica. An "Alliance of Consensus" was imposed upon Dorak, and the mortified dominion was easily brought under the control of the occupying Bartolican carbineers. For all the setbacks of the previous two months, Bartolica now controlled the entire northern half of Mounthaven. Stanbury even called for a truce with the middle dominions of Cosdora and Senner, and offered generous reparations for what was described as an accidental attack on Vernal. With Yarron further reduced in area and looking as if it might really fall, the two dominions did not relish the idea of facing Bartolica alone. It was not until Sartov flew to Cosdora and conferred with the Airlord that the shaky alliance against Bartolica was shored up.

As a result of the attack on his regal, Sartov now flew everywhere in an armed trainer gunwing with two seats. He was still able to work, even if the space was cramped. Early in July he flew across from Wind River to Vernal, right across the edge of the Red Desert and the tramway linking eastern Yarron with Bartolica. There was little to be seen from such a height, yet the hatchings on his maps showed it to be occupied and that was all that mattered.

He was met at Vernal's wingfield by Thedser, the Cosdoran Airlord, who said that he was gratified to see him alive.

"The Airlord of Senner sends his apologies," Thedser explained. "His people are lacking in unity at the best of times, and some of his regional chiefs want to go over to the Bartolicans to gain advantage in their tribal disputes."

"That is like factions of chickens enlisting the aid of a dirkfang cat against their peers."

"They were his words, almost precisely," said Thedser. "I am anxious to hear what you propose next for our little alliance, but, ah, first I would like to go somewhere more comfortable and private."

Thedser was glancing at Sartov's flyer as they walked.

"This man has the very highest of security clearances," Sartov assured him.

"Airlord Sartov, what I want to discuss is only for the ears of a head of state."

"Airlord Thedser, this man *is* a head of state. May I introduce Airlord Maybaron of Dorak, the leader of the Dorakian resistance?"

It proved to be a fruitful meeting. It was agreed that

Bartolica's greatest strength was that it could act like a single entity, concentrating all of its resources at precisely the right place and time. A widespread campaign of resistance would not win any battles, but it would prevent Stanbury from concentrating his resources and winning any battles for himself. They also agreed on a massive campaign against Callwalker infiltrators.

"But how do we break their coordination?" asked Thesder. "We don't even know how they achieve it."

"I do," replied Sartov.

Two Airlords and the Sennerese Archwarden stared back at him.

"Well?" asked Thesder.

"For now, trust me," replied Sartov.

After the meeting Sartov was resting in his rooms when one of his guards rapped at the door.

"I want no more visitors," Sartov called, sitting on the edge of his bed with one boot already off.

"The man insists on seeing you, Lordship. He says he is a guildsman."

"Tell him to make an appointment for the morning. I have a quarter hour free at noon."

The guard went away, but was soon back.

"Airlord Sartov, he says it concerns repairs to your most precious sailwing."

Sartov froze, his trousers at his knees.

"Tell him I'm on my way. We can talk in the garden of fountains."

The garden of fountains was designed especially for people to talk with no fear of being overheard. Sartov's visitor was tall and angular, and might have been in his late twenties. With his voice masked by the gurgling and tinkling of water, he introduced himself as Sair Kalward.

"Say your words," said Sartov as they paced slowly amid the lamplit columns of splashing water.

"Earlier this month one of your wings shot down an

extremely advanced sailwing which had no markings on it. No markings at all."

"Departures from the forms of air chivalry are common enough in this war," replied Sartov. "What of it?"

"So you have this aircraft now?"

"I admit nothing, sair Kalward. I am an airlord, you are a guildsman—supposedly. Tell me more."

"Reports to hand say that the wing came down largely intact about five miles from a tramway to Wind River. They also say that your men carried the thing out in sections because it was designed to break apart that way. It is now in a tent at the edge of Wind River wingfield, and guarded by carbineers with shoot-to-kill orders. Is all of that correct?"

"I am yet to hear something of interest, sair Kalward. More facts, if you please."

"I have no more facts as such, Lordship, but I can tell you one thing for certain. The wing had engines unlike any you have ever seen before, and controls that have baffled your finest and most learned guildsmen. There are no fuel tanks, and the structure is at least four times lighter than your finest sailwings."

"Tell me something that I do not know."

"The sailwing is powered by electrical essence, and the dead flyer's hair looked like long, fine feathers when put under a magnifier. My hair does as well, and I know how to repair it."

Sartov assimilated all this without pausing as he paced, but his heart was racing.

"You say you are a guildsman and a Callwalker. Why should I let you near your own wing? Why would you repair it for us?"

"Because us aviads, Callwalkers as you quaintly describe us, are no more united than you humans. These wings are all old technology. We can repair and maintain them, but they are impossible for us to build from scratch. At present a renegade faction has all of our sunwings. The

sun powers them, you see, but they can store reserves to
fly by night as well."

"Go on."

"The wing that you have is a ferry, it is used to ascend
to the truly huge sunwings that can fly around the very
world itself. Your wings cannot fly so high. With our captured ferry you can storm aboard one of those sunwings
that your flyers have seen from time to time."

Sartov was keeping a very strict inventory of what was
being said. Kalward had given little away, had made an
unverifiable offer, and clearly wanted the electrical sailwing back very badly.

"Apart from the fact that I have something that you
want, what incentive do I have to trust you?" Sartov asked.

"Lordship, Bartolica could never have crushed your fair
dominion without help from, ah, Callwalkers. I offer you
a chance of stanching the supply of those Callwalkers.
Does the thought not appeal to you?"

"*You* could be one of the rogue Callwalkers. Can you
prove otherwise?"

"No, but if you were to take me back to Wind River I
would be but one among thousands. Your guildsmen could
watch me work instead of attempting damaging experiments themselves. When it came time to test the wing, well
it has seating for two, remember?"

"How long have you been here?" asked Sartov.

"In Vernal? Oh about two days."

"No, I meant in Mounthaven?"

"Eleven months."

"Eleven months . . . So you were here all along," said
Sartov, in a tone of speculation mixed with malice. "When
the Callwalkers were sabotaging the defenses of our cities,
town, and estates, you had the people we needed to stop
them. The Bartolicans would not have got past Akemore
before we started to push them back. Why didn't you help
earlier?"

"We have very limited facilities to travel all the distance

from Australica, and we started coming over later than the renegades. There is only a handful of us here, including myself. Thanks to your campaign against the Callwalkers in Yarron, most of us have had to flee to refuges where humans would not be . . . comfortable."

Sartov stopped. His eyes moved to focus on a brass model gunwing mounted above one of the fountains, but otherwise he stood motionless. Kalward fidgeted as the silence lengthened. Sartov's eyes slowly returned to fix upon him.

"I shall take you back to Wind River in my trainer, but with a gun pressed against your head all the way. When you work on the, the sunwing, you will be under guard at all times."

"I see. Anything else?"

"You are to do one thing and one thing only, sair Kalward or whoever you really are. You must get the sunwing airworthy and show us how it can be flown."

"They need maintenance as well. My people—"

"I'm sure the Guild of Airframe Fabricators can manage under your good instructions. Just get it working."

7 July 3961: Wind River

Four days later Sartov was back in Wind River, along with the Airlords of Cosdora and Dorak. The occasion was the thousandth anniversary of Yarron's foundation, and envoys from Senner and Deanery were there as well. The actual ceremony was held on the wingfield, with thirty gunwings and sailwings on patrol overhead. The only color in the gathering was the flight jackets of those gathered to listen. Sartov stood on a low dais and had to shout through a megaphone to make himself heard above the engines. That was no matter, however, as the text would be spread far and wide within very short order.

He started with the usual words on Yarron's history, glories, and triumphs against terrible odds.

"The adversities over which we have triumphed are greater than you may imagine. You may wonder how Yarron was so badly mauled in the war, so as to be reduced to this little fastness in the mountains. The truth is that the Bartolicans have made contact with a new race of people, a race immune to the Call. Callwalkers."

He paused for emphasis, for the statement was indeed unbelievable. Rumors had been circulated to add credibility to the idea, but this was the first time that an official pronouncement had been made on the subject.

"There are not many of them, for they come from a very remote place and the journey here is difficult. We are not even sure why they favor Bartolica over any other dominions, except perhaps that Bartolicans are sufficiently stupid to trust an ally with such an immense potential for betrayal."

The gibe brought a ripple of laughter, and in a curious way added credibility to Sartov's words.

"Throughout our long and glorious history there have been many legends and tales of magicians, elementals, and even the bigfoot being able to resist the Call. Never once has any proof been tendered, however. Now I can give you proof!"

Kalward was brought up onto the dais in irons. An orderly set up a folding table and field microscope for all to see. Sartov called for a representative from the crowd to come forward, and a junior airframe guildsman soon found himself standing beside the Airlord.

"Take your knife, cut a few strands of my hair, and put it under the microscope," Sartov ordered.

He obeyed. The orderly helped the man with adjusting the slide and bringing it into focus on the black and grey strands.

"I see strands like big, scaly ropes," he reported.

"Now do the same with some of your own hair."

The guildsman did as he was told, and reported the same result.

"Do the same with some strands of this man's hair," ordered Sartov, pointing to Kalward.

Kalward flinched away as the strands of his hair were cut. The guildsman peered into the eyepiece.

"They're like long, fluffy feathers!" he exclaimed.

Sartov suspended the address and let dozens of others clamber up onto the dais to see for themselves. Kalward's hair was pulled and his scalp examined while carbineers looked on vigilantly. Over twenty minutes passed before Sartov began speaking again.

"As you have seen, this man has hair like very fine feathers, and as we all know, birds of all sizes are immune to the Call. He came to me from Bartolica, proposing a scheme which might have robbed us of our most secret and effective of weapons. Now he is our prisoner, a living testament to the real reason for Bartolica's victories. Go to your units, take hair from everyone, and examine it beneath a physician's microscope. Should you find any with the look of a feather, kill the featherhead at once! Show no mercy, do not hesitate."

The term "featherhead" suddenly became the most feared and despised word in the Yarronese vocabulary, and it quickly spread to Cosdora and Senner as well. Of over five hundred people seized and shot over the ensuing week only sixty proved to be real aviads, but gradually better testing standards and regulations reduced the number of innocent executed to almost nil. Kalward was kept in close confinement and subjected to intensive study and questioning. He was not allowed anywhere near the sunwing.

Most important of all, the legendary ability of Bartolican commanders to pick where Yarronese forces were most vulnerable suddenly diminished, and every front became a stalemate. For the Yarronese it was a most welcome relief in a year of continual setbacks and disasters. For the Bartolicans it meant the end of the cavalcade of victories that had fueled the morale of their war effort and bound the large and diverse dominion together. For all that, however, Bartolica was still ruler of half of Mounthaven. That was enough to ensure Stanbury's credibility in the short term, but strategically he knew that he was vulnerable.

9 July 3961: Bartolica

The attack on the Bartolican palace had a profound effect on the politics of the entire region. Within Bartolica itself, the north and central regions allied with Samondel at once, but the east and southwest were more reluctant. Thus Stanbury needed a new unifying factor. In the southwest the garrisons were strengthened against a counterattack from the wilderness deserts of Senner, and warden patrols regularly reported intense nomad activity to the south. The upgrade of Bartolican strength was purely to retain central control, however, and was of limited use against outside attack.

Strategically speaking, the Wind River stronghold seemed the least of Bartolica's problems. Once the hysteria from the super-regal attack had subsided, the strategic staff ascertained that the attack had been a superbly coordinated and executed effort by a very small number of gunwings. The main factor favoring the Yarronese attackers had been the Bartolicans' very complacency. Stanbury took steps to change all that.

A massive program was commenced to build two hundred enhanced gunwings, sailwings, and regals, and everyone who could fly an aircraft was put through combat training—including guildsmen, mechanics, and carbineers. Stanbury's strategy, like Sartov's, was always to keep his enemies busy. Eastern Bartolica was starved of resources while carrying much of the campaign to subdue the growing rebel activity in Dorak. The central government concentrated on the difficult war of attrition against Senner and Cosdora, wearing down the newly constructed fortified garrisons and building garrisons of their own. On the other hand, sensible military planning and minor, bloody battles did not have as much public appeal as the swift, decisive defeat of Median or the fall of Yarron's capital. Something major was needed, something as inspiring as the destruction of Wind River.

"Wind River is an annoyance that we can well do without," Stanbury declared to Archcarbineer Carabas as they looked over a papier-mâché diorama of the whole of Mounthaven.

"Wind River is also behind some very impressive natural barriers needing few defenders," said Carabas. "The Wind River Range, and the Red Desert. To the north the Dorak rebels are working with them, and in the east the approaches are difficult and they are well dug in."

"Pah. My agents estimate that they have less than ten thousand souls in Wind River. Our carbineers alone outnumber their entire population."

"My agents put the unaccounted Yarronese higher than that, Archwarden. After what happened at Median and the western cities, the field officers reported that a lot of women had joined the combatants, so one must deduce that—"

"That they are desperate enough to field women," concluded Stanbury in triumph. "It is a sure sign of defeat."

"Well, we could attack from the east, striking along the torn-up tramway from Bonneville to Riverton. It would be slow, as most of their forces are there, they are dug in securely, and there are Dorakians with them too."

"In short, a difficult, unrewarding, and costly campaign. Those huge Yarronese regals have been strafing our steam trams and trains as they cross the Red Desert. Between them and the Dorakian rebels we are lucky if three trains in five reach the east of Yarron. Not a day passes without an attack on our sailwings in Bartolican airspace, and even our gunwing flocks have been mauled in full view of the conquered towns and cities."

"Well, their flyers are very good, and are generally led by the Air Carbineers. They also began experiments with nontraditional wings long before we did. Meantime our wardens and guildsmen still resist innovations."

"Yes, I know. It is ironic that in the very act of destroying their airpower I turned loose such an unchivalric monster. Still, monsters can be slain just as dead as mice. I intend to mount an attack on Wind River from the air."

Carabas blinked.

"The air?"

"Yes. The air."

Carabas considered a diplomatic reply, then decided against it. There were too many valuable aircraft at stake.

"Archwarden Stanbury, with all possible respect and deference might I remind you that the Yarronese air defenses are as tight as a duck's backside. Even if our flocks got through, we know little about their targets."

"Ah, but that is where you are wrong. Bartolican sailwings have been secretly developed that can fly higher than any Yarronese wing. Their flyers have mapped targets: wingfields, workshops, steam tram marshaling yards, storehouses, bridges, and compression spirit barrel pits."

"I have never heard of such sailwings."

"You are a carbineer. I would be alarmed if you had."

Carabas had in fact written the specifications for those sailwings, but only three men in that entire hemisphere knew that. Stanbury was not one of those men. Carabas' problem was that Stanbury was planning a desperate gamble to win back the initiative in the war, while his own requirement was to merely harvest as many undamaged aircraft as possible from wherever they might not be missed. If Carabas had his own way, the war would be kept festering along inconclusively for years and major air battles would be avoided at all costs.

Stanbury unrolled a map and spread it over a nearby

table. The geography was of the Wind River area, but few of the marks and shadings looked familiar to Carabas.

"The wardens would never consent to something as crass as dropping bombs," Carabas pointed out doubtfully. "They'd not let their squires do so either."

"No, but some of the new Air Guild flyers have already been bombing towns in Dorak," Stanbury assured him, pointing out several pins in the surface of the diorama.

"There will be deaths. One gunwing in five will be lost."

"Good, then we shall put the wardens from the southwest and southeast in the first wave. Not all of our enemies are on the other side of the front."

"But why do it at all?" pleaded Carabas.

"Because Yarron is nothing without its gunwings. Senner is massing its nomad carbineers to strike us from the south, as people have been telling me in every tactical advisory meeting for three weeks. If we can disable Yarron's wingfields for even a fortnight we can hit the nomads with everything we have from the air. The Cosdorans hate such unchivalric clear air fighting, so we are unlikely to see them help unless Yarron gives a lead."

"My carbineers can help in following up against the nomads on the ground," said Carabas, trying to rally some enthusiasm.

Stanbury smiled broadly and selected three pins representing three thousand of the Bartolican carbineers each. He stuck them into the papier-mâché at a tram stop on the Dorak-Bartolica border, just west of the Wind River Range. Carabas watched as he traced a path with a pair of dividers.

"Your carbineers will march north to Jackson Lake and then east through this pass to Gannett and Wind River. In three days you will be engaging the Yarronese, and in four Sartov's head will be dangling from your utility belt."

Back in his own chambers again, Carabas had made up his mind by the time his aviad courier, Traffon, arrived with the latest dispatches. As the courier was shown in,

Carabas was drinking tepid green tea from the terraced hills near Denver and reclining on a giltbead couch.

"Even in the Overmayor's palace there was never luxury such as this," Carabas said with a gesture to the elegant Aubenton tapestries and rich furnishings. "Throughout the surviving civilizations the world round, there is no people quite so good at living in comfort as the Bartolicans."

"Some might call it decadance, sair Carabas," replied Traffon respectfully but firmly.

"You judge them harshly. They live well, but work hard and fight fiercely. After the Miocene Arrow strikes, I shall make Condelor my capital and this will be my palace."

"It will require a lot of upkeep."

"Which slaves from Mexhaven will provide."

They walked across to stand looking out over the palace wingfield. A line of gunwings stood ready to ascend at short notice, and guildsmen were moving about with a portable furnace that piped hot air over the compression engines.

"When will I know what the Miocene Arrow is, and when it will be fired?" asked Traffon.

"When it no longer matters, when it is over. If you are caught and tortured you must say nothing because you know nothing. Too many of our people have been caught, and not all have been killed."

"I have heard that they are being tortured by being mated with Yarronese beauties to breed aviads," Traffon responded.

"It may be true, it may not. From Kalward's reports it is evident that the Yarronese are not particularly friendly toward us Callwalkers."

"Nevertheless, he is in a position of trust."

"Only because they think that the ferrywing has value. Before long they will realize that it is not a weapon, and that it will take a century of applied research and reverse engineering to duplicate its technologies. By then Kalward should have arranged the theft of a sample of their superb long-range wings, but in the meantime we must protect the facilities at Wind River from damage. Inform Sair Kalward about an impending Bartolican air attack. Tell him to find some way to alert the Yarronese."

"Surely the warning would create greater losses," warned Traffon. "The Yarronese will be geared up for a fearful battle."

"No. From what I have been told, the Yarronese have nothing major to hit. Everything is in tents and hardened bunkers, and they even have mockup gunwings to tempt Bartolicans to waste their ammunition. With luck they will have all their real wings and equipment dispersed and hidden, and will not bother to send up any serious opposition."

Samondel and Alion were on a palace balcony, watching the scurrying guards search the palace. A pack of terriers was barking at the edge of a canal.

"It has already been said that foreign merchants are spying on us, my love," Samondel said softly, her hand on Alion's.

"It is hardly a surprise, my lady. Bartolica has occupied three dominions and is at war with another two."

"You are said to be in league with the spies," she said with a face full of concern rather than accusation.

"My lady, what do I have to do to prove my good faith and loyalty?"

"There are traces of infiltrators at work in the palace. Papers have been disturbed in the office of the Archwarden himself, and the terriers have found strange scents that lead nowhere."

"The terriers ignored my scent when I was taken to them," Alion pointed out with complete confidence.

"They say you may have let others in."

"*They, they, they,* it is always *they*! This is impossible. I ruin my life to save you, yet I am still under suspicion."

"Oh not from me, Alion," she assured him, slipping her

arm about his waist. "Stanbury still talks and grumbles, though. I am the Lady Airlord, and he never ceases to remind me that you are an enemy warden."

"I am a nobleman who deserted his own airlord in the name of chivalry!" Alion snapped, whirling away from her and clenching his fists. "In a way I am more worthy than all those others in your court. Throw me in irons, then, or have me shot. I saved you, that's all that matters. Chivalry asks no fee."

They were interrupted by the shift captain of the guards, arriving with his report. He glanced at Alion with plain unease as Samondel checked the report with the laborious care of a novice. Alion turned full on, folded his arms, and faced him. The captain let his hand rest on the stubby assault carbine slung from his shoulder. Alion put a hand out and began to stroke Samondel's hair without taking his eyes off the captain. The captain lost color, but did not move until Samondel signed the report and returned it to him.

"He hates me," said Alion once the door had closed. "He specifically."

"He is a commoner," Samondel replied serenely.

"Stanbury is a noble," Alion countered.

"And I am Airlord," Samondel countered again, then stifled any possible reply with a long and tender kiss.

15 July 3961: Wind River

The Bartolican flocks rallied for visibility as much as strategic advantage. From all over occupied Yarron and eastern Bartolica they flew in fives of twenty, with their mufflers minimized for maximum noise on the ground. All together there were two hundred gunwings and sailwings, and another fifteen regals, amounting to over a third of the Bartolican wingfleet's engines. The flock rallied over the Sweetwater River. Standing orders were to return to Bartolica if operational, and to Median if badly hit. The idea was that losses would not be evident to the Bartolican public. The mission would involve little more than two hundred miles of flying, yet half of that would be after the battle that was sure to take place over Gannett.

The first hour was quiet as the sub-flocks approached over the Red Desert. They watched their shadows travel over mile after mile of dry wilderness with their engines throttled right back. When they reached Wind River, the Yarronese flocks that were expected to meet them never materialized. Wind River was as they had expected, with new, unpainted buildings, huge tents, and a vast wingfield. The surprise was complete as they attacked, but the groundfire was nevertheless fierce. Two regals blew holes in the wingfield with their two-hundred-pound bombs, while sailwings dropped firebombs on the tents and buildings. The wardens in the patrolling gunwings grew bored and began diving to rake likely-looking targets with their reaction guns. As the tents burned, the outlines of burning aircraft were visible beneath them.

At Gannett it was different. The Yarronese gunwings were in the air by the time the Bartolican flock arrived, and the forty triwing gunwings were a fast, fresh, and dangerous force to contend with. Again the damage on the ground was extensive, yet all but two of the regals were cut down as they lumbered in to attack. By the time it was Riverton's turn, the ground attack force was exhausted and the gunwings were short on compression spirit. The attack was confined to a few firebombs dropped from a thousand feet; then the Bartolicans rallied into a single flock to return across the desert.

All in all the gunwings came out of it well. Only nineteen were lost of the Bartolican flocks, and fourteen of defending Yarronese. The problem was that the sailwings had taken most of the groundfire damage, and it was these which now had to struggle to Median. Undamaged Yarronese sailwings ascended from Riverton's wingfield, pouring

into the sky and setting upon the struggling, weaker part
of the Bartolicans' combined flock. Fully two-thirds of the
day's casualties were lost here, above the Red Desert, yet
on the day it seemed not to matter. The wardens in their
gunwings had a triumphant return, and the Yarronese had
lost two of their three bases. Stanbury declared a great
victory in the name of the Lady Airlord, and celebrations
in the capital featured an evening of fireworks, a parade
of carbineer bands, and a free barrel of ale for the public
delivered to every tavern.

In fact, the bomb craters in the Wind River and Gannett
wingfields had been repaired within an hour of the attack,
and many of the buildings and tents destroyed had been decoys. Most of the Yarronese wings were dispersed under
earthwork bunkers, and all of the super-regals had been
away attacking the bridge over the Bighorn River at White-
field. They landed intact amid the supposed devastation.

Sartov always made sure that the enemy could never
turn his own tactics against him.

None of that was of any interest to the revelers in Condelor, however. Wardens of every faction swore that a
great victory had been won, and Stanbury was again in
favor. In the temporary throne hall the former Yarronese
Airlord was given a pardon for atrocities against Bartolican
carbineers at Forian as a gesture of goodwill, but he was
then forced to listen as testimonies were declared by dozens of wardens to the Lady Airlord.

16 July 3961: Condelor

Serjon sat up on his stone bunk as he heard the tramp of
guards' feet in the distance. The door of the cell next to
his creaked open and slammed shut. The tramp of feet
receded again.

"What was it this time?" asked Serjon.

"Big victory," rasped Virtrian. "Wind River and Gannett were bombed by the biggest flock ever assembled."

"So they are in Bartolican hands now?"

"Oh no, they were just set a-burning, and craters blasted in the wingfields."

Serjon considered this for some time, then took off his prison shirt and examined his injured arm. The splint was off by now, and the last of the stitches had been removed. Grasping the bars of the door at their highest point, he began raising and lowering himself slowly. His arm gave him some discomfort, but was again functional. After a short rest he began to do pushups on the flagstone floor.

Something does not make sense, Serjon thought as he worked in the darkness. There was nothing much to bomb in those places. He had flown out of Gannett and Wind River for weeks. There were a lot of wings kept there, but little in the way of buildings. All compression spirit was in underground barrel stores, most wings were in earth and timber bunkers, and even the engine shops were underground. Sartov always got the refugees and even idle carbineers digging. Gopher Sartov, they called him. Quite a lot of decoy sites were built too, and they looked passably convincing from the air.

"What did they say of Riverton?" Serjon puffed as he began a bracket of squat-kicks.

"Why, nothing."

Odd, that's the biggest supply base of all, though Serjon. "Are you sure that this is not some great hoax?" he asked.

"I've heard a lot of wardens boasting in my time, Serjon. These seemed genuine."

"Well, if you're convinced then I am too."

"By my herald's red plush."

That was their private code for lies. Outside, the celebrations went on all through the night, but an air pageant planned for the next day was canceled when a Call's approach was announced by a belltower.

16 July 3961: Wind River

"Magical devices, yet no evidence for these devices," Sartov said as Rollins sat bound to a chair before him in a partitioned annex of the command tent at Wind River. "This does me no service if I cannot use such a weapon myself."

"Then you do not believe me?" asked Rollins.

"Your papers and your story answer a lot of questions. The pedal device, wires on poles and metal boxes might allow communications over vast distances, and the calculor machine might be able to work out all possible solutions for any battle and select the right one. That would explain how Stanbury crushed two-thirds of Yarron with a few tramloads of carbineers who had never fought together before."

"But that is the whole truth!"

"But Sair Rollins, your story and papers are like a verbal account of a gunwing by a Mexhaven envoy to some noble in Veraguay. It explains a great deal, but it does not help me to build my own."

Rollins looked down at the cords that bound him to the chair, thinking not so much how to convince the Airlord of Yarron to believe him but of how to please him.

"Lordship, when I was a student I had a rival for the affections of a girl," he began.

"Didn't we all," replied Sartov, but rather than walking out he sat on the corner of a trunk and inclined his head.

"I was a far better student, but my rival was the third son of a warden and had more money. He gave her moss-work gold bangles, scarves of silk from dyed parachute offcuts, and even had his brothers give her sailwing rides. I had better prospects, yet could she wait for prospects? It was war, Lordship. I hated him, despised him, I swore an oath that he would never have her."

"And you killed him."

"Yes. I came from a poor area, Lordship. A priest recognized my talent early and gave me a good education, but my streetmates taught me the way of the knife. I challenged my rival to a blood duel and he stupidly agreed. We met alone in an alleyway at night, and I slew him with the first thrust of my knife. Call's curse, how was I to know that the stupid toad had brought his brothers to help dispose of my body? Those future wardens ran away screaming bloody murder. I ran too, and now I am here."

"True or not, what is the lesson?" asked Sartov, glancing at his watch.

"I did not have riches, but I did not need them to keep my rival from my sweetheart. You do not have signal machines and calculors, but you do not need them to stop the black trams taking Yarron. You do not need their secrets to stop them."

Sartov sat thinking on what was fundamentally good advice. Eventually he slipped from the edge of the trunk and walked to the entrance of the tent.

"You do not think by the rules, sair Rollins, you are the right sort of man for these times," he called back. To the guards at the entrance he said, "Untie my new adviser and tell my aide to arrange papers for him."

16 July 3961: Condelor

Alion was soon confronted with a serious test of his loyalty to Bartolica and Samondel. He was sent just north of Condelor to a wingfield where a new and very large gunwing was being tested by Bartolican guildsmen. Its wings were thirty-five feet across and it had two large, powerful compression engines driving tri-bladed propellers. Captured Yarronese gunwings had been put through simulated war duels with it, yet there was one important element missing: a Yarronese warden.

Alion was put into the air in an assortment of gunwings against the Sandhawk, as it was called. His flight experience proved to be of value, as Yarronese were trained to get in close with quick, accurate bursts of fire rather than the Bartolican approach of heavier fire at a safe distance. One day of intensive tests passed. Alion ate in the cafeteria, then went to his tent. He felt exhausted and barely able to move a muscle as he collapsed onto his field bunk.

17 July 3961: Condelor

Unlike the Airlord Abdicate, Serjon was never taken from his cell and never spoken to by the guards. When he heard a guard approaching he assumed that they were coming for Virtrian and did not even get off his bunk. He stopped at Serjon's door. Serjon assumed that the next meal had arrived early and watched for the slot at the floor to slide up. To his surprise he heard the turning of a key in the door's lock.

"As you live, Wingcaptain Serjon, make no sound," a soft, piping voice pleaded in the near-darkness.

Serjon did as he was told, and a moment later the door swung open. He walked to the door and was seized firmly by the arm and guided out into the corridor, where the single lamp revealed a man dressed as one of the kitchen hands. Beneath the lamp was a tray of bread and cheese that was to have been his next meal. The figure began to remove his kitchen oversmock.

"Wear this, Wingcaptain, and walk down the passageway. Take the fourth archway on the left, then the right branching of that passage and climb the stairs that lie about four paces beyond. At the top of the stairs is the guardroom."

"The guardroom!"

"Keep your voice down! A guard will come out and seize you as you pass, then abuse you for taking a wrong turn. Do not fight back, he is with us. He will drag you to the outer door and kick you out into the service cloisters. You will be met there by an old woman with a mop and bucket. Go with her."

"What about you?"

"I shall be found in your cell, bound with strips of blanket and gagged with a rough-made wad. A pick-wire will be in the lock. I shall say that you had tinkered the lock open before I arrived, and that you took me by surprise as I made to push your tray beneath the door."

"They may not believe you."

"Then I shall die. Now go."

Serjon dutifully pulled the oversmock on over his head and made his way along the passageways as he had been instructed. At the guardroom he was seized, beaten, and flung out into a sunlit cloister, where he lay genuinely stunned for a moment. The scullion met him there, and he was escorted through at least a half mile of the labyrinth beneath the royal palace of Condelor until he found himself pulling a garbage wagon along the artisans' access road. A few minutes after crossing the swinging bridge over the canal, the Yarronese fugitive was put aboard a steam tram dressed in a stonemason's leathers and carrying a sling of facing tools. He took a seat between two nattily dressed merchants.

"Hie, brother, be to Parratar wingfield?"

Another dressed as a mason had spoken, but Serjon just nodded wearily rather than betray his Yarronese accent. The other man had spoken the prearranged rendezvous phrase.

After a half-hour journey due north the steam tram stopped and Serjon alighted with his new companion. They were on the edge of a training wingfield which had been converted for the gunwings that were now assigned to defend the capital.

"Bear to those tents yonder, sair Feydamor," said the real mason and they began walking.

"May I ask what is going on?" Serjon asked as they trudged the path of broken stone, their shadows lengthening with the late afternoon sun.

"There is a resistance, even in the mighty capital of Bartolica itself. We rescued your companion Warden Alion from the wreckage of his gunwing before it burned—"

"Alion!"

"Alas, we're few in number and did not reach your mighty wing's wreckage until the carbineers had found you. The warden bravely feigned defection to Bartolica, then spied for us in the palace so we could rescue you."

Serjon considered the new pieces in his puzzle. He had been shot at by one of his escorts, yet Alion had showed loyalty to him. That meant Bronlar had opened fire on the super-regal when he had returned to fire rockets into the palace grounds. Bronlar? It was unthinkable.

Once they reached the guildsmen's tents and buildings of the wingfield they entered a tent where a warden's flight furs and embroidered leathers were laid out. Serjon changed clothes for the fourth time since he had left his cell, and when he emerged he was met by a guildsman from a flight crew. The man said a few curt but deferential words in Bartolican, and from his attitude Serjon realized with a start that he was not with the resistance. He replied "Good," in Bartolican, then to his relief the guildsman gestured for him to follow.

They walked in silence out to where a twin-engine gunwing was warming up for what seemed to be a night training flight. It was a big aircraft, and had sleek lines. Serjon was saluted and shown to the steps at the front of the cockpit. Evidently he was the student in a training flight. As Serjon climbed up and strapped himself in he heard what seemed to be the crackle of shots above the chugging of the compression engine.

Others now approached through the gloom across the wingfield, and Serjon noticed that one of them was being supported by two of his companions. "Dar-kay? Dar-kay?"

the chief guildsman called—"What's this? What's this?" in Bartolican.

Abruptly there was another burst of automatic small-arms fire, and the four guildsmen standing beside the trainer went down. The men of the resistance hauled a body up the steps to the cockpit.

"This Alion, he hit in fight," someone cried in heavily accented Yarronese above the compression engines.

"How bad?" Serjon called back.

"Hit in leg, fall, hit head. We bandage."

"Alion, can you hear me?" Serjon called back as the body was strapped into the instructor's seat.

"He stunned. Go! You fly."

"But I can't reach back to help him from—"

"You fly. Go, go, go! You stay, all die. Go!"

Serjon ran his hands over the controls as the canopy was slid back into place; then he snapped down the catches from inside. The control layout was fairly standard, except for the two engines. The flightstrip's boundary lanterns were alight as he gunned the compression engines and trod the right brake to turn the gunwing trainer. Away in the darkness there were more shots, some of them from re-action guns of a heavy caliber. The gunwing gathered speed, rotated, then lifted into the air. Serjon wound the wheels up the moment they had left the ground.

It being early in the evening, Mirrorsun was rising in the east. Serjon made several estimates based on Mirror-sun, the stars, and the time of year and banked into a course for the Wind River Range.

"Alion!" he called back. "Hie there, Alion! Can you hear me? Are you all right?"

There was no answer. By turning as far as the seat would allow and stretching his arm back Serjon was able to reach Alion's wrist. The skin was warm, and there was a steady pulse. He had been shot in the thigh, which had been roughly bandaged with a ragged piece of cloth. There was blood seeping out of the fabric, but not an alarming amount.

Flying northeast over the mountains, Serjon flew through cloud for a time, then caught sight of the glinting waters of Bear Lake in a gap. It was not a long flight, only 150 miles or so, and he had studied the terrain in detail in preparation for the raid that had brought the war to Condelor. The clouds continued to clear, and soon after their first hour in the air he was able to make out Green River in Mirrorsun's light. Ahead was the southernmost lip of the Wind River Range, but as he got closer to free Yarronese territory, so did Serjon's problems grow. There would be no landing lights at any wingfield, and there would be shots fired if he did manage to find one by Mirrorsun's glow.

There was another way, however. The Sweetwater River became visible, and Serjon began to recognize some of the bends and stretches from his orientation training. A dispersal wingfield was close by. The night was calm and Mirrorsun shone down from the southeast, a pale but steady beacon. Serjon wrenched back on a handle that ignited a trail flare while the gunwing was still high. That would draw shots from anyone on the ground, but it could not be helped.

Water is flat, he kept telling himself as he threw two levers to kill the compression engines. The gunwing bounced amid a burst of spray, skipped, bounced more heavily amid a bigger splash, then lurched to an abrupt stop on a shoal just beneath the surface. Serjon immediately snapped the canopy open, but the gunwing was stuck fast and they were safe.

17 July 3961: Wind River

Alion moaned as he revived. His head was throbbing, and there was a stabbing, insistent pain in his right thigh. He tried to move, but his limbs felt as if lead weights had been strapped to them. As far as he could tell he was in a tent and it was daylight, yet everything around him seemed familiar while out of place. In the distance he could hear compression engines. So, he was still at the training wing-field north of Condelor, yet what had happened to him?

A field nurse entered. She was dressed in a neat but plain brown uniform with a red cross at either side of her collar.

"Warden Alion, you're awake at last!" she exclaimed in Yarronese when she saw that his eyes were open.

Yarronese. Now Alion was even more confused. He decided to groan rather than speak, and he clumsily moved his hand to the bandage on his forehead.

"Try not to move," she said as she knelt beside the stretcher and gently moved his hand back to his side. "You were shot in the escape from Bartolica, then Wingcaptain Feydamor crash-landed the stolen gunwing in the Sweet-water River. Such an ordeal! Were you awake for any of it?"

Alion thought for a moment, then decided that confusion was his best ally. He rolled his head from side to side on the pillow.

"Well now, the same Bartolican resistance fighters who had been sheltering you also managed to free the Wingcap-tain Feydamor from the Bartolicans. I thought it was so noble of you, defecting to the Bartolicans to free your flockleader. What happened to you, how did you get shot?"

"Bartolican adjunct . . . heard me speak Yarronese. Slip of the tongue. Shot him, then . . . all went black."

"Oh, how brave, you were very lucky," she gushed. "Your Bartolican friends carried you to the trainer gun-wing where the wingcaptain was waiting, and now you are home again."

It slowly became clear to Alion what had happened. His liaison with the Lady Airlord was looked upon with ex-treme displeasure in Bartolica, yet he was also a hero to

Samondel. What better way to be rid of him than to have him turn traitor? At that very moment someone would be telling her what a despicable turncoat he was, how he had feigned love for her to rescue Serjon.

Serjon had hardened during his time in the Bartolican cell. Rank no longer impressed him, and he was all too aware of his current high status. Sartov had expected more. Bubbling effusion, an enraged outburst, anything but uneasy politeness.

"I appreciate your, ah, initiative in the bombing of Condelor," said the Airlord when they were at last alone. "It was an act of bravery and loyalty beyond my wildest dreams. Even had I thought of such a raid I could never have ordered you against the stronghold of Bartolica with just two gunwing escorts."

"I would have been happier with no escorts, after what happened," said Serjon with all the warmth of a slipstream in winter.

Sartov was aware that something odd had taken place after the bomb had plunged into the Bartolican throne hall. He now faced up to Serjon, hoping that whatever words followed would not damage the war effort.

"I have read a disturbing synopsis of your report, Wingcaptain Feydamor. It says that one of your escorts fired upon your wing as you made your second attack."

Serjon nodded. "My dome gunner was killed instantly, and all three starboard engines shut down. I think that rockets hit them. Reaction gun bullets tore past me, but none hit. I managed to get the wing under partial control. The flight guildsman was unhurt, but in the nose. The outer port engine seized, I lost control. The flight guildsman was calling my name as the streets and housetops raced past below. Then we crashed. I remember pain, breaking spars, fire, and then water rising all around me. Bartolican carbineers cut me free and laid me on a stone road. I saw the triwing Slash fly overhead, then ... I think someone kicked me in the head."

Sartov shifted in his chair. "There were two gunwings flying escort behind you," he pointed out. "Which of them opened fire?"

"How am I to know, Lordship? I was delivered from captivity by Warden Alion. I returned to find Bronlar Jemarial a hero and your liaison to Cosdora. What would you think?"

"Both deny shooting at you. I have a testament from Bronlar describing her part in the bombing and war duel that followed, but it says nothing about how the superregal was shot down. Alion has made a statement. He denies it too. It might have been a triwing captured by the Bartolicans."

"And painted sufficiently like Slash or Princess to fool my tail gunner?"

Sartov got to his feet and walked over to the trestle table where his maps and briefing cannisters were. He picked up a small box and opened it.

"This is the daystar," he said as he looked into the box. "It was to be yours posthumously for extreme bravery in the defense of Yarron. Note that it has a red background, because it is meant to be posthumous. Now it will have to be made blue."

"I'm sorry to cause inconvenience."

"A member of the Guild of Medalliers is preparing another."

"Have you spoken to Warden Alion yet?"

"No, but what—"

"Now it is my turn to ask questions and I want the answer to this one: who shot me down over Condelor, and from behind?"

Nobody else could have spoken to an Airlord like that, but Serjon already had a legend built that would live for centuries and outlast the reputations of most Airlords.

"An inquiry of the Warden Inspectorate will be called

this very hour," Sartov assured him. "Now, can I arrange anything for you? Leave to see your father in Gannett? A new flight jacket and a comfortable bed? Company in the latter?"

"I want a patrol gunwing and a place on the duty roster," Serjon replied.

Sartov nodded with considerable relief and called in his clerk.

18 July 3961: Wind River

It was the following day before Alion was able to get up, and by then Serjon was in the air again and on active duty. Alion was able to walk only with a crutch, but the wound to his thigh had not been serious as gunshot wounds go. Sartov arrived in the early afternoon, and Alion met the Airlord of Yarron in the wingfield adjunct's tent. After an exchange of formalities Sartov ordered the other officials out.

"What can you tell me about the Bartolican resistance?" asked Sartov, leaning forward. His manner was more one of eagerness than suspicion.

"They . . . are Bartolicans, mainly. They are against the war, and are opposed to the Archwarden, Stanbury."

"Can you give me names, or contact codes? Where were you held?"

"I am sorry, Lordship, I cannot. I was kept in basements and unlit rooms. As for names, why one of the resistance told me that he knew not a single name that was not a codeword."

Sartov sat back and clapped his hands together. "It makes sense, yes. Without such secrecy they would not last long . . . yet it would be helpful to be in contact. What do you remember of the attack on the palace?"

"Everything that I saw, Lordship."

Sartov picked up a report and read what he already knew off by heart.

"Wingcaptain Feydamor was fired upon from behind. He did not see the gunwing responsible, but he is adamant that it was not groundfire. What happened, Warden Alion? Tell it in *your* words."

"Ah, as I saw it, the super-regal bombed the palace. As I flew through the cloud of debris. I was hit by either groundfire or flying stone. I nursed Princess clear of the palace grounds, then crash-landed in a street. I ignited the destruct flare and left Princess burning."

"That was brave and resourceful. And the resistance found you before the vigilance brigades?"

"Yes. It was just luck."

"Were there any other gunwings in the sky during the second attack against the palace? Had the Bartolicans ascended by then?"

"Lordship, I did not even *see* the second attack on the palace. I noticed one triwing in a war duel, but quite far away."

"You are certain?"

"Yes, Lordship."

This was not what Sartov had wanted to hear. The attack on the Bartolican wardens and nobility had unified both warden and artisan classes throughout Yarron and all its allies. The attack had been so spectacularly successful that it was touted as a sign of divine approval for the Yarronese cause. The Bartolicans had even tried to emulate it in an attack against Cosdora, but that scheme had gone badly wrong and left the Bartolicans looking stupid as well as unchivalric. Yarronese attacked in the open, bravely and directly: Bartolicans did it by stealth and secret bombs.

To have suspicion and dissension surfacing now would do no good to the war effort. Sartov stood up and folded his arms behind his back.

"From what you say, it is clear that Semme Jemarial was the only one in a position to shoot down the super-regal, yet she is currently our military liaison to Cosdora. Guilty or not . . ."

Sartov's voice trailed off as he considered the constraints and options. Serjon was the greatest Yarronese hero for decades, and perhaps the greatest ever. Alion had saved him from a Bartolican prison. Bronlar had brought Cosdora into the war on Yarron's side, and the Cosdorans would not hear a word against her. Either Bronlar or Alion had shot down Serjon, and the evidence pointed to Bronlar. The palace gardens were apparently full of women when Serjon had attacked, and that might have aroused her sense of chivalry. It might also have aroused Alion's, for that matter. Who was to know?

That afternoon Sartov told Serjon that groundfire had been deemed responsible for the crash of the super-regal by the presiding Warden of the Inspectorate after consultations with him. Serjon had added an unmarked sailwing and a Bartolican warden to his tally by then, and was in a fighting mood. They went walking along the flightstrip for privacy, and a mild wind tugged at their clothing and floated their voices away.

"The word must be that groundfire brought you down," insisted Sartov. "Any other conclusion would damage Free Yarron's war effort."

"Yarron's freedom can't be founded on lies. Chancellor Virtrian saw a gunwing shoot at me."

"Chancellor Virtrian might have been mistaken. Besides, he is imprisoned in Condelor and obviously not available to testify, and we have only your word on what he said. Yarron can be weakened by truth for its own sake. Accept and proclaim my word, Flockleader Feydamor, we cannot let anything detract from Yarron's triumph at Condelor."

"Yarron's triumph at Condelor was nothing but a breach of discipline on my part," Serjon snapped angrily. "How would you like me to proclaim *that* to the guildsmen, artisans, wardens, and carbineers of the ground and air? It's just as I confessed to you yesterday: I broke off and flew against Condelor on my own initiative out of sheer revenge for the Bartolican atrocities at Opal and the other estates of western Yarron. Never forget that, Lordship."

"And what about now? I have my sources, and my sources tell me that you once propositioned Bronlar Jemarial and she refused you! That could be a reason to besmirch her name with this accusation. Do you destroy everything that displeases you, including Semme Jemarial?"

Serjon's face reddened with shame, but his eyes were wide with tethered anger.

"I am Serjon Warden Killer, as I was then. Why would I want one scrawny little rat wearing registration wings when I had my choice of every maid in Casper—and most of their mothers. I accuse someone of shooting the super-regal down. Only Bronlar and Alion qualify."

Alion was approaching in the distance, limping along on his crutches. Sartov beckoned to him and waited until he was within earshot before he replied to Serjon.

"What would you suggest doing about the incident at Condelor, Flockleader Feydamor?" he asked, his voice even and reasonable in spite of the agitation in his face.

"Proclaim an inquiry."

"Is that all?"

"It would ruin her name," said Alion, entering the exchange for the first time.

"You are honorably lenient toward her, but then she did not shoot at you from behind," retorted Serjon.

"She may have been strafing the Bartolican nobles too," protested Alion. "The super-regal may have got in the way."

"Impossible!" insisted Serjon. "Besides, she has testified that she did not join in the second attack."

"Neither did I!" cried Alion.

"Well, *somebody* shot at me!"

"That is for a formal hearing of the Warden Inspectorate

to determine," interjected Sartov. "Until then, I want no more discussion on this matter. Yarron must see unity among its heroes."

"Even when they shoot each other in the back?"

"The Warden Inspectorate will decide if that really happened."

"Well, meantime the suspects must be removed from the active list."

"You are talking about two of my best warriors. No!"

"Lordship, this is dishonesty, this is against every wardenly principle."

"Not so, Flockleader. This is a path to wartime justice. Reject it and you betray your wardenate, guild, flocks, dominion, and airlord. Accept it and you will get what you want. If—and I say if—the Inspectorate finds that a Yarronese shot at you, then Alion and Bronlar will certainly be suspended, subject to a deeper investigation."

Serjon looked from the Airlord to Alion and then back to the Airlord. None of this satisfied him, yet it was clearly as much of a concession as he could hope for. Standing with them on the flightstrip, he felt exposed and hunted, as if a rogue gunwing were about to appear and strafe him.

"Very well, Lordship, have it your way."

19 July 3961: Vernal

Sartov had one further log to roll into Serjon's path. He flew to Cosdora and secretly asked the Airlord to refuse the extradition of Bronlar. On the way back from the capital, he stopped at Vernal where Bronlar was training a group of young flyers in the new Yarronese way of war dueling. When she landed after a demonstration of power dives, she found that an improvised ceremony had been thrown together. Sartov had brought a daystar medal with him, and very soon the eight-pointed decoration was hanging from a silk ribbon around her neck while three of her guildsmen played the Yarronese anthem on flute, fiddle, and guitar. Nobody thought it odd that Sartov took her aside for a walk beside the flightstrip when the ceremony was over.

"I have just heard that Serjon and Alion are alive and safe!" Bronlar said excitedly. "That's even better than the daystar. When can I—"

"Semme Jemarial, you do not hail a noble without being hailed," Sartov pointed out. His voice was patient, but his expression grim. "You salute or bow, then wait to be hailed. The only exception is if you are the closest of friends, and have made a magistrate's declaration."

Bronlar fiddled with the daystar, abashed. "I'm sorry, Lordship. Formality is not enforced on this wingfield, especially now that we're trying to encourage unchivalric methods of air combat. One gets into new habits easily."

"Flockleader Serjon Feydamor, Air Carbineer First Class, has accused one of his escort of shooting down his super-regal over Condelor. Warden Alion Damaric helped to rescue him from Condelor, supporting the case against *you*."

His words had the impact of a carbine butt to the head. Bronlar gasped, stopped, and gripped the daystar with both hands.

"No! No! I broke off to attack the palace wingfield after the first pass. I fought till my guns were empty, I claimed clear air victories. You have to believe me, the whole of Condelor saw it happen."

"The people of Condelor are being less than cooperative about supplying witnesses to Yarronese inquiries just now. Serjon, Alion, or you may be telling a monstrous lie. Alion rescued Serjon, and is well known for his sense of honor and commitment to chivalric fighting, so few suspect him. Serjon may have concocted the story himself to cover some secret. He is very odd about broken mirrors and the position of the Sentinels amid the constellations, not to mention a fear of thirteen bordering on mania. I happen to think that groundfire brought the super-regal down, but I was not there."

Bronlar slowly unclenched her hands from around the daystar. There was blood where the points had dug into her skin.

"This charge brings death as a sentence for the guilty," she said in a small, quavering voice. "What is to become of me? Do I return to Wind River and face the Warden Inspectorate?"

"No, you stay here and train Cosdorans for now. The Cosdoran Airlord has agreed to refuse to release you from your current work, and no inquiry can be held until you are present. Feydamor is back on active duty, and with luck he may be killed before the war ends and an inquiry can be held."

"With *luck* he may be *killed*?" Bronlar echoed.

Sartov looked at his watch, then cross-waved both arms above his head. Distant guildsmen backed a steam trolley to his gunwing and spun the compression engine into life.

"I must go now, Semme Bronlar. I admit that I seem harsh and devious, but what more can I do? Feydamor is adamant that one of his escort shot him down and is demanding an inquiry. His seventy-four victories and the bombing of Condelor's palace have made him a hero of such stature that even as his airlord I cannot force him into silence."

"So, I might face a line of carbineers with assault carbines?"

"That is unlikely." Sartov took an envelope from his pocket and handed it to Bronlar. "Here is a transcript of his charges, Warden Alion's statement, and my assessment. Study it carefully."

Sartov walked Bronlar back to the staging area and quickly ascended into the late-afternoon sky. The congratulations and celebrations from the Cosdoran guildsmen and flyers lasted into the evening, and Bronlar lost herself in a reverie of light red wine, dancing, and ballads by the local bards. The revel paraded Bronlar the two miles into Vernal on a galley cart and continued in the largest tavern at the expense of the adjunct. He also rented a room so that Bronlar could spend one night in the comfort of a real bed with a feather mattress. It was early in the morning when Bronlar left the taproom and climbed the stairs to the circumbalcony. She paused at the railing before the door to her room, staring up at Mirrorsun, its band of nothingness amid the stars, and the stars themselves. After what could have been any length of time, Ryban called her name and approached with her embroidered flight jacket.

"You left this below," he began.

"Oh, good, grats. I'd best not lose it."

He draped the jacket over the rail and stared out into the night with her.

"Bronlar, I thought you looked sad tonight, for all your triumph."

"It was bought by the deaths of others, Ry. Should I be happy?"

"I—I worried about you. I hope you don't mind, but I found papers in your jacket and—Oh Semme Bronlar, he's a monster, how could he do such a thing?"

Bronlar took the jacket and draped it over her shoulders; then she put an arm around Ryban as if it were she who was comforting him.

"He's jealous of you," said Ryban. "He wanted to be the only hero of that raid, but then he crashed and Alion had to rescue him."

"Do you really think that? Do you think I'm innocent?"

"Pah, of course. Some carbineer hit him with a lucky shot."

Ryban drew Bronlar closer to him and they both looked at the sky for a few minutes more.

"You're shivering," said Ryban.

Bronlar turned and glanced into the door that she had opened but not entered. She shuddered. Her flight jacket fell to the floor.

"I'm scared to go in there," she admitted. "It's the blackness."

"I'll go first and light the lamp."

He picked up her flight jacket and stepped through the door. Bronlar entered too and took his arm.

"No, I dread the blackness of sleep. Nightmares of those I killed, nightmares of gunwings shooting at me . . . and now nightmares of Serjon leading a Yarronese firing squad. The bed should be a cloud of balm to restore me, but it's become a pit of horrors."

Ryban put his arms around her and held her tightly.

"You should relax more, learn to live, Bron."

"What do you mean?"

"You play so hard at being neither youth nor girl that your true self presses all the harder at the inside to escape. You are a girl of nineteen, a lovely girl of nineteen."

She clung to him, aware that her nipples were erect and her pulse was racing. The floor seemed to spin and precess beneath her feet. There was an odd taste in her mouth.

"This is an . . . unpleasing time for me," Bronlar found herself saying. "The others . . . I shouldn't."

"I'm proud of you, are you proud of me?" he asked, sounding slightly hurt.

"Of course."

"Then damn what the others think. I offer only to stay with you, to help you fight away the nightmare blackness. Would Serjon do such a thing?"

"I never let him."

"Ho ha, then if only he could see us now!" said Ryban with a curious twist of triumph in his voice. His thigh pressed gently but insistently between Bronlar's legs, pushing, pushing rhythmically. Bronlar found that she could not pull away.

"I'll shield you from Serjon's guns even if he be above us," Ryban said, "though he'd care more for another Bartolican gunwing to add to his tally."

A skilled duelist, she thought. His words held deference,

but his body courted her. He has done this before, he is even good at it . . . but why not trust experience? Words coursed through her mind. Why am I doing this? Why am I *not* doing this? Tomorrow I might be dead. What does it feel like? Who will ever know? Safeish time of the month?

"I've fought too much," sighed Bronlar. "Shield me tonight."

Ryban reached down between them, caressing her curves, then pulled a brass button from the fly of his trousers.

"Take this," he said, "it's a Cosdoran custom."

Bronlar dropped the button into her jacket pocket, then let the jacket drop to the floor again.

At that moment Serjon was in fact flying a night gunwing and firing his reaction guns at a black, unmarked sailwing above the tramway through the Green River Basin. The enemy flyer was keeping low, just above the rails, and blending with the shadows on the ground. Serjon climbed a little to get a better perspective. Mirrorsun was in a bad position, but—

An explosion lit up the countryside as the black, unmarked sailwing hit a black, unmarked steam tram. Serjon circled, wrestled with his conscience, then decided to claim both sailwing and steam tram.

He was glad of the taste of blood. Earlier that evening he had been told by the presiding Warden of the Inspectorate that Bronlar would be granted asylum in Cosdora until the end of the war. Faced with diplomatic obstructions apparently beyond even Sartov's control, Serjon sullenly accepted that no more could be done.

Ryban awoke to find Bronlar already out of bed and partly dressed, and water was splashed about the dresser stand where she had washed hastily. Outside the sky was growing light. She looked around as Ryban sat up in bed. In the morning light he could see that she had nicely proportioned breasts on a wiry figure. She hastily buttoned her shirt to hide her breasts.

"Not so modest," he crooned. "I've been there already."

"This was a bad idea," Bronlar said in a tense voice. "The other guildsmen will not take to it well."

"But this is not just affectionate fun, this is the beginnings of love," said Ryban as he slipped out of the bed and padded over. "They must be made to understand."

"This was not love, it was revenge. It was not fun either, it hurt—both times."

Ryban stood next to Bronlar and put his arm around her. "Virgins always find it painful the first few times. Why I can tell you—"

Bronlar twisted away from him. She lifted her glittering flight jacket from the floor and draped it over her shoulders.

"At the end of the war I may take steps to find out if it improves with practice, Guildsman Ryban. Until then I am no longer available to be courted. Is that clear?"

She managed to come across as vulnerable yet dangerous at the same time, like some small, cornered thing that was all needle teeth and razor claws. Ryban deferred to her.

"Bronlar, I'm in love with you. Would I do anything that you did not wish?"

Not trusting him with a parting kiss, Bronlar walked shakily through the door and made her way to the stairs. What she had done with Ryban had solved nothing, she decided as she walked back to the wingfield. Far from keeping the nightmares back, it had brought guilt, confusion, and regret to burden her further. Well, it was a lesson, she concluded. A lesson like the bullet hole she had once found in her gunwing's headrest.

19 July 3961: Condelor

In Condelor the Lady Airlord Samondel was heartbroken by the second desertion of Alion. As Archwarden Stanbury told it, the whole romance had been a sham to get him familiar with the palace so that he could arrange the escape of his wingcaptain. He had not shot down the huge regal at all, it had been the combined firepower of a hundred palace guards and their assault carbines that had smashed its engines and dropped it out of the sky. Faced with betrayal on this sort of scale, Samondel was easy prey. After she had endured a series of carefully orchestrated admonitions by her advisers, Stanbury approached her in a far more conciliatory tone.

"They should all be ashamed of themselves," said the Archwarden. "Those who deceived you and those who now blame you for being deceived."

The Lady Airlord did not reply for some time. She was sitting on a wide marble rail with her back against a pillar, wearing the embroidered breeches and flight jacket of a warden. The gold circlet of the Airlord was on her head, blending with her ruddy hair, which cascaded over the rail and down to the flagstones of the gallery. Her legs were drawn up against her body and her arms were wrapped about them. Stanbury walked up and looked over the edge of the rail. The drop to the flagstones below was at least seventy feet.

"I was never groomed for the throne," she said eventually. "It was such a good life, being a girl at court. I led parades, I was celebrated, people loved me for myself." She looked up at Stanbury. "Why has it turned so horrible, Archwarden?"

"The Airlord of Greater Bartolica has power, Ladyship, more power than any other airlord in the known world.

People are drawn to power, especially in the hands of someone of goodwill but little experience."

"You mean me."

"Only friends can be trusted with bad news. All others will bend it to suit themselves."

"I met Alion at the coronation last year, we exchanged coy letters, he even dedicated a duel to me. When he shot down the monster sailwing he seemed to sacrifice everything to save me."

"More faith could be placed in the palace defenses, Ladyship. My inspectors said the damage came from beneath, not from behind. Warden Damaric saw his friend shot down and bravely decided to try to save him. He defected, lied about protecting you, then used you to free the monster Feydamor after one of the most hideous crimes against chivalry in all the annals of Mounthaven."

Samondel looked away across the palace roofs to the city beyond.

"I have thought a lot about abdicating," she said, as if to her people.

"You have a good heart, my lady. All that you need is experience."

"And how much damage will I do as I gain that experience, Archwarden? I want to be left in the shadows to learn while someone else makes wise decisions about affairs of state. Archwarden, I cannot even manage an affair with . . ."

Stanbury glanced about slowly, and was rewarded with nods from four of the Inner Guard who were visible. Their right hands rested on polished reaction guns slung from their shoulders, and they watched each other as much as for threats from assassins. Clearly there would be no better privacy than this at any time and in any place.

"I could manage affairs of state very effectively as your consort, Ladyship," he said with what he hoped was both deference and concern.

Samondel's hair swirled out in a red fan as she turned

her head to face him. Her face was a study in shock at first.

"You are twice my age, sair Archwarden."

It was a mild reaction, the best that Stanbury could have hoped for under the circumstances.

"I was not proposing a love match, Ladyship," he replied with his eyes cast down to the flagstones. "In matters of state I have a great deal of experience, however. Under my hand, Greater Bartolica's rule has extended across the entire north of Mounthaven, remember?"

"You would make a better airlord than me," Samondel said, her voice flat and lifeless again.

"I would be but a regent, Ladyship, were I to marry you. When you felt ready to rule, you could declare the marriage unconsummated."

"But—"

"I shall testify the same, and the marriage will be declared void. You need never do more than put your hand on my arm during public appearances."

Samondel slipped down from the railing and took Stanbury's hand in both of hers.

"Sair, sair, you do not know what you are proposing. The courtiers would ridicule you, rumors would spread about you being impotent, homosexual, or poxed. Your reputation would be ruined in a day."

"Any warden's career can be ended in a single day, Ladyship. All it takes is a duel."

"Yes, yes, but a duel is honorable."

"Where the good of Greater Bartolica is concerned, even honor is not too precious to sacrifice."

Samondel pulled back and released his hand, now gazing down at the flagstones as well.

"Make an announcement for us, noble Archwarden Stanbury. I shall marry you and sign the regency to my new consort. With time, perhaps it will not be necessary to dissolve our marriage."

Stanbury walked away through the corridors feeling as

if he knew what it was like to fly without the need of an aircraft. Not only had she agreed, she might even consider a permanent union. That would remove the need to push her aside at some time in the future, an act which was always tricky with such a public figure. The announcement of their engagement was a welcome relief in diplomatic circles, while in the court the coming marriage seemed a glorious affirmation of life after so much death.

22 July 3961: Condelor

The Call took Virtrian as he sat in his cell within the Condelor palace. His eyes glazed over; then he stood up and shuffled to the west wall of his cell. Here he mindlessly tried to find a way through it, as he had done at least twice a week for nearly three months. He was oblivious of everything around him, and even though he could still eat and drink by reflex, he would remember nothing when he awoke in three hours.

Ten minutes passed. The door to his cell clanked open and a figure in nondescript robes entered with a strangely designed harness. With some difficulty the woman slipped the harness over Virtrian's hands and head. It was designed to choke if the wearer struggled too hard to go with the Call. Outside, she led him away after locking the door to his cell. The guards were all in the grip of the Call and their terriers had been shot dead as the woman came past with her prize.

Virtrian awoke bound and gagged. He was somewhere outside the dungeons, that was immediately apparent. There was carpet on the floor, and the walls were plastered and draped. A robed and veiled figure sat across the room, watching him stir.

"Welcome back, Sair," said a contralto voice in Yarronese. "You will forgive the gags and bindings, but people have been known to get a little excitable when they wake

after being rescued during a Call. They cry out in amazement, shout that it is impossible, all that sort of thing. We
are still in Condelor, and as soon as your escape is noticed
there will be guards and carbineers everywhere."

She got up and sauntered across to him with a slight
mincing gait in her steps.

"I am going to remove your gag now, sair Virtrian.
Kindly refrain from shouting."

Virtrian nodded. She removed the cloth.

"Who are you?" asked Virtrian.

"An enemy of your enemy. I am Theresla, a former
servant of the Veraguay envoy, and I am a fugitive, like
you."

"I've heard of the envoy. Yarron's former envoy mentioned her in his reports. So you are from Veraguay too?"

"No, I am from a continent on the other side of the
Earth," replied Theresla. "I am also a Callwalker."

From the look on Virtrian's face it was clear that he did
not believe a word that she said, but she had rescued him
from a Bartolican cell and that was difficult to explain by
any other means. Another woman now entered, and Virtrian thought that he knew her from some diplomatic function years ago.

"I'll untie you now," she said. "Please do everything
that we say. My name is Laurelene Hannan, wife of the
late Inspector General."

Once freed, Virtrian watched as Theresla and Laurelene
unveiled themselves. Laurelene brought tea and fresh
grapes, and assured him that a hot lunch would not be long
in arriving. Theresla began eating pickles. They were in
the house of the Inspector General, and there was an outlook over the palace. As they sat eating lunch a bell began
jangling in the distance. The tiny figures of guards could
be seen scurrying about on the palace walls.

"Some warder just tried to give me my slops," Virtrian
concluded. "Will they search here?"

"Eventually, perhaps," said Laurelene.

"By then you will be someone else, sair Virtrian," said Theresla.

"I know it may seem like a stupid question, but why did you free me?" he asked.

"I need a flyer," said Theresla.

"Lies," snorted Laurelene. "She was sorry for you. So was I."

"But I *do* need a flyer," retorted Theresla, sounding hurt.

"Your escape discredits the Archwarden," said Laurelene. "It has been decided that discrediting the Archwarden is more important than shooting down a hundred Bartolican gunwings, so here you are. You will be safe here for now. I have already had one of my maids dressing up as a man and being accidentally seen by visitors. There are tales going about concerning me having a secret lover."

"But, but—"

"You don't have to share either of our beds, of course. I am hardly an enticing mistress—"

"But older women are said to be more grateful," Theresla interjected.

"Besides, Semme Theresla has habits that might alarm you," Laurelene countered.

At her words Virtrian realized that Theresla was not eating meatballs but whole roast mice. She noticed his stare.

"I marinate them in a secret recipe before cooking them so the bones are rendered crumbly," Theresla assured him. "Try one?"

Virtrian declined.

24 July 3961: Occupied Senner

Two days later, in occupied Senner, several divisions of nomad carbineers launched a coordinated attack on a string of Bartolican garrisons under the cover of Cosdoran gunwings. Only five of the twelve garrisons fell to the initial onslaught, but the others were left under siege and isolated. The nomad commanders all had microscopes and sample slides of aviad hair. All prisoners were screened very carefully, and three were shot without explanation.

Although it was meant as no more than a test of resolve on the part of the allies, it proved to be a good guide to the state of Bartolican resolve as well. Fast courier sailwings escaped north with word of what was going on, but no flocks of gunwings swarmed out of the north in response. The allies' wings bombed the garrisons during a Call and Sennerese nomads swarmed over trapfields on the trailing edge of the Call. Still no flocks of Bartolican gunwings droned across the desert from the northern skies.

"Give them time," counseled Triglaw, the military liaisory from Cosdora counseled the Sennerese Archwarden. "They are merely luring your forces north until they are overextended, and then there will be a monumental counterattack. That is the Bartolican way. Overwhelming advantage and a battleground of their own choice. Our gunwings report major buildups of gunwings, heavy sailwings, and carbineers south of Condelor."

Sriek hak-Hale gazed down at the map woven into the rug on the floor of his tent. Coloured blocks denoted garrisons, troops, and wingfields.

"Sartov promised that he would begin a mighty diversion in two days," the Sennerese Archwarden replied.

"Pah. He says he will be our salvation, but he tells nothing of what he will do. You should trust the word of an ally that has sailwings and gunwings over this battlefield."

"Senner may have only nine wardens in gunwings, but we use those few to great effect," hak-Hale pronounced as he reached out to adjust the disposition of two blocks. "Our own wardens report no buildup of Bartolican carbineers, only the wings."

"Are you calling me a liar?"

"No, but your own people may be deceiving you."

"I have fought duels over less."

"Then challenge, if you have a mind to. My feeling is that you value victory over Bartolica more than a squabble over some minor point of honor. Duels are a luxury of peacetime, sair Triglaw."

The liaisory did not reply.

"As I was about to say," continued hak-Hale, "my own feeling is that you do not want Senner to overwhelm the undefended southernmost parts of Bartolica before your own carbineers take Evanston and are free to march west."

"Such accusations are not the basis for an alliance. Many of our wardens and squires have died flying cover for your nomad carbineers."

"But many more of my carbineers have died taking the garrisons. I have made my decision, sair Triglaw. We shall trust the eyes of our own wardens and advance across the Bartolican border. If it is a trap, we shall fight bravely and take many Bartolicans with us as we die. If not, we shall drive them into the Salt Lake or shoot them down, then end the war all the faster."

25 July 3961: Condelor

The royal palace of Condelor was subjected to a search without precedent in that entire century after the escape of Airlord Abdicate Virtrian. Although a great deal of stolen and hoarded property was discovered and several people were found in bedrooms where they had no business, the Airlord Abdicate of Yarron was not among their number. The guards who had been on duty in the palace dungeon complex were tortured according to the double-blind method, but their confessions established only that they were lying to avoid further pain.

There were thirty other prisoners who had been left to their fate in the dungeons. Only the Airlord Abdicate was missing, and it was abundantly clear to Stanbury that he had been freed during a Call.

"Why were you keeping him alive?" demanded the aviad chief of his Inner Guard, Paraville. "Surely he was better dead?"

"I sought to keep him as a symbol of Bartolican victory," said Stanbury. "Victories are so transitory, they fade in the memory without visible symbols. Where were your 'special forces' during the Call?"

"They were engaged in . . . important but routine duties elsewhere in the palace."

"Spying on my own people, you mean."

"Most of my people are in the field, fighting!" retorted Paraville firmly but quietly. "Dozens, hundreds have died due to Sartov's featherhead hunt. There are but six on duty in Condelor, including me, and do not forget that we spy as much for you as for ourselves. There is sedition among your own people, Archwarden, or have you forgotten it?"

Stanbury swept the reports from his desk with his arm.

"Useless!" he cried. "What is going wrong? Victories were so easy to pluck from the fields and skies until a few weeks ago. People wanted to have me assassinated because they thought anyone could be archwarden and oversee a procession of triumphs. Now they want me to be archwarden so that they can blame me for everything that goes wrong."

"But little has gone wrong. The bombing of the palace was a tragic accident, and the escape of the Airlord Abdicate does nothing for the Yarronese war effort. Impressions of defeat are all that you see, you are just a pessimist."

"Impressions are everything!" Stanbury retorted, the veins of his temples standing out alarmingly. "The four regions that are Greater Bartolica are held together by impressions. One impression is that a girl of nineteen with no experience of combat or dueling is their airlord. The Sennerese are advancing north even as we speak, and the carbineers defending the capital are from Pocatello. Pocatello!"

Stanbury seized Paraville by the lapels of his coat, then pushed him backward. The aviad stumbled back over a chair but recovered without falling. He slowly righted the chair and set it neatly on a rug.

"The Pocatello carbineers are as loyal as any."

"They are shopkeepers and artisans, recruited or impressed mere weeks ago. There's not a one of them who would not march back to his wife and a bowl of carbonara pasta if given a chance. Put a line of nomads before them and they'd *run* back. Were it not for the Bartolican gunwings the nomads would be swarming through the suburbs by next month."

Stanbury had personally ordered a flock of ninety Bartolican gunwings to provide support to the garrisons in Senner, and reports were returned that they had turned the tide for now. In fact there were no Bartolican gunwings flying over Senner. Somewhere in the chain of command it had been decided that perfectly good gunwings could not be risked in fighting when carbineers could slow the enemy down first. Besides, the aviad supreme command had decided that Bartolica was losing the war, and was now useful as nothing more than a supply of gunwings. Stanbury would be furious when he found out, but in a fortnight he would probably be in a cell or dead so it hardly mattered. In the meantime Kalward had infiltrated the Yarronese base at Wind River, where the really useful, long-range wings were being built. He would prove his loyalty by restoring the solar powered ferrywing to working order, and after that the radical aviads would have a new client.

8 | FAILING IN LOVE, AGAIN

24 July 3961: Wind River

Jeb Feydamor had still been in mourning for his dead stepson and heir when Serjon had returned from Condelor alive. Like many others in the chivalric guilds, Feydamor was torn between praise for the boy's courage and condemnation for his attack on the Condelor palace.

Of more immediate concern was the stolen Sandhawk that Serjon had flown from Bartolica. Two days after Serjon's return Feydamor was examining the aircraft as head of an assessment crew. It had been dragged clear of the stream where it had landed, but no effort had been made to repair it or remove parts for more detailed inspection. The big compression engines were by the Milarvis guild and had an extremely good weight-to-power ratio. The wings were well over the old limit, while the airspeed indicator was calibrated to an ambitious 250 mph.

"The Bartolicans seem convinced that the old limits can be exceeded safely," Feydamor dictated to a clerk who was following him about with a board. "The airframe is made of an extremely light and strong laminate-ashwood and silk combination."

His fellow guildsman Terrica came around from the other side of the sailwing.

"Under the control of an experienced warden this thing could match all but our most advanced prototypes," Terrica said, and the clerk hastily switched to another board.

"What we really need to know is just how many of these Sandhawks have been built."

"Very few, perhaps two or three," said Feydamor. "This thing must have cost as much as twenty standard gunwings. It has processes and materials in it that are just not practical, and it must be a nightmare to tune and maintain. It might be fast, tough, and light, but it's of no use in a war. The engine's fuel consumption on boost must be three times that of our triwing gunwings."

Terrica reached up and ran his hand along the leading edge of the wing until he touched the gun barrel.

"If it can destroy twenty or thirty of our gunwings for every Sandhawk lost, surely this is a good bargain. Any accountant would approve."

"Believe me, Terrica, I could design engines to run almost as well as these for a quarter the cost. This one has polished and engraved access covers, hollow reamed struts, dynamic pitch control, and more. This is the sort of thing that a committee of guildsmen might come up with. It's impractical. Our young heroes picked the wrong gunwing to steal. If the Bartolicans kept with such a design they would soon be defeated by bankruptcy."

Feydamor stood back and stared at the big gunwing with his hands on his hips.

"Pack up and get back to the utility cart," he said to the clerk. "Sair Terrica and I will be there soon."

"What do we report on this thing?" asked Terrica when they were alone.

"Declare that we have learned its secrets and have a half dozen of the local militia posted to guard it until the Northwind Campaign is over. After that it can be dragged to the nearest wingfield by a couple of compression carts and be made flightworthy—if anyone can be bothered. Believe me, sair, this thing is of no military use to anyone."

26 July 3961: Wind River

Two days later the Northwind Campaign was ready to be launched. Almost the entire force of Sartov's Air Carbineers was ready to depart in the half-light before dawn, and the steam engine trolleys were being dragged from aircraft to aircraft at the run by frantic guildsmen.

"So, you have your own super-regal now," Serjon said to Ramsdel. "Are you also against me for accusing Bronlar of what she did?"

Ramsdel wrapped his glittering green and gold arms about himself as if cold, yet the day was pleasantly warm.

"You were there, I was not and I make no judgments. I heard you reprimanding two of your flock yesterday. You were almost hysterical."

"The idiots flew behind me after I'd given strict orders about *never* flying behind me."

"But it's traditional to cover one's leader—"

"Not when the leader is me! I can look after myself, my victories say as much. My flock must only fly in a tiered line."

A super-regal thundered down the flightstrip and rose into the blue sky, drowning all conversation for some moments.

"This was a terrible decision," Serjon said grimly as they watched the second super-regal beginning to move. "I warned the Airlord but he would not listen."

"About what?" asked Ramsdel.

"The date. This is July twenty-sixth, and twenty-six is twice thirteen—"   He got no further. Ramsdel put his fingers between his lips and gave a piercing whistle. Immediately a dozen flyers and wardens converged on Serjon, pinned his arms, lifted him from the ground and dunked his head into a quenching trough. This done, they departed without a word.

Serjon shook himself like a wet terrier. Only Ramsdel was still standing beside the trough as he wiped the water from his eyes and dusted drops from the fraying gold embroidery of his flight jacket.

"Wha—What in the name of Hell's Call was that for?" Serjon gasped.

"That was your bad luck for the day," Ramsdel replied in a very earnest tone. "Now nothing can go wrong with the battle."

Northwind struck the Bartolican-held tramway precisely between Median and Green River, in a remote part of the Red Desert. The super-regals and regals parachuted a hundred carbineers down beside the rails, where they began tearing up the sleepers and rails and piling them into a fortification.

Meantime the gunwings attacked the marshaling yards at Median and Green River, destroying many trams and starting fires in the compression spirit stores. The two air battles over the provincial cities meant that the super-regals and regals managed to make five ferry runs that day, dropping another three hundred carbineers, six cart cannons, and two galley carts at the break in the tramway. Two forts were established, one mile apart, both from piles of sleepers and rails. The ferry flights continued through the night and all through the next day, and by dusk on the 27th there were a thousand men defending the two improvised forts. All were well supplied with food and ammunition and securely dug down against any attack.

The following day the super-regals bombed other stretches of tramway while gunwings shot up steam-tram-drawn trains that were being rushed from as far away as Forian with carbineers. The air battle was almost continuous, aided by the continuing fine, clear weather. Sartov was using a month's accumulation of compression spirit each day, but after four days the Bartolican relief forces were still unable to run trams more than five miles west of Median. A column of eight thousand carbineers began marching west, but a wingfield had been carved out of the desert at what was now called Fort Sartov. Precious compression spirit was ferried in, and the defending gunwings no longer had to make the half-hour flight from the Wind River wingfield.

A column of two thousand Yarronese militia had begun marching straight across the Red Desert for Fort Sartov on the evening before the first attack, and after five days they had crossed the sixty miles of wilderness to the outpost. Day by day the Bartolican air attacks grew heavier, and Sartov began to cut back on flights. Yarronese losses had been acceptable, but the reserves of compression spirit were running down. Sartov even resorted to sending his flyers over a hundred miles southwest to Vernal in Cosdora, where the Airlord had stockpiled compression spirit and ammunition in response to his request. All the Cosdoran aircraft were by now covering a massive ground attack by Senner on Condelor and holding off the Airlord's Militia Flock of Greater Bartolica.

The master plan was Sartov's, even though his Yarronese carbineers and air carbineers had such a difficult task. A series of attacks by his militias in occupied eastern Yarron had lured heavy Bartolican reinforcements over the Red Desert during the previous fortnight, so that more than a third of all Bartolican carbineers were east of Median when the tramway was cut. Now the Dorak resistance lashed out, destroying nine key tramway bridges on the morning of the 26th and attacking dozens of trams. Dorak also became impassable to Bartolicans.

A Call came to Sartov's aid as it swept over the advancing column of Bartolican carbineers. His sailwings attacked the helpless carbineers while gunwings battled in the sky above. It was unchivalric, but it was the way pioneered by Bartolica. The sun set on the 30th of July with twenty thousand Bartolican Carbineers still cut off from Condelor. Serjon had eighty-nine victories painted on the side of his gunwing, with another thirty-seven unconfirmed.

Ramsdel was made a warden after nursing his super-regal back over the Red Desert with all his crewmen dead and two engines on fire.

The climax came on the first day of August, when the Yarronese and Bartolican carbineers clashed just to the north of Fort Sartov. The Bartolicans had a numerical advantage and better weapons, but the Yarronese had better morale. The battle was on open ground in midmorning, and by the late afternoon their combined casualties exceeded four thousand killed or wounded. The result of the battle was inconclusive. The Yarronese retreated to the sanctuary of Fort Sartov and Fort Virtrian while the Bartolicans debated whether to lay siege or continue on to Green River. The following day the Yarronese heavy sailwings attacked with racks of reaction guns bolted to their wings, pinning the Bartolicans down. The Fort Sartov break in the tramway was holding.

Over in the west the combined ground forces of Senner, Cosdora, and another four newly allied dominions had begun a march on Condelor on Serjon's unlucky July 26th. Thirty-nine thousand carbineers, nomads, militiamen, and Montrassian exiles began a forced march of a hundred miles that had Condelor as its destination. The flocks that were to have struck the Sennerese had been diverted to the battle above the Red Desert, leaving just one hundred gunwings and sailwings to defend Condelor against the combined flocks of Cosdora, Senner, Omelgan, Pangaver, and Charlsand. The flocks mauled each other in the air, but neither could break free to provide ground support for the carbineers. Deprived of aviad support, air superiority, and battle calculor coordination, the outnumbered Bartolican carbineers were unable to halt the advance. After eight days of skirmishing, the allied column faced the Condelor city militia of fifteen thousand at the Ogden ruin. The battle lasted five hours, during which the Condelor militiamen were routed. The allied carbineers fanned out to encircle

Condelor while Stanbury frantically called for fresh carbineers to be sent from the regional capitals.

That same day Stanbury was married to the Lady Airlord Samondel in the royal palace of Condelor. In the skies above the gunwings of six dominions battled while heavy reaction guns in the palace gardens shot at those enemy aircraft that got too close. Bronlar was allowed back into action in the sky above Condelor on that day, and shot down her thirty-fifth Bartolican aircraft as the city's bells began to peal for the royal marriage.

Soon after the Northwind had begun, the resistance cells in Yarron mounted a series of suicidally intense assaults on the well-guarded and camouflaged sidings where the black trams were kept by day. Not one siding in five actually had a black tram there, but the Yarronese intelligence was limited and everything had to be hit. The attackers were armed with ballistic rockets designed for gunwings but dropped with instructions to make improvised shoulder-launchers. Hundreds of Yarronese and Bartolican carbineers died, but the Bartolicans also lost seven black trams, destroyed along with the twenty decoys that were hit. Serjon's accidental victim had been the other.

Sartov posted a reward of a million gold crendars for each of the remaining black trams. Dread of the black trams was instantly replaced by blind greed. Confronted by an ambush a fortnight after Northwind began, the commander of MC-1 set off the self-destruct charges and jumped clear. He was lynched before the fire had begun to die down. The driver and stoker of MC-3 shot the aviad crew, released the components, and derailed the tram into a shallow ravine. A carefully placed rockslide covered the prize, and the pair melted into the nearby forest to await the end of the war and their reward. They were never seen again.

4 August 3961: Wind River

The ceremony for awarding medals to Serjon and Alion
was postponed while the fighting raged on the two fronts,
but by August 4th a courier sailwing brought news of the
victory at the battle of Ogden. Amid the celebrations it
was also discovered that Bronlar's reply to the charges
against her had been included in the sealed bag.

She testified that she had left the super-regal to attack
the palace wingfield when Serjon had turned for his second
run against the palace. The next time she saw the super-
regal it was lying half submerged in a Bartolican canal. As
far as she was concerned, only Alion would have been in
a position to open fire on his own wingcaptain—whether
accidentally, deliberately, or not at all. The Wind River
Warden Inspectorate did not take long to consider the evidence. Alion was exonerated, while Bronlar's evidence
was declared to be "outside reasonable trust." A full investigation was ordered for when Bronlar could be summoned to appear in person. The Airlord of Cosdora now
intervened, saying that he would allow Bronlar to be tried
only by the new Council of Allied Airlords. Sartov was
secretly delighted to have the matter out of his hands and
agreed, although with public reluctance.

No sooner was this settled than Kalward sent a petition
to Sartov complaining about his continued confinement.
Sartov summoned Jeb Feydamor, and when the guildmaster arrived at his tent he handed him the petition and asked
him to read a circled section aloud.

" 'I originally surrendered myself for the purpose of repairing the sunwing, yet for four weeks I have been confined and subjected to almost continual examination and
interrogation. Airlord of Yarron, I most humbly beseech
you to allow me to work on the sunwing at the first pos-

sible opportunity, and subject to whatever scrutiny that you wish. Your loyal ally, Pyter Kalward.' "

Feydamor handed the petition back.

"That is all he has to say," Sartov said as he put the petition in a gilt-embossed folder.

"Ignore it, Lordship" was Feydamor's opinion.

"Have you made any progress with the sunwing?"

"Nearly all of our resources have been dedicated to Northwind, Lordship," Feydamor replied without a pretense of apology. "Some of the more obvious structural damage has been repaired with splints, and the wheel assembly is again usable."

"That is all that you have done? Nothing important has been made to actually work as yet?"

"No, Lordship."

"It is still in pieces, you say?"

"Yes, Lordship."

"My first thought was that Kalward might set off some self-destruct device, but if it is in pieces, how much damage can he do? Let him work on the engines first, in fact let him demonstrate them in working order to you before you will sanction the sunwing being reassembled. Assign a dozen guards to watch with you, but remember that this work is only to be done if you have time after tending the gunwings fighting over the Red Desert."

"Understood, Airlord."

The next day Sartov presented the daystar medal to Alion as he rested between patrols over Fort Sartov, and he also promoted Serjon to flock commander. Serjon had refused to accept a medal that had also been awarded to Bronlar or Alion, so he just watched and scowled. Sartov scowled back, but Alion determinedly maintained no expression at all.

Feydamor approached his son as the crowd was dispersing after the ceremony. The guildmaster had a scrap of paper in his hand and stared at it thoughtfully as they walked.

"If I remember anything about this glorious day it will be that a tailor's pin was sticking into my side for the whole of the presentation," Serjon said before his father could speak.

"Serjon—"

"And do you know why? Thirteen pins left by that excuse for a tailor! Gah, how I miss Ramsdel's work. I had my suspicions so I went right through the coat and trousers and counted them. Flock commander! That means a higher allowance, and I can afford to have a proper flight jacket run up with gold thread, plush, silk and velvet. Ramsdel suggests raised moonflowers in curved teardrops with leaves that curve off the lines. He says it impresses the girls, they think flowers on dueling dress is a sign of a man's tenderness within. I now have some discretion about who I have flying with me, be they wardens, squires, or commoners."

"Serjon, do you recognize this?" Feydamor interrupted as he held out the scrap of paper.

Serjon's smile vanished at once and the tone of his voice plunged.

"Where did you get this?" he demanded. "This is the one from Opal, the one who raped . . . Where did you get this?"

"The Airlord assigned a Bartolican featherhead to help me work on some very secret captured equipment."

"It's called a sunwing ferry, word has leaked. It was shot down over the wilderness to the east but is not seriously damaged. The technology is so far ahead of ours that you have not been able to make sense of the controls or engines yet, except that they are powered by the essence of sunlight. It was built in separate modules, *thirteen* modules if my sources are right. How am I doing so far?"

"Flawless, my son."

"So whose pennant bar was this char rubbing done from? Was it the featherhead's?"

"Yes. His name is Kalward. Yesterday morning he began work on one of the electrical essence engines, and showed us how to make it operate. He left his coat on the rack and I decided to search it for sabotage tools. I noticed the bars on his collar and made this rubbing. They seemed familiar, you see, but one was obviously a recent copy by a less skilled artisan."

Serjon drew the original out of a pocket and compared it to the rubbing. They were identical.

"The hand of my dead sister accuses you," Serjon hissed, his eyes unfocused. "Where is he now?"

"Resting in the prison blockhouse. He was showing us how to make the control flaps move by using a box with an intelligence inside—"

"I want him shot!" Serjon shouted. "I'll denounce him to the Airlord! I have evidence, I saw what he did. A featherhead! The Airlord was right about them, they prey on us like cats upon chickens, but *this* chicken has had enough."

"The Airlord wants the sunwing—"

"Damn the sunwing! I want him shot. Today!"

5 August 3961: Wind River

It was true to say that Sartov did not like Kalward, either personally or as what he represented. He was one of a type who gained position and power by manipulation rather than ability, and even worse the tall, spindly man was of a species designed to do just that. The aviad was brought to the Airlord's tent an hour after the ceremony honoring Serjon and Alion, and the guards were sent away after securing him to a heavy bench by leg shackles.

"The war has suddenly turned in your favor, Lordship," he said as Sartov entered alone.

"For a man held in isolation you seem well informed," replied Sartov, barely concealing his annoyance as he swept his field cloak open and sat down.

"There is more to the sun-powered sailwing than you realize. It contains a device for communicating at vast distances, and I have been in contact with my people in Condelor every day since I arrived here."

This time Sartov really was alarmed. He made no attempt to conceal it.

"What do you mean?" he asked, sitting forward with his fists clenched.

"Just that your carbineers and gunwings are holding the tramway through the Red Desert against everything that Bartolica can throw against them, and that the Dorak resistance has paralyzed the northern tramways. The carbineers of Senner and Cosdora are actually advancing on the mighty and beautiful Condelor while wardens and gunwings of six dominions tear each other to pieces in the skies above. Do you know what they are saying in what is left of the Bartolican court?"

"They can say what they like, it will change nothing."

"They say that Colandoro and others are about to join your alliance and that you intend to besiege the Bartolican carbineers in your own country while you crush Condelor. The three northern regions want to withdraw from Greater Bartolica and sue for peace."

Sartov was beginning to regain his nerve. With considerable relief he realized that Kalward had not been allowed near the device until after the Northwind campaign had been unleashed in the Red Desert. Had he been able to transmit word of a massive Yarronese buildup, had the attack been stopped, had the tramway stayed open . . . battle-hardened carbineers now stalled at Median would have been poured into the defense of Condelor.

"This tells me nothing of value," Sartov said more calmly. "Any of my wardens, flyers, and guildsmen could operate your machines with a month of the right training. Unless we can build them ourselves they are useless. What do you want?"

"I want you to know that you are playing with vast and

dangerous forces that could easily destroy you."

"Indeed. So where are those forces being supplied from since you stupidly murdered Highliber Zarvora and cut off the shipments of sunwings and night goggles from Mirrorsun?"

Now it was Kalward's turn to be surprised. Sartov pressed the advantage.

"I put it to you that you want to steal Mounthaven wings and weapons because *our* forces are vast and dangerous compared to the toys Mirrorsun has dropped to you."

"I can win the war for you," said Kalward. "The Bartolicans were fat and lazy, but the Yarronese—"

"I have already won, and without your help," Sartov pointed out. "In the meantime I have a problem with *you* in particular. In the first days of the war, Pyter Kalward, several dozen west Yarronese estates were overrun by Bartolican carbineers. The few witnesses to survive and escape told of entire families murdered, of girls and women raped and mutilated, of halls full of bodies and of everything that could not be carried away being burned. Templates, machines, tools, diagram archives, compression engines, reaction guns, and even the guildmasters were crammed onto steam trams and made to vanish. In the hand of one dead girl was found this."

Sartov opened his hand to reveal Kalward's pennant bar of the Bartolican Merchant Carbineers. The aviad officer considered it for a dozen heartbeats.

"So? She was going to die anyway," Kalward began, but was cut short as Sartov ripped the bar's pin across his cheek. Beads of blood welled and dribbled down his skin.

"You place the secrets of the sunwing in peril," Kalward warned as he slowly turned his head back to face Sartov.

In reply Sartov flung back the tentflap and pointed outside to what seemed to be a single wing with a five-bladed propellor in the base of its V body.

"That aircraft is out latest gunwing, featherhead. It has a range of nine hundred miles even without pod tanks and a *cruising* speed of two hundred miles per hour. We do not need your pathetic sunwings. They are clever toys, but that Skyfire out there is a *weapon*!"

"Skyfire. Not a poetic name."

Sartov ignored him. "Unlike the Bartolican's Sandhawk it is cheap to build and easier than a gunwing to fly. Even its controls are standard. Keep your secrets, sair Kalward, keep them and take them to the grave and to hell beyond. We need nothing from unchivalric slime like you."

Kalward was marched back to the blockhouse jail. Meantime Sartov came under attack from one of his own flyers.

"You mean to let him go?" cried Serjon, almost in tears with outrage.

"Boy! Respect the Airlord," warned Jeb Feydamor.

"He commanded the carbineers that wiped our estate and families from the map, he raped and murdered at least one of my sisters and you want to let him go?" Serjon continued without heeding his stepfather.

"The featherheads have been taking vast numbers of gunwings and sailwings during the confusion of this war," Sartov explained, choosing to ignore the outburst. "We need to know where that base is located. Kalward will be allowed to escape in one of our new Skyfire gunwings, but will be followed by three other Skyfires with pod tanks."

"He's a depraved murderer—"

"He is senior enough to know where the base is located, and I think that he would certainly like to deliver a new Skyfire there."

"Lordship, what are we fighting for if not for justice to be done?" Serjon pleaded.

"We are fighting for Yarron!" Sartov shouted back. "When Yarron is again more than a few dozen tents in the wilderness, well we can have so much justice that you can hire an advocate to sue your peers for lingering too long in the privy, but until then we have to fight the enemy with whatever means we can."

"You don't win wars by condoning murder," Serjon began.

"Silence!" Sartov shouted. "One more word and you will be taken to the presiding Warden of the Inspectorate and charged with treason. Now get back to your flock and prepare for your next patrol. Say nothing of this, understand?"

Serjon was still furious, but was not stupid enough to defy an airlord.

"Yes, Lordship," he replied, then bowed stiffly and left the tent.

"And you, sair Feydamor, what is your opinion?"

"The featherhead should die," Feydamor replied firmly.

"I meant what is your opinion of what I want to do? That featherhead carries the secret of hundreds of missing wings, our missing guildmasters, and who knows what else?"

"He should still die."

"The featherhead base needs to be found and wiped out, else they will establish a dominion in the Callscour lands and in ten years be flying out of the east and bombing Yarron. I want that base, sair Feydamor. Then and only then can he be killed."

Kalward had been waiting for weeks, but the dozens of aviad infiltrators and Bartolican agents that he had been counting on had not managed to breach Wind River's security. Sartov was still protecting him, but sooner or later the hothead Warden Killer would find a way to kill him. It was time to select the best prototype wing on the base and fly east, so that his time in Wind River would not be a complete waste. He checked his hidden snaplock wire as soon as he was returned to the prison blockhouse. Four hours later a Call shrouded the wingfield in silence, except for the sound of a compression engine that had been left idling out on the flightstrip. Kalward picked the lock within minutes; it was part of his training on the other side of the world.

Hastily he opened his cell door and took the guard's assault carbine. He emptied a clip while killing a dozen Call-immune terriers that were roaming outside the block-house, then stood outside contemplating what to do. He could try to find Sartov and kill him, but that was also a good way to waste time and there were a lot more terriers loose, looking for anyone not insensible with the Call. He had a lot of scope for starting fires, but the compression spirit dumps were widely dispersed, and the Call wardens on patrol would fly over to investigate. Over on the flight-strip, however, was a prototype Skyfire gunwing for the taking. Through some oversight its engine had been left idling.

The Skyfire was shaking with the barely idling engine as Kalward ran up. Distant terriers noticed him and came hurtling over on their short legs, but he was in the cockpit before they arrived. As Sartov had said, the controls were standard, but it was also fully fueled. He could be in the air in a moment, and no patrolling gunwing or sailwing would be able to catch him. Kalward settled into the leather seat of the shuddering Skyfire and fastened the can-opy, then gunned the engine. It was warm and flight-ready.

Jeb Feydamor awoke as the Skyfire rose above the Call layer. He was bound securely in the stores hold of the aircraft, just as his guildsmen had left him. The Call made him struggle to follow its allure, but his struggles were mindless. Now that he could think he did not stay bound for long.

He bent over and pulled at a knot with his teeth. It came undone easily, as had been intended. In a moment Fey-damor's hands were free. He untied his legs, then drew his knife. The bulkhead behind the flyer's armored seat was lacquered canvas, and he gently cut a flap open. Pulling a length of wire from his pocket he eased himself up. With one fluid motion he looped the wire over the flyer's head and pulled it against his throat.

Kalward wheezed as he grasped at the wire with gloved hands. He thrashed and fought with incredible strength for such a thin man, punching holes in the fabric and smashing at the controls. The Skyfire began to bank more and more steeply but Feydamor held on grimly, cutting the wire deeper and deeper into the aviad's throat. The Skyfire was standing on its port wingtip and dropping fast by the time Kalward went limp. Feydamor struggled past the flyer's seat and reached out for the stick, settling the Skyfire back into level flight before struggling all the way into the cockpit. Kalward's head was all but severed and an apron of blood covered his chest and lap. His eyes bulged as if in surprise.

Putting the Skyfire into a turn, Feydamor returned it to the wingfield, cut power, and parachuted out. He watched the flying wing go into a shallow dive, but was on the ground and in the Call's grip before it crashed amid the distant hills in a little puff of flame.

The flyers of the Skyfires that were to have followed Kalward noted in their logbooks that his aircraft had attempted to lose them amid the hills but had crashed. No report was made of a parachute.

Feydamor landed in a stand of trees east of the wingfield, but still under the Call. His parachute acted as an effective Call anchor, and when the Call passed he followed its trailing edge back onto the wingfield to be greeted by knowing looks and discreetly raised thumbs by nearly everyone who caught sight of him.

Sartov made only the most feeble of attempts to hide his suspicion of Feydamor's role in the aviad's death, but he never mentioned the incident again.

10 August 3961: Condelor

Three days after the death of Kalward a flock of forty
gunwings ascended from the wingfields around Condelor,
all fully fueled and armed. As far as the adjunct was concerned they were to assemble over the city and strike at
the gunwings that were covering the advance of the allied
carbineers. Instead they turned east and flew out over the
mountains. The adjunct of the palace wingfield lay on the
ground with tears of rage in his eyes, beating the dust with
his fists and cursing all cowards to hell, but the damage
was done. The flock included the only five operational
Sandhawks in Bartolica.

Stanbury later announced that the flock had flown east
to smash the Yarronese air cover at Fort Sartov and allow
the tramway link to be reopened through the Red Desert.
The attack never came. The wings landed at Median, and
Flockleader Carabas demanded that they be refueled for
an attack on Forts Sartov and Virtrian. When they ascended they flew due east.

Sartov had been slow to react, but this ultimately gave
him his advantage. A new Skyfire was sent to overfly Median. It found the flock as it was ascending and followed
them as they flew almost due east again. It flew over Kennyville and the Laramie Mountains, then over the Callscour frontier. An hour later and ninety miles inside the
Callscour region, they landed.

The wingfield was nothing of note from the air. There
were no tents or buildings, but there appeared to be compression spirit stockpiled here and there. By the time the
Skyfire was forced to turn back the first gunwings were
ascending and flying due east again. If they noticed the
high-flying intruder they showed no sign of it.

"They landed there, at the Alliance ruin, but they ascended as soon as they had refueled," Sartov said to his

Advisory Board of Wardens as he read the report of the sailwing flyer that night. "Somewhere to the east there must be a far bigger base of featherheads."

In Greater Bartolica, the desertion of the flock alarmed the regional governors past endurance. By the next morning they had withdrawn their wardens and squires from the wingfields of the capital, and were evacuating their carbineers as fast as the steam-tram-drawn trains would allow. New borders were established and announced to the advancing allies by leaflets dropped by high-flying sailwings. Condelor was being thrown to the advancing enemy as a blood sacrifice.

The Sennerese nomads' elite spearhead carbineers marched into Condelor on August 12, 3961. Unlike Forian, there was little resistance to the fall of Greater Bartolica's capital. Laurelene, Theresla, Darien, and Virtrian watched the first wave of nomads running through the streets in skirmishing order, checking buildings and firing occasional shots. Their uniforms were dusky, like the deserts that they had boiled out of, and their manner was very professional.

"Ah, they are here at last," Theresla observed, looking down into the street. "Good, they are good. My own people are like this, as free as the fingers of a hand yet as tight as a fist."

"Proud Bartolica, brought to this," said Virtrian without emotion.

"Proud Bartolica was defeated the day that Stanbury turned against Dorak," said Theresla. "Yours are small, poor dominions. They are not kept at peace by the warden system, they are kept at peace by the lack of resources to go to war. The carbineers that should be defending this city are fighting their way back here through Yarron, but it's too late now."

The firing intensified from the direction of the palace, and there was an explosion at the gates. An improvised bridge was wheeled along the Grand Road of Processions to span the moat, and the invaders swarmed across. Gun-wings circled overhead, alert for anyone trying to escape by air, but all the sailwings and gunwings on the palace wingfield had been either shot up and destroyed or grounded with white flags flying above them. There was another flurry of shots.

"The Archwarden's personal guard, perhaps," ventured Virtrian. "Why do they bother?"

"You bothered, back in Forian," said Theresla.

"Back in Forian I had what was left of Yarron behind me. This is just death for its own sake."

The shooting died away to sporadic exchanges, and Theresla, Darien, and Virtrian sat down to quailmeat and groundnut pastries. Condelor had fallen so quickly that luxuries were still available.

"Ah, they seem to be among the palace buildings now, I can see smoke," Virtrian observed.

"Is the palace afire?" asked Theresla.

"No, I suspect that smoke pots are being hurled by the Sennerese nomads to choke the defenders. They don't want to damage what is liable to be their new capital and palace."

For Stanbury the nightmare had come true at last. His mighty war beast had fallen on its face after being denied its meals of blood. At dawn on the 12th of August he ran about the palace with two dozen of his Inner Guard, collecting gold coins in bags and burning documents. His wife Samondel found herself roused from her bed and bundled into a flying suit by maids acting on Stanbury's orders; then she was taken out into the corridor to meet with her husband.

"What is this about, where are we going?" she asked.

"Condelor is about to fall, but we are not going to fall with it. There are still enough loyal carbineers and wardens in eastern Yarron to set up New Bartolica and defend it forever."

They hurried out by a side door and through the palace gardens while sailwings and gunwings swooped overhead and cart cannons boomed in the distance. The flag of capitulation already flew over the palace wingfield, but Stanbury had another escape planned. At Festival Park the tentcloth façade of a house on the perimeter was drawn away to show an advanced Sandhawk-class prototype, one more than capable of ascending with Stanbury, Samondel, and their combined weight in gold as well.

A steam starter engine was already fired up and as soon as the Inner Guard pushed the Sandhawk out it was engaged to the compression engines. The propellor began to spin and the guardsmen cleared the gravel path across the center of the path of debris as Stanbury and Samondel climbed into the cockpit and strapped themselves in.

A stutter of reaction-gun fire sounded without warning, and shots tore up the ground before the Sandhawk. A second, sustained burst hammered into a compression engine. The guardsmen began exchanging fire with drably uniformed carbineers who emerged from bushes and nearby buildings as the Sandhawk began to roll forward. Bursts from at least six reaction guns focused on the engines and wings. Guards shot down the carbineers and were shot down themselves. Compression spirit began to pour down onto the path, the engines spluttered and lost power, but it did not actually die. Sparks from flying rounds set the spilled fuel ablaze and the Sandhawk began to trail smoky flames and streams of burning compression spirit.

In hindsight it would have been better for Stanbury to have abandoned the Sandhawk then and there, and stay under the protection of his Inner Guard, but he still thought to escape. The struggling compression engines drove the Sandhawk down along the path, but it did not even approach the ascent speed. What it did manage to do was take Stanbury and Samondel some distance down the wide path and well away from their loyal Inner Guard. The blazing gunwing rolled amid the trees, trailing fire and smoke until its wheels hit an ornamental rock wall. The aircraft collapsed into a flowerbed in a cloud of smoke and burning fragments. Stanbury and Samondel struggled clear within moments, but the carbineers were waiting for them.

The survivors of the Inner Guard could not see that the Bartolican leaders were being led clear of the burning wreck. The remaining fuel exploded. Burning wreckage and gold coins showered down over the park, and there was a prolonged lull in the firing. Now the reaction guns started up again, but this time the Inner Guard's survivors were covering their own retreat, having assumed that their Lady Airlord and Archwarden were dead.

"Bind them and take them to the Sunflower Street refuge," a familiar voice called. "There's any number of hotheads who would kill them out of revenge."

"Hannan!" exclaimed Stanbury, recognizing the Inspector General beneath the lampblack grease on his face.

"Search both of them," he continued, ignoring Stanbury. "Remove everything, especially papers and code cards."

"You're betraying me, your own airlord!" Samondel cried, her terror giving way to outrage.

"It's odd, Ladyship, I was about to say the same about you and your people," replied Hannan.

"Did your secret masters reward you well?" asked Stanbury.

"You should know best what rates secret masters pay, sair Archwarden."

Drawn by the explosion and smoke, Sennerese nomads soon arrived at the park. They were slowed far more by the gold coins littered about than any squad of resistance carbineers could have managed. An hour later Hannan approached a Sennerese carbineer captain with articles of general surrender signed by Samondel, and by the late afternoon the fighting for the capital was over. Samondel and Stanbury were led back to the palace in shackles by Sennerese carbineers and nomads, while rockets trailing green and red smoke signaled that the capital had fallen and the

Lady Airlord was in custody. Some of the sailwings overhead broke away at once to report the news home.

Samondel and Stanbury had a busy night as they signed
decrees ordering occupation forces in Montras and Dorak
to hand the government back to the local nobles and begin
an orderly withdrawal. The carbineers and wardens in Yarron were still fighting, however, and they were ordered to
simply surrender. In the latter case many of the local units
mutinied. Sartov's diplomats eventually negotiated their
withdrawal in return for safe passage across the Red Desert
and on to the newly autonomous regions of what had been
Greater Bartolica.

13 August 3961: Condelor

The Airlord of Montras was freed from his cell in the
palace on the night of the surrender, and he immediately
allied himself to Sartov. The next morning the allied airlords began arriving in their regals, each with a formation
of gunwings trailing smoke in their colors and resplendent
in their wardenate livery. The Sennerese Airlord landed
first, and was followed by the Airlords of Cosdora and
Dorak. The other alliance airlords arrived later in the
morning, and finally at noon the huge shape of a super-
regal appeared in the northeast. The olive-green monster
circled the city twice with its escort of battle-worn, brown
and green dapple gunwings, then came in for an impressive
landing on the hastily cleared palace wingfield. Sartov
stepped out to cheers of adulation from wardens and commoners alike. In a tribute to those who had brought him
the victory, he wore a flight jacket of his Air Carbineers.

A Council of Alliance Airlords was assembled at once,
with Airlord Abdicate Virtrian elected as their Proclaimant.
Justice was as swift as it was firm. The first of the Bartolican nobles were brought before the council later that
very afternoon, and the first of the death sentences were

passed by Virtrian before the summer sunset had begun to splash gaudy colors across the horizon.

Strangely, Samondel was treated leniently by the council. She had been in power for only a short time, and had been little more than a figurehead during that period. Stanbury was a different matter.

The council's hearing of the Archwarden's case began after the evening meal. A series of lists of charges were read out by each of the Airlords, most to do with breaches of the code of chivalry prevailing in Mounthaven. As it stood, Stanbury could have been executed several hundred times over.

"I plead the defense of peer reaction," he declared to Virtrian, who was now sitting in judgment on Samondel's throne. "There is not an airlord present who has not violated some principle of war duel chivalry that should carry the death penalty. Airlord Sartov ordered the bombing of this very palace, and his wings do not wear chivalric livery but cowardly green and brown disguise paint. Why am I condemned while he is allowed to sit in judgment?"

"Not an airlord present breached a chivalric principle without first being shown the way by yourself, Archwarden Stanbury," Virtrian replied. "The plea of peer reaction is denied."

"Honorable Proclaimant, I petition that two wrongs cannot be added together and called justice."

"Unless I am mistaken, and subject to correction by my honorable colleagues, defense against unjust attack is allowable under both common law and chivalric codes. Defense against unjust and unchivalric attack renders codes of conduct for war duels null. Petition declined."

"In that case, I have nothing more to say, Honorable Proclaimant."

Virtrian leaned forward on the throne. "Archwarden Stanbury, in the unlikely event that you do not understand your position, let me explain it to you again. You are charged with multiple breaches of the Mounthaven Code

of Chivalric War and are being judged by nine of Mounthaven's sixteen airlords. That is a majority, so a unanimous
verdict of guilty carries enough legal weight to execute
even a head of state. If your plea is guilty, you are granted
the right to take your own life as a gift to the dead. If you
plead innocent and are found guilty, then your entire government down to flock commander rank will be executed
along with you. Again I say to you, sair Stanbury, what is
your plea?"

"I have nothing to say, Honorable Sair."

Virtrian turned to the nine airlords sitting to his right.

"The refusal to enter a plea is taken as one of innocence,
just as suicide is taken as a plea of guilt. I must reluctantly
decree that we assume a plea of innocence and proceed
with a trial."

Sartov stood up. "I propose that Archwarden Stanbury
be taken to Median, where some of the worst atrocities of
the war took place. This council can then see direct evidence of the charges, and hear from those whose lives were
shattered."

"Are any against that?" asked Virtrian. Three were
against, the rest in favor. "In that case I decree that Archwarden Stanbury be transported to the city of Median in
Yarron, where this council will reconvene on a date to be
fixed. All in favor? Against? Carried six to three. What
other business?"

"I move that this council rise for the night," moved Sartov.

The motion was carried unanimously.

While Stanbury's hearing was taking place, Serjon landed
in his drably painted gunwing, at the head of his new flock.
The darkened wingfield became a whirl of activity as the
dozen gunwings were accommodated. Then, to the amazement of the adjunct and all others on the wingfield, two
super-regals droned out of the north, circled like bats the
size of dragons, then landed. Thirty-six stiff, cold but smil-

ing guildsmen emerged and wearing field support jackets. They formed into twelve groups of three at a command from Ramsdel, each with his warden, squire, or flyer. At another command they marched for the pennant pole where the adjunct waited.

"Flock Commander Serjon Feydamor of the ninth Yarronese Air Carbineers," Serjon declared to the adjunct. "I have instructions from the Council of Alliance Airlords to assume authority over this wingfield."

The adjunct bowed and accepted his credentials. A Bartolican warden held up a lantern as he read Serjon's papers. He returned the credentials and took a folder of his own from an aide.

"I, Warden Grant Dennian of the Palace Air Guard, accept your authority," the adjunct said as he handed Serjon the folder. "Do you wish me to continue in my role as adjunct?"

"Yes, by all means. Now please make tents, tools, and supplies available to my Air Carbineers and their field guildsmen."

The truth was that the adjunct had not expected to be left in his position. The legendary Warden Killer, with ninety-seven victories confirmed, was no more than a polite but haggard boy. He stayed with the adjunct to make arrangements for the arrival of five Skyfire gunwings from Wind River in the morning. Warden Damaric would be leading this small but elite flock, and they were to be kept under heavy guard by Dorakian carbineers.

"It is also my intention to search for stolen Yarronese gunwings, tools, and guildmasters," he told the adjunct as he removed his flight jacket and gave it to one of his guildsmen. "I want a tour of inspection of all Condelor's wingfields, starting with this one."

"Very good, Commander Serjon. What hour would suit you best? Dawn, while things are quiet, or after breakfast when more people are about to help?"

"Now, Sair Adjunct," Serjon said firmly as he rubbed his eyes.

"But commander, it's nearly ten P.M. You have been two hours in the air. There are no lamps lit in some of the—"

"Then bring a lantern, Sair Adjunct. I want to start now."

There were few surprises as the inspection of the gunwing halls and maintenance tents got under way. The adjunct expected Serjon to pause at some experimental wings that were in the early stages of flight testing, but he gave them scarcely a glance. Several wrecks of Alliance wings held his attention longer, but he quickly went on to the next gunwing hall. Here there were three complete Yarronese gunwings and five sailwings amid the Bartolican wings under repair, but they were older, standard models.

In Gunwing Hall 11 Serjon stopped in front of the most recent Yarronese gunwing to fall into Bartolican hands. It had been kept under tarpaulins, and nobody was allowed near it. Serjon stood and stared when the tarpaulins were thrown aside.

"Is there something the matter, Commander Feydamor?" asked the adjunct.

"Is this a joke?" Serjon replied in a hoarse, contorted voice.

"What do you mean, Commander? This is a captured Yarronese gunwing. We have had it since May, and the mark on my manifest shows that it was landed here by a defector."

"A defector? What was his name?"

"That has been left blank on the register, sair Feydamor. It had been marked for destruction by fire, but with all the confusion and the rapid Sennerese advance we have had more important things to attend. Now all such orders are yours to review."

"It is completely intact," breathed Serjon.

"Indeed. Do you like it? Your guildsmen could check it for flight status."

"He *lied* to me, he lied to *everyone*!" shouted Serjon in Yarronese with his eyes squeezed closed. "He played us like puppets, then he tried to *burn* us!"

The adjunct and his staff remained silent, aware that something was seriously wrong.

"Do not touch the gunwing," Serjon rasped more quietly in Bartolican, pointing to the main double doors with a trembling hand. "Now leave me alone."

Once the doors had been rolled shut the sound of smashing glass and splintering wood came to them from within the gunwing hall. After a few minutes Serjon came out, looking unsteady and disheveled. He was holding a length of pipe, which he dropped as he reached the adjunct.

"It would not do for a commander to display unseemly or unstable behavior in front of a vanquished enemy officer, would it Sair Adjunct?"

"No, Commander."

"Clean up in there, then call my guildsmen. Tell your people that I shall kill anyone going within ten feet of Princess."

"Yes, Commander."

Glass from broken beakers and stills was everywhere, and the smell of compression spirit was heavy on the air. Serjon had smashed up a spirit testing bench, wrenching it from the wall mountings and reducing it to a pile of kindling. Once the hall had been swept clean Serjon examined the gunwing in great detail, starting at the propellor and finishing at the rudder. He took notes, copied guild marks and serial numbers, documented and sketched damage, then allowed his own guildsmen to bring it to flight status.

At first light Serjon's guildsmen had the gunwing on the flightstrip with its engine chugging. Serjon took Princess into the air, circled the palace several times, then landed. The gunwing was rolled to an earthwork buffer where the reaction guns were fired into the soil. The bullets were then dug out and examined. The adjunct watched as Serjon

completed the report, then handed it to one of his guildsmen. The man set off in the direction of the palace.

"Get Princess back into Gunwing Hall Eleven, now!"
Serjon barked as the adjunct went up to him. He looked
as if he had not slept at all during the night. "I have already
arranged for a dozen Dorakian carbineers to stand guard."

"Is the gunwing so very special?" asked the adjunct as
he waved some of his own guildsmen over.

"It shot me through the heart," Serjon replied, then made
for the ablutions screens.

Half an hour later the flock of five Skyfire gunwings arrived over Condelor. With their powerful tandem-radial
engines roaring and the clean lines of their single-wing
configuration, they had crowds running across to them as
they taxied up to the guild tents. Warden Alion Damaric
presented his credentials to the adjunct, then left the big
gunwings in the care of the guildsmen that had arrived the
previous day. They were only there for the victory flypast,
and would then return to Yarron. Sartov did not want his
best technology being studied and copied. The adjunct began filling him in on all that had happened the previous
day.

"If the Archwarden pleaded innocent, then the Lady Airlord must share his sentence," the adjunct concluded as
they stood before the pennant pole.

"True. He must have great faith in his innocence to
plead thus. He is to be paraded above the city in one of
the super-regals in the flypast this morning, then flown to
Median to be put on trial before his victims."

"So soon?"

"Pah, can't have him around here with the confusion of
the celebrations. Loyalists will try to free him, won't they?
In Median the guard is liable to be tighter."

Serjon found Alion as the warden was supervising the
painting of a new pennant plaque for himself.

"Can you spare the time for a few words, sair Warden?" asked Serjon crisply.

"Only a few, sair Commander," said Alion, looking distracted and impatient. "I am to be in the victory flypast above the city in just twenty minutes."

"Oh good, then you can use your old triwing, Princess," said Serjon in a voice so cold that it could have iced over wings on a midsummer's day.

Alion lost color but replied smoothly and without any pause.

"Princess was destroyed, shot down over Condelor and burned. I crawled from the wreck just before—"

Serjon backhanded Alion across the face and he went reeling back, crashing over the artist's table. Serjon was upon him at once, breaking a light chair over his back and kicking him about the shoulders and head until a crowd of bewildered Dorakian carbineers pulled them apart.

"Your old triwing is in Gunwing Hall Eleven!" cried Serjon in a fury. "It's completely intact and still bears Yarronese guild seals. It never crashed, it never burned, and it has barely any groundfire damage. You landed at the palace of your own free will, damn you, confident that you would not be shot at. That would only be the case if you had proved disloyalty to Yarron by shooting at *my superregal*. I had several others examine Princess, they are all ready to testify that it is yours."

The carbineers slowly released them and stood back.

"Come with me," Serjon snarled.

Alion closed his eyes. "Leave me alone," he whispered.

"I'll not say it again," warned Serjon in a voice like the clacking of the safety release on a reaction gun.

Alion shambled forward, but did not come within reach of Serjon. They began to walk and soon Alion had only his accuser for company on the wingfield. An uncharacteristically cold wind was blowing for August, and Serjon's greatcoat flapped free.

"I want to die," Alion moaned, then stopped and sank to his knees with his hands clasped.

"For *that* all you need is a bucket of water and the willpower to keep your head in for long enough."

"Would you accept the revenge of the aggrieved?" pleaded Alion. "Would you shoot me down in a duel?"

"I want no duel with you," replied Serjon. "You are clearly unchivalric and I would not dignify you with an honorable death. Get up and walk."

He pointed to the line of Yarronese Skyfire gunwings being refueled for the flypast.

"After the flypast, go," ordered Serjon. "You may have enough compression spirit to reach a neutral domain, and then again you may not. If you land here again, then Airlord Sartov will have some very hard questions for you after he opens his mail this afternoon."

"That's . . . generous of you. Why are you doing this for me?"

"I am not doing this for *you*, I am trying to get your filthy body out of my sight. You shot me down, then you caused me to be rescued—for whatever reasons you had. Now I give you your own freedom in turn, so that I can be free to hate you. Go. If ever I meet you again I shall surely kill you, Warden Alion Damaric."

"Serjon, I swear by my honor that I was only trying to distract you from firing into the crowds of Bartolican nobles. I never sought to kill you. I could see Samondel at your mercy—"

"Tell me, Warden Alion, just what is your word and honor worth? You are very adept at proclaiming and defending your honor, but it's a pity you have no honor in the first place."

"It's you who has no honor!" Alion retorted. "You're just a killer."

"Warden Killer is my name, and I do not pretend to be otherwise."

Serjon turned and walked away in the direction of the

maintenance tents. As Alion got to his feet the distant onlookers hurriedly dispersed, although whispering and
glancing back at him as they went.

Harkli da' Mik looked up from his orders log to see a
senior warden from Yarron arriving. The man bowed
curtly and presented a sealed envelope. The seal was that
of the Yarronese Airlord, and was countersealed by that
of the Airlord of Senner. Harkli broke the seals and took
out the letter. It was in Yarronese. He made a show of
studying the letters, not willing to admit that he could not
read the language.

"So, is the prisoner ready for transfer?" asked the warden.

"Do you wish to check our arrangements?" asked Harkli
in turn.

The warden nodded and they walked to a tent where a
squad of nomad carbineers stood guarding Stanbury and
Samondel.

"I was told there would only be one prisoner," said the
warden.

"Hah, this place is bedlam, it's a wonder the couriers
get any messages through at all. Both Archwarden and
Lady Airlord are to be flown over the city in chains, then
taken to Median. Their destinies are linked, if you know
what I mean."

Stanbury noted the arrival of the Yarronese warden at the
flap of the tent, but did not hear the Sennerese conversation
regarding his fate. Four carbineers unchained him and
locked light shackles to his wrists and ankles. He shuffled
out between the carbineers and behind Samondel. She
walked with her head down, listless and unaware of what
was happening, her hair tangled and loosely bound back.
She had not spoken to him since the previous evening.
Carbineers, flyers, and guildsmen lined his path, staring
and scowling but silent. Over near the flightstrip wardens

were waving their arms and shouting while adjuncts ran about with maps and weather briefing slates. The engines of four of the Skyfire gunwings and a super-regal were idling. Stanbury was impressed by the machines, in spite of where they were taking him.

Harkli folded his arms and whistled with relief as the four Skyfire gunwings roared into the sky. They began to circle the palace and wingfield complex as the super-regal began to move down the dispersal path. The super-regal reached the far end of the flightstrip, turned, then stood unmoving. Harkli could make out the figure of the flight guildsman and two carbineers climbing out of the hatch in the underside. They walked over to a wheel and began examining it.

"Oh no, not a mechanical failure!" groaned Harkli. "Not with the escort already in the air."

Just then he heard someone hail the wingfield adjunct in Yarronese. The tall, thin youth was the new commander, by the bar colors at his collar. After a moment both the adjunct and commander came running over, calling to him urgently.

"Where are the Bartolican leaders?" demanded the adjunct in Sennerese.

"There in the super-regal, as per these orders," replied Harkli, taking his orders from his coat and offering them to the adjunct.

The adjunct read for a moment, cried out in horror to the commander then turned back to Harkli.

"This is the seating layout for tonight's formal declaration of the war's end!" the adjunct barked angrily. "What is going on here?"

"But the Lady Airlord Samondel and Archwarden Stanbury are in the guard of the super-regal's wingcaptain—"

"*There's* the wingcaptain!" shouted the adjunct, pointing to a man in white underwear running toward them at the head of several wingfield guards.

Harkli turned back to the super-regal. Dark shapes fell out of the hatch; then the hatch was pulled shut from inside. The compression engines revved up to full power and the huge wing began to roll forward.

"Stop that wing!" Harkli shouted in Sennerese. "Shoot! Shoot out its engines!"

By chance there were no Sennerese guards in the immediate vicinity, and none of the Bartolican guildsmen or Dorakian carbineers spoke Sennerese. As Harkli drew his sidearm and dashed out onto the flightstrip he heard the adjunct translating at the top of his voice. The commander ran up beside Harkli, his own pistol out. Together they emptied their clips at the sailwing as it roared past, already airborne.

Serjon turned and ran back to the guildsmen, shouting for his gunwing to be started and fueled at once.

"The devious bastard, he managed to get away with both of them!" he shouted to the adjunct as he flung off his dress cap and checked that the gunwing being prepared was armed.

"But there are four Skyfire gunwings escorting him, how can he escape them?" asked the adjunct. "They are the fastest wings in the sky."

"Very easily! That super-regal can fly four thousand feet higher than even the Skyfire gunwings, and it has a greater range!"

The steam trolley was wheeled up and backed to the compression engine of the remaining Skyfire gunwing. As it spluttered into life and began to warm, Serjon began a preflight check of the controls. The adjunct watched the super-regal circling the wingfield with the four Skyfire gunwings, climbing all the while.

"Send a runner to the tents, tell them to get the remaining super-regals into the air with a full load of fuel and ballistic rockets—and experienced wardens flying them. Give them a bearing of . . . well, track him until he's out of sight. Tell him to look for my Skyfire, I'll be trailing him at whatever height I can manage, and—What bearing is he taking, anyway?"

The adjunct had his binoculars to his eyes. "He's still circling, but gaining height slowly."

"That makes sense, he wants to get to safety before— Hie! What's that at the end of the flightstrip?"

From his vantage in the cockpit Serjon had seen four figures standing beside the long grass at the end of the flightstrip, just where the super-regal had stopped.

"Adjunct! Send a dozen guards down the flightstrip. Warden Alion dumped Archwarden Stanbury along with his guildsman and guards. He's only got the Lady Airlord Samondel aboard."

Serjon slumped back with relief, but he was still tense and angry. Alion had abducted Samondel in his escape, and that had not been part of the bargain. The super-regal was at about 4,000 feet now, but was still circling. There was high cloud, he could easily hide amid that, once he gained enough altitude. A group of carbineers reached the end of the flightstrip.

"They have Stanbury," said Serjon to the adjunct.

"That's a relief. It seems we have an embarrassment rather than a catastrophe."

At that moment there was a change in the sound from the compression engines above them as the gunwings began to disperse like dark sparks from a pinwheel. Above their compression engines' noise there was a much louder, sharper note.

"The super-regal is diving," whispered Serjon, stating the exceedingly obvious.

"Run for your lives, he's coming down here!" the adjunct was shouting.

Serjon was well behind the others, having had to clamber out of his Skyfire first and shuffle along in heavy flying boots. All the while the howl of the compression engines above grew louder, the pitch rising as the super-regal picked up speed. Fighting down his panic Serjon slowed, looked up and took a bearing on the plummeting V-shape above him. A year of desperate fights had taught him to estimate speeds and courses with instinctive accuracy. He quickly realized that he was safe, but the super-regal was still plunging earthward.

The ground shook as the super-regal smashed into a gunwing hall and detonated its full load of compression spirit in a thunderclap of flame and roiling smoke. Dirt and smoking debris rained down on Serjon as he crouched with his hands over his head. The devastated gunwing hall had collapsed outward and was rimmed with wreckage and burning gunwings. The adjunct came running up to Serjon, his field glasses still in his hand.

"Did either of them bail out?" Serjon asked.

"I checked just a moment ago, no," he answered.

The fire guildsmen were now on the way, pushing water wagons and pumps, and waving people back from the ruin. The adjunct turned his field glasses back down the flight-strip.

"At least they have—Good Lord! It's the Lady Airlord Samondel!"

Serjon began to walk toward the burning gunwing Hall, the confused adjunct trailing behind.

"That's Gunwing Hall Eleven, isn't it," said Serjon. "That just has to be Gunwing Hall Eleven."

The adjunct glanced about hurriedly. "It is Gunwing Hall Two, sair. On the roof it is written in Old Anglian classical numerals. It looks like eleven to confuse non-Bartolican enemies, but it is really two."

Now it was Serjon's turn to glance from hall to hall. To either side of the annihilated hall were 01 and 03. The halls were arrayed in staggered ranks, to further confuse any attacking super-regal bomber after what had happened early in May. There were three rows of four. The second last row at the north left corner was XI, but the number at the south right row was II.

"Just like eleven," laughed Serjon, stopping and sitting in the gravel of the dispersal path.

"I beg your pardon, Commander?"

"The stupid, upper-class, arrogant, cowardly, vindictive bastard," laughed Serjon. "The *stupid*, vindictive bastard."

Serjon rocked back and forth, laughing until the tears ran down his face. The adjunct squatted beside him, patting him on the back and unsure of what to do next. He looked up to see the Skyfire gunwings descending and preparing to land, then beckoned for a medic.

"Sair Commander, sair, tell me what is the matter," he asked, turning back to Serjon.

"Nothing is the matter, Sair Adjunct. Everything could have been, but nothing is."

Late that morning at special sitting of the Council of Alliance Airlords, the Airlords pronounced that Stanbury had probably died as a result of a pact of honor between himself and the Yarronese Warden Alion. While there were multitudes of unanswered questions, they concurred that Stanbury had died within an aircraft, apparently taking his life honorably. His act of honorable behavior meant there would be no trial, there would be no mass executions. The presence of Alion's undamaged gunwing in Gunwing Hall 11 was quite another matter. In a vote that went against Sartov, the council voted the inquiry into the shooting down of Serjon's super-regal to be an interdominion matter and it was reopened immediately. Because technically they were only investigating Alion's previous testimony, Bronlar was not required to be present. Clerks and liaisories hurried about fetching records, guildsmen, and witnesses. As Virtrian was a witness, it was decided that Bartolica's most senior resistance leader, Inspector General Vander Hannan, should be the Proclaimant.

Sitting in an anteroom in the palace that he had once bombed, Serjon was painfully aware that he had given virtually no thought to Bronlar since he had set eyes on Prin-

cess. Alion had shot him down. Alion had to be humbled,
Alion had to be humiliated, Alion had to be annihilated.
Now he was dead. Bronlar had endured a month of sus-
tained accusation and vilification from the mighty Serjon
Warden Killer, the flyer who could even shout at Airlord
Sartov and get away with it, the flyer who had refused a
daystar medal because she had been awarded one. Now
what of Bronlar?

Serjon felt very small, sitting beneath the vaulted ceiling
of marble and redstone which was older than his family's
guild status. He could fight, but he could also be wrong.
Murals of Bartolican wardens in their various hours of triumph mocked him. They were remembered with honor, as
he would be. Bronlar had been wronged by Alion, after
all, the evidence suggested as much. He could testify that
Alion had admitted guilt to him, but that could be seen as
a crass attempt to clear Bronlar's name by an unprovable
accusation. The evidence suggested as much. Alion had
defected to the Bartolicans, that had been proved, and was
a strong point against him. Why am I thinking this way,
Serjon wondered. Some flyers had brought home rumors
that Bronlar had slept with at least one Cosdoran guildsman, while Serjon . . . He squeezed his eyes shut and
grated his teeth as he forced an admission out from deep
within himself.

"I was saving myself for her, and I still am," he told a
dispirited-looking Bartolican warden who sat with his
flight jacket unbuttoned and his collar open.

"Di nys tik Yarronese," he replied.

"Sc'ay di appologor," said Serjon.

There was really only one thing to do, he decided. If he
really loved Bronlar he had to clear her name, and at any
cost. Alion's love had run to any sacrifice, after all. Alion
had chosen death and the prospect of eternal dishonor for
saving the girl that he loved. Serjon noticed that his hands
were cold and moist as he dragged himself toward his only
possible decision. He would give up far, far more for Bron-

lar. A footman arrived to take him to the council.

Serjon's testimony before the council was superficially no different from what he had stated in Wind River. He said he had been fired on by one of his escort, and that a Yarronese triwing had overflown the wreck of the super-regal. Virtrian and several Bartolican witnesses testified that they had seen a gunwing firing on the super-regal, but none remembered its identifiers. Virtrian had remembered two gunwings, however.

"Chancellor Virtrian," prompted the red advocate, "did you see anything else that could have identified which of the gunwings stayed with the super-regal, and ultimately shot it down on the second attacking run?"

"The super-regal banked to the port, and the lead broke off to starboard and flew toward the palace wingfield. The other closed in and fired."

"That suggests that Semme Jemarial attacked the super-regal," concluded the red advocate. "After all, the traitor Damaric surrendered at the wingfield."

"Commander Feydamor, have you anything to add to what has been said by these witnesses?" prompted Vander when the red advocate had sat down.

Sweat trickled down Serjon's ribs as he composed his words. It was not going well for Bronlar. He was going into battle as surely as if he were in a gunwing. Alion had challenged him to fight for his beloved's honor by his very suicide. Beloved. Serjon had never admitted that Bronlar was his beloved until a few minutes earlier, he had been too busy hating Bartolicans. He had desired her, but . . . how long had he loved her? Time to stop hating, he decided.

"None, Your Honor, but may I restate my testimony to clarify the facts?" Serjon asked.

Vander turned to the white and red advocates, but they had no objections.

"Proceed."

"For the second run on the palace I banked the super-regal, then straightened out to attack with ballistic rockets and reaction guns. I saw nothing of my either of my escorts. My guildsman was in the nose, and was not in a position to observe the escorts, my dome gunner said nothing and my rear gunner just cursed."

Serjon looked down and frowned.

"I . . . can remember it as clearly as if it just happened." Serjon paused, beads of perspiration now on his forehead, his hands gripping the dock's rails and his knuckles white. "My rear gunner said 'Damn traitorous bitch!' I shouted back 'Keep those pipes clear!' We, I—ah, continued the run on the palace gardens, strafing the Bartolican nobles in the gardens with my racks of reaction guns. There was double blast from ballistic rockets hitting my starboard wing. I was told later that a fragment of propellor hit the dome, killing the dome gunner. Oil pressure and power in all my starboard engines died. I heard the clang of shells hitting metal. The rear gunner gave a cry of pain and I heard no more from him. The super-regal lost height very rapidly after that. I crashed in a wide street and came to rest in a shallow canal. A Yarronese hybrid triwing overflew the wreck."

"This testimony is more detailed than that before the Warden Inspectorate in Wind River," Vander pointed out.

"The sights of Condelor and the testimonies of other witnesses has pried more detail loose from my memory," explained Serjon.

In the gallery above the council Ramsdel suddenly stood up and hurried out of his row to an official. The man went across to the moderator and whispered a few words. The moderator went to the Proclaimant, who looked from Serjon to the gallery, then called for a suspension of five minutes. The Airlords agreed.

As the council reconvened Serjon was called to the stand again by the white advocate, and asked to repeat what his rear gunner had said during the attack.

"The words were 'Damn traitorous bitch!' " Serjon repeated.

"You are certain of that?"

"As certain as I am that my bomb hit the throne hall window."

"And you are certain that he called out before the supposed rogue gunwing opened fire."

"Yes. About five seconds before."

"Five seconds! A gunwing can fly a thousand feet in five seconds. Why did you not say this before?"

"It's hard to estimate time under fire. After returning to Condelor and seeing the distances between reference points around the palace I realized the true interval."

"Your witness," he said to the red advocate, but his opponent had no questions for Serjon.

Ramsdel was called next.

"You flew a gunwing on the day the super-regals went into action for the first time," began the white advocate, "yet you were trained as a super-regal wingcaptain."

"Yes, I was one of the reserve wingcaptains."

"And you knew Vortiel, Commander Feydamor's rear gunner, quite well."

"We flew nine practice missions in super-regals," Ramsdel responded.

"When he became excited, what was his reaction?"

"He yelled 'Ding, damn!' over the pipe. It was usually when he got a fright when we flew too low, or when he hit a target kite."

"What else did he yell under stress?"

"Nothing else, sair. That is why I was so surprised that Flockleader Feydamor heard him shout 'Damn traitorous bitch!' "

"Could it be, Warden, that he was not cursing, but that he was *commenting* on Semme Bronlar Jemarial leaving the super-regal, because she could see a threat that he could not? Might it not have been because she banked away to the right, to starboard, toward the wingfield well before an escort gunwing opened fire on the super-regal at extreme range?"

Ramsdel nodded emphatically. "Yes, Sair Advocate, that is very likely the case. A lot can happen in five seconds."

The wingfield adjunct was called.

"Could the triwing Slash have overflown the super-regal's wreck after attacking the palace wingfield, while the triwing Princess had gone on to land at the palace wingfield?"

"Yes, sair Advocate."

The white advocate called for Serjon to return to the dock.

"Tell us truthfully, Commander Feydamor, why did you not testify to the Warden Inspectorate at Wind River about your rear gunner's words and that the interval between his words and the rockets hitting was so long?"

Serjon swallowed. "It . . . the words." He stopped, staring down at the front of the dock.

" 'Damn traitorous bitch!' . . . one . . . two . . . three . . . four . . . five . . . Bang!" prompted the white advocate. "Quite an interval, even under fire."

"I forgot—No!" Serjon's shout brought everyone to the edge of their seats. He swayed, steadied himself, then went on. "I thought the interval unimportant, it . . . complicated a clear case against Semme Jemarial. When Alion supposedly rescued me I became convinced that she had done the shooting, but when I saw Warden Damaric's undamaged gunwing at the palace wingfield, I realized . . . that he had lied. That is why I now present them before this council."

There was bedlam in the observers' gallery. Serjon was close to collapse, but he refused Vander's offer of an adjournment. The red advocate had many questions, but Serjon's expanded testimony was enough for the nine airlords. After a thirty-minute deliberation they reached a verdict. Vander rose to address the white and red advocates.

"This Council of Airlords has decided by a majority of

eight to one abstention in favor of the white advocate's client, Semme Bronlar Jemarial."

The cheering that erupted was tolerated by the Airlords, but Vander soon called for order so that the rest of the verdict could be heard.

"The Airlord of Cosdora has granted Semme Bronlar Jemarial immediate release from her duties, and all nine airlords of the council hereby extend an invitation for her to fly here on the nineteenth day of this month for the grand banquet to celebrate our victory over Greater Bartolica."

Vander paused, and looked across to where Serjon sat with his head bowed.

"Flock Commander Serjon Feydamor, the Airlords have voted unanimously to condemn your behavior in withholding evidence. Normally you would face charges, but given your previous good record, your dedication to Yarron's welfare, and your role in hastening the war's end, the charges have been withdrawn on the following conditions: that you forfeit all rank above that of flyer, that you enter Airlord Sartov's personal service as a courier flyer, that you forfeit one half of your family wealth to the family of Semme Bronlar Jemarial, and that you dictate an unconditional apology to Semme Bronlar Jemarial which will be published in full throughout all of Mounthaven.

"Do you accept these terms, sair Feydamor, or do you wish to have a separate hearing?"

"I accept the terms, Your Honor," said Serjon clearly.

Serjon's ordeal was not over yet. That afternoon a second hearing opened on the question of whether ground fire or Alion's guns had actually brought down the super-regal. Several witnesses, fellow Yarronese prisoners who had been with Virtrian, thought that Alion's gunwing had fired in the direction of the super-regal, but could not be sure that Alion had hit it. The surviving Bartolican carbineers who had been first at the super-regal's wreckage testified that all the visible bullet holes were at the rear. Finally the results of the morning's exhumation of the rear gunner's grave became available and were presented. One round had struck his knee, run the length of his thigh and lodged in his pelvis. The guildmark on the base of the round showed it to be from one of Alion's reaction guns. Bronlar was doubly exonerated, and the verdict went unanimously against the dead warden.

"Warden Alion Damaric's house will have its hereditary articles of flight reduced to the status of squire, and nine-tenths of its wealth will be confiscated," Vander announced. "One-tenth will go to the cost of this council. The council also finds that Warden Alion Damaric deliberately tried to crash a stolen super-regal into Gunwing Hall Eleven, so as to destroy evidence that would have proved his defection and helped clear Semme Bronlar Jemarial. Thus Sair Serjon Feydamor and Semme Bronlar Jemarial are declared to be aggrieved parties. Sair Feydamor will be given two-tenths of Warden Alion's estate, while Semme Bronlar Jemarial will receive the remaining six-tenths plus the title of Warden Bronlar Jemarial."

When Condelor had fallen Bronlar had been stationed at Kamastone wingfield at the western edge of Cosdora. Farrasond, Lesh, and Torak were there as her field guildsmen, and it was in fact Bronlar who had first brought news of Greater Bartolica's fall on the 12th of August. At the spontaneous revel that night she confessed to Farrasond that Ryban was likely to be a problem when she returned to Vernal. The young guildmaster was very sympathetic. Ryban had something of a reputation as a seducer, although he appeared to have behaved himself in the month since he slept with Bronlar.

Farrasond was similar in stature to Ryban, but much stronger. The quiet, dedicated guildmaster worked hard, believed in chivalric honor, and even aspired to becoming a squire one day. He also adored Bronlar, and condemned both Serjon and Ryban for taking advantage of her. He said that gossip around the guild tents had it that Serjon had parachuted into Condelor before it had fallen, in order to seek witnesses to support him against Bronlar. It was quite by accident that he had found evidence to clear her.

"So much hate!" moaned Bronlar. "Why? What did I do to him?"

"You once rejected Feydamor, and now he knows about you having Ryban's button."

"How?" gasped Bronlar.

"People know, people talk—Ryban has been dropping broad hints and winking. Then there's the maid who changed the bed linen at Vernal, idlers in the street the next morning, guildsmen who crouched with an ear to the keyhole."

Bronlar shuddered, horrified at what they might have heard.

"Cosdoran guildsmen chat with Yarronese flyers, Semme, so word must have reached Wind River. Feydamor can't have you, so he wants to destroy you."

Later that night Bronlar took the cod-button and virginity of her guildmaster, and resolved to try to return his adoration with love. Four days later Bronlar flew west to Vernal to collect her notes for the hearing before the Council of Alliance Airlords that she knew would be soon.

As soon as she landed at Vernal, Ryban was told that Farrasond was now her lover, and that the liaison had to be honored. He protested, pleaded, and even accused her of forsaking him for someone more senior, but Bronlar had been stung by what Farrasond had said: Ryban had been boasting. Although miserable, she still had pride. Ryban denied the accusation, but then what else would he do?

Bronlar was about to enter her tent on Vernal wingfield when a sailwing appeared out of the north with white and green flares burning like intense stars against the night sky. It was a courier's colors, and the engine had the sound of a Yarronese radial. It circled the wingfield three times as the flyer took firm bearings from the beacon torches and checked the wind's direction from a flare trailing white fumes. A permission rocket was sent up, and then the adjunct hurried across to meet the courier as he landed. Bronlar sauntered over to the pennant pole, where any announcements would be made.

The sailwing came toward the waving torches of a wing-field directant, then stopped with the compression engine ticking over. The flyer handed out a folder to the adjunct even before he had clambered out himself.

"Call for a translator, Old Anglian to Cosdoran," the adjunct cried as he ran across to the lamps beside the pennant board.

Ryban called "Aye, that I can," as he strode forward. He began to read, then gave a whoop of joy.

"Bronlar, find Bronlar!" he cried, running for the tents and waving the dispatch.

"I'm here," called Bronlar, and Ryban skidded, slipped and fell, then came scrambling back to her.

"It's all over, you're pronounced innocent, you're a warden, you're rich! Feydamor confessed that he was lying! He's even been forced to write you this apology."

He flung a page to the ground and jumped on it, then threw the other papers into the air. Bronlar shrieked with surprise, then joined hands with Monterbil and Ryban and danced in circles around the trampled paper. She kissed the adjunct and her guildsmen, then stood with her arms around Ryban's neck as he read fragments of the dispatch.

"Tell me, what, how?" she asked.

"A bullet from Warden Alion's guns was found in the body of the tail gunner of the super-regal when it was exhumed. Feydamor had to confess. He's been broken down to flyer and lost most of his family's wealth to you."

"Here's his confession!" cried the prancing Monterbil, wiping the seat of his trousers with the paper.

"Darling Bronlar, I never doubted you for a moment," said Ryban.

Bronlar squeezed her arms around Ryban's neck and

kissed him full on the lips, then danced a few steps of a Cosdoran jig on the dispatch before seizing Monterbil and kissing him as well. Someone produced a flask of mountain whisky and Bronlar took a swig. Monterbil began playing a reel on his flute. More whisky was brought out from caches being kept to celebrate the end of the war.

The courier from Condelor walked over through the darkness, and behind him the white tips of his propellor described a flickering white circle. He bowed to the adjunct, the torchlight glinting off the panes of his goggles, then said something to him.

"The courier requires a reply for the council, Warden Jemarial," the adjunct said as he stepped into the light before the pennant board. "And he says you are expected to fly to Condelor by the nineteenth of the month to be honored at a banquet."

"Tell them to piss on Feydamor!" she laughed, kicking at the paper on the ground.

"Semme! That is not the response of a warden to the Council of Alliance Airlords."

"Then thank them for their wisdom and justice, and oh I don't know! Say anything! I'll go to Condelor when I've thanked my friends here and given them a revel to end all revels with Serjon Feydamor's money." She kissed Ryban again. "Friends like these supported me in my deepest need while Feydamor threw shit at me, so they come first. Tonight we revel!"

The adjunct scribbled out a formalized version of Bronlar's thanks, and explained that it would take her a day or two to prepare for the flight to Condelor. The adjunct managed to get her signature with some difficulty, then he countersigned it and handed it to the courier. The courier bowed to the adjunct, the lamplight flashing on the panes of his goggles.

"We'll all go to Yarron and live on the Damaric estate," Bronlar shouted above the music.

"The *former* Damaric estate," Monterbil corrected her.

"Then you can challenge Feydamor to a duel."

"No she can't, he's only a commoner without rank!" cried Ryban.

Out in the darkness the courier sailwing suddenly revved up and turned sharply on a braked wheel, blowing dust and gravel back over those by the pennant board.

"Hie, damned wardenling!" shouted Monterbil.

"Adjunct, don't give him a clearance flare until he comes back to apologize," added Ryban.

The adjunct lit a red lantern and began walking over to the flightstrip. Out in the darkness the courier gunned his compression engine. The adjunct stared for a moment then began to run forward, waving his lantern.

"Stop! You're ascending with the wind!" he shouted, but the sailwing was already beginning its ascent run.

The sailwing roared past along the path defined by the strip-side beacon lamps. After rolling nearly the entire length of the strip it lumbered into the air, banked sharply to miss a nearby ridge that Mirrorsun barely outlined, then turned north. The adjunct stood staring, his lantern a red point of light in the darkness.

"Hie there loon, where'd you buy your certificate?" Monterbil shouted in the direction of the sailwing.

By now word of Bronlar's good fortune was spreading through the tents of the wingfield and more guildsmen and flyers were running over to the pennant board.

"And would you like me to shield you again tonight?" Ryban said in Bronlar's ear as they danced.

Bronlar jammed a flask of whisky upside down into the waist of his trousers. "Fuel up your engine and keep it warm for me," she cried back for all to hear.

A mile to the northwest Serjon's sailwing was gaining height rapidly as he checked his bearings by Mirrorsun's light and his compass.

"Six guildsmen, the adjunct, Bronlar, me, a directant, and three wingfield carbineers: that's thirteen," he whispered miserably. "No wonder she took it so badly."

He held a glowbar to the fuel float. Enough for about a hundred and forty miles, but Condelor was ten farther than that. Evanston was closer, but no, that would never do, the dispatch from Bronlar was there in his flight jacket pocket, eating away at his soul like an oil fire in the engine bay. He had to deliver it at once, to get it away from him. It was Condelor or nothing.

The adjunct of the palace wingfield at Condelor had begun his round of the strip-side beacon lamps when he thought he heard an engine. It died, even as he turned his head from side to side to get the direction. He shrugged, concluding that whoever it was had landed at one of the outlying wingfields. He had checked the level of oil in the first of the midfield beacon lamps and was setting out for the second when there was a squeal of wheels at the end of the flightstrip. The shape of a sailwing rolled out of the darkness, silent except for the rumble of its wheels on the surface.

Abandoning his oil trolley the adjunct ran after the sailwing as it slowed.

"Hie, you're lucky to be alive!" the adjunct shouted as he reached the aircraft.

The flyer jumped to the ground in the darkness and held up what appeared to be a folder.

"Sair, I am actually unlucky to be alive but I have to make the best of it," Serjon replied. "Flyer First Class Serjon Feydamor, returning from Cosdora with the reply of Warden Bronlar Jemarial."

"Feydamor! You didn't have to return tonight!"

"Oh yes I did. Is the adjunct still awake?"

"I am the adjunct."

"Sair Adjunct, your pardon. Please accept a dispatch from Warden Jemarial to the Council of Alliance Airlords. Now then, might I impose upon your charity to help me push this thing back to my guildsmen's tent?"

It took twenty minutes for the pair of them to push the

sailwing onto a dispersal track and over to the tents. The Yarronese field guildsmen were asleep as they arrived at the tent, but Serjon was not inclined to wake them.

"I shall sign the Descents Register, then go to my room in the palace," said Serjon as they walked away.

"Your guildsmen will be surprised in the morning."

"The work of *guildsmen* is to keep one flying, Sair Adjunct, not to tell one how to fly," Serjon replied with undisguised loathing.

"I guess that you had an exchange of words with guildsmen in Vernal?" asked the adjunct knowingly.

"I exchanged few words, but I *heard* a great deal and saw even more. Goodnight to you, Sair Adjunct, and my thanks for your help with my sailwing."

"Sair Feydamor, a moment longer!" the adjunct called after him.

"Yes?"

"I . . . ah, I saw your super-regal bomb the palace. Even though you were the enemy, I still want to say that it was superlative flying, and bravery beyond imagining."

Serjon bowed to him in the dim light. "Strange that the only kind words for Serjon Feydamor should come from a former enemy."

"Tomorrow I should like to buy you a drink."

"I do not drink, Sair Adjunct, but I can watch as you have one for me."

"Sair Feydamor, ah, did you, ah, *care* for Warden Jemarial?"

"That I did, sair, but I only realized it today, and today was far too late. Now, I should like to be alone with my nightmares for a few hours, so I shall bid you goodnight."

Being an aviad, Theresla was in a difficult position in postwar Condelor. She represented the very beings that caused the war and it would take no more than a sample of her hair to expose her, yet she had also rescued Virtrian from the palace dungeons.

Sartov was standing in a doorway that opened into the space and ruin that had once been the throne hall when Virtrian arrived with Theresla beside him. The bomb that had brought down the roof of the throne room had worked with strange precision, leaving the back and side walls weakened but partially intact.

"One bomb and a war was lost," he said as he turned back to Virtrian. "What did you think when you saw the super-regal fly overhead, Virtrian?"

"I thought that Bartolican propaganda had outsmarted itself yet again, Lordship. Then when the throne hall's roof collapsed I knew that the war was over."

"And you, mysterious Semme, did you see it happen too?"

"Only from a distance. I was hiding from the authorities at the time, after all."

"I have heard a lot about you. You seem to have talents and capabilities that would not spread thinly over a dozen agents and spies. I assume that you are from . . . over there, wherever that is."

Theresla was dressed as a Bartolican woman, with voluminous skirts reaching down to chunky high-heeled boots, frilly ruffs at the wrists and shoulders, cutaway cleavage, and a scarf trailing from her throat. Her body was a lot thinner than suited the Bartolican taste, but then Sartov was not a Bartolican. Would that I look as young in my fifties, thought Sartov, then wondered if the Callwalkers aged more slowly than humans. He also noticed that her breath was ripe with something like rotted flesh: a predator's breath.

"I am from the same continent as those you call featherheads and Callwalkers, but I represent a minority faction," she explained in Old Anglian. "Those who are at work here wish to rule humans, but my people think that the future of our race would be better served by doing things for ourselves. Slavers are parasites. Unfortunately the temptation to dominate is very great when one's kind can resist the Call and all others cannot."

"So, they came here after conquering their own continent," Sartov probed.

"Nothing of the sort. There are few aviads even in Australica, some tens of thousands, and even these are balanced by factions with different and competing aims."

"This is all very plausible, Semme, but I am a good storyteller too—it is a talent common among leaders. I could conjure half a dozen conspiracies to cover what has happened in Mounthaven before and during the war. What have you done for Yarron, apart from show compassion to Virtrian? If it comes to that, why did you take so long to release him? Was it that you wanted to make sure that Yarron was winning first, so that you could be with the winners? Perhaps all of you featherheads work for the same master, but some are planted on the other side, just in case."

"I'll not plead, Lordship," said Theresla with no concern in her manner. "What will it take to convince you? Who will you believe?"

"I'd believe a man named Glasken. He came to me when Yarron was all but crushed. He gave me secrets to allow us to fight back and win."

"Glasken is dead," said Theresla with an even stare and an impassive expression.

Sartov was moved by the news. He looked over the ruins of the Bartolican throne room where a thousand people had died not three months earlier. It had been war, there were always casualties, yet the Mounthaven way had once been to confine casualties to those whose place it was to fight. Glasken had been one of the fighters, even though he could not fly . . . that somehow made it easier for Sartov to accept.

"I am sorry to hear that, he was a fine man. Unfortunately, Semme, that means it will be all the harder for you to—"

"But you may speak with him. Sair Virtrian, please leave us."

When Virtrian had gone Theresla touched the band beneath the scarf at her neck, and at once thin whirls of light motes gathered out of nowhere, thickening, solidifying and stabilizing until they became—

"Glasken!" Sartov exclaimed.

"Death is a very unexciting state, Lordship," the faintly glowing spectre declared. "Try to put it off if you possibly can."

For the purpose of this appearance Glasken was in his early fifties again, but with the gunshot wounds that had killed him and a great deal of blood on his clothing. He was dressed as a monk, which was a little touch that Sartov recognized from what he had said back in Sheridan.

"Glasken, are—are you all right?" gasped Sartov, at a loss for any more sensible words.

"I'm dead, Lordship," the image replied, spreading his hands wide. "It really did hurt."

"But, but, what are you?" Sartov stammered.

"I am a copy of the inner soul of Glasken. My body lies rotting in a monastery grave near Denver, which is quite a pity because there are two or three bits that I rather miss."

There was a certain fatalism about the manner of the image, but it still came across as unquestionably Glasken.

"This is some trick of the ancient guildsmen," Sartov said to Theresla.

"Yes, it certainly is!" Theresla responded. "A trick which keeps the essence of what was Glasken sufficiently alive to speak with you. What is your word, Lordship? There are others we can go to."

Sartov turned back to Glasken.

"Say your words, sair Glasken, I shall give them a fair hearing."

"I can say little more than Theresla can tell you. My image lives within Mirrorsun's structure, but I have access to little of its resources. I am like a king's pet cat: existing in luxury and free to come and go at will, but with little power and even less understanding of what is going on around me. Mirrorsun is studying me, Lordship. It has had no direct contact with humans. It is ruled by the image of Highliber Zarvora, and she can hardly be described as human. Trust Theresla. Give her the freedom to search the Condelor palace from tower top to dungeon, give her a squad of carbineers to break down doors and carry things about, force Bartolican clerks, servants, and flunkies to answer her questions. There is more to the Callwalkers' Miocene Arrow plan than we yet know, and that ignorance may kill us—or kill you, at least. It has already killed me."

Sartov felt uneasy about trusting Theresla, but Glasken and he had an odd kinship. He reached out a friendly hand, but it passed through the image of Glasken's arm. Sartov jerked back a step, and nearly toppled out into the nothingness of the old throne hall.

"Would that include the location of the second featherhead wingfield?" he asked, trying to maintain his dignity in front of the smirking Theresla.

"Friend and benefactor, that is the one thing I *can* help with. I have a lovely view of the earth from Mirrorsun, and can resolve objects as small as a single gunwing. Many, many gunwings have been landing at a place named Sioux City on your Archaic Anglian maps. Most stay there."

A meeting of the Council of Alliance Airlords was convened very soon after Sartov had heard what Glasken had to say. Sartov reported that he had the location of not just one but two aviad bases in the eastern Callscour lands. One was at a ruin a mere three hours' return flight from the wingfields of Forian, but this was just a staging field for the main wingbase. At the Sioux City ruin was an enormous wingfield, restored by the aviads and now housing four hundred stolen gunwings and sailwings from Yarron, Bartolica, Montras, and Dorak.

"But, but a round trip to drop firebombs would be nine hours," spluttered the Cosdoran airlord. "Nearly all of that would be over Callscour lands, and the furthermost two hundred miles would be over territory not seen by human eyes for two thousand years."

"My super-regals can fly for ten hours without refueling, Lordship," Sartov assured him.

"Very impressive, Airlord Sartov, but those things lumber along at one hundred miles per hour. Even a couple of armed sailwings could bring one down, and you suggest that there are four hundred wings at the Sioux City ruin."

"My guildsmen have developed techniques to massively extend the range of gunwings and sailwings. *Any* gunwings and sailwings, not just those of Yarron. Starting with six hundred aircraft we could provide an escort of perhaps a hundred gunwings over the target."

Sartov now told of how the aviads were gathering a massive stockpile of guildsmen and wings to take south to Hildago and other dominions in Mexhaven. These were already under aviad domination, he had been told, but even worse was that they were in rich country compared to Mounthaven. They already supplied over half the compression spirit used by the Mounthaven wardens, and much of the flight-rated wood, cloth, and metal besides. If they ever learned to build and fly their own wings they could reduce Mounthaven to a client backwater in years, if not months.

After another hour of debate the council gave a guarded approval to one single, massive attack on the two aviad bases, but there was still the problem of the fragmented Bartolican regions. They had some hundreds of wings operational, and that was a dangerous vulnerability to leave unattended when the best of the victors' wings were going to be at Forian for no less than a fortnight.

"There is no question of it, we shall have to bring the

Bartolican Regions in with us," concluded Sartov.

"What!" exclaimed the Dorakian Airlord, who had had bitter experience of working together with Bartolicans. "They would turn against us, they—"

"Would be outnumbered," Sartov pointed out. "We would reduce their numbers in domestic defense by just as much as ours. More importantly, we might also gain their trust and make them less likely to huddle together for fear of us."

"Why stop at the Bartolican regions, why not send to all Mounthaven's dominions?" the Airlord of Omelgan suggested.

"Towervale has only five gunwings and they have not been in action since 3917," the Pangaver Airlord said dismissively.

"But Friscon and Colandoro both specialize in long-range wings, yes, that is a good thought," Sartov decided. "Tomorrow I shall send a courier to the former Bartolican regions and another five to the remaining neutral dominions. In a few weeks we could well have a thousand wings ready to ascend from the wingfields of Forian."

17 August 3961: Vernal

Carbineer Carlen Hongraz was standing guard between the tents and gunwings. After twenty-four hours of nearly continuous revelry he was glad that the guildsmen and flyers of Vernal had finally exhausted themselves. Carbineers on the guard roster were less lucky, and had to stay sober. Still, Hongraz had sipped some firedew and had a brief dance with the first female warden in all Mounthaven, so in a sense he counted himself lucky. The carbineer glanced at one tent in particular.

"Ryban's far luckier, sharing her tent," he said to himself, vocalizing his thoughts.

As if cued by his whisper, angry voices began to come from the tent.

"I say no more!" insisted the unseen Bronlar.

"To the Call with Feydamor and saving his thirteen!" Ryban cried back. "I'm full nozzle again."

"Well take it to Ma Gertie's in town! This is personal."

"I deserve better."

"So do I! You're rough, and it still hurts."

"I'm insulted."

"You should be *honored*, with what you've had."

"What *I've* had? Sharing you with Farrasond?"

"Get out of my tent."

"*My* tent? *My* tent? Last night it was *our* tent! I'm not going until I—Argh!"

Ryban burst from the tent as if pushed, and he rolled naked on the ground clutching his groin. With a glance to the carbineer, he got up and ran off among the other tents, most of which already had heads poking out in Mirrorsun's light. The adjunct hurried over, his feet bare and his coat over his star-pattern pyjamas. Rummaging sounds were coming from Bronlar's tent.

"Have, ah, they been arguing?" the adjunct asked Hongraz.

"Aye, that appears so, Sair Adjunct," Hongraz replied nervously.

Bronlar crawled out of her tent, hastily dressed and carrying her flight bag. Both adjunct and carbineer backed away a few steps, each hoping to leave the other to speak to her, then stood facing the advancing warden side by side.

"Warden Jemarial, giving notice of leaving for Evanston, Montras," she said as she reached the adjunct.

"It's close to midnight," began the adjunct.

"Evanston is a capital, and has flightstrip beacons burning all night. I want to spend the day in the markets there before I go on to Condelor for the victory banquet."

"Yes, I see," said the adjunct, taking a notepad from his

coat. "New, fine clothes for the banquet, and perhaps presents?" he said as he scribbled the ascent notes.

"Just clothes. As of a few minutes ago I finished making my present, and I want to keep it safe."

The steam engine was fired up by Bronlar's guildsmen while the adjunct's men ran along the flightstrip lighting the beacon lamps. At a few minutes to midnight she pushed Slash's throttle forward and the gunwing ascended into the wind, turned northeast, and was gone. Slowly the wingfield began to blend back into the night as lamps were extinguished and guildsmen returned to their tents.

Hongraz watched as the adjunct hung an annotated pennant on the pole.

"I saw that Lesh fueled her gunwing instead of Ryban," said the adjunct to the carbineer. "Did you happen to hear what was going on?"

"I heard the warden say 'No more,' then Sair Ryban called out something like 'To the Call with Feydamor and saving his thirteen' and that he was full nozzle. After more words along that course she threw him out with his moon full."

The Vernal adjunct leaned against the pennant pole, shaking his head.

"Ryban will be slow to show his face tomorrow. He must have forgotten that she hates Serjon Warden Killer more than she favors any guildsman."

19 August 3961: Condelor

Even though he had been one of the principal contributors to the defeat of Greater Bartolica, Serjon was not invited to the allies' victory banquet on the night of August 19th. Late afternoon found him wandering the Condelor palace grounds, tracing on foot the approach paths of his superregal on that day in early May. Most of the bushes, paths, statues, ornamental walls, and flowerbeds were etched into his mind, but the people were missing. The palace gardens were almost deserted as everyone prepared themselves for the great revel that would see the end to the most savage and damaging war since the wardenate system had been established in some long-gone century.

Suddenly Serjon stopped and blinked. A girl in a blue promenade gown with long, flame-red hair was standing where one like her had been framed in his canopy's forward pane on the day he had flown his super-regal against Bartolica's heart. Airlord Samondel.

"Might I have a word?" she asked in accented but clear Yarronese.

"Who am I to withhold words, Ladyship?" he replied. "Have as many as you will."

"Would the truth about Alion be of interest to you, Serjon Warden Killer?"

Serjon regarded her for a tense, chilly moment. Was there sarcasm in her voice? She also sounded as weary as he did. Perhaps he was the only one she could trust with the truth. He wondered if he could take its weight.

"I suspect the truth is worse than the Airlords' verdict," he answered.

"Indeed it is. Are you interested, Serjon Warden Killer?"

"Just flyer now, Ladyship, and I am not interested. I'm tired of hurting, and I'm very tired of being hurt."

Serjon strolled on without another word. Presently he noticed that Samondel was walking beside him.

"I, I . . . apologize for calling you Warden Killer," she offered.

For an airlord this was a considerable concession. Serjon hung his head, but held up his arm for her hand as he kept strolling. Samondel put her hand on his forearm, and choked down a sob with a deep breath.

"When he pushed me from the super-regal Alion said 'Never forget what I did for you, Samondel. Always remember that I did it for love.' Then he pulled the hatch shut. In that moment I would have given the world to have loved him, but I could not. He died without knowing, that was all I could give him."

Serjon stopped, and Samondel walked around in front of him. Alion and Samondel, Serjon and Bronlar. Two halves of two great, tragic, and one-sided loves. She kept her hand on his forearm, then took his hand in both of hers.

"Serjon Feydamor, Alion died honorably."

"He died trying to destroy Gunwing Hall Eleven, where evidence clearing Warden Jemarial of *his* crime was in storage. Fortunately he bungled the attempt."

Samondel had not known this, and was at a loss for words. Alion had died for her, but not without malice. They walked in silence for a way, about a yard apart and both staring at the red gravel path at their feet.

"The Sennerese Airlord's son has proposed a betrothal with me," Samondel revealed.

"Congratulations."

"Remove Condelor from Greater Bartolica and there is no Greater Bartolica."

"Good."

"I rejected him. Sennerese nobles treat their women like furniture. They see both stupidity and beauty as alluring in a woman."

"Taste is nature's justice."

"Are you pleased that my dominion has been destroyed? Does it satisfy you to have revenge for the invasion of Yarron?"

Serjon stopped again and turned on her.

"Yes, Ladyship, all of that pleases me a great deal. It pleases me for the seventy-eight thousand Yarronese who died on their own soil at the hands of your carbineer murderers. Less than five thousand Bartolicans have died on Bartolican soil, remember? I have seen a whole hall littered with the bodies of raped and murdered Yarronese women at Opal after the Bartolicans passed through. I have seen the flower of Yarronese chivalry dead beneath the ruins of a hall brought down by a bomb hidden by Bartolica's featherhead mercenaries. So many cold hands, I'm so sick of the touch of cold hands. With Condelor and the surrounding farmlands as part of Senner, your realm will shrink to a tiny mountain domainlet the size of Montras. Mounthaven will be the better for it."

Samondel pouted, then looked at him through her red eyelashes. "I am pleased too, Serjon. You saved us."

The answer could have been taken a number of ways, but Samondel was unused to intelligent duelspeak after months as airlord, and Serjon was too tired to take it at anything more than face value.

"The Sennerese prince offered me an alliance almost the size of Greater Bartolica. It wrenched me, but I said no."

"If you do not like the direction of your life, Ladyship, then take the controls into your own hands and fly it in one that suits you better. Hone your flying, *really* lead what's left of your people as an airlord."

"I don't even have a gunwing."

"Borrow Starflower while I'm gone. Just don't use over-boost until new compression rings are settled—oh, and the port gun has a tendency to jam unless you lock the release down really hard."

Samondel folded her arms beneath her breasts and drew them up until the setting sun cast a deep shadow in her cleavage.

"You're taking me seriously," she said with her head inclined.

"I know a few jokes, if you prefer. What's black and crisp and sits at the bottom of a crater?"

"I—I—"

"A court herald after his first solo flight."

Samondel laughed before she could help herself. "I am to attend tonight's banquet as an act of reconciliation and peace. I would like to enter with you."

"Grats, Semme, but I'm specifically not invited. I shall

eat at a tavern, then try to find bawdy women with warm hands."

"Really?" Samondel exclaimed.

"Well, so far they've not found me. Now I must go. I apologize for trying to kill you, Ladyship."

"And I'm sorry for your mother and sisters. I did not know, truly, I did not know."

The setting sun cast shadows a hundred feet in length from the Airlord of the new domain of Highland Bartolica and the greatest flyer in Mounthaven's history. Both stood with her hands clasped before them.

"Tomorrow you must go to my guildsmen, I'll speak to them first," Serjon said earnestly, his heart suddenly opening to her. "Take up Starflower, get flight time. Be more than a bauble, be a fighting airlord, be proud of yourself, Ladyship. I don't adore you as Alion did, but I do like you, Ladyship, and, and—"

"Samondel to you, my brave and chivalric friend."

She reached up and drew Serjon's face down with her fingertips beneath his jaw, then she kissed him softly on the lips as the sun dropped and their shadows lengthened across the palace gardens to be greater than the highest spires of the palace.

"That . . . could cause unseemly talk in court," said Serjon, brushing her cheek with his fingers nevertheless.

"Let them talk. I have been thinking a lot since Condelor fell, Serjon. It ripped my heart out to admit it, but you saved the people of Bartolica from the featherheads by what you did. My people. I wanted to hate you but I could not, and now . . . I may not be a bawdy woman, but my hands are very warm."

After a moment the astonished Serjon realized that his mouth was open. He closed it.

"I am very tired of hating," he managed, wondering whether the words were even vaguely appropriate.

"Then it is time to stop."

*   *   *

At dusk a lone gunwing droned out of the southeast, a green approach flare burning at its underside. The flight-strip beacon lamps were alight, and a permission rocket streaked up and stabbed brilliantly through the dark. The gunwing landed on its first approach and taxied to the wing halls. The adjunct was back from the Flying Swinelet by then, where he had enjoyed dinner but missed Serjon. He noted that it was a Yarronese triwing gunwing of recent design—in fact one identical to that still stored in Gunwing Hall 11 and another that stood before Serjon's maintenance tent.

The victory banquet was by then in full cry in the Condelor palace. Bartolican servants and retainers were doing their best to adapt to the new circumstances of Condelor, but had to use lists to keep track of people and titles for the hundreds of unfamiliar guests.

Serjon stood swaying at the door to Samondel's chambers, far across the palace. They had emptied a small jar of her finest sherry together in the hours past.

"Until this evening I did not drink," Serjon confessed.

"Oh no! You should have told me."

"It seemed a worthy occasion to start." He waved a strand of her red hair at her nose. "You must gain flight time, it would be good for your soul. You need something more than beauty to be proud of."

"My flying is a joke," she answered, pulling her hair over her bare breasts and shivering with cold. "I took four months to ascend solo."

Serjon removed his unbuttoned flight jacket and draped it over her shoulders. "Sorry for, ah, the awkward ascent just now," he mumbled.

"What comparison have I?" she replied, hugging him into her hair. "Besides, I think I liked it better for having a partner who knows no better than me. You were very considerate, it was nothing like I had feared."

"Keep my jacket," he offered. "Wear it to the banquet, say it is a gift from Serjon Warden Killer who broke Stanbury's grip on your people. That will be very good for inter-dominion relations."

"But—"

"I have a spare, not as nice but adequate. Goodnight now, beautiful and gentle Samondel."

They kissed again, then Samondel pulled the door closed. Serjon's head was wobbling like a mis-tuned radial compression engine as he made his way back to his rooms in just shirt, trews, and boots. He glanced at his watch, which showed a minute past nine. As he turned into the corridor where his room was, he saw a servant girl knocking on his door and calling out in Bartolican.

"You won't find me in there," he said in Yarronese, knowing only too well why she was at the door.

She bowed low to him, exposing a wide expanse of flawless white cleavage. She was dressed in a Yarronese-style apron-robe that was convincing but chunky in its execution, obviously a hasty attempt to please her new masters. In a few years she might have a weight problem, he speculated, but for now her figure seemed healthy and generous.

"Come please, if it is your pleasure," she said in strangled Yarronese.

"I speak Bartolican, Montrassian, Yarronese, Dorakish, Old Anglian, and a little more Cosdoran than is good for me," Serjon replied. He was tired, tipsy, genuinely happy for the first time in years, and uninterested in doing anything that required effort.

"Sair, will you please come with me?" the girl now said in Bartolican. "A very important warden wishes to speak with you."

Serjon entered his room to fetch his spare embroidered flight jacket, but did not do up the buttons when he had put it on. He straightened his collar and scarf, rubbed his shoes against his trousers, then followed the girl. She took his arm and guided him some distance through the corridors of the palace.

"Are you a warden, Sair Serjon?" she asked as they walked.

"Not a warden, only a free flyer. Free means nobody has to support me, but I work for the Airlord of Yarron just now."

"Oh, that is important."

"Maybe so, but I am not."

The girl took a while to assimilate this, but frowned as she caught the meaning.

"I am Seyret, sair, a baker's daughter. I am very sorry about the invasion of Yarron. Big mistake."

Serjon burst out laughing, then stumbled over a Dorakian rug on the marble flagstones.

"Think nothing of it, Semme Seyret."

"If you like, I will sleep with you and help make up for everything."

Even though it was not the first such offer made to Serjon since he had landed in Condelor, he still felt an involuntary thrill run through him. Many Bartolican women were looking for favors, protection, and patronage among the victors, and he now understood what was on offer.

"Your offer flatters me, but I'm very tired," Serjon responded without needing to act. "My head spins and aches."

"Oh! Are you wounded?"

"It's an old wound, to my heart. I have been applying sherry to it."

She stopped at a roped off section of a heavily decorated and pillared corridor. The doorway beyond the heavy red rope barrier led into a pit of blackness through which a cool, pleasant breeze was blowing in the late summer night.

"You will wait here, please," said Seyret with a curtsey, and then she hurried back the way they had come.

Serjon waited, staring out over the pit of rubble lit by torches affixed to high poles. With a start he realized that it was the ruins of the throne hall. This corridor had once led onto some staircase for the Bartolican airlord to make a grand entrance, but both staircase and Airlord were no more now. The occupation forces had torn down the façades and coverings erected by Stanbury and bared the destruction for all the citizens of Bartolica to see. Bootsteps clacked on the stone floor in the distance behind Serjon. Steadily, remorselessly, they drew closer. They stopped.

"All your own work?" a female voice behind him asked, this time in perfect Yarronese.

"Bronlar, good evening," he said without turning.

She approached another three steps.

"What? No welcoming embrace for your long-lost wing cover?"

Serjon slowly turned, his arms hanging limp and his jacket still open. Bronlar was in a parade uniform and was wearing her daystar. There was a well-healed but alarming scar that ran from her left temple down in front of her ear and ended at her jawbone.

"If I thought an embrace would help I would give one," he said as he let his gaze drop to her boots. "But hugs are as cheap as words, and they mean no more."

Bronlar took a step to one side and leaned against a pillar, folding her arms across the double row of brass buttons that fastened her coat.

"When I got word that you had accused me of shooting your super-regal down I thought my world had ended," said Bronlar. "I cursed, I cried, I even took a guildsman to my bed and gave him my virginity. Remember it? The one I would not give to you last October?"

"We've not been introduced," said Serjon, feeling giddy and aware of the drop behind him.

"Weeks later I found out that you had lied in your testimony! By then I had a second lover."

"I'm sorry."

"I'm sure you are. We really enjoyed doing it."

"I'm sorry that I accused you thus."

Serjon's reactions were those of total defeat, but Bronlar did not want him vanquished without a satisfying fight. This was to be a war duel, not a strafing run.

"Why did you accuse me at all?" she demanded, growing annoyed and impatient.

"The evidence pointed to you."

"The evidence? The evidence? You had no evidence, I had no trial, deliberation, or judgment, yet you shot those lies at me. If I had been in Yarron at the time I would have been before a firing squad within a week."

"True. But you were not, and now I have cleared your name."

"And I might have been a month *dead* by now! I kept imagining myself dead: tied to a post, blindfolded and shot full of gaping holes. You know, I found that taking lovers helped remind me that I was still alive. I have had lovers, I learned that willing girls have a far easier time of it than boys. Would you like to be my next lover? It would be the thirteenth time that I have done it! It's an unlucky number but I've saved it for you."

Serjon winced at the word thirteen. "You needn't have bothered, I'm already unlucky."

Serjon's bland reaction to his nemesis number took Bronlar by surprise. She now sauntered forward and past Serjon, stopping at the red rope and looking out over the ruins of the Bartolican throne room.

"When I first heard that you had accused me . . ." She stopped, jaw clamped and breathing heavily through her nostrils. "I decided that you did not like sharing this . . . this triumph. I hate you, Serjon! Do you understand that?"

"Only too well," replied Serjon softly, his voice flat.

"I used to write your name on scraps of paper and fling them into the privy pit before I squatted."

"That seems reasonable."

Serjon's penitence was beginning to try her patience.

"Reasonable? Reasonable? I don't want it to seem reasonable, sair Feydamor, I want it to hurt you! What does it take to hurt you?"

"Nothing much, it's not hard. You're already doing it."

"Don't bother begging for pity."

"I'm not."

"Damn you, Feydamor! Were it not for your slip of the tongue before the Airlords' council I would *still* stand accused. I would not be able to walk into that banquet on the other side of the palace and sit in honor at the Yarronese table. Why did you stay silent for so long?"

"I had no decisive evidence—"

"You *did*, damn you!" shouted Bronlar, furious. "You withheld your gunner's words, words that would have cleared me. All because you trusted some scum-piss warden boy."

"As soon as I had proof that he lied about crashing his gunwing, I came to doubt everything else that he had sworn in evidence."

"But your testimony about the tail gunner cursing me for a stupid bitch would have proved that it was *I* who broke off, and that I was too far away to have shot at you. You knew that! You hated me because you thought I broke and ran! Well *I* hate *you*! I hate you so much that I spread my legs for my guildsmen so that I could walk in here and fling their cod-buttons at your feet!"

She reached into her pocket and tossed two brass cod-buttons at Serjon's feet. They rolled to the edge of the pavement, near the gap where the old throne hall had been. Serjon watched as they skittered, then looked up directly at Bronlar's face.

"Does that hurt?" shrieked Bronlar. "Two lovers, Feydamor! I had my revenge, and it felt good all *twelve* times."

The changed look on Serjon's face cut her short. It frightened her, but she misunderstood what was behind his expression.

"You're hurt, now I can see it, and you hate me too.

That's better. Thirteen. That's my gift to you! Thirteen! What can you give me in return? Can you do better than that? Two lovers and twelve times?"

Serjon straightened, adjusted his collar, then clasped his hands over his belt buckle and stared unblinking into Bronlar's face. The patient resignation was gone.

"Well before your next little gift I'd like to give you a truth," he said, each word a clipped, hissing snap. "My only lie was to the Council of Alliance Airlords. The tail gunner shouted nothing down the pipe when you broke off. Nothing! Understand? Nothing! As soon as I so much as suspected that you were innocent I lied to clear your name, *Warden* Bronlar Jemarial, I lied to the Alliance Council itself. I found Princess undamaged in Gunwing Hall Eleven and I *assumed* the worst about Alion. I had no more evidence, he might have just turned tail and defected, but my faith in you was stronger so I lied to clear you and abased myself. That lie brought upon me undeserved guilt, disgrace, demotion, fines, and the contempt of nearly everyone whose regard I value. Worst of all, it has brought me two grinning, gleeful little cod-buttons."

For a brief eternity there was silence between them. Sounds of the distant banquet echoed through the passageways and cloisters, people were laughing and shouting and a band was playing Yarronese marching tunes.

"What? You're lying now!" she retorted. "The rear gunner's grave was dug up on the day of your testimony. A bullet from Alion's guns was found in his corpse. You changed your testimony as soon as you found out."

"I suggest that you read the Airlords' dispatch more carefully. It is all written there, quite clearly. The rear gunner's corpse was dug up *after* my testimony was given. It's there in flawless Old Anglian, followed by my apology in plain, unambiguous Yarronese."

"No, I—it was translated for me, word for word," said Bronlar, still aggressive in her tone but now visibly shaken.

"By who? Some chubby little pudding of a Cosdoran

guildsman wearing a pottery gunwing, anxious to paint me blacker than the devil's turds, fill you full of whisky, and slip your drawers down? I lied to clear your name, Bronlar! I *lied* as soon as I became suspicious of Alion."

"Serjon!" He had started to walk away, but she strode after him and seized his arm. "Serjon Feydamor, wait! How did you know what Ryban looked like?"

He shook his arm free.

"Because I personally flew in with the Airlords' dispatch! I was desperate to give you the good news. I'd realized that I loved you by then, but you'd already decided to take whoever was to hand. I missed most of what was being said at first because my compression engine was ticking over, but when I came near the pennant board you were kissing everything in guildsmen's overalls and shouting 'Piss on Feydamor!' or words to that effect. When I ascended it was with the wind and I nearly hit a mountain."

He paused for her reply, but the shocked Bronlar clearly did remember that all had been as he said. It was a direct hit to her engine, and now the chivalric thing to do was break off the duel.

"Now leave me alone," Serjon concluded. "I'll not cross your path again if I can help it. I have my own lover now." For the last two hours, at least, he added to himself.

"Serjon, you bastard, you're still lying!" she shrieked, seizing his arm again. "I know you're lying. I'll prove it. Come with me!"

"Let me go!" he shouted back, shaking her loose. "There's nothing to prove and there's nothing between us."

"No! I want your damn filthy lies dragged out for everyone to see. I'm not finished with you!"

"Go nail some poor yoick for your thirteenth hump, there's a banquet hall full of heroes to choose from—"

Bronlar had meant to slap his face with an open hand but a year of war and death had trained her to instinctively hit with a fist. The slap that had become a right cross landed between Serjon's cheek and jaw, then caught his nose. Serjon fell, striking his head on a column. He lay still. Bronlar spat on him, scooped up her two brass buttons, and strode off down the corridor.

The palace echoed a great deal, and although Bronlar tried to walk in the direction of the sounds of the banquet, she seemed to get no closer. Several servants that she met spoke only Bartolican; then she cried out in joy to see Kanoshi in the distance. The former adjunct of Middle Junction wingfield was reeling but exuberant as she ran up and embraced him.

"Damn this palace, I can't find the banquet," she laughed.

"I'll take you there now," he cried jovially. "I had to deliver some dispatches to the adjunct for delivery flights tomorrow. The Airlords have been signing 'em on the very banquet table."

"Would Sair Feydamor the younger be one of the couriers?"

"The same," he replied with a nudge of his elbow. "The mighty Warden Killer is now a courier to the new Bartolican dominions. I hope he doesn't mind being spat on."

"Kanoshi, you speak and read Old Anglian," she said as he tried to guide her down the corridor.

"Only when I have to."

She drew some folded, wrinkled sheets of paper from her boot and handed them to him.

"What happened, has someone been dancing on these?" he exclaimed.

"If you please, could you clear up a little misunderstanding by translating these for me? As a second opinion."

"Translating—but it's nine-thirty, Semme, the toasts will be soon and I have to show you to your place at the Yarronese table."

"Kanoshi, I'll enjoy the banquet at lot more, and I'll even do it in your company if you translate this and lay a troublesome ghost for me now."

She winked at him, and Kanoshi blushed.

"Ah yes, I see—well no, I don't see but I, ah, see well enough to . . . translate. It's written in Old Anglian, the scribes of the council use it as a common language. Now let me see . . ."

He began reading the Old Anglian back in Yarronese. Bronlar paid close attention, and leaned forward eagerly with an arm draped around his neck as the adjunct reached a critical passage.

" '*Serjon Feydamor changed his testimony to exonerate you by mentioning details that he had not included in the previous testimony. Later that day the body of the tail gunner was exhumed and a bullet was recovered from the pelvic region. This was determined to be from the guns of Warden Alion's gunwing, adding weight to Serjon Feydamor's second testimony. Serjon Feydamor was ordered to pen the following apology to you—*' "

"*Later that day,* you said!" she exclaimed, suddenly feeling a pang as if she had been flayed internally by shards of flying glass. "Are you absolutely sure it says *Later that day?*"

"Not only does it say that in plain Old Anglian, Semme, but I was there at the Council of Alliance Airlords on that very day. First Serjon testified, then around lunch the body was dug up. Within an hour the bullet was found and—"

Bronlar had gone chalk-white with horror.

"Tell me," she whispered, "has Serjon ever parachuted into Condelor—like before the occupation?"

"Never, Bronny. He's only been shot down once, and that was in the super-regal. Why last week he told me in Wind River that he's only used a parachute in training."

"You're sure?"

"Absolutely positive! I worked as deputy adjunct at Wind River, which is his home wingfield. I signed him in every day from when he escaped Condelor until he returned here with twenty gunwings after the surrender."

"They all lied," whispered Bronlar. "Except for Serjon. He said he loved me. Loved. Used to."

"Semme Bronny, what—"

"SERJON!"

She snatched the pages out of Kanoshi's hands and ran back the way she had come through corridors still echoing with her cry.

"But Semme Bronlar, it's nine-thirty-five!" he called after her. "The banquet! The toasts!"

This time it was even harder for Bronlar to find her way around. She seized servants that she found and demanded the way to the demolished throne hall. Eventually she was shown to the new, temporary throne hall. Again she ran through the corridors, shrieking and cursing, clutching the dispatch and calling for Serjon. Another ten minutes passed before she reached the place where she had hit him.

There was blood on the floor in darkening pools, and smears leading away that thinned to nothing. There were two sets of footprints in the blood: those of Serjon's dress boots and smaller, feminine slippers. She followed the trail as far as she could, calling to him with a voice that had grown ragged, harsh and weak.

"Serjon, love, listen to me, please. Give me a minute, give me a heartbeat."

If Serjon heard, he did not come. She went back to the pools of blood and smeared it on her hands and face. Her tortured, knotted stomach finally gave up the struggle with what she had eaten in Evanston, and she threw up down the front of her uniform. Two Dorakian guards found her writhing on the floor, contorted with cramps. She was unable to speak and was smeared with vomit.

"Ho ha, too much drinking!" chuckled one.

"Ho yes, we have ways for curing of too much drinking," the other replied.

They picked Bronlar up by the arms and legs and carried her away.

"Silly girl dress in warden's uniform after jumpy-humpy, yes?"

"Ho yes, and somewhere is warden wearing skirts and apron. Ho ha!"

Outside in the palace gardens, Bronlar was dumped into a shallow fountain. The guards stayed to laugh, then turned back for the palace. She crawled out of the fountain and collapsed on the grass, shivering and retching. Pounding through her mind was a single, horrifying thought: three fatal nights ago in Cosdora she had not asked anyone else to check Ryban's translation. Nobody had asked anybody to check, they all *wanted* to believe what Ryban said.

"And you were there in the very flesh," she whispered to the grass beside her lips. "I could have reached out and touched you. You must have wondered why I took the good news so badly. You must have wondered why, why, why, why, why . . . ?"

She raised her head enough to gaze at the lights of the palace. Her hands and face were clean now. Although the Airlords' dispatch to her was wet, the lacquering that was applied to all dispatch papers had prevented the ink from running.

"Serjon, oh Serjon! I couldn't even keep a few smears of your blood. But I have your apology, and I shall keep it beside my heart forever."

Serjon had revived with his head on Seyret's lap. She was wiping blood out of his eyes. His forehead hurt like fire, as did his jaw and nose.

"Serjon, can you hear me? Are you in bad pain?"

He pushed at her as he tried to sit up. The columns swayed and wavered before his eyes as he looked around. Blood began streaming from his nose, and he pinched it with one hand.

"Best that you go," he mumbled.

"But Serjon, you are hurt."

"Good. I want to die."

"You are hurt," she said, holding him steady. "You need to be tended."

Taking a flask from her apron she dabbed a little firedew whisky on a handkerchief and wiped the gash on his forehead. He winced, but did not resist. She had a gentle, warm touch, and was wearing a subtle, pleasant scent. Serjon was cheered, in spite of himself.

"Funny, but I don't feel so desolate anymore," he said.

"Your pardon?"

"I mean . . . I feel better. You have a nice touch, like a nurse."

Seyret unbuttoned her blouse and to Serjon's surprise placed his hand against a soft, warm breast featuring a particularly large and hard nipple.

"It is a nursing thing. Arousal of the male feelings makes the pain less."

Serjon smiled. "Clever. It works well."

"I will hold your pain away all night? Yes?"

"Please, Semme. I'm in disgrace. If you want protection or favors, one of the wardens would be a much better prospect for you."

"Wardens need no help. You need help. Come, I shall help you walk."

As she helped Serjon back to his assigned room in the palace hostelry they heard Bronlar screaming Serjon's name and other incoherent words in the distance.

"The madwoman!" gasped Seyret. "What can I do? She knows where your room is."

"Samondel," whispered Serjon. "Find Airlord Samondel's room. She will help."

The hall where the banquet was to be held had been decked out with the Yarronese, Cosdoran, Dorakian, Sennerese, and Montrassian battle pennants, and the colors of every noble present were strung between the walls. Bartolican banners were draped as tablecloths, while some Bartolican tapestries on heroic themes were on the floor as carpets. Everyone was dining from palace silver, while the Airlords and their consorts who were present had gold plates and goblets. Two woodwind bands alternately played the marching songs and anthems of the victor dominions, and all the servants were dressed as wardens of Greater Bartolica.

The toasts were nearly over as Samondel entered the banquet wearing Serjon's flight jacket and with her hand upon Serjon's arm. Serjon's face and shirt were still streaked with blood, and his forehead was unbandaged. The entire hall plunged into a silence as deep as if a Call had just swept past. The pair walked a short distance between the rows of tables; then Serjon stumbled over the edge of a tapestry and Samondel caught him. They walked the rest of the way to the council's high table with Serjon's arm around her shoulders.

"My apologies for being late, Lordships," Samondel declared as she came to a stop before the assembled airlords. "There was an incident. Sair Feydamor came to my defense. He was good enough to lend me his flight jacket, too."

"Who did this?" demanded Sartov, rising from his seat. "Floor marshal, take note. Airlord Samondel, who attacked you? My people?"

"Many people have suffered through Bartolica's fault, Lordship. Let them go, but grant me one favor."

"Just ask."

"Let Sair Feydamor stay with me for what remains of the banquet."

20 August 3961: Condelor

The sun was above the horizon when Serjon arose and began washing himself at the handbasin. Samondel had already left for the palace wingfield with a note for his guildsmen to prepare Starflower for her use, and as he dried himself he heard the sound of his radial compression engine in the distance. Seyret entered with the clothing and bag from his room, and she reported that Bronlar did not appear to have gone there. Samondel and he had talked about the servant as they lay together. She was in an occupied city, and she was Bartolican.

"How can I repay your kindness?" he asked Seyret. "I have some gold, if that would help," he offered.

"Oh but I have money saved. The lady warden who hit you gave me one silver dori, too."

Serjon ran his fingers through his hair as he considered all this.

"I'm sure I can do better than that, but what would you like most of all, Seyret? Her Ladyship suggested that you might want to go home. She was curiously coy about it."

"Oh yes, I would like to go home," exclaimed Seyret, hugging a stack of clean towels to herself. "I come from Pocatello, but Pocatello is in a new dominion now. If I stay here, well, Sennerese men are horrible, bad for the likes of Seyret. I need border papers to go home, but after the war, well, border papers now cost five times more than all my savings. Papers are hard to get, too, whether one is a noble or commoner."

Her voice had become stiff and controlled, as if she was hiding something. What have they done to you, he wondered as he laced his boots and cast about for the clean shirt that Seyret had brought. He thought again of his mother and sisters, then knew that he could not hate her either. She had warm hands, she was alive.

"Well, I can't get you papers, and few will do Serjon Feydamor any favors, but . . . last night you helped me when I was trailing flames and spinning earthward. Perhaps I can give you something in return. Tell me, have you ever been flying?"

Seyret gasped. "Sair! Flying is for the nobles! I am not a noble. Definitely. I am a baker's daughter."

"Nonsense. Flying is for anyone who is friends with a flyer."

*   *   *

Bronlar was waiting at the pennant pole when Serjon emerged from between two maintenance tents with Seyret. She was speaking with the adjunct, who looked distracted and uncomfortable.

"The mad woman, the mad woman!" squealed Seyret as she caught sight of Bronlar.

Starflower roared overhead as Samondel practiced a roll. Serjon put an arm around Seyret and kept walking until he reached the adjunct and presented his credentials.

"Nice calm day for a flight, Sair Adjunct?" Serjon said cheerily in Yarronese, ignoring Bronlar except for a crisp salute.

"Too true, Sair Feydamor. Wish I was up there, like Her Ladyship."

"Sorry to have missed you last night."

"None's the harm."

"I'm touring the three new Bartolican capitals. This fine lady here is to, shall we say . . . see me off. So to speak."

"What fine lady, Sair?"

Serjon nodded as the adjunct smiled knowingly and stared into the distance.

"I owe you yet another favor, Sair Adjunct."

The adjunct laughed as he handed the dispatches to Serjon. "Just return safe, my friend."

Serjon began to walk to the line of sailwings with Seyret, but Bronlar hurried after him.

"Serjon, it's me. Why don't you speak?" she asked, also in Yarronese.

Serjon stopped dead, turned, and saluted again.

"Warden Jemarial, I'm not your peer. By chivalric law you have a right to beat me if I hail you first, and I'm in no mood or condition to be beaten."

Bronlar spread her hands, and there were tears on her cheeks below the dark circles beneath her eyes.

"Serjon, Serjon, I grant you eternal permission to hail me. You and nobody else beneath my peer level. Should any other flyer, squire, or guildsman hail me I'll flay the skin from them!"

"Warden Jemarial, kindly put that in writing and get it endorsed by a magistrate. Until then I cannot afford to believe you. Now, may I pass?"

"I sat on my gunwing all night," Bronlar said desperately. "A chaplain was good enough to sit within sight, he will testify that no man approached me."

"You don't have to go to those lengths to prove you're saving thirteen for me," said Serjon, rubbing the bruise on his face. "I'm not so desperate."

Bronlar curled over slightly, her stomach again cramping. Her vigil of devotion had become another gibe at Serjon, and she was close to despair.

"Serjon, I apologize, you were right, I admit it."

"I'm always right, people never listen."

"Please, please, please, *listen*! I tried to find you last night, I tried to apologize but you were gone."

"I was at the banquet, one of the Airlords spoke on my behalf and got me admitted. Now can we please get past, Warden Jemarial? I'm on Airlord Sartov's business and you're frightening my little friend here."

Bronlar was in fact smaller than Seyret. She stood before the Bartolican girl and bowed. It was the crisp bow of a warden to a noblewoman. Seyret shrank back behind Serjon, still convinced that Bronlar was mad. The conversation had been in Yarronese until now, and was too fast for her to follow. Now Bronlar spoke in awkward but rehearsed Bartolican.

"Semme Seyret, I do, ah, for frightening, apologize. Grats you for, ah, tending Serjon, for service of. Very dear, to me, he is. Badly hurt, I had him?"

Summoning up all her courage, Seyret managed, "Yes, Warden Jemarial. As a matter of fact he was hurt, and badly."

Bronlar squeezed her eyes shut and more tears trickled down her cheeks as she bowed again.

"Serjon, when you return I shall have the declaration for you, all signed by a magistrate," she said in Yarronese.

"No hurry. I'll be gone ten days at least," he said lightly.

"I'll have done it this morning. I already had a testimony done to Airlord Sartov, about how you gave false testimony to clear my name. Serjon, the truth will be known to all Mounthaven in this very hour, I—"

"You what?" he barked, his words like gunshots.

"I cleared your name."

"You swore as a warden that I lied to the council! That means an automatic charge of perjury, and more. Even if I'm not dragged out and shot I'll be broken so low that I'll not even be allowed onto a wingfield to carry out the nightsoil."

Serjon turned and put his arm around Seyret, saying, "Hurry, we have little time left," in Bartolican as he led her around Bronlar.

"Wait Serjon, I can help with anything!" Bronlar cried as she went after them.

"Warden Jemarial, I would *really* appreciate it if you would help your Cosdoran knobby-boy guildsmen in *exactly* the same way you have helped me," Serjon said as he walked. "It's a terrible thing to wish on them, but I'm feeling vindictive this morning."

Desperate, she slapped her hands against her forehead. "Tell me what to do, anything!"

"Stop walking after me."

Bronlar stopped dead, as if she had come to a stone wall.

Serjon kept walking briskly away with Seyret hurrying along beside him.

"Serjon, I'll make it up to you," Bronlar called after them.

"Go screw your reaction guns," muttered Serjon without turning.

His field guildsmen were waiting beside a sailwing, whose compression engine was already chugging. Serjon signed for the borrowed aircraft.

"I wish to take a passenger," Serjon said as he handed back the clipboard.

"That is not permitted on an airlord's business, Squire Feydamor," his guildmaster warned.

"It is important to this Bartolican girl, very important."

"What girl?" replied the guildmaster, staring straight past Seyret as he handed her his coat.

The sailwing was one of the newer, larger types, and it had no trouble ascending with Seyret's weight and a full load of fuel. Seyret sat in the front seat, squealing whenever the sailwing bounced or tilted in the early morning thermals over the boundary between desert and mountains, and exclaiming with delight at the view.

After an hour Serjon began circling a regional city, and he fired two colored flares as a patrol warden approached to investigate. The Bartolican sailwing displayed unfamiliar colors, but after a brief exchange of wingdip code they began to descend together. The perspective was all muddled for Seyret, who thought they were over another part of Condelor. The wheels squeaked on the flightstrip and Serjon taxied to the couriers' line near the pennant pole. In the distance they could see officials hurrying about and pointing.

"That was magical," Seyret cooed as they came to a stop.

"It's better than servicing other people's compression engines," replied Serjon as he starved the engine of spirit. "Best leave the guildmaster's coat with me."

"But I'd like to thank him."

"I'll pass on your thanks," said Serjon as he slid the canopy forward.

A line of officials and armed guards waited as Serjon helped Seyret out of the sailwing. Seyret realized there was something wrong. This was not Condelor.

"Welcome to Pocatello, sair, uh—" began the adjunct in Bartolican as Serjon walked forward.

Seyret turned with a shriek of joy, dropped the coat, and

flung her arms around Serjon. She was unable to speak or release him as Serjon held a folder out to the adjunct with his free hand.

"This is from the Council of Alliance Airlords, convened in Condelor," he explained. "Please take it to Airlord Designate Mostiron."

"Of course, Warden . . ." He looked at the dispatch note and swallowed. "Feydamor!"

"Just Feydamor. And this girl has a bakery to find. Could I have a diplomatic pass to escort her there?"

"You can have a pass, to be sure, but why would she want to go to a bakery before seeing her family?"

"Please explain," asked Serjon.

"Her grandfather, the Airlord Designate, would be offended if this dispatch arrived before she did. Semme Sey-Rettelliar Mostiron, welcome home to the new dominion of Eastgarde. Squire Feydamor, this is the most noble of gestures by your Alliance Council."

"It's . . . nothing, really," replied Serjon, dumbfounded.

"Come home, meet my family," gasped Seyret between sobs of relief and joy. "You will be welcome."

"Seyret, I'm just a courier."

"Please, you're a hero here, you brought me home, you freed Bartolica from Stanbury and the featherheads: you deserve a welcome and by the Call I'll make sure you get one."

"A hero? I've shot down seventy-four of your wardens, ninety-seven of your wings. They call me Warden Killer. This trip was assigned to me as punishment! Ten days of cold shoulders and isolation, ten days of widows trying to tear my eyes out."

Seyret turned to the adjunct. "Escort us at a distance, there are words we must have on the way to the Governor's palace."

The story was voiced about that Serjon had discovered Seyret's secret by accident, and had immediately arranged to be the flyer on a courier mission that would take him to Pocatello. He had placed himself at risk of very serious charges when he returned, Seyret told her grandfather, but he had done it so that she could be returned to the arms of her fiancé, Warden Prolean.

"You, the greatest air warrior in the history of Mounthaven chivalry, would sacrifice it all for the honor of a girl?" marveled the old man.

"It is the Yarronese way," Serjon replied, thankful that Alion would never hear his words and realizing now what Samondel had been suggesting.

The Airlord Designate of what had been East Region in Bartolica needed several days to assess the dispatch and discuss it with his wardens. Serjon became the toast of the city, and spent his time being feted by the Bartolican wardens, some of whom had even fallen to his reaction guns. He was also given a great deal of attention by the women of the new court. Presently he flew on to Evansburg in the north and Hedria in the west, and wherever he landed his reception was no less enthusiastic.

20 August 3961: Condelor

By special favor of the Cosdoran Airlord, two regals had been made available to fly the guildsmen of Bronlar's ground crew to Condelor. She had made the request herself by courier two days earlier, and the Airlord was inclined to deny her nothing. The regals landed three hours after Serjon and Seyret had left, and the guildsmen tumbled out in high spirits, singing the drinking songs of the Cosdoran highlands and dancing jigs as their travel kits were unloaded and Monterbil played tunes on his flute. Farrasond alone was subdued.

The adjunct appeared in the distance, marching at the head of a squad of Dorakian carbineers. They were smartly turned out in red uniforms with ochre epaulettes on swallow coats cut back at the waist to show off their large brass belt buckles. They carried assault carbines whose wood-work had been inlaid with silver tracery. The squad stopped with the mechanical precision of a powerful machine; then the adjunct strode forward and stopped before Farrasond, who was in his guildmaster's jacket.

"Guildmaster Farrasond of Vernal?" barked the adjunct crisply in Cosdoran.

"Aye, that be me," he drawled, aware that the show of glitter was meant for him and his guildsmen.

"Accept this from the magistrate of Palace Precinct!" the adjunct said crisply, handing over a leather document sheaf.

Farrasond glanced inside, but it was only a translation of the dispatch that the Council of Alliance Airlords had sent to Bronlar, along with some other papers with seals.

"Well, much obliged, but this can wait until we've caught up with Bronlar," said Farrasond.

"Take us to see her, if ye will," said Ryban. "She's anxious to see *one* of us."

The adjunct turned on the spot and marched back the way he had come. The guards fell in behind when he passed them.

"Rude bastards," sneered Monterbil. "Aye, but I saw her marking from the air, I'll take us to her gunwing."

They began to walk, but noticed very quickly that nobody was paying them the slightest attention. Monterbil asked several guildsmen the way to Bronlar's gunwing and tents, but they either ignored them entirely or gave them an odd sign: a thumb crossed over an open palm.

"Feels like I should know that sign," said Farrasond.

Bronlar was sitting on the lower left wing of her triwing gunwing when they finally came upon her amid the maze of little aircraft. She was hunched over, glaring at something in the distance, and did not appear to notice them as they approached.

"Ah, Semme Hero Bronlar, they made us work to find

you," began Monterbil, trotting up to her with his arms extended.

Bronlar slipped from the wing and brought a heavy parade cane around and down in a vicious swipe that slashed across Monterbil's left cheek and laid it open. The force of the blow knocked him to the ground, and she stood over him, slashing at his head and hands.

"Hail a warden, will you?" she screamed. "I'll teach you respect, you guildsman slime!"

Thekam, Lasser, and Rewlon rushed forward and seized Bronlar by the arms, but suddenly carbineers in red and ochre uniforms burst upon the scene and there was a brief, deadly stutter of assault carbines on reaction setting. Thekam, Lasser, and Rewlon fell dead beside Monterbil's cowering form, expertly excised from Bronlar, who remained standing and unhurt.

The other Cosdoran guildsmen stood frozen, scarcely daring to breathe. Bronlar looked down at Monterbil, then gave him one additional slash that pulped his left ear and left him stunned. She looked through the guildsmen as if they did not exist, then hailed the adjunct who had arrived with the Dorakian carbineers.

"A good day to you, Sair Adjunct," she said in a voice that might have scratched piston rings. "Do you have business with me or Warden Ramsdel's guildsmen?"

"I have heard that unaccounted personnel are on the wingfield, Warden Jemarial. I mean to keep them in sight, lest a disturbance take place."

Bronlar was pacing slowly among the guildsmen now. Sweat streamed down Ryban's face as he stood trembling, frantically trying to think of what may have happened to cause such a nightmare, and of why the wingfield adjunct was ignoring their very existence. Bronlar circled Ryban slowly, staring into the distance all the while. She was wearing a new green flight jacket sewn with masses of glittering gold and semiprecious stones. Her collar was encrusted with jade pentagons for each of her victories in the air, and she was wearing a sharp, heady perfume.

Black bars of a girl faithful to her absent lover were
painted on her lips. Which absent lover, wondered Ryban?
Her lips and the veins of her neck were engorged with
blood, and stood out in a way that he found strangely sensual. An erection began pressing against his trousers. Bronlar was lusting . . . for who, for what . . . and she kept
lingering near him. Never having fought in clear air, he
did not know that sexual lust and battle lust were not separated by very much.

"Warden, dearest Bronlar—" he managed.

"Slime does not hail a warden!" she shouted as she
whirled and slashed his face with her cane.

Bronlar laid open Ryban's ear, cheek, and lips; then, as
he raised his hands to his face she swung it up between
his legs. The shock alone made Ryban topple and Bronlar
slashed at his face and hands as he fell then stood beating
him blindly for another half minute. The adjunct came forward holding a cloth that smelled of compression spirit.

Bronlar wiped her hands and cane in the towel, then
thanked the adjunct and returned to her gunwing and sat
on the lower port wing. The adjunct remained, watching
with his squad of carbineers, who were standing alert. The
safety catches of their assault carbines were off and the
sliders set to reaction. Farrasond slowly put his hand into
his coat, aware that several assault carbines were probably
trained on his head. Even more slowly he withdrew the
folder that the adjunct had given him a few minutes ago,
before the very world itself had been transformed into the
depths of hell. The other Cosdoran guildsmen stood pet-
rified while he read. Quite a large crowd of guildsmen,
wardens, carbineers, medics, and nurses had gathered by
now. Even the wingfield chaplains of several denomina-
tions were watching from a distance.

"Sair Ryban, these are translations of the dispatch that
you translated for Warden Jemarial back in Cosdora," Farrasond said in a cold, level voice. "They have been signed,

dated, and timed as of late last night by the scribe and countersigned by a magistrate. The dispatch has been translated into Yarronese, Cosdoran, Montrasic, Dorakish, and Sennerese. There is also a sworn statement from the Council of Alliance Airlords' office that these faithfully match and reflect the official records. There is not a word missing—or misplaced."

Farrasond continued to read in silence. The adjunct snapped his fingers and the bodies of Thekam, Lasser, and Rewlon were dragged away to a waiting nightsoil cart. The carter made a show of putting on his gloves before heaving them up; then he pushed the cart downwind of Bronlar and out of sight.

"Warden Jemarial," said the adjunct, "may I speak as a peer about Air Carbineer First Class and hero of ninety-seven victories in clear air war duels, Flyer Serjon Feydamor?"

"You may, Sair Adjunct. Even the sound of his name cheers me."

"I saw that you spoke with him before he ascended this morning. Was it a cordial parting?"

"No, Sair Adjunct. He took my most desperate attempt at apology very badly."

"I am sorry to hear that."

"But I have something of him, the original of his apology to me, penned by his own hand. It is the only thing left to me of my darling, lost Serjon, so I wear it cupped around my left breast, close to my heart. It caresses my skin every hour, minute, and second of the day."

The sheer horror of Bronlar's sudden and devastatingly unqualified worship of Serjon was too much for Ryban. His bowels failed him and he fouled himself noisily. Farrasond suddenly snapped out of the trance in which he had been reading the translated dispatch, and he flung himself on Ryban, seizing him by the hair.

"Pick up that dispatch and read it!" he shrieked as he

smashed Ryban's face into the wingfield surface over and over. "Read it! Read it aloud! Read it!"

Ryban's hands were trembling so badly from Bronlar's beating that it was some moments before he could unfold the papers and find the Cosdoran translation. He began to read through broken teeth, word for word. He got through the preliminaries slowly, knowing and dreading what was to come. A tiny detail loomed ahead like a mountain, a detail that detracted from Serjon's undoubted guilt. It was an inconvenient detail that he had bent aside four days earlier.

" *'Serjon Feydamor changed his testimony to exonerate you by mentioning details that he had not included in the previous testimony. Later that day the body of the tail gunner was exhumed and a bullet was recovered—'* "

"*Later that day?*" bellowed Farrasond. "You never read those words to Warden Jemarial! Monterbil told me so too, *and* the adjunct of Vernal." He smashed Ryban's face into the ground again. "You didn't even read the sentences in that order!"

"The, the light was b-bad," said Ryban. "In jubilation . . . must have misarranged the, the sense, the g-grammar. An honest mistake, I swear."

"You read it to us *five times* that night!" Monterbil reminded him from where he lay. "You wanted to get her spirits soaring so that she would land in your bed again."

Farrasond took two cod-buttons from the folder and held them up.

"You failed her, just as surely as if you ignored a bent valve or a clogged filter. You warped the translation. The rest of you were *stupid* enough not to check his work. As a result Warden Jemarial's heart fell out of the sky and crashed to its death! Listen, all of you. The adjunct's folder also contained the severance certificates of our articles of service, and there is a nullity endorsement from the Airlord of Cosdora. We do not exist! We are legally dead. Anyone can shoot us down who feels inclined to waste a bullet."

Farrasond stood up, walked over to Monterbil, and kicked him in the ribs.

"Get up," he ordered. "Stand with the others."

The guildsmen moved slowly, aware that the guns of the carbineers were tracking their every move. He pointed to Ryban.

"Seize him," Farrasond ordered, tossing the two brass buttons into the air and catching them.

The guildsmen fell upon Ryban, and the shrieking went on for a very long time. Monterbil and Farrasond were later killed by demobilized carbineers while the guildsmen were fleeing through Condelor, but the remaining three escaped into the countryside and east into the mountains. They were never heard of again.

Half an hour later Samondel returned with Serjon's gunwing, to get compression spirit for another ascent. She noticed odd scraps of bloody meat on the ground near Serjon's area and decided to complain.

"They attract birds, and birds mean birdstrike," Samondel said huffily to a wingfield directant, remembering a passage from some book of wingfield procedures.

"No bird would bother, Ladyship," replied the directant, "but I shall have them cleaned up."

Suddenly Samondel gasped with shock and danced sideways. Serjon's guildsmen were servicing Princess prior to bringing it back into operational service, but lying beside one wheel was a severed human head. The nostrils were sealed with two brass buttons, the lips had been sewn shut, and the cheeks bulged ominously.

"That—" began Samondel, pointing with one hand while the other covered her mouth. "What—I mean, who?"

"He learned by experience that while heroes are only human, they are very dangerous and not to be toyed with, Ladyship. Experience is a costly school, but there are always fools willing to pay the fee."

*　　*　　*

Ten days after leaving Condelor, Serjon was back at Pocatello to receive a dispatch containing the joint response
of the three Bartolican rulers. Seyret met him at the wingfield as his sailwing was being refueled.

"If things do not prosper for you in Yarron, the new
dominions will always welcome you," she assured him.

"I did not get ninety-seven clear air victories by running
away," Serjon said, his manner more alive than it had been
before. "Just in case I never return here, however, may I
say that you were a quite exquisite hostess, Seyret."

"If all goes well, promise to return."

"I do promise."

He turned to check if the fuelers' guild was done with
his sailwing. Seyret took him by the arm after glancing
about to see that they were still out of anyone's earshot.

"Bronlar came here three days ago, we had a long talk."

Serjon swallowed, and was dismayed to feel his warm
glow of well-being chilling beneath a crust of ice.

"Was she . . . civilized?"

"She explained everything: every lie, misunderstanding,
accident, betrayal, and plot. She needed to talk to someone,
Serjon, to have someone understand. I heard about every
lie she was told, every grunt and thrust her guildsmen
gave, and everything else she has done since the night of
the banquet in Condelor's palace. She has made it up to
you, Serjon, I believe that and you should too."

He looked to his sailwing again. A fueler was standing
with a completion flag while other guildsmen were wheeling a steam trolley over to start the compression engine.

"So what now? Will you hate me too if I don't love
her?"

"Serjon, you could go over to the pennant pole and piss
on my fiancé's boot and I'd still love you. All I ask is that
you soften a little for Bronlar, and I ask that as your
friend."

Serjon went down on one knee and kissed her hand, then
returned to his sailwing. Seyret's fiancé now joined her

and they stood together watching him taxi away to the flightstrip.

"Did he listen?" asked the young warden.

"He listened," replied Seyret, "but he may not have heard."

THE DOOMSDAY FLOCK

30 August 3961: Condelor

Serjon landed at the Condelor palace wingfield in brilliant sunshine and taxied to the crowded marshaling area. The adjunct was waiting, along with his field guildsmen. Off to the north Samondel was putting Starflower through spin recoveries in the blue sky. Serjon presented the dispatches from the north and was in turn presented with a folded, sealed sheet of paper.

"This is a summons to appear before the council of Alliance Airlords on six charges, most seriously that of perjury," the adjunct said, his face a mask.

"Perjury?" asked Serjon, even though he knew the answer.

"Perjury in your testimony in favor of Warden Jemarial."

"I see," replied Serjon calmly. "All right, then, I know the way."

Bronlar was waiting close by, and came running over as soon as the adjunct had signed for the courier bag. Her face, her voice, her every gesture was a picture of relief and happiness.

"Serjon, Serjon, I have the magistrate's declaration!" she cried.

"Now what?" he asked with a glance to the clouds.

"I declared you a peer, free to hail me," she replied, sounding hurt that he had not remembered or even put a hand out to her.

"Ah, yes. Well that assumes that I *want* to hail you. Now then, the council of Alliance Airlords has some stern words for me, so I must be off."

"Serjon, I flew to Denver and brought Lombrosh, the famous advocate, back with me. He's been working on the charges against you as your white advocate. He had two withdrawn and reduced another three to fines—which I paid. They were five thousand gold circars, but I paid."

Serjon stopped, genuinely surprised for once. "Is this another trick?"

"No, no, Lombrosh is over there with all the papers and briefs. You only have to answer perjury, and he has some powerful cases in precedent that could reduce the mandatory sentence to another fine and loss of rank. The nightmare is over, I promise."

Although ruthless in clear air combat, Serjon was not a vindictive man. Being a somewhat kindly romantic besides, he was unable to sustain his already waning bitterness.

"It's good to have you back, Little Sister, but the nightmare's still alive and flying," he warned. "Come now, introduce me to your advocate."

They began walking, Bronlar clutching the embroidered fabric of his sleeve tightly.

"Have you passed thirteen onto some poor yoick as yet?" he asked.

"I've vowed to let nobody but you touch me, ever again."

"So you won't lift your thirteen curse?"

"Serjon, I *can't*! But nobody else will ever touch me.

Ever. Once I feared the lonely blackness of my bed, now it is a blessed refuge and fortress."

The sharp-witted, bearded advocate from Denver briefed Serjon to plead not guilty and to cite a defense of a chivalric conspiracy, which apparently had a precedent going back to a case two centuries earlier. Guildsmen stood to rigid attention as the three of them passed, and a sphere of silence seemed to travel along with them.

Within half an hour Serjon was standing before the five airlords who were currently in the palace, with a packed gallery of onlookers behind him.

"You have heard the charge, brought by Airlord Sartov after being given testimony by Warden Bronlar Jemarial," said Proclaimant Virtrian. "How do you plead?"

"Guilty, as charged."

The white advocate from Denver dropped to his seat with his head in his hands and Bronlar squeezed her eyes shut. There was a flurry of hushed whispers from the gallery, and the red advocate returned to his seat.

"In that case, there is nothing else to do but pronounce sentence," Virtrian declared. "Free Flyer Serjon Feydamor, you are guilty of perjury before the council of Alliance Airlords, albeit in extenuating circumstances. In reparation you are to be discharged from the courier duties in the Airlord's Gunwings, and will forfeit all reparations from the estate of former Warden, the late Alion Damaric. Do you accept the sentence without question?"

Serjon shrugged. "Yes, I do accept it."

"In that case, the sentence is pronounced," Virtrian declared.

Virtrian sat down, nodding to Sartov. Sartov rose to his feet, holding papers with the crest of the new dominion of Eastgarde. He shook out his robes before speaking.

"Sair Feydamor, speaking as your Airlord, if I find you hauled up before me one more time on any matter regarding love, hate, honor, betrayal, your lovers' good or bad names, or amorous hanky panky in general I swear I'll send you to a chain gang in the Red Desert and you'll stay there long enough to grow a beard down to your knees.

"Moving on to more important matters, I have a request from the Airlord Designate of Eastgarde before me. He requests that you be made the new Warden Liaisory between Yarron and Eastgarde, Highland Bartolica, and the other new dominions. His request is rather emphatic. Are you willing to accept this position?"

"Lordship, to be Warden Liaisory one has to be a warden," said Serjon, his composure suddenly shaken.

"You have been discharged from my personal service, nothing more. As you are the son-expedient of the late Warden Remat Jannian, whose other sons are dead, you can inherit the title at my discretion and I *really do want Eastgarde's goodwill*! What say you?"

"Accepted, Lordship," replied Serjon after hurriedly deciding that there was no alternative.

"Will you take the name Jannian?"

"Feydamor, Lordship, if you please."

"Your choice, Warden Feydamor."

"May I keep my Air Carbineer gunwing and field guildsmen until I can find a sponsor?"

"Why do you want a sponsor?" asked Sartov as he shuffled the papers he held. "The moment that you became a warden you were awarded *nine hundred thousand* gold circars in war duel reparations from wardenly families in Eastgarde, and further sums will be forthcoming from the other new dominions. You shot seventy-four wardens out of the sky, Warden Serjon Feydamor. The cost of your gunwing has been deducted already, and I have the invoice here. Your guildsmen volunteered to work for you for free but I suggest that you pay them, now that you are richer than any other Yarronese—myself included."

Ramsdel took Serjon aside while the council was making a number of other pronouncements.

"What did I miss while I was away?" Serjon asked.

"Have you heard nothing?"

"Only that Bronlar got me an expensive advocate who had some of the less serious charges dropped. Oh, and that she swore that nobody else will ever raise her coattails and lower her drawers but me—which is unlikely because, ah . . ."

"I know about the thirteen business. Did you know that she's barely sane?"

"What? But I've spoken with her. She seemed distraught but coherent."

"Her guildsmen were flown in from Cosdora, a special boon by the Cosdoran Airlord. She beat two of them to a pulp for daring to say hullo first—including the chubby one who had deflowered her and lied about the trial. Three more were shot by wingfield carbineers for trying to hold her back. The other Cosdoran guildsmen laid hold of the chubby one, jammed two brass cod buttons up his nose then stuffed his mouth with his own—well, he choked to death, then they—brrr, you don't want to know. The rest were endorsed as nullity, declared *ney vitiar mondinil*: the walking dead. Two were shot dead on the outskirts of Condelor, the other three may have reached the mountains."

Serjon folded his hands and thought for a time.

"None of that is beyond the law, strictly speaking. Wardens can beat any guildsman for negligence, undue familiarity, or insolence. I'd certainly class tricking her into jiggery as undue familiarity."

"It's far, far worse. Just . . . just wait, and watch. I need to find a very brave friend."

Bronlar stood before the council soon after that, and stated that she had been disgracefully negligent in the discipline of her guild crew. This had led her to make an unlawful assault on Warden Liaisory Serjon Feydamor. Virtrian fined her one gold circar and told her to take all such cases to the Yarronese civil magistrates in future. She returned to stand near where Serjon was sitting, obviously wanting to leave with him when the council rose. An ashen-faced guildsman from Ramsdel's crew shuffled forward and inclined his head to speak. Serjon was close enough to hear his whisper.

"That was a brave thing to do, Warden Jem—"

Bronlar screamed with rage, seized the guildsman, and whirled him around, slamming him against the advocate's dock. She punched him twice in the face before he went down, and had seized the council's winged mace to strike him before Serjon managed to tackle her and pin her arms.

"Let go! He hailed me!" Bronlar shouted hysterically as Serjon dragged her back. "That guildsman filth hailed me, I demand reparation in the letter of chivalric law!"

"Strictly speaking, the law is with her," said Serjon as he and Ramsdel sat in the Flying Swinelet nursing untouched goblets of wine.

"She thrashed eleven guildsmen thus before the word spread," Ramsdel explained. "Today is twelve."

"Of course I'll pay your fine and compensate your guildsman. That was a brave, loyal thing for him to do."

"Pah, he agreed that you needed to see her at her worst. He's all right. Only some bruising and loose teeth."

"Don't the Airlords frown upon this? Why, they just sat there while she was beating him."

Ramsdel explained how the airlords were trying to restore some of the credibility of chivalric law, which had been weakened seriously in the war between Bartolica and Yarron. They could not censure Bronlar without bringing in reforms, and in a way she served to show the citizens of Mounthaven how lenient their wardens really were in practice but how powerful in principle. The air and ground carbineers had done their work, and now they were expected to accept the leash again. Making Serjon a warden was part of the same conspiracy. He was a hero, therefore he had to be a noble.

That evening Serjon and Ramsdel assembled a field ground crew for Bronlar, after asking her to promise to merely report lapses by the guildsmen rather than thrashing them instantly. He also gave Starflower to Samondel, and bought Princess for himself. What with all that had happened, he did not want her to be in Alion's former gunwing. After dinner at one of the serveries near the palace Serjon and Bronlar strolled the gardens by a canal as the sky darkened and Mirrorsun rose. Bronlar clung to Serjon's sleeve all the time, and when they were far from the nearest strollers she shyly drew out a small pubic comb of jade inlaid with gold. The inlay spelled Serjon's name.

"When in Bartolica, do as Bartolicans," she suggested as she offered him the love comb.

"You know I can't accept this," said Serjon gently.

"Yes. I just want you to know it is here," replied Bronlar without rancor. "Did you collect many on your tour?"

"I was offered thirty."

"And you bedded them all?"

"What I did or did not do is between me and my conscience. I will admit that sex is wonderful, though. I know it now."

"With you, perhaps."

"I did ask you first, Bronlar. Last October—but not as nicely as Matthew Ryban, it seems."

"Will nothing I do scour that turd's stink away?"

"You raised the subject, Little Sister, and I'll not take all the blame myself." Bronlar began to sniffle, and he hastily put an arm around her. "Was it so very bad?"

"It was the day I got my medal, my daystar. The little turd kept slithering about me saying wise and knowing nothings, and showing concern. It was so fast, he was so anxious to get it all in and shooting—and it hurt, it really did! There was another guildsman besides, yet another who seduced by being pathetic. So much guilt, hate, death and mess, I wonder why we bother living sometimes. Call's touch, how I hate pathetic men. The very sight of seeing one cringe and simper makes me want to take out my cane and beat and beat—"

"Shush, don't think upon it."

"I'm sorry I made you bleed over Samondel, I seem to spoil—"

Serjon exclaimed and bounced up from the stone seat. He backed away until he stopped against a columned stone rail, then eased himself up to sit with his arms folded, looking at the glinting brass caps on the toes of Bronlar's boots.

"What did Seyret tell you?" he asked in the weak voice of a condemned prisoner before a magistrate.

"Your nose began bleeding in bed, and it was all in Samondel's hair before you realized. You spent a half hour trying to stop the bleeding, while Samondel washed her hair and Seyret was called in to change the bed linen. By then it was after midnight. You said you had better lie underneath in case your nose bled again—"

"That's enough!" exclaimed Serjon, his hands to his ears. "She should be a sailwing war scout if she can report with that sort of detail and accuracy."

"From what she told me, you were very well—"

"I said enough! Please! Hell's Call, I should be in a merchant's catalogue: semi-automatic, ideal for extreme conditions, does not jam when damaged, fast reload, low maintenance, can be adjusted to suit any user—"

He stopped when he realized that Bronlar was laughing. He had not seen her laugh since . . . he could not remember. For a time he sat with his elbows on his knees and his chin on his fists, keeping a studiously glum expression on his face.

"Did it hurt you too, the first time?" she asked.

"This is positively the last question on all this. No, it doesn't hurt boys."

Bronlar rose, squeezed his hand, and leaned her head against his.

"Virgins and rakes are a bore, I've had both, so I ought to know," she admitted. "What do you think?"

"I said last question, and I meant it," he replied, all the

while wondering what she found so boring about virgins.

"On the night of the banquet I found a magistrate, canceled my guildsmen's articles, and posted proclamations of status and cause before the clock struck eleven. Now I know I had some hours free of them before you lay with someone else. That's important."

"Why?" he asked, not daring to tell her the truth about what had been done, and when.

"Because I changed the past a little, I cheated fate just a tiny bit by . . . by really hurting and humiliating someone who had hurt you. Now all that I want is you back. If I die for you will that be enough?"

"You'd hardly be good company in bed, Bronlar. You'd be cold and stiff, and you'd smell."

"But would that purge my thirteen?"

"Little Sister, if you died for me yet remained living, yes—but only then."

He returned to the stone bench and watched Mirrorsun rise between the spires of the palace. Bronlar was frowning with thought while Serjon counted the thirteen surviving spires. A bell began to toll in the distance.

"A Call," Serjon said. "It's probably stopped for the evening, and just outside the city."

"If you were falling without a parachute and I flew past without a parachute, I could jump and cling to you for a minute or so. I could give my life for you, we would be dead yet still alive."

"Yes . . . but in the circumstances, I'd probably not get it up."

"But if that is good enough, then there must be other ways."

"If you're thinking of getting yourself declared *ney vitiar mondinil* then forget it. That's a death sentence, not death itself. Are you sleeping at the palace?"

"Yes. I refuse to be near guildsmen, especially at night. I have a large room with a double bed. I'm fond of luxury, now, it's beyond the reach of commoner guildsmen. East

Southern, Third Floor, Suite Seven. There's a glorious
view of sunrise over the mountains. Knock twice three if
you—"

"I'll take your word for it."

"I—I'll avoid your room, Serjon. I'd not want you embarrassed, if . . . you know. Samondel. I've told nobody
that you sleep with her."

"Grats. Her position is delicate."

"If you please, though, I've had an uncomfortable ten
days wearing your apology."

She took his hand and guided it beneath her coat, shirt,
and singlet to her left breast. Serjon caressed the soft skin
for a moment, then drew out the paper between his fingers.
With hardly a glance he folded it and slipped it into her
jacket pocket.

They kissed each other's cheeks in the cold light of Mirrorsun, then walked shivering to the palace with their arms
linked. At the hostelry wing's door they kissed goodnight
again while the Dorakian and Montrassian guards stared
ahead into the darkness and scarcely dared to breathe.
When they had gone their separate ways, the guards turned
to each other.

"That her? Mad devil warden?" asked the Montrassian.

"Devil warden, yes," replied the Dorakian. "You say
nice day, *hullo*, *look good*: she beat you to jerky."

"Then who is boy? Airlord or brave idiot?"

"Serjon Warden Killer."

"Ah, Warden Killer. Explains all."

Later that night Serjon lay half smothered in Samondel's
hair. Both of them were sleepily contented and discussing
the traumas and triumphs of the day past.

"So you have a truce with Warden Jemarial?" Samondel
asked.

"So it seems. She is in a mess, but I am trying to help."

"I was a mess, and you helped me. Nobody else would
have, nobody but one as . . . interesting as you."

Samondel's flying had improved dramatically, and she

could now shoot up target kites over the Salt Lake. The scattered remnants of Bartolican flocks were rallying around her as they returned from Yarron, and she had even persuaded Sartov to let some of them keep their gunwings.

"How would your wardens take to us . . . being thus?" he asked.

"Badly, but it is not their business."

"You are their airlord, so it *is* their business. We had best keep our voices down."

The airlords had repaired to their inner chambers once Serjon's hearing was over. They examined the responses that he had brought back, and they were all in broad agreement.

"Unanimous," Sartov declared as the papers were passed around. "The new airlords of Eastgarde, Northreach, and Middle Bartolica will be here by this afternoon. Airlord Samondel will attend too."

"They cannot be part of this council," warned the Airlord of Senner.

"Of course not. That is why we have to make our decision now, before they arrive. Have you read my briefing folders?"

The Airlord of Dorak opened his leather and gilt folder and held up one of the sheets.

"You claim that there are four hundred wings hidden in the Callscour lands by these featherheads that we keep finding everywhere."

"Between three hundred and five hundred, I cannot be sure. It is hard to distinguish between real losses and theft. I have been able to gather in scattered reports from eastern Yarron and the records of the Bartolican occupiers, but it all turns out the same. Gunwings and sailwings have been heading east out over the Callscour frontier and not returning. The headings converge on a circle twenty miles across, and my Skyfire flyers have found a refueling wingfield at the Alliance ruin. The storage wingfield lies far beyond."

"It makes sense," added the Airlord of Cosdora. "In spite of their losses and the number of wings they captured, they always had flyers in abundance."

"There is a related matter that I am concerned about, too," said Sartov, unrolling a large map. "The late envoy from Veraguay showed me the plans of a grand scheme when I was stationed here last year. It was a system of tramways running from Veraguay to Calgary. Our isolation would end, our gunwing skills would leak out and we would be just a gaggle of poor dominions in these cold, arid mountains. I always opposed that link to Alberhaven, and now I want work on it stopped."

"But the southern dominions are hundreds of years behind us in weapons skills, and they have no gunwings," the Cosdoran Airlord protested.

"The southern dominions have immense populations and resources, they could easily dominate us. The featherheads now have hundreds of gunwings and sailwings in the Callscour lands. Worse still, they abducted dozens of our best artisans, while trying to make it look as if they were slaughtered with their families. My thought is that somewhere in Hildago there are estates where Yarronese guildsmen are teaching the skills of making airframes, compression engines, and reaction guns. They may think that they are the Yarronese exiled resistance, and how are they to know otherwise?"

"Impossible!" exclaimed the Airlord of Dorak. "Guildsmen are bound by oaths as sacred as our belief in chivalric war."

"Those beliefs were shaken by the Bartolican invasion of Yarron. The danger is real, my peers. Our only hope is an armada of gunwings, sailwings, and regals that can shatter their stockpile before Hildago flyers can be trained. Otherwise they will fly over the southern desert, smash the local wardens aside, and establish a bridgehead. The tramway over the Callscour lands will supply them better than us, and Hildago carbineers will pour in."

"Pah, such a tramway is too thin a line for supplies," scoffed the Dorak Airlord.

"The deserts are stable, and very kind to tramways," Sartov countered.

"And they may have started already," exclaimed the Cosdoran Airlord, thumping the arm of his chair.

"Precisely."

"But this circle is at double the return range of our gun-wings," the Cosdoran pointed out.

"That can be accommodated. After a year of flying great distances under great duress, we Yarronese can teach you much about using four hundred wings to double the range of another two hundred. What is most important is that we act within two weeks at most."

"Two weeks—ah yes, the weather will close in after that," said the Cosdoran.

"Quite so. Now, can we have a vote?"

The vote was unanimous, and later that day the three Bartolican Airlords joined the alliance. As a cover for the operation, an immense victory festival was proclaimed at Forian and voiced about as the greatest gathering of wings and wardens in history. Even neutral airlords were briefed about the real agenda, however, and they began to prepare their best wings.

"Well, here we are again," said Sartov as he grasped wrists with Vander in his rooms after the council meeting.

"Who could believe what fifteen months can do," said Vander.

They sat down facing each other over a low table, but did not touch the drinks that had been set out for them.

"Of all Bartolicans to find in the resistance I least ex-pected the Inspector General," Sartov said, his voice slur-ring with fatigue now that he was relaxing in trusted company. "But of all Bartolicans to find in the resistance, I most expected Vander Hannan."

"Was it as bad as the rumors we heard?"

"Worse. On several wardenate estates the guildmasters were taken away on a tram, then everyone remaining was murdered. Some of the women were kept alive for a time, and of those a handful escaped—and I do mean a handful. Five out of three thousand. They wanted the wings, supplies, and guildmasters, nothing more. All who might have slowed them down or harassed them were killed. Seventy-eight thousand other Yarronese died, a third of them in battle, the rest of starvation, exposure, disease, or vandalized Call facilities."

"Why did they do it? Just to steal flight skills?"

"Yes, and to arm Mexhaven against us. Mexhaven has resources and sheer numbers of people that we can only dream about, and they can easily control Mexhaven's courts. Arm Mexhaven with gunwings and Mounthaven becomes a gaggle of poor client dominions."

A Yarronese carbineer announced that Theresla had arrived, and she was shown in at once. She was carrying a heavy arrow of metal, about two yards long and as thick as her arm. It was painted black, except for the edges of the thick barb, which gleamed bright with honing. Hanging from her shoulder was an artists' portfolio which bulged with papers that had hastily been stuffed into it.

"This is the Miocene Arrow behind Operation Miocene Arrow," she said as she set the missile down on the low table.

Sartov picked it up and examined it with the eyes of experience. The barb at the head was sharp enough to shave with, while metal fins framed a rocket nozzle at the tail. Noting a seam, at the base of the barb, he unscrewed it and found a short fuse. It was clearly not meant to kill people. A gunwing would be a more likely target, but why have a sharpened barb? A tram rocket? Again, why the sharpened barb just to punch through wood? The blade implied a living target to slice through, but such a creature would have to be as big as a tram. No such creature had existed since the Call had wiped out elephants.

"I found this in a palace workshop leased to the Guild of Armorers," said Theresla. "Searching this place is a lot easier now that I no longer have to stay out of sight, and have the authority to chop through locked doors. There are several hundred of these, all packaged up and marked for shipment to Forian Central wingfield. From the guild numbers I would say that five boxes of twelve were sent before the Red Desert tramway was cut, but they are easy to make."

"They do not look to be practical as weapons," Sartov concluded and handed the pieces to Vander.

"I think I know," he said, barely glancing at them before replacing them on the table.

Theresla set her portfolio on the floor and opened it. There were diagrams for the black arrows marked GRE-NADE ROCKET, and launching rails designed to fit beneath wings. Other papers had sketches of fish between four and ten times the length of human-scale figures, but it was a sheaf of pages that Theresla extracted and handed over to Sartov.

"This is a copy of an ancient document," she explained. "The original was in Archaic Anglian, but Darien has rendered this version into Old Anglian."

The first page bore only the words "The Chronicle of James Brennan." Sartov riffled through the other pages.

"This will take an hour, and I don't have an hour," said Sartov. "Ten minutes is all I could spare to meet with Sair Vander, and that's almost gone. I'm so busy in Condelor that I get four hours of sleep a night, and even have a clerk taking down dictation as I stand having a piss."

"This concerns a Callwalker plan to kill every human in both North and South America," said Theresla, twirling a lock of bushy hair around her finger.

"Explain," prompted Sartov when she did not elaborate.

"Read," prompted Theresla, indicating the sheaf of paper with her little finger.

"I think I know what she means, Alveris," Vander said

to Sartov, holding his forehead in his hand and rocking back and forth. "With enough of those grenade harpoons they could kill many Callers of the Call, provoking them to extend the Callscour lands over Mounthaven, Mexhaven, and Alberhaven. The Call can be varied, make no mistake. Politics, resources, even compassion for us by reformer Callers is what keeps these Callhavens preserved. With the Callhavens smothered in permanent Call as well the Callwalkers could then take possession of our entire civilization by doing nothing more than walking in and sitting down."

"He has read this chronicle, so he understands," said Theresla. "Can you spend an hour to save the fifteen million souls of Mounthaven?"

Sartov made as if to reply, then turned to the first page of the chronicle. He began to read, scanning the words and turning the pages quickly; then he stopped and looked up at Vander.

"This is hard to follow," he protested.

"That is because it is real. There is a glossary attached."

Sartov turned back to the first page and began to read more slowly.

At the end of an hour Sartov understood that the Call came from several species of immense, seagoing mammals that had once been hunted by humans. In Greatwinter times grenade harpoons attached to ropes had been used to kill them and reel them in, but the thing on the table was merely meant to kill. It would be fired from gunwings over water when the massive creatures surfaced for air, and would sink deep into their flesh and explode. After a few thousand had died it would seem to the cetezoids that the humans were killing them to destroy the Call, and they would strike back. Theresla began to fill in some gaps in the story.

"Mountains are difficult to sustain a continuous Call over—especially the Callscour type of Call that is almost continuous. The Call sweeps are thought to keep humans in their place and sufficiently disrupted to be harmless, but give the cetezoids and their servant species enough incentive and they can do anything. They take to murder of their own kind about as well as a Yarronese airlord."

"How do you know this?" asked Sartov, riffling through the pages he had just read.

"I have lived for years at the sea's edge, I am a Callwalker, after all. The language of the cetezoids and their client species is not a real language, it is a sharing of concepts, feelings, and images. One has to be in the water to do it, and to be proof against the Call."

"Answer me this. You say Australica is one immense Callhaven, with only a band of Callscour land at the rim. Why is it worse on the American continents?"

"Politics and fear. The cetezoids have developed twenty-eight major political groupings over the past two centuries. As well, the ancient dominion of the United States was the most powerful and advanced of the human states, and so the cetezoids hit it a lot harder than minor dominions like Australica."

"Nothing is free in this world," Sartov said as he picked up the harpoon rocket and examined it again. "What do you want?"

Theresla began to pack up her papers and sketches. "I have a proposal for the council of Alliance Airlords, but I shall need a super-regal for a very long journey."

Sartov now looked to Vander. "Sorry, old friend, but you are not an airlord. Can you wait outside?"

Vander went outside and sat down in one of the Bartolican armchairs. The chair was designed to be sprawled in rather than sat upon, and Vander was too tense to sprawl. He stood up again and paced before the door, watched by the two Yarronese guards. Suddenly there were raised voices behind the varnished pine paneling, then angry shouting. Sartov flung the door open, reaction pistol in hand, and called the guards in. When Vander finally got a clear view of the room's interior he could see Theresla gagged and being bound as she lay on the floor. The Callwalker was not struggling.

"She went too far!" declared Sartov as he stood at the door, his face almost purple with fury. He turned back to the guards. "Tell the warders of the palace dungeons that her gag must stay on at all times. She can live on soup sucked through a straw."

Sartov stayed until the guards had bound Theresla, then followed as they carried her away. Vander walked with him.

"I'd kill her, but she knows how to repair the sunw—a very advanced artifact that I have at Wind River."

"But what did she say?"

"What she said about the cetezoids may be true or may be exhaust, it doesn't matter," said Sartov as they walked the polished stone floor and thick carpets to the stairs. "If we destroy the featherhead wingbases and their stolen wings we thwart their Operation Miocene Arrow. If the Airlords think that they are merely keeping the wings out of the hands of Mexhaven nobles and their peons, they will fight just as hard for us. Let it go at that."

"But what did she say?" demanded Vander again.

Sartov stopped and rounded on him, his reaction pistol raised but pointed to one side. The guards carrying Theresla stopped too, but he told them to take her down to the dungeons and have her put in a muffled isolation cell. He stood in silence with Vander as they left, then slowly turned back for his rooms.

"She proposed the end of all that you and I stand for!" he explained to Vander. "Yarron just lost seventy-eight thousand lives in the struggle to remain Yarronese and free, and I am not about to let those lives be wasted. If you knew, I would . . . no, I would probably not shoot you, but as sure as the Pope of Mexhaven is a Catholic you would join her in that cell. Now leave! Go to your house,

I'll come around and apologize when I am fit company again. Go!"

Alone again, Sartov called for a clerk, then sat at a bureau and scratched out a death warrant for Theresla. He sealed it with his ring when the clerk had poured out a puddle of hot wax.

"Call me a coward, Vander, but I couldn't let you know that I gave such an order," Sartov said as he twirled the propellor of a model gunwing of solid gold mounted above the bureau.

The new Yarronese supervisor of the Condelor palace dungeons read Sartov's instructions a second time before calling five carbineers down from the old guardroom. He set them to work prising up a dozen flagstones, then digging a shallow grave.

"Not you, Horrey," he said, taking one of them aside and handing him a drawstring hood and a key. "Put that on the woman in Isolation Six, and make sure there's a bullet hole in it when you carry her out."

Horrey put the hood under his arm and checked the revolver at his waist. "The grave will take another half hour to dig," he mentioned, letting the implication float on the air.

"Do as you will, just leave the gag on."

Horrey clattered down the steps to the isolation cells and drew open the outer door to that marked with a 6. A lantern burned in the short passage beyond. He closed the outer door. These cells were for political prisoners who might shout truths that even guards could not be allowed to hear without joining them, but the woman Theresla was gagged and bound hand and foot so it hardly mattered. He frowned at the thought of the bindings as he lifted the lantern from its peg, then decided that he could bend her over the stone bunk rather than untying her legs. Horrey drew the inner door's shutter aside and peered through the bars. The woman was bound and gagged, but lying stark naked on the bunk!

"Aht, but those buggers who brought her in here were quick," he muttered as he unlocked the inner door.

Warily pushing the door open he glanced about the tiny cell. In one corner was piled the woman's clothing, while she lay naked and gleaming in the lantern's light on the bunk, regarding Horrey with wary, frightened eyes.

"Well now, would you be cold?" he said as he set the lantern down and bent over her. "You're going to be colder when I carry you out of here, but first—"

The pile of clothing on the floor lashed out with a pair of bound legs, kicking Horrey in the backside with great force. He pitched forward, striking his head on the stone wall and slumping through the image on the bunk and onto the floor where he lay still. The clothing lost a dark fuzziness to reveal the fully clothed but still bound and gagged Theresla snaking backward over the floor to Horrey. She scrabbled blindly with her fingers until his knife came free, then jammed it into the join between two flagstones and began rubbing her bonds against the edge.

The ropes and gag binding the image on the bunk dissolved; then Theresla's face transmuted into Glasken's.

"You know, I've always like getting my hands on women, but this is a bit extreme," he said as he experimentally fondled a breast.

Theresla freed her hands then unbound her ankles before undoing the gag. She quickly went through Horrey's pockets and found both drawstring hood and death warrant. She examined his head.

"Depressed fracture of the skull," she concluded as she began pulling off his clothes. "Get a good look at his face, Glasso, my life depends on it."

"May I point out that he is about two inches taller than you?" said the image on the bunk as Glasken's face grew a handlebar mustache and became Horrey's.

"And may I point out that you fabricated the image of

a body about thirty pounds heavier than mine!" snarled Theresla as she drew the hood over Horrey's head. "I was simply mortified!"

She rolled Horrey's body on its back, placed a knee on his chest, and fired his pistol at the hood. The sharp crack was all the louder for being in the tiny stone cell.

"Was he dead already?" asked Glasken.

"That's between me and my conscience."

"Poor fool, but he's lucky. My existence is pointless nothingness, I can't even hope for the release of death. The real Glasken is probably swapping jokes with the devil, but what am I doing?"

"Helping me get out of here alive," muttered Theresla impatiently.

Ten minutes later Theresla knelt in Horrey's uniform, trying to push and pound his large feet into her small boots. The hooded and skirted guardsman on the floor would not bear close inspection, but it would probably not come to that. The image on the bunk dissolved into just Horrey's face, which moved through the air and backed onto that of Theresla.

"Remember to let me do all the talking," warned Glasken. "Remember too, that this image loses substance in daylight. Once out of here you're wearing your own face."

From the annotation on the death warrant and what Horrey had said when he came in, Theresla decided to carry the skirted body out of the cell on her shoulder. The Yarronese supervisor was there as she climbed the stairs with the body. Blood dripped from the hood as she walked, and Horrey's face was impassive.

"Any problems?" asked the supervisor.

"Had better," Glasken said with Horrey's voice, and Theresla's eyes bulged with impotent fury beneath the holographic mask.

To Theresla's relief the supervisor led the way to the grave in the floor. She eased the body face down into the grave with some care, not wanting to expose Horrey's hairy legs and lack of breasts. A bucket of lime was poured over the corpse, and the four guardsmen began filling in the grave.

"Are you all right?" the supervisor asked what passed for his carbineer.

"Need a drink," replied Horrey's voice.

"Then go. Take an hour, but make it up this evening."

Out on the streets of Condelor, Theresla had her own face exposed to the world by the bright sunlight. Feeling like a rabbit that could hear terriers in the distance, she made straight for the tramway depot and used all Horrey's money to bribe the immigration inspector to let her board a tram for Yarron. There had been no money left for a ticket, but she agreed to work as a relief stoker.

"What did you mean, 'Had better'?" she asked as the tram rattled over points and turned east at Ogden's ruin.

"Man talk," piped a voice in her ear. "You had to pass as a convincing man."

"Suppose you're right. I owe you the ultimate debt, Fras Glasken."

"It's a pity I'm dead or I might take you up on that."

Theresla left the tram at Green River, and hitched a ride in empty trucks being drawn by a tram going north. She talked her way past the Dorakian border guards, and finally left the tramway at Jackson Lake. From here she set out to walk the ninety miles to Wind River wingfield after stealing a pack, bedroll, and supplies during a Call.

In the fortnight that it took Theresla to travel from Condelor to Wind River, over seven hundred wings from fourteen dominions had gathered at Forian. Every airworthy regal in Mounthaven was there, as well as the three surviving super-regals. Serjon was almost continually in the air, liaising with the new Bartolican dominions. Bronlar took over his place as Sartov's personal liaison, and saw Serjon only infrequently. Men now gave her a wide berth, and one free guildsman apprentice was flogged for merely touching the seat of her gunwing. Nobody dared to praise her, and even among her peers she would speak only to Ramsdel—and only when on a wingfield, in full view.

10 September 3961: Wind River

The guards at the Wind River perimeter jumped up in surprise when a figure came walking in from the darkness, but in the lanternlight it turned out to be Guildmaster Feydamor. He had been out walking, he said, now that there was enough time to be alone again. Even though it was his second excursion for the day, nobody was inclined to question the acting adjunct of the wingfield any further. The cloaked figure had Feydamor's face and voice, so he was let through.

Once in among the tents the face dissolved into Theresla's, and she drew out a dispatch with a seal on it. Shown into Feydamor's tent by a surprised and confused aide, Theresla explained that she had parachuted into the wingfield from a sunwing, and that she was on Sartov's business. If the guildmaster had given the seal more than a glance he would have seen that it did not have the sharp, crisp lines of the Airlord's real seal, but his night vision was not good and he saw what he expected to see.

Sartov's order was that Theresla be allowed to work on the sunwing immediately, but he imposed strict limits on what she could do. Most conspicuously, she was not allowed to lay a hand upon the sunwing without having a gun against her head. Wind River was practically deserted as a result of the Forian gathering, and Feydamor had been made acting adjunct and commander of the three interceptor gunwings, two sailwings, and four hundred staff and carbineers who were left. Every guildsman except Feydamor had been moved to Forian.

"Well, first thing in the morning," began Feydamor as he looked up.

"Now," said Theresla firmly.

"Now? It's ten o'clock at night!"

"Now."

She started by having all the scattered modules of the sunwing brought back together. True to her eccentric reputation, she called for several bags of beet sugar, a water cart, two hundred blankets, and a special detail of carbineers to rip canvas tents into strips. As if the modules of the sunwing were patients in an infirmary, she splinted and wrapped the broken pieces together, then soaked them in sugary water. The large areas of torn fabric were sewn together by tentmakers; then Theresla covered the repairs with sugar-soaked blankets. Feydamor noticed that the blankets soon got quite warm and gave off steam. More carbineers were detailed to apply more sugar water or patrol the rows of modules with sprayers.

After two days of work Theresla began carefully peeling off the blankets and bandages. To Feydamor's astonishment, the breaks and rips had healed like skin and bone. Theresla gently removed the stitching in what had been rents and applied more strips of sugar-soaked cloth to the little rows of holes. All the while Feydamor sat on a folding chair with a reaction pistol, watching and dictating notes to a clerk. More carbineers were called in to carry the modules about and interlock them with each other. Presently the sunwing was a whole aircraft again.

Feydamor watched nervously while Theresla sat in the cockpit and brought a screen within a frame to life. She tapped at colored squares inscribed with Old Anglian words, stroked images in the screen, and even spoke to the sunwing. Feydamor was no stranger to people who spoke to compression engines to coax more performance out of them, but the guildmaster nearly dropped his reaction pistol when the sunwing suddenly replied in Archaic Anglian. Theresla told it to speak Old Anglian instead.

"System diagnostic enabled," reported a clear contralto voice.

"What?" exclaimed Feydamor.

"This will take six minutes, so please sit back and relax."

"It spoke to me!" exclaimed Feydamor.

"It likes you," suggested Theresla.

"But it's a machine."

"True. But don't you like machines too?"

Feydamor had realized by now that such conversations were liable to lead nowhere. Theresla climbed out of the cockpit and ordered the sunwing dragged out of the tent and into the sunlight, where it was tied down against a light breeze. As the carbineers washed the last of the sugar from its skin she ate something small and furry that she took from a jar of pickle.

"The sunwing is in very good condition," she reported as she stretched like a cat that had been watching a mousehole for too long. "When the diagnostic is complete we can spin the electric engines and even do taxi and flight trials."

"No flight trials, not even taxiing," said Feydamor firmly. "The Airlord wants all such trials done tethered to a sailwing, with three gunwings flying escort. It says so in his dispatch."

Theresla had written such strict instructions because otherwise the supposed dispatch from Sartov would have been out of character. Now she shrugged and looked around as if searching for something. This put Feydamor on his guard, but he could see nothing unusual. There were the guild tents, carbineers, guards for various facilities, the three gunwings and two sailwings, and the pen complex of the two hundred terriers awaiting release before the next Call.

The remaining tests did not take long. The sunwing reported that its systems were all operational, and on Theresla's command it flexed all its control surfaces and finally spun up the engines for a few minutes. Finally satisfied, she ordered the aircraft left in the sunlight and began to read through the notes made by Feydamor's clerk.

"This is good, but you need these notes expanded if you want to keep the sunwing in good repair," Theresla finally said. "Come over to the tent and out of the wind."

Feydamor felt the tension drain out of him as they got clear of the sunwing, and even holstered his reaction pistol. Inside the maintenance tent Theresla spread the notes out on a bench and asked Feydamor to send all the guards and carbineers away. They had barely begun to work when the inner Calltower's bell began to ring.

"Damn! Five minutes," sighed Feydamor as he set his drop-anchor.

"Wait, this won't take long."

"Semme, you have to get to the cage for your own good. At a half-minute to the Call the terriers are released. They are trained to scent aviads. They will tear you to pieces if you are outside."

"Ten seconds, give me ten seconds. Just look here."

"Very well, what—"

Theresla's elbow slammed into Feydamor's jaw as he leaned over and he collapsed silently across the bench. With fluid precision she removed his reaction pistol, checked the magazine, released the safety catch, then rummaged in his pockets and removed four more clips of ammunition and a heavy-caliber carbineer's revolver.

"Four minutes, Sair Guildmaster," called a guard from outside as Theresla bound down her hair and pulled on Feydamor's greatcoat. By the three-minute warning bell she had his boots on as well, and had pulled his body under the bench. The guildmaster's peaked hat was a snug fit over her bound hair, but there was no mirror to check the overall effect. At the two-minute bell she strode from the tent just as a guard came to check on them.

"Guildmaster, the featherhead needs to be caged," the guard warned, but Theresla only jerked her thumb back to the tent and kept walking.

The wingfield was making an orderly transition to secure for the Call, but the terriers were still caged. Theresla walked straight for the three guards who were preparing to do the release. Through the mesh the dogs were bounding about excitedly in anticipation of three hours of freedom on patrol. As she neared the wire they caught her scent and started barking and lunging frantically. One of the guards noticed.

"Sair Guildmaster, the scent of that featherhead is on you and making the dogs—"

Theresla swept the coat open and sprayed the guards with bullets, dropping them before they had time to reach for their weapons. Theresla dropped too, pretending to be a victim. Others began to shout and point, and the dogs behind the wire mesh went into a frenzy. Theresla changed the clip on her reaction pistol as she crawled toward the bodies, then rolled over and fired at the guards and carbineers who were running across.

Lying behind the bodies of the guards, Theresla shot another three carbineers before the others dropped to the ground or ran. The minute bell rang automatically above the cacophony of barking from the dog cages; then Feydamor staggered out of the tent and shouted for the carbineers to charge Theresla before the Call arrived. Theresla looked up as she heard a clang from the gate to the dog pens and she saw the bolt being drawn back by a pulley: there was an automatic clockwork fail-safe mechanism!

She drew her knife and stood up amid a torrent of bullets, then jammed it into the race under the bolt. She fell, shot in the abdomen; then the Call blanketed the fighting, leaving only the barking of the terriers, which were still locked in their cages.

13 September 3961: Forlan

Before first light on September 14 the weather seers decreed that calm conditions were likely for the day to come.

Hundreds of compression engines began chugging into life and Forian's wingfields were alive with lanterns and torches. No attempt was being made at secrecy as the exercise was meant to be a victory air show, and the citizens of the recently liberated capital crowded the highest buildings and ruins to see the great pageant begin.

"I see that Samondel is leading the Highland Bartolicans against the staging wingfield," Bronlar said to Serjon as they stood reading their orders.

"It's a matter of honor. She is compared to you at every turn, so she must prove her bravery."

"Is your liaison with her still secret?"

"As of two nights ago our liaison has been amicably ended," said Serjon as he folded his orders and put them into his flight jacket. "It's a story I have heard before: she feels that she must be one of the boys in order to lead them."

"That's stupid. Do you want me to tell her what being one of the boys did to me?"

"Best not to. She also wants to be free to hate the featherheads that we are attacking, and being with me was warming her heart a little too much. It's her path, and she must fly it if she wishes to."

First six gunwings ascended, then six sailwings. These would stay on patrol in case any attack materialized while the huge super-flock was streaming into the air. Next came a triwing regal behind three sailwings. The crowd expected the trio to ascend in formation, but as they began rolling along the flightstrip it became clear that they were tethered to the regal. Rockets on the sides of the regal were fired as they gained speed, and the ungainly assembly struggled into the air with the compression engines at full throttle and the rockets streaming fire. The onlookers applauded, but by now another regal and three sailwings were lining up. The second group ascended, then a third and a fourth. Gunwings began ascending too, each towed by a sailwing.

They banked to fall in with the regals and headed east.

The thirteenth regal and its sailwings sat ready, spun the compressions up to full throttle, and began moving. Thirteen. The onlookers held their breaths, prayed or shouted "Lift! Lift! Lift!" in a chant as the rockets fired. The regal left the flightstrip, dropped back and bounced, rolled to the left, then straightened and steadied, and finally began climbing. Cheers broke out from everyone who had been within view.

It was now twenty minutes into the mass ascent, and the eastern horizon was beginning to glow with dawn and utterly clear of cloud. The fourteenth regal rolled into place, the sailwings pulled the tow-ropes taut, then they rolled forward. At the line across the flightstrip the port rocket fired—but not the starboard!

Incredibly the regal staggered into the air, its compression engines on overboost. For a few moments it gained height, but almost together the rocket flared out and one engine seized from being too long on overboost. The additional drag pulled the sailwings closer together until two collided. The flyer in the regal released his two bombs and the cables, but could not avoid the lines and debris streaming back at him. The bombs hit the ground and exploded as the tangled sailwings crashed into trees. Live ammunition! nearly every onlooker in the city exclaimed. This was not just a show. The regal banked, lost height, leveled and clipped something and erupted into an oily ball of flame. The surviving sailwing flew out to join the escort group.

The fifteenth regal had been revving up even before its predecessor had met its fiery death, and it ascended and passed through the cloud of smoke as it banked and gained height behind its trio of towing sailwings. Regal twenty-two's middle sailwing lost power when the group was barely in the air, but this time the lesson of regal fourteen came to the rescue. The wingcaptain released all three sailwings at once and banked away from the flightstrip, then released a cloud of small bombs. These were incendiaries, and they hit with brilliant plumes of flame as the middle sailwing flopped down onto the flightstrip, skidded and caught fire in a long, smoky smear. The flyer limped to safety.

Groundrunners had the debris clear and sand on the flames in less than two minutes as the last two regals sat chugging patiently, then they were aloft and turning east. Now the climax was about to begin. The first of the three super-regals was hauled into position while all eyes were watching the last regals rise higher and catch the sunlight of the dawn that had not yet reached the ground.

Powered by six engines and fourteen booster rockets, the super-regals needed no towing sailwings to ascend. The first lifted into the air on a huge cloud of roiling smoke. The still air had not dispersed the rocket fumes before the second super-regal began its run with rockets roaring and six engines at full throttle, and the onlookers shouted and cried prayers aloud as it flew invisible through the cloud, then cheered as it emerged intact.

The sky to the east was now a mass of pairs of sailwings and gunwings, and last of all a thin line of sailwing pairs straggled after the flock. The sound of the engines lessened, and was presently reduced to those of the circling patrol gunwings. Those with field glasses cried out that the vast flock of multi-dominion wings was flying northeast, and was showing no signs at all of turning back.

Sirens began to wail, sirens that heralded the declaration of a full mobilization alert in wartime. Militia and merchant carbineers ran for their weapons, and shops and stalls that had just opened for business quickly closed and packed up. It was only now that criers were sent about with their bells, proclaiming that the massive show of wing power was not just a spectacle to mark the end of the war, but a strike at an enemy far deadlier than the Bartolicans.

By the time the sun rose the city was tense and full of excitement. What enemy was there to the northeast? There is no dominion in all of Mounthaven that did not have wings or regals in that massive flock, so the threat had to be from outside—yet the only other known Callhavens were to the north and south. Callwalker featherheads?

"Fifteen wings lost in ascent, and two of them regals," said Sartov as he stood beside his own gunwing, staring east.

"Out of seven hundred that is not a bad start," said the wingfield adjunct.

"Out of the two hundred and thirty meant to get as far as the Sioux City ruin, it is more significant."

"Lordship, are you sure it is wise to fly in the second wave?" the adjunct asked his airlord, firmly and directly.

"It is not wise, Sair Adjunct, but it is important to *me*. If Samondel can lead her Bartolicans to the staging wingfield, then why not me? When the first wings begin to return, send out the five observer floatwings at one-hour intervals. I want a good report on what damage we did at the Alliance ruin."

Feydamor awoke with the sky dark and the whine of the sunwing's engines in his ears. He was strapped into the front seat of the sunwing's cockpit and his hands were firmly tied between his legs. Mirrorsun was low on the horizon.

"I see that you are awake, Sair Feydamor," said Theresla from the seat behind him.

Feydamor tried to turn, but he was tied too tightly to get a good view of her. The air was cool and musty inside the cockpit, like a bedroom on a winter's morning, but there was no condensation on the inside of the curving canopy.

"So, you fly to warn your featherhead friends about tomorrow?" Feydamor said sullenly.

"Sair Feydamor, that vague glow to the east is the beginnings of *sunrise*, not the end of sunset. This is already tomorrow. Work out the rest for yourself, I've no mind for chatter."

Her tone was irritable and tense, which was quite out of character. Sunrise. Were she speaking the truth he must have been insensible for at least fourteen hours, and Mirrorsun would be setting in the west. The sky was clear as he glanced at the constellations, and he soon found the Condor and the Boxkite. Sure enough, they were indeed headed due west. Craning his neck over he could just discern a range of mountains far ahead.

"That's the Wasatch Range, we're going to Condelor," Feydamor concluded.

"That was once known as the Sierra Nevada Mountains, and Condelor is five hundred miles behind you. You are the first human to set eyes on them for nearly two thousand years."

Her reply silenced Feydamor for several minutes more. They were so far west into Callscour country that it did not bear contemplating by anyone who wanted to remain sane. A super-regal could make a trip like this—in fact Theresla had originally demanded a super-regal to make a long trip west, Feydamor now remembered from a letter from Sartov.

"The headwinds have been bad," Theresla commented as the foothills passed beneath them. "We were blown a way south, but that will give us a good view of the San Francisco abandon."

"Abandon?"

"My word for ruined city."

"Travel broadens the mind," muttered Feydamor.

"I estimate that we have another two hours, maybe three, before turning back. Would you like to see Forian?"

"You said Forian is nearly a thousand miles behind us."

Swirling motes of light began to dance and gather in the space before Feydamor, and he recognized the projection image that Glasken's machine could make. It expanded until it was a holographic sphere ten feet across that enclosed the nose of the sunwing. It showed a wingfield by night, but aswarm with torches, lanterns, and hurrying guildsmen. There was even sound, but it was faint and mostly smothered by the whine of the sunwing's electric engines.

"Sair Virtrian is wearing Glasken's collar, Laurelene passed it on to him. Whatever he sees is what we see."

The view was from the noseplate of a super-regal waiting in a queue to turn onto a flightstrip. Off to starboard another super-regal was spinning its engines up to full power; then its rockets were lit and it began to roll forward belching smoke and flames until the edge of the plate cut off the view.

"They're up, they're up!" called the tiny voice of someone over the super-regal's communications pipe.

"This is the attack beginning," said Feydamor. "But where is the dawn?"

"We are an hour ahead of them. The attack has been getting into the air for the past forty minutes."

"So they did it, they really did it. The greatest superflock in the history of Mounthaven is going into battle."

They watched until Virtrian's super-regal heaved itself into the air, then were treated to a view of Forian from above as the huge aircraft banked and turned northeast. Escorting gunwings and sailwings formed up into an escort around it, but Feydamor noticed that they were tied together in bunches. One or two sailwings were towing each gunwing, and they were all loaded with pods of extra compression spirit. The sky was lightening at Forian now, and they could see unencumbered gunwings with extenders flying past in separate flocks. These would be the force flying for the Alliance ruin's Callwalker base. One bore a starflower on its side.

Turbulence from the mountains below began rocking the sunwing, but they flew blindly on with the view above eastern Yarron before their eyes.

"How many did you kill back at Wind River?" Feydamor asked as he tried to rub an itch against the padding of his seat.

"Nine," replied Theresla.

"At least three of them were my friends," he said after waiting for words of apology but getting none. "They all had lives before them. You sneaked up in my clothes and you murdered them."

"They were in the way."

"Ah, but I forgot, humans are just so many meat birds to you featherheads."

"They were about to release two hundred guard terriers onto the base, and I could not have gotten both you and me into the sunwing with that pack of aviad killers trying to have me for afternoon tea."

"What is so important that you could squander nine lives so readily?"

"Forty-five million lives in four Callhavens, Sair Feydamor."

"Lies and cheap dramatics," he retorted.

"If they had died defending the sunwing from a Bartolican attack would you be so sanctimonious?"

That caught Feydamor unprepared. He sat sullenly for a time; then Theresla switched off the holographic sphere and they now looked down on a wide, sunlit valley. The sunwing was dropping slowly, and some of the overgrown ruins were visible. Ahead of them was an immense, dark expanse of flatness.

"Most of San Francisco is under water now," explained Theresla. "With the end of Greatwinter the sea level rose and changed all the coastlines. Little that we do or build is truly lasting, Sair Feydamor."

Dark lines of ancient bridges ran under the water, and stumps of buildings protruded like giant rock crystals. Large, dark shapes moved just below the surface of the water.

"Those fish, they must be immense," gasped Feydamor.

"They are not fish, but they are immense."

*   *   *

Ramsdel was wingcaptain of the second super-regal, and through strict security he was the only one aboard to know the target. Not long after they crossed the North Platte River he whistled into the pipes and cleared his throat.

"Gentlefolk, this is your wingcaptain speaking. I would like to draw your attention to the pall of smoke rising over the ruin known on the old maps as Alliance. That is the advance flock of gunwings and heavy sailwings paying an unannounced visit on a featherhead waystation that traffics in stolen merchandise. That merchandise is the gunwings and sailwings of Yarron, Bartolica, Dorak, and Montras that were misplaced in the recent war.

"Our objective is a ruin by the name of Sioux City, which lies just inside the five-hundred-mile operational radius of this thing. With a lot of luck and no headwinds, and with the use of towing sailwings that go only part of the way, just over two hundred of our regals and gunwings should reach the featherheads' base at Sioux City, where they have stored as many as four hundred wings. Now if you are the praying type, start praying that there are a lot less than four hundred featherheads that can fly and fight out at Sioux City, because sure as our Airlord's Yarronese we're in trouble if we hit odds of two to one when we're four hundred miles from the nearest edge of the Callscour frontier. Any questions?"

The attack on Alliance was met by twenty gunwings stationed there for contingency defense. It did not destroy the aviads' primitive radio tower before a transmission could be sent, but luckily for the Mounthaven flock the sheer boldness of the attack defeated even the aviad imaginations. The commander at the Sioux City wingfield assumed that the attack was to disable Alliance and no more. A spare but unmanned wingfield had been cleared at the Chadron abandon, just sixty miles to the north, and it would not take much to get it operational. A Sandhawk ascended, with instructions to fly to Chadron to ensure that it had not been attacked as well, then to turn south and check the damage at Alliance.

Theresla switched the holograph sphere back into life. To port of the super-regal was a column of smoke rising not quite straight up from an olive-green plain. From the barely discernible dots of distant gunwings in the foreground Feydamor could tell that it was from an immense fire.

"What did they keep there?" Virtrian's voice asked. "That's a huge fire for a few dozen gunwings to start."

"Compression spirit," explained a voice over the pipe. "They took the stolen wings there and refueled them for the trip to the Sioux City ruin."

"Maybe it's a bigger base than we thought."

"No, I say it's a few interceptor gunwings, a dozen featherheads, and thousands of barrels of compression spirit. A close, easy target, not like what's in store for us in three hours."

Theresla switched off the sphere and looked out over the ocean that now presented an unbroken line before the canopy.

"I am going to release your hands now, Sair Feydamor. Do not take advantage of your freedom, I still have your reaction pistol and I am in a very scratchy mood."

Feydamor saw a hand caked with blood reach past his seat and release the knot on the bindings of his hands. She teased the bindings loose, then withdrew her hand and left him to do the rest himself.

"You're wounded," he observed, noting fresh blood on the cords.

"Do I get a daystar?"

"How did it happen?"

"Some dog fanciers were in my way back at Wind River. I was shot just below the ribs."

"But that was sixteen hours ago."

"Correct. I had a great deal of trouble dragging you to

the sunwing and getting it into the air while bleeding all over the place. I took forty standard units of warden-heart. That dulled the pain and cheered me up a lot."

"Forty units!" cried Feydamor. "Ten in one day can kill a man."

"But I am a woman, and an aviad, either or both seems to make a difference. Since then I have been taking one unit of warden-heart every hour. I also have some coagulant gel, all the way from a place called Glenellen. It's helped me hoard what blood I still have left."

"You must let me tend you," Feydamor said as he unbuckled his straps, but Theresla ordered him to stay where he was.

"I have a meeting to attend, but you are not required there. When I am gone you may want to appoint Darien as the envoy from Australica to Mounthaven. She understands your language and is expert at tapping code on those modulated induction radios. She is human, if that makes any difference."

"When you are gone?"

"I've told the sunwing to take you to Forian. The Wind River folk are liable to shoot at this thing if it returns unannounced."

"But I can't fly it."

"It knows the way, and it will train you once I am gone. There's rations and water in the pannier lockers to the lower left of your seat. Explain where we went and what I did to Airlord Sartov, if he is interested."

"Explain it? I don't have the slightest idea what is happening. What—"

There was a hiss like air escaping a seal under pressure; then the access hatch on the starboard side slid down in a long, flat concertina. Theresla said simply "Goodbye!" and tumbled out.

Feydamor cried out incoherently as the hatch slid shut again and the sunwing began to bank and it turned to fly east. Theresla's parachute billowed open, but she hung limp in the harness as it descended. She was carrying something about a yard long with a barb at one end and fins at the other.

"Theresla!" shouted Feydamor, trying to activate the concertina hatch again.

"Thank you for choosing to train on the Boeing-Aerospatiale Albatros Mark 2," declared the cheery contralto voice of the sunwing.

"Go back! She's wounded, she's falling to the water!"

"We are programmed to fly to Forian today, and you have been nominated for introductory training during the flight. At the end of the trip you will have a limited permit for supervised flight, ascent, and landing."

The parachute reached the water and collapsed. Large, dark shapes began converging once she hit the surface.

"Do you wish to familiarize yourself with the basic methods of flight control?"

"Flap off."

"According to your profile, you are an engineer with some flight training. Do you wish to discuss your skills with me before I assemble a tailored tutorial?"

"Leave me alone."

"I register that you have elected to enjoy the view for now. In one hour I shall get back to you and we shall return to familiarizing you with the Boeing-Aerospatiale Albatros Mark 2."

Several of the shapes in the water were far bigger than the collapsed parachute, but it was becoming difficult for Feydamor to keep it in view as the sunwing completed its turn. Now he saw that the back seat, floor, and sides were awash with the Callwalker woman's blood, and several roughly opened field trauma kits were littered about. His reaction pistol was on the floor, but his greatcoat and boots had gone into the ocean with Theresla.

Serjon and Bronlar were both in gunwings, both armed with nothing more than their reaction guns and additional fuel pods. Mile after mile of sand hills rolled by below as the two hundred nine wings droned east at a steady 100 mph. By noon the country below was distinctly greener. They were over what had been the farmlands of northeast Nebraska two millennia before.

By now they were reduced to a single towing sailwing each, but as the Elkhorn River came into view below Serjon moved from vague apprehension to the Serjon who had ninety-seven victory symbols repainted on the side of Princess. Undoing his harness and leaning as far forward as he could, he engaged the priming levers, then sat back and strapped in again. A small, black knob beckoned, but if it did not work the first time he was out of the fight and dead. After running through the checklist in his mind again he cast around for anything resembling thirteen in his field of view, then seized the knob and pulled back firmly.

There was a sharp blast as the charge went off, and the propellor began to spin, aided by the slipstream. Cautiously Serjon spun his compression engine up from idle to cruise speed and slack began to show in the tow rope. He reached up and tugged at another small lever, this one protruding from the upper wing. The tow rope detached, and immediately the sailwing banked to port and the flyer waved. Bronlar's gunwing was already flying free. Most engines had started—but not all. One towline remained attached to a gunwing whose engine remained stubbornly inert. Suddenly the flyer detached the tow rope, glided for a moment, then leaped from his gunwing and trailed parachute silk.

"What do you expect, flying to a war duel on the thirteenth day of the month," Serjon said to the tiny, descending figure.

Serjon looked away, checking the sky for enemy aircraft. Down in the Callscour lands the man would die within days, if not hours. He checked his map, then marked a flyer down at the appropriate grid reference. The rest of the super-flock formed up around their designated regals and super-regals. Nine were in the close escort, the rest were either general air support or were ground attack and armed with ballistic rockets.

Carabas ascended in a long-range Sandwing prototype more by luck than acumen. It had occurred to him that the first Sandhawk might not get a good look at the super-flock that the combined dominions had assembled, and he was curious to see it for himself. Once in the air he climbed to 10,000 feet and pushed the Sandhawk's speed to 300 miles per hour. The humans were sure to be using a variety of range-extension technologies to strike over such a distance, and the key to the Miocene Arrow's success was extreme endurance.

He was not disappointed. Carabas was just thirty miles into his flight when he saw a vast flock below him. Fortunately the experimental Sandhawk was equipped with a miniaturized induction transmitter, and he tapped out a warning to the Sioux City wingfield's adjunct at once.

ASCEND ALL GUNWINGS. ATTACK FLOCK OF SIXTEEN DOZEN WINGS APPROACHING. ESTIMATE QUARTER HOUR TO ARRIVAL.

After a moment an acknowledgment peeped in his headset. Carabas began a leisurely spiral to gain height, so that he could watch the attack in safety. While annoying, this was an ideal chance to study an extreme-range attack on surface-level targets. After the flock was gone, he would put his contingency plan into action and evacuate the base. Several Mexhaven rulers would be very pleased to provide shelter for Callwalkers, their captive Mounthaven guild-masters, and a large flock of operational aircraft.

Feydamor was staring blankly at the sunwing's little frame screen, which was rolling arcane images in one corner and flashing numbers in the opposite. Theresla had been gone two hours, yet the little cabin was still scented with her blood. A senseless and filthy way to die, he thought over and over.

The screen suddenly blinked and flashed into a full-color image of—Glasken! He looked much younger.

"I came back to say goodbye, Fras Feydamor," Glasken's voice said above the whining of the electric engines.

"Sair Glasken, it's good to see you! Rumor had it that you died."

"I am dead, Fras. I died a messy and exceedingly painful death."

"But, but what are you now? *Where* are you?"

"That's beyond your comprehension, Jeb, but for me it's a good approximation of Hell."

"The devil you say!"

"Yes, there is a devil here, and her name is Zarvora. Jeb, listen carefully: Laurelene had a baby at Denver. Your son."

"What? No!"

"That's what I always used to say. She thinks kindly of you, Jeb, and you two could be very happy together. She should be in Forian with the baby by now. She is reluctant to approach you, so go to her instead. Make a new life together in the new world."

"New world?"

"Theresla reached the, ah, creatures that speak the Call, Jeb. She can speak their language, she told them that the aviads were going to slaughter them with barbed spear-bombs from gunwings."

"What?"

"The aviads wanted to provoke them into intensifying the Call in Mounthaven, annihilating all humans and leaving it clear for them to take over. They would then use it as an arms factory and wipe out humans everywhere else in the world. Theresla told them that a balance between aviads and humans was needed. The Call-creatures listened to her, and Sartov's worst nightmare has just come true."

Feydamor felt a chill in spite of the warm, stuffy air in the cabin.

"Nightmare? What do you mean?"

"You will soon find out. My cohesion, my . . . my sanity is slipping, Jeb, but I can make one last contact with Laurelene. What shall I tell her?"

"Tell her—tell her yes. But what about Theresla?"

"She is dead, her collar told me that after her last words to me. I am dead too. Goodbye."

Glasken's image winked out before Feydamor could speak again.

"Sartov's worst nightmare," said Feydamor, shivering as he wondered what it might be.

Virtrian studied the terrain below against his map as the flock approached Sioux City's ruins.

"Fifteen miles," he called.

"Where's that Missouri River then?" asked the dome gunner.

"Mind on the job, or you'll be drinking it."

"Number One Super has vapor from his inner port engine," piped the rear gunner. "Not much, but it's a long walk home."

"Signaling now," Ramsdel piped back.

The super-regal dipped to the left three times and to the right once. Behind them each wing dipped to the right and left as they checked for the fire he had signaled. Super-regal One remained steady for a time.

"He's feathered it," piped the rear gunner.

"Ten miles," Virtrian called.

"Starting to drop, secure stations," ordered Ramsdel.

"Nine miles."

"Commence release check. Bombardier, release incendiary rack levers IR Alpha and IR Beta."

It was times like these that Virtrian desperately wished for his missing arm instead of a tapered hook. "Releases confirmed."

"Bombardier, release safety catch on drop levers IR Alpha and IR Beta."

"Releases confirmed, ready to drop."

"Just supply the standard responses if you please. Releasing reaction gun rack to starboard. Releasing gun rack to port."

"Eight miles."

"Rear and dome gunners, release the safety catches on your reaction guns."

"Releases confirmed," they answered in turn.

"Target acquired!" cut in Virtrian. "Immense, ancient wingfield. Gravity towers, rows of wings, rows of tenting."

"What heading?"

"Six degrees to starboard, range would be . . . estimated point five miles."

"Igniting pathfinder flare and altering course."

Yellow smoke streamed from the super-regal. It turned, leading the rest of the super-flock after it.

"Five miles. Interceptors ascending, others already high. Groundfire to port."

"Keep the pipes clear for the bombardier," warned Ramsdel as the low-flying super-regal began to buck in the slight turbulence.

"Four miles—bear two degrees to port, we have a gravity tower surrounded by tenting."

"Your call, bombardier," Ramsdel replied.

"Two miles, hold it steady."

"Two gunwings, coming in from the sun, under fifteen."

"Deal with them and shut up!" called Ramsdel.

Two gunwings overhauled the super-regal, one already trailing vapor, both with their reaction guns blazing. A Cosdoran gunwing sped after them; then they were gone.

"One mile."

They swept over the perimeter. Reaction guns spat fire from the ground. The tail gunner fired back in reply.

"Your target!"

There was a slight lurch as the incendiary bombs fell

away; then the five reaction guns on each wing erupted in a line of fire that converged on the gravity tower ahead of them. It burst into smoky flames then exploded and flung dark, acrid smoke into their path as Ramsdel climbed and banked.

"Estimate five, maybe six aircraft destroyed, hard to say through the tents," reported the rear gunner. "The gravity tower and compression spirit dumps are burning."

"Now listen up," piped Ramsdel. "We wait until the others have had a run, then we have another. Commence secondary release check."

The super-flock had managed to offset the immense distance with near-complete surprise. The defenders at Sioux City knew that the super-regals could reach as far as there and still return, but they expected them to be alone. Some aviad flyers even speculated about forcing a few of them down relatively intact. The appearance of sixteen dozen gunwings was nothing less than magical to them, and some even thought that they were suicides, operating right at the end of their reserves and about to crash.

Bronlar was in the second strike flock. Serjon had gone ahead with ten other gunwings to prepare the way for the super-regals by breaking up the formations of aviad interceptor wings that were positioning themselves to go down after the super-regals. When Bronlar arrived the air was already filled with individual battles, with the aviads outnumbered but fresher and more alert. Bronlar fired a deflection burst at an unmarked Cosdoran guild gunwing that climbed past her gunsights, then broke away and settled behind an aviad that was firing at one of her flock. She caught him quite unaware, and left the engine smoking and the flyer dead. Another gunwing dived on her but overshot, only to find himself stopping the bullets of her reaction guns. He bailed out in a panic.

As she turned to find the rest of the flock Bronlar realized that most of the defenders of this huge wingbase were probably trainees, flyers who had never fired a shot in anger before.

Bronlar made a fast pass at a rising aviad formation, then realized that she still had her drop tanks attached. Reluctantly she switched to her main tanks and dropped her pods as she turned back, boosting her compression engine as she scanned the sky. Ahead an aviad gunwing was climbing to get behind Ramsdel's super-regal, unprotected by any companion. Bronlar closed the gap and fired at the edge of her guns' effective range, but enough shells impacted to panic the inexperienced aviad. He broke off and dived almost vertically to escape, but Bronlar knew that her first duty was to protect the super-regals and she let him go. Inexperience in the enemy gave her a victory, for he had forgotten how low to the ground they were fighting. By the time he began trying to pull out of his dive he was flying too fast and too low, and his gunwing buried itself in what had been a cornfield two millennia earlier.

Three other gunwings joined her, including Serjon's. Immediately Bronlar knew something was wrong. Serjon was supposed to have turned back by now. Aviad gunwings approached in open order. Serjon dropped back, dived, and attacked an unmarked Yarronese triwing. It broke off and turned inside his attack, but Serjon was faster. He turned and climbed; the triwing doubled back and fired head-on, dueling-style. Serjon's shells hammered into the triwing's compression engine. A puff of black smoke trailed out of the triwing, to be followed by the aviad trailing a parachute. Serjon broke off. He's already overstayed his time over the target, Bronlar thought with relief as Serjon turned west.

A wave of the new heavy sailwings was sweeping over the aviad wingfield firing incendiary rockets at the wing tents, but there were already dozens of fires burning and the question was now becoming one of finding targets amid the devastation. Bronlar noticed another aviad gunwing pursuing the heavy sailwings as they climbed and she came around in a tight circle, winding up her feed springs and switching to new ammunition belts as she closed.

She fired, but instantly there were bullets flying through the fabric all around her. She wove, slamming her feet against the rudder pedals and twisting the stick about. The aviad hung on skillfully, firing only as needed. Bronlar was already close to the ground, so there was little scope for evasion. Ahead of her was another gunwing, a Yarronese triwing. It approached head-on; it began firing.

Bronlar wrenched her gunwing to port and put it into a tight turn that almost had her down among the burning aircraft and tents. For a moment she wondered that the Call did not take her for dropping so low; then she was climbing again. She was just in time to see her attacker slam into the wingfield some distance away. Off to the west a triwing was struggling to gain height. That was her rescuer, and he was breaking for home. She checked her watch. Her five minutes over the target had already stretched to six, and the third wave of gunwings would be arriving by now. She looked warily around, then fell in behind the triwing that had saved her.

He had gained his kill by collision, as far as Bronlar could see. Part of the upper port wing was trailing fabric and smashed ribs, and there was some damage to the middle wing too. He would not make it, it was only a question of where he came down. The starboard wing array was high—and the name was Princess! Bronlar's heart missed a beat. Serjon!

In spite of Bronlar's fears there was no pursuit. Once clear of Sioux City they were in clear air. Off to port were three heavy sailwings flying in cover formation. Bronlar noticed that they were slowly pulling ahead. Serjon's mangled wings had raised the drag of his gunwing, and he was trying to conserve the remaining spirit in his tanks. Another gunwing overhauled them, this one trailing a streamer of smoke. It vanished into the distance ahead, but after another half hour Bronlar noticed a pillar of smoke amid the sand hills. She noted the position on her issue map and made an entry in her flight log, but she doubted that it would serve as more than a note of the flyer's resting place. It was now two hours since they had left the battle at the aviad wingbase.

A subtle difference in the color of the sand below traced an ancient rail track. Far off to port two regals passed them, apparently undamaged. Bronlar was startled to see another two dozen pairs of sailwings and gunwings heading east. On impulse she rolled Slash to signal that the fight had been going their way when she had broken off. Not long after that she noticed a pall of smoke slanting east and centered on the Alliance ruin. At that distance she could not distinguish whether any wings were still attacking. Then it struck her like a blow to the plexus: there was now a headwind blowing out of the west.

She checked her compression spirit levels, but the float tubes showed adequate fuel for another hour and a half of flight. From the slant of the column of smoke she estimated the wind to be no more than 10 mph. Bronlar was safe, but then her gunwing was intact and she had not spent double her allotted time over the target as Serjon had. A river passed below, then another, then a chimney-shaped outcrop of rock. On her map Bronlar noted that Serjon was heading slightly north of the line to Forian. He was headed straight for the closest stretch of Callscour frontier: he knew that he was desperately short of compression spirit. They passed what was called Hogback Mountain on her copy of the ancient map, and Bronlar wondered what a hog might have looked like. Something very different from the tiny pigs of contemporary Mounthaven, she was sure of that. She glanced at her issue map again. Twenty-five miles, only a quarter of an hour from safety. If he lasted just minutes more, Serjon could practically glide to the Callscour frontier's edge.

Bronlar looked up to see that Serjon's propellor was feathered, and the gunwing had lost a lot of height.

The Horse River lay ahead. Bronlar estimated 400 feet as they passed over a subtle change in the color of the trees that marked an ancient road; then there was a uniform carpet of scrubby treetops. The Horse River came into view, along with the overgrown remains of a small cluster of buildings.

Serjon was losing height more quickly now, he was less than a hundred feet from the treetops. Twenty-three miles, so near yet so far, Bronlar thought in dismay. The stricken gunwing began to weave to avoid the highest branches. The standing Call of the area should have seduced away his control already, but . . . No Call! Bronlar realized with a start that they were over a pause in the Call. It was one of the rare breaks that rippled over the Callscour lands every three days or so. They never lasted more than about forty minutes, but here there was one and so here was a chance for Serjon.

Serjon's aircraft banked, straightened, then lined up a sandbank beside a river. Bronlar noted that he was winding his wheels down. A belly landing on the water near the sandbank would be safer—but of course! If the sand was sufficiently firm for him to touch down and roll to a stop then Bronlar could land, take him aboard, and ascend again. He was testing the surface, he knew she would follow him down for a rescue. Love and pride welled up in her chest. The gunwing's wheels touched, gouged; then the undercarriage collapsed and Princess cartwheeled into the shallows and came to rest amid an arc of spray. Serjon struggled out of the wreck and onto the sandbar as Bronlar circled. Still no Call, thought Bronlar as Serjon waved, gesturing her to fly east and leave him.

"Only one thing to do," Bronlar said aloud, winding

As Bronlar straightened and eased the throttle back Serjon's waving became frantic. Back and forth, his arms crossed above his head: *Don't land, danger*. Ah well, even being alive is dangerous, she thought as she descended. The grooves in the sand from Serjon's wheels were deep, it was loose and coarse. There was no hope. Bronlar's grip tightened on the throttle . . . then she pulled it back. The compression engine slowed to an idle, the gunwing's wheels bumped sand, dug in, bent, snapped, and collapsed.

Bronlar's gunwing continued straight on its belly until it came to rest. Serjon came running up and pulled up the canopy as she released it.

"Are you all right?" he panted as he helped her out.

"That ruined my average," she said, patting the side of the gunwing.

Dried blood from a gash above his hairline smeared his face. Bronlar remembered a long flight of her own with a similar wound. She climbed out of Slash.

"Didn't you see me waving you off?" demanded Serjon, allowing himself to be angry now that he knew she was all right. "The sand is coarse, loose—hopeless for wheels."

"I knew that, I saw the grooves left by your own wheels."

"You what? Don't you know where we are? These are still the Callscour lands, this break in the Call has barely a half hour left! *This is the thirteenth day of the month!*"

"I knew that too, Serjon. In a few minutes the Call will beckon us east for three days or more, even if we are tethered to my gunwing. In the meantime the dirkfangs will eat us alive, but we shall feel nothing until we awake in the afterlife."

He took her by the shoulders and tried to shake the dreaminess out of her voice.

"Bronlar! Are you mad? You mean to say that you landed even though you knew this would happen?"

"I was totally certain that this would happen, Serjon

Feydamor," she replied, looking into his bloodshot, wind-reddened eyes.

At a loss for words, Serjon sank to the sand. Bronlar knelt beside him and put an arm over his shoulders. Serjon clutched at his hair, his mouth open. Slowly he began to relax, as if he had surrendered to something akin to the Call.

"The dirkfangs may not notice us out here on the sand-bank," suggested Bronlar.

"And a floatwing may happen past when there is next a break in the Call," countered Serjon, hopeless and wretched.

Two small birds flew overhead, screeching and striking at each other.

"Some fool is always starting a war in the air," observed Serjon.

"Who do you think will win?"

Serjon shrugged. "The bird with the black streak along its belly."

"I mean the war. Us or the featherheads?"

"Oh, we'll win. The featherheads are just parasites. If we could beat Bartolica we can beat anyone. Yarron was transformed into a disease that sapped Bartolica's strength. There will be more fighting now, because all the other dominions will become like Yarron."

"Such a stupid reward for all our suffering, sacrifice, and bravery," sighed Bronlar.

She looked down at the watch on her wrist.

"We must have caught the leading edge of this break. It's over fourteen minutes since you crash-landed."

"My maps showed that we are twenty-three miles from the nearest point on the Yarronese Callscour frontier. We're just five miles from the Hawk Springs ruin, and beyond it is an ancient road going due west to the frontier. It's no more than a day's walk."

"It's unfair, I know."

They sat in silence as a scatter of sailwings and gunwings droned past in the distance. They even saw the two super-regals flying west. Bronlar stroked Serjon's hair smooth.

"You should have stayed up," Serjon said, his voice bleak and distant.

"I did not want you to die alone, Serjon. You were my friend, and I want my friend back."

"Bronlar? You can't mean that."

"But I do. I prepared the most cruel dilemma possible for you. It was for revenge, nothing more, and it made me lose you just when you drifted into reach. Now that you are falling toward death alone, the least I can do is be company for your fall."

"But damnall, you could have done that by circling overhead! I've faced death alone before."

"But not certain death. You gave up your honor, rank, and property when you lied to clear my name. Now here is my life, to atone for hating you. I'm here to die with you, Warden Serjon Feydamor, and it's really too late for you to do anything about it."

Serjon's head jerked around, his face contorted with an expression of pure horror.

"My—my words in Condelor," he whispered. "Die for me, give your life for me . . . some drivel like that."

" 'Little sister, if you died for me yet remained living,' " Bronlar quoted precisely.

Serjon buried his face in his hands. "I've killed you," he moaned between his palms.

"But does thirteen—"

"To hell with thirteen! Thirteen ruled my life and thirteen forced me to kill you. Thirteen be damned! Thirteen be humped!"

Minutes passed, and still there was no Call. They sat side by side in the wet sand. A light breeze sighed through the trees, and some distance away on the riverbank a wild emu minced into view and paused to regard the first humans of its experience. Bronlar stroked the back of Serjon's neck, then took his wrist and felt his pulse.

"Clammy skin, lost blood, high pulse, rapid breathing—you may be in shock. Do you feel nauseous?"

"We're about to die, what does it matter? I hated you flying into danger beside me, I hated the idea of you dying."

"We shared danger. What other lovers can say that?"

"Gah, we're friends, not lovers. Lovers pull off their drawers and play nozzle-in-the-fuel-tank. Friends are people who are not good enough to be lovers."

"Serjon, how can you say that?" cried Bronlar. "People are *dead* because they pissed on our friendship. Since 9:35 P.M. on 19th August 3961 I have been your . . . your lover designate. All that stood between us was your thirteen, my faithfulness to you, and one very pretty Airlord."

Serjon dabbed one of his cuts open, and with the blood on his fingers wrote 13 on his trouser leg.

"Well, *do* something to me!" he barked at the number.

He spat on it when no thunderbolt struck him down. He skipped thirteen stones over the calm surface of the river.

"It's good to die free of thirteen," he declared.

"So . . . how do you feel about consummating a long and badly managed courtship?" Bronlar asked.

He put an arm around her shoulders. "I got this far at Casper last October. I know others have been a lot farther since then, but I'd love it if you didn't push my arm away this time."

Bronlar squeezed him with all her strength, and fire stabbed his chest where a rib had been cracked in the crash-landing. He did not cry out.

"Serjon, I . . . I . . . I want to say something pretty and poetic, but I am no poet: do—ah, do you want to move beside my gunwing, in the shade, ah, before we undress and . . . ?"

He shook his head. "Bronlar, any moment now the Call

die with dignity—not with our drawers at our ankles. Force the dirkfangs to unwrap us."

"You are a gentleman, Sair Thirteenth Time," she said, kissing his ear.

After a moment she reached down into her flight breeches and drew out a tiny jade comb which she offered to Serjon. He took it from her and savored the musky scent about it, then kissed it and put it in his coat pocket.

"I don't give buttons," said Serjon firmly.

"Good. It's a filthy, primitive tradition."

Still no Call came as they sat with their heads together. A dirkfang began to yowl a challenge close by, and Serjon fired two shots into the air from his pistol. The dirkfang crashed away through the bushes. Serjon pulled Bronlar against him and delicately kissed her lips. The kiss lingered and lingered, as if tempting the Call to tear them apart.

"They say love is like a wineglass, Serjon. Once shattered it can never be made whole, yet here we are with the broken glass perfect."

"Let's not drop it again—Is that an engine?"

"Yes, but what does it matter?"

"It matters, it matters!" he shouted, standing up and waving his arms. "That's Rowley, the engine of Finwings the Third, a *floatwing*! I flew it at Wind River. It's used as an observer, but it can land on *water*!"

Serjon fired a smoke flare. The floatwing passed overhead at three hundred feet, then descended when the flyer saw the two figures waving beside the wrecked gunwings. He selected a clear stretch of river and made a smooth landing.

"Just as well we stayed dressed," Bronlar said as they waded out into the shallows.

The floatwing turned back and started for the sandbank.

"Ascend as soon as we're aboard!" Serjon shouted as he and Bronlar splashed toward the floatwing. "There's been no Call for nearly forty minutes. The next one must be right on us."

"Take your ease, young sair," the flyer called back. "There's been no Call in the Callscour lands for more than five hours. Something's changed. The whole world's changed! The Call has ceased completely."

Carabas had started to descend when he heard the desperate transmission from his wingfield.

CALL HAS CEASED. REPEAT. CALL HAS CEASED.

At once Carabas knew that something was seriously wrong. There had been a break passing over the wingfield when he had ascended, and that had been over an hour ago. He tapped out his orders.

INITIATE CONTINGENCY PLAN MEXHAVEN. RE-PEAT. INITIATE CONTINGENCY PLAN MEX-HAVEN.

The attack flock would be back in a few hours, and this time the super-regals would be crammed with carbineers. Still, a few hours were enough.

UNDER FIRE. GUILDSMEN'S COMPOUND BREACHED IN ATTACK. GUILDMASTERS LOOSE AND HAVE TAKEN GUARDS' ARMORY. AT LEAST A DOZEN FLYERS SURVIVED CRASHES AND HAVE JOINED GUILDMASTERS.

Carabas considered the scene below him. One flightstrip was free of craters, but wreckage needed to be cleared away before it could be used.

INITIATE PLAN MEXHAVEN. ACKNOWLEDGE, he tapped, then waited.

Far below he could see a new plume of smoke over the transmitter building. There was no reply. Carabas never took long to reach a decision. He plugged a new coil into his induction transmitter and tapped out a message to the nearest sunwing. His heart sank. It reported being not far from Condelor, some seven hundred miles away. Carabas ordered it to turn due east at once, then turned the Sand-hawk west, abandoning his work of the past five years to the unexpectedly tenacious humans.

Serjon and Bronlar were debriefed as soon as they landed at Forian. The aviad bases had been wiped out, but around the same time the Call had vanished from the Callscour lands. Surviving flyers were being picked up or dropped food, water, and extra flares all the way to Sioux City, and the super-regals had already been sent back carrying two dozen battle-hardened carbineers each to secure the main aviad wingfield. Some flyers had seen dozens of figures waving to them at Sioux City's ruins, and names painted on the flightstrips. They were the missing guildmasters, and Bronlar's father was among them. Bronlar and Serjon did not get out until after dusk, by which time Serjon was dizzy with fatigue and the blood that he had lost.

"I have rooms in a hostelry that was restored for the use of Bartolican wardens during the occupation," Bronlar said as they walked from the adjunct's tent. Serjon was un-steady on his feet and leaning on her.

"I'm open to suggestions," replied Serjon; then he sud-denly straightened and fumbled to adjust his flight jacket's collar.

Sartov appeared out of the darkness, at the head of at least ten Airlords and escorted by a large squad of carbi-neers. He noticed the pair at once, for all Serjon's effort to remain utterly still and blend with the shadows. Sartov stopped. Everyone else stopped. The Airlord of Yarron reached into his pocket and drew out something on a loop of silk.

"Warden Feydamor, this is your daystar medal," Sartov declared, holding out the medal on its loop of silk ribbon. "To use an Old Anglian word, take this fucking medal or I shall blast your head off and award it to you posthu-mously."

"Ah, that would require changing the enamel background to red," the Cosdoran Airlord pointed out.

"Quite so," said Sartov. "Take it for *my* sake, Serjon. Don't make a fool of me in front of the Council of Alliance Airlords."

"Again," added the Cosdoran.

Serjon saluted, said, "Yes, Lordship," then bowed his head. Sartov lowered the silk loop over Serjon's cap and hung Yarron's highest decoration on his neck.

"Samondel said to tell you 'Two gunwings confirmed,' " Sartov whispered in his ear before Serjon stepped back.

The airlords walked on. Serjon sat down in the grass, waiting for his head to stop spinning while Bronlar removed the ribbon and pinned the daystar to the throat of his collar. Presently they began walking again.

"I've never held hands before," Bronlar confessed as they left the wingfield. "It makes me feel like I'm walking on clouds."

"What?" laughed Serjon. "In spite of doing the ultimate with two—"

"That's nothing, that's done out of sight. You have to be proud of someone to walk down a street holding hands with him."

"I . . . I do believe it's my first time too," Serjon said after thinking carefully, surprised that it was true.

A huge celebration had erupted throughout Forian. Gunshots, flares, and bells were going off all through the siege-ravaged city, and bonfires with effigies of Stanbury and stylized Callwalkers atop were ablaze. In the newly renamed Virtrian Square were thousands of revelers, all singing, dancing, and drinking around a great central bonfire. Many more had spilled out into the side streets, and it was a party of these who encountered Serjon and Bronlar. A big, burly carbineer caught sight of them and pointed.

"Eh, here's two Air Carbineers wi'out a drink!" he bellowed, and immediately the group of drunken, cheering men and women began to converge.

"Yer a sweet young pair," said a gap-toothed backwoods

trapper turned carbineer who was barely able to stand for the drink. "Daystars," muttered someone else in awe.

"You got flight jackets, were you in today's attack?" a girl wearing a carbineer's hat asked.

"Aye, we plucked some feathers," called Serjon.

"And is the Call really stopped?" cried a guildsman as he held out a beer bottle to them.

Serjon nodded, but declined the bottle. Although Bronlar was tense, she did not fly into a rage. Her mania was under control now, even if the presence of guildsmen set her on edge and brought a dangerous gleam to her eyes.

Just then the big carbineer realized that Bronlar was a warden as well as a girl—and there was only one female Yarronese warden in existence.

"Warden Jemarial!" he gasped, going down on one knee.

Silence rippled out from the couple behind a dozen whispered exclamations.

"Beggin' yer pardon, Semme, but will ye touch me carbine—so I can tell me wife and young'uns?" the carbineer asked, holding out a battered Harlington automatic.

Bronlar shuddered at being addressed by a commoner, but again made no outburst. "Don't demean yourself," she said tersely, and walked on.

"She's been in the air for ten hours, sair, she's a little scratchy," Serjon said to the disappointed carbineer, then he shook his hand.

"Eh sair, did she get any today?" asked the guildsman.

"Three, all confirmed."

"That's forty kills! Three cheers for Warden Jemarial!"

Bronlar leaned against a wall with her arms folded, ignoring the cheers.

"And you, young sair: were you victorious today?" the girl asked.

"Only seven, it's not my best but the range—"

"Serjon, I'm getting cold!" Bronlar called from farther

down the road where she was still standing and tapping a foot. "Are you to bed or the revel?"

"Coming! A long peace to you, gentlefolk," Serjon called as he left them for Bronlar. Hand in hand they walked down the street and were lost amid the shadows. The group stood stunned, gaping after them until they were gone.

"That was him, wasn't it?" said the big carbineer.

"Serjon Warden Killer," breathed the guildsman. "Warden Killer himself! Ninety-seven plus seven is one hundred and four confirmed victories!"

"They were so sweet," slurred the trapper with tears in his eyes.

"Pity he's taken," said the girl in the carbineer's hat.

"He shook my hand, Warden Killer himself," cried the big carbineer as the group set off to tell anyone who would listen.

"Nobody's ever going to believe us," warned the guildsman.

Nobody noticed the ferrywing come sweeping silently in to land at the darkened Forian Central wingfield, so it was not fired upon. Feydamor asked the adjunct about his family as he climbed out of the cockpit, but was interrupted by Sartov, who came running over from the briefing tent near the pennant pole.

"You did it, you got it working!" Sartov exclaimed, running his hands along the smooth, tough fabric. "Tell me how."

"For that we need privacy," said Feydamor as they grasped wrists.

An aide was sent out to search for Laurelene and the baby as Sartov and Feydamor retired to an annex of the command tent. They were brought mugs of coffee by an aide, then left alone.

"Your stepson survived the raid on the Callwalker wingfields, I saw him a while back," said Sartov. "He was with